Mayne Reid

The Maroon

A Novel

Mayne Reid

The Maroon
A Novel

ISBN/EAN: 9783337002152

Printed in Europe, USA, Canada, Australia, Japan

Cover: Foto ©Andreas Hilbeck / pixelio.de

More available books at **www.hansebooks.com**

THE MAROON.

A Novel.

By CAPTAIN MAYNE REID,

AUTHOR OF "THE SCALP HUNTERS,"—"THE RIFLE RANGERS,"—"THE
TIGER HUNTER,"—"THE WAR TRAIL,"—"THE WHITE CHIEF,"
—"THE HUNTER'S FEAST,"—"THE WILD HUNTRESS,"—"THE
WOOD RANGERS,"—"WILD LIFE,"—"THE MAROON,"—
"OSCEOLA THE SEMINOLE,"—"THE WHITE GAUNT-
LET,"—"THE HEADLESS HORSEMAN,"—
ETC., ETC., ETC.

NEW YORK:

G. W. Dillingham, Publisher,

SUCCESSOR TO G. W. CARLETON & CO

MDCCCXCII.

CONTENTS.

CHAPTER I.

A JAMAICA SUGAR PLANTATION.

A sugar plantation, and one of the finest in the " land of springs," is the estate of "Mount Welcome;" it is situated about five miles from Montego Bay, in a broad valley, between two rounded ridges. These ridges, after running parallel for more than a mile, and gradua\y increasing in eleva tion, at length converge with an inward sweep into a stupendous hill, that fairly merits the name which it bears upon the estate—the " mountain."

Both the ridges are wooded almost down to their bases ; the woods, which consist of shining pimento trees, ending on each side in groves and island copses, pleasantly interspersed over a park-like greensward.

The " great house " or " buff " of the estate—Mount Welcome itself—stands under the foot of the mountain, just at the point of union between the two ridges, where a natural table or platform, elevated several feet above the level of the valley, had offered a tempting site to the builder.

In architectural style it is not very different from other houses of its kind, and after the same fashion as the well-known planter's dwelling of the West Indies. One storey—the lower one, of course—is of strong stone mason-work; the second and only other being simply a wooden " frame " house set on the top of the stone-work, and roofed with Ameri-can " shingles."

The side and end walls of this second storey cannot with propriety be termed walls : since most part of them are occupied by a continuous line of Venetian shutters—the " jalousies " of Jamaica.

These impart a singular cage-like appearance to the house, at the same time contributing to its coolness—a quality of primary importance in a tropical climate.

Outside in the front centre a flight of broad stone steps, resting upon arched mason-work, and bordered by strong iron balustrades conducts to the level of the second storey—the real dwelling-house : since the ground floor is entirely occupied by store-rooms, magazines, and other " offices."

The entrance door is from the landing of the aforesaid *escalier*, and conducts at once into the " hall," a spacious apartment, of crucifix-shape, running clear across the building from side to side, and end to end. The current of air which enters at the openings of the jalousies, passing constantly through this apartment, renders it at all times delightfully cool, and the lattice-work serves to mellow the glare of light which, under the sky of the tropics, is almost as disagreeable as the heat. The uncarpeted floor, moreover, composed of the hardest sorts of native wood, and subjected to a diurnal polish, contributes to increase the coolness.

The great hall is the principal apartment of the dwelling. It is dining and drawing-room in one, where side-boards and cheffoniers may be seen in juxta-position with lounge chairs, fauteuils, and ottomans—a grand chandelier in the centre suspended over all.

The bed-chambers occupy the square spaces to one side of the cross; and these also have their jalousied windows to admit the air, and exclude, as much as possible, the sultry rays of the sun.

In Mount Welcome House, as in all other country mansions of Jamaica, a stranger would remark a want of correspondence between the dwelling itself and the furniture which it contains. The former might be regarded as unsubstantial and even flimsy, for in reality it is so. But it is this very character which renders it appropriate to the climate, and hence the absence of substantiality or costliness in the style or materials of the building.

The furniture, on the other hand—the solid tables of mahogany, and other ornamental woods—the shining carved sideboards—the profuse show of silver and finely cut glass that rests upon them—the elegant couches and chairs—the glittering lamps and candelabras—all combine to prove that the *quasi* meanness of the Jamaica planter's establishment extends no farther than to the walls of his house. If the case may be considered a cheap one, the jewels contained in it are of the rarest and costliest kind.

Outside, the great house of Mount Welcome looks grand enough. Its broad façade, in which the deep green of the jalousies contrasts prettily with the white of the surrounding walls—the massive stone stairway in front—the wooded mountain sweeping up and forming a back-ground of variegated green—the noble avenue of nearly a mile in length, with its double rows of tamarinds and cocoa palms, leading up in front—all contribute to produce a picture of almost palatial grandeur, especially when viewed from the lower end of the valley.

Nor does a nearer view detract from the splendour of this picture. The platform on which the house is built affords space for a large garden and shrubbery, extending rearward to the mountain-foot, from which they are separated by a high wall of stone.

This mountain is a conspicuous feature of the landscape. Not so much from its height; for there are others of equal elevation near to it, and further off, though still within sight, many far higher. Even the famed "Blue Peak" is visible, towering hundreds of feet abeve the sur rounding summits.

Nor is it conspicuous from being isolated. On the contrary, it is only a spur of that vast elevated chain of hills, that separated by deep gorge-like valleys, and soaring thousands of feet above the level of the Caribbean Sea, are known as the "Blue Mountains of Jamaica."

Covering almost the entire area of the island, which is thus broken into an endless succession of gigantic corrugations, Jamaica presents a surface rough and irregular as the crumpling upon a cabbage-leaf, and "land of mountains" would be a title as appropriate as its ancient Indian appellation, "the land of fountains."

The one which overlooks the estate of Mount Welcome is only two thousand feet above sea-level; but what renders it remarkable is the geometrical regularity of its outlines, and, still more, its singularly shaped summit.

Viewed from the valley below, it presents the appearance of an exact and somewhat acute cone, up to within about fifty yards of its top. There the sloping outline ends, the line on each side thence trending vertically upward, and abruptly terminating in a square table-top, forty or fifty feet in diameter. In general appearance, this truncated summit is not unlike that of the famed "Cofre di Perotè" of Mexico.

The sloping sides of the mountain are densely wooded, especially that fronting the estate of Mount Welcome, to which is presented a broad frowning *facade*, thickly clothed with a forest that appears primeval.

Alone at its top is the mountain tree-less. There it is bare and bald as the crown of a Franciscan friar ; but only the square coffer-like summit, which, being a mass of solid rock, repels the approach of the vegetable giants that crowd closely around its base, some of them stretching out their huge arms as if to strangle or embrace it. One only has succeeded in scaling its steep rampart-like wall. A noble palm—the *areca* —has accomplished this feat, and stands conspicuously upon the table top, its plumed leaves waving haughtily aloft, like a triumphant banner over some conquered castle.

The rock itself presents a singular appearance. Its seamed and scarred surface is mottled with a dark glaze, which during the sunlight, and even under the mellower beams of the moon, gives forth a corruscation, as if the light were reflected from scale armour.

To the denizens of the valley below it is known as the *Jumbe Rock*—a name characteristic of the superstitious ideas attached to it—since "Jumbé" is the Coromantee appellation for his Satanic majesty. Though constantly before their eyes, and accessible by an hour's climbing up the forest path, there is not a negro on the estate of Mount Welcome, nor on any other for miles around, that would venture alone to visit the Jumbe rock ; and to most, if not all of them, the top of this mountain is as much of a *terra incognita* as the summit of Chimborazo.

This terror of the Jumbé rock does not altogether owe its origin to a mere superstition, but has been partly inspired by the rémembrance of a horrid history: for the rock has been the scene of an execution, which for cruel and cold-blooded barbarity rather deserves to be called a crime.

That table-summit, like the blood stained temples of the Moctezumas has been used as an altar upon which a human sacrifice has been offered up. Not in times long past, neither by the sanguinary priesthood of Azteca, but by men of white skin and European race, cruel and ferocious as they. A black victim has there breathed his last. If that lone palm could speak, it might tell a wild tale of woe, as testified by the bones that lie scattered around its root—the chief sustenance of its vigorous verdure! The tree is silent; but for all that the story has been told: no legend either, but a veritable history; and one of such an atrocious character as needs to stand in a chapter by itself.

CHAPTER II.

THE MYAL-MAN.

In Jamaica, a few years previous to the period when our tale opens, there was much agitation on the subject of " obeah-ism."

The practise of this horrid art had become appallingly common—so common that upon almost every extensive estate in the island there was a " professor," of it, in other words, an " obeah-man." " Professor," though often used in speaking of these charlatans, is not a correct title. To have *professed* it—at least in the hearing of the whites—would have been attended with peril; since it was punishable by the death penalty. Practitioner is a more appropriate appellation.

These mysterious doctors were almost always men—very rarely women—and usually natives of Africa. Universally were they persons of advanced age and hideous aspect; the uglier the more successful in the pursuit of their criminal calling. There was a class of them distinguished as " myal-men," whose chief distinction consisted in their being able to restore life to a dead body. Such was the belief of their ignorant fellow slaves, who little suspected that the defunct subject had been only dormant, not dead: his death-like slumber having been secretly brought about by the myal-man himself, assisted by a prescription of the branched " calalue"—a species of *caladium.*

I cannot here enter into an explanation of the mysteries of Obi, which are simple enough *when understood.* I have met it in every land where it has been my lot to travel; and although it holds a more conspicuous position in the social life of a savage, it is also found in the bye-lanes of civilisation.

The reader, who may have been mystified about its meaning, will perhaps understand what it is, when I tell him that the *obeah-man* of the West Indies is simply the counterpart of the " medicine man" of the North American Indians, the " piuche" of the South, the " rain maker" of the Cape, the " fetish man" of the Guinea coast, and known by as many other titles as there are tribes of uncivilised men

It is the first dawning of religion on the soul of the savage ; but even when its malignant spirit has become changed to a purer aspiration after eternal life, it still lingers amidst the haunts of ignorance, its original form almost unaltered—*witchcraft.*

To the statement before made—that on every large plantation there was an obeah-man—the estate of Mount Welcome was no exception. It, too, was blessed, or rather cursed, by a follower of the art, an old Coromantee negro—Chakra by name—a man whose fell and ferocious aspect could not have failed to make him one of the most popular of its practi-tioners ; and such, to his misfortune, had he become.

He had long been suspected of having poisoned the former owner of the estate, who had made an abrupt and mysterious exit from the world His fate, however, was not much lamented, as he bore the reputation of being a cruel slave-master. The present proprietor had least reason to regret it : since it gave him possession of an estate he had long coveted. It was more chagrin to him, that since entering upon the enjoyment of the property, several of his most valuable slaves had terminated their existence suddenly, and in a manner which could only be accounted for by the supposition that Obi had had a finger in their fate.

Chakra, the myal-man, was suspected of causing their deaths, arraigned and brought to trial.

The judges were three—three justices of the neighbourhood—for that number was sufficient to pass the death-sentence upon a slave. The president of the court was the man's own master, Loftus Vaughan, Esq., proprietor of Mount Welcome, and *custos rotulorum* of the precinct.

The substance of the crime charged against Chakra was "practising the arts of Obi." The charge had no reference to the death of the former master of Mount Welcome ; but to those of the slaves that had occurred more recently upon the estate, as also upon the plantations of the other two justices who officiated at the trial.

The proofs were not very clear ; but were deemed sufficiently so by the court to warrant a conviction.

Strange to say that of the three justices, the man's own master—the president of the court—appeared the most anxious to bring the trial to this termination. So anxious indeed, that he used every effort to over-rule the opinions of the other two ; his superior position giving him a certain power of controling the decision. One of them had actually pro-nounced himself in favour of an acquital ; but after a whispering con-sultation with the custos, he suddenly retracted his former opinion, and gave his vote for the verdict.

There was a rumor at the time, that Loftus Vaughan, in this trial, was actuated by meaner motives, than either a stern love of justice, or the desire to put down the practise of Obi. There was a whisper abroad of some secrets—family secrets with which the Coromantee had become acquainted—some strange transaction, of which he was the sole living witness ; and of such a character, that even the testimony of a negro would have been an inconvenience ; and it was suspected that this and not obeah-ism was the crime for which Chakra had to answer with his life. The rumour, as is too often the case, may have been a scandal—a slander. Whether or not, the Coromantee was condemned to die. The trial was not more irregular than the mode of execution, decreed for the wretched criminal. He was to be taken to the top of the Jumbé rock, chained to the palm tree, and there left to perish ! It may be asked why this singular mode of execution was selected ? Why was he not hung upon the scaffold, or burnt at the stake—a custom not unusual demned criminals of his class?

The answer is easy. As already stated, at this particular period much unpleasant feeling prevailed on the subject of obeah-ism. In al- most every district mysterious deaths had occurred, and were occurring —not only of black slaves, but of white masters, and even mistresses— all attributed to the baneful influence of Obi.

The African demon was ubiquitous, but invisible. Everywhere could be witnessed his skeleton hand upon the wall, but nowhere himself. It had become necessary to make a conspicuous example of his worship- pers. The voice of all planterdom called for it; and the myal-man, Chakra, was selected for that example, in the belief that his fearful fate would terrify the votaries of the vile superstition to their very hearts' core.

The Jumbé rock suggested itself as the most appropriate place for the execution of the Coromantee. The terrors with which the place was al ready invested—added to those now to be inspired by the fearful form of punishment of which it was to be the scene—must exert a beneficial effect on the superstitious understandings of the slaves, and for ever de- stroy their belief in Obeah and Obboney. With this design was the myal-man escorted up to the summit of the Jumbé rock; and like a mod- ern Prometheus, chained there. No guards were placed over him—none were required to stay near the spot. His chains, and the terror inspired by the act, were deemed sufficient to prevent any interference with his fate. In a few days, thirst and hunger, aided by the vultures, would perform the final and fatal ceremony—as surely as the rope of the hang- man, or the axe of the executioner.

It was long before Loftus Vaughan ascended the mountain to ascertain the fate of the unfortunate negro, his *ci-devant* slave. When, stimulated by curiosity—and, perhaps, a motive still stronger—he at length, accom- panied by his overseer, climbed to the top of the Jumbé rock, his hopes and expectations were alike confirmed. A skeleton, picked clean by the John crows, hung suspended to the stem of the tree !

A rusty chain, turned around the bones, kept the skeleton in place ; though the fore-arms had become disconnected at the elbow joints, and would have fallen but for the support thus afforded.

Loftus Vaughan had no inclination to dwell long upon the spot. To him the sight was fearful. One glance, and he hurried away; but far more fearful—far more terrifying—was that which he saw, or fancied he saw, in passing homeward down the forest path—either the ghost of the mya.-man, or the man himself !

CHAPTER III.

LOFTUS VAUGHAN, ESQUIRE.

LOFTUS VAUGHAN was a widower, as generally supposed, with but one child—a daughter. Kate was the name of this young lady, at least, it was the name she bore among her friends and acquaintances. Another name might occasionally be heard—" lily Quasheba." This only on the

lips of some of the older negroes of the estate, and never in the presence
of Mr. Vaughan—who had sternly forbidden it to be pronounced.

There were doubts of the young girl having ever received either of
these names at the baptismal font: partly arising from the circumstance
that none of Mr. Vaughan's friends had witnessed the ceremony, and
partly from a general knowledge of the fact, that the mother of Mr.
Vaughan's daughter had been a *slave*—the slave Quasheba.

Hence originated the *alias*—hence the doubts as to the performance
of the baptismal rites, and hence, too, other doubts of Mr. Vaughan's
being—according to the ordinary acceptation of the term—a *widower*.

It was certain, nevertheless, that the slave Quasheba was dead—dead
long ago. She died on that same day just eighteen years ago, when the
" lily Quasheba" first saw the light. This was a circumstance known to
everybody on the estate old enough to have remembered it.

It was not known to every body—though one knew it—that, previous
to the appearance of " lily Quasheba," in fact previous to Mr. Vaughan's
coming into possession of Mount Welcome and its human chattels—there
had been a " lily Cubina " from the same mother; a boy, notwithstanding
the *feminal* orthography of the name. It was known to the same individual that this child was darker than its mother, the quadroon Quasheba.

There was nothing strange in this last circumstance. The presump-
tion is, that its father was either himself a quadroon or a mulatto. In
the former case the child would be, according to the nice distinction of
race observed in Spanish America—a quadroon of the kind called *tente
en el aire* (suspended in the air); by the latter supposition it would be a
" Sambo"—*salto atras*—that is, instead of being white by its paternity,
it would exhibit a retrogression towards the negro.

Whether the father of this child was mulatto or quadroon, or whether
its complexion was darker than that of the mother, was only known to
one individual upon the plantation of Mount Welcome—and that one
was not Mr. Vaughan himself. It was several years after its birth, that
this gentleman became proprietor of the estate, and owner of the slave
Quasheba.

Equally ignorant was he, that the beautiful quadroon—who had won
his heart, become sole mistress of his affections, and, afterwards, mother
of his child—had ever erred in this fashion—had ever been pressed in
the arms of another, and that other a mulatto—like herself, a slave.
When Mr. Vaughan became lord and master of the slave Quasheba, there
was no evidence of this damning fact—no " lily Cubina " to call her
mother—for the boy, almost upon the instant of his birth, had mysteriously disappeared.

Well would it have been for Mr. Vaughan had he remained in happy
ignorance of these hideous truths. Better for Chakra had he kept them
to himself: for it was the myal-man who knew.

The crime of the quadroon mother—even her double error—must be
looked upon with a lenient eye. It was not just to judge her by the
standard of other lands and other times, and pronounce her too flippant-
ly one of the fallen. She only followed the fashion—the universal
fashion—of the time and of the place; and that was often proved too
powerful for the most virtuous principle. If there was guilt in her con-

duct surely it is the white man who deserves reprehension, since he it is who established the custom by which she fell.

As to the history of Mr. Vaughan himself, it differed but little from that of hundreds who have made Jamaica their home ; nor was the amount of his criminality in this connection greater than might be charged against most of his fellow-planters of the time. Originally only a needy adventurer—the son of an English provincial shopkeeper—he nad come out to Jamaica in the capacity of " book-keeper ;" in other words, he had been brought out by an old friend of his father, not to keep books, but merely to form one of that curious staff of idle " dummies " to be seen on every extensive estate, and whose presence there is explained by an insular law—which compels the planter to have a resident white man for every fifty slaves upon his domain.

The shopkeeper's son, however, did not long remain a book-keeper. Being of an active and aspiring turn, he soon rose to the rank of *over-seer*, and at the death of his patron was appointed " attorney" of the estate—a Jamaica phrase of no *legal* signification, but meaning simply manager, or agent. The natural desire of a Jamaica attorney, like that of his litigious homonyme,. is to accumulate riches—usually by the easiest and most unscrupulous method. To this rule the *ci-devant* book-keeper did not prove an exception ; and, after a few years spent in the management of his deceased patron's estate, he became wealthy enough to purchase a plantation for himself—a splendid one, too—Mount Welcome. Notwithstanding the rapidity with which his fortune had been made, he had preserved his reputation from the charge of any considerable embezzlement. Nothing was alleged against him farther than the legitimate *six per cent.*, and such other trifling *peculia* as are considered. only fair game among Jamaica attorneys. Indeed, one of those who does not, in a few years, swallow up the total property of his employer—especially where that employer chances to be a trustee, and the trust held for a *minor*—is a *rara avis* in the island, and esteemed a remarkably honest man.

Such a man was Loftus Vaughan ; and not only had he given satisfaction in the management of his former patron's estate, but the minor, for whom he had managed it, and who was now of age, had implored him to continue his stewardship.

As for Mr. Vaughan, he no longer stood in need of patronage. Mount Welcome, unencumbered, was his own property ; and this was one of the finest estates in the island, quite equal to that of which he still continued the management.

Mr. Vaughan had risen in rank in proportion as he had prospered in riches. First a vestry-man of the parish, afterwards a justice of the peace, he was, at the period when our story commences—and had been sometime before—chief-magistrate of the district, with the title, " Custos rotulorum." Surely, this was dignity sufficient for the son of a provincial shopkeeper !

The domestic relations of Mr. Vaughan had been of a less respectable character ; at least, they would appear so to the mind of an European. But, in those days, the social circle of Jamaica was superlatively tolerant ; and but little, if indeed any, account was made of such a relationship as that which existed between him and the slave-quadroon. So long as the quadroon had been regarded in the light of a *temporary* wife, there was not the slightest scandal. On the other hand, had Mr. Vaughan rendered the connection permanent, by a marriage—which elsewhere might have been to his credit—he would have been at once *tabooed*, and rigorously excluded from society.

Indeed, at one time, he came near being the victim of such a social exclusion: a report having got abroad that he had privately married his slave !

It was not true in fact; but, to do him justice it was so in intention, both to have married and manumitted her.

This laudable design he had procrastinated from time to time—until death stepped in, and placed the act beyond his power.

Then, more than ever, did he feel regret for his negligence—more than regret—remorse.

Moreover, this negligence had left his offspring illegitimate ; in Jamaica, at that time, a phrase of peculiar significance, and far more comprehensive than elsewhere.

Had the mother been white, it would have signified less. The daughter would still have been illegitimate ; but she could have inherited her father's property by *testamentary disposition*. Not so the "lilly Quasheba." No will that her father could devise would make Kate Vaughan the heiress of his estate ! She was a *mustee* (*quinteroon* sometimes called), and therefore still one remove from being free of the negro disabilities. The cruel statute of 1762 applied to her case. Beyond £2,000 currency she could not inherit *even by will*. All the rest of her father's property must go to the heir-at-law—the nearest of his own kin.

Loving his daughter as he did, and determined on making her his heiress, this would have been a terrible dilemma, had there been no way of escaping from it. Fortunately there was, and Mr. Vaughan well knew it. The same assembly that had passed the flagitious statute had also provided a means by which, in certain exceptional cases, it could be avoided : that is, a man of great wealth and influence might be favoured by a *special act*.

As Loftus Vaughan was just such a man, he of course knew he could procure the act at any time, and fully intended doing so; but the same spirit of procrastination that had withheld him from performing his duty toward the mother, was again the cause of his neglecting that which he owed to the child—her child and his. To procure the special statute would require him to make a journey to the capital—perhaps a lengthened sojourn there—the solicitation of assembly men, and much worry and expense. The prospect of all these troubles caused him from time to time to delay the execution of his project ; and, although he had never for a moment entertained a thought of abandoning it, still did it remain unperformed.

In this condition were his family affairs at the period our narrative commences. "Lilly Quasheba," though gifted with every natural charm, educated, accomplished, and refined—in short a lady—was still the daughter of a slave !

CHAPTER IV

A JAMAICA DEJEUNER.

On a tranquil morning in the fair month of May—fair in Jamaica, as elsewhere on the earth—a large bell ringing in the great hall of Mount Welcome announced the hour of breakfast. As yet there were no guests
around the table, nor in the hall—only the black and coloured domestics,
who, to the number of half a dozen, had just come up from the kitchen
with trays and dishes containing the viands that composed the meal.

With one exception, these servants—all boys or young men—were
habited in the scantest costumes—coarse osnaburg trousers, and striped
cotton shirts, being all they wore. The exception to this rule was a burly
and pompous black man, with trim shining whiskers, who, in authoritative
voice and gesture, directed the movements of the others. The full suit
of livery which he wore betokened him the butler of the establishment
—who, like all others of his elevated rank, insisted upon prompt obedience from his subordinates.

Though but two chairs were placed by the table—and the disposition
of the plates, knives, and forks indicated that it had been set for only
that number of guests—the profusion of dishes, thickly covering the
snow-white damask cloth, might have led one to suppose that a large
party was expected.

It was emphatically a *dejeuner a la fourchette*. There were cutlets
plain, and with *sauce piquante, cavished* fish, *entrees* of devilled fowl and
duck, broiled salmon, and the like. These were placed around the table,
while a cold ham on one dish, and a tongue ditto on another, occupied
the centre. Of "bread kind," there were mealy yams—some mashed
with milk and butter, and dished up in shapes—roast plantains, hot rolls,
toast, cassada cakes, and sweet potatoes. But that a splendid silver tea
service, and a large glittering urn were conspicuous on the table, the
spread might have been mistaken for a dinner, rather than the matutinal
meal. The hour—nine o'clock A. M.—also precluded the idea of its being
dinner. Whoever were to be the guests at this table, it was intended
they should fare sumptuously. So did they every day of their lives ; for
there was nothing occasional in that morning's meal. Both the style and
the profuseness were of diurnal occurrence. Soon after the tones of the
bell had ceased to vibrate through the hall, they for whom the summons
was intended, made their appearance—entering from opposite sides, not
together, but one coming in a little after the other.

The first was a gentleman of somewhat over middle age and height, of
a hale complexion, and full, portly form.

He was dressed in a suit of nankeens, jacket and trousers, both of
ample make, the former open in front, and displaying a shirt bosom of
finest white linen, the broad plaits of which were uncovered by any vest.
A wide turn-down collar was folded back, exhibiting a full development
of throat—which, with the broad jaws of ruddy hue, appeared clean and
freshly shaven.

From a fob in the waistband of his trousers hung a massive gold chain,
with a bunch of seals and watch keys at one end ; while at the other

was an immense chronometer watch of the old-fashioned "guinea gold," with white dial, upon which the black figures were conspicuously painted. The watch itself could be seen; as, on entering, the wearer had drawn it out of its fob with a view of ascertaining whether his servants were punctual to the minute: for the gentleman in question—who was no other than Loftus Vaughan, Esq.—was a very martinet in such matters.

After casting a scrutinising glance at the display of viands, and apparently satisfied with what he saw, the master of Mount Welcome seated himself before the table, his face beaming with a smile of pleasant anticipation.

He had scarce taken his seat when a fair apparition appeared entering from the further end of the hall—a young virgin-like creature, looking as fresh and rosy as the first rays of the Aurora.

She was habited in a dress, or rather an undress, of purest white ; a morning wrapper of fine lawn, that, fitting closely behind, displayed the waving *contour* of her back. In front, however, the dress fell in loose folds, scarce, however, concealing the full, bold outline of her bosom ; and thence draped gracefully downward, so as to leave nothing visible but the tips of a pair of tiny satin slippers, alternately showing themselves like white mice, as she glided over the polished surface of the floor.

Her throat, full and finely rounded, was encircled with a string of amber beads ; and a crimson blossom—the beautiful flower of the Quamoclit—glittered amidst the ample folds of her hair. This, of a rich chestnut colour, was parted on the forehead, and carried in a curving sweep over cheeks that rivalled the radiance of the rose.

It would have required an experienced eye, one well acquainted with the physiological characteristics of race, to have told that that young girl was not of the purest Caucasian blood. And yet the slight undulation of the hair ; a rotund rather than an oval face ; eyes of darkest umber, with a light gleaming perpetually in the pupils—a singular picture-like expression in the colouring of the cheeks—were all characteristics, that proclaimed the presence of the *sang melée*.

Slight indeed was the *taint*, and it seems like profanation to employ the phrase, when speaking of a creature so beautifully fair—for beautifully fair was the daughter of Loftus Vaughan.

This, then, was the "lilly Quasheba," the child of the erring and ill-starred quadroon. "Little" was no longer an appropriate word for one just stepping over the threshold of womanhood, and whose large, finely-developed form created in the mind of the beholder an impression of the majestic rather than the diminutive.

On entering the hall, the young girl did not proceed directly to seat herself ; but, gliding behind the chair occupied by her father, she flung her arms around his neck, and imprinted a kiss upon his forehead. It was her usual matutinal salute ; and proved that on that morning they had met for the first time. Not that it was the first appearance of either: for both had been much earlier abroad—up with the sun, indeed, as is the universal custom in Jamaica. Mr. Vaughan had entered the hall from the front door, and the Leghorn hat and cane carried in his hand, told that he had been out for a walk—perhaps to inspect the labour going on at the " works," or ascertain the progress made in his extensive cane-fields. Kate, on the contrary, might have been seen entering the house some half-hour before, in riding costume—hat, habit, and whip—proving that her morning exercise had been taken on horseback. After saluting her father as described, the young lady took her seat in front of the great urn, and commenced performing the duties of the table.

In this she was assisted by a girl apparently of her own age, but of far different appearance. Her waiting-maid it was, who, having entered at the same time, had taken her station behind the chair of her mistress.

There was something strikingly peculiar in the aspect of this young girl—as well in her figure as in the colour of her skin. She was of that slender classic shape which we find in antique sculptures, like the forms of the Hindoo women known in England as " ayahs" and differing altogether from the negro outline. Her complexion, too, was not that of a negress—still less of a mulatto or quadroon. It was an admixture of black and red, resulting in a clear chestnut or mahogany colour, which, with the damask tincture upon the cheeks, produced an impression not unpleasing.

Nor were the features at all of a negro type. On the contrary, far removed from it. The lips were thin, the face oval, and the nose of an aquiline cast, such as may be traced on Egyptian sculptured stones, or such as might yet be seen in living forms in the land of the Arabs. Her hair was not woolly, though it differed altogether from the hair of a European. It was straight, and jet black, yet scarcely reaching to her shoulders. Not that it had been shortened by the scissors, for it appeared to be at its fullest growth, and, hanging loosely over her ears, it imparted a youthful appearance to the brown-skinned damsel.

She was far from ill-looking; and, to an eye accustomed to her " style," she may have appeared even handsome. Her elegant shape, exposed by the extreme scantiness of her costume, a sleeveless robe, with a Madras kerchief worn à la toque upon her head; the graceful attitude, which seemed natural to her either when in motion or standing poised behind the chair of her mistress; the quick glance of her fine, fiery eye; and the pearl-like whiteness of her teeth, all contributed to make up a picture that was far from common-place.

This young girl was a slave —the slave Yola.

CHAPTER V.

TWO LETTERS.

INSTEAD of being in the middle of the floor, the breakfast table had been placed a little to one side of the entrance door, that, with the jalousies thrown open, the fresh air might be more freely felt, while at the same time a view could be obtained of the landscape outside. A splendid view it was, comprising the valley from end to end, with its long palm-shaded avenue, a reach of the Montego river, the roofs and spires of the town, the shipping in the bay and roadside, the bay itself, and the blue Caribbean beyond.

Striking as was this landscape, Mr. Vaughan just then felt no inclination to look upon it. He was too busy occupied with the rich viands upon the table ; and when he did find time to glance over the window-sill, his glance extended no further than to the negro "gang" at work among the canes, to see if his drivers were doing their duty.

The eyes of Miss Vaughan were oftner directed to the outside view. It was at this hour that one of Mr. Vaughan's servants usually returned from Montego Bay, bringing the letters from the post-office. There was nothing in her manner that betrayed any inward anxiety, but simply that lively interest which young ladies in all countries feel when expecting the postman—hoping for one of those little letters of twelve sheets with closely written and crossed lines most difficult to decipher, and yet to them more interesting than even the pages of the newest novel.

The landscape without appeared to possess more interest for the girl Yola, or rather was it the water that lay beyond. Now and then, when her attendance was not required at the table, her eyes wandered to the distant sea with a strange dreamy expression, as if her thoughts were carried away over the wide expanse to the far land of her nativity—that African home from which she had been forced into captivity, and sold as a slave.

Whatever impatience Miss Vaughan may have felt for the arrival of the post, it was soon to be appeased.

Only a few minutes after the ringing of the breakfast bell, a dark object in the avenue proclaimed the approach of Quashie, the post-boy ; and shortly after, an imp-like negro lad upon the back of a rough pony galloped up to the front entrance ; and flinging his bag to the butler, who had met him at the bottom of the stair, turned off towards the stables. If the fair Kate expected a billet, she was doomed to disappointment. There were only two letters in the bag, with a newspaper, and all three were for Mr. Vaughan himself. All bore the English post-mark ; and the superscription of one of the letters was by him at once recognised—a pleasant smile stealing over his features as he broke open the seal. A few moments sufficed to make him master of its contents, when the smile increased to a look of vivid gratification ; and, rising from his chair, he paced for sometime back and forward, snapping his fingers, and ejaculating, " Good—good ! I thought so !"

His daughter regarded this behaviour with surprise. Gravity was her father's habit, at times amounting to austerity. Such an exhibition of gaiety was rare with Loftus Vaughan.

" Some pleasing news, papa ?"

" Yes, you little rogue ; very."

" May I not hear it ?"

" Yes—no—no—not yet awhile."

" Oh, papa ! It is very cruel of you to keep it from me. I promise I shall share your joy."

" Ah ! you will when you hear the news—that is, if you're not a little simpleton, Kate."

" I a simpleton, papa ? I shall not be called so if to be joyful is all that's needed to spare me the reproach."

"Why, you'd be a simpleton if you don't be joyful—never mind, child—
I'll tell you all about it by-and-by. Good, good!" continued he, still
cracking his fingers in a sort of ecstatic frenzy. "I thought so—I knew
he would come."

"Ah! you expect some one, papa?"

"I do. Guess who it is!"

"How could I? You know I am unacquainted with your English
friends, and I see the letter bears an English post-mark."

"Not with their names? You have heard their names, and seen letters
from some of them?"

"Oh, yes, I often hear you speak of one—Mr. Smythje—a very odd
name it is. I would'nt be called Smythje for the world."

"Ta, ta, child! Smythje is a very pretty name, especially with Montagu before it. Montagu is magnificent. Besides, Mr. Smythje is the
owner of Montagu Castle."

"Oh, papa! how can that make the name sound any better? Is it he
whom you expect?"

"Yes, dear. He writes to say that he will come by the next ship—the
Sea Nymph she is called. She was to sail a week after the letter was
written, so that we may look out for his arrival in a few days. Gad! I
must prepare for him. You know Montagu Castle is out of repair. He
is to be my guest; and, hark you, Kate!" continued the planter, once
more seating himself at the table, and bending towards his daughter, so
that his *sotto voce* might not be overheard by the domestics, "you must
do your best to entertain this young stranger. He is said to be an accomplished gentleman, and I know he is a rich one. It is to my interest
to be friendly with him," added Mr. Vaughan, in a still lower tone of
voice, and as if in soliloquy, but loud enough for his daughter to hear
what he said.

"Dear papa!" was the reply, "how could I be otherwise than polite to
him? If only for your sake——"

"If only for *your own*," said the father, interrupting her, and accompanying the remark with a sly look and laugh. "But, dear Kate, continued he, "we shall find time to talk of this again. I must read the
other letter. Who on earth can it be from? Egad! I never saw the
writing before."

The announcement of the projected visit of Mr. Montagu Smythje
with the trumpet-like flourish of his many accomplishments—which
Kate Vaughan had not now listened to for the first time—appeared to
produce in the heart of the young quinteroon no very vivid emotions of
pleasure—at least, there was no evidence that it did so. She had received it with perfect indifference, not seeming to care much one way or
the other. If there was a balance, it was rather against him: for it so
chanced that much of what she had heard in relation to this gentleman
was not at all calculated to prepossess her in his favour. And she had
heard a good deal about him, both from her father and her father's acquaintances: for the lord of Montagu Castle was often the topic of
after-dinner talk.

In Jamaica, Mr. Montagu Smythje was only known by repute: for
during all the years of his minority—even from infancy - he had been a

resident of London. He was, in truth, a "cockney," not only by breed‐
ing, but by birth—for he was not the son of the deceased proprietor of
Montagu Castle, but only his nephew and heir.

We have said that Kate Vaughan had heard nothing of this young man
to create within her an interest in her favour, but rather the reverse.
She had heard that he was an exquisite—a fop in fact—perhaps of all
other characters the one most repulsive to a young creole : for, notwith‐
standing the natural disposition of these to become enamoured of fine
personal appearance, it must be accompanied by certain qualities of mind
if not of the highest morality, or even intellectuality, yet differing alto‐
gether from the frivolous accomplishments of mere dandeyism.

Nature, that inspires the creole girl to give her *whole heart away, and
without any reserve,* has also taught her to bestow it with judgment. In‐
stinct warns her not to lay her precious offering upon an altar unworthy
of the sacrifice.

There was another circumstance calculated to beget within the heart
of Kate Vaughan a certain feeling of repulsion towards the lord of
Montagu Castle ; and that was the conduct of her own father in regard
to this matter. From time to time—when speaking of Mr. Montagu
Smythje—he had made use of certain expressions and inuendoes, which,
though uttered in ambiguous language, the young girl very easily com‐
prehended.

The heart of woman is quick, as it is subtile, in the understanding of
all that relates to the disposal of itself ; and that even at the earliest age
of maidenhood. It is prone to repel any effort that may be made to
guide it from its natural inclinations, and rob it of its right to choose.

Mr. Vaughan, in his ignorance of these rather recondite truths, was
erecting a barrier to his own designs, all the while he fancied he was
successfully clearing the track of presumptive obstructions, and making
the path smooth and easy.

At match-making Mr. Vaughan was but a bungler : for it was evident
that match-making was in his mind.

"Never saw the handwriting before," said he, in repetition, as he broke
open the seal of the second letter.

If the contents of the first epistle had filled him with joy, those of the
second produced an effect directly the opposite.

"'Sdeath !" exclaimed he, crushing the letter, as he finished reading it,
and once more nervously springing to his feet. "Dead or living, that ill‐
starred brother of mine seems as if born to be a curse to me ! While
alive, always wanting money ; and now that he is dead sending his son, a
never-do-well, like himself, to trouble, and, perhaps, disgrace me."

"Dear father !" said the young girl, startled more by his wild demeanor
than what he was saying—for the words were muttered in a low voice,
and rather in soliloquy—"has the other letter brought unpleasant news ?"

"Ah ! that it has. You may read for yourself."

And once more seating himself, he tossed the unwelcome epistle across
the table, and re-commenced eating with apparent voracity—as if by this
means to tranquillise his perturbed spirit.

Kate took up the rejected letter, and smoothing out the crumples ran
her eyes over the contents

The perusal did not require much time : for, considering that the letter
had made such a long journey, its contents were of the shortest :

DEAR UNCLE,   *London, June* 10, 18—,
    I have to announce to you the melancholy intelligence that your brother,
my dear father, is no more. His last words were, that I should go over to
you ; and, acting in accordance with his wish, I have taken passage for
Jamaica. The ship is the Sea Nymph, and is to sail upon the 18th instant,
I do not know how long we shall be at sea, but I hope it will prove a short
voyage : as my poor father's effects were all taken by the sheriff's officer, and
I am compelled, for want of money, to take passage in the *steerage*, which I
have been told is anything but a luxurious mode of travelling.   But I am
young and strong, and no doubt shall be able to endure it. Yours affectionately,   HERBERT VAUGHAN.

CHAPTER VI.

POOR FELLOW.

WHATEVER effect the reading of the letter may have had upon Kate
Vaughan, it certainly did not produce indignation. On the contrary, an
expression of sympathy stole over her face as she mastered the contents
of the epistle ; and on finishing it, the phrase " poor fellow !" dropped as
if involuntarily, and just audibly, from her lips. Not that she knew anything of Herbert Vaughan, more than the name, and that he was her
cousin ; but the word *cousin* has an attractive sound, especially in the ears
of young people, equalling in interest—at times even surpassing—that of
sister or brother. Beyond doubt, the affection felt for a blood relation is
an instinct of our nature ; and though it may at times be outraged, and become an antipathy—where avarice, or some other passion, gains predomi-
nance—the antipathy is the exception, and not the rule.
    In the case of Loftus Vaughan, worldly ambition, combined with ava-
rice, had usurped the dominion of his heart, and destroyed every vestige
of fraternal affection. Under the influence of these baneful passions, he
had long since ceased to care for his kin ; and even the paltry sums which
from time to time, he had transmitted to his less fortunate brother,
had been wrung from him by repeated and earnest solicitation, and given
with grudging reluctance.
    There were no such passions in the heart of his daughter to misguide
its instincts, and mislead them out of their true channel ; and though she
could know very little of the nature of the relationship, the word
" cousin" had awakened within her those natural instincts of endearment
which it usually calls forth. Herbert Vaughan was the only one who
stood to her in this relationship ; and indeed with the exception of this
young man and her own father—now that that father's brother
was dead —she knew of no other relative she had upon earth. Neither her mother, nor her mother's kindred, had ever been known to
her. She had neither brother nor sister ; and Herbert Vaughan was not

only her cousin, but her only cousin. This state of comparative orphanage, may have strengthened the instinctive tie which nature prompted her to feel. There was another circumstance calculated to exert a similar influence. Though surrounded by every luxury, and waited on by troops of slaves, still there was a want; and one which she could not otherwise than be sensible of.

Her father's friends were all *dining* friends, and all of the opposite sex. Their wives, sisters, and daughters were rarely ever seen at Mount Welcome : and when by chance they did present themselves, their behaviour proclaimed that they were there as the friends of Mr. Vaughan rather than of his daughter. Between them and Miss Vaughan there was a certain restraint—a coldness of demeanour on their part—which, although not observable to one unacquainted with Jamaican " society," nevertheless existed.

The young girl knew it herself—though ignorant of the cause, and in her innocent simplicity not caring to inquire into it. Happily she had never been told of the *taint* in her blood, and knew not that there was a stigma attached to the appellation of " lilly Quasheba." So far had kind fortune withheld from her this humiliating knowledge.

Still was she conscious of a certain social isolation—a lack of real friends ; and this, no doubt, contributed to impress her heart as it had also done her features, with a character of self-possession and self-reli ance but little corresponding with her age.

It had also strengthened the ties of tenderness which attached her to her father. And might it not have invested with a certain interest the word *cousin ?*

Whether it did, or whether it was mere childlike compassion for misfortune, certain it is that Kate Vaughan, as she laid aside the letter, was heard to pronounce the phrase, " poor fellow !"

Though uttered, as we have said, in a tone almost inaudible, the words reached the ears of her father.

" Poor fellow !" he repeated, turning sharply to his daughter, and regarding her with a glance of displeasure. " I am surprised, Kate, to hear you speak in that strain of one who has done nothing to deserve your compassion. An idle, good-for-nothing fellow—just as his father was before him. And only to think of it—coming over here a *steerage* passenger, in the very same ship with Mr. Montagu Smythje ! 'Sdeath ! What a disgrace ! Mr. Smythje will be certain to know who he is— though he is not likely to associate with such *canaille.* He cannot fail to notice the fellow, however ; and, when he sees him here, will be sure to remember him. Ah ! I must take some steps to prevent that. Poor fellow, indeed ! Yes, poor enough, but not in that sense. Like his father, I suppose, who fiddled his life away among paint-brushes and palettes instead of following some profitable employment, and all for the sake of being called an artist ! Poor ! fiddlestick ? Bah ! Don't let me hear the words again !"

And as Mr. Vaughan ended his ill-natured harangue, he tore the wrapper off the newspaper, and endeavoured, among its contents, to distract his mind from dwelling longer on the unpleasant theme of the epistle, or him who had written it.

The young girl, abashed and disconcerted by the unusual violence of the rebuke, sat with downcast eyes, and without making any reply. The red colour had deepened upon her cheeks, and mounted to her forehead ; but, notwithstanding the outrage done to her feelings, it was easy to see, that the sympathy she had expressed for her poor but unknown cousin was felt as sensibly as ever.

So far from having stifled or extinguished it, the behaviour' of her ather was more likely to have given it increase and strength : for the adage of the " stolen waters " is still true ; and the forbidden fruit is as tempting now as upon the morning of creation. As it was in the begin ning, so will it ever be.

CHAPTER VII.

THE SLAVER.

A HOT West Indian sun was rap. dly declining towards the Caribbean Sea —as if hastening to-cool his fiery orb in the blue water—when a ship, rounding Pedro Point, in the island of Jamaica, stood eastward for Montego Bay. She was a three-masted vessel—a barque—as could be told by the lateen rig of her mizenmast—and apparently of some three or four hundred tons burden. As she was running under one of the gentlest of breezes, all her canvas was spread ; and the weather-worn appearance of her sails denoted that she was making land at the termination of a long ocean voyage. This was further manifest by the faded paint upon her sides, and the dark, dirt-coloured blotches that marked the position of her hawse-holes and scuppers.

Besides the private ensign that streamed, pennon-like, from her peak, another trailed over her taffrail ; which, unfolded by the motion of the vessel, displayed a blue starry field with white and crimson stripes. In this case the flag was appropriate, both in its stripes and their colour. Though proudly vaunted as the flag of the free, here was it covering a cargo of slaves : the ship was a *slaver*.

After getting fairly inside the bay, but still at a long distance from the town, she was observed suddenly to tack ; and, instead of continuing on towards the harbour, made for a point on the southern side, where the shore was uninhabited and solitary.

On arriving within a mile of the land she took in sail, until every inch of canvas was furled upon her yards. Then the sharp rattling of the chain, as it dragged through the iron ring of the hawse-hole, announced the dropping of her anchor. A few moments after the vessel swung round, and, drifting till the chain cable became taut, lay motionless upon the water.

The object for which the slaver had thus anchored short of the harbour will be learnt by our going aboard of her—though this was a privilege not granted to the idle or curious : only the initiated were permitted to witness the spectacle of which her decks now became the theatre : only such as had an interest in the disposal of her cargo.

Viewed from a distance, the slaver lay apparently inert; but for all that a scene of active life was passing upon her deck—a scene of rare and painful interest. The barque carried a cargo of two hundred human beings—"bales," according to the phraseology of the slave-trader. These bales were not exactly alike. It was, as her skipper jocularly styled it, an "assorted cargo"—that is, one shipped on different points of the African coast, and, consequently, embracing many distinct varieties of the Ethiopian race. There was the tawny, but intelligent Mandingo, and by his side the Jolof of ebon hue; there the fierce and warlike Coromantee, alongside the docile and submissive Pawpaw ; the yellow Ebo, with the visage of a baboon, wretched and desponding, face to face with the cannibal Moco, or chained wrist to wrist with the light-hearted native of Congo and Angola.

None, however, appeared of light heart on board the slaver. The horrors of the "middle passage" had equally affected all ; until the dancing Congese, and the Lucumi, prone to suicide, seemed equally to suffer from dejection. The bright picture that now presented itself before their eyes —a landscape gleaming with all the gay colours of tropical vegetation— was viewed by them with very different emotions. Some seemed to regard it with indifference ; others it reminded of their own African homes, from which they had been dragged by rude and ruffian men ; while not a few gazed upon the scene with feelings of keen apprehension—believing it to be the dreaded *Kocmi*, the land of the gigantic cannibals—and that they had been brought thither *to be eaten !*

Reflection might have convinced them that this would scarcely be the intention of *Tobon-doo*—those white tyrants who had carried them across the ocean. The hard, unhusked rice, and coarse maize corn—their only food during the voyage—were not viands likely to fatten them for the feast of Anthropophagi ; and their once smooth and shining skins now exhibited a dry, shrivelled appearance, from the surface coating of dandruff, and the scars of the hideous *cra-cra.*

The blacks among them, by the hardships of that fearful voyage, had turned ashen-grey, and the yellows of a sickly and bilious hue. Males and females—for there were many of the latter—appeared to have been alike the objects of ill-usage, the victims of a starved stomach and a stifled atmosphere.

Some half a dozen of the latter—seen in the precincts of the cabin — presented a different aspect. These were young girls, picked from the common crowd on account of the superiority of their personal charms ; and the flaunting vestments that adorned their bodies—contrasting with the complete nudity of their fellow-voyagers—told too plainly why they had been thus distinguished. A horrid contrast—wantonness in the midst of woe ?

On the quarter-deck stood the slave-skipper—a tall, lathy individual of sallow hue—and, beside him, his mate—a dark-bearded ruffian ; while a score of like stamp, but lower grade, acting under their orders, were distributed in different parts of the ship.

These last, as they tramped to and fro over the deck, might be heard at intervals giving utterance to profane oaths, as often laying violent nands upon one of their unfortunate captives, apparently out of the sheer wantonness of cruelty.

Immediately after the anchor had been dropped, and the ropes belayed and coiled in their places, a new scene of this disgusting drama was entered upon. The living " bales," hitherto restrained below, were now ordered, or rather driven, upon deck—not all at once, but in lots of three or four at a time. Each individual, as he came up the hatchway, was rudely seized by a sailor, who stood by with a soft brush in his hand and a pail at his feet; the latter containing a black composition of gunpowder, lemon-juice, and palm-oil. Of this mixture the unresisting captive received a coating, which, by the hand of another sailor, was rubbed into the skin, and then polished with a " danbybrush," until the sable epidermis glistened like a newly-blacked boot.

A strange operation it might have appeared to those who saw it, had they not been initiated into its object and meaning. But to the spectators there present it was no uncommon sight. It was not the first time those unfeeling men had assisted at the spectacle of a slaver's cargo *being made ready for market !*

One after another were the dark-skinned victims of human cupidity brought from below, and submitted to this demoniac anointment—to which one and all yielded with an appearance of patient resignation, like sheep under the hands of the shearer. In the looks of many of them could be detected the traces of that apprehension felt in the first hours of their captivity, and which had not yet forsaken them. Might not this process be a prelude to some fearful sacrifice ? Even the females were not exempted from this disgusting desecration of God's image ; and one after another were passed through the hands of the operators, with an accompaniment of brutal jests, and peals of ribald laughter !

CHAPTER VIII.

JOWLER AND JESSURON.

Almost on the same intant that the slave-barque had dropped anchor, a small boat shot out from the silent shore ; which, as soon as it had got fairly out into the water, could be seen to be steering in the direction of the newly-anchored vessel.

There were three men in the boat, two of whom were plying the oars. These were both black men—naked, with the exception of dirty white trousers covering their limbs, and coarse palm-leaf hats upon their heads.

The third occupant of the skiff—for such was the character of the boat —was a white, or more properly, a *whitish* man. He was seated in the stern-sheets, with a tiller-rope in each hand ; and steering the craft—as his elbows a-kimbo, and the occasional motion of his arms testified. He bore not the slightest resemblance to the oarsmen, either in the colour of his skin, or the costume that covered it. Indeed, it would not have been easy to have found his counterpart anywhere either on land or at sea.

At the first glance an entire stranger would have pronounced him a *char acter;* and those who knew him more intimately did not hesitate to call him a *queer* character. He appeared to be about sixty years old—he might have been more or less—and had once been white; but long exposure to a West Indian sun, combined with the numerous dirt-filled creases and furrows in his skin, had darkened his complexion to the hue of leaf tobacco. His features, naturally of an angular shape, had become so narrowed and sharpened by age as to leave scarce anything in front; and to get a view of his face it was necessary to step to one side and scan it *en profile.* Thus viewed, there was breadth enough, and features of the most prominent character—including a nose like the claw of a lobster —a sharp, projecting chin—with a deep embayment between, marking the locality of the lips : the outline of all suggesting a great resemblance to the profile of a parrot, but still greater to that of a Jew—for such, in reality, was its type. When the mouth was opened in a smile—a rare occurrence, however—only two teeth could be detected within, standing far apart, like two sentinels guarding the approach to the dark entrance within. This singular countenance was lighted up by a pair of black watery orbs, that glistened like the eyes of an otter ; and eternally glistened, except when their owner was asleep—a condition in which it was said he was rarely or never caught.

The natural blackness of his eyes was rendered deeper by contrast with long white eyebrows running more than half way around them, and meeting over the narrow ridge of the nose. Hair upon the head there was none—that is, none was visible—a skull-cap of whitish cotton-stuff covering the whole crown, and coming down over both ears. Over this was a white beaver hat, whose worn nap and broken edges spoke of long service.

A pair of large green goggles, resting on the humped bridge of his nose, protected his eyes from the sun ; though they might perhaps have been worn for another purpose—to conceal the villanous expression of the eyes that sparkled beneath them.

A sky-blue cloth coat, whitened by long wear, with metal buttons, once bright, now changed to the hue of bronze ; small-clothes of buff kersey-mere glistening with grease, long stockings ; and tarnished top-boots, made up the costume of this unique individual. A large blue cotton umbrella rested across his knees : as both hands were occupied in steering the skiff.

The portrait here given—or, perhaps, it should be styled profile—is that of Jacob Jessuron, the slave-merchant ; an Israelite of the Portuguese breed, but one in whom it would not be truth to say—there was " no guile." The two oarsmen were simply his slaves. The little craft had put out from the shore—from a secluded spot at a distance from the town, but still within view of it. It was evidently rowed at its best speed. Indeed, the steersman appeared to be urging his blacks to the exertion of their utmost strength : as though for some reason he wished to arrive on board at the very earliest moment possible.

Moreover, from time to time, he was seen to twist his body half round and look towards the town—as though he expected or dreaded to see a rival boat coming from that quarter, and was desirous to reach the barque ahead of her.

If such was his design, it proved successful. Although his little skiff was a considerable time in traversing the distance from shore to ship—a distance of at least a mile—he arrived at the point of his destination with-out any other boat making its appearance.

" Sheep ahoy !" shouted he, as the skiff was pulled up under the larboard quarter of the barque.

" Ay, ay !" responded a voice from above.

" Ish that Captain Showler I hearsh ?"

" Hilloo ! who's there ?" interrogated some one on the quarter-deck ; and the moment after, the sallow face of Captain Aminidab Jowler presented itself at the gangway.

" Ah ! Mister Jessuron, that you, eh ? Determined to have fust peep at my blackeys ? Well ! fust kim, fust served ; that's my rule. Glad to see you, old fellow. How d' doo ?"

" Fusht-rate !—fusht-rate ! I hopsh you're the shame yourshelf, Captin Showler. How ish you for cargo ?"

" Fine, old boy ! Got a prime lot this time, All sizes, colours, and *sexes* too ; ha ! ha ! You can pick and choose to suit yourself, I reckon. Come climb aboard, and squint your eye over 'em !"

The slave merchant, thus invited, caught hold of the rope ladder let down for his accommodation ; and, scrambling up the ship's side with the agility of an old ape, stepped upon the deck of the slaver. After some moments spent in hand-shaking and other forms of gratulation—proving that the trader and merchant were old friends, and as thick as two thieves could possibly be—the latter fixed the goggles more firmly on the ridge of his nose, and commenced his inspection of the " cargo."

CHAPTER IX.

THE FOOLAH PRINCE.

ON the quarter-deck of the slaver, and near the "companion,' stood a man of unique appearance—differing, not only from the whites who composed the crew, but also from the blacks and browns who constituted the cargo. His costume, attitude, and some other trivial circumstances, proclaimed him as belonging neither to one nor the other. He had just stepped up from the cabin, and was lingering upon the quarter-deck.

Having the *entrée* of the first, and the privilege of remaining upon the second, he could not be one of the " bales " of this human merchandise ; and yet both costume and complexion forbade the supposition that he was of the slaver's crew. Both denoted an African origin, though his features were not of a marked African type. Rather were they Asiatic, or, more correctly, Arabian ; but, in some respects, differing also from Arab features. In truth, they were more nearly European ; but the complexion again negatived the idea that the individual in question belonged to any of the nationalities of Europe. His hue was that of a light Floren-tine bronze, with a tinge of chestnut.

He appeared to be about eighteen or nineteen years of age ; tall, and well proportioned, and possessed the following characteristics :—A fine arched eyebrow, spanning an eye full and rotund ; a nose slightly aquiline ; thin, well-modelled lips ; white teeth—whiter from contrast with the dark shading on the upper lip—and over all an ample *chevelure* of jet-black hair, slightly curling, but not at all woolly.

In nothing did he differ more from the dark-skinned helots of the hold than in his costume. While none of these had any clothing upon their bodies, or next to none, he, on the contrary, was splendidly apparelled—his face, throat, arms, and limbs, from the knee to the ankle, being the only parts not covered by a garment. A sort of sleeveless tunic of yellow satin, with a skirt that just reached below his knees, was bound around his waist by a scarf of crimson China crape, the ends of which, hanging still lower, were adorned with a fringe work of gold. Over the left shoulder rested loosely another scarf of blue *burnous* cloth, concealing the arm over which it hung ; while half hidden beneath its draping could be perceived a scimitar in its richly-chased scabbard, and with a hilt of carved ivory. A turban on the head, and sandals of Kordofan leather upon the feet, completed his costume.

Notwithstanding the Asiatic character of the dress, and the resemblance of the wearer to those East Indians known as Lascars, he was a true African—though not of that type which we usually associate with the word, and which suggests a certain *negroism* of features. He was one of a people entirely distinct from the negro—the great nation of the Foolahs (Fellattas)—that race of shepherd warriors whose country extends from the confines of Darfur to the shores of the Atlantic—the lords of Sockatoo and Timbuctoo—these fanatic followers of the false prophet who conspired the death of Laing, and murdered Mungo Park upon the Quorra. Of such race was the individual who stood on the quarter-deck of the slaver.

He was not alone. Three or four others were around him, who also differed from the wretched creatures in the hold. But their dress of more common material, as well as other circumstances, told that they were his inferiors in rank—in short, his attendants. The humble mien with which they regarded him, and the watchful attention to his every look and gesture, proclaimed the habitual obedience to which they were accustomed ; while the turbans which they wore, and their mode of salutation—the *salaam*—told of an obeisance Oriental and slavish.

To the richness of this young man's attire was added a certain haughtiness of mien, that proclaimed him a person of rank—perhaps the chieftain of some African tribe.

And such, in reality, he was—a Foolah prince, from the banks of the Senegal.

There, neither his presence or appearance would have attracted more than passing observation ; but here, on the other side of the Atlantic, on board a slave-ship, both required explanation.

It was evident he was not in the same category with his unfortunate countrymen " between decks"—doomed to perpetual captivity. There were no signs that he had been treated as a captive, but the contrary.

How, then, was his presence on board the slave barque to be accounted for ? Was he a passenger ? or in what relationship did he stand to the people that surrounded him ?

Of such a character, though differently worded, were the interrogatories put by the slave merchant, as, returning from the fore-deck, after completing his inspection of the cargo, his eyes for once fell upon the young Fellatta.

" Blesh my shtars, Captain Showler !" cried he, holding up both hands, and looking with astonishment at the turbaned individuals on the quarter-deck. " Blesh my shtars !" he repeated ; " what ish all thish ? S'help my Gott! theesh fellows are not shlaves, are they ?"

" No, Mister Jessuron, no ; they ain't slaves, not all on 'em aint. That 'ore fine fellow, in silk and satin, air a owner o' slaves hisself. That cro's a prince."

" What dosh you say, Captain Showler ? a prince ?"

" Ye aint 'stonished at that, air ye ? 'Taint the fust time I've had an African prince for a passenger. This yeer's his Royal Highness the Prince Cingues, son o' the Grand Sultan of Footatoro. The other fellows you see thar by him are his attendants—courteers as waits on him. That with the yellow turban's ' gold stick ;' him in blue's ' silver stick ;' an' t'other fellow's ' groom o' the chamber,' I s'pose."

" Sultan of Foota-toro !" exclaimed the slave merchant, still holding up the blue umbrella in surprise ; "King of the Cannibal Islandsh ! Aha, a good shoke, Captain Showler ! But, serious, mine friend, what for hash you tricked them out in thish way ? Won't fetch a joey more in the market for all theesh fine feathers."

" Seerus, Mister Jessuron, they're not for the market. I sw'ar to ye the fellur's a real Afrikin prince."

" African fiddleshtick !" echoed the slave merchant, with an incredulous shrug. " Come, worthy captin, what'sh the mashquerade about ?"

" Not a bit of that, ole fellur ! 'Sure ye the nigger's a prince, and my passenger—nothing more or less."

" S'help you Gott ish it so ?"

" So help me that !" emphatically replied the skipper. " It's just as I've told ye, Mister Jessuron."

" Blesh my soul !—a passenger, you shay ?"

" Yes ; and he's paid his passage, too—like a prince, as he is."

" But what's hish business here in Shamaica ?"

" Ah ! that's altogether a kewrious story, Mister Jessuron. You'll hardly guess his bizness, I reckon ?"

" Lesh hear it, friend Showler."

" Well, then, the story air this : 'Bout twelve months ago an army o' Mandingoes attacked the town of old Foota-toro, and, 'mong other plunder, carried off one o' his daughters—own sister to the young fellur you see there. They sold her to a West India trader, who, of course, brought the girl over here to some o' the islands ; which one ain't known. Old Footatoro, like the rest o' 'em, thinks the slaves are all fetched to one place ; and, as he's half besides himself 'bout the loss of this gurl—she war nis favourite, and a sort o' a court belle among 'em—he's sent the brother to search her out, and get her back from whoever hez purchased her on this side. There's the hul story for you."

The expression that had been gathering on the countenance of the Jew, while this relation was being made to him, indicated something more than a common interest in the tale—something beyond mere curiosity—at the same time he seemed as if trying to conceal any outward sign of emotion, by preserving, as much as possible, the rigidity of his features."

" Blesh my soul !" he exclaimed, as the skipper had concluded. " Ash I live, a wonderful sthory ! But how ish he ever to find hish sister ? He might ash well look for a needle in a hay-shtack."

"Wal, that's true enough," replied the slave skipper. "As for that," added he, with an air of stoical indifference; "tain't no business o' mine. My affair was to carry the young fellur acrost the Atlantic, an' I'm willin' to take him back on the same terms, and at the same price, if he kin pay it."

"Did he pay you a goodsh price?" inquired the Jew, with evident anxiety as to the answer.

"He paid like a prince, as I've told you. D'ye see that batch o' yellow Mandingoes by the windlass yonder?"

"Yesh—yesh."

"Forty there air—all told."

"Well?"

"Twenty on 'em I'm to have for fetchin' him across. Cheap enough, ain't it?"

"Dirt cheap, friend Showler. The other twenty?"

"They are his'n. He's brought 'em with him to swop for the sister, when he finds her."

"Ah, yesh! if he finds the girl."

"In coorse, if he finds her."

"Ach!" exclaimed the Jew, with a significant shrug of his shoulders; "that will not be an easy bishness, Captin Showler."

"By Christopher Columbus, old fellow!" said the trader, apparently struck with an idea; "now I think of it, you might give him some help in findin' o' her. I know no man more likely than yourself to be able to pilot him; you know everybody in the island, I reckon. No doubt he will pay you well for your trouble. I'm anxious he should succeed. Old Foota-toro is one of my best sources of supply; and if the girl could be found and taken back, I know he would do the handsome to me on my next trip to the coast."

"Well, worthy captin, I don't know that there's any hope, and won't hold out any to hish royal highnesh, the prince. I'm not as able to get about ash I ushed to was; but I'll do my besht for you. As you shay, I might do something towardsh putting him in the way. Well, we'll talk it over; but let ush first settle our other bishness, or all the world will be aboard. Twenty, you shay, are his?"

"Twenty of them 'ere Mandingoes."

"Hash he anything besides?"

"In cash? no, not a red cent. Men and women are the dollars of his country. He hes the four attendants, you see. They air his slaves like the others."

· "Twenty-four, then, in all. Blesh my soul! What a lucky fellow ish this prince. Maybe I can do something for him; but we can talk it over in the cabin, and I'm ready for something to drink, worthy Showler."

"Ha!" exclaimed he, as, on turning round, he perceived the group of girls before mentioned. "Blesh my soul! Some likely wenches. Just the sort for chambermaids," added he, with a villanously significant look. "How many of that kind hash you got, my good Showler?"

"About a dozen," jocularly responded the skipper; "some splendid breeders among 'em, if you want any for that bizness."

"I may—I may. Gad! it's a valuable cargo—one thing with another! Well, let ush go below," added he, turning towards the companion.

" What's in your locker ?   I musht have a drink before I can do bishness
Likely wenches !   Gad—a valuable cargo !'

Smacking his lips, and snapping his fingers as he talked, the old repro-
bate descended the companion stairway—the captain of the slaver follow
ing close behind him.

We know not, except by implication, the details of the bargaining that
took place below.   The negotiation was a secret one—as became the nature of any transaction between two such characters as a slave-dealer and
slave-stealer.

It resulted, however, in the purchase of the whole cargo, and in so
short a time, that just as the sun sunk into the sea, the gig, cutter, and
long-boat of the slaver were lowered into the water ; and, under the darkness of night, the " bales" were transported to the shore, and landed in
the little cove whence the skiff of the slave merchant had put out.

Amongst them were the twenty Mandingoes, the attendants of the
prince, and the " wenches," designed for improving the breed on Jessuron's
plantation : for the slave merchant was also a land proprietor and planter.

The skiff was seen returning to the shore, a cable's-length in the wake
of the other boats.   Now, however, a fourth personage appeared in it,
seated in the stern, face to face with the owner.   The gaily-coloured costume, even in the darkness, shining over the calm, shadowy surface of the
sea, rendered it easy to recognise this individual as the Foolah prince.
The Jew and the Moslem—the wolf and the lamb—were sailing in the
same boat.

CHAPTER X.

A HANDSOME OFFER.

On the day after the slaver had landed her cargo, and at a very early
hour in the morning, Mr. Vaughan, looking from the front window of his
house, perceived a strange horseman approaching by the long avenue.

As the stranger drew nearer, his horse appeared gradually to trans
form himself into a mule ; and the rider was seen to be an old gentleman
in a blue coat, with metal buttons, and ample outside pockets—under
which were breeches and top-boots, both sullied by long wear.   A dam-
aged brown beaver hat upon his head, with the edge of a white cotton
nightcap showing beneath it ; green goggles upon the nose ; and a large
blue umbrella, instead of a whip, grasped in the right hand, enabled Mr
Vaughan to identify one of his nearest neighbours, the penn-keeper
Jessuron, who, among other live stock, was also known as an extensive
speculator in slaves.

" The Jew ?" muttered Mr. Vaughan, as soon as the sharp features of
the Israelite were recognised.   " What can *he* want at this early hour ?
Some slave stock for sale, I suppose.   That looked like a trader I saw
yesterday in the offing, and he's sure to have the first lot.   Well, he
won't find a market here.   Fortunately, I'm stocked.   Morning, Mr
Jessuron !" continued he, hailing his visitor from the top of the stairway
" As usual, you are early abroad.   Business, eh ?"

"Ach, yesh, Mishter Vochan! Bishness must be minded. A poor mansh like me can't afford to shleep late theesh hard times!"

"Ha! ha! Poor man, indeed! That's a good joke, Mr. Jessuron! Come, alight! Have you breakfasted?"

"Yesh, thanks, Mister Vochan. I always breakfasht at six."

"Oh, that is early! A glass of swizzle, then?"

"Thanks, Mishter Vochan; I will. A glash of shwizzell will be better sea anything else. Itsh warm thish mornings."

The swizzle, a mixture of rum, sugar, water, and lime-juice, was found in a large punch-bowl that stood upon the sideboard, with a silver ladle resting across the rim, and glasses set around it. This is a standing drink in the dwelling of a Jamaica planter—a fountain that never gets dry, or always renewed when exhausted.

Stepping up to the sideboard, where he was attended to by the butler, the penn-keeper briskly quaffed off a tumbler of the swizzle; and then, smacking his lips, and adding the observation, "Tish good," he returned towards the window, where a chair had been placed for him beside that of his host.

He had already removed his beaver, though the white skull-cap—not over clean, by-the-bye—was still permitted to keep its place upon his head.

Mr. Vaughan was a man possessed of considerable courtesy, or, at least, an affectation of it. He remained silent, therefore, politely waiting for his guest to initiate the conversation.

"Well, Mishter Vochan," began the Jew, "I hash come over to see you on a shmall bishness—a very shmall bishness it is, and shcarcely worth troubling you about."

Here the Jew hesitated, as if to put some proposition into shape.

"Some black stock for sale? I think I've heard that a cargo came in yesterday. You got part, I suppose?"

"Yesh, yesh, I bought a shmall lot, a very shmall lot. I had'nt the monish to buy more. S'help me —— ! the shlaves ish getting so dear ash I can't afford to buy. This talk about shtoppin' the trade ish like to ruin ush all. Don't yoush think so, Misher Vochan?"

"Oh! as for that, you need'nt fear. If the British Government should pass the bill, the law will be only a dead letter. They could never guard the whole of the African coast—no, nor that of Jamaica neither. I think Mr. Jessuron, you would still contrive to land a few, eh?"

"Ach, no, Mishter Vochan! dear, oh dear, no! I shouldn't venture againsht the laws. If the trade ish stop, I musht give up the bishness. Shlaves would be too dear for a poor Jewish man like me to deal in : so s'help me —— ! they're too dear ash it ish."

"Oh, that's all nonsense about their getting dearer! It's very well for you to talk so, Mr. Jessuron ; you have some to sell, I presume?"

"Not now, Mishter Vochan, not now. Possbible I may have a shmall lot in a day or two, but joosht now I haven't a shingle head ready for the market. Thish morning I want to buy, instead of shell."

"To buy! From me, do you mean?"

"Yesh, Mishter Vochan, if you're dishposed to shell."

"Come, that's something new, neighbour Jessuron. I know you're

always ready for a trade; but this is the first-time I ever heard of you
buying off a plantation."

" Well, the truth ish, Mishter Vochan, I have a cushtomer who wants
a likely wench for waiting at hish table.   Theresh none among my shtock
he thinks good enough for hish purposh; I was thinking you hash got
one, if you could shpare her, that would suit him nisnely."

" Which do you mean ?"

" I mean that youngsh Foola wench ash I sold you lasht year- j наl
after crop time."

" Oh ! the girl Yola ?"

" Yesh, that wosh her name.   Ash you had her dirt sheep, I don't miな l
giving you shomethings on your bargain—shay ten pounds currenshy ?'

" Poh, poh, poh !" replied the planter, with a deprecating shrug. " That
would never do, even if I meant to sell the girl ; but I have no wish to
part with her."

" Shay twenty, then ?"

" Nor twice twenty, neighbour.   I would'nt, under any circumstances,
take less than two hundred pounds for Yola.   She has turned out a most
valuable servant——"

" Two hunder poundsh !" interrupted the Jew, starting up in his chair.
" Osh ! Mishter Vochan, theresh not a black wench in the island worth
half the monish.   Two hunder poundsh ! Blesh my soul, that ish a prishe !
I wish I could shell some of my shtock at that prishe ! I give any two I
hash for two hunder poundsh."

" Why, Mr. Jessuron, I thought you said just now slaves were becoming very dear !"

" Dear, yesh ; but that's doublish dear.   S'help me ——! you don't mean
it, Mishter Vochan ?"

" But I do mean it ; and even if you were to offer me two hundred——"

" Don't shay more about it," said the slave merchant, hurriedly interrupting the hypothetic speech ; " don't shay more ; I agreesh to give it. Two
hunder poundsh !—blesh my shtars ! it'll make a bankrup' of me."

" No, it will not do that : since *I* cannot agree to take it."

" Not to take two hunder poundsh ?"

" No—nor twice that sum, if you were disposed to offer it."

" Gott help ush, Mishter Vochan ; you shurely ish shokin ? Why can
you not take it ? I hash the monish in my pocket."

" I am sorry to disappoint you, neighbour ; but the fact is, I could not
sell the girl Yola at any price, without the consent of my daughter, to
whom I have given her."

" Mish Vochan ?"

" Yes—she is her maid, and I know that my daughter is very fond of
her.   It is not likely she would consent to the girl's being sold."

" But, Mishter Vochan, you shurely don't let your daughter shtand between you and a good bargain ? Two hunder pound is big monish,—big
monish, Mishter Vochan.   The wench ish not worth half the monish, and,
for myshelf, I wouldn't give half ; but I don't want to dishappoint a good
cushtomer, who'se not so particular ash to the prishe."

" Your customer fancies the girl, eh ?" said Mr. Vaughan, glancing significantly at his guest. " She is very good looking—no wonder. But if

that be the case, I may as well tell you, I should myself not be inclined to part with her; and, as for my daughter, if she suspected such a purpose, all the money you have got, Mr. Jessuron, would'nt reach the price."

"S'help me ——, Mishter Vochan, you're mishtaken. The cushtomer 1 speak of never shet hish eyes on the wench. Itsh only a waiting-maid he wants for hish table; and I thought of her, ash she'sh joosht what he describes. How do you know that Mish Vochan might not consent to let her go? 1 promish to get her another young girl ash good or better ash Yola."

" Well," replied the planter, after a moment's reflection, and apparently tempted by the handsome offer, " since you seem so determined upon buying her, I'll consult my daughter about it; but I can hold out very little hope of success. I know that she likes this Foolah. I have heard that the girl was some king's daughter in her own country; and I am as good as certain Kate won't consent to her being sold."

" Not if *you* wished it, Mishter Vochan?"

" Oh, if I insisted upon it, of course; but I give my daughter a sort of promise not to part with the girl against her wish, and I never break my word, Mr. Jessuron—not to my own child."

With this rather affected profession, the planter walked out of the room, leaving the slave merchant to his reflections.

" May the devil shtrike me dead if that man ishn't mad!" soliloquised the Jew, when left to himself. " S'help me ——, if he isn't! refuse two hunder pound for a neger wench as brown as a cocoa-nut shell! Blesh my shtars!"

" As I told you, Mr. Jessuron," said the planter, returning to the hall, " my daughter is inexorable. Yola cannot be sold."

" Good morning, Mishter Vochan," said the slave merchant, grasping his hat and umbrella, and making for the door. " Good morning, shir; I hash no other bishness to-day."

Then, putting on his hat and grasping his umbrella with an air of spiteful energy he was unable to conceal, he hurried down the stone steps, scrambled upon the back of his mule, and rode away in sullen silence.

" Unusually free with his money this morning," said the planter. looking after him. " Some shabby scheme, I have no doubt. Well, I suppose I have thwarted it; besides, I am glad of an opportunity of disobliging the old rascal: many's the time he has done as much for me."

CHAPTER XI.

JUDITH JESSURON.

In the most unamiable of tempers did the slave speculator ride back down the avenue. So out of sorts was he at the result of his interview, that he did not think of unfolding his blue umbrella to protect himself from the hot rays of the sun, now striking vertically downwards. On the contrary, he used the *parapluie* for a very different purpose—every now and then belabouring with it the sides of his mule, as if to rid himself of his spleen by venting it on the innocent mongrel.

Nor did he go in silence, although he was alone. In a kind of involven
dark soliloquy he kept muttering, as he rode on, long strings of phrases
denunciatory of the host whose roof he had just quitted. The daughter,
too, of that host came in for a share of this muttered denunciation, which,
at times, assumed the form of a menace.

Part of what he said was spoken distinctly, and with emphasis :—
" The dusht of my shoosh, Loftish Vochan—I flingsh it back to you!
Gott for damsch! there wash a time when you would be glad for my two
hunder poundsh. Not for any monish? Bosh! Grand lady, Mish Kate
—Mish Quasheby! Ha! I knowsh a thing—I knowsh a leetle thing. Some
day, may be, yourshelf sell for lesh as two hunder poundish : ach! I not
grudgsh twice the monish to see that day !

" The dusht of my shoosh to both of yoush !" he repeated, as he cleared the gate entrance. " I'sh off your grounds, now, and, if I hash
you here, I shay you something of my mind—something as make you sell
your wench for lesh as two hunder poundsh! I do so, some time yet,
pleash Gott. Ach !"

As he uttered this last exclamation with a prolonged aspirate, he raised
himself erect in his stirrups, and, half turning his mule, shook his umbrella in a threatening manner, towards Mount Welcome, his eye accompanying the action with a glance that expressed some secret but vindictive
determination.

As he faced back into the road, another personage appeared upon the
scene—a female equestrian who, trotting up briskly, turned her horse, and
rode on by his side.

She was a young girl, or rather a young woman—a bright beautiful
creature, who appeared an angel by the side of the demon-like old man.

She had evidently been waiting for him at the turning of the road ; and
the air of easy familiarity, with the absence of any salutation as they met
told that they had not long been separated.

Who was this charming equestrian.

A stranger would have asked this question while his eye rested upon
the object of it with mingled feelings of wonder and admiration at such
rare beauty—wonder at beholding it in such rude companionship !

It was a beauty that need not be painted in detail. The forehead of
noble arch, the scimetar-shaped eye-brows of ebon blackness, the dark
brown flashing pupils, the piquant prominence of the nose, with its spiral
surving nostrils, were all characteristics of Hebraic beauty—a shrine before which both Moslem and Christian have oftimes bent the knee in hum
blest adoration.

Twenty cycles have rolled past—twenty centuries of outrage, calumny,
and wrong—housed in low haunts—pillaged and persecuted—oft driven
to desperation—rendered roofless and homeless—still amid all, and in
spite of all, lovely Judah's dark-eyed daughters, fair as when they danced
to the music of cymbal and timbrel, or, to the accompaniment of the
golden-stringed harp, sang the lays of a happier time.

Here, in a new world, and canopied under the occidental sky, had
sprung up a very type of Jewish beauty ; for never was daughter of
Judah lovelier than the daughter of Jacob Jessuron—she who was now
riding by his side. A singular contrast did they present— this fair maid

tc that harsh-featured, ugly old man—unlike as the rose to its parent thorn.

Sad are we to say, that the contrast was only physical: morally, it was, like father like daughter. In external form Judith Jessuron was an angel; in spirit—and we say it with regret—she was the child of hei father.

The truth of our avowal will be readily deduced from the dialogue that on the moment of their meeting commenced between them.

" A failure ?" said she, taking the initiative. " Oh ! I needn't have ask ed you : it's clear enough from your looks—though, certes, that beautiful countenance of yours is not a very legible index to your thoughts. What says Vanity Vaughan ? Will he sell the girl ?"

" No."

" As I expected."

" S'help me, he won't !"

" How much did you bid for her ?"

" Osh ! I'sh ashamed to tell you, Shoodith."

" Come, old rabbi, you needn't be backward before me. How much ?"

" Two hunder poundsh."

" Two hundred pounds ! Well that is a high figure. If what you've told me be true, his own daughter isn't worth so much. Ha ! ha ! ha !"

" Hush, Shoodith, dear ! Don't shpeak of that—for your life don't shpeak of it. You may shpoil all my plansh !"

" Have no fear, good father. I never spoiled any plan of yours yet— have I ?"

" No, no ! You hash been a good shild, my daughter !—a good shild s'help me——, you hash !"

" But tell me, why would the custos not sell ? He likes money almost as well as yourself. Two hundred pounds is a large price for this cop- per-coloured wench—quite double what she's worth."

" Ach, Shoodith dear it wash not Vochan hishelf that refused."

" Who then ?"

" Thish very daughter you speaksh of."

" She !" exclaimed the young Jewess, with a curl of the lip, and a con- temptuous twist of her beautiful nostril, that all at once changed her beauty into very ugliness. " She, you say ? I wonder what next ? The conceited *mustee;* herself a slave !"

" Shtop—shtop, Shoodith," interrupted the Jew, with a look of uneasi- iess. " Keep that to yourshelf, my shild. Shay no more about it—at leasht, not now, not now. The trees may have ears, Shoodith."

The burst of angry passion hindered the fair Judith from making re- joinder, and for some moments father and daughter rode on in silence.

The latter was the first to re-open the conversation.

" You are silly, good father," said she, " in offering to buy this girl at all."

" Ay—what would you shay ?" inquired the old Jew, as if the interro- gatory had been an echo to his own thoughts. " What would you shay ?"

" I would say that you are silly, old rabbi Jacob, and that's what I do say."

"Blesh my soul! What dosh you mean, Shoodith?"

"Why—dear, dear father! you're not always so dull of comprehension. Answer me: What do you want the Foolah girl for?"

"Osh! You know what I wants her for. Thish prinsh will give hish twenty Mandingoes for her. There ish no doubt but she's hish sister. Twenty good shtrong Mandingoes, worth twenty hunder poundsh. Blesh ny soul! it'sh a fortune!"

"Well, and if it is a fortune, what then?"

"If it ish? By our fathers! you talk of twenty hunder poun' ash if monish was dirt."

"My worthy parent, you misunderstand me."

"Mishunderstand you, Shoodith?"

"You do. I have more respect for twenty hundred pounds than you give me credit for. So much, as to advise you to *get it.*"

"Get it! why, daughter, that ish shoosh what I am trying to do."

"Ay, and you've gone about it in such a bungling fashion, that you run the risk of losing it."

"And how would you go about getting it, mine Shoodith?"

"By *taking it.*"

The slave merchant jerked upon the bridle, and pulled his mule to a stand—as he did so darting towards his daughter a look half-puzzled, half-penetrating.

"Good father Jacob," continued she, halting at the same time, "you are not wont to be so dull-witted. While waiting for you at the gate of this pompous sugar planter, I could not help reflecting; and my reflections led me to ask the question: what on earth had taken you to his house?"

"And what answer did you find, Shoodith?"

"Oh, not much; only that you went upon a very idle errand."

"Yesh, it hash been an idle errand; I did not get what I went for."

"And what matters it if you didn't?"

"What mattersh it? Twenty Mandingoes mattersh a great deal—twenty hunder poundsh currenshy. That ish what it mattersh, Shoodith, mine darling!"

"Not the paring of a Mandingo's toe-nail, my good rabbi Jessuron."

"Hach! what shay you, mine wise Shoodith?"

"What say I? Simply, that these Mandingoes might as well have been yours without all this trouble. They may be yet—ay, and their master too, if you desire to have a prince for your slave. I do."

"Shpeak out, Shoodith; I don't understand you."

"You will presently. Did you not say that Captain Jowler has reasons for not coming ashore?"

"Captain Showler! He would rather land in the Cannibal Islands than in Montego Bay. Well, Shoodith?"

"Rabbi Jessuron, you weary my patience. For the Foolah prince, as you say he is, you are answerable only to Captain Jowler. Captain Jowler comes not ashore."

"True—it ish true," assented the Jew, with a gesture that signified his comprehension of these preliminary premises.

"Who, then, is to hinder you from doing as you please in the matter of these Mandingoes?'

" Wonderful Shoodith!" exclaimed the father, throwing up his arms, and turning upon his daughter a look of enthusiastic admiration. "Wonderful Shoodith! Joosh the very thing ;—blesh my soul!—and I never thought of it."

" Well, father ; luckily it's not too late. I have been thinking of it. I knew very well that Kate Vaughan would not part with the girl Yola. I told you she wouldn't ; but, by-the-bye, I hope you've said nothing of what you wanted her for ? If you have ——"

" Not a word, Shoodith ! not a word !"

" Then no one need be a word the wiser. As to Captain Jowler ——"

" Showler daren't show his face in the Bay ; that'sh why he landed hish cargo up the coast. He'll be gone away in twenty-four hours."

" Then in twenty-four hours the Mandingoes may be yours—prince, at tendants, and all. But time is precious, papa. We had better hasten home at once, and strip his royal highness of those fine feathers, before some of our curious neighbours may come in : people will talk scandal, you know. As for our worthy overseer ——"

" Ah, Ravener ! he knowsh all about it. I wash obliged to tell him ash we landed."

" Of course you were ; and it will cost you a Mandingo or two to keep his tongue tied : that it will. For the rest, there need be no difficulty. It won't matter what these savages may say for themselves : fortunately, there's no scandal in a black man's tongue."

" Wonderful Shoodith!" again exclaimed the admiring parent. " My precious daughter, you are worth your weight in golden guinish ! Twenty-four shlaves for nothing, and one of them a born prinsh ! Two thous- and currenshy ! Blesh my soul ! It ish a shplendid profit—worth a whole year's buyin' and shellin'."

And with this honest reflection, the slave merchant hammered his mule into a trot, and followed his " precious Shoodith "—who had already given the whip to her horse, and was riding rapidly homeward.

CHAPTER XII.

THE STEERAGE PASSENGER.

A the third day after the slaver had cast anchor in the Bay of Montega, a large square-rigged vessel made her appearance in the offing ; and head-ing shoreward, with all sail set, stood boldly in for the harbour. The Union Jack of England, spread to the breeze, floated freely above her taff-rail ; and various boxes, bales, trunks, and portmanteaus, that could be seen on her deck—brought up for debarcation—as well as the frank, man-ly countenances of the sailors who composed her crew, proclaimed the ship to be an honest trader. The lettering upon her stern told that she was the " Sea Nymph, of Liverpool."

Though freighted with a cargo of merchandise, and in reality a mer-chantman. the presence on board of several individuals in the costume of landsmen, denoted that the Sea Nymph also accommodated passengers

The majority of these were West India planters, with their families, returning from a visit to the mother country—their sons, perhaps, after graduating at an English university, and their daughters on having received their final *polish* at some fashionable metropolitan seminary.

Here and there an " attorney"—a constituent element of West Indian society, though not necessarily, as the title suggests, a real limb of the law. Of these, however, there might have been one or two, and an unpractised disciple of Esculapius—both professionally bent on seeking fortune, and with fair prospects of finding it, in a land notorious for crime as unwholesome in clime. These, with a sprinkling of nondescripts, made up the list of the Sea Nymph's cabin passengers.

There were but few in the steerage. They who are compelled to adopt that irksome mode of voyaging across the Atlantic have but little errand to the West Indies, or elsewhere to tropical lands—where labour is monopolised by the thews and sinews of the slave. Only three or four of this class had found passage on board the Sea Nymph ; and yet, among these humble voyagers was one destined to play a conspicuous part in our story.

The individual in question was a young man, in appearance of twenty or twenty-one years of age. In stature he was what is termed " middle height," with limbs well rounded and tersely set, denoting activity and strength. His complexion, though not what is termed *brunette*, was dark for a native of Britain, though such was he. His features were nobly defined, and his whole countenance sufficiently striking to attract the attention of even an indifferent observer. Dark brown eyes, and hair of like colour waving luxuriantly over his cheeks, were characteristic points of gracefulness ; and, take him all in all, he was one that might justly be pronounced a handsome young fellow.

His dress, though neither rich in quality nor cut in the newest fashion, was, nevertheless, becoming to him, and did not detract from the graces which Nature had somewhat lavishly bestowed upon his person. It was a costume not at all rustic, but rather such as might be worn by some young student, whose poor but fond parents had pinched themselves, to provide for him an education superior to that of the common parochial school, and a dress becoming the position which they sought for him.

The garments he wore were his best, put on for the first time during the voyage, and for the grand occasion of *landing*. Nor did the young fellow make such a mean appearance in them. Their scantiness only served to exhibit the fine *tournure* of his body and limbs ; and the dark blue tunic frock, with black braid, skirting down over a pair of close-fitting tights, and Hessian boots, gave him rather a *distingue* air, notwithstanding a little threadbarishness apparent along the seams.

The occupation in which the young man was engaged betrayed a certain degree of refinement. Seated upon the fore-mast head, in the blank leaf of a book, which appeared to be his journal, he was sketching the harbour into which the ship was about to enter ; and the drawing though merely intended as an outline limning, exhibited no inconsiderable degree of artistic skill.

For all that, the young man was *not* an artist. Professionally, indeed, and to his misfortune, he was nothing. A poor scholar without trick or trade by which he might earn a livelihood, he had come c it to the West Indies, as young men go to other colonies, with that sort of indefinite hope that Fortune, in some way or other, might prove kinder abroad than she had been at home.

Whatever hopes of success the young colonist may have entertained, they were evidently neither sanguine nor continuous. Though naturally of a cheerful spirit, as his countenance indicated, a close observer might have detected, now and then, a certain shadow upon it.

As the ship drew near to the shore, he closed the book, and sate scanning the gorgeous picture of tropical scenery now, for the first time, disclosed to his eyes.

Despite the pleasant emotions which so fair a scene was calculated to call forth, his countenance betrayed some anxiety—perhaps a doubt as to whether a welcome awaited him in that lovely land upon which he was looking.

CHAPTER XIII.

THE CABIN PASSENGER.

ANOTHER passenger of the Sea Nymph, with whom our readers must necessarily become acquainted, was also a young man, apparently of the same age as the one already introduced. Only in this, and the circumstance that both were Englishmen, did they resemble each other. In all other respects they were signally unlike. In complexion, colour of the hair, eyes, and beard, each presented a complete contrast to the other. The former has been described as of dark complexion; the latter was fair-skinned—pre-eminently so—with hair of a light yellowish hue, having the appearance of being artificially curled, and slightly darkened with the gloss of some perfumed oil. The whiskers and moustache were nearly of the same colour, both evidently cultivated with an elaborate assiduity, that proclaimed excessive conceit in them on the part of their owner. The eyebrows were also of the lightest shade; but the colour of the eyes was not so easily told; since one of them was kept habitually closed, while a glancing lens, in a frame of tortoise-shell, hindered a fair view of the other. Through the glass, however, it appeared of a very light grey, and decidedly "piggish." The features of this individual were regular enough; though without any striking character, and of a cast rather effeminate than vulgar. Their prevailing expression was that of a certain superciliousness, at times extending to an affectation of sardonism.

The dress of the young man was in correspondence with the foppery exhibited in the perfumed locks and eye-glass. It consisted of a surtout of broadcloth, of a very light drab, with a cape that scarce covered the shoulders; a white beaver hat; vest and pants of spotless buff kerseymere; kid gloves on his hands; and boots, bright as lacquer could make them, on his feet—all items of apparel made in a style of fashion, and worn with an air of *savoir faire* that loudly proclaimed the London exquisite.

The affected drawl in which the gentleman spoke, whenever he condecended to hold communion with his fellow-passengers confirmed this character—a fop of the first water.

It need not be added that our exquisite was a cabin passenger—in this respect also differing from his less favoured *compagnon du voyage;* and the marked obeisance which was paid him by the steward and cabin boys of the Sea Nymph, gave evidence of his capability to bestow a liberal largess. Even the blunt skipper treated him with a certain deference, which proved his passenger to be a person either of wealth or distinction, or, may be, both.

Let us bid adieu to circumlocution, and at once declare who and what he was. Yclept Montagu Smythje—a presumed improvement upon *Smith*—the individual in question was a youth of good family and for-tune ; the latter consisting of a magnificent sugar estate in Jamaica—left him by a deceased relative—to visit which was the object of his voyage.

The estate he had never seen: as this was his first trip across the At-lantic ; but he had no reason to doubt the existence of the property. The handsome income which it had afforded him, during several years of his minority, and which had enabled him to live in magnificent style in the West End of London, was a substantial proof that Montagu Castle—such was the name of the estate—was something more than a castle in the air. He had been virtually its owner for several years ; but up to the attainment of his majority—a very recent event—the property had been managed by a trustee, resident in the island : one Mr. Vaughan, himself a sugar planter, and next neighbour to the original lord of Montagu Castle.

Mr. Smythje had not come over the water with any intention of settling upon his Jamaica estate "Such an ideaw," to use his own phraseology, " nevwaw entawed my bwain. To exchange London and its pwesywas for a wesidence among those howid niggaws—deaw, no ; aw could neywaw think of such a voluntawy banishment—that would be a baw— a decided baw !"

After this fashion did Mr. Montagu Smythje declare himself to his fel-low-passengers of the Sea Nymph, as he explained to them the object of his voyage.

" A meaw twip to see something of the twopics, of which aw've heard extwaor'nary stories—have a look at my sugaw plantation and niggaws —dooced nyce cwib, they say, but sadly out of repawa and hot— aw, hot as the infawnal regiaws."

To say the truth, Mr. Smythje could scarce tell why he was making this trip. It was not the obedience to the promptings of any inclination that he had consented to seperate himself, even temporarily, from his " deaw London," and its gay delights ; nor had he the slightest curiosity to see the goose that laid his golden eggs, so long as the eggs themselves were transmitted safely to his banker in London. It was partly at the in-stigation of his friends—who fancied that an absence from the gay metro-polis might do something to cure him of certain proclivities towards dis-sipation to which he was too recklessly giving way—and partly at the solicitation of his Jamaica trustee, that he had adventured on this voy-age.

Another motive, which he himself proclaimed—perhaps as power'ul —was his "desiaw te see some of those Queole queetyaws," whom he had heard too be "dooced pwetty." Even the sober guardian, Mr Vaughan—as if well comprehending the character of his ward, though never having seen him—had made use of this lure in his letter of invitation, though only in an incidental and extremely delicate manner. It argued well for the trustee's integrity—thus courting, as it were, a personal inspection of the estate in trust. Perhaps, however, he might have been actuated by some motive not quite so creditable!

One fact may here be mentioned : the young proprietor, during his stay in the island, was to be the guest of Mr. Vaughan, on the plea that Montagu Castle having been for years uninhabited, was not in a fit state for the reception of its distinguished owner. The trustee had not deemed it worth while to go to the unnecessary expense of putting it in order, since only a temporary residence was intended. His own house was to be placed at the service of his ward in trust during the latter's sojourn in the island. There he would find ample accommodation; since the mansion of Mount Welcome was one of the largest in Jamaica, while the family of its proprietor was one of the smallest : Mr. Vaughan having but one child—an only daughter.

——

CHAPTER XIV.

LOFTUS VAUGHAN ON THE LOOK-OUT.

EVERY day, after that on which he had received the two English letters, and almost every hour during daylight, might Loftus Vaughan have been seen, telescope in hand, at one of the open windows of his house, sweeping with his glass the roadstead and offing of Montego Bay. The object of this telescopic observation was, that he might descry the Sea Nymph refore she had entered the harbour,-in order that his carriage should be at the port to receive the distinguished Smythje on his landing. At this period there were no steamers trading across the Atlantic punctual to a day and almost to an hour. Though the letter of advice had been written ten days before that on which the Sea Nymph was to sail, there could be no calculation made upon such uncertain data as winds and waves ; and the ship which carried Montagu Smythje might arrive at any hour.

That some distinguished guest was expected, was a fact that had rendered itself conspicuous to every domestic in the establishment of Mount Welcome. Every day saw some article or articles of costly furniture brought home from the " Bay ;" and the chambers of the " great house " were being freshly decorated to receive them.

The house wenches, and other in-door servants, were furnished with new dresses, some even with liveries—an unusual piece of finery in Jamaica—while shoes and stockings were forced upon feet that, perhaps, had never felt such *impedimenta* before, and whose owners would have been only too glad to have escaped the torture of wearing them.

It need scarcely be said that the planter was undergoing all this extravagant expenditure for the reception of Mr. Montagu Smythje, and him alone. Had it been only his own nephew that was expected, no such continuous look-out would have been kept for him, and no such preparations made to do him honour on his arrival.

Neither do M. Vaughan's motives require explanation: the reader will ere this have surmised them. He was the father of a daughter, ready at any moment for marriage. M. Montagu Smythje was, in his eyes, not only eligible, but highly desirable, specimen for a son-in-law. The young man was possessed of a splendid property, as Mr. Vaughan well knew; for the worthy planter was not only custos rotulorum, but for many long years had been custos of Montagu Castle. He could tell its value to a shilling " currency." It lay contiguous to his own. He had often looked with a longing eye upon its broad acres and its black retainers; and had imbibed a desire, amounting indeed to a passion, to possess it—if not in his own right, at least in that of his daughter. The union of the two estates, Mount Welcome and Montagu Castle, would make a magnificent domain—one of the richest in the island. To accomplish this object had long been the wish of Loftus Vaughan. It had grown and grown upon him, till it had become the most cherished purpose of his heart. Let us not conceal a more creditable motive that Mr. Vaughan had for desiring this union. He had been too long in Jamaica to be ignorant of the true social position of his daughter. However beautiful and accomplished Kate Vaughan was; however much her father loved her—and, to do him justice, his paternal affection was of the strongest—he knew—he had observed it, and knew—that between her and the young gentleman of his acquaintance—that is, those who would have been eligible—there was that social barrier, the *taint*. Often had he reflected upon it, and with bitterness. He knew, moreover, that young Englishmen, especially on their first arrival in the island, made light of this barrier; in fact, altogether disregarded it, until corrupted by the "society" of the place.

In his match-making designs the Jamaica planter was not more of a sinner than hundreds of other parents, both at home and abroad; and there is this much in his favour: that, perhaps, his affection for his daughter, and the desire of ennobling her—for by such an alliance would the *taint be extinguished*—were the chief motives for the conduct he was pursuing.

Unfortunately, it becomes our duty to record other traits in his character, with acts springing from them, that cannot be characterised as otherwise than *mean*.

Mr. Vaughan, despite his vigorous prosecution of the business of life, despite the energy that had enabled him to grow rich, was still only a weak-minded man. Like many men of humble birth who had risen to rank and fortune, he had become the "beggar set on horseback;" far more jealous of aristocratic honours than those who are born to them; an advocate for hereditary privileges, ever on the *qui vive* to battle for them; in short, a true specimen of "plush."

In these peculiarities, the character of Mr. Vaughan does not stand out in such bold relief. His counterparts are common enough, even at this later day. We can see them in hundreds around us. In the " upper house," among our "law lords," most of whom, and the basest born of them, are the stoutest advocates of aristocratic privilege. In the streets we have our "Sir Peters" and " Sir Roberts," bearing the broad arrow of trade side by side with the fire-new patent of nobility.

studied courtesy with which Mr. Vaughan was preparing to re-
the lord of Montagu Castle was in strong contrast with the dis-
,y he had designed for his kinsman.
were the offsprings of mean motives ; but in the latter case, both
and the intention were paltry beyond parallel. The announce-
in the nephew's letter that he had taken a *steerage passage* had been
his uncle a source of bitter chagrin. Not that he would have cared a
.. it about the thing, had the young fellow voyaged in any other vessel
than the Sea Nymph, or had he travelled unrecognised. What troubled
Mr. Vaughan was the fear, that this fact might become known to Mr.
Montagu Smythje ; and thus creat in the mind of the latter a suspicion
of his, the planter's, respectability.

The dread of this *expose* so preyed upon Mr. Vaughan's mind that, had
it been possible, he would have denied the relationship altogether.

He had conceived a hope that this recognition might not take place
during the voyage : building his hope on the character of the aristocratic
cockney, which he knew to be a type of supercilious pride. Confiding
in the faith that nothing might transpire on board ship to make Mr.
Smythje acquainted with the relationship, he was determined there should
be no chance on shore. To preclude the possibility of such a thing, he
had conceived a design as childish as it was cruel : his nephew was to
be kept out of the way.

The plan of action he had traced out long before the arrival of the Sea
Nymph. Mr. Montague Smythje was to be met at the landing, and at
once hurried off to Mount Welcome. Herbert Vaughan was likewise to
be conducted thither ; and also direct. It was not desirable he should be
left to make inquiries in the town, where his uncle was universally
known, and where a disclosure of his relationship to the poor steerage
passenger would have been equally unpleasant to the proud planter.

A different means of transport was to be provided for the expected
visitors, and their transit was arranged to take place at different times—
to avoid the possibility of an encounter on the road. Furthermore, on
the arrival of Herbert upon the plantation, he was not to proceed to the
dwelling of his uncle, but was to be taken by a private road to the house
of the overseer—which stood in a secluded corner of the valley, nearly
half a mile distant from the " Buff."

Here he was to remain as the guest of the overseer, until such time as
his uncle could find a way of disposing of him—either by procuring
some employment for him at Montego Bay, or the situation of book-keeper
on some distant plantation.

The execution of the programme thus prepared was intrusted to the
overseer of Mount Welcome estate—a man every way worthy of such a
confidence, and, like most of his calling, capable of schemes even still
less commendable.

With this ingenious contrivance did Mr. Vaughan await the arrival of
his guests.

* * * * * * *

It was upon the eighth day after receiving his letters of advice, and
about the hour of noon, that the planter, playing as usual with his telescope, perceived in the offing of Montego Bay, and standing in for the
port, a large square-rigged vessel—a ship

It might be the Sea Nymph, and it might not; but taking into consideration the time and some other circumstances known to Mr. Vaughan, the probabilities were that it was the expected vessel.

Whether or no, the planter was determined that the programme he had so ingeniously sketched out should not be spoiled by any mismanagement in the performance; and its execution was ordered upon the instant.

Bells were rung for a general muster of the domestics; a horn was sounded to summons the overseer; and, in less than half an hour afterwards, the family barouche—a handsome equipage, drawn by a pair of splendidly caparisoned horses—was on the road to the Bay, with the overseer on horseback, riding as an escort behind it.

In rear of this went a wagon, to which eight large oxen were attached; and behind the wagon appeared an escort *sui generis:* a rough negro boy, mounted on the shaggiest and scraggiest of steeds, who was no other than the post-boy already mentioned—the identical Quashie.

Quashie was not now on his usual diurnal duty: his present errand was one of a far more important character.

At this moment the great hall of Mount Welcome exhibited a scene that, to the eye of a stranger to West Indian customs, might have appeared curious enough.

Scattered over the floor, at certain distances from each other, were some six or eight negro girls, or " wenches," as there called, most of them being of the younger brood of the plantation. All were down on their knees, each one having by her side, and within reach of her hand, an orange freshly cut in halves, some bees' wax, and a portion of the fibrous pericarp of a cocoa-nut.

The floor itself was without carpet of any kind, and, instead of being of plain deal, it presented a mosaic of hard woods, of different colours—among which might be recognised the mahogany and heart-wood, the bread-nut, and bully-tree.

To give the tesselated surface a polish was the business of the dark damsels on their knees; for that purpose were the oranges and cocoa-husks provided.

To an islander the sight was one of common, indeed, daily occurrence. The polish of his hall floor is a matter of pride with a Jamaica planter; as much so as the quality or pattern of his drawing-room carpet to a householder at home; and every day, and at the same hour, the dark-skinned housemaids make their appearance, and renew their glitter of the surface, whose gloss has been tarnished by the revels of the preceding night.

The hour set apart for this quaint custom is just before laying the cloth for dinner—about three or four o'clock; and that they may not sully the polish while carrying in the dishes, these barefooted Abigails adopt a plan that deserves mention on account of its originality.

Each having provided herself with two small pieces of linen or cotton cloth, spreads them out upon the floor, and then places a foot upon each. As the toes of a West Indian house wench are almost as prehensile as her fingers, she finds no difficulty in " cramping " the cloth and holding it between the " big-toe " and its nearest neighbour; and with this simple *chaussure*: she is enabled to slide over the floor, without in the least degree

" smoutching " its gloss, or leaving any sign of her passage over the shining surface.

While such a busy scene was transpiring in the great hall of Mount Welcome, one of a different character, but of equal activity, was going on in the kitchen of the establishment. This " office " stood a little apart from the main dwelling, communicating with the lower storey of the latter by a covered passage. Along this, black and yellow wenches could be seen constantly going and returning, each with her load—a haunch o venison, a ham of the wild hog, a turtle, ramier pigeons, and mountain crabs, all on their way to the spit, the stew-pan, or the chafing-dish.

A similar sight might have been witnessed at Mount Welcome any other day in the year, but perhaps with a less abundant variety in the materials, and with not half so much movement among the staff of wenches pertaining to the *cuisine*—whose excited manner in the performance of their specific duties testified, as much as the variety of luxuries lying around, that on this particular day a repast of the most sumptuous kind was expected from their hands.

The custos did not leave the preparations to be made without his own personal surveillance. From the time that the ship had ben descried he was everywhere—in the stable, to look after the sable grooms ; in the kitchen, to instruct the cooks ; in the great hall, to inspect the polish of the floor ; and, at last, on the landing outside, standing, telescope to his eye, and looking down the long avenue, where the carriage containing his distinguished vistor might at any moment be expected to appear.

CHAPTER XV.

KATE AND YOLA.

In one corner of the mansion of Mount Welcome—that which was farthest removed from the din and clangor of the kitchen—was a small chamber richly and elegantly furnished. The light was admitted into it on two sides through jalousied windows, that, when open, left a free passage from the floor to a little balcony outside, with which each of the windows was provided.

One of them looked to the rearward, commanding a view of the back garden, and the wooded steep beyond ; the other opened to the left side of the house, upon the shrubbery grounds that extended in that direction as far as the foot of the ridge. Even had there been no one in this little chamber, the style and character of its furniture would have told that the person to whom it appertained was one of the gentler sex. In one corner stood a bed with carved posts of yellow lancewood, from which hung what at first sight might have been taken for white muslin curtains, but which, on closer scrutiny, were seen to be the gauze-like netting of a "mosqueto bar." The size of the bed told that it was intended for but one individual : its habitual occupant was therefore unmarried.

In the bay of one of the windows stood a dressing table *of papier-mache*, inlaid with mother-of-pearl ; and upon this was placed a mirror of] circular shape on a stand of the finest Spanish mahogany In front of the mirror was a variety of objects of different forms—among which might be noticed the usual implements of the toilet, with many of those little articles of *luxe* and *vertu*, that bespeak the refined presence of women. Other piece of furniture in the room were three or four Chinese cane chairs ; a small marqueterie table ; a work-box of tortoiseshell veneer, on a pedestal of like material ; and a little cabinet of ebony wood richly inlaid with buhl.

There was neither mantel nor fire-place—the climate of eternal summer precluding all necessity for such a thing. The window curtains were of a thin transparent muslin, with a pattern of pink flowering woven in the stuff, and bordered with a fringe of alternate pink and white tassels. The breeze, blowing in through the open lattice-work of the jalousies, kept these light hangings almost continually in motion, imparting an aspect of coolness to the chamber, heightened by the glossy smoothness of the hard wood floor, which glistened like a mirror.

No one could have glanced into this little apartment, without being struck with its costly yet chaste adornment. Rich and elegant howev)r, as was the case, it was no more than worthy of the jewel which it was accustomed to contain. It was the bedroom and boudoir of "lilly Quasheba," the heiress *presumptive* of Mount Welcome.

But few were ever favoured with a glance into that luxurious chamber. It was a sacred precinct into which curious eyes were not permitted to penetrate. Its polished floor was not to be trodden by vulgar feet. With the exception of her father, no man had ever intruded into that virgin shrine ; and he, only on rare and extraordinary occasions. Even to the domestics it was not free access. Only one could enter it unbidden—the brown-skinned hand-maid of its mistress.

* * * * * *

On that same day—shortly after the ringing of the bells had announced the arrival of the English ship, and while the dusky domestics were engaged, as described, in their ante-prandial preparations—two individuals occupied the chamber in question. One was the young lady to whom the apartment appertained–the other her maid Yola. They were in different attitudes : the former seated upon one of the Chinese chairs in front of the window, while the maid was standing behind, occupied in dressing her mistress's hair.

The girl was just entering upon her task—if we may so designate that which might have been esteemed a pleasure. Already the complicated machinery of combs and hair-pins lay strewed over the table ; and the long chesnut-coloured tresses hung in luxuriant profusion around those shoulders of snow, in whose velvet-like epidermis there appeared no trace of the *taint*.

Involuntarily the maid ceased from her task, and stood gazing at her young mistress with a look of instinctive admiration.

"Oh! beautiful!" exclaimed she, in a low, murmured voice; "you beautiful, missa!"

"Tut, Yola, 'tis only flattery of you to say so. You are as beautiful as I ; only your beauty is of a different order No doubt, in your country you would be a great belle ?"

KATE AND YOLA. 51

"Ah, missa, you belle anywhere—black man—white man—all you think a belle, all you admire."

"Thank you, Yola! but I shouldn't particularly desire to be the object of such universal admiration. For my part, I dont know one male biped in whose eyes I care to appear attractive."

"Perhaps missa no say so when come young buckra from Inglis country."

"Which buckra?—there are two of them expected from the English country."

"Yola not hear two come. Massa, he speak only one."

"Oh, you've heard speak of one only. Did you hear his name mentioned?"

"Yes; he grand man—Sultan of Mongew. Other name Yola hear—she no sabbey speak it."

"Ha! ha! ha! I don't wonder at that. It's as much as I 'sabbey' myself to pronounce that second name, which I presume to be *Smythje*. Is that the name you heard?"

"That is, missa—he berry fine gentl'man, he beauty man. The overseer massa tell so."

"Ah, Yola; your master is a man, and men are not always the best judges of one another's looks. Perhaps the Sultan of Montagu, as you call him, might not be such a pattern of perfection as papa describes him. But, no doubt, we shall soon have an opportunity of judging for ourselves. Did you hear your master tell the overseer nothing about another buckra that is expected?"

"No, missa. One only he speak of—he same one of Mongew Castle."

A low ejaculation, expressive of disappointment, escaped the lips of the young creole, as her head settled down into an attitude of silent reflection, her eyes turned upon the shining floor at her feet. It is not easy to tell why she put the last interrogatory to her maid. Perhaps she had some suspicion of her father's plans. At all events, she knew there was some mystery, and was desirous of penetrating it. The maid was still gazing upon her, when all at once the dark Arab-like features of the latter assumed a changed expression—the look of admiration giving place to one of inquiry, as if some idea had occurred to her.

"Allah!" muttered the girl, as she gazed earnestly in the face of her mistress.

"Well, Yola," said the latter, attracted by the exclamation, and looking up at her attendant, "why do you exclaim Allah? Has anything occurred to you?"

"Oh! beauty missa! you so like one man."

"I like a man? I resemble a man? Is that what you mean?"

"Yes, missa."

"Well, Yola, you are certainly not flattering me now. Who might this man be? I pray you tell me."

"He man of the mountains—Maroon."

"Oh! worse and worse! I resemble a *Maroon?* Gracious me! Surely you are jesting, Yola?"

"Oh! missa, he beauty man; roun' black eyes that glance like fire-flies —eyes like yours—berry, berry like you eyes, missa."

"Come, silly girl!" said the young lady, speaking in a tone of reproval more affected than real; "do you know that it is very naughty of you, to compare me to a Maroon?"

"Oh! Missa Kate, he beauty man—berry beauty man."

"That I doubt very much; but even were it so, you should not speak of his resembling me '

"Me pardon, missa. I not more so say."

"No, you had better not, good Yola. If you do I shall ask papa to sell you."

This was said in a tone of gentle raillery, which told that the intention of carrying out the threat was far from the speaker's thoughts.

"By-the-bye, Yola," continued the young lady, "I could get a good price for you. How much do you suppose was offered for you the other day."

"Missa Kate, I know not. Allah forbid me you ebber leave. If you no more my missa, I care not more to live."

"Thanks, Yola," said the young creole, evidently touched by the words of her maid, the sincerity of which was proved by the tone in which they were spoken. "Be not afraid of my parting with you. As proof that I shall not, I refused a very large sum—how much can you guess."

"Ah! missa, I worth nothing to no one but you. If I you leave I die."

"Well, there is one who thinks you worth two hundred pounds, and has offered that for you."

"Who he, missa?"

"Why—he who sold you to papa—Mr. Jessuron."

"Allah protect poor Yola! Oh! missa Kate, he bad master; he berry wicked man. Yola die—Cubina kill her! Yola self kill if she sold back to wicked slave-dealer! Good missa!—oeauty missa!—you no sell you poor slave?"

The girl fell upon her knees at the feet of her young mistress, with her hands clasped over her head, and remained for some moments in this attitude.

"Don't fear my selling you," said the young lady, motioning the suppliant to rise to her feet; "least of all to him, whom I believe to be what you have styled him, a very wicked man. Have no fear for that. But tell me, what name was that you pronounced just now? *Cubina*, was it not?"

"Yes, missa, Cubina,"

"And, pray who is Cubina?"

The brown maid hesitated before making reply, while the crimson began to show itself on her chesnut-coloured cheeks.

"Oh! never mind!" said her young mistress, noticing her hesitation. "If there's any secret, Yola, I shall not insist upon an answer."

"Missa, from you Yola not have secret. Cubina he mountain man—Maroon."

"What! is he the Maroon I am supposed to resemble?"

"True missa, he same."

"Oh! I see how it is then—I suppose that that accounts for you thinking *me* beautiful? This Cubina, no doubt, is a sweetheart of yours?"

Yola hung her head without making reply. The crimson spread more widely over the chesnut.

"You need not answer, good Yola," said the young creole, with a significant smile. "I know what your answer *ought* to be if you spoke your mind. I think I have heard of this Cubina. Have a care! these Maroons are a very different sort of men from the coloured people on the plantations. Like me, he is! ha! ha ha!" and the young beauty glanced coyly at the mirror "Well, Yola; I'm not angry with you, since it is your sweetheart with whom I am compared. Love, they say, is a wonderful beautifier; and no doubt Master Cubina is, in your eyes, a perfect Endymion.

"Come!" added she, after a pause and another spell of laughter, "I fear we have been wasting time. If I'm not ready to receive this grand guest, I'll get into trouble with papa. Haste, Yola! and dress me out in a style becoming the mistress of Mount Welcome."

With a peal of merry laughter at the air of grandeur she had thus jestingly assumed, the young lady bent down her head, submitting her magnificent *chevelure* to the manipulation of her maid.

CHAPTER XVI.

TWO TRAVELLERS FOR THE SAME BOURNE.

MR. MONTAGU SMYTHJE had voyaged all the way from Liverpool to Jamaica, without ever having set his foot one inch over that line which separates the sacred precinct of the quarter-deck from the less respected midships and for'ard part of the vessel. Beyond the main mast he had not been. Thus, rarely—except when the ship was sailing close upon a wind —did the tarry frequenters of the forecastle come between the breeze and Mr. Smythje's nasal susceptibility.

As the Sea Nymph was not a regular packet, or "royal liner," but only an ordinary merchant vessel incidentally carrying a few passengers, no very strict rules were observed as to quarter-deck privileges. Of course, the common sailors were not allowed to violate the usual custom; and these only visited the quarter-deck, when the necessities of duty, more imperious than the most despotic skipper, required their presence there. The steerage passengers, however, with the exception that they might not enter the cabin, had the freedom of the whole vessel; and might lounge along the poop, or pace the quarter-deck itself if so inclined. Most, indeed all, of them, with one exception, had from time to time felt this inclination, and taking advantage of the favour allowed them—in fine weather passing the greater part of their time abaft the binnacle, or elsewhere around the cabin. The one exception to this rule was the young man already mentioned and described—the amateur artist.

During the long voyage of six weeks, he had never set foot on the quarter-deck, nor, indeed, was he much to be seen upon deck. As a general thing he kept himself below; though when the weather was temptingly fine, he might be observed silently climbing the shrouds, and seating himself on the fore-mast head—where book in hand, he would remain for hours together.

The spritsail yard, too, was another favourite locality with him ; and there, stretched along the furled sail, he would lie, gazing down into the blue water, as if watching the movements of the turquoise-hued dolphins that might be seen almost constantly gliding beneath, as if deputed by Neptune to form an escort to the ship.

It was not that the young fellow was of a gloomy or solitary disposition, for at other times he might be seen diving down through the trap-like hatchway of the forecastle ; and the clear ring of his voice, mingling in jest and laughter with those of the jolly Jack tars, proved that his natural inclination was neither saturnine nor anti-social.

That he was a great favourite with " Jack" was certain.

Evidence of this is found in the fact that, while crossing the " line" (Jack regards the tropic of Cancer as the " line," when the real one, the equator, does not come within the limits of his voyage)—while crossing the line, Neptune did not insist on shaving him with his rough razor ; although he was too poor to have escaped the operation by bribing the barbers of the sea-god. The god was less lenient with Mr. Montagu Smythje, who was compelled to pay no less than six bottles of rum, with sundry plugs of tobacco, to preserve his elegant whiskers and moustaches from the pollution of tar and " tub fat." Why the young steerage passenger thus kept himself clear of the quarter-deck, and shunned communion with the denizens of the cabin, was a mystery to those who chanced to speculate upon the circumstance ; though after all, there was not much mystery about his behaviour. Doubtless, he was actuated by a certain personal pride, and felt humiliated by his inferior position as a steerage passenger—a feeling natural enough, though, perhaps, not very commendable. He knew the allowance of the quarter-deck to those of his class was a courtesy, not a privilege ; and being one of those independent spirits who refuse to accept that which they cannot claim as a right, he had declined to avail himself of the quarter-deck courtesy.

Since he had never been aft, and Mr. Montagu Smythje had as religiously abstained from venturing forward, it was not likely that much conversation had passed between the two. In truth, there had not been any—not even the exchange of a word—during the whole voyage.

Of course the two young men had often seen each other, and were perfectly familiar each with the other's face. Smythje had even noticed the peculiarity of his fellow-voyager, in keeping apart from the rest, and had pronounced him a " demned queeaw fellaw"—a description which the latter—in thought, if not in speech—had no doubt reciprocated.

The cockney exquisite, moreover—notwithstanding the paucity of his reflective powers—had gradually become inspired with a certain degree of curiosity as to who and what the " queeaw fellaw" might be. More than once he had put this question to the captain and others ; but all these, equally with himself, were ignorant of the antecedents of the steerage passenger.

" Know nothing about him," said the blunt skipper; " nothing whatever. Came aboard the day before we sailed, with an old portmanteau, paid his passage money, and took possession of his berth—that's all I know."

" Demned queeaw fellaw !" reiterated Mr. Smythje, for the twentieth time. " Aw—aw—should ask himself if thaw was an oppawtunity ; but the odd animal nevaw comes this way—aw cawnt undawtake a jawney up yawndaw—the place smells abawmnably of taw."

The " oppawtunity" thus desired turned up at length ; but only at the eleventh hour. In the very last hour of the voyage—just as the Sea Nymph was heading in to the harbour—the passengers of all degrees walked towards the ship's head in order to get a better view of the glorious landscape now unfolding itself before them ; and the exquisite, yielding to a curiosity so general, went forward among the rest. Having gained an elevated standpoint upon the top of the windlass, he adjusted his glass to his eye, and commenced ogling the landscape, whose details were now near enough to be distinguished. Not for long, however, did Mr. Smythje remain silent, for he was not one of a saturnine habit. The fair scene had inspired him with a poetical fervour, which soon found expression in characteristic speech.

" Dooced pwetty, 'pon honaw !" he exclaimed ; " would make a splendid dwop scene faw a theataw. Don't you think so, my good fwend ?" added he, addressing himself somewhat presumingly to a person who was standing by his side.

" Really, my good fwend," replied the person addressed, and who chanced to be the young steerage passenger, " I think that altogether depends upon the subject that may have been chosen for your dwop-scene." Notwithstanding the satirical wording of the reply, it was uttered without any evidence of ill-nature. On the contrary, a good-humoured smile curled upon the lips of the speaker, at the same time that he fixed his eyes upon the exquisite, with a somewhat quizzical expression.

" Aw—haw—it is yaw, my young fellow," said the latter, now for the first time perceiving to whom he had made his appeal. " Aw, indeed !" he continued, without appearing to notice the cynical attitude which the other had asumed. " Aw ! a veway stwange individwal !—incompwehensibly stwange. May aw ask—pawdon the liberty—what is bwinging yaw out heaw—to Jamaica, aw mean ?"

" That," replied the steerage passenger, slightly nettled at this rather free style of interrogation, " which is bringing yourself—the good ship Sea Nymph."

" Aw, haw ! indeed ! Good—veway good ! But, my deaw saw, that is not what aw meant."

" No ?"

" No, aw ashow yaw. Aw meant what bwisness bwings yaw here P'waps you have some pwofession ?" .

" No, not any, I ashow yaw."

" A twade, then ?"

" I am sorry to say I have not even a twade."

" No pwofession : no twade ! what the dooce daw yaw intend dawing in Jamaica ? P'waps yaw expect the situation of bookkeepaw on a pwantation, or niggaw dwiver. Neithaw, aw believe, requiaws much expewience, as aw am told, the bookkeepaw has pwositively no books to keep—haw ! haw ! and showly any fellaw, howevaw ig-iowant, may dwive a niggaw. Is that yaw expectation, my worthy fwend ?"

" I have no expectation, one way, or another " replied the young man,

in a tone of careless indifference. " As to the buisness I may follow out
here in Jamaica, that, I suppose, will depend on the will of another."

" Anothaw! aw!—who, pway ?"

" My uncle."

" Aw, indeed! yaw have an uncle in Jamaica, then ?"

" I have—if he be still alive."

" Aw—haw! yaw are not sure of that intewesting fact? P'waps
yaw've not heard from him wately ?"

" Not for years," replied the young steerage passenger, his poor prospects now having caused him to relinquish the satirical tone he had assumed. " Not for years," repeated he, " though I've written to him, to
say that I should come by this ship."

" Veway stwange! And, pway, may I ask what bwisness yaw uncle
follows ?"

" He is a planter, I believe."

" A sugaw plantaw ?"

" Yes—he was so when we last heard from him."

" Aw, then, p'waps he is wich—a pwopwietor. In that case he may
find something faw yaw to daw bettew than niggaw-dwiving ; make yaw
his ovawseeaw ? May aw know yaw name !"

" Quite welcome. Herbert Vaughan is my name."

" Vawn! repeated the exquisite, in a tone that betrayed some newly
awakened interest; " Vawn, do aw understand yaw to say ?"

" Herbert Vaughan," replied the young man, with firmer emphasis.

" And yaw uncle's name ?"

" He is also called Vaughan. He is my father's brother—or rather
was—my father is dead."

" Not Woftus Vawn, Esq., of Mount Welcome !"

" Loftus is my uncle's baptismal appellation, and Mount Welcome is, I
believe, the name of his estate."

" Veway stwange! incompwehensibly stwange! D'yaw know, my
young fellaw, that yaw and aw appeaw to be making faw the same pawt.
Woftus Vawn, of Mount Welcome, is the twustwee of my own pwoperty
—the veway fellaw to whom aw am consigned. Deaw me! how dooced
stwange yaw and aw should be guests-undaw the same woof !" The remark was accompanied by a supercilious glance, that did not escape the
observation of the young steerage passenger. It was this glance that
gave the true signification of the words, which Herbert Vaughan interpreted as an insult. He was on the point of making an appropriate rejoinder, when the exquisite abruptly turned away—as he parted drawling out some words of leave-taking, with the presumptive conjecture
that they might meet again.

Herbert Vaughan stood for a moment looking after him, an expression
of high contempt curling upon his lip. Only for a short while, however,
did this show itself ; and then, his countenance resuming its habitual
expression of good nature, he descended into the steerage, to prepare
his somewhat scanty baggage for the debarkation.

CHAPTER XVII.

QUASHIE.

In less than half an hour after the brief conversation between Mr. Montagu Smythje and the young steerage passenger, the Sea Nymph had got warped into port, and was lying alongside the wharf.

A gangway-plank was stretched from the shore : and over this, men and women, of all shades of colour, from blonde to ebony black, and of as many different callings, came crowding aboard ; while the passengers sick of the ship and everything belonging to her, hastened to go ashore.

Half-naked porters—black, brown, and yellow—were wrangling over the luggage—dragging trunks, boxes, and bags in every direction but the right one, and clamouring their gumbo jargon with a volubility that resembled the jabbering of apes.

On the wharf appeared a number of wheeled vehicles, that had evidently been awaiting the arrival of the ship—not hackneys, as would have been the case in a European port, but private carriages—some of them handsome "curricles," drawn by a pair, and driven by black Jehus in livery : others only gigs with a single horse, or other two wheelers of even an inferior description, according to the wealth or style of the individual for whose transport each had been brought to the port.

Wagons, too, with teams of oxen—some having eight in the yoke— stood near the landing-place, waiting for baggage : the naked black driv ers lounging silently by the animals, or occasionally calling them by their names, and talking to them just as if their speeches had been understood.

Among the different carriages ranged along the wharf, a handsome barouche appeared conspicuous. It was attached to a pair of cream-coloured horses, splendidly harnessed. A mulatto coachman sat upon the box, shining in a livery of lightest green, with yellow facings ; while a footman, in garments of like hue, attended at the carriage step, holding the door for some one to get in.

Herbert Vaughan, standing on the fore-deck of the Sea Nymph—as yet undecided as to whether he should then go ashore—had noticed this magnificent equipage. He was still gazing upon it, when his attention was attracted to two gentlemen, who, having walked direct from the vessel, had just arrived by the side of the carriage. A white servant followed them ; and behind were two negro attendants carrying a number of parcels of light luggage. One of the gentlemen and the white servant were easily recognised by Herbert: for both had been his fellow-passengers. They were Mr. Montagu Smythje and his valet. The other, who appeared to act as chaperone, was of the island, and the two negro attendants were his. Herbert now recalled the odd expression made use of, but the moment before, by the fop—that he was "consigned" to the proprietor of Mount Welcome. Was the carriage from Mount Welcome ? And was the bland-looking gentleman, who accompanied it, his uncle ? No—the man was too young for that ? and, moreover, his rather well-worn coat, and common duck trousers would scarcely become the owner of such an equipage ? Herbert turned round and looked for some one, to

whom he might address an inquiry. Plenty of islanders were aboard—
whites as well as coloured people—but most of them were far off—amid-
ships, or on the quarter-deck. Only one veritable *native* was within
speaking distance—a negro boy of such clumsy and uncouth appearance,
that the young man hesitated about putting his interrogatory—hopeless
of obtaining an intelligible answer.

As he scrutinised the darkey with more care, a certain twinkling of
his cyes bespoke more intelligence than Herbert had at first given him
credit for. Moreover, the boy was eyeing him with a fixed regard - as
if courting an inquiry, or desirous of making one himself.

Herbert resolved to seek from this source the information he required.

" Well, my lad ;" said he, in a kindly tone ; " can you tell me whose
carriage that is up yonder—the one with the cream-coloured horses, and
coachman in green livery ?"

" Yaw ! yaw !" replied the young darkey, exhibiting his ivories in a
broad grin ; dat yonna massr b'rouche. Ebberybody know dat b'rouche
—ebberybody in da Bay."

" What massa ?"

" Why, *my* massr, sartin sure."

" And what might be your massa's name ?"

" Him name ? da great house him name—Moun' Welc'm'—big plantation ob da sugar."

" It is Mr. Vaughan's carriage, then ?"

" Ya, sa, Massr Va'n—great buckra."

" Is that Mr. Vaughan himself—he that is now mounting his horse ?"

" Massr Va'n—no. Da's only de oberseeah. He met the grand buckra
who come by big ship. Dey drive out na Moun' Welc'm'. Dar dey go !
Hoop ! how Cudjo whip up dem hosses !"

The carriage having received Mr. Montagu Smythje, and the footman
having mounted the box—leaving the rumble to the English valet—was
driven off at full speed, the overseer following on horseback as an escort.
Herbert watched the receding vehicle, until a turn in the road hid it
from his view ; and then, dropping his eyes towards the deck, he stood
for some moments in a reflective attitude, revolving in his mind some
thoughts that were far from agreeable. He had, for the time, forgotten
the darkey ; though the latter still remained by his side, gazing upon
him with a marked look of interrogation. Herbert was reflecting upon
his own situation. No one there to meet *him* and bid him welcome !
What could it mean ?

Had his uncle not received his letter ? Surely it must have miscar-
ried ? In that case, how should he act ? Inquire the way to Mount
Welcome, and set out for it at once ? At once it must be : for he had no
money—not a crown to pay for a lodging in the town. He would have to
walk, too, from the lack of the wherewith to hire a horse. And then, on
his arrival, how should he be received ? At Mount Welcome was he to
find a welcome ? He knew nothing of his uncle's disposition towards
him. For years the planter had not deigned to correspond with his
father—with himself, never ; knew nothing of himself, and he, coming
penniless, poorly clad, and, worse than all, without calling or profession
—what reception could he expect ?

The countenance of the young adventurer became clouded under the influence of these thoughts ; and he stood silently gazing upon the deck with eyes that saw not.

"Sa !" said the negro boy, interrupting his reflections.

"Ha ! you there yet ?" rejoined Herbert looking up and perceiving with some surprise that the darkey was regarding him with a fixed stare " What might you want, my lad ? If it be money, I have none to give."

" Money, sa ? wharra fo Quashie want money ? He do wha' masser bid! Young buckra ready go now ?"

" Ready to go ! whore ? what mean you, boy ?"

" Go fo da great house."

" Great house ! Of what great house are you speaking ?"

" Moun' Welc'm'. so—Masser Va'n. You fo Masser Va'n, sa ?"

" What !" exclaimed Herbert in surprise, at the same time scanning the darkey from head to foot, " how do you know that, my boy ?"

" Quashie know dat well 'nuff. Cappen ob da big ship, obaseeah say so Obaseeah point out young buckra from de waff—he send Quashie.fetch young buckra to Moun' Welc'm'. Ready go now, sa ?"

" You are from Mount Welcome, then ?"

" Ya, sa—me hoss-boy da, an' pose-boy—fetch pony for young Englis buckra. Obaseeah he bring b'rouche for grand Englis' buckra. Baggage dey go in de ox-wagon. '

" Where is your pony !"

" Up yonna, sa ; on de waff, sa ; ready go, sa !"

" All right," said Herbert, now comprehending the situation of affairs. "Shoulder that portmanteau, then, my lad, and toss it into the wagon. Which road am I to take !"

· " Can't miss um road, sa—straight up da ribber till you come to do crossin'. Dar you take de road dat don't lead to da leff—you soon see Moun' Welc'm', sa."

" How far is it !"

" 'Bout fo' mile, sa—reach dar long 'fore sundown ; pony go like do berry lightnin'. Sure you keep to da right by da crossin'."

Thus instructed, the young steerage passenger left the ship—after bidding adieu to the friendly tars, who had treated him so handsomely during his irksome voyage. With his gun, a single-barrelled fowling-piece, on his shoulder, he strode over the platform, and up the wooden wharf. Then detaching the pony from the wheel of the ox-wagon, to which it had been tied, he threw himself into the saddle, and trotted off along the road pointed out as the one that would conduct him to Mount Welcome.

CHAPTER XVIII.

TRAVELLING AT THE TAIL.

THE excitement produced by the sudden change from ship to shore—the stir of the streets through which he had to pass—the novel sights and

sounds that at every step saluted his eyes and ears—hindered Herber
Vaughan from thinking of anything that concerned himself.
Only for a short time, however, was his mind thus distracted from
dwelling on his own affairs. Before he had ridden far, the road—hither·
to bordered by houses—entered under a dark canopy of forest foliage ;
and the young traveller, all at once, found himself surrounded by a per
fect solitude. Under the sombre shadow of the trees, his spirit soon re
turned to its former for*boding ; and, riding more slowly over a stretch
of the road where the ground was wet and boggy ; he fell into a train of
thoughts that was far from pleasant. Indeed, the gloomy expressi**
they produced upon his features proclaimed them exceedingly painful
The subjects of his reflections may be easily guessed. It was but
natural his mind should dwell on the reception he was likely to meet at
the hands of his kinsman ; and, from what had already transpired, he
could draw no very favourable augury of what was to come.
He had not failed to notice—how could he !—the distinction made between himself and his fellow-voyager. While a splendid equipage had
been waiting for the latter—and his landing had been made a sort of
ovation, under the superintendance of the head manager of his uncle's
estate, assisted by servants in shining liveries—how different was the
means of transport provided for him ! No word of welcome, nor even
recognition, from the overseer—so obsequious to his fellow-passenger !
And yet, there was proof positive that his letter had been received in
due course. The presence of the scraggy, ill-conditioned, and poorly-
caparisoned cob—with the intelligence he had gathered from the uncouth groom who brought it to the Bay—were evidence of his being ex·
pected by his uncle.
The young man felt the humiliation—not slightly, but keenly ; and
the longer he dwelt upon the circumstance, the more mortified did he
become.
" By the memory of my father !" muttered he, as he rode on, " it is an
insult I shall not overlook : an insult to him, more than to myself. But
for the fulfilment of his dying wish, I should not go one step farther ;"
and as he said this, he drew his rough roadster to a halt, as if half resolved to put his hypothetic threat into practice. " Perhaps," he continued, again moving forward with a more hopeful air, " perhaps there may
be some mistake ! But no," he added, with a strong emphasis on the
negative monosyllable, " there can be none ! This shallow fop is a young
man of fortune—I a child of misfortune ;" and he smiled bitterly at the
antithesis he had drawn ; " that is the reason why such a distinction has
been made between us. Be it so !" he continued, after a pause. " Poor
as I am, this churlish relative will find me as proud as himself. I shall
return him scorn for scorn. I shall demand an explanation of his behaviour, and the sooner I have it the better."
As if stimulated by a sense of the outrage, as also by a half-formed
purpose of retaliation, the young adventurer gave the whip to his shaggy steed, and dashed onward at full gallop. The cob needed no very
violent driving. Had its head been turned in the opposite direction, the
case might have been different ; but the animal knew it was going homeward ; and the attractions of its own crib acted as the stimulus to a more

rapid speed than the flagellation of whip or the pricking of spurs could have produced. For a full hour was this gallop continued, without pause or slacking. The road was a wide one, much tracked by wheels ; and, as it ran in a direct course, the rider took it for granted he was keeping the right path. Now and then he caught a glimpse of water through the trees—no doubt the river mentioned in the directions given him by the darkey. The crossing at length came in sight, causing him to desist from his rapid gallop—in order that he might ford the stream. There was no appearance of a bridge. The water, however was only knee deep ; and, without hesitation, the pony plunged in, and waded over. Herbert halted on the opposite bank : for there appeared in front of him a dilemma. The road forked. The negro boy had warned him of this— telling him at the same time to take the one that *didn't* lead to "da leff;" but, instead of two "tines" to the fork, there were *three*!

Here was a puzzle. It was easy enough to know which of the three not to take—the one that *did* lead to " da leff ;" but which of the other two was to be chosen, was the point that appeared to present a difficulty in the solution. Both were plain, good roads ; and each as likely as the other to be the one which would conduct him to Mount Welcome.

Had his rider left the pony to its own guidance, perhaps it would have chosen the right road. In all likelihood he would have done so in the end ; but, before determining on any particular line of action, he thought it better to look for the wheels of the carriage that he knew must have passed in advance of him.

While thus cogitating, the silence occasioned by his momentary halt was all at once interrupted by a voice—that sounded at his very side— and the tones of which he fancied were not new to him.

On suddenly turning in the saddle, and looking in the direction whence the voice appeared to proceed, what was his astonishment on beholding the negro boy—the veritable Quashie !

" Da, sa! das da crossin' me you tell 'bout; you no take by de leff— dat lead to ole Jew penn; nor da right—he go to Mon'gew Cassel; de middle Massr Va'n road—he go strait na Moun' Welc'm'."

The young traveler sat for some moments without speaking, or making reply in any way—surprise holding him as if struck by paralysis. He had left the boy on the forward deck of the ship, to look after his luggage ; and he had seen him—he could almost swear to it—still on board, as he rode away from the wharf ! Moreover, he had ridden a stretch of many miles—most of the way at full gallop, and all of it at a pace with which no pedestrian could possibly have kept up ! How, then, was he to account for the presence of Quashie ?

This was the first question that occurred to him ; and which he put to the darkey, as soon as he had sufficiently recovered from his surprise to be able to speak.

" Quashie foller young buckra—at him pony heels."

The answer went but a short way towards enlightening the " young buckra ;" since he still believed it utterly impossible for any human being to have travelled as fast as he had ridden.

" At the pony's heels ! What, my blackskin! do you mean to say you have run all the way after me from the landing-place ?"

" Ya, sa, dat hab Quashie do."

" But I saw you on board the ship as I started off? How on earth could you have overtaken me?"

" Yaw, massr, dat wa' easy 'nuf. Young buckra, he start off; Quashie, he put him porkmantle in da ox-cart and foller. Buckra, he go slow at fuss, Quashie soon cotch up, and den easy run 'long wi' da pony—not much in dat, sa."

" Not much! Why, you imp of darkness, I have been riding at the rate of ten miles an hour, and how you've kept up with me is beyond my comprehension! Well, you're a noble runner, that I must say! I'd back you at a foot-race against all comers, whether black ones or white ones. The middle road, you say?"

" Ya, sa, dat de way to Moun' Welc'm'; you soon see de big gate ob de plantation."

Herbert headed his roadster in the direction indicated; and moved onward along the path—his thoughts still dwelling on the odd incident.

He had proceeded but a few lengths of his pony, when he was tempted to look back—partly to ascertain if Quashie was still following him, and partly with the intention of putting a query to this singular escort.

A fresh surprise was in store for him. The darkey was nowhere to be seen! Neither to the right, nor the left, nor yet in the rear, was he visible!

" Where the deuce can the imp have gone?" inquired Herbert, mechanically, at the same time scanning the underwood on both sides of the road.

" Hya, sa !" answered a voice that appeared to come out of the ground close behind—while at the same instant the brown mop of Quashie, just visible over the croup of the cob, proclaimed his whereabouts.

How the boy had been able to keep up with the pony was at length explained : he had been *holding on to its tail !* There was something so ludicrous in the sight, that the young Englishman forgot for a moment the grave thoughts that had been harassing him ; and, once more checking his steed into a halt, gave utterance to roars of laughter. The darkey joined in his mirth with a grin that extended his mouth from ear to ear —though he was utterly unconscious of what the young buckra could be laughing at. He could not see anything comic in a custom which he was almost daily in the habit of practising—for it was not the first time Quashie had travelled at the tail of a horse.

CHAPTER XIX.

ON TO MOUNT WELCOME.

JOURNEYING about half a mile farther along the main road, the entrance gate of Mount Welcome came in sight. There was no lodge—only a pair of grand stone piers, with a wing of strong mason-work on each flank, and a massive folding gate between them. From the directions Herbert had already received, he might have known this to be the entrance to his uncle's plantation ; but Quashie, still clinging to the pony's tail, removed all doubt by crying out—

" Da's da gate, buckra gemman—da's de way fo' Moun' Welc'm'."

On passing through the gateway, the mansion itself came in sight—its white walls and green jalousies shining conspicuously at the extreme end of the long avenue ; which last, with its bordering rows of palms and tamarinds, gave to the approach an air of aristocratic grandeur.   Herbert had been prepared for something of this kind.   He had heard at home that his father's brother was a man of great wealth; and this was nearly all his father had himself known respecting him.   The equipage which had transported his more favoured fellow-voyager—and which had passed over the same road about an hour before him—also gave evidence of the grand style in which his uncle lived.   The mansion now before his eyes was in correspondence with what he had heard and seen.   There could be no doubt that his uncle was one of the grandees of the island. The reflection gave him less pleasure than pain.   His pride had been already wounded ; and, at that moment, he would have preferred a hovel and a hearty welcome to the hospitality of a palace so churlishly extend- ed to him.   Even before landing—before embarking, we might say—he had indulged in no very sanguine expectations of being well received. He could then reason only from his own father's experience.   Now he had other *data :* in the difference of the reception already accorded to his fel- low-voyager and himself ; and, as he looked up the noble avenue, he was oppressed with a presentiment that some even greater humiliation was in store for him.

He knew not what family his uncle had : his father had never heard— not even whether he had been married.   To the English relatives of Loftus Vaughan, his ' mésalliance ' with the quadroon, Quasheba, had never been reported ; nor much else that related to him since his migration to Jamaica.

Herbert was therefore approaching the house utterly ignorant upon those points—not knowing whether his uncle was childless, or whether, on his arrival, he might encounter a large family circle.

Naturally enough, his mind speculated upon the probability of his hav ing some cousins, and very naturally did he feel a curiosity to be satisfied on this head.   Could Quashie give him the desired information ?   The boy was still clinging to the pony's tail, and Herbert resolved to interro- gate him.

" Quashie ! that's your name, is it ?"

" Ya, sa ; Quashie da pose-boy."

" Post-boy ! you carry the letters, then ?"

" Ya, sa ; to pose-office in da Bay, an toddars back fo' da great house."

" Whose letters do you carry ?"

" Massr letter, be sure, sa ; sometime be letter for young missr."

" Which young missr ?"

" Lor, sa ! why you axe ?   Sure, dar only be one young missr—Missr Kate, massr own daughter."

" One cousin, at least," soliloquised Herbert, rather satisfied at the success of his indirect questioning, " and that of the right sex," he con- tinued ; " I wonder if there be any males in the family.   Quashie ?"

" Hya, sa."

" Do you ever have letters for Miss Kate's brother ?"

"Missr Kate brodder? She hab no brodder, sa; I nebber seed um."
"Oh! I meant her father."
"Lor, sa! Quashie jess say jess now he bring letter for Massr Va'n. Mose all de letters fo' massr."
"Only one cousin," again soliloquised Herbert. "Under other circumstances this might have been interesting; but now——Tell me, Quashie Was it your master himself who gave you directions about conducting me to Mount Welcome; or did you have your orders from the overseer?"
"Massr no me speak 'bout you, sa; I no hear him say nuffin."
"The overseer, then?"
"Ya, sa, de obaseeah."
"What did he bid you do? Tell me as near as you can; and I may make you a present one of these days."
"Gorry, massr buckra! I you tell all he say, 'zactly as he say um. 'Quashie,' say he, 'Quashie,' he say, 'you go down board de big ship; you see dat ere young buckra'—dat war yourself, sa—' you fotch 'im up to de ox wagon, you fotch 'im baggage, too; you mount 'im on Coco'—da's de pony's name—'and den you fotch him home to my house.' Da's all he say—ebbery word."
"To *his* house? Mount Welcome, you mean?"
"No, young buckra gemman—to da obaseeah house. And now we jess got to da road dat lead dar. Dis way, sa! dis way!"
The darkey pointed to a bye-road, that, forking off from the main avenue, ran in the direction of the ridge, where it entered into a tract of thick woods.
Herbert had checked the pony to a halt, and sat gazing at his guide, in mute surprise.
"Dis way, sa!" repeated the boy. "Yonner's 'im house. You see wha da smoke rises, jess ober de big tree?"
"What do you mean, my good fellow? What house are you talking of?"
"Da obaseeah house, sa!"
"What have I to do with the overseer's house?"
"Wees agwine da, sa."
"Who? You?"
"Bof, sa; an' de pony too."
"Have you taken leave of your senses, you imp of darkness?"
"No, sa; Quashie only do what him bid. Da obaseeah Quashie bid fotch young buckra to him house. Dis yeer's da way."
"I tell you, boy, you must be mistaken. It is to Mount Welcome I am going—my uncle's house—up yonder!"
"No, buckra gemman, me no mastake. Da obaseeah berry partikler 'bout dat. He toll me you no for da great house—da Buff. He say me fotch you to 'im own house."
"Are you sure of that?"
Herbert, as he put this interrogatory, leant forward in the saddle, and listened attentively for the reply,
"Lor, buckra gemman! I's sure ob it as de sun in de hebbens dar I swa' it, if you like"

On hearing this positive affirmation, the young Englishman sat for a moment, as if wrapt in a profound and painful reflection. His breast rose and fell as though some terrible truth was breaking upon him, which he was endeavouring to disbelieve.

At this moment, Quashie caught the rein of the bridle, and was about to lead the pony into the bye-path.

"No!" shouted the rider, in a voice loud as thunder. "Let go, boy! let go! or I'll give you the whip! This is *my* way."

And, wrenching the rein from the grasp of the guide, he headed the pony back into the avenue.

Then, laying on the lash with all his might, he kept on, at full gallop, 'n the direction of the "great house."

CHAPTER XX.

A SLIPPERY FLOOR.

THE carriage conveying Mr. Montagu Smythje from Montego Bay to Mount Welcome had passed up the avenue and arrived at the great house, just one hour before Herbert Vaughan, mounted on his rough roadster, and guided by Quashie, made his appearance at the entrance-gate of the plantation. Herbert, keeping his eye fixed on the house as he advanced, could see no one neither in front nor on the landing, nor in the windows, though the Venetian shutters stood wide open.

This absence of every human being from the front part of the dwelling very naturally suggested to the young man a reflection. His uncle, and all his domestics as well, were occupied inside with the aristocratic and honoured guest—no one was looking out for him.

This conjecture was not far from the truth. His uncle was not even thinking of him. Having taken the precautions already explained, the planter was no longer apprehensive of a *contretemps*. Mr. Smythje had arrived at half-past three, P. M. Four was the regular dining hour at Mount Welcome: so that there was just neat time for the valet to unpack the ample valises and portmanteaus, and dress his exquisite master for the table. All this had been done before the young steerage passenger came within view of the house—all this, and more. The dinner had been placed upon the table; the bell had summoned the guests; Mr. Vaughan had presented the honoured stranger to his daughter Kate; and the three—father, daughter, and, in Mr. Vaughan's view the presumptive son-in-law—had seated themselves at the table.

As only three covers had been placed, the number of guests was complete, and the dinner commenced. No one else appeared to be expected, and no one was mentioned as missing. It had been the aim of Mr Vaughan to make the introduction of Mr. Smythje to his daughter as effective as possible. He was sage enough to know the power of first appearances. For that reason, he had managed to keep them apart until the moment of meeting at the dinner table, when both should appear under the advantage of a full dress. So far as the impression to be made on Mr. Smythje was concerned, Mr. Vaughan's scheme was perfectly successful. His daughter really appeared superb—radiant as the crimson quamoclit that glistened in her hair; graceful as nature, and elegant as art, could make her. Even the heart of the cockney felt, perhaps for the first time in his life, that true sentiment of admiration which beauty, combined with virgin modesty, is almost certain to inspire.

For a moment, the remembrance of the ballet-girl, and the lewd recollections of the *bagnio*, were obliterated; and a graver and nobler inspiration took their place. Even vulgar Loftus Vaughan had skill enough to note this effect; but how long it would last—how long the plant of a pure passion would flourish in that uncongenial soil, was a question which it required an abler physiologist than Loftus Vaughan to determine. The sugar-planter chuckled as he noted his success. Smythje was smitten, beyond the shadow of a doubt.

Had the calculating father been equally anxious to perceive a *reciprocity* of this fine first impression, he would have been doomed to a disappointment. As certainly as that of Mr. Smythje was a sentiment of admiration, so certainly was that of Kate Vaughan a feeling of 'degoût;' or, to speak in more moderate terms, one of indifference.

Worst sign of all—worst for the hopes of Montagu's lord—from the moment she became seated at the table, Miss Vaughan was all mirth and smiles. The guest appeared gratified by this genial amiability. Ah, Smythje! you were not then in the *coulisse* or the green-room. Your deductions were deceitful. Had you known as much as I, you would have preferred a frown. In truth, the Londoner had made a most unfortunate 'début,' A *gaucherie* had happened in the ceremony of introduction—just at that crisis moment when all eyes are sharply set, and all ears acutely bent in mutual *reconnoisance*. Mr. Vaughan had committed a grand error in causing the presentation to take place in the grand hall. Ice itself was not more slippery than its floor; and the consequence was unavoidable. Had the cockney been upon skates, he might have performed to satisfaction: for many winters had seen him upon the Serpentine, running figures of 8.

As it was, however, his patent pumps were frictionless upon the polished floor of a Jamaica dining-hall; and, essaying one of his most graceful attitudes, he came down like a "thousand of bricks" at the feet of her he simply intended to have saluted. In that fall he had lost everything—every chance of winning Kate Vaughan's heart. A thousand acts of gracefulness, a thousand deeds of heroism, would not have set him up again after that fall. It was a clear paraphrase of the downfall of Humpty Dumpty—the restoration alike hopeless, alike impossible.

Mr. Montagu Smythje was too well stocked with self-complacency to suffer much embarrassment from a *lapsus* of so trifling a character. His valet had him upon his feet in a trice; and with a "Haw-haw!" and the remark that the floor was "demned swippawy," he crept cautiously to his chair, and seated himself. The dinner proceeded. Though the Londoner had been all his life accustomed to dining well, he could not help a feeling of surprise at the plentiful and luxurious repast that was placed before him.

Perhaps in no part of the world does the table groan under a greater load of rich viands than in the West Indian islands. In the prosperous times of sugar planting, a Jamaican dinner was deserving of the name of feast. Turtle was the common soup, and the most sumptuous dishes stood thickly over the board. Even the ordinary every-day desert was a spread worthy of Apicius ; and the wines—instead of those dull twin poisons, port and sherry—were south-side madeira, champagne, claret, and sparkling hock—all quaffed in copious flagons, plenteous as small beer

These were glorious times for the white-skinned oligarchy of the sugar Islands—the days of revel and rollicky living, before the wedge of Wilberforce split the dark pedestal which propped up their pomp and prosperity.

A dinner of this good old-fashioned style had Loftus Vaughan prepared for his English guest. Behind the chairs appeared troops of coloured attendants, gliding silently over the smooth floor. A constant stream of domestics poured in and out of the hall, fetching and removing the dishes and plates, or carrying the wine decanters in their silver coolers. Young girls, of various shades of complexion—some nearly white—stood at intervals around the table, fanning the guests with long peacock plumes, and filling the great hall with an artificial current of delicious coolness.

Montagu Smythje was delighted. Even in his " deaw metwopolis " he had never dined so luxuriously.

" Spwendid, spwendid—'pon honaw ! A dinaw fit fwo a pwince."

So complimented he his West Indian entertainer.

Mr. Vaughan, on his part, was gratified by the progress of events. He saw that his preparations had not been thrown away. He had succeeded in his purpose—to make a good first impression upon his visitor ; and, as far as human foresight could penetrate into the future, all would go well. He no longer doubted—how could he ?—that the estates of Montagu Castle and Mount Welcome would at some, and no very distant, day be united in one magnificent domain.

Kate was behaving admirably ; though about her behaviour he had less solicitude. It had never entered into his calculations to consult *her* will in his match-making designs. As his daughter she owed him obedience. Perhaps the thought occurred to him that she owed it in a double sense ; *since he was both her father and her master.*

Kate, however, was giving him no reason to complain of her conduct. She was acting just as he desired ; and the same smiling affability that had made such favourable impression on the newly arrived guest, equally deluded the belief of the fond parent.

Ah, Loftus Vaughan? You may have known how to ratoon your golden canes—you may have been deeply skilled in the crystallisation of sugars—but those signs that indicate the instinctive inclinings of a maiden's heart were things too subtle for your comphchension !

CHAPTER XXI.

THE COMING CLOUD.

THE dinner passed smoothly. The savoury dishes had been tasted, and

carried off; and the table, now arranged for *dessert*, exhibited that gorgeous profusion such as a tropic clime can alone produce—where almost
every order of the botanical world supplies some fruit or berry of rarest
excellence. Alone in the tropic regions of the New World may such
variety be seen—a *dessert table*, upon which Pomona appears to have
poured forth her golden *cornucopia*.

The cloth had been removed from the highly polished table, and the
sparkling decanters were once more passed around. In honour of his
guest, the planter had already played free with his own wines, which
were all of most excellent quality. Loftus Vaughan was at that momen'
at a maximum of enjoyment.

Just at that very moment, however, a cloud made its appearance on the
edge of the sky. It was a very little cloud, and still very far off; but,
for all that, a careful observer could have seen that its shadow was reflected on the brow of Loftus Vaughan.

We have spoken figuratively in calling the object that caused this
shadow a cloud, and placing it in the sky. Literally speaking, it was an
object on the earth, of shape half human, half equine, that appeared near
the extreme end of the long avenue, moving towards the house.

When first seen by Loftus Vaughan it was still distant, though not so
far off but that, with the naked eye, he could distinguish a man on horseback.

This apparition appeared to produce an instantaneous effect upon him.
A shadow settled upon his forehead; and from that moment he might
have been observed to turn about in his chair, at short intervals casting
uneasy glances upon the centaurean form that was gradually growing
bigger as it advanced.

This apparently mysterious change in the behaviour of Mr. Vaughan
was easily accounted for. He had recognised the approaching horseman,
or rather the pony on which he was mounted. He knew the rider to be
his nephew: for the overseer had already reported the arrival of Herbert Vaughan by the Sea Nymph.

For a time the expression was far from being a marked one. The looks
that conveyed it were furtive, and might have passed unnoticed by the
superficial observer. They had, in fact, escaped the notice both of his
daughter and his guest; and it was not until after the halt at entrance of
the by-path, and the horseman was seen coming on directly for the house,
that the attention of either was drawn to the singular behaviour of Mr.
Vaughan. Then, however, his nervous anxiety had become so undis-
guisedly patent, as to elicit from Miss Vaughan an ejaculation of surprise,
while the cockney involuntarily exclaimed, "'Bless ma soul!" adding the
interrogatory—

"Anything wrong, sir?"

"Oh! nothing!" stammered the planter; "only—only—a little surprise
—that's all."

"Surprise, papa! what has caused it? Oh, see; yonder is some one on
horseback—a man—a young man. I declare it is our own pony he is
riding; and that is our Quashie running behind him! How very amusing! Papa, what is it all about?"

"Tut! sit down, child!" commanded the father, in a tone of nervous

perplexity. " Sit down, I say ! Whoever it be, it will be time enough
to know when he arrives. Kate ! Kate ! 'tis not well bred of you to in
terrupt our dessert. Mr. Smythje, glass of madeira with you, sir ?"
" Plesyaw !" answered the exquisite, turning once more to the table,
and occupying himself with his glass.

Kate obeyed the command with a look of reluctance and surprise. She
was slightly awed, too ; not so much by the words, as the severe glance
that accompanied them. She made no reply, but sat gazing with a mysti
fied air in the face of her father, who, hob-nobbing with his guest, affected
not to notice her.

The pony and his rider were no longer visible, as they were now too
close to the house to be seen over the sill of the window, but the clatter-
ing hoofs could be heard, the sounds coming nearer and nearer.

Mr. Vaughan was endeavouring to appear collected, and to say something ; but his *sang froid* was evidently assumed and unnatural ; and, being unable to keep up the conversation, an ominous silence succeeded.
The sound of the hoofs ceased to be heard. The pony had arrived under
the windows, and come to a halt. Then there were voices—earnest and
rather low. These were succeeded by the noise of footsteps on the stone
stairway. Some one was coming up the steps. Mr. Vaughan looked aghast.
All his fine plans were about to be frustrated. There was a hitch in the
programme—Quashie had failed in the performance of *his* part.

" Aha !" ejaculated the planter, with delight, as the smooth, trim countenance of his overseer made its appearance above the landing. '' Mr.
Trusty wishes to speak with' me. Your pardon, Mr. Smythje—only for
one moment."

As he said this, he rose from his seat, and hastened to meet the overseer before he could enter the room. The latter, however, had already
stepped inside the doorway ; and, not being much of a diplomatist, had
bluntly declared his errand—in *sotto voce,* it it true, but still not la
enough to hinder a part of his communication from being heard. Among
other words, the phrase, " your nephew," reached the ears of Kate—at
that moment keenly bent to catch every sound.

The reply was also partially heard, though delivered in a low, and apparently tremulous voice—" Show him—kiosk—garden—tell him—there
presently."

Mr. Vaughan turned back to the table with a half-satisfied look. He
was fancying that he had escaped from his dilemma, at least, for the
time ; but the expression he perceived on the countenance of his daughter restored the suspicion that all was not right.

Scarce a second was he left in doubt, for almost on the instant that the
words were uttered, Kate cried out, in a tone of pleased surprise—

" Oh ! papa, what do I hear ? Did not Mr. Trusty say something about
' your nephew ?' After all, has cousin come ? Is it he who——"

" Kate, my child," quickly interrupted her father, and appearing not to
have heard her interrogatory, "you may retire to your room. Mr.
Smythje and I would like to have a cigar ; and the smoke don't agree
with you. Go, child—go !"

The young girl instantly rose from her chair, and hastened to obey the
command—notwithstanding the protestations of Mr. Smythje, who looked

as if he would have preferred her company to the cigar.   But her father
hurriedly repeated the " Go, child, go !" accompanying the words with
another of those severe glances, which had already awed and mystified
her.
    Before she had passed fairly out of the great hall, however, her
thoughts reverted to the unanswered interrogatory ; and as she crossed
the threshold of her chamber, she was heard muttering to herself, " I
wonder if cousin be come ?"

CHAPTER XXII.

THE KIOSK.

A PORTION of the level platform on which Mount Welcome was built extended to the rear of the dwelling ; and was occupied, as already described, by a garden filled with rare and beautiful plants.   Near the midst
of this garden, and about a dozen paces from the house, stood a small
detatched building, the materials of which were ornamental woods of
various kinds, all natives of the island, famed for such products.   The
pieces composing this cottage, or "kiosk," as it was habitually called, had
all been cut and carved with skillful care ; and the whole structure had
been designed as a representation of a miniature temple, with a cupola
upon its top, surmounted by a gilded and glittering vane.
    Inside there were neither stairs nor partitions—the whole space being
occupied by a single apartment.   There were no glass windows, either ;
but all round the walls were open, or closed with Venetian blinds, the
laths of which were of the finest mahogany.   A Chinese mat covered the
floor, and a rustic table of bamboo cane pieces, with some half dozen
chairs of like manufacture, constituted the principal part of the furniture.
On the aforesaid table stood an inkstand of silver, elaborately chased,
with plume pens pertaining to it.   Some writing paper lay beside, and on
a silver tray there were wafers, red sealing-wax, and a signet seal.   An
escritoire stood on one side ; and two or three dozen volumes placed
upon the top of this, with a like number thrown carelessly on chairs,
formed the library of Mount Welcome.
    Some magazines and journals lay upon the centre table, and a box of
best Havannahs—open and half used—showed that the kiosk served occasionally for a smoking-room.   It was sometimes styled the " library," t
though its purposes were many.   Mr. Vaughan, at times, used it for the
reception of visitors—such as might have come upon an errand of business—such, in short, as were not deemed worthy of being introduced to
the company of the grand hall.   Just at the moment when Kate Vaughan
quitted the dinner-table, a young man was shown into this detached
apartment, Mr. Trusty, the overseer, acting as his chaperone.
    It is not necessary to say that this young man was Herbert Vaughan.
    How Herbert came to be conducted thither is easily explained.   On
learning from Quashie the destination designed for him—aggrieved and
angry at the revelation—he had hurried in hot haste up to the house.   To

Mr. Trusty, who was keeping guard at the bottom of the stairway, ho announced his relationship with Mr. Vaughan, and demanded an interview
—making his requisition in such energetic terms, as to disturb the habit-
nal *sang-froid* of the overseer, and compel him to the instantaneous delivery of his message.

Indeed, so indignant did Herbert feel, that he would have mounted the
steps and entered the house without further parley, had not Mr. Trusty
put forth his blandest entreaties to prevent such a terrible catastrophe.

" Patience, my good sir !"· urged the overseer, interposing himself be
tween the new comer and the stairway ; " Mr. Vaughan will see you, pre
sently—not just this moment; he is engaged—company with him. The
family's at dinner."

So far from soothing the chafed spirit of the young man, the announco
ment was only a new mortification. At dinner, and with company—the
cabin passenger, of course—the ward—not even a relative—while he, the
nephew—no dinner for him ! In truth, Herbert recognised in this incident a fresh outrage !

With an effort, he surrendered the idea of ascending the stairs. Poor
though he was, he was nevertheless a gentleman ; and good breeding
stepped in to restrain him from this unbidden intrusion, though more
than ever did he feel convinced that an insult was put upon him, and one
that almost appeared premeditated.

He stood balancing in his mind whether he should not turn upon his
heel, and leave his uncle's house without entering it. A straw would
have brought down the scale. The straw fell on the negative side, and
decided him to remain. On being conducted to the kiosk, and left to
himself, he showed no wish to be seated ; but paced the little apartment
backward and forward, in a state of nervous agitation.

He took but slight heed of aught that was there. He was in no mood
for minutely observing—though he could not help noticing the luxurious
elegance that surrounded him ; the grandeur of the great house itself;
the splendid *parterres* and gardens filled with plants and flowers of exquisite beauty and fragrant perfume. These fine sights, however, instead
of soothing his chafed·spirit, only made him more bitterly sensible of his
own poor fortunes, and the immeasurable distance that separated him
from his proud, rich uncle.

Through the open sides of the kiosk he merely glanced hastily at the
grounds ; and then his eyes became bent upon the great house, directed
habitually towards an entrance at the back, that by a flight of steps conducted into the garden. By this entrance he expected his uncle would
come out, and in angry impatience did he wait his coming.

Had he seen the soft eyes that were, at that moment, tenderly gazing
upon him from behind the lattice-work of the opposite window, perhaps
the sight would have gone far towards soothing his irate soul. But he
saw them not. The jalousies were closed ; and though, from the shadowy
interior of the chamber, the kiosk and its occupant were in full view, the
young Englishman had no suspicion that he was at that moment the object of observation—perhaps of admiration—by a pair of the loveliest
eyes in the island of Jamaica.

After turning for the twentieth time across the floor—at each time

scanning the stairs with fresh impatience—he somewhat spitefully laid
hold of a book, and opened it, in the hope of being able to kill time over
its pages. The volume which came into his hands—by chance, for ne
had not chosen it—was but little calculated to tranquillise his troubled
spirits. It was a digest of the statutes of Jamaica relating to slavery—
the famous, or rather infamous, *black code* of the island.

There he read, that a man might mutilate his own image in the person
of a fellow-man—torture him, even to death,—and escape with the punishment of a paltry fine! That a man with a black skin, or even white
if at all tainted with African blood, could hold no real estate—no office
of trust! could give no evidence in a court of law—not even had he been
witness of the crime of murder! That such a man must not keep or ride
a horse ; must not carry a gun, or other weapon of defence ; must not defend himself when assaulted ; must not defend wife, sister, or daughter
—even when ruffian hands were tearing them from him for the most un-
holy of purposes! In short, that a *man of colour* must do nothing to
make himself different from a docile and submissive brute!

To the young Englishman, fresh from a Christian land—at that period
ringing with the eloquent denunciations of a Wilberforce, and the phi-
lanthropic appeals of a Clarkson—the perusal of this execrable statute-
book, instead of producing tranquillity, only infused fresh bitterness into
his soul ; and stamping his foot fiercely upon the floor, he flung the detested volume back to its place.

At this moment—just as he had reached the maximum of reckless defiance—a noise was heard in the direction of the great house ; and the
door of the stair landing was seen to turn on its hinges.

Of course, he expected to see a surly old uncle, and was resolved to
be as surly as he.

On the contrary, and to his pleased surprise, he beheld in the doorway
a beautiful young girl bending her eyes upon him with an affectionate
look, and as if courting recognition!

A sudden revulsion of feeling passed through his whole frame ; his
countenance changed its angry expression to one of admiration ; and
unable to utter a word, he remained silently gazing on this lovely apparition

---

CHAPTER XXIII.

A BOLD RESOLVE.

Far better would it have been for Mr. Vaughan—at least, for the success of his schemes of a matrimonial alliance—had he adopted an honourable course with his nephew ; and at once introduced him, openly and
above board to his table, his daughter, and his aristocratic guest. Had
he known before dinner, what he was made aware of in less than five
minutes after it, he would, in all likelihood, have adopted this course. It
would have spared him the chagrin he was made to feel, on Mr. Smythje
reporting to him the encounter he had had on board ship ; which he pro-

ceeded to do, the moment after Kate had been so unceremoniously dismissed from the hall.

Smythje had also overheard the communication of the overseer—the word "nephew," at least—and this recalled to his mind—not without some unpleasant remembrance of the satire from which he had suffered —the steerage passenger who had treated him so brusquely on board the Sea Nymph.

The miserable bubble was burst ; and the onus of a somewhat bungling explanation was put upon the shoulders of the pompous planter— into whose heart a bitter drop of gall was infused by the disclosure. As the deception could be sustained no longer, the relationship was necessarily acknowledged ; but the spark of ire thus introduced boded a still more unwelcome reception to the unlucky nephew. The planter partially cleared himself of the scrape by a false representation. In other words, he told a lie, in saying that his nephew had not beeen expected. Smythje knew it was a lie, but said nothing ; and the subject was allowed to drop. Loftus Vaughan was a common man ; and the course he had followed— shallow and self-defeating—was proof of an intellect as low as its morality.

By his shabby treatment of his nephew, he was investing that young man with a romantic interest in the eyes of Kate, that, perhaps, might never have been felt, or, at all events not so rapidly. Misfortune—especially that which springs from persecution—is a grand suggestor of sympathy ; that is, when the appeal is made to noble hearts ; and the heart of Kate Vaughan was of this quality.

Moreover, this surreptitious dealing with the poor relative—smuggling him into the house like a bale of contraband goods—was sufficient of itself to pique the curiosity of those whom it was meant to mystify. So far as Kate Vaughan was concerned, that very effect it produced ; for, on leaving the dining-room—from which, to say the truth, she was only too happy to escape—the young girl glided at once to that window that opened out upon the garden ; and, parting the lattice with her fingers, looked eagerly through.

In the brief undertone that had passed between her father and the overseer, she had heard the command, " Show him to the kiosk ;" and she knew that the kiosk was within view of her chamber window. She was curious to see what in all her life she had never beheld—a *cousin ;* and her curiosity was not baulked. Her cousin was before her eyes, pacing the little apartment to and fro, as described.

With his blue braided frock, buttoned tightly over his breast ; glittering Hessian boots on his well-turned limbs ; his neat three-cornered hat set lightly over his brown curls ; he was not a sight likely to terrify a young girl—least of all a cousin. Even the bold, somewhat fierce, expression upon his countenance, at that moment reflecting the angry emotions that were stirring within him, did not in the eyes of the young creole, detract from the gracefulness of the noble face before her. What impression did the sight produce ? Certainly not terror—certainly not disgust. On the contrary, she appeared gratified by it : else, why did she continue her gaze, and gaze so earnestly ? Why became her eyes filled with fire, and fixed, as by some fascination ? Why did her young bosom

4

heave and fall, as if some new, undefinable emotion was for the first time germinating within it? For some moments she remained in the same attitude, gazing steadfastly and silent. Then, without turning, there escaped from her lips, low murmured, and as if by an involuntary effort, the interrogatory:—

"Yola! is he not beautiful?"

"Beautiful, missa," repeated the maid, who had not yet beheld the ·bject for whom this admiration was meant; "who beautiful?"

"Who? My cousin, Yola."

"You cousin—what is cousin, young missa?"

"Look yonder, and see! That's a cousin."

"I see a man."

"Ah! and saw you ever such a man?"

"True, missa; never see man look so—he surely angry, missa?"

"Angry?"

"Berry angry. He go back, he go forward, like hyena in 'im cage."

"He is only impatient at being kept waiting. My word! I think he looks all the better for it. Ah! see how his eye flashes. Oh! Yola, how handsome he is—how different from the young men of this island. Is he not a beautiful fellow?"

"He curled hair, like Cubina?"

"Cubina! ha! ha! ha! This Cubina must be a very Proteus, as well as an Adonis. Do you see any other resemblance, except in the hair? If so, my cousin may, perhaps resemble me."

"Cubina much darker in de colour ob de skin, missa."

"Ha! ha! ha! that is not unlikely."

"Cubina same size—same shape—'zactly same shape."

"Then, I should say that Cubina is a good shape; for, if I know anything of what a man ought to be, that cousin of mine is the correct thing. See those arms! they look as if he could drag down that great tamarind with them! Gracious me! he appears as if he intended doing it! Surely he must be very impatient! And, after his coming so far, for papa to keep him waiting in this fashion! I really think I should go down to him myself. What is your opinion, Yola? Would it be wrong for me to go and speak with him? He is my cousin."

"What am cousin, missa?"

"Why cousin is—is—something like a brother—only not exactly—that is —it's not quite the same thing."

"Brudder! Oh, missa! if he Yola brudder, she him speak; she care for no one be angry."

"True, Yola; and if he were my brother—alas! I have none—I should do the same without hesitation. But with a cousin, that's different. Besides, papa don't like this cousin of mine—for some reason or another. I wonder what can he have against him. I can't see; and surely it can be no reason for my liking him. And, surely, his being my cousin is just why I should go down and talk to him.

"Besides," continued the young girl, speaking to herself rather than to the maid, "he appears very, very impatient. Papa may keep him waiting —who knows how long, since he is so taken up with this Mr. Montagu what's his name? Well, I may be doing wrong—perhaps papa will be

angry—perhaps he won't know anything about it! Right or wrong, I'll
go! I *shall* go!"

So saying, the young creole snatched a scarf from the fauteuil; flung it
over her shoulders; and, gliding from the chamber, tripped silently along
the passage that conducted towards the rear of the dwelling.

CHAPTER XXIV.

THE ENCOUNTER OF THE COUSINS.

OPENING the door, and passing out, Kate Vaughan paused timidly upon
the top of the stairway that led down into the garden. Her steps were
stayed by a feeling of bashful reserve, that was struggling to restrain
her from carrying out a resolve, somewhat hastily formed. Her hesitancy was but the matter of a moment; for on the next—her resolution
having become fixed—she descended the stairs, and advanced blushing-
ly towards the kiosk.

Herbert had not quite recovered from surprise at the unexpected
apparition, when he was saluted by the endearing interrogatory—

"Are you my cousin?"

The question, so 'naively' put, remained for a moment unanswered:
for the tone of kindness in which it was spoken had caused him a fresh
surprise, and he was too much confused to make answer. He soon found
speech, however, for the hypothetical reply:—

"If you are the daughter of Mr. Loftus Vaughan——"

"I am."

"Then I am proud of calling myself your cousin. I am Herbert
Vaughan, from England."

Still under the influence of the slight, which he believed had been put
upon him, Herbert made this announcement with a certain stiffness of
manner, which the young girl could not fail but notice. It produced a
momentary incongeniality, that was in danger of degenerating into a
positive coolness; and Kate, who had come forth under the prompting
of an affectionate instinct, trembled under a repulse, the cause of which
she could not comprehend. It did not, however, hinder her from courteously rejoining:—

"We were expecting you—as father had received your letter; but not
to-day. Papa said not before to-morrow. Permit me, cousin, to welcome you to Jamaica."

Herbert bowed profoundly. Again the young creole felt her warm
impulses painfully checked; and, blushing with embarrassment, she
stood in an attitude of indecision. Herbert, whose heart had been melting like snow under a tropic sun,·now became sensible that he was committing a rudeness, which, so far from being natural to him, was costing
him a struggle to counterfeit. Why should the sins of the father be
visited on the child, and such a child? With a reflection kindred to this
the young man hastened to change his attitude of cold reserve.

"Thanks for your kind welcome!" said he, now speaking in a tone of affectionate frankness; "but, fair cousin; you have not told me your name."

"Catherine—though I am usually addressed by the shorter synonym, Kate."

"Catherine! that is a family name with us: my father's mother, and your father's too—our grandmamma—was called Kate. Was it also your mother's name?"

"No; my mother was called Quasheba."

"Quasheba that is a very singular name."

"Do you think so cousin? I am sometimes called Quasheba myself —only by the old people of the plantation, who knew my mother. Lilly Quasheba they call me. Papa does not like it, and forbids them."

"Was your mother an Englishwoman?"

"Oh, no! she was born in the island, and died while I was very young —too young to remember her. Indeed, cousin, I may say I never knew what it was to have a mother!"

"Nor I much, cousin Kate. My mother also died early. But are you my only cousin?—no sisters nor brothers?"

"Not one. Ah! I wish I had sisters and brothers!"

"Why do you wish that?"

"Oh, how can you ask such a question? For companions, of course."

"Fair cousin! I should think *you* would find companions enough in this beautiful island."

"Ah! enough, perhaps; but none whom I like—at least, not as I think I should like a sister or brother. Indeed," added the young girl, in a reflective tone, "I sometimes feel lonely enough!"

"Ah!"

"Perhaps, now that we are to have guests, it will be different. Mr Smythje is very amusing."

"Mr. Smythje! Who is he?"

"What! you do not know Mr. Smythje? I thought that you and he came over in the same ship? Papa said so; and that you were not to arrive until to-morrow. I think you have taken him by surprise in coming to-day. But why did you not ride out with Mr. Smythje? He arrived here only one hour before you, and has just dined with us. I have left the table this moment, for papa and him to have their cigars. But, bless me, cousin! Pardon me for not asking—perhaps you have not dined yet?"

"No, cousin Kate," replied Herbert, in a grave tone; "nor am I likely to dine here, to-day."

The storm of queries with which, in the simplicity of her heart, the young creole thus assailed him once more brought him back into that train of bitter reflection, from which her fair presence and sweet converse had for the moment rescued him. Hence the character of his reply.

"And why, cousin Herbert?" asked she, in a tone of marked surprise. "If you have not dined, it is not too late. Why not here?"

"Because"—and the young man drew himself proudly up—"I prefer going without dinner to dining where I am not welcome. In Mount Welcome, it seems, I am *not* welcome."

"Oh, cousin——"

The words, ana tne appealing accent were alike interrupted. The door upon the landing turned upon its hinge, and Loftus Vaughan appeared in the doorway.

"Your father?"

"My father!"

"Kate!" cried the planter, in a tone that bespoke displeasure, "Mr Smythje would like to hear you play upon the harp. I have been looking for you in your room, and all over the house. What are you doing : ut here?"

The language was coarse and common—the manner that of a vulgar man flushed with wine.

"Oh, papa! cousin Herbert is here. He is waiting to see you."

"Come you here, then!" was the imperious rejoinder. "Come, Mr. Smythje is waiting for you."

"Cousin! I must leave you."

"Yes : I perceive it. One more worthy than I claims your company Go! Mr. Smythje is impatient."

"It is papa."

"Kate! Kate! are you coming? Haste, girl! haste, I say!"

"Go, Miss Vaughan! Farewell!"

"Miss Vaughan? Farewell?"

Mystified and distressed by those strange-sounding words, Kate Vaughan stood for some seconds undecided and speechless; but the voice of her father again came ringing along the corridor—now in tones irate and commanding; obedience could no longer be delayed ; and, with a half-puzzled, half-reproachful glance at her cousin, the young girl reluctantly parted from his presence.

CHAPTER XXV.

A SURLY RECEPTION.

AFTER the young creole had disappeared within the entrance, Herbert re· mained in a state of indecision as to how he should act. He no longer needed an interview with his uncle for the sake of having an explanation. This new slight had crowned his convictions that he was there an unwelcome guest, and no possible apology could retrieve the ill-treatment he had experienced. He would have walked off on the instant without a word; but, stung to the quick by the series of insults he had received, the instinct of retaliation had sprung up within him, and determined him to stay—at all events, until he could meet his relative face to face, and reproach him with his churlish conduct. He was recklessly indifferent as to the result.

With this object, he continued in the kiosk—his patience being now baited with the prospect of that slight satisfaction. He knew that his uncle might not care much for what he could say ; it was not likely such a nature would be affected by reproach. Nevertheless, the proud young man could not resist the temptation of giving words to his defiance, as the only course by which he could mollify the mortification he so keenly felt.

The tones of a harp, vibrating through the far interior of the dwelling faintly reached the kiosk; but they fell on his ear without any soothing effect. Rather did they add to his irritation; for he could almost fancy the music was meant to mock him in his misery.

But no : on second thoughts, that could not be. Surely, that sweet strain was not intended to tantalise him. He caught the air. It was one equally appropriate to the instrument and to his own situation. It was the " Exile of Erin."

Presently a voice was heard accompanying the music—a woman's voice —easily recognisable as that of Kate Vaughan.

He listened attentively. At intervals he could hear the words. How like to his own thoughts !

> " ' Sad is my fate,' said the heart-broken stranger :
> ' The wild deer and wolf to the covert can flee;
> But I have no refuge from famine and danger—
> A home and a country remain not to me.' "

Perhaps the singer intended it as a song of sympathy for him ? It cer tainly exerted an influence over his spirits, melting him to a degree of tenderness.

Not for long, however, did this feeling continue. As the last notes of the lay died away in the distant corridor, the rough baritones of the planter and his guest were heard joining in loud laughter—perhaps some joke at the expense of himself, the poor exile ? Shortly after this, a heavy footstep echoed along the passage. The door opened; and Herbert perceived that it was his uncle, who had at length found time to honour him with an interview.

Though so joyous but the moment before, all traces of mirth had dis appeared from the countenance of Loftus Vaughan, when he presented himself before the eyes of his nephew. His face, habitually red, was fired with the wine he had been drinking to the hue of scarlet. Never- theless, an ominous mottling of a darker colour upon his broad massive brow foretold the ungracious reception his relative was likely to have at his hands.

His first words were uttered in a tone of insolent coolness :—

" So you are my brother's son, are you ?"

There was no extending of the hand, no gesture—not even a smile of welcome !

Herbert checked his anger, and simply answered—

" I believe so."

" And pray, sir, what errand has brought you out to Jamaica ?"

" If you have received my letter, as I presume you have, it will have answered that question."

" Oh, indeed !" exclaimed Mr. Vaughan, with an attempt at cynicism, but evidently taken down by the unexpected style of the reply. " And what, may I ask, do you purpose doing here ?"

" Have not the slightest idea," answered Herbert, with a provoking air of independence.

" Have you any profession ?"

" Unfortunately, not any."

" Any trade ? I suppose not ?"

" Your suppositions are perfectly correct."

" Then, sir, how do you expect to get your bread ?"

" Earn it, the best way I can."

" Beg it, more likely, as your father before you : all his life begging it, and from me."

" In that respect I shall not resemble him. You would be the last man I should think of begging from."

" S'death ! sirrah, you are impertinent. This is fine language to me, after the disgrace you have already brought upon me."

" Disgrace ?"

" Yes, sir, disgrace. Coming out here as a pauper, in the steerage of a ship ! And you must needs boast of your relationship—letting all the world know that you are my nephew."

" Boast of the relationship !" repeated Herbert, with a smile of contempt. " Ha ! ha ! ha ! I suppose you refer to my having answered a question asked me by this pretty jack-a-box you are playing with. Boast of it, indeed ! Had I known you then as well as I do now, I should have been ashamed to acknowledge it."

" After that, sir," shouted Mr. Vaughan, turning purple with rage— " after that, sir, no more words. You shall leave my house this minute."

" I had intended to have left it some minutes sooner. I only stayed to have an opportunity of telling you what I think of you."

" What is that, sir ? what is that ?"

The angry youth had summoned to the top of his tongue a few of the strongest epithets he could think of, and was about to hurl them into his uncle's teeth, when, on glancing up, he caught sight of an object that caused him to check his intention. It was the beautiful face of the young creole, that appeared through the half-opened lattice of the window opposite. She was gazing down upon him and her father, and listening to the dialogue with an anguished expression of countenance.

" He is *her* father," muttered Herbert to himself; " for *her* sake I shall not say the words ;" and, without making any reply to the last interrogatory of his uncle, he strode out of the kiosk, and was walking away.

" Stay, sir !" cried the planter, somewhat surprised at the turn things had taken. " A word before you go—if you *are* going."

Herbert turned upon his heel and listened.

" Your letter informs me that you are without funds It shall not be said that a relative of Loftus Vaughan left his house penniless and unprovided. In this purse there are twenty pounds currency of the island Take it; but on the condition that you say nothing of what has occurred here ; and, furthermore, that you keep to yourself, that you are the nephew of Loftus Vaughan."

Without saying a word, Herbert took the proffered purse ; but, in the next moment, the chink of the gold pieces was heard upon the gravel walk as he dashed the bag at the feet of his uncle.

Then turning to the astonished planter, and measuring him with a look that scorned all patronage, he faced once more to the path, and walked proudly away.

The angry " Begone, sir !" vociferated after, was only addressed to his back, and was altogether unheeded. Perhaps it was even urheard, for the expression in the eyes of the young man told that his attention was occupied elsewhere.

CHAPTER XXVI.

THE JEW PENN.

As he walked towards the great house—with the design of going round it to get upon the avenue—his glance was directed upwards to the window where that beautiful face had been just seen. The lattice was now closed ; and he endeavoured to pierce the sombre shadows behind it. Oh ! for one word—one look—though it might be a look of sórrow, perhaps of reproach !

There was no look met his—no eyes were glancing through the lattice.

He looked back, to see if he might linger a moment. His uncle was in a bent attitude, gathering the scattered pieces of gold. In this position the shrubbery concealed him.

Herbert was about to glide nearer to the window, and call out the name of Kate Vaughan, when he heard his own pronounced, in a soft whisper, and with the endearing word " cousin " prefixed.

Distinctly he heard " Cousin Herbert." Not from the lattice above did the words proceed, but as if spoken around the angle of the building.

He hastened thither : for that was his proper path by which to arrive at the front of the house.

On turning the wall, he looked up. He saw that another window opened from the same chamber. Thence came the sweet summons, and there shone the face for which he was searching.

" Oh, cousin Herbert! do not go in anger. Papa has done wrong— very wrong, I know ; but he has been taking much wine—he is not himself. Good cousin, you will pardon him ?"

Herbert was about to make reply, when the young creole continued :— " You said in your letter you had no money. You have refused father's—you will not refuse mine ? It is very little. It is all I have Take it !"

A bright object glistened before the eyes of the young man, and fell with a metallic chink at his feet. He looked down. A small silk bag containing coin, with a blue ribbon attached, was lying upon the ground. He raised it, and holding it in one hand, hesitated for a moment—as if he had thought of accepting it. It was not that, however, but another thought that was passing in his mind,

His resolve was soon taken.

" Thanks !" said he. " Thanks, cousin Kate !" he added, with increas-. ing warmth. " You have meant kindly, and though we may never meet again——"

" Oh, say not so !" interrupted the young girl, with an appealing look.

" Yes," continued he, " it is probable we never may. Here there is no home for me. I must go hence; but, wherever I may go, I shall not soon forget this kindness. I may never have an opportunity of repaying it—you are beyond the necessity of aught that an humble relative could do for you; but remember, Kate Vaughan! should you ever stand in need of a strong arm and a stout heart, there is one of your name who will not fail you!

"Thanks!" he repeated, detaching the ribbon from the bag, and flinging the latter, with its contents, back through the lattice. Then, fastening the ribbon to the breast button of his coat, he added: "I shall feel richer with the possession of this token than with all the wealth of your father's estate. Farewell! and God bless you, my generous cousin!"

Before the young creole could repeat her offer, or add another word of counsel or consolation, Herbert Vaughan had turned the angle of the building, and passed suddenly out of sight.

While these scenes were transpiring upon the plantation of Mount Welcome, others of still more exciting nature were being enacted on that which adjoined it—the property of Jacob Jessuron, slave-merchant and penn-keeper.

Besides a " baracoon " in the Bay, where his slaves were usually exposed for sale, the Jew was owner of a large plantation in the country, on which he habitually resided. It lay contiguous to the estate of the custos Vaughan—separated from the latter by one of the wooded ridges already mentioned as bounding the valley of Mount Welcome.

Like the latter it had once been a sugar estate, and an extensive one; but that was before Jessuron became its owner. Now it was in the condition termed *ruinate*. The fields where the golden cane had waved in the tropic breeze were choked up by a tangled " second growth," restoring them almost to their primitive wildness. With that quickness characteristic of equatorial vegetation, huge trees had already sprung up, and stood thickly over the ground—logwoods, bread-nuts, cotton, and calabash trees, which, with their pendent parasites, almost usurped dominion over the soil. Here and there, where the fields still remained open, instead of cultivation, there appeared only the wild nursery of nature—glades mottled with flowering weeds, as the Mexican horn-poppy, swalloworts, West Indian vervains, and small *passiflorae*.

At intervals, where the underwood permitted them to peep out, might be seen stretches of " dry wall," or stone fences, without mortar or cement, mostly tumbled down, the ruins thickly trellised with creeping plants—as convolvuli, cereus, and aristolochia; cleome, with the cheerful blossoming *lantana ;* and, spreading over all, like the web of a gigantic spider, the yellow leafless stems of the American dodder.

In the midst of this domain, almost reconquered by nature, stood the " great house "—except in size, no longer deserving the appellation. It consisted rather of a *pile* than a single building—the old " sugar-works " having been joined under the same roof with the dwelling—and negro cabins, stables, offices, all inclosed within an immense high wall, that gave to the place the air of a penitentiary or barracks, rather than that of a country mansion. The inclosure, however, was a modern construction—an afterthought—designed for a purpose very different from that of sugar-making.

Garden there was none, though evidence that there *had been* was seen everywhere around the building, in the trees that still bloomed: some loaded with delicious fruits, others with clustering flowers, shedding their incense on the air. Half wild, grew citrons, and *avocado* pears, sop and custard apples, mangoes, guavas, and pawpaws; while the crown-like tops of cocoa-palms soared high above the humbler denizens of this wild orchard, their recurvant fronds drooping, as if in grief at the desolation around.

Close to the buildings stood several huge trees, whose tortuous limbs, now leafless, rendered it easy to identify them. It was the giant of the West Indian forests—the silk-cotton tree (*Eriodendron anfractuosum*). The limbs of these vegetable monsters—each itself as large as an ordinary tree—were loaded with parasites of many species; among which might be distinguished ragged *cactacæ*, with various species of wild pines (*bromeliæ*), from the noble *vriesia* to the hoary, beard-like "Spanish moss," whose long streaming festoons waved like winding-sheets in the breeze— an appropriate draping for the eyrie of the black vultures (John Crows) perched in solemn silence upon the topmost branches.

In the olden time this plantation had borne the name of "Happy Valley;" but during the ownership of Jessuron, this designation—perhaps deemed inappropriate—had been generally dropped; and the place was never spoken of by any other name than that of the "Jew's Penn."

Into a "penn" (grazing farm) Jessuron had changed it, and it served well enough for the purpose: many of the old sugar fields, now over-grown with the valuable Guinea grass, affording excellent pasturage for horses and cattle.

In breeding and rearing the former for the use of the sugar estates, and fattening the latter for the beef markets of the Bay, the industrious Israelite had discovered a road to riches, as short as that he had been travelling in the capacity of slave dealer; and of late years he had come to regard the latter only as a secondary calling. In his old age, too, he had become ambitious of social distinction, and, for this reason, was de-sirious of sinking the slave merchant in the more respectable profession of penn-keeper. He had even succeeded so far in his views as to have him-self appointed a justice of the peace—an office that, in Jamaica, as else-where, is more distinctive of wealth than respectability.

In addition to penn-keeper, the Jew was also an extensive spice-culti-vator, or rather spice gatherer: for the indigenous pimento forests that covered the hills upon his estate required no cultivation—nothing farther than to collect the aromatic berries, and cure them on the *barbacoa*.

Though changed from a plantation to a penn, the estate of Jacob Jes-suron was not less a scene of active industrial life.

In the fields adjacent to the house, and through the glades of Guinea grass, horses and half-wild cattle might be seen in turns neighing and bellowing, pursued by mounted herdsmen, black and half-naked.

Among the groves of pimento on the hills, gangs of negro wenches could be heard screaming amd chattering continually, as they picked the allspice berries from the branches; or, poising the filled baskets on their heads, marched in long, chanting files towards the *barbacoa*.

Outside the gate-entrance, upon the broad avenue leading to the main

road, negro horse-tamers might every day be observed, giving their first
lessons to rough colts fresh caught from the pastures ; while inside the
grand inclosure, fat oxen were slaughtered to supply the markets of the
Bay—huge, gaunt dogs holding carnival over the offal—while black
butchers, naked to the waist, their brown arms reeking with red gore, ,
stalked over the ground, brandishing blood-stained blades, and other instruments of their sanguinary calling.

Such scenes might be witnessed diurnally on the estate of Jacob Jessuron ; but on the day succeeding that on which the slave merchant had
made his unsuccessful errand to Mount Welcome, a spectacle of a somewhat rarer kind was about to be exhibited at the penn.

The scene chosen for this exhibition was an inner inclosure, or court-
yard, that lay contiguous to the dwelling—the great house itself forming
one side of this court, and opening upon it by a broad verandah, of a
dingy, dilapidated appearance.

' Vis-à-vis ' with the dwelling was another large building, which shut in
the opposite side of the court—the two being connected by high, massive
walls, that completed the quadrangle. A strong, double gate, opening
near the centre of one of these walls, was the way out—that is, to the
larger inclosure of the cattle-penn.

From the absence of chimneys and windows, as well as from its plain
style of architecture, the building that stood opposite the dwelling-house
might have been taken for some large granary or barn, But a peep into
its interior at once controverted this idea. Inside were seen groups of
human beings, of all colours, from ebony black to jaundice yellow, in all
attitudes—seated, standing, or lying upon the floor—and not a few of
them, in pairs, manacled to one another. Their attitudes were not more
various than the expression upon their faces and features. Some looked
sad and sullen ; some glanced fearfully around, as if waking from horrid
dreams, and under the belief that they were realities ; others wore the
vacant stare of idiotcy ; while here and there a group—apparently regardless of past, present, or future—chattered in their barbaric language,
with an air of gaiety that bespoke the most philosophic *insouciance.*

The building that contained them was the baracoon—the storehouse of
the slave merchant. Its occupants were his stores !

The " stock " had been recently replenished by the cargo of a slave
ship, but there were also some old " bales " on hand ; and these were in
the act of entertaining the new comers, and initiating them into the ways
of the place. Their means of showing hospitality had been limited—as
testified by the empty calabashes and clean-scraped wooden platters that
lay scattered over the floor. Not a grain of rice, not a spoonful of the
pepper-pot, not a slice of plantain was left. The emptiness of the vessels
showed that the rations had been as short, as the viands were coarse and
common,

Outside, in the yard, were many groups, happier to escape from the
stifled atmosphere of their crowded quarters ; though that was freedom
when compared with the 'tween-decks of the *middle passage.*

Each group was gathered around some old hand—some compatriot
who had preceded them across the great sea—and who, himself initiated
into slavery under a western sky, was giving them some notions of what

they had to expect. Eager looks of all, from time to time directed towards the verandah, told that they were awaiting some event of more
than ordinary interest.

There were white men in the court-yard—three of them. Two were
of dark complexion—so swarth that many of the coloured slaves were as
fair-skinned as they. These last were lounging by the stairway of the
verandah—one of them seated upon the steps. Both were sparely clad
in check shirts and trowsers, having broad-brimmed palmetto hats on
their heads, and rough buckskins on their feet and ankles.

Each carried a long rapier-like blade—a *machete*—hanging over his hip
in its leathern sheath; while a brace of fierce dogs—looped in cotton
rope leashes, attached to belts worn around their waists—crouched upon
the ground at their feet.

The faces of these men were clean shaven, a pointed chin-tuft, or
"bigots," alone being left; and the hair on the heads of both was close
cropped. Their sharp, angular features were thus fully displayed, denoting a high order of intelligence, which might have produced a pleasing effect, but for the pronounced expression of cruelty which accompanied it.

The exclamations that from time to time escaped from their lips, with
the few words of conversation that passed between them, spoke of a
Spanish origin. Their costumes, their arms and accoutrements—their
comrades, the fierce dogs—plainly proclaimed their calling, as well
as the country whence they came. They were 'cacadores de negros'—
negro-hunters of Cuba.

The third white man who appeared in the court-yard differed essential
ly from these—not so much in colour, for he was also of swarth complexion—but in size, costume, and calling. A pair of horseskin riding-
boots reached up to his thighs, on the heels of which appeared heavy
spurs, with rowels three inches in diameter. A sort of monkey jacket of
thick cloth—notwithstanding its unsuitableness to the climate—hung
down to his hips, under which appeared a waistcoat of scarlet plush,
with tarnished metal buttons, and a wool comforter of the same flaming
colour. Crowning all was a felt hat; which, like the other articles of
his dress, gave evidence of exposure to all weathers—sun and rain, storm
and tornado.

A thick shock of curling hair, so dark in colour as to pass for black ; a
heavy beard, jet black, and running most of the way around his mouth ;
amber-coloured eyes, with a sinister, shining light that never seemed to
pale ; lips of an unnatural redness gleaming through the black beard ; and
a nose of aquiline oblique, were the points in the personal appearance of
this man that most prominently presented themselves.

The effect of their combination was to impress you with the conviction
that the individual in question belonged to the same nationality as the
proprietor of the penn. Such was in reality the case : for the bearded
man was another of the race of Abraham, and one of its least amiable
specimens. His name was Ravener, his calling that of overseer : he was
the overseer of Jessuron. The symbol of his profession he carried under
his arm—a huge cart-whip. He had it by him at all hours—by night, as
by day—for, by night, as by day, was he accustomed to make use of it.

And the victims of his long lash were neither oxen nor horse— they were men '

No sparing use made he of this hideous implement. " Crack, crack!" was it heard from morn to eve , " crack, crack!" from eve to midnight; if need be, from midnight to morning again ; for some said that the over- seer of Jessuron never slept. " Crack, crack!" did he go through the court-yard, proud to show off his power before the newly arrived ne- groes—here and there swinging his long bitter lash among the groups, as if to break up and scatter them in sheer wantonness!

CHAPTER XXVII.

A FIERY BAPTISM.

It was about twelve o'clock in the day. Jessuron and his daughter had just stepped forth into the verandah, and taken their stand by the balus- trade looking down into the court. The countenances of both betrayed a certain degree of solicitude ; as if they had come out to be witnesses to some spectacle of more than common interest.

The house wenches and other domestics, trooping behind them with curious looks, showed that some rare scene was to be enacted. A small iron furnace, filled with live coals, had been placed in the courtyard, near the bottom of the steps. Three or four sullen-looking men—blacks and mulattoes—stood around in it lounging attitude. One of these stoop- ed over the furnace, turning in the fire what appeared to be a soldering iron, or some other instrument of a brazier. It was not that however, as the spectators well knew. All who beheld it recognised the dreaded *branding iron:* for every one present, the whites and newly arrived Africans excepted, had, ere now, felt its hot, seething fire in their flesh. These last had already learnt what was preparing for them ; and stood re- garding the preparations, most of them with looks of silent awe. Some Coromrantees there were among the number, who looked on with reckless indifference, chatting as gaily—and, at intervals, laughing as loudly—as if they awaited the beginning of some merry game. Little did these courageous sons of Ethiopia—whose sable skins bore scars of many a native fray—little cared they for the scorching of that red brand.

It was not long before the inhuman spectacle commenced. The entrance of Jessuron and his daughter was the cue to begin ; and the bearded over- seer, who was master of the ceremonies, had only been waiting till these should make their appearance. The man, from experience, knew that his master always gave his personal superintendance when such a scene was to be enacted. He knew, moreover, that his master's daughter was equally accustomed to assist at these interresting ceremonies !

" Go on, Mishter Ravener!" cried the Jew, reaching the front of the verandah. " Thesh first," he added, pointing towards a group of Eboes— who stood trembling with apprehension in the corner of the yard. At a sign from the overseer, who was one of the taciturn sort, a number of old negroes—evidently used to the business laid hands upon the Eboes and led them up to the furnace.

As the victims were brought near to the fire, and saw the red iron glowing amid the coals, fear became more vividly depicted upon their faces, and their frames shook with a convulsive terror. Some of them, the younger ones, screamed aloud, and would have rushed away from the spot—had they not been held in the grasp of the attendants. Their appeals, made by the most pitiful looks and gestures, were answered only by unfeeling jeers and shouts of laughter in which the old Jew himself joined—in which, incredible to relate, joined his beautiful daughter! Not was it a mere smile which appeared on the face of the fair Judith; clear laughter rang from her lips, exhibiting her regular rows of pretty white teeth—as if some fiend had assumed the form of an angel!

The Eboes were led forward, and held firmly by the assistants, while their breasts were presented to receive the brand. The red hot iron flashed for a moment in the eyes of each; then fell with a dull clap upon the clammy skin. Smoke ascended with a hiss, followed by the smell of roasting flesh. A struggle, some wild cries, and the operation was over. The slave was marked with those indelible initials, to be carried with him to his grave. One by one the Eboes received this terrible baptism, and were led away from the ground. A batch of Pawpaws—from the Whidaw country—came next. They were brought up one by one, like the Eboes; but altogether unlike these was their behaviour. They neither gave way to extreme fear, nor yet displayed extraordinary courage. They appeared to submit with a sort of docile resignation: as though they regarded it in the light of a destiny or duty. The operation of branding them was a short work, and afforded no mirth to the by-standers; as there was no ludicrous display of terror to laugh at. This facile disposition renders the Whidaw people the most valuable of slaves. A group of Coromantees were now to undergo the fiery ordeal. These bold and warlike indigenes of Africa, evinced, by their attitudes and actions, the possession of a moral nature altogether different from that either of Pawpaw or Eboe. Instead of waiting to be led forward, each stepped boldly up, as he did so, baring his breast to receive the red brand, at which he glanced with an air of lordly contempt.

One young fellow even seized the iron from the grasp of the operator, and turning it in his hand, struck the stamp firmly against his breast, where he held it until the seething flesh told that a deep imprint had been made. Then, flinging the instrument back into the furnace, he strode away from the spot with the air of a triumphant gladiator! At this moment there occurred a pause in the proceedings—not as if the drama was ended, but only an act. Another was still to come.

Ravener stepped up to the verandah, in front of the place where Jessuron and his daughter stood. With the former, or indeed with both, he communicated in a voice just audible, but not as if with any design of concealing what he said—only because he was at no time a loud-talker.

The two man-hunters were the only persons there he might have had any care to be cautious about; but these were at the moment busy with their dogs, and not heeding aught that was going on. Branding a batch of negroes was no new sight to them; and they were spectators, merely from having, at the moment, nothing better to do.

" Which next ?" was, the question put by Ravener to the Jew ; " the Mandingoes ?"

"Either them, or the prinsh," replied Jessuron ; " it don't mattei which ish marked first."

" Oh, the prince first, by all means !" suggested the amiable Judith with a smile of satisfaction. " Bring him out first, Mr. Ravener ; I'm cu· rious to see how his royal highness will stand fire."

The overseer made no reply ; but, taking the wish of the young lady for an order, proceeded to obey it.

Stepping across the court, he opened a door at one corner that led into a room separate from that in which the slaves had been lodged. The overseer entered the room. In a few minutes he came out again, bring· ing with him an individual who, by his dress, it would have been difficult to recognise as the young Fellata seen on board the slaver, but whose noble mien still rendered it possible to identify him ; for it was he.

Changed, indeed, was his costume. The turban was gone, the rich silken tunic, the sandals and scimetar—all his finery had been stripped off; and, in its place, appeared a coarse Osnaburg shirt and. trowsers —the dress of a plantation negro. He looked wretched, but not crest- fallen. \

No doubt he had by this time learnt, or suspected, the fate that was in store for him ; but, for all that, his features exhibited the proud air of a prince ; and the glances which he cast upon the overseer by his side, but oftener upon Jessuron—whose instrument he knew the othei to be—were those of concentrated anger and defiance. Not a word es- caped his lips, either of protest or reproach. This had all passed before —when the first rude assault had been made upon him, to deprive him of his garments and the adornments of his person. T! e hour of recrimi- nation was past. He saw he had no alternative but submission, and he was submitting—though in angry and sullen silence. He knew not what was now intended to be done to him. He had been shut up in a window- less room, and saw nothing of the spectacle that had just passed. Some new outrage he anticipated ; but of what nature he could not give a guess. He was not allowed to remain long in ignorance. Ravener, roughly grasping him by the wrist, led him up to the furnace. The iron by this time was ready, glowing red hot among the coals. The operator stood watching for the signal to use it ; and this being given, he seized the instrument in his grasp, and poised it aloft. .The prince now per- ceived the intention, but shrank not at the sight. His eyes were not upon the iron, but, gleaming with a fire like that of the furnace, were now di· rected upon the face of the old Jew—now upon that of the angel-like demon at his side. The Jew alone shrank from the glance . his daughter returned it with a mocking imperturbability. In another instant the red brand hissed as it burnt into the flesh of the Fellata's bosom. Prince Cingtûes was the slave of Jacob Jessuron ! As if the terrible reality had now for the first time burst upon him, the young man leaped forward with a cry ; and before any one could oppose his progress, he had bound- ed up the steps and entered the verandah. Then, rushing along the gal- lery, to the spot occupied by Jessuron and his daughter, he sprang up like a tiger, and launched himself forward upon the Jew. As he clutched the latter by the throat, both came together to the ground, and rolled over and over in the writhings of a desperate struggle. Fortunate

It was for the slave merchant that his victim had been disarmed : else that moment would have been fatal to him. As it was, he came very near being strangled; and had it not been for Ravener and the two Spaniards, who hastened to his rescue, the betrayal of the Foolah prince would have been the last treason of his life. Overpowered by numbers, and by the brutal strength of the overseer, Cingûes was at length secured, and the throat of the slave merchant was extricated from his death-like clutch.

"Kill him!" cried the Jew, as soon as he found breath to speak. "No, don't kill him yet," added he, correcting himself, "not joosh yet, till I punish him fust! an' if I don't punish him—ach!"

"Flog the savage!" shouted the beautiful Judith; "make an example of him, Mr. Ravener; else those others will be rising upon us in the same style."

"Yesh, flog him! that'll do to begin with. Flog him now, good Rave-ner! Give him a hundred lashes thish minute!"

"Ay, ay!" responded the overseer, dragging the victim down the steps; "I'll give him his full dose—never fear you!"

Ravener was as good as his word. The spectacle that followed was even more horrible to behold than that which has been described; for the punishment of the lash is among the most fearful of exhibitions.

The young Foolah was tied to a post—one that stood there for the purpose. A strong *headman* wielded the cruel *quirt;* and as the last stripe was administered, completing that horrid hundred, the poor victim sank, fainting and bloody, against the stake!

The occupants of the verandah showed not the slightest signs of hav-ing been moved to pity by this horrid spectacle. On the contrary, both father and daughter seemed to draw delight from it, and instead of retir-ing when the fearful scene was over, both, seemingly with perfect uncon-cern, remained to witness the *finale* of the day's work—the marking of the Mandingoes!

CHAPTER XXVIII.

A COUCH OF SILK COTTON

On parting from the presence of his fair cousin, and, at the same time, from the house of his inhospitable relative, Herbert Vaughan struck off through the shrubbery that stretched towards the ridge on the right.

Notwithstanding the storm that was raging in his breast, a reflection had occurred to him, which hindered him from going by the main avenue. Suffering from a keen sense of humiliation, he had no desire to meet with any of his uncle's people; since the very slaves seemed to be privy to his false position. Still less desirious was he of being observed, while making the long traverse of the avenue, by eyes that might be directed upon him from the windows of the great house. On reaching the limits of the level platform, he leaped a low wall, that separated the shrubbery from the outer fields; and then, under cover of the pimento groves, com-menced ascending the slope of the ridge.

For some time the conflicting emotions that were stirring in his soul hindered him from anything like tranquil reflection. Conflicting, I say; for two very opposite sentiments had been aroused by the two individuals with whom he had just held interviews; opposite as darkness from day—as sorrow from joy—perhaps, as hate from love. The conflict might have lasted longer, had there been an opportunity to give way to idle emotions; but there was not. The young man felt too forlorn and friendless to indulge in the luxury of passionate thought; and, on this account, the sooner did the storm subside. His first reflection, after calm had been partially restored, was, " Whither ?" and the answer, " To Montego Bay."

What he should do on his arrival there was not so easily answered. He had no longer a claim for shelter on board the ship—though no doubt the friendly fellows of the forecastle would have made him welcome as ever to a share of their " bunks" and sea biscuits. But Herbert knew that the hospitality of the Sea Nymph was not theirs to bestow; and, even if it had been, it could not long avail him.

To return to England again, and by the same ship, might have entered his thoughts; but that was out of the question. It had cost him twenty pounds, and his last shilling, to come out. It would have required the same amount to pay his passage back—therefore the idea was not to be entertained for a moment. Perhaps the thought of returning did not enter his mind ? Perhaps he would not have gone back, had a free passage been offered him? Neither of these suppositions is improbable. Notwithstanding the ill-treatment he had received from his uncle—notwithstanding the now desperate situation of his affairs—there was something, he scarce knew what, that hindered him from hating Jamaica—ay, even from hating Mount Welcome, the scene of his greatest humiliation! On reaching the crest of the ridge, and before plunging into the deep forest that stretched away on the other side, he endeavoured, through an opening in the trees, to catch a view of those white walls and green jalousies. In that glance there was more of regretfulness than anger—an expression of despair, such as may have appeared on the face of the fallen angel when gazing back over the golden palings of Paradise. As the young man turned away, and entered under the sombre shadows of the forest, the expression of despair seemed to become deeper and darker. To make Montego Bay—to seek in it such humble home as might offer—to wait there till his poorly-stocked portmanteau, now on its way to Mount Welcome, should be returned to him—these were the simple plans that suggested themselves. His mind was still too much on the rack to permit of his dwelling upon any ulterior purpose.

He walked on through the woods, without taking much heed as to the direction in which he was going. Any one who could have seen him just then might have supposed that he had lost his way, and was wandering.

It was not so, however. He knew, or believed, that by keeping to the left of his former course, he would get out upon the main road, by which he had reached the entrance gate of Mount Welcome. In any case, he could not fail to find the river he had already crossed; and, by following it downward, he would in time arrive at the town. With this confidence, falso as it may have been, he was not wandering—only absorbed in thought—in common parlance, absent-minded. But this absence of mind lasted so long, that it led to the result it resembled : he lost his way in reality. The trees hindered him from seeing the sun—now low down. But even if a view of the golden orb had been afforded him, it would have served no purpose: since, on riding out to Mount Welcome, he had taken no note of the relative directions between it and the Bay. He was not much disconcerted by the discovery that he had lost himself. The reflection, that in Montego Bay he would be no better off, hindered him from greatly regretting the circumstance. He had not the means to command the shelter of a roof—even in the midst of a whole city full—and the chances were he might find none better than that which was above him at the moment—the spreading fronds of a gigantic " ceiba," or cotton-tree.

At the time that this reflection crossed his mind, the sun had gone quite down : for the cotton-tree stood upon the edge of an opening where he could see the sky above him, and he perceived that it was already tinged with the purple of twilight. To find his way in the darkness would be no longer possible, and he resolved for that night to accept the hospitality of the " ceiba."

It had even spread a couch for him : for the seed capsules had burst upon its branches, and the pale-brown staple thickly covered the ground beneath, offering a couch that, under the canopy of a West Indian summer sky, was sufficiently luxuriant.

Was there a supper as well? Herbert looked around—he was hungry. Not a morsel had he eaten since breakfast, only a piece of mess-pork and a brown wormy biscuit, on parting from the ship. Hunger had already made itself felt. During his wanderings, having his gun with him, he had looked out for game. Had any appeared, he was too good a sportsman to nave let it escape. But none had shown itself—neither beast nor bird. The woods seemed deserted as himself. He could hear the voices of birds—all strange to his ear—he could see bright-winged creatures fluttering among the trees ; but none near enough for the range of his fowling-piece. Now that he had come to a halt, and having nothing better to do, he took his stand, watching the open glade. Perhaps some bird might yet show itself, passing from tree to tree, or flying about in pursuit of prey. It was the hour for owls. He felt hungry enough to eat one.

Neither owl nor night-jar came in sight ; but his attention was attracted to an object edible as either, and which promised to relieve him from the pangs he was suffering.

Close by the cotton-tree stood another giant of the forest—rivalling the former in height, but differing from it as an arrow from its bow. Straight as a lance, it rose to the height of an hundred feet. It was branchless, as a column of polished malachite or marble—up to its high summit, where its green, feather-like fronds, radiating outward, drooped gracefully over, like a circlet of reflexed ostrich plumes.

A child could have told it to be a palm, but Herbert knew more : he had heard of the noble " mountain cabbage" of Jamaica—the kingly *areca oredoxia*. He knew that in the centre of that circlet of far-stretching fronds—in that crown—there was a jewel that had often proved more precious than gems or gold : for often had it been the means of saving human life. How was this jewel to be obtained? Like all crowns, it was placed high—far above the reach of ordinary mortals. Young and active though he was, and a climber at school, he could never " swarm up" that tall, smooth shaft. Without a ladder an hundred feet in length, it would not be possible to reach its summit. But, see ! the palm-tree stands not alone. A great black lliana—a parasite—stretches tortuously from the earth up to the crown, where its head is buried among the feathery fronds, as if it were some huge dragon in the act of devouring his victim. Herbert stood for a moment reconnoitering this grand stay-cable, that, trailing from the summit of the palm, offered, as it were, a natural ladder for ascending it. Hunger stimulated him to the attempt ; and, resting his gun against the trunk of the ceiba, he commenced climbing upwards. With out much difficulty, he succeeded in reaching the top, and making his way among the huge *pinnæ* of the leaves—each in itself a leaf of many feet in length. He arrived at the youngest of them all—that still enfolded in the envelope of the bud, and which was the object for which he had climbed. With his knife he separated the summit leaf, flung the mass to the earth, and then, descending to the bottom of the tree, made his sup per upon the raw but sweet and succulent shoots of the mountain cab bage. Supper over, he collected a quantity of the strewn fleece of the silk-cotton, and placing it between two of the great buttress-like root spurs of the tree, constructed for himself a couch, on which, but for some hard thoughts within, he might have slept as softly and soundly, as upon a palliasse of white goose feathers and a mattress of eider.

CHAPTER XXIX.

THE TREE FOUNTAIN.

THAT he did not sleep soundly may be attributed solely to his anxieties about the morrow : for the night was mild throughout, and the composi tion of his improvised couch kept him sufficiently warm. His cares, however, had rendered his spirit restless. They were vivid enough to act even upon his dreams—which several times during the night awoke him, and again, finally, just after the break of day.

This time, on opening his eyes, he perceived that the glade was filled with soft blue light ; and the quivering fronds of the cabbage-palm—just visible where he lay—had caught the first trembling rays of the sun. Only there, and among the summit branches of the *ceiba* far o'ertopping the *spray* of the surrounding forest, was the sun yet visible. Everything else was tinted with the blue grey of the morning twilight. Herbert could sleep no longer ; and rose from his forest lair, intending to make an immediate departure from the spot. He had no toilet to make—nothing to do further than brush off the silken floss of the tree-cotton that ad hered to his clothes, shoulder his gun and, go. He felt hungry, even more than on the preceding night ; and, although the raw mountain-cabbage offered no very tempting 'dèjeuner,' he determined, before starting, to make

another meal upon it—remembering, and very wisely acting upon, the
adage of a " bird in the hand." There was plenty left from the supper
to serve him for breakfast; and, once more making a vigorous onslaught
on the *chou de palmiste*, he succeeded in appeasing his hunger. But another appetite, far more unpleasant to endure, now assailed him. In
truth, it had assailed him long before, but had been gradually growing
tronger; and was now unendurable. It was the kindred appetite, thirst;
which the cabbage of the palm, instead of relieving, had, from a certain
icridity in its juice, only sharpened—till the pain amounted almost to
torture. The sufferer would have struck off into the woods in search of
water. He had seen none in his wanderings; still he had the hope of
being able to find the river. He would have started at once, but for an
idea he had conceived that there was water near the spot where he
had slept. Where? He had seen neither stream nor spring, pond nor
river; and yet he fancied he had seen water—in fact he felt sure of it!
In a very singular situation he had seen it—so thought he at the time—
since it was over his head in the top of the cotton tree! On the previous evening, while up on the crown of the cabbage-palm, he had glanced
slantingly across, among the branches of the *ceiba*. These, as with all
great trees in the tropical forests, were loaded with parasites—*oriesias*,
long, ragged-looking cacti, bromelias, epiphytical orchids, and the like.
Tillandsias too, of the kind known as " wild pines," sat snugly in the
forks, or on the upper surfaces of the great limbs, flourishing as luxuriantly as if their roots rested in the richest soil. Among them was conspicuous the most magnificent of the genus, the noble *Tillandsia lingu-
lata*, with its spike of gorgeous crimson flowers projecting from the
midst of its broad sheathing leaves. It was in the convexities of these
huge leaves that Herbert had observed something which did not belong
to the plant—something he believed to be *water*.

It would cost but a few seconds' time to confirm or refute this belief
—a climb among the branches of the *ceiba*. Another huge parasite, from
the same root as the former, trended tortuously up to the limbs of the
silk cotton-tree, here and there touching and twisting around them. Its
diagonal direction rendered it easy of ascent; and Herbert, impelled by
his desire to drink, commenced climbing it.

Ere long, he had succeeded in reaching a main fork of the *ceiba*, where
nestled one of the largest of the wild pines. He had not been deceived.
In the convexity formed by its huge ventricose leaves was the natural
reservoir he had noticed—the gatherings of dew and rain, which the
rays of the sun could never reach.

At his approach, the green *hyla* sprang out from this aerial pool; and
leaping, frog-like, from leaf to leaf—protected from falling by the clammy
sponge-disks of its feet—soon disappeared amid the foliage. It was this
singular creature whose voice Herbert had heard throughout the live-
long night; and which, in constant chorus with others of its kind, had
recalled to his memory the groaning and working of the Sea Nymph in
a storm.

The presence of the tree-toad, in this its natural haunt, did not deter
the young man from drinking. Raging thirst has no scruples; and,
bending over one of the leaves of the *tillandsia*, he placed his lips to the

cool water, and freely quenched it. The labour of scrambling up the
lliana had taken away his breath, and to some extent fatigued him. Instead, therefore of descending at once—which he knew would cost him
effort equal to that of the ascent—he determined to rest for a few minutes upon the large limb of the *ceiba* on which he had seated himself.

"Well!" muttered he, in satisfied soliloquy, "if the people of this
island have proved inhospitable, I can't say the same of its trees. Here
are two of them—three, if I include the parasite—almost the first I have
encountered. They have yielded me the three necessaries of life—meat
drink, and lodging—lodging, too, with an excellent bed, a thing not so
common in many a human hostelry, What more is wanted? Under
such a sky as this, who need care to have walls around, or a roof over
him? Verily, to sleep here, *sub Jove*, is rather a luxury than an incon
venience? And, verily," continued he, "were it not that I should feel
rather lonely, and that man is designed to be a social animal, I might
pass my whole life in these great woods, without work or care of any
kind. No doubt there is game; and I was told at home there were no
game laws—so I might poach at pleasure. Ha! game? What do I see?
A deer? No! a hog? Yes, hog it is; but such a singular fellow—prick
ears, red bristles, long legs, and tusks. A boar! and why not a wild
boar?"

There was no reason why it should not be, since it *was* one—a wild
boar of the Jamaica forest—a true descendant of the Canarian hog, transported thither by the Spaniards.

The young Englishman never having seen a wild boar in its native
haunts, put the question conjecturally; but a moment's observation of
the animal convinced him that his conjecture was correct. The short
upright ears, the long head, hams, and legs, the shaggy neck and frontlet,
the foxy red colour, the quick short step as it moved onward—all these
points, combined with a certain savage air which Herbert noticed at a
glance, satisfied him that the animal under his eyes was not one of the
domestic breed, but a genuine wild hog of the woods. The grunt, too,
which the creature uttered as it moved across the glade—short, sharp,
and fierce—had but slight resemblance to the squeaking sounds of the
farm-yard. A wild boar beyond a doubt!

On perceiving this noble head of game, and so near him, Herbert's
first reflection was one of extreme regret. How unlucky that he should
be up in the tree, with his gun upon the ground! Had the piece only
been in his hands, he could have shot the boar from where he sat, and
right easily too: for the creature had actually come to a stand under the
ceiba, and so fairly under him, that if he had been provided with a stone,
he could have dropped it right upon its back. It was very tantalising;
but the young man saw it would be impossible to get hold of his gun
without giving the alarm. To attempt descending from the tree, or even
to make a movement upon the branch, would be sufficient to send the
boar scampering from the spot: of course never to be seen more. Conscious of this, Herbert preferred remaining upon his perch—the silent
spectator of a scene of wild Nature, to which chance had so oddly introduced him.

CHAPTER XXX.

THE HOG-HUNTER.

THE boar had stopped over the 'débris' of Herbert's breakfast—some fragments of the mountain cabbage which the young man had left upon the ground. Switching its feathered tail, and uttering a short grunt, expressive of satisfaction, the animal proceeded to snap up the scattered pieces, crunching them between its formidable grinders. All of a sudden the tranquil tableau became transformed into a scene of a more exciting nature. As Herbert continued to gaze, he saw the boar suddenly make a start, jerk its muzzle high in the air, at the same instant uttering a peculiar cry. It was a cry of alarm, mingled with angry menace—as testified by the bristles upon its back, which had suddenly shot up into an erect spinous mane.

Herbert looked for the enemy. None was in sight—at least to his eyes. The boar, however, had either seen or heard something : for he was evidently upon the strain to spring off. Just then, a loud report reverberated through the glade, a bullet hissed through the air, and the animal with a shrill scream turned over upon its back, the blood spouting from a wound in its thigh. Herbert saw that the boar was not killed, but only crippled by the loss of a leg. In an instant the animal was on his feet again, and upon the other three might have easily escaped ; but rage appeared to hinder it from attempting flight! It retreated only a few paces, taking its stand between two of the buttresses of the *ceiba*—on the very spot where Herbert had passed the night. There—protected on both flank and in the rear—and uttering fierce grunts of defiance—it stood awaiting its enemy.

Herbert looked in the direction whence the shot came, expecting to see the individual who had fired it. He had not long to wait. In an instant after the hunter appeared rushing across the glade towards the disabled game. Sword in hand came he, and without any gun! Herbert presumed that the empty piece must have been left behind him. The young Englishman was struck with the peculiar appearance of the Jamaica sportsman ; but he had little time for observing it, before the latter was directly under him. In a dozen quick strides the hunter had crossed the glade, reached the roots of the cotton tree, and became engaged in a deadly struggle with the wounded boar.

Notwithstanding the damage done to it, the creature was still a formidable antagonist ; and it required all the address of the hunter—habile though he appeared to be—to avoid contact with its terrible tusks. Each alternatively charged upon the other—the hunter endeavouring to thrust the quadruped with his long blade, while the boar in his turn would repeatedly rush towards his antagonist, suddenly rear himself upon his hind legs, and strike upwards with his armed and grinning muzzle. It was one of the fore-legs of the animal that had been broken by the shot ; but the wound, although greatly disabling it, did not hinder it from making a protracted and desperate defence. The spurs of the cotton-tree rising on each side proved its best protectors, hindering its assailant from turning its flanks and piercing it in the side. The combat, therefore, was face to

face; and the blade of the hunter, repeatedly thrust forward, as often
glanced harmlessly from the hard skull, or glinted with a metallic ring
against the tusks of the boar. For several minutes did this singular con
test continue—the young Englishman all the while watching it with lively
interest; but without giving the slightest signs of his being a spectator.
Indeed, the scene was so exciting, and had come under his eyes so unex
pectedly, that he was for a time held speechless by sheer surprise. As
soon as he had recovered from this, he would have made his presence
known, and hurried down to the assistance of the hunter; but the thought
quickly occurred to him that any movement on his part might distract
the attention of the latter, and expose him to danger from his fierce anta
gonist. His sudden descent from the tree—which would have brought
aim down almost on the shoulders of the man—could not otherwise than
disconcert the latter, and perhaps put his life in peril: for, had the hunter
faltered for a moment, or desisted from the attack, the boar would un
doubtedly have charged after him.

Herbert, himself a sportsman, comprehended all this with a quick instinct; and, with a prudent resolve, determined to keep quiet and remain
where he was. At that instant the struggle between biped and quadruped was brought to a termination. The hunter—who appeared to possess
all the craft of his calling—put in practise a *ruse* that enabled him to give
his antagonist the *coup de grace*.

It was a feat, however, accompanied by no slight danger; and so adroitly did the hunter perform it, as to create within the mind of his English
spectator both surprise and admiration. Thus was the feat accomplished.
In charging forward upon his human adversary, the boar had incautiously
ventured beyond the flanking buttresses of the tree. In fact, the hunter
had enticed the animal outward—by making a feint of retreating from the
contest. Just then—and before the brute could divine his intention—the
hunter rushed forward, and, throwing all his strength into the effort,
sprang high into the air. Quite clearing the quadruped, he alighted in
the angle formed by the converging spurs of the tree!

The boar had now lost his position of defence; though that of the
hunter for the moment appeared desperate. He had calculated his
chances, however; for before the enraged animal—hindered by its hanging limb—could face round to assail him, he had lunged out with his long
blade, and buried it up to the hilt between the creature's ribs. With a
shrill scream the boar fell prostrate to the earth—the red stream from his
side spurting over and spoiling the improvised mattress of cotton-tree
dock, upon which Herbert had passed the night.

CHAPTER XXXI.

THE RUNAWAY.

UP to this moment the young Englishman had done nothing, either by
word or gesture, to make known his presence. Now, however, he was
about to descend and congratulate the hunter upon a feat that had filled

him with admiration. A fancy passing through his mind at the moment, determined him to remain where he was a little longer ; and in obedience to this fancy, he sat gazing down upon the successful sportsman at the bottom of the tree.

To say the least, the appearance presented by this individual was picturesque—especially so to the eyes of an Englishman unacquainted with West Indian costumes ; but, in addition to picturesqueness of attire, there was something.in the features of the man that could not fail to make a remarkable impression upon the beholder.

The impression was decidedly pleasing, though the face that produced it was not that of a *white* man. Neither was it the face of a black man ; nor yet the yellow countenance of the mulatto. A shade lighter than the last, but still not so light as the skin of a quadroon ; but, like many quadroons, there was a dash of crimson in the cheeks. It was this colouring of the cheeks, perhaps, combined with a well-rounded, sparkling iris, that imparted the agreeable expression.

The man was young. Herbert Vaughan might have guessed him about his own age, without being many months astray ; and in point of size and shape, there was no great dissimilitude between them. In the colour of their hair, complexion, and features, there was no resemblance whatever. While the face of the young Englishman was of the oval type, that of the West Indian hunter was rotund. A prominent, well-cut chin, however, hindered it from degenerating into any expression of feebleness ; on the contrary, firmness was the prevailing cast of the features ; and the bold, swelling throat was a true physical index of daring. His complexion has been told. It only remains to say that it betokened a ' sang-melée' between African and Caucasian, which was further confirmed by the slight crisping that appeared among the jet black curls of hair thickly covering his head. The luxuriance of these curls was partly kept in check by a head-dress, that Herbert Vaughan would have been less surprised to see in some country of the East: for, at the first glance, he had mistaken it for a turban. On closer examination, however, it proved to be a brilliant kerchief—the Madras check—ingeniously folded around the forehead, so as to sit coquettishly over the crown, with the knot a little to one side. It was a *toque*—not a turban.

The other articles of dress worn by the young hunter were an outer coat, or shirt, of sky-blue cottonade, cut somewhat-blouse fashion ; an undershirt of fine white linen, ruffled and open at the breast ; trowsers of the same material as the coat ; and buff-coloured boots of roughly-cleaned cowskin. There were straps and strings over both shoulders, all crossing each other on the breast.

From the two that hung to the right side were suspended a powder-horn, and skin shot-pouch. On the same side hung a large calabash canteen, covered with a strong network of some forest withe, to protect it from injury. Under the left arm was a carved and curving cow's horn, evidently not for holding powder, since it was open at both ends. Below this, against his hip, rested a black leathern sheath—the receptacle of that long blade still reeking with the blood of the boar.

, This weapon was the macheto—half sword, half hunting-knife—which with its straight, short blade, and haft-like hilt of grey horn, it is to be found in every cottage of Spanish America, from California to the " Land of Fire." Even where the Spaniards have been, but *are* no longer—as in Jamaica—the universal machete may be seen in the hands of hunter and peasant—a relic of the conqueror colonists.

* * * * * * * *

Up to the moment that the boar was laid prostrate upon the ground, he in the *toque* had been kept too well employed with his fierce game to find time for looking at anything else. It was only after dealing the death blow to his adversary that he was able to stand erect, and take a survey around him.

In an instant his eye fell upon the gun of the young Englishman, and then the white pieces of palm-cabbage upon which the boar had been browsing.

" Hoh!" exclaimed he, still gasping for breath, but with a look that betrayed surprise ; "a gun! Whose ? Some runaway slave who has stolen his master's fowling piece ? Nothing more likely. But why has he left the piece behind him ? And what has started him away from here ! Surely not the boar ? He must have been gone before the animal got up ? *Crambo !* a richer prize than the pig, if I could only have set eyes upon him ! I wonder in which direction he has tracked off. Hish ! what do I see ? The runaway ! yes—yes, it is he! He is coming back for his gun ? *Crambo ?* This is unexpected luck, so early i' the morning—a slave capture—a *bounty !*

As the hunter hurriedly muttered these concluding phrases, he glided with stealthy tread between the two buttresses ; and having placed himself in the extreme angle of their convergence, remained perfectly still— as if waiting the approach of some one who was advancing towards the tree.

Herbert, from his perch, looked for the new comer thus announced, and saw him with surprise—surprise, not at his appearance, which was expected, but at the attitude in which he was advancing, and the wild aspect of the individual.

A young man of a copper red colour, with straight black hair, shaggily tossed and drawn over his brows, as if some one had been tearing it from his head ! His face, too—a fine one, notwithstanding its mahogany colour —appeared freshly lacerated ; and his whole body also bore the marks of nhuman abuse! The coarse cotton shirt that covered his shoulders was blotched with blood ; and long, crimson-coloured stripes running across his back, looked like the imprints of an ensanguined lash. The shirt was his only clothing—every rag he wore. Head, throat, legs and feet were all uncovered. The attitude in which he was advancing was as peculiar as his costume. When Herbert first set eyes on him he was *crawling* upon his hands and knees, yet going with considerable speed. This led to the belief that his crawling position was assumed rather with a view towards concealment, than from the inability to walk erect. This belief was soon after confirmed, for on entering the glade the young man rose to his feet, and trotted on—but still with body bent—towards the *ceiba*. What could he want there ? Was he making for the huge tree as a haven of safety from some deadly pursuers ? Herbert fancied so.

The hunter believed he was coming back for his gun—having no suspicion that the real owner of the piece was just over his head.

Both remained silent; though from motives that had no similitude to each other.

In a few seconds' time, the fugitive—for his actions proved him one—had reached the bottom of the tree.

"Halt!" cried the hunter, showing himself round the buttress, and stopping in front of the new comer. "A runaway, and my prisoner!" The fugitive dropped upon his knees, crossed his arms over his breast, and uttered some phrases in an unknown tongue—amongst which Herbert could distinguish the word "Allah." His captor appeared equally at fault about the meaning of the words; but the attitude of the speaker, and the expression upon his countenance, could not be mistaken: it was an appeal for mercy.

"*Crambo!*" exclaimed the hunter, bending forward, and gazing for a moment at the breast of the runaway—on which the letters "J. J." were conspicuously branded—"with that tattoo on your skin, I don't wonder you've given leg-bail to your master. Poor devil! they've tattooed you still more brutally upon the back."

As he said this—speaking rather to himself than to the creature that knelt before him—the hunter stretched forth his hand, raised the shirt from the shoulders of the runaway, and gazed for a while upon his back. The skin was covered with purple wales, crossing each other like the arteries in an anatomic plate!

"God of the Christian!" exclaimed the yellow hunter, with evident indignation at the sight, "if this be your decree, then give me the fetish of my African ancestors. "But no," added he, after a pause, "J. J. is *not* a Christian—he cares for no God."

The soliloquy of the hunter was here interrupted by a second speech from the suppliant, spoken in the same unknown tongue.

This time the gesture signified that it was an appeal for protection against some enemy in the rear: for the pitying looks of his captor had evidently won the confidence of the fugitive.

"They are after you—no doubt of it," said the hunter. "Well, let them come—whoever are your pursuers. This time they have lost their chance; and the bounty is mine, not theirs. Poor devil! it goes against my grain to deliver you up; and were it not for the law that binds me, I should scorn their paltry reward. Hark! yonder they come Dogs, as I'm a man! Listen! the bay of a bloodhound! Ha-a-a! Those villanous man-hunters of Batabano! I knew old Jessuron had them in his pay. Here, my poor fellow, in here!" and the hunter half-led, half-dragged the fugitive over the carcass of the wild boar, placing him between the buttresses of the *ceiba*. "Stand close in to the angle," he continued. "Leave me to guard the front. Here's your gun: I see it is loaded. I hope you know how to use it? Don't fire till you're sure of hitting: we'll need both blade and shot to save ourselves from these Spanish dogs, who will make no distinction between you and me Not they Crambo! there they come!"

The words had scarce issued from the speaker's lips, when two large dogs broke, with a swishing noise, out of the bushes on the opposite side of the glade—evidently running on the trail of the fugitive.

The crimson colour of their muzzles showed that they had been baited with blood—which, darkening as it dried, rendered more conspicuous the white fang-like teeth within their jaws.

They were half hound, half mastiff; but ran as true-bred hounds on a fresh trail. No trail could have been fresher than that of the flogged fugitive; and, in a few seconds after entering the glade, the hounds were up to the *ceiba*, in front of the triangular chamber in which stood the runaway and his protector.

These dogs have no instinct of self-preservation—only an instinct to discover and destroy. Without stopping to bark or bay—without even slackening their pace—both dashed onward, bounding into the air as they launched themselves upon the supposed objects of their pursuit.

The first only impaled himself upon the outstretched *machete* of the yellow hunter; and as the animal came down to the earth, it was to utter the last howl of his existence.

The other, springing towards the naked fugitive, received the contents of the fowling-piece; and, although the gun was loaded only with small bird-shot, at such close quarters it proved equal to a bullet; and the second dog sank lifeless by the side of his comrade.

CHAPTER XXXII.

A COMBAT DECLINED.

THE spectator in the tree began to fancy that he was dreaming. Within the short space of twenty minutes he had been the witness of a greater number of exciting events, than he might have seen, in his own country during the same number of years! And yet he had not witnessed the *finale* of the drama. The gestures of the runaway, and the speeches of his captor, had already warned him that there was another act to come; and, from the attitudes of both, it was evident that that act would be performed on the same stage, without any change of scene.

As yet the young Englishman saw no particular reason why he should cease to be a spectator, and become an actor, in this West Indian drama. That the yellow hunter should kill a wild boar, capture a runaway slave, and afterwards shield both his captive and himself from a brace of bloodhounds, by killing the fierce brutes, was no affair of his. The only thing that concerned him was the unceremonious use that had been made of his fowling-piece; but it is scarce necessary to say, that the young Englishman, had he been asked, would have freely lent the piece for such a purpose.

Nothing, however, had yet transpired to tempt him from a *strict neutrality;* and, until something *should*, he determined to preserve the passive attitude he had hitherto held.

Scarce had he come to this determination, when the new actors appeared upon the scene. They were evidently expected both by the fugitive and his protector. both of whom, after the defeat of the dogs stood looking towards the thicket whence the animals had issued.

Of the new comers there were three. One, the foremost, and apparently the leader, was a tall, black-bearded man in a red plush waistcoat, and high-topped horseskin boots. The other two were lean, lithe-looking fellows in striped shirts and trowsers, each wearing a broad-brimmed palm-leaf hat that shadowed a sharp Spanish physiognomy.

The bearded man was armed with gun and pistols. The others appeared to be without firearms of any kind ; but each carried in his hand a long rapier-like blade, the sheath of which hung dangling from his hip. It was the *machete*—the same kind of weapon as that which the yellow hunter had but the moment before so skilfully wielded.

On perceiving the tableau under the tree, the three new comers halted —and with no slight surprise depicted in their looks. The men of Spanish face appeared more especially astonished—indignation mingling with their surprise—when they beheld in that grouping of figures the bodies of their own blood-hounds stretched dead upon the sward !

The bearded man, who, as we have said, appeared to be the leader, was the first to give speech to the sentiment that animated all three.

" What game's this ?" he cried, his face turning purple with rage. " Who are you that has dared to interfere with our pursuit ?"

" *Carajo !* who's killed our dogs ?" vociferated one of the Spaniards.

" *Demonios* ! you'll pay for this with your lives !" cried the other, raising his *machete* in menace.

" And what if I have killed your dogs ?" rejoined the yellow hunter, with an air of *sang froid,* which won the silent applause of the spectator " What if I have ? If I had not killed *them,* they would have killed *me.*'

" No," said one of the Spaniards ; " they would not have touched you. *Carramba!* they were too well trained for that—they were after *him.* Why did you put yourself in the way to protect him ? It's no business of yours."

" There, my worthy friend, you are mistaken," replied he in the *toque,* with a significant sneer. " It is my business to protect him—my *interest* too : since he is my captive."

" *Your* captive !" exclaimed one of the men with a glance of concern.

" Certainly, he is my captive ; and it was my interest not to let the dogs destroy him. Dead, I should have got only two pounds currency for his head. Living he is worth twice that, and mileage money to boot; though I'm sorry to see by the ' J. J.' on his breast that the mileage money won't amount to much. Now what more have you to say, my good gentlemen ?"

" Only this," cried the man with the black beard, " that we listen to no such nonsense as that there. Whoever you may be, I don't care. I suspect who you are ; but that don't hinder me from telling you, you've no business to meddle in this affair. This runaway slave belongs to Jacob Jessuron. I'm his overseer. He's been taken on Jessuron's own ground : for this is on it. You can't claim the captive, nor yet the bounty. So you'll have to give him up to *us.*"

" *Carrambo, si* !" vociferated both the Spaniards in a breath, at the same time that the three advanced towards the runaway—the bearded overseer pistol in hand, and his two comrades with their *machetes* drawn, and ready to be used.

" Come on, then !" cried the hunter, in a taunting tone—as he spoke making signs to the runaway, whose gun he had re-loaded, to stand to his defence.

"Come on! but, remember! the first that lays hand upon him or me is a dead man. There are three of you, and we are but two—one already half dead with your inhuman cruelty."

"Three against two! that's not a fair fight!" cried the young English man, dropping down from the tree, and ranging himself on the weaker side. "Perhaps it'll be a better match now," added he, taking a pistol from under the breast of his coat, and cocking it as he did so—evidently with the intention of using it on the person of the overseer, should the latter attempt to proceed with the affray.

This addition, to the number of the combatants, equally unexpected by both parties, in both created surprise. But, when it was seen on which side the new comer had placed himself, other emotions took the place of surprise—one party regarding him with looks of joyful gratitude, while the other viewed him with feelings of dire hostility.

His advent having nearly equalised the strength of the adverse parties, as it had their numbers, produced, as is not unusual in such cases, a withdrawal from the battle—the bearded overseer, and his two swarthy coadjutors, at once dropping down from their attitude of menace to one of parley.

"And who are you, sir?" demanded the first, with as much arrogance as he could throw into his manner. "Who, sir, may I inquire, is the white man who thus places himself in opposition to the laws of the island? You know the penalty, sir; and by *my* word, you shall pay it!"

"If I have committed a breach of the laws," replied Herbert, "I presume I shall have to answer for it. But I have yet to learn what law I have broken; and I don't choose that you shall be my judge."

"You are aiding in the escape of a slave!"

"That's not true," interruped the yellow hunter. "The slave is already captured; he could not have escaped; and this young gentleman, who is as much a stranger to me as to you, I am sure, had no intention of assisting him to escape."

"Bah!" exclaimed the overseer; "we care not for your talk—we deny your right to capture him; and you had no business to interfere. We had already tracked him down with the dogs; and should have had him without any help from you. He is *our* prize, therefore; and I again demand of you to give him up."

"Indeed!" sneeringly responded the yellow hunter.

"I make the demand," continued the other, without noticing the sneer, "in the name of Jacob Jessuron—whose overseer I've told you I am."

"Perhaps, were you Jacob Jessuron himself, I might resist it," rejoined the hunter, coolly, and without any appearance of braggadocio.

"You refuse to surrender him, then?" said the overseer, as if making his final demand.

"I do," was the firm reply.

"Enough—you shall repent this; and you, sir," continued the deputy of Jessuron, turning a fierce look upon Herbert, "you shall answer before a magistrate for the part it has pleased you to play in this transaction. A pretty white man you for the island of Jamaica! A few more of your sort, and we'd have a nice time, with our niggers. Don't fear, mister, you'll see me again."

" I have no particular desire," rejoined Herbert ; " for certainly," continued he, with a provoking jocularity, "an uglier looking face than yours I have never set eyes upon ; and it could be no pleasure to me to look upon it again."

"Confusion!" cried the overseer. " You'll repent that insult before you're a month older—curse me if you don't !'

And with the dreadful menace the ruffian turned and walked sullenly away.

" *Cospita !*" cried one of the Spaniards, as the two hastened to follow their leader. " My brave dogs ! Ah, *demonio !* you shall pay dearly for them. Two hundred *pesos* each—not a *cuartito* less !"

' Not a *cuartito* for either !" responded the yellow hunter, with a mocking laugh. " Haven't I proved that they are not worth it ? With all your boasting of what your bloodhounds could do, look at them now. ' *Vaya !* my fine fellows ! Go back to your own country, and hunt runaway negroes there. Here you must leave that game to those that know how to manage it—*the Maroons !*"

Herbert observed that the hunter, on pronouncing this last word, drew himself up with an air of majestic pride as he did so, glancing scornfully at the ' caçadores.'

An angry " *Carrai !*" simultaneously hissed from the lips of both, was the only reply made by the two Spaniards ; who, at the same instant, turned their backs upon the *ceiba*, and followed their leader across the glade.

In a few moments the three had entered the underwood, and became lost to the view of those who remained by the tree—the young Englishman, the yellow hunter, and the red runaway.

CHAPTER XXXIII.

THE MAROONS.

As soon as they were gone, the hunter turned towards Herbert, his eyes sparkling with gratitude.

" Master !" said he, making a low obeisance as he spoke, " after, tnat words are but a poor way of offering thanks. If the brave white gentleman, who has risked his life for a coloured outcast, will let me know his name, it will not be forgotten by *Cubina, the Maroon*."

"Cubina, the Maroon !"

Struck by the oddness of the name and title—as he had already been by the appearance and behaviour of him who bore them—Herbert repeated the phrase mechanically, rather than otherwise,

" Yes, that is my name, master."

The young Englishman, though not yet enlightened as to the odd appellation, was too well bred to press for an explanation.

" Pardon me," said he, " for not directly replying to your request. I am an Englishman ; my name Vaughan—Herbert Vaughan.'

"By that name, master, I take it you have relatives in the island. The owner of Mount Welcome estate——"

"Is my uncle."

"Ah! then, sir, anything a poor Maroon hunter could do for you would not be much. All the same, you have my thanks; and if——; but, master," continued the speaker, suddenly changing his tone, as if in obedience to some instinct of curiosity, "may I make bold to ask why you are afoot so early? The sun is not yet ten minutes above the trees, and Mount Welcome is three miles distant. You must have tracked it here in the dark—no easy matter, through these tangled woods?"

"I passed the night here," replied the Englishman, smiling; "that was my bed, where the boar is now sleeping."

"Then the gun is yours, not his?"

The hunter nodded interrogatively towards the runaway, who standing some paces off, was regarding both the speakers with glances of gratitude, not, however, unmingled with some signs of uneasiness.

"Yes, it is my gun. I am very glad the piece was not empty: since it enabled him to destroy the fierce brute, that would otherwise have had him by the throat. Wretched as the poor fellow appears, he handled his weapon well. What is he, and what have they been doing to him?"

"Ah, Master Vaughan! By those two questions, it is easy to tell you are a stranger to the island. I think I can answer both—though I never saw the young man before. Poor wretch! The answers are written out upon his skin, in letters that don't require much scholarship to read. Those upon his breast tell that he's a slave—the slave of J. J.: Jacob Jessuron. You'll excuse me from giving my opinion of *him*: since he's a magistrate of the parish, and a friend of your uncle the custos."

"What have they done to you, my poor fellow?" asked Herbert of the runaway — his compassion hindering him from waiting for the more roundabout explanation of the Maroon.

The blood-bedaubed creature, perceiving that the speech was addressed to him, made a long rejoinder; but in a tongue unknown both to the hunter and Herbert. The latter could distinguish two words that he had never heard before—"Foolah" and "Allah"—both of which occurred repeatedly in the speech.

"It's no use asking him, Master Vaughan. Like yourself, he's a stranger to the island; though, as you see, they've already initiated him into some of its ways. Those brands upon his breast are nearly fresh—as one may tell by the inflamed skin around the letters. He's just landed from Africa, it appears. As for the marks upon his back—those have been made by a plaything the white planters and their overseers in these parts are rather too fond of using—the cartwhip! They've been flogging the poor devil, and, *Crambo!* they've given it to him thick and sharp."

As the Maroon made this remark, he raised the blood-stained shirt, exposing to view that back so terrible reticulated. The sight was sickening. Herbert could not bear to gaze upon it; but averted his eyes on the instant.

"Fresh from Africa, you say? He has not negro features."

"As to his features that don't signify. There are many African tribes

who are not negro-featured. I can tell from this that ne is a Foolah. I
hear him use the word when he talks."

"Yoy—Foolah! Foolah!" cried the wretched young man, on hearing
pronounced the name of his people; and then he continued in a strain
of the same tongue, accompanied by much gesticulation.

"I wish I knew his language," said the hunter. "I know he's a
Foolah. It is some reason why I should take an interest in him; and
maybe if only for that I might——"

The speaker paused, as if he had been talking to himself; and then
continued the soliloquy only in thought. After a pause he resumed
speech.

"Crambo! little would tempt me *not* to restore him to his master."

"And must you?"

"I must. We Maroons are bound by a treaty to deliver up all runaways we may take; and if we fail to do so—that is, *when it is known;*
but these villains of old Jessuron know I have him——"

"You will receive a bounty, you say?"

"Yes. They will try to deprive me of that; but it isn't the bounty
would tempt me in this case. There is something about this young
fellow——My word! he *is* like her!—ay, as if he were her brother!"

The last speech was involuntary, and delivered as if in soliloquy.

"Like her! Like whom?" demanded Herbert, with a puzzled look.

"Your pardon," replied the hunter. "I was struck with a resemblance
between this poor fellow and one whom I know:——but, Master
Vaughan," he continued, as if wishing to change the subject, "you have
not said how you came to be all night in the woods? You were hunting yesterday, and lost your way?"

"True, I lost my way; but not exactly while hunting."

"Perhaps that is all the sort of breakfast you have had?" and the
Maroon pointed to some pieces of the cabbage that still lay on the turf.

"I have both supped and breakfasted upon the palm. I had climbed
the tree for water, when the boar came up to break his fast upon what
remained of it."

The Maroon smiled at this explanation of some circumstances by
which even he had been mystified.

"Well," said he, "if you are not anxious to return at once to Mount
Welcome, and will give me five minutes' time, I think I can provide you
something better than raw cabbage."

"I am not particularly in a hurry about getting back to Mount
Welcome. Perhaps——I may never go back!"

These words, combined with the manner of the young Englishman as
he uttered them, did not escape the notice of the intelligent Maroon.

"Something strange in this young man's history," said he to himself,
though he had the delicacy not to demand an explanation of the ambiguous speech just made. "Well, it's not my affair, I suppose!"

Then, addressing himself to Herbert, he said aloud—

"Do you agree, Master Vaughan, to eat a forest breakfast of my providing?"

"Indeed, with pleasure," answered Herbert.

"Then I must ring for my servants."

As he said this, the hunter raised the curved horn that was suspended under his left arm ; and, placing the small end to his lips, blew a long, tremulous blast.

It had scarce ceased reverberating through the woods, when similar calls—to the number of a dozen or more—were heard ringing in reply! So like were they to that given by the yellow hunter, and to one another that for a moment Herbert believed them to be echoes !

"That should procure us company, and something to eat, master," said the Maroon, allowing the horn to drop back to its place.

"Hark!" he continued, the instant after, "there are some of my fellows! I thought they could not be far off. You see these vultures would not have had it all their own way, since my hawks were so near! Not the less am I beholden to you, Master Vaughan. I did not think it worth while to call my people. I knew these three poltroons would not venture beyond a little swaggering talk. See! they come !"

"Who ?"

"The Maroons !"

Herbert heard a rustling among the bushes on the opposite side of the glade ; and, in another instant, about a dozen armed men emerged from the underwood, and advanced rapidly towards the *ceiba.*

CHAPTER XXXIV.

A FOREST BREAKFAST.

The young Englishman gazed upon the advancing troop with keen curiosity. There were about a dozen of them, all black men, or nearly all—only one or two of them showing any admixture of colour. There was not a dwarfish or deformed figure in the party. On the contrary, every man of them possessed a tall stalwart form, strong muscular limbs, a skin shining with health, and eyes sparkling with a vigorous brilliance that betokened an innate sense of freedom and independence.

Their erect, upright carriage, and free, forward step, confirmed the belief, which Herbert had already formed, that these black men were not *bondsmen.* There was nothing of the slave either in their looks or gestures. But for the colour of their skins, he would never have thought of associating such men with the idea of slavery. Armed as they were with long knives and guns, some of them with stout spears, they could not be slaves. Besides, their equipments told that they were hunters—and warriors, if need be. All of them had horns, with pouches suspended over their shoulders ; and each was provided with a netted calabash for water, like that of the yellow hunter, already described.

A few carried an equipment altogether different, consisting of a small pannier of withe-work, or palm-fibre neatly woven. It rested upon the back, where it was held in place by a band of the same palm sinnet, crossing the breast, and another brought over the forehead, which sustained a portion of the weight. This pannier was the "cutacoo"—the depository of the "commissariat," or such other articles as were required in their wild forest rambles

With regard to their costume, that was "bizarre,' though not unpicturesque. No two were dressed alike, though there was a certain idiosyncrasy in their attire, which proclaimed them all of one following The "toqued" "bandanna" was the most common head-dress — a few having palm-leaf hats. Only some of them had a shirt with sleeves others wanted a complete pair of trousers; and one or two were naked from the waist upward, and from the thighs downwards—the white cotton loin-cloth being the unique and only garment! All of them had their feet and ankles covered: as the stony and thorny paths they were accustomed to tread rendered necessary. The "chaussure" was the same in all; and appeared to be a tight-fitting jack-boot, of some species of raw hide, without seam or stitching of any kind! The reddish bristles standing thickly over its surface, proclaimed the character of the material. It was the skin of the wild hog: the hind leg of a boar, drawn upon the foot while fresh and warm, as it dries tightening over the instep and ankle like an elastic stocking. A little trimming with the knife is all that is necessary for this ready-made moccassin; and once on, it is never taken off till the wearing of the sole renders necessary a refit. Drawing on his boots, therefore, is no part of the diurnal duties of a Jamaica hog-hunter.

I have said that Herbert Vaughan regarded the new comers with a feeling of curiosity as well as surprise. It was no wonder he did so The mode in which they had been summoned into his presence, their echoing answers to the horn signal, and their prompt, almost instantaneous appearance, formed a series of incidents that more resembled what might have been witnessed upon the stage of a theatre than in real life; and had the yellow hunter been a white man, and he and his followers clad in Lincoln green, the young Englishman might have fancied himself in Sherwood Forest, with bold Robin "redivivus," and his merry men gathering around him!

What could these men be? So interrogated himself Herbert Vaughan. Brigands with black skins? The arms and accoutrements gave some colour to the supposition that it was a band of sable robbers. "Maroons," the yellow hunter had called them; and he had used the same title in speaking of himself.

Herbert had often heard the word; had met with it in books and newspapers; but was not acquainted with its true signification. Maroon! runaway negro, as generally understood; but the men before him did not correspond to that definition. Though negroes, they had not the appearance of being runaways. On the contrary, the yellow hunter had just made a declaration that forbade this belief. They could not be run aways.

"This white gentleman has not eaten breakfast," said Cubina, as they came up. "Well, Quaco! what have the men got in their cutacoos?"

The individual thus appealed to was a jet black negro of large dimensions, with a grave yet quizzical cast of countenance. He appeared to be a sort of lieutenant: perhaps the "Little John" of the party.

"Well, worthy captain," answered he, saluting the yellow hunter with a somewhat awkward grace; "I believe there's enough, one thing with another—that be, if the gentleman has got a good appetite, and 's not too nice about what he eats."

"What is there? Let me see!" interrupted Cubina, as he proceeded to inspect the panniers. "A ham of wild hog barbecued," continued he, turning out the contents of a cutacoo. "Well, that to begin with—you white gentry are rather partial to our barbecued hog! What else! a brace of soldier crabs. So far, good; ah! better still, a pair of ramier pigeons, and a wild guinea fowl. Who carries the coffee and sugar?"

"Here, captain," cried another of the cutacoo men, throwing his pannier to the ground, and drawing out several bags which contained the necessary materials for coffee-making.

"A fire, and be quick!" commanded Cubina, evidently the captain of this black band.

At the word given a tinder was struck, dry leaves and branches quick-ly collected, and a sparkling, crackling fire soon blazed upon the ground. Over this was erected a crane—resting horizontally on two forked sticks —which soon carried a brace of iron pots suspended in the blaze. With so many cooks, the process of preparing the meat for the pots was very short and quick. The pigeons and guinea fowl were singed as fast as feathers would burn; and then being "drawn and quartered," were flung in torn fragments into the largest of the pots.

The soldier crabs shared the same fate; and some pieces of the wild hog ham. A handful of salt was added, water, a few slices of plantain, eddoes, calalue, and red capsicum—all of which ingredients were supplied from the cutacoos.

A strong fire of dried sticks soon brought the pot to a furious boil; and the lieutenant Quaco—who appeared also to act as *chef de cuisine*—after repeatedly testing the contents, at length declared that the *pepper-pot* was ready for serving up.

Dishes, bowls, cups, and platters made their appearance—all being shells of the calabash, of different shapes; and as soon as Herbert and the captain were helped to the choicest portions of the savoury stew, the re-mainder was distributed among the men: who, seating themselves in groups over the ground, proceeded to discuss the well-known viand with an avidity that showed it was also their breakfast.

The *pepper-pot* was not the sole dish of the *déjeuner*. Pork steaks, cut from the carcass of the freshly-slain boar, were added; while plantains and "cocoa-fingers," roasted in the ashes, contributed a substitute for bread not to be despisingly spoken of.

The second pot boiling over the fire contained the coffee; which, quaffed from the calabashes, tasted as fine as if sipped out of cups of the purest Sévres porcelain.

In this "al-fresco" feast the poor captive was not forgotten, but was supplied among the rest—the colossal Quaco administering to his wants with an air of quizzical compassion.

CHAPTER XXXV.

CAPTAIN CUBINA.

BREAKFAST over the Maroons gathered up their traps, and prepared to depart from the spot.

Already the wild boar had been butchered, cut up into portable flitches and packed away in the cutacoos.

The wales upon the back of the runaway had been anointed by the hand of Quaco with some balsamic cerate ; and by gestures the unfortunate youth was made to understand that he was to accompany the party Instead of objecting to this, his eyes sparkled with a vivid joy. From the courtesy he had already received at their hands, he could not augur evil. Whatever might be their intention, their chief had delivered him for the time ; and from enemies, whose fiend-like treatment of him was indelibly stamped upon his person. He knew that he could not well fall into more unfeeling hands, than those from which he had escaped. Satisfied on this score, he regarded his new acquaintances in the light of deliverers. Had he known their true character and calling, it might have hindered him from falling into that happy illusion.

The Maroons, out of respect to their chief—whom they appeared to treat with submissive deference—had moved some distance away, leaving Captain Cubina alone with his English guest. The latter, with his gun shouldered, stood ready to depart.

" You are a stranger in the island ?" said the Maroon, half interrogatively. "I fancy you have not been living along with your uncle ?"

" No;" answered Herbert. " I never saw my uncle before yesterday afternoon."

" Crambo !" exclaimed the hunter captain in some surprise ; " you have just arrived, then ? In that case, Master Vaughan—and that is why I have made bold to ask you—you will scarce be able to find your way back to Mount Welcome. One of my people will go with you ?"

" No, thank you. I think I can manage it alone."

Herbert hesitated to say that he was not going to Mount Welcome.

"It is a crooked path," urged the Maroon; "though straight enough to one who knows it. You need not take the guide to the great house with you ; though Mr. Vaughan, I believe, does not object to our people going on his ground, as some other planters do. You can leave the man when you get within sight of the place. Without a guide, I fear you will not find the path."

" In truth, Captain Cubina," said Herbert, no longer caring what idea his words might communicate to his Maroon acquaintance, " I don't wish to find the path you speak of. I'm not going that way."

" Not to Mount Welcome ?"

" No."

The Maroon remained for a moment silent, while a puzzled expression played over his features. " Only arrived late yesterday—out all night in the woods—not going back ! Something strange in all this."

Such were the quick reflections that passed through his mind.

He had already noticed an air of distraction—of dejection, too—in the countenance of the stranger. What could it mean? The gay ribbon knotted in the button-hole of his coat—what could that mean? Captain Cubina was of the age, and perhaps just then in the very temper, to observe all matters that appeared indications of a certain soft sentiment; and both the blue ribbon and the thoughtful attitude were of that signification. The Maroon captain knew something of the white denizens of Mount Welcome—more, perhaps, of those with a coloured skin. Could the odd behaviour of the young Englishman be attributed to some family difficulty that might have arisen there?

The Maroon mentally answered this interrogatory for himself, with the reflection that something of the kind had occurred.

Perhaps Captain Cubina was not merely guessing? Perhaps he had already listened to some whisper of plantation gossip: for electricity itself can scarce travel faster than news in the negro *quarter!* If the hunter captain had any suspicions as to the real position of his woodland guest, he was polite enough not to express them. On the contrary, he waived the opportunity given him by Herbert's ambiguous rejoinder, and simply said—

"If you are going elsewhere, you will need a guide all the same. This glade is surrounded by a wild stretch of tangled woods. There is no good path leading anywhere."

"You are very kind," answered Herbert, touched by the delicate solicitude of this man with a coloured skin. "I wish to reach Montego Bay; and if one of your men would set me on the main road, I should certainly feel under great obligations. As to rewarding him for his trouble, beyond thanking him, I am sorry to say that circumstances just now have placed it out of my power."

"Master Vaughan!" said the Maroon, smiling courteously as he spoke, "were you not a stranger to us and to our customs, I should feel offended. You speak, as if you expected me to present you with a bill for your breakfast. You seem to forget, that, scarce an hour ago you threw yourself before the muzzle of a pistol to protect the life of a Maroon—a poor outcast mulatto of the mountains? And now—but I forgive you. You know me not——"

"Pardon me, Captain Cubina; I assure you——"

"Say no more! I know your English heart, sir—still uncorrupted by vile prejudices of caste and colour. Long may it remain so; and whether Captain Cubina may ever see you again, remember! that up yonder in the blue mountains"—the Maroon pointed as he spoke to the purple outline of a mountain ridge, just visible over the tops of the trees —"up yonder dwells a man—a coloured man, it is true, but one whose heart beats with gratitude perhaps as truly as that of the whitest; and should you ever feel the fancy to honour that man with a visit, under his humble roof you will find both a friend and a welcome."

"Thanks!" cried the young Englishman, stirred to enthusiasm by the free friendship of the Maroon. "I may some day avail myself of your hospitable offer. Farewell!"

"Farewell!" responded the mulatto, eagerly grasping the hand which Herbert had held out to him. "Quaco!" he cried, calling to his lieutenant, "conduct this gentleman to the main road that leads to the Bay. Farewell, Master Vaughan, and may fortune favour you!"

It was not without regret that Herbert parted with this new friend;
and long time was he following upon the heels of Quaco, before ne ceased to reflect on the circumstances that had led to his making so singular
an acquaintance.

CHAPTER XXXVL

QUACO THE GUIDE.

QUACO being one of the taciturn sort, made no attempt to interrupt Herbert's meditations until the two had walked together for more than a
mile. Then, however, some matter upon his mind brought the negro to
a halt, and the commencement of a conversation.

"Two tracks from here, buckra. We can follow either; but dis to the
right am the shortest—the best road, too."

" Why not take it, then ?"

" O—a, master ; there may be reasons."

" What! for avoiding it ?"

" Ya—a !" replied Quaco, in a thoughtful, drawling tone.

" What reasons, friend ?"

" Don't you see the roof of a house—just over the tops of them paw-
paws ?"

" Yes—what of that ?"

" That's the baracoon."

" The baracoon ?"

" Ya—the house of Jew Jessuron."

" And what if it be ?"

" Ah, buckra, what if it be ? If we take the path to the right we must
pass the Jew's house, and some of his people sure see us. That John
Crow's a justice of the peace, and we may get in trouble."

" Oh! about the affair of the runaway, you mean ? Your captain said
he belonged to a Mr. Jessuron."

" As much 'bout the dogs, as the man. Captain had a right to clair
the runaway as his catch ; but these Spanish cusses 'll make a muss 'bout
the dogs. They 'll say our captain killed them out o' spite—that they 'll
swa to ; since it's well known we mountainee men don't like such inter-
lopers here, meddlin' with our business."

" But neither you nor I killed the dogs ?"

" Ah, bucrka, all the same—you helped—your gun helped kill the
dog. Besides you hindered the John Crows from pecking the hawk."

" For what I have done I am not afraid to answer before a justice, be
it this Mr. Jessuron, or any other," said the young Englishman ; conscious
of having acted rightly in the part he had taken in the quarrel.

" Not much justice to be expected from Justice Jessuron, master. My
advice be to keep out of the hands of justice as long 's can ; and that we
can only do by taking the road to the left."

" Will it be much out of our way ?" asked Herbert ; not caring to
greatly inconvenience himself for the reasons set forth by his compan
ion.

"Nothing to signify," answered Quaco, though not speaking very truth-fully: for the path he intended to take was really much longer than the one leading by Jessuron's house.

"In that case," assented Herbert, "take which way you please."

Without further parley, Quaco strode forward on the path branching to the left—as before, silently followed by him whom he was guiding. The track they had taken ran entirely through woods—in some places very difficult to traverse on account of the thorny thickets as well as the unevenness of the ground, which caused the path to be constantly ascending, or trending rapidly downward. At length, however, they arrived at the summit of a high ridge, and were moving onwards amidst groves of pimento, more open than the forest from which they had emerged.

From the top of the ridge, Herbert saw a large house shining against the verdant back-ground of the landscape, which he at once recognised as the Mansion of Mount Welcome. They were not going towards the house, but in a diagonal direction, which would bring them out on the avenue near the entrance gate.

Herbert called out to his guide to make halt. The young man did not like the idea of entering upon the avenue, lest he might encounter some of his uncle's people—a circumstance which he should not wish to have reported at the great house. He therefore requested Quaco to conduct him by some way lying more to the right—so that he might reach the main road without being seen from Mount Welcome.

The guide yielded compliance, though not without a little grumbling reluctance—as he turned off, muttering some words about giving "as wide a berth as possible to the baracoon."

He obliqued, however, into a new direction; and after another traverse through the woods, Herbert had the satisfaction of finding himself on the main road leading to Montego Bay. He would not have known it but for the guide, as he had only travelled this road as far as the gate of Mount Welcome; and the point at which he had now reached it was a half-mile further on. Better for him if he had left Quaco to his own judgment, and permitted himself to be conducted by the path which the guide had originally intended to take. By doing so, he would have reached the road at a point nearer the town, and in all probability have avoided an encounter of a most disagreeable kind.

On the main road he had no farther need of a guide, and Quaco was just on the point of taking leave of him, when at that moment a party of horsemen suddenly made its appearance round a bend in the road. There were six or seven in all; and they were riding forward at a rapid pace, as if bent upon some serious business. At the first sight of these strangers, Quaco shot like an arrow into the underwood—calling upon the buckra to follow his example. Herbert, however, disdaining to hide himself, remained standing in the middle of the road. Seeing his determination, Quaco returned to his side—as he did so, clamorously protesting at the imprudence of his 'protege.'

"Don't like their looks," muttered the Maroon, as he glanced apprehensively towards the horsemen, "It might be—by the Great Accompong it is!—that harpy Ravener, the overseer of Jessuron. Now, buckra, we's in for it! No use tryin' to escape 'em now."

As Quaco finished speaking the horsemen rode forward on the ground —one and all halting as they came to the spot where the pedestrians were standing.

"Here's our fellow," cried the bearded man at their head, whom Herbert easily identified. "Just dropped upon him like a duck upon a June bug. Now, Mr. Tharpey, do your duty! We'll hear what this young gentleman's got to say before the justice."

"I arrest you, sir," said the person appealed to as Mr. Tharpey. "I am head constable of the parish—I arrest you in the name of the law."

"On what charge?" demanded Herbert, indignantly.

"Mr. Ravener here will bring the charge. I've got nothing to do with that part of it. You must come before the nearest justice. I reckon the nighest justice from here is the custos Vaughan?"

This half interrogatory of the constable was addressed not to Herbert, but to his own followers. Though it was spoken rather in an undertone, the young man heard it with sufficient distinctness, and with very little complacency. To be carried back into the presence of his uncle—whom he had so lately defied—and in the character of a felon; to be brought, under such humiliating circumstances, before the eyes of his fair cousin—before the eye-glass of his late fellow-passenger— was a prospect that could not fail but be unpleasant. It was a sort of relief then when Ravener—who appeared to use some guiding influence upon the constable, and his *posse comitatus*—overruled the suggestion that Mr. Vaughan was the nearest magistrate, and claimed the honour for Jacob Jessuron, Esq., of the Happy Valley.

After some discussion between the parties upon this moot legal point, the overseer's opinion was adopted; and it was determined that the case should be carried before Justice Jessuron. Both Herbert and Quaco were then formally arrested in the name of the king, and marched off in custody—not without some very vociferous protestations on the part of the latter, with a long string of threats that he would some day make both constable and overseer pay for this outrage upon the person of a Maroon.

CHAPTER XXXVII.

A JAMAICA JUSTICE.

JESSURON, ESQUIRE, held court in the verandah of his dingy dwelling-house, where we have already seen him assisting at a different spectacle. He was now seated, with a small table before him, covered with a piece of green baize, and carrying a gold snuff-box, an inkstand, pens, and some sheets of paper. A book or two lay upon the table, one of which, by the lettering upon its cover, proclaimed its title and character—*The Jamaica Justice.* It was bound in black leather—a colour sufficiently emblematic of the chief subject on which it treated: for more than four-fifths of the laws and regulations it contained related to creatures with black skins.

The justice was in full costume, as the occasion required—that is, he wore his best blue body coat with gilt buttons, his drab smallclothes, and top-boots. The white beaver had been laid aside ; as the sanctity of justice requires even the judge's head to be uncovered. With Judge Jessuron, however, the uncovering extended only as far as the hat. The white cotton skullcap still remained upon his cranium : justice in Jamaica not being so rigorous as to exact its removal. With the spectacles well set upon his nose, and his thin face screwed into an expression of pompous importance, Squire Jessuron sat behind the baize-covered table that constituted the *bench*.

He was sole justice present; but, of course, it was merely a " preliminary inquiry before a magistrate." To have tried a white criminal on the serious charge brought against Herbert Vaughan, would have required a fuller bench—at least three magistrates, and one of them a custos.

Jessuron's power could go no farther than to *commit* the presumed criminal to prison, until a more formal process should be organised against him.

Herbert had been brought up in front of the table—his captor, the constable, and one or two of the *posse* standing behind him. On the right side appeared Ravener, backed by the two Spanish *cacadores ;* the last-mentioned worthies no longer—as had formerly been their constant custom—attended by their canine companions. Quaco had been left in the yard below—unguarded—since there was, in reality, no charge against *him*. There was one other witness to this magisterial trial—the daughter of the justice himself. Yes, the fair Judith was present—as on all important occasions ; but this time not conspicuously so. On the contrary, she was seated in a window that opened on the verandah, her beautiful face half concealed behind the netted fringe-work of the curtains. The position enabled her to observe what was passing without formally exposing her own person to view. Her face was not altogether hidden ; and her white shining forehead and dark lustrous eyes, gleaming through the gauzy muslin that veiled them, only appeared more piquantly attractive. It was evident, from her actions, that the gentle Judith had no intention of remaining unseen. There were several rather good-looking young men in the party that accompanied the constable—dashing fellows he had picked up by the way—and who desired nothing better than a lark of this kind. From the moment that these had entered the courtyard, the fair mistress of the mansion had been almost constantly at the window.

It was only, however, after the people had got grouped in the gallery, that she took her seat behind the curtain and entered upon a more minute inspection of their faces and persons. She was not long engaged in this game, when a change might have been observed passing over her countenance. At first her eyes had wandered from face to face with rather a sneering, cynical expression—such as the Jewess well knew how to put on. All at once, however, her gaze became fixed, and the contemptuous smile gradually gave place to a look of more serious regard. By following the direction of her eyes the object of this regard could easily be discovered. It was the " prisoner at the bar !"

What was the meaning of that gaze ? Sympathy for the accused ?

She knew why the young man was there. Ravener had already informed her father of all that had transpired, and the daughter had heard the

tale. Was it a generous pity for the position in which this unknown
youth was placed, that was now stirring within the breast of the fair
Judith, and had produced that sudden change in the expression of her
countenance? Hers was hardly the soul for such a sentiment.

Certainly, however, was she actuated by some motive different from the
common: as the trial progressed she no longer looked stealthily from behind the curtain; but having drawn it to one side, she directed her full
glance on the stranger, and kept her eyes fixed upon him, apparently regardless of any observation which her conduct might call forth. Her
father, whose back was towards her, saw nothing of this; though it was
not unnoticed by the others--Ravener, in particular, appearing to suffer
annoyance at the act.

The young Englishman—though little disposed at that moment to the
contemplation of aught beyond his own unpleasant position—could not
help observing the beautiful face directly opposite to where he stood;
nor did he fail to notice the peculiar glance with which he was being regarded.

Was the old man, before whom he stood on trial, the father of that fair
creature at the window? Such was his interrogative reflection as he
glanced inquiringly from the one to the other. If so, the frowns of the
father were in striking contrast with the soft, sympathetic looks directed
upon him by the daughter! Herbert could not hinder himself from making
the observation.

Some time had been occupied by the overseer in telling his story—to
substantiate the charge he had made. That done, the prisoner was put
upon his defence.

" Young man!" said the justice, " you have heard what this witness
alleges against you. What hash you to say in your defence? and first tell
ush what's your name?"

" Herbert Vaughan."

Jessuron re-adjusted his spectacles, and looked at the prisoner with
some show of surprise. The by-standers—stolid constable and all—
seemed a little startled. Quaco, whose colossal form rose above the rail-
ings in the background, uttered a grunt of satisfaction on hearing the
young man's name—which he had not known before—a name all-powerful
in the district, being that of the mighty custos himself!

There was one upon whom the words appeared to produce an impression different from that of mere surprise. A glance of anger shot from
the dark eyes of the Jewess as she heard it pronounced, and the look of
sympathy for the moment disappeared. Evidently, to her the name was
distasteful

" Herbert Vochan?" repeated the justice. " Might you be any kinsh-
man of Mishter Vochan of Mount Welcome?"

" His nephew," was the laconic reply.

" Ah! hish nephew! Blesh my soul! is that true?"

This announcement, as testified by his speech, produced a sudden com-
motion in the mind of the Jew-justice. From some little that was known
of his secret hostility towards his neighbour of Mount Welcome—Ravener knew more than a little—it might have been expected that the discovery of the relationship of the prisoner would have put him in high
glee. To be sitting in judgment upon the near kinsman of the custos—

of a serious crime, too—was a proud position for Jacob Jessuron, who
could remember many a slight he had received from the haughty lord of
Mount Welcome.   What a splendid revanche!

Certainly the manner of the justice, on learning who was before him,
seemed to indicate that such were his reflections.   He rubbed his skinny
hands together; helped himself from his gold snuff-box; gleefully smiled
from behind his glasses, which were once more shifted upon the sharp
ridge of his nose; and then, bending his face forward over the table, he
remained for some moments smiling, but silent and thoughtful; as if considering how he should proceed.

After a time he raised his eyes and freshly scrutinised the prisoner—
who had already returned an affirmative answer to his last query.

"Blesh my soul!—I never knew that Mishter Vochan had a nephew!
You are from England, young mansh?   Hash your uncle any more English nephews?"

"Not that I am aware of," replied Herbert, frankly.   "I believe I am
his only relative of that kind—in England, at least."

The proviso in this reply betrayed a significant fact: that the young
man was not very well acquainted with the family affairs of his colonial
kinsman.   The astute justice did not fail to note this deficiency in the
nephew's knowledge.

"How long hash you been in Shamaica?" asked he, as if endeavouring
to arrive at an explanation of some point that was puzzling him.

"A night, and part of two days—in all, about sixteen hours," replied
Herbert, with scrupulous exactness.

"Blesh my soul!" again exclaimed the justice; "only sixteen hours!
It'sh a wonder you're not at your uncle's house?   You has been there?"

"Oh, yes," answered Herbert, carelessly.

"You come to shtay at Mount Welcome, I supposh?"

Herbert made no reply to this interrogatory.

"You shleep there last night?   Excush me, young man, for ashking
the question, but as a magistrate——"

"You are perfectly welcome to the answer, *your worship*," said Herbert,
laying a satirical emphasis on the titular phrase; "I did *not* sleep there
last night."

"Where did you shleep?"

"In the woods," answered Herbert.

"Moshesh!" exclaimed the Jew-justice, raising his spectacles in surprise.   "In the woods, you shay?"

"In the woods," re-affirmed the young man; "under a tree; and a very
good bed I found it," he added, jocosely.

"And did your uncle know of thish?"

"I suppose my uncle knew nothing about it, and as little did he care,"
replied Herbert, with a reckless indifference as to what answer he gave.

The bitter emphasis on the last words, with the tone in which they
were delivered, did not escape the acute observation of Jessuron.   A
suspicion had arisen in his mind, that there was something amiss in the
relationship between the young man and his uncle; to the comprehension of which the answer of the former, aided by a knowledge of the
character and affairs of the latter, was gradually giving him a clue.   A
secret joy sparkled in his sunken eyes as he listened to the last answer

given. All at once he discontinued the direct examination of the prisoner; and, signing to Ravener and the constable to come nearer, he became engaged with these two worthies in a whispering conversation. What passed between the trio the young Englishman could not tell, nor indeed any one else who chanced to be present. The result, however, was to Herbert as pleasant as unexpected. When Jessuron again returned to address him, a complete change appeared to have taken place in his manner; and instead of the frowning justice, Herbert now saw before him a man who appeared more in the character of a friendly protector—bland, smiling, almost obsequious!

"Mr. Vochan," said he, rising from his magisterial seat and extending his hand to the prisoner, "you will excush the rough treatment you hash had from theesh people. It ish a great crime in thish country—helping a runaway shlave to eshcape; but as you hash joosh landed, and cannot be ekshpected to know our shtatutes, the law deals mershifully with a firsht offence. Besides, in thish instance, the runaway—who ish one of my own shlaves—did not eshcape. He ish in the hands of the Maroons, and will soon be brought in. The punishment I inflict upon you—and I shall inshist upon its being carried out—ish, that you eats your dinner with me, and—I think that ish punishment enough. Mishter Ravener," added he, calling to his overseer, and at the same time pointing to Quaco, "take that good fellow and see that he ish carred for. Now, Mr. Vochan! pleash to step into the housh, and allow me to introshuce you to my daughter Shoodith."

It would have been contrary to all human nature had Herbert Vaughan not felt gratified at the pleasant turn which this disagreeable affair had taken; and perhaps this gratification was enchanced at the prospect of the proposed introduction. Indeed, no man, however cold his nature, could have looked upon those lovely eyes—so long watching him from the window—without wishing a nearer acquaintance with their owner.

The angry glance had been evanescent. It was gone long before the conclusion of the trial scene; and as the young Englishman—in obedience to the invitation of his *ci-devant* judge—stepped across the verandah, the fair face, retreating from the window, seemed suffused with the sweetest and most sympathetic of smiles.

CHAPTER XXXVIIL

AN UNEXPECTED PATRON.

THUS had the chapter of accidents that conducted Herbert Vaughan to the penn of Jacob Jessuron come to a very unexpected ending. But the end was not yet. There was more to come—much more. We have seen how the prisoner became the guest of his judge—being sentenced by the latter to dine with him, Nor did the former find the penalty a severe one, as his host had incidently hinted it might be. On the contrary, the young Englishman found himself seated before a table far better provided than anything to which he had been accustomed at home and not much inferior to that which he might have seen spread at Mount Welcome—had it been his good fortune to dine there.

Nor was a fine dinner a rarity on the table of Jacob Jessuron. Grasping and avaricious as was this West Indian Israelite, and somewhat neglectful of external appearance—as indicated by his rather shabby dress—he was, nevertheless, addicted to luxurious living ; and, though with less parade, as fond of good eating and drinking as the owner of Mount Welcome.

Not that in his *menage* he eschewed ornament altogether. His establishment was genteel, his domestics numerous and well equipped—of late years more than formerly : on account of the advance which he had made both in wealth and social position.

Herbert, therefore, dinned well ; and was, of course, no little gratified by the unexpected hospitality shown him by the Jew-justice—the more so when he contrasted it with the niggardly behaviour of his own uncle. He took it for granted that it was to his uncle's name he was indebted for the honours that were being done to him—a mere neighbourly feeling of the penn-keeper for the great sugar-planter.

" They are friends," thought Herbert, " and this kindness to me is the offspring of that friendship."

The reflection did not give him pleasure, but the contrary. He felt himself in an awkward position — the recipient of a hospitality not meant for himself, but for one who had injured him ; and who although his own relative, he now regarded as his enemy. Had the reflection occured to him sooner, he would have declined the invitation to dine—even at the risk of giving offence. But the thing had come upon him so unexpectedly, that he had not thought of the peculiar position in which he was placing himself with regard to his uncle. He thought of it now, and uneasily. His uncle would hear of it—no doubt,

soon—and would be able to accuse him of taking advantage of his name.
The thought caused Herbert a very unpleasant feeling. Perhaps he
would have cared less had there been no one but his uncle to be cogniz-
ant of the false position. But there was. His short and troubled visit
to Mount Welcome had made Herbert Vaughan acquainted with one
whose remembrance was likely for a long time to exert an influence over
his thoughts, even though lips as red, and eyes, perhaps, as brilliant as
hers, were now smiling courteously upon him. The memory of his cousin
Kate was still mellow ; he could fancy her soft, sweet voice yet ringing in
his ears ; the warm glow of her virgin presence seemed hanging like a
halo around him ; all these urging him to preserve the heroism of his
character, if only for the sake of standing well in her estimation.
     Influenced by these considerations, he resolved to throw off the mask
with which circumstances had momentarily invested him, and declare the
true position in which he stood to his haughty relative. It was not until
the conclusion of the dinner—after the daughter of his host had retired
smilingly from the table—that the young Englishman unburdened himself.
Then—perhaps a little prompted by the wine—he made a full confession
of the disagreeable circumstances existing between himself and the master of Mount Welcome. Was it the wine—somewhat freely pressed upon
him—that hindered him from perceiving the displeasure which his communication had produced upon his hearer ? Was there any displeasure ?
Herbert did not perceive it, if there was. On the contrary, had the young
man been closely observant, he might have noticed an effect altogether
of an opposite character. Behind the green goggles, he might have seen
those deep, dark, Israelitish eyes sparkling with a fiendish joy at the revelation he had made.
     Though Herbert did not perceive this, he could not help being consci-
ous that his confession had not done much injury to himself in the eyes
of his entertainer. The Jew was certainly not less courteous than before
but, if anything more profuse in his proffers of hospitality. Indeed, before another hour had passed over his head, the homeless adventurer came
to know that in his Hebrew host—in his judge, who, but a short while
ago, had been trying him for a serious misdemeanour—he had found a
sympathetic friend ; at all events, a patron and protector ! The young
Englishman could not be otherwise than convinced of this, by the conversation that followed, and the consequences resulting from it.
     " I'm exsheedingly sorry, young Mishter Vochan," said the Jew, some
time after his surprise at Herbert's revelations had apparently subsided
—" exsheedingly sorry I ish—to hear that you and your uncle ish not on
good terms. Ah ! well ; we mush hope for the better ; and, ash I am one
of Mishter Vochan's humble friendish, possibly I might do something to
recoushile your little quarrel. Dosh you not intend going back to Mount
Welcome !"
     " Never. After what has passed, never !"
     " Ach ! yoush musht not be too ravengeful. Mishter Vochan ish a
proud man ; and I mush say he hash behaved badly—very badly ; but still
he ish your uncle."
     " He has not acted as such."
     " That ish true—very true—thish fine gentleman you shspeak of shtill

that ish no reason why Mishter Vochan should treat hish own nepnew sho
shabby. Well, well—I am sorry—exsheedingly sorry. But, Mashter
Herbert," continued the penn-keeper, interrogating his guest with evident
interest, " what *dosh* you intend to do ? I supposh you hash monish of
your own ?"

" I am sorry to say, Mr. Jessuron, I have not."

" No monish at all !"

" Not a shilling," affirmed Herbert, with a careless laugh.

" That *ish* bad. Where dosh you think of going—since you shay you
will not return to Mount Welcome ?"

" Well," said Herbert, still preserving his air of jocularity, " I was
making for the port again, when your worthy overseer and his friend in-
tercepted me—luckily, I may say, since, but for their intervention, I
should in all likelihood have gone without dinner to-day—at all events, I
should not have dined so sumptuously."

" A wretched dinner, Mashter Vochan—a misherable dinner to what
your uncle could have given you. I'm but a poor humble man con-pared
with the cushtos ; but what I hash ish at your service any time."

" Thanks !" said Herbert ; " I know not, Mr. Jessuron, how I shall ever
repay you for your hospitality. I must not tax it any longer, however.
I see, by the sun, it is time I should be making for the Bay."

As Herbert spoke, he was rising to take his departure.

" Shtop, shtop !" cried his host, pushing him back into his chair ; " not
to-night, Mashter Vochan, not thish night. I can t promish you ash fine
a bed as yoush might get at Mount Welcome, but I think I can give you
a better as you shleep in lash night—ha, ha ! You musht stay with ush
thish night, and Shoodith will make yoush some music. Don't shay a
word ; I takesh no refushal."

The offer was a tempting one ; and, after some further pressure, Herbert acquiesced in it. He was partly influenced by the poor prospect of
a lodging which the Bay afforded him ; and, perhaps, a little from a desire
to hear the promised music. The conversation was continued, by his
host putting some further interrogatories. How did Herbert intend to
employ himself in the Bay ? What prospect had he of employment ; and
in what line ?

" I fear not much in any *line*," replied the young man, answering both
questions in one, and in a tone of sarcastic despondence.

" Hash you no professhion ?"

" Alas, no !" replied Herbert. " It was intended by my father I should
have one ; but he died before my education was completed ; and my col-
lege—as is too often the case—has taught me little more than a knowledge
of dead languages."

" No ushe—no ushe, whatever," rejoined the intelligent Israelite.

" I can draw a landscape," pursued the young man, modestly, " or paint
a portrait tolerably well, I believe—my father himself taught me these
accomplishments."

" Ah ! Mashter Vochan, neither ish of the shlightest ushe here in
Shamaica. If you could paint a housh, or a wagon, it would bring you
more monish than to make the likeneshes of every face in the island.
What saysh you to the situation of book-keeper ?"

" Unfortunately, I know nothing of accounts. The very useful science of book-keeping—either by double or single entry—I have not been taught."

"Ha! ha! ha!" replied Jessuron, with an encouraging chuckle, " you ish what we, in Shamaica, call green, Mashter Vochan. You musht know that a book-keeper here hash no books to keep—neither day-books nor ledgers. He doesh not even put a pen to paper."

" How is that, Mr. Jessuron ? I have heard the statement before, though I did not comprehend what was meant by it."

" Then I musht explain, Mashter Vochan. There ish a law here which makes all proprietors of shlaves keep a white man on hish estate for every fifty blacksh. A very shilly law it ish ; but it ish a law. Theesh white supernumeraries are called book-keepers : though, ash I've told you, they keepsh no books. Now you undershtand what it meansh."

" Then what duties do they perform ?"

" Oh ! that depends on circumsthances. Some look after the shlaves, and some do thish and some that. But, egad ! now I think of it, Mashter Vochan, I am myshelf in need of a book-keeper. I have joosh bought a new lot of blacksh, and I musht not break the law. I am ushed to give my book-keepers fifty poundsh a year, cutrenshy ; but if you would be content to acchept such a berth, I would make the salary—on account of your uncle—a hundred poundsh a year. You would also be found in everything elsh. What dosh you shay, Mashter Vochan ?"

The unexpected proposal caused the young Englishman to hesitate and reflect. Not long, however. His forlorn, homeless situation presented itself too forcibly to his mind, to detain him long in doubt as to what an-swer he should make. A hundred a year, though it was " currency," was more than he was likely to obtain elsewhere—far more than he had ex-pected. And for this there was apparently no very arduous duties to be performed. It is true he knew nothing whatever of the man who pro-posed to employ him. He had not failed to notice his Jewish and some-what forbidding physiognomy ; but after the kind treatment he had al-ready experienced at the hands of this man, he could not augur very ill of him. After all, what signified who might be his master, whether Jew or Gentile ? He was not in a position to be over-scrupulous about whose bread he should eat. These reasons and reflections passing rapidly through his mind, urged him to the acceptance of the proposal made by his host. There was another reflection that occurred to him ; and though so faint and vague, that he was scarce conscicus of its existence, yet it was a motive for his remaining, stronger than all the rest. With or with-out the others, it would have decided him to give an affirmative answer.

After a little more fencing about the conditions—which Herbert deem-ed only too generous—he accepted the situation ; and from that hour the Happy Valley became his home

CHAPTER XXXIX.

A PLOTTING PARENT.

Jacob Jessuron was never known to be generous without expecting some reward. Never did he fling out a sprat, without the expectation of catching a salmon.

What object had he in view in thus becoming the patron and protector of the young Englishman—an outcast adventurer, apparently incapable of making him any return? Why such liberal conditions; unasked, and to all appearances unmerited—for, to say the truth, Herbert Vaughan was not the stuff for a *slave-driver*, a term almost synonymous with that of *book-keeper*.

No doubt the Jew had some deep scheme; but in this, as in most other matters, he kept his thoughts to himself. Even his " precious Shoodith" was but half initiated into his designs upon this special subject : though a conversation, which occurred between father and daughter, had placed before the latter some data calculated to assist her in guessing at them.

The date of this dialogue was upon the morning after Herbert's arrival at the penn; and it referred chiefly to the treatment which the new book-keeper was to receive from the denizens of the Happy Valley, but more particularly at the hands of Judith herself.

" Show the young man every kindness, Shoodith dear! Don't shpare pains to please him."

" Why particularly *him*, my worthy parent ?"

" Hush! mine Shoodith! Shpeak low, for the luf of Gott! Don't let him hear you talk in that shtyle. Theesh young Englishmen are not ushed to our free ways. I hash a reason for being friendly to him."

" What! because he is the nephew of Vanity Vaughan ? Is that your reason, rabbi?"

" I shay, shpeak low ! He's in his shleeping room, and may hear ush. A single word like that you shay might shpoil all my plans."

" Well, father, I'll talk in whispers, if you like. But what *are* your plans ? You'll let *me* know them, I suppose ?"

" I will, Shoodith, but not shoos now. I hash an idea, mine daughter —a grand idea, it ish ! And if all goes right, you, Shoodith, will be the richest woman in Shamaica."

" Oh, I have no objection to that—to be the richest woman in Jamaica, with a prince for my footman! Who won't envy Judith Jessuron, the daughter of the slave-merchant ?"

" Shtay ! a word about that, Shoodith dear. In hish presence we musht say as little ash possible upon the subject of shlaves. He musht see no shlave-whipping here—at least till he comes ushed to it. Ravener mushi be told to behave himself. I knowsh of more than one young English-mans who left hish place joosh for that thing. He needn't go among the field handsh at all. I'll take care of that. But, dear Shoodith ! every thing depends on you ; and I knowsh you can, if you will."

" Can what, worthy father ?"

" Make this young fellow satishfied to shtay with ush."

The look which accompanied these words betokened some other mean-ing than what they might have literally conveyed.

" Well," replied Judith, affecting to understand them literally, " I fancy there will not be much difficulty about that. If he's as poor as you say, he'll only be too well pleased to get a good situation, and keep it, too, I should think."

" I'sh not so sure about that. He'sh a young man of a proud shpirit. That ish proved by hish leaving his uncle ash he has done—without a shil ling in hish pocket—and then to defy the cushtos faysh to faysh ! Blesh my soul ! what a foolish young fellow he ish ! He must be managed, Shoodith, dear—he must be managed; and you're shoost the girl to do it."

" Why, father, to hear you talk, one would think that this poor young Englishman was a rich sugar estate—to be managed for some grand profit——"

" Aha !" exclaimed the other, interrupting her ; " maybe yesh—maybe he ish a rich sugar estate. We shee—we shee."

" Now, had it been the grand guest of Mount Welcome," continued Judith, without heeding the interruption ; " had it been this lord of Mon-tagu Castle that you wished me to manage"—at the word the Jewess smiled significantly—" I might have come nearer comprehending you."

" Ah ! there is no schance there—no schance whatever, Shoodith."

" No chance of what ?" abruptly inquired the Jewess.

" Why, no schance of—that ish——"

" Come, worthy rabbi, speak out ! You needn't be afraid to tell me what you're thinking : for I know it already."

" What wash I thinking, Shoodith ?"

The father put this question rather with a view to escape from an ex-planation. The daughter instantaneously answered.

" You were thinking, and I suppose still are, that I—your daughter, the child of an old nigger-dealer as you are—would have no chance with this aristocratic stranger who has arrrived—this Mr. Montagu Symthje. That's your thought, Jacob Jessuron ?"

" Well, Shoodith, dear ! you know he ish to be the guesht of the cushtos ; and the cushtos, ash I hash reason to know, hash an eye to him for hish own daughter. Mish Vochan is thought a great belle, and it would be no ushe for ush to ashpire——"

" She a belle !" exclaimed the Jewess, with a proud toss of her head, and a slight upturning of her beautiful spiral nostril ; " she was not the belle of the last ball at the Bay—not she, indeed ; and as for aspiring, the daughter of a slave-dealer is at least equal to the daughter of a slave—a slave herself, as I've heard you say."

" Hush, Shoodith ! not a word about that—not a whisper in the hearing
of thish young man. You know he ish her cousin. Hush !"

" I don't care if he was her brother," rejoined the Jewess, still speaking in a tone of spiteful indignation—for Kate Vaughan's beauty was
Judith Jessuron's especial fiend ; " and if he were her brother," continued
she, " I'd treat him worse than I intend to do. Fortunate for him, he's
only her cousin ; and as he has quarrelled with them all, I suppose—has
he said anything of *her* ?"

" Of hish cousin Kate, you mean ?"

" Why, who should I mean !" demanded the daughter, bluntly. " Ther:
is no other *she* in Mount Welcome the young fellow is likely to bo talk
ing about ; nor you either—unless, indeed, you've still got that copper
coloured wench in your head. Of course, it's Kate Vaughan I mean.
What says he of her ? He must have seen her—shor: as his visit seems
to have been ; and, if so, you must have talked about her last night—
since you sat late enough to have discussed the whole scandal of the
island. Well ?"

With all this freedom of verbiage, the Jewess seemed not to loose sight
of the original interrogatory ; and her frequent repetition of it was
rather intended to conceal the interest with which she looked for the answer. If her words did not betray that interest, her looks certainly did :
for, as she bent forward to listen, a skilled observer might have detected
in her eyes that sort of solitude which springs from a heart whence the
love passion is just beginning to appear—budded but not yet blooming.

" True, Shoodith, true," admitted the slave merchant, thus bantered by
his own bold offspring. " The young man did shpeak of hish cousin ; for
I hash a wish to know what wash hish opinion of her, and ashked him.
I wash in hopes he had quarrelled with her too ; but ach no—he hashn't,
he hashn't."

" What might that signify to you ?"

" Moch moch, daughter Shoodith ; a great deal."

" You're a mysterious old man, father Jacob ; and, though I've been
studying you for a score of years, I don't half understand you yet. But
what did he say of Kate Vaughan ? He saw her, I suppose ?"

" Yesh. He had an interview with hish cousin. He saysh she behaved very kind to him. He'sh not angry with *her*. S'help me, no !"

This information appeared to produce no very pleasant impression upon
the Jewess ; who, with her eyes downcast upon the floor, remained for
some moments in a thoughtful attitude.

" Father," she said, in a tone half serious, half in simplicity, " the young
fellow has got a bit of blue ribbon in his button-hole. You have noticed
it, I suppose ? I am curious to know what he means by wearing that. Is
it an order, or what ? Did he tell you ?"

" No. I noticed it ; but, ash he shayed nothing about it, I did not ashk
him. It'sh no order—nothing of the kind. Hish father wash only a poor
artisht."

" I wonder where he procured that piece of ribbon ?" said Judith,
speaking in a low tone, and half in soliloquy.

" You can ashk him for yourself, Shoodith. There ish no harm in that."

" No, not I," answered Judith, suddenly changing countenance, as if ashamed of having shown the weakness of curiosity. "What care I for him or his ribbon ?"

"No matter for that, Shoodith, dear ; no matter for that, if yoush can make him *care for you.*"

"Care for *me!* What, father! do you want him to fall in love with me ?"

"Joosh that—joosh so."

"For what reason, pray ?"

"Don't ashk now. I hash a purpose, you shall know it in good time, Shoodith. You make him in luff with you—over head and earsh, if you like."

The counsel did not appear displeasing to her who received it. Anything but displeasure was in her looks as she listened to it.

"But what," asked she, after a reflective pause, and laughing as she spoke, "what if, in luring him, I should myself fall into the lure ? They say that the tarantula is sometimes taken in its own trap ?"

"If you succeed in catching your fly mine goot shpider Shoodith, that won't signify. So much the better ish that. But fusht catch your fly. Don't let go the shtrings of your heart, till you hash secured hish ; and then you may do as you pleash. But hush! I hear him coming from hish shamber. I musht go and bring him in to hish breakfasht. Now, Shoodith dear, show him every reshpect. Shower on him your sweetest of shmiles!"

And terminating the dialogue with this parental injunction, Jacob Jessuron walked off to conduct his guest into the great hall.

"Ah! worthy father !" said Judith, looking after him with a singular smile upon her countenance " for once you may find a dutiful daughter ; though not for you or your purpose—whatever that may be. I have my suspicion of what it is. No, not for that either—grand destiny as it may be deemed. There is something grander still—a passion perilous to play with ; and just for that peril shall I play with it. Ha—he comes! How proud his step! He looks the master, and you, old Israelite, his overseer —his book-keeper—ha! ha! ha!

"Ach !" she exclaimed, suddenly checking her laughter, and changing her smile to a frown ; "the ribbon! he wears it still! What can it mean? No matter now! Ere long I shall unravel the skein of its silken mystery --even if this heart should be torn in the attempt!"

CHAPTER XL.

ANOTHER OF THE SAME.

At that same hour, a scene of remarkable parallelism was passing at Mount Welcome. Loftus Vaughan was holding dialogue with his daughter, as Jacob Jessuron with Judith—the subject very similar, the motives of planter and penn-keeper equally mean

Smythje was still abed. In his "dwea metwopolis," matutinal hours he had never known ; and probably, in all his life, had never looked upon the rising of the sun. The ordinary hour of a Jamaica 'déjeûner' would have been far too early for him; so, knowing his habits, the courteous custos had ordered each morning the postponement of the meal—till his guest should give some signs of restored wakefulness. No one was per- mitted to disturb either his dreams or his slumbers, till Morpheus had made a voluntary exit from his chamber; and then his valet, Thoms, who had charge of the important vigil, would enter, and return with the an- nouncement that his master would presently show himself.

On this, the second morning after his arrival, the cockney was lying late as usual. The planter and Kate had paid their tribute to the skies several hours before. Both had been abroad—though on different errands —and had now met in the great hall, at the hour at which they had been accustomed to have breakfast. No breakfast appeared upon the table, although the cloth was laid in readiness. None must appear until the dis- tinguished guest should condescend—not to come *down*, since his cham- ber was on the same floor—but to come *out*. As for the young creole, she cared little about the change of hours for the morning or any other meal. She was too young to have contracted habits that called for indulgence. With Mr. Vaughan the thing was different, and he found the postpone- ment of his breakfast a somewhat serious inconvénience. In order to re- medy it, in some measure at least, he had ordered a cup of coffee and a biscuit, with which he was breaking his fast. when Kate entered the room. Occasional glances, half expectant, half anxious, which he had cast along the corridor—the direction in which Kate must come—beto- kened some purpose: either that he expected a communication, or had one to make. The latter was the more likely, as the young creole, on entering, manifested herself in an interrogative manner.

"You have sent for me, papa? Breakfast is not yet ready?"

"No, Catherine," replied Mr. Vaughan, gravely, "it is not for that."

The grave tone was not needed. The "Catherine" was enough to tell Kate that her father was in one of his serious moods: for it was only when in this vein that he ever pronounced her baptismal name in full.

"Sit down there!" he said, pointing to a faisceul in front of where he was himself seated. "Sit down, my daughter, and listen : I have some- thing of importance to say to you."

The young lady obeyed in silence, and not without a little of that re- luctant *gaucherie*, which patients display when seating themselves in front of a physician; or a naughty child composing itself to listen to the parent- al lecture.

The natural gaiety of "lilly Quasheba" was not easily restrained ; and though the unusual gravity depicted in her father's face might have checked it, the formality with which he was initiating the interview had an opposite effect. At the two corners of her pretty mouth might have been observed a strong tendency towards a smile.

Her father did observe this ; but, instead of reciprocating the smile, he returned it by a frown.

"Come, Catherine!" said he, reprovingly, "I have called you out to talk over a serious matter. I expect you to listen seriously, as becomes the subject I am about to introduce."

"Oh! papa; how can I be serious till I know the subject? You are not ill, I hope?"

" Tat ᵪ—no. It has nothing to do with my health—which, thank Providence, is good enough—nor yours neither. It is our wealth, not our health, that is concerned—our wealth, Catherine!"

The last phrase was spoken with emphasis, and in a confidential way, as if to enlist his daughter's sympathies upon the subject.

' Our wealth, papa? I hope nothing has happened ? You have had no losses ?"

" No, love," replied Mr. Vaughan, now speaking in a fond, parental tone ; "nothing of the sort, thanks to fortune, and perhaps a little to my own prudence. It is not losses I am thinking about, but gains."

" Gains !"

" Aye, gains, you little rogue! gains which you can assist me in ob- taining."

" I, papa ? How could I assist you ? I know nothing of business—I am sure I know nothing:"

" Business! ha! ha! It's not business, Kate. The part which you will have to play will be one of pleasure—I hope so, at least."

" Pray tell me what it is, papa ? I am sure I'm fond of pleasure. Every- body knows that."

"Catherine!" said her father, once more adopting the grave tone, " do you know how old you are ?"

" Certainly, papa ! at least, what I have been told. Eighteen—just past last birthday."

" And do you know what young girls should, and generally do, think about, when they come to be of that age ?"

Kate either affected or felt profound ignorance of the answer she was expected to make.

" Come !" said Mr. Vaughan, banteringly, "you know what I mean, Catherine ?"

" Indeed, papa, I do not. You know I keep no secrets from you : you taught me not. If I had any, I would tell you."

"I know you're a good girl, Kate. I know you would. But that is a sort of a secret I should hardly expect you to declare—even to me, your father."

" Pray what is it, papa ?"

" Why, at your age, Kate, most girls—and it is but right and natural they should—take to thinking about a young man."

" Oh! that is what you mean ? Then I can answer you, papa, I have taken to thinking about one."

" Ha !" ejaculated Mr. Vaughan, in a tone of pleased surprise; " you have, have you ?"

" Yes, indeed," answered Kate, with an air of most innocent 'naiveté ' I have been thinking of one—and so much, that he is scarce ever out of my mind."

" Ho !" said the custos, repeating his exclamation of surprise, and rather taken aback by a confession so unexpectedly candid. " Since how long has this been, my child ?"

The answer was listened for with some anxiety.

"Since how long ?" rejoined Kate, musingly.

" Yes. When did you first begin to think of this young man ?"

"Oh! the day before yesterday, after dinner—ever since I first saw him, father."

"*At* dinner you first saw him," said Mr. Vaughan, correcting his daughter. "But no matter for that," he continued, gleefully rubbing his hands together, and not noticing the puzzled expression upon Kate's countenance. "It might be, that you did not think of him in the first moment of your introduction. It's not often people do. A little bashfulness has to be got over. And so, then, Kate, you like him *now*—y:o think you like him now?"

"Oh! father, you may be sure I do—better than any one I ever saw—excepting yourself, dear papa."

"Ah! my little chit, that's a different sort of liking—altogether different. The one's love—the other is but fillial affection—each very well in its place. Now, as you're a good girl, Kate, I have a bit of pleasant news for you."

"What is it, papa?"

"I don't know whether I should tell you or not," said the custos, playfully patting his daughter upon the cheek; "at least, not now, I think. It might make you too happy."

"Oh! papa! I have told you what you wished me; and I see it has made you happy. Surely you will not conceal what you say will do the same for me? What is the news?"

"Listen, then, Kate!" and Mr. Vaughan bending forward, as if to make his communication more impressive, pronounced in a whisper, "He reciprocates your feeling—*he likes you!*"

"Father, I fear he does not," said the young creole, with a serious air.

"He does—I tell you so, girl. He's over head and ears about you. I know it. In fact, I saw it from the first minute. A blind man might have perceived it; but then a blind man can see better than a young lady that's in love. Ha! ha! ha!"

Loftus Vaughan laughed long and loudly at the jest he had so unexpectedly perpetrated: for at that moment he was in the very mood for merriment. His dearest dream was about to be realised. Montagu Smythje was in love with his daughter. That he knew before. Now his daughter had more than half admitted—in fact, quite confessed—that she liked Smythje; and what was *liking* but *love?*

"Yes, Kate," said he, as soon as his exultation had to some extent subsided, "you are blind, you little silly—else you might have seen it all. His behaviour would show how much he cares for you."

"Ah! father, I think that his behaviour would rather show that he cares not for either of us. He is too proud to care for any one."

"What! too proud? Nonsense! it's only his way. Surely he has not shown anything of that to you, Kate?"

"I cannot blame him," continued the young girl, still speaking in a serious tone. "The fault was not his. Your treatment of him, father—you must not be angry at me for telling you of it—now that I know all, dear papa—was it not enough to make him act as he has done?"

"My treatment of him!" cried the custos, with a self-justifying but puzzled look. "Why, child, you rave! I could not treat him better, if I was to try ever so. I have done everything to entertain him, and make him feel at home here. As to what *he* has done, it's all nonsense about his pride: at least, with us he has shown nothing of the kind. On the contrary, he is acting admirably throughout the whole matter. Certainly, no man could behave with more politeness to you than Mr. Smythje is doing ?"

" Mr. Smythje !"

The entrance of this gentleman at the moment prevented Mr. Vaughan from noticing the effect which the mention of his name had produced: an unexpected effect, as might have been seen by the expression which Kate's features had suddenly assumed.

But for that interruption—hindering the " éclaircissement' which, no doubt, his daughter would on the instant have made—Mr. Vaughan might have sat down to breakfast with his appetite considerably im paired.

His guest requiring all his attention caused him to withdraw suddenly from the dialogue ; and he appeared neither to have heard the exclamatory repetition of Smythje's name, nor the words uttered by Kate in a lower tone, as she turned towards the table :—

" *I thought it was Herbert !*"

CHAPTER XLI.

A SWEETHEART EXPECTED.

THE departure of the young Englishman, under the conduct of Quaco, was a signal for the black band to disperse. At a sign from their chief, they broke up into knots of two or three individuals each, and went off in different directions—disappearing amid the underwood as silently as they had emerged from it.

Cubina alone remained in the glade, the captured runaway cowering upon a log beside him. For some minutes the Maroon captain stood resting upon his gun—which one of his followers had brought up—his eyes fixed upon the captive. He appeared to be meditating what course he should pursue in relation to the unfortunate slave ; and the shadow upon his countenance told that some thought was troubling him.

The runaway on his side was regarding his captor with a look half cheerful, half apprehensive ; or rather, with these expressions alternating, as he observed similar changes on the countenance of the other. His hopes, however, outweighed his fears. Though unable to comprehend what had occurred, and ignorant of the motives of the Maroon in rescuing him from his pursuers, he knew that he had escaped from merciless men, to fall into the hands of others that appeared not only merciful, but friendly. Had he known that just then his captor was debating with himself, as to whether he should deliver him up, and to the very men from whom he had rescued him, or their equally merciless master—could he have conjectured that this was the subject of that silent cogitation, of which he was a witness, his apprehensions would have been stronger than his hopes,

The Maroon captain felt himself in a dilemma: hence his hesitating and reflective attitude. His duty was in conflict with his desires. From the first the face of the captive had interested him; and now that he had time to scan it more narrowly, and observe its noble features, the idea of delivering him up to such a cruel master, as him whose initials he bore upon his breast, became all the more repugnant. Duty demanded him to do so. It was the law of the land—of the treaty by which the Maroons were bound—and disobedience to that law would be certain to meet with punishment stringent and severe. True, there was a time when a Maroon captain would have held obedience to this law more lightly; but that was before the conquest of Trelawny town—or, rather its traitorous betrayal—followed by the basest banishment recorded among men.

That betrayal had brought about a change. The Maroons who had avoided the forced exile, and still remained in the mountain fastnesses, though preserving their independence, were no longer a powerful people —only a mere remnant, whose weakness rendered them amenable, not only to the laws of the island, but to the tyranny and caprice of such planter justices as might choose to persecute them. Such was the position of Cubina and his little band, who had established their home in the mountains of Trelawney. With the Maroon captain, therefore, it was a necessity, as well as a duty, to deliver up the runaway captive. Failing to do so, he would place his liberty in peril. He knew this, without the threat which Ravener had fulminated in such positive terms. His interest also lay in the line of his duty. This also he could understand. The captive was a prize, for which he would be entitled to claim a reward—the *bounty*. Not for a moment was he detained by this last consideration. The prospect of the reward would have had no weight with him whatever; it would not even have cost him a reflection, but that, just then, and for a very singular purpose, Cubina required money.

Thus, there were three powerful motives in favour of restoring the slave to his master—duty, necessity, and self-interest. But one nobler than all was stirring within the breast of the yellow hunter—humanity. Would it prevail over the other three?

Some words he had let drop before the departure of Herbert—a hypothetical threat of disobedience to the laws—might lead to the hope that it would.

As he stood gazing upon his captive, this threat was repeated in a kind of involuntary soliloquy, while another motive was revealed by an additional phrase or two that escaped from his lips.

"*Crambo!*" he muttered, using an exclamation of the Spanish tongue, still found in a corrupted form among the Maroons; "he is as like to Yola as if he was her brother! I warrant he's of the same nation—perhaps of her tribe. Two or three times he has used the word *Foolah*. Besides, his colour, his shape, his hair, are all like hers. No doubt of it, he's Foolah."

The last word was uttered so loudly as to reach the ear of the runaway.

"Yah! Foolah, Foolah!" he exclaimed, turning his eyes appealing upon his captor. "No slave—no slave!" added he, striking his hand upon his breast as he repeated the words.

"Slave! no slave!" echoed the Maroon, with a start of surprise; "that's English enough. They've taught him the word. No slave! what can he intend by saying that?"

"Foolah me—no slave!" again exclaimed the youth, with a similar gesture to that he had already made.

"Something curious in this!" muttered the Maroon, musingly. "What can he mean by saying he is no slave—for that is certainly what he is trying to say? Slave he must be: else how did he get here? I've heard that a cargo was landed the day before yesterday, and that the old Jew got most or all of them. This young fellow must be one of that lot. Very likely he's picked up the words aboard ship. Perhaps he is speaking of what he was in his own country. Ah! poor devil! he'll soon find the difference here.

"*Crambo!*" continued the Maroon, after a pause, in which he had been silently regarding the countenance of the newly-arrived African. "It's a shame to make a slave of such as he—an hundred times more like a freeman than his master. Ah! *Dios! Dios!* it's a hard row he'll have to hoe. I feel more than half tempted to risk it, and save him from such a fate. But that I want this money——"

As this half determination passed through the mind of the Maroon, it was accompanied by a noble and proud expression of features.

"If they had not seen him in my possession," he continued to reflect; 'but the overseer and those Spanish poltroons know all, and will—— Well, let them—at all events, I shall not take him back till I've seen Yola. No doubt she can talk to him; if he's Foolah she can. We'll hear what he's got to say, and what this 'no slave' means. Ha!" exclaimed the speaker, now uttering his soliloquy aloud, and glancing upward to the sky, "the time has been passing. What! noon? It is within a few min utes. Yola should soon be here. Twelve o'clock was her hour. Oh! I must have him out of sight, and these dead dogs, too, or my timid pet will be frayed. There's been so much doing about here—blood and burning fires—she will scarce know the old trysting-place. Hark, you Foolah! Come this way, and squat yourself in here, till I call you out again."

To the runaway the gestures of his captor were more intelligible than his words. He understood by them that he was required to conceal himself between the buttresses of the *ceiba*; and, rising from the log, he readily obeyed the requisition.

The Maroon captain seized the tail of one of the dead bloodhounds: and, after trailing the carcase for some distance across the glade, flung it into a covert of bushes. Returning to the *ceiba*, in a similar manner he removed the other; and then, cautioning the runaway to remain silent in his concealment, he awaited the approach of her whose assignation had been fixed for the hour of noon.

CHAPTER XLII

A LOVE SCENE UNDER THE CEIBA.

THE lover who is beloved need never fear disappointment. True to her tryst, and punctual to the time, did the expected sweetheart make her appearance within the glade.

With shy but graceful step, she advanced towards the *ceiba*, and with sufficient firmness of mein to show that she came not in doubt. A smile, confident and slightly coquettish, dancing in her dark eyes, and playing upon her prettily curved lips, told of a love already plighted—at the same time betokening free faith in the vows that had been exchanged.

Cubina stepped forth to receive her; and the lovers met in the open ground, at some distance from the tree. Their demeanour at meeting told that it was not their first assignation, but that ofttimes before had they come together in that same rendezvous.

The presence of the runaway—not seen, however, from the spot—did not hinder Cubina from saluting his sweetheart with a kiss, nor prevent him from enfolding her for a moment in his arms.

That spasm of exquisite pleasure passed, the dialogue began. The girl spoke first.

"Oh, Cubina! news I have tell."

"Come, my love—what news? Ah! you are looking grave, Yola; your news are not very joyful, I fear?"

"No, no joyful—bad news."

"Let me hear them, love. Something Cynthy has been saying to you. You shouldn't heed what that girl say."

"No, Cubina, I no care what her mo tell. I her know, wicked, bad girl. Not Cynthy say that thing me trouble now. Miss Kate me tell."

"Ah! something Miss Vaughan has told you. I wouldn't look for bad news from her. But what is it, dear Yola? Maybe, after all, it's nothing?"

"Ah! yes, Cubina, something. I fear me keep from you long, long time."

"Keep you from me? Surely Miss Vaughan don't object to your meeting me?"

"No—no! that. Something I fear me hinder from be——"

"Be what?" inquired the lover, seeing that his sweetheart hesitated to pronounce some word, the thought of which was causing her to blush. "Come, dear Yola, don't fear to tell *me!* You know we're engaged. There should be no secret between us. What were you going to say?"

In a low, murmured voice, and looking lovingly in his eyes as she
spoke, the girl pronounced the word "marry."

"Ho! ho!" exclaimed the lover, in a confident tone. "I think nothing
can occur to hinder that—at least, for a very long time, I have now nearly a hundred pounds laid by, and a lucky capture I've just made this
morning will help still further to make up that sum. Surely the custos
will not require more than a hundred pounds; though if you were once
mine," continued the speaker, casting a look of smiling fondness upon
his sweetheart's face, "all the money in the world wouldn't tempt me to
part with you. I hope," added he, speaking in a jocular air, "a hundred
pounds will be enough to make you *my slave?*"

"You slave, Cubina?"

"Yes, Yola, as I am yours now."

"Ah—that way, Yola yours; yours ever—evermore."

"I will believe you, dear girl," rejoined the lover, gazing, with a gratified look, in the face of his beloved. "I am very happy to think that in
that way you are mine; and that I have, as you assure me, your heart and
soul. But, dearest Yola, so long as another is the owner of your body—
not with the right, but the power to do, aye,—indeed, almost as he might
please—for who can hinder these proud planters from committing crimes
of which they are their own judges? Ah! Yola, girl, it is fearful to reflect on their wicked doings. This very morning I have come across a
sample of their cruelty; and when I think of you being in the power of
one, it makes me feel as if every hour was a day until I can obtain your
freedom. I am always in fear lest something may happen to hinder me.

"Just to-day I am in high hopes," continued the lover, evincing the
truth of his words by a pleasant smile. "I have succeeded in raising
nearly the hundred pounds; and the bounty I expect to receive for the
runaway I have caught will make it quite that."

The girl returned no reply to this speech of her lover, but stood gazing upon him silently, and as if half reproachfully. Something of this
kind he read, or fancied he read, in her looks.

"What, Yola, you are not satisfied with what I have said? You reproach me? Ah! true. I confess it is not a very creditable way of procuring your purchase-money. *Maldito?* what can I do? We Maroons
have no other way of raising money, except by hunting the wild hogs,
and selling their barbecued flesh. But that barely gives us a living
Crambo! I could never have got together a hundred pounds in that way
So do not reproach me, dear Yola, for what I've done. I assure you it
goes against my grain, this man-hunting business. As for the young fel
low I caught this morning, I'd risk a good deal rather than give him up-
if it wasn't for the purpose of procuring your freedom. For that I must
have the hundred pounds, which it is to be hoped will be enough to
satisfy your master."

"Ah, Cubina!" replied his slave-love, with a sigh, "that the bad news
I you bring. Hundred pound no massa care. Only two days go, he
offer twice so much for poor slave Yola."

"Two hundred pounds offered for *you!*" exclaimed the Maroon, with a
start of surprise, his brow becoming suddenly clouded. "Is that what
you mean, Yola?"

"Ah, yes!" answered the slave, repeating her sad sigh.

"And who—who is he?" demanded the lover, in a quick, earnest tone, a gleam of jealous thought flashing from his dark eyes, like forked lightning across a clouded sky.

He knew that no man would have bid two hundred pounds for a slave —even for Yola—without some wicked motive. The girl's beauty, combined with the extravagant offer, would have suggested the motive to one disinterested in her fate. How much more was it calculated to arouse the suspicions of a lover!

"A white man?" continued he, without waiting for the reply to his first question. "I need not ask that. But tell me, Yola, who is he that wants so badly to become your owner. You know, I suppose?"

"Missa Kate me tell all. He Jew—wicked white man! Same who me take from big ship; he me first sell Massa Vaughan."

"Ha!" sharply ejaculated the lover, "that old John Crow it is. Wicked white man you may well call him. I know the old villain well. *Crambo!* what can he want with her?" muttered the Maroon, musingly, but with a troubled mien. "Some vile purpose, to a certainty? Oh, sure!" Then once more addressing himself to his slave sweetheart—

"You are certain, Yola, the old Jew made this offer?"

"So me say Missa."

"Two hundred pounds! And Mr. Vaughan refused it?"

"Missa Kate no allow Massa Vaughan me sell. She say, 'Never!' Ah! young missa! she good—bery, bery good! No matter what money he give, she never let wicked white man take Yola. She so say many time."

"Miss Kate—true, Yola. She is good, she is generous! It must have been her doing, else the custos would never have refused such a tempting offer. Two hundred pounds! It is a large sum. Well, I must begin again. I must work night and day to get it; and then, if they should refuse *me.* Ha! what then?"

The speaker paused, not as if expecting a reply from her who stood by his side, but rather from his own thoughts.

"Never mind!" continued he, his countenance assuming an expression partly hopeful, partly reckless. "Have no fear of the future, Yola. Worst come worst, you shall yet be mine. Aye, dearest, you shall share my mountain home, though I may have to make it the home of an outlaw!"

"Oh!" exclaimed the young girl, slightly frayed by the wild look and words of her lover, her eye at the same instant falling upon the red pool where the hounds had been slain. "Blood, Cubina?"

"Only that of some animals—a wild boar and two dogs—just killed there. Don't let that frighten you. You must be brave, my Yola: since you are to be the wife of a Maroon! Ours is a life of many dangers."

"With you Yola no fear. She go anywhere—far over the mountains —to Jumbé Rock—anywhere you tell her go, Cubina."

"Thanks, dearest! Maybe, some day, we may be forced to go far over the mountains—in *flight, too,* Yola. But we shall try to avoid that. If not, then you will fly with me—will you not?"

"What Cubina do, Yola do same; where he go, she go."

The passionate promise was sealed by a kiss, followed by an interval of sacred silence.

" Enough, then !" said the lover, after the pause had passed. " As a last resource, we can do that. But we shall hope for the best; and, maybe, some good fortune may befal.

"My followers are true, and would help me ; but, alas ! all are poor hunters like myself. Well, it may take some time before I can call you my own fearlessly, in the face of the world—longer, maybe, than I ex- pected. Never mind for that ; we can meet often. And now, dear Yola, listen to what I am going to say to you—listen, and keep it in your mind! If ever a white wretch insults you—you know what I mean ?—if you are in danger of such a thing, as you would have been, were old Jessuron to become your master—aye, and who knows how, where, or when ?—well, then fly to this glade and wait here for me. If I do not come, some one will. Every day I shall send one of my people to this place. Don't fear to run away. Though I may not care to get into trouble about a com- mon slave, I shall risk all to protect you—yes, my life, dearest Yola !"

" Oh, Cubina !" exclaimed the girl, in passionate admiration. " Oh, brave, beauty Cubina ! you not fear danger ?"

" There is no great danger in it," returned the Maroon, in a confident tone. "If I had made up my mind to run away with you, I could soon take you beyond the reach of pursuit. In the Black Grounds we could live without fear of the tyranny of white men. But I don't want to be hunted like a wild hog. I would rather you should become mine by honest means—that is, I would rather buy you, as I intend to do ; and then we may settle down near the plantations and live without fear. Perhaps, after all, the custos may not be so hard with me as with the old Jew—who knows ? Your young mistress is kind, you have told me : she might do something to favour our plans."

" True, Cubina—she me love ; she say never me part."

" That is well : she means, she would not part with you against your will. But if I offer to buy you, it would be a different thing. Perhaps you might let her know all, by and by, after a while ; but I have some- thing to learn first, and I don't wish you to tell her till then. So keep our secret, dear Yola, for a little longer. And now !" continued the Maroon, changing his tone, and turning towards the ceiba as he spoke, "I've got something to show you. Did you ever see a runaway ?"

" Runaway !" said the girl ; " no, Cubina—never."

" Well, my love, there's one not far off; he that I said I had captured this morning—only a little while ago. And now I'll tell you why I've kept him here : because I fancied that he was like yourself, Yola."

" Like me !"

" Yes ; and that is why I felt for the poor fellow something like pity : since it is to this cruel old Jew he belongs. From what I can make out, he must be one of your people ; and I'm curious to know what ac- count he will give of himself."

" He Foolah, you think ?" inquired the African maiden, her eyes spark- ling with pleasure at the anticipation of seeing one of her own race.

" Yes ; I am as good as sure of that. In fact, he has called himself a Foolah several times, though I can't make out what he says. If he is one of your tribe, you will be able to talk to him. There he is !" •

Cubina had by this time conducted his sweetheart round the tree, to that side on which the runaway was concealed between the two spurs.

The young man was still crouching within the angle, close up to the trunk of the *ceiba*. The moment the two figures came in front of him, and his eyes fell upon the face of the girl, he sprang to his feet, uttering a cry of wild joy. ᵧ

Like an echo, Yola repeated the cry ; and then pronouncing some hurried phrases in an unknown tongue, rushed together, and became folded in a mutual embrace !

Cubina stood transfixed to the spot. Surprise—something more—held him speechless. He could only think :—

" She knows him ! Perhaps her lover in her own land !"

A keen pang of jealousy accompanied the thought.

Rankling it remained in the breast of the Maroon, till Yola, turning from the fond embrace, and pointing to him who had received it, pronounced the tranquillising words :—

" *My brother !*"

CHAPTER XLIII.

SMYTHJE IN SHOOTING COSTUME.

SEVERAL days had elapsed since that on which Mr. Montagu Smythje became the guest of Loftus Vaughan ; and during the time neither pains nor expense had been spared in his entertainment. Horses were kept for his riding—a carriage for his driving—dinners had been got up—and company invited to meet him. The best society of the Bay and the neighbouring plantations had been already introduced to the rich English exquisite—the owner of one great sugar estate, and—as society began to hear it whispered—the prospective possessor of another.

The matrimonial projects of the worthy custos—that had been suspected from the first—soon became the subject of much canvass and discussion.

It may be mentioned—though it is scarce necessary—that in his designs upon Smythje, Mr. Vaughan was not left all the field to himself. There were other parents in the planter fraternity of the neighbourhood blessed with good-looking daughters ; and many of them, both fathers and mothers, had fixed their eyes on the lord of Montagu Castle as a very eligible sample for a son-in-law. Each of these aspiring couples gave a grand dinner ; and, in turn, trotted out their innocent lambs in presence of the British " lion."

The exquisite smiled amiably upon all their efforts—adopting his distinguished position as a matter of course.

Thus merrily passed the first fortnight of Smythje's sojourn in Jamaica.

On a pleasant morning near the end of this fortnight, in one of the largest bed-chambers of Mount Welcome house—that consecrated to the reception of distinguished strangers—Mr. Montagu Smythje might have been seen in front of his mirror. He was engaged in the occupation of dressing himself, or, to speak more correctly, permitting himself to be dressed by his *valet de chambre*.

In the extensive wardrobe of the London exquisite there were dresses for all purposes and every occasion : suits for morning, dinner, and
evening ; one for riding, and one for driving ; a shooting dress, and one
for the nobler sport of the chase ; a dress for boating, "à la matelot ;" and
a grand *costume du bal.*

On the occasion in question, Mr. Smythje's august person was being
enveloped in his shooting dress ; and, although a West India sportsman,
or an English squire, would have smiled derisively at such a "rig," the
cockney regarded it with complacency as being "just the thing."

It consisted of a French tunic-shaped coatee of green silk velvet, trimmed with fur ; a helmet-shaped hunting cap to match ; and a purple
waistcoat underneath, embroidered with cord of gold bullion.

Instead of breeches and top-boots, Mr. Smythje fancied he had im-
proved upon the costume by encasing his limbs in long trousers. These
were of dressed fawn skin, of a straw colour, and soft as the finest
chamois leather. They fitted rather tightly around the legs, notwithstanding that the wearer was rather spindly in that quarter. Moreover,
they were strapped at the bottoms, over a pair of brightly shining lac-
quered boots—another error at which a true sportsman would have
smiled.

No matter for that. These little eccentric innovations on the shooting
costume of the time were *designed* on the part of Mr. Smythje : who
looked upon himself as by right a fashionable original—since his very
handsome fortune enabled him to set the style among a limited circle of
his acquaintances in great Cockneydom.

Theoretically considered, the dress looked well enough. Practically,
it would have suited only for the stage of a theatre—whence, no doubt,
the idea of the costume had been taken.

The suit had never seen service in the field ; but was being donned,
for the first time, since coming from the fingers of the tailor. Not a stain
tarnished the delicately soft fawn skin trousers—not a crease could be
seen in the smooth nap of the velvet tunic. Vest and all were new and
fresh, as just drawn out of a band-box.

The object, for which Mr. Smythje was thus having his person apparelled, was a shooting excursion to the hills ; which he designed making in order to vary his pleasures, by committing havoc among the
ramier pigeons and wild guinea fowl which, he had been told, abounded
there. To show himself in his splendid shooting costume was another
motive, perhaps, of equal moment ; but this was known only to his valet
—a personage too accomplished to disclose the fact, that in his eyes his
master had long ceased to be a hero.

The projected expedition was not any grand affair by appointment—
merely an ordinary, improvised thing. The sportsman intended going
alone—as the custos on that day had some important business at the
Bay ; and Mr. Smythje, by a ramble through the neighbouring woods,
fancied he might kill the time between breakfast and dinner pleasantly
enough. This was all that was intended ; and a darkey to guide him all
that was needed.

"Weally !" remarked he, in a moment of enthusiasm, as he stood before
his glass, and addressing himself to his valet, " these queeole queetyaws

aro chawming- positively chawming! Nothing in the theataw or opewa
at all to compare with them. Such lovely eyes, such 'divine figaws, and
such easy conquests! By jove! aw can count a dozen alweady! Haw,
haw!" added he, with a self-gratulatory chuckle, "it's but natywal that—
dawn't yaw think so, Thoms?"

"Parfectly natyeral, your honner," replied Thoms, with just enough of
an Irish brogue to show he was a Welshman.

Either the lady-killer was not content with his twelve easy conquests,
and wished to have the number more complete by making it "a baker's
lozen"—either this, or he was uncertain about his victory over one of the
twelve—as would appear by the dialogue that followed between him and
his confidential man.

"Hark, yaw, Thoms," said he, approaching the valet in a more serious
way ; "yaw are an exceedingly intelligent fellow—yaw are, 'pon honaw."

"Thank your honner. It's keepin' your honner's company has made
me so."

"Nevaw mind—nevaw mind what—but I have observed yaw intelligence."

"It's at your honner's humble service."

"Ve-well, Thoms ; ve-well! I want you to employ it.,'

"In what way, your honner? anything your honner may desire me to
do,"

"Yaw know the niggaw girl—the brown girl with the tawban, aw
mean?"

"Miss Vaghan's waitin'-maid?"

"Exactly—ya-as. Yolaw, or something of the sawt, is the queetyaw's
name."

"Yis—Yowla ; that's her name, your honner."

"Well, Thoms, aw pwesume you have excellent oppowtunities of hold
Ing convawsation with haw—the niggaw, aw mean?"

"Plenty of oppurtunity, your honner. I've talk'd with her scores of
times."

"Good. Now, the next time yaw talk with haw, Thoms, I want yaw to
. pump haw."

"Pump her! what's that, your honner?'

"Why, dwaw something out of haw!"

"Feth! I don't understan' your honner."

"Not undawstand! yaw are stoopid, Thoms."

"Keeping your honner's company——"

"What, fellaw? keeping my company make yaw stoopid?"

"No, your honner; ye didn't hear me out. I was goin' to say, that
keeping your honner's company would soon take that out o' me."

"Haw—haw—that's diffwent altogethaw. Well, listen now, and aw'l
make yaw undawstand me. Aw want yaw to talk with this Yolaw, and
dwaw some seekwets out of haw."

"Oah!" answered Thoms, dwelling a long time upon the sound, and
placing his forefinger along the flat side of his nose. "*Now* I comprehend
your honner."

"All wight—all wight."

"I'll manage that, don't fear me ; but what sort of sacrets does your honner want me to draw out af her ?"

"Aw want yaw to find out what she says about me—not the niggaw, but haw mistress."

"What the negur says about her mistress ?"

"Thoms, yaw are intolawably stoopid this mawning. Not at all—not at all ; but what haw mistress says about me—me."

"Oh ! fwhat Miss Vaghan says about your honner ?"

"Pwecisely."

"Faith ! I'll find that out—every word af it."

"If yaw do, Thoms, aw shall be your debtaw faw a guinea."

"A guinea, your honner !"

"Ya-as ; and if yaw execute yaw commission clevawly, aw shall make it two—two guineas, do yaw heaw ?"

"Never fear, your honner. I'll get it out of the negur, if I should have to pull the tongue from between thim shinin' teeth af hers !"

"No, Thoms—no, my good fellaw ! There must be · no woodness. Wemember, we are guests heaw, and Mount Welcome is not an hotel. You must work by stwategy, not stwength, as Shakespeaw or some other of those skwibbling fellaws has said. No doubt stwategy will win the day."

And with this ambiguous observation—ambiguous as to whether it referred to the issue of Thoms's embassy, or his own success in the wooing of Miss Vaughan—Mr. Montagu Smythje closed the conversation.

Thoms now gave the last touch to the sportsman's toilet, by setting the hunting-cap on his head, and hanging numerous belts over his shoulders —among which were included a shot-pouch, a copper powder-horn, a pewter drinking flask with its cup, and a hunting-knife in its leathern sheath.

"Pon honaw ! a demmed becoming costume !" exclaimed the exquisite, surveying himself from head to foot in the mirror. "A killing costume— decidedly spawtsman-like. Yaw think so, Thoms ?"

"Pe cod ! it is all that, your honner."

"I must see my fwends, and say good-bye befaw starting out. Aw ya-as, sawtinly I must."

And so saying, the exquisite strode stiffly from the apartment—his tight-fitting fawnskins hindering any very supple movement—and wended his way towards the great hall, evidently in the hope of encountering the fair queetyaw Kate in his killing costume.

CHAPTER XLIV.

A COCKNEY SPORTSMAN.

THAT Mr. Montagu Smythje had obtained the interview he sought, and that its result had gratified him, might be inferred from the complaisant smile that played upon his countenance as he sallied forth from the house. Moreover, in crossing the two or three hundred yards of open ground which separated the dwelling from the wooded slope of the ridge, he walked with an exalted, gingerly step—occasionally glancing back over his shoulder, as if conscious of being observed.

He *was* observed. Two faces could be seen at a window, one of which Mr. Smythje knew well enough to be that of Kate Vaughan. The other, of darker hue, was the face of the maid Yola.

Both were set in smiles. It did not matter to Mr. Smythje whether the maid smiled or not; but he fondly fancied he could distinguish a pleased expression on the countenance of the mistress. He was at too great a distance to be certain; but he had little doubt of its being a look of intense admiration that was following him through his fine paces.

Had he been near enough to translate the expression more truly, he might have doubted whether he was the object of so much admiration; and had the remark made by Yola to her mistress reached his ear, with the clear ringing laughter it called forth, his doubts would have had a melancholy confirmation.

"He berry gran, missa !" said the maid. "He like cock-a-benny turned yellow-tail !"—a plantation proverb, which, translated into plain English, means, that the coarse and despised little fish, the "cock-a-benny," had become metamorphosed into the splendid and esteemed species known among the negroes as the "yellow-tail."

As the sportsman neither heard the remark nor the laugh it elicited, he was enabled to carry his self-esteem into the woods unhurt and undiminished.

At his heels walked an attendant—a negro boy, whose sole costume consisted of an Osnaburgh shirt, with a huge game bag slung over his shoulders, and hanging down to his hams. It was the veritable Quashie, post-boy, horse-boy, and factotum.

Quashie's duties on the present occasion were to guide the English buckra to the best shooting ground among the hills, and carry the game when killed. As there was no dog—pigeon and *pintado* shooting not requiring the aid of this sagacious animal—Quashie was to act also as finder and retriever.

For a full mile over hill and dale, through "brake, brush, and scaur," tramped the ardent sportsman, and his Ethiopian attendant, Quashie, keeping like a shadow at the heels of the grand buckra. Still not a head of game had as yet been bagged. Ramiers were scarce and shy, and as for the beautiful speckled hen—the exotic *Numida meleagris*—not as much as the crest of one could be seen. Their shrill shreek, like the filing of a frame saw, could be occasionally heard " skirling"afar off in the woods; and the hope of getting sight of one enticed the sportsman still further into the forest.

Another mile was passed over, and another hour spent, almost equally unfruitful in events. A few ramiers had been sighted and shot at; but the thick corselet of feathers, that covers the bold breasts of these beautiful birds, seemed impenetrable to the shot of a gun; at least, they proved so to the double-barrelled "Manton" of the London sportsman.

Another mile traversed—another hour spent—still nothing bagged!

His want of success did not hinder the sportsman from growing hungry; and, at the end of his third mile, he began to feel a certain void about the epigastric region that called for viands. He knew that the bag which Quashie carried contained a luncheon, that had been carefully provided and packed by the major-domo of Mount Welcome. It was time to examine this luncheon ; and, seating himself under the shadow of a spreading tree, he directed the darkey to draw it forth.

Nothing loth was Quashie to respond to this request; for the weight of the bag, which he had been wincing under for some hours, and its distended sides, promised pickings for himself—after the grand buckra should satisfy his hunger.

Certainly there appeared enough for both, and to spare : for on " gutting" the game bag, a whole capon was turned out upon the grass, with sundry slices of bread, ham, and tongue, and all the paraphernalia of salt, pepper, and mustard.

A bottle of claret was found at the bottom of the bag; which, in addition to the flask of *eau de vie* that the sportsman himself carried, and which he now laid aside to disencumber him, was liquid enough to wash down the savoury solids which the thoughtful steward had provided.

A knife and fork was also turned out ; and, as Mr. Montagu Smythje was more habile in the handling of these weapons than he was in the use of a gun, in a trice the capon was cut into convenient pieces. In an equally short space of time, many of these pieces disappeared between his teeth, in company with sundry slices of the ham and tongue.

Quashie was not invited to partake ; but sat near the grand buckra's feet, wistfully watching his movements, as a dog would his master similarly occupied.

As the masticatory powers of the cockney sportsman appeared to be of no mean order, Quashie's look began to betray astonishment, mingled with a growing dread, that the " oughts" he might be called upon to eat would be neither very numerous nor very bulky. Half the capon had already disappeared, with a large proportion of the odd slices of the ham and tongue!

" I b'lieve de dam buckra glutton za gwine eat um all up—ebberry bit!' was Quashie's mental, and not very good-humoured, soliloquy. " Ay, an drink 'um up too—ebbery drop !" continued he, in thought, as he saw

Mr. Smythje quaff off a full cup of the claret without taking the vessel from his lips.

Shortly after, another cup was poured into the same capacious funnel: for the exercise he had undergone, combined with the warmth of the day had rendered the sportsman drouthy.

To the great chagrin of Quashic, and the no small mortification of Smythje himself, a worse misfortune than that of its being drunk befel the remainder of the claret. On setting down the bottle, after filling his cup for the second time, the sportsman had performed the act in an unskilful manner. The consequences was that the bottle, losing its balance toppled over; and the *balance* of the claret trickled out upon the grass.

Both Quashie's temper and patience were put to a severe test; but the buckra's appetite being at length appeased, the 'débris' of the feast—still a considerable quantity—remained for Quashie's share; and he was directed to fall to and make his best of it.

The darkie was not slow in complying with the order; and, from the manner in which he went to work, it was evident, that unless Mr. Smythje should make better shooting after luncheon than he had done before it, the game bag would go back to the house much lighter than it had left it.

While Quashie was masticating his meal, the refreshed sportsman—his spirits elevated by the claret he had quaffed—bethought him of taking a stroll by himself. There was no time to be wasted—as the contigency of having to return to Mount Welcome with an empty bag had already begun to suggest itself; and after the sanguine expectations which his grand sporting costume must have given rise to—assisted by some little bravedo he had indulged in while leave-taking—his failing to fulfil these expectations could not be otherwise than humiliating.

He resolved, therefore, to return to his shooting with a more serious earnestness, and, if possible, make up for the deficiencies of the morning.

It was now one o'clock, and he had yet three hours to the good, before it would be necessary to face homeward. Dinner was to be on the table at five; for since his arrival at Mount Welcome, Mr. Vaughan had changed the hour for that important meal from three to five—to accommodate the fashionable habits of his aristocratic guest.

Slinging on his horn and pouch, and laying hold of his gun, the sportsman once more started off, leaving his retriever busily employed in polishing off the "drumsticks" of the capon.

CHAPTER XLV.

STALKING A TURKEY

IT almost seemed as if the divine patron of the chase—the good St. Hubert—had regarded the spilt wine as an oblation to himself, and, in return had consented to give the sportsman success.

Scarce had the latter advanced two hundred yards from the spot where he had launched, when his eyes were gratified by the splendid spectacle of a flock of large, fine-looking birds. They were upon the ground, in an open field or glade of several acres in extent, by the edge of which the sportsman had arrived.

They were sitting, or rather standing, close together; and had Mr Smythje not been so terribly flurried by the sight, he might have observed that they were clustered round the skeleton of a pig or some other animal—from whose bones the flesh had been stripped as cleanly as if intended for a museum.

As Smythje's knowledge of natural history was confined to what he had picked up in a stray visit to a London menagerie, it never occurred to him what kind of birds they were, or what they might be doing there.

At first he had taken it for granted they were the Guinea hens he was in search of; but, on looking at them more particularly, he began to doubt whether they were Guinea hens. The latter—at least the tame ones he had seen about Mount Welcome—were all bluish and speckled; whereas the birds now in view were of a uniform *black*. Perhaps the wild Guinea fowls might be a different breed from their tame cousins, and this would account for the want of resemblance in the colour of their plumage.

While making these conjectural reflections, he noticed another peculiarity about the birds. They had all of them naked necks and heads, of a reddish or flesh colour—just like turkeys.

" Haw! tawkeys they are! By Jawve! a flock of wild tawkeys!"

The London exquisite had heard, somehow or somewhere, that the wild turkey was indeginous to America, and, of course, also to Jamaica —since Jamaica is part of America.

However erroneous the deduction, the reasoning satisfied Smythje; and, firmly convinced that he saw before him a flock of wild turkeys, he determined on taking measures to *circumvent* them.

They were still at too great a distance to offer any chance for a shotgun ; and, in order to get nearer, he dropped down upon his knees, and

commenced creeping behind the low bushes that grew around the glade.
His delicate fawn-skin inexpressibles were likely to suffer damage by
this mode of progression; and he now felt the inconvenience of the
straps; but so desirous was he of success, that the total destruction of
both straps and trousers would not have deterred him from proceeding.
He thought only of the chagrin of returning to Mount Welcome with an
empty game bag, and the glory of going back with a full one.

Instead of crouching among the shrubs—in the idle contempt to conceal his person from the observation of the birds—had he
walked straight forward to them, in all probability he would have succeeded in getting a shot. This is the more probable: since the birds
instead of being *turkeys*, were only *turkey-buzzards* (or " John Crows," as
they are called in Jamaica); and, knowing themselves to be under the
protection of a statute of the island, they would have taken no more notice of the sportsman than if he had been a cow straying among them.

The fact, however, of his being, a cockney—which the Jamaica "John
Crows" could not have failed to observe—combined with the sly manner
of his approach, aroused their suspicions; and, taking the alarm, one and
all of them rose up into the air, and flapped sluggishly away.

They did not fly far: most of them alighted on the adjacent trees; and
one in particular perched itself on the top of a stump which could not
be more than a hundred yards from the spot where Smythje was kneeling.

This bird—apparently the finest of the flock—now monopolised the
attention of the sportsman to the exclusion of all the rest.

He saw that a pot shot at the flock was no longer possible, as they
were scattered over the trees; and he thought it better to content himself with a single bird. Even one of these large creatures would make
a bag not to be bantered about. A wild turkey—and a cock bird at that
would be worth half a dozen of Guinea hens, or a half-score of *ramier*
pigeons.

To insure success, the sportsman still kept to his knees, and crawled
forward cautiously. If he could only make thirty yards in advance,
he knew his gun was good for the other seventy—the complement of the
hundred, at which distance he guessed the turkey to be from him.

In fine, the thirty yards were accomplished, and still the turkey remained upon its perch.

The gun was brought to bear upon the bird; Joe Manton did the work;
and, simultaneous with the "bang," the turkey was seen to tumble over,
disappearing as it did so from the top of the stump. The overjoyed
sportsman hastened forward to secure his game; and soon arrived at
the spot where he expected to find it. To his surprise, it was not there!

The others had all flown away; had it gone along with them?

Impossible! He had seen it fall, and without a flutter. It must have
been shot quite dead? It could not have come to life again? He searched all about—going round the stump at least a dozen times, and carefully
scrutinising every inch of the ground for a score of yards on each side
—but no turkey could be found!

Had the unlucky sportsman been at all doubtful of the fact of his having killed the bird, he would have given up the search in despair. But

upon this point he was as certain as of his own existence; and it was that which rendered him so pertinacious in his endeavours to find it. He was determined to leave neither stick nor stone unturned; and to aid him in the prosecution of his search, he called loudly for his retriever Quashie.

But to his repeated calls no Quashie came; and Mr. Smythje was forced to the conclusion that the darkey had either gone to sleep or had strayed away from the spot where he had been left. He had some thoughts of going back to look for Quashie; but, while he was meditating on the matter, an idea occurred to him, which promised to explain the mysterious disappearance of the bird.

The stump upon which the " turkey" had been perched could scarcely be termed a *stump*. It was rather the trunk of a huge tree, that had been abruptly broken off below the limbs, and still stood some fifteen or twenty feet in height, erect and massive as the tower of some ruined castle. Though quite a dead wood, and without any branches of its own, it was, nevertheless, garnished with verdure. A complete matting of vines that grew around its roots, and parasites that sprang from its decaying sides, inclosed it all around with a tortuous trellis work—so that only near its top could the shape of the old tree be distinguished.

At first the sportsman supposed that his game had dropped down among the ragged shrubbery that clustered around the tree; but he had searched the whole of this with elaborate minuteness, and in vain.

It had now occurred to him—and this was the idea that promised *eclaircissement* spoken of—that the bird had never fallen from the stump, but had dropped dead upon the top of it, and there might still be lying !

The diameter of the dead wood, which at its broken summit, was some five or six feet, rendered this conjecture probable enough; and Smythje resolved upon putting it to the proof, by climbing to the top. He would have appointed Quashie to the performance of this feat; but Quashie was *non esset inventus*.

Several thick cable-like vines, that struggled up to the summit of the dead wood, promised an easy means of ascent; and, although the cockney could climb about as dexterously as a shod cat, he fancied there could be no great difficulty in attaining the top of that stump. Throwing aside his gun, he entered enthusiastically upon the attempt.

The feat was not so easy of performance but that it cost him an exertion. Stimulated, however, by the desire to *retrieve* his game, and the reflections about the game bag, already alluded to, he put forth his utmost energies, and succeeded in reaching the summit.

His conjecture proved correct. There lay the bird—not *on* the stump, but *in* it—at the bottom of a large cylinder-shaped concavity, which opened several feet down the heart of the dead wood. There it was dead as the tree itself.

The sportsman could not restrain himself from uttering a cry of joy— as he saw his fine game at length secure within his reach.

It proved not exactly within his reach, however: as, upon kneeling down and stretching his arm to its full length, he found that he could not touch the bird, even with the tips of his fingers.

That signified little. It would only be necessary for him to descend

into the cavity, and this he could easily do : as it was wide enough, and
not over four feet in depth.

Without further reflection, he rose to his feet again, and leaped down
into the hole.

It would have been a wiser act if he had remember the prudent counsel of the paternal frog, and looked before leaping. That was one of the
most unfortunate jumps Mr. Smythje had ever made in his life. The
brown surface upon which the bird lay, and which looked so deceptive
solid, was nothing more than a mass of rotten heartwood, honeycomb
with long decay. So flimsy was it in structure, that, though supporting
a dead bird, it gave way under the weight of a living man ; and the lord
of Montagu Castle shot as rapidly out of sight as if he had leaped feet
foremost from the mainyard of the Sea Nymph into the deepest sounding
of the Atlantic!

CHAPTER XLVI.

SMYTHJE EMBARRASSED BY HIS BOOTS.

RAPID as was the pitch, and dark the abyss into which it was made, the
sportsman was not killed. Neither was he much hurt, for the " punk"
through which he had pitched, though not firm enough to support him,
had offered some resistance to the velocity of his descent ; and towards
the bottom he had settled down more gradually.

But though neither killed nor yet stunned by the fall, he was for
awhile as completely deprived of his senses as if he had been both.
Surprise had bereft him not only of the power of speech, but of thought
as well ; and for some moments he was as quiet as Jack after being jerked into his box.

After a time, however, feeling that, though badly scared, he was not
much hurt, his consciousness began to return to him; and he made a
scramble to recover his legs ; for, in going down, he had somehow got
doubled up in a sort of tailor fashion.

He found his feet after an effort ; and, as he saw that light came from
above, he raised his eyes in that direction.

It took him some time to make out the exact character of the place in
which he was : for a thick " stoor" was swimming around him, that not
only impeded his sight, but, having entered his mouth and nostrils, had
inducted him into a violent fit of sneezing.

The dust, however, gradually thinned away ; and Smythje was enabled
to " define his position."

Above his head was a clear circular patch, which he knew to be the
sky ; while all around him was a dark brown wall that rose many feet
beyond the reach of his outstretched arms. He became conscious that
he was standing in the concavity of a huge upright cylinder, with a surface of corrugated rotten wood rising all around him.

As his senses, grew clearer—and also the atmosphere—he arrived at a
better comprehension of the mishap that had befallen him. He did not,

at first, regard it in the light of a *misfortune*—at least not a very heavy one—and he was rather disposed to laugh at it as a ludicrous adventure.

It was not till he began to think of climbing out, and had actually made the attempt, that he became aware of a difficulty hitherto unsuspected; and the contemplation of which at once inspired him with a feeling of alarm.

A second attempt to get out was unsuccessful as the first; a third equally so; a fourth had no better issue; a fifth was alike a failure; and after the sixth, he sat down upon the rotten rubbish in a state bordering on despair.

Well might he have exclaimed:

"*Facilis descensus Averni, sed revocare gradum.*"*

The mind of Mr. Smythje was now under the influence of an indescribable awe; which for some time held mastery over it and hindered him even from reflecting.

When reflection came to his aid, it was only to make more certain the fearful reality of his situation. The more he reflected upon it, the more he became convinced of the peril into which his rash leap had precipitated him.

It was not simply a slight mishap—a ludicrous adventure he no longer saw it in that light. Neither was it a mere misfortune; but a positive danger—the danger of his life!

Yes, his life was most certainly in danger; and he was not slow in arriving at this knowledge. The chain of inductive reasoning that led to it was but too palpably clear—every link of it—from premises to conclusion. If he could not help himself out of the prison, in which by his unlucky leap he had incarcerated himself, who was to help him?

Hope could not dwell long upon Quashie. The darkey had been left some distance off; and since he had not answered to his calls, he must be asleep or straying? In either case, or even if awake and still on the ground of the bivouac, what chances would Quashie have of finding him?

Could the boy follow his tracks to the tree? Very unlikely. Smythje remembered that most of the ground over which he had come was covered with wild guinea grass, upon which neither his feet nor his knees would leave any impressions. Its elastic culms would spring up again, as soon as he had passed over them, leaving but little evidence of his passage; enough, perhaps, for a skilled hunter to have tracked him; but not sufficient for a loutish negro lad—a stable boy of the plantation. And if Quashie should fail to take up his track, what chance was there of the boy's finding him? None at all; or only one in a thousand.

Who else was to find him, if not Quashie—! who else? Who was likely to come that way?

Not a soul! The tree that contained him stood in the midst of a wild tract—a solitary forest all round—no roads, no paths—he had observed none. He might be there for a month without a human being approaching the place; and a week would be enough to destroy him! Yes, in one week, or far less, he might expect to die of starvation? perhaps sooner than that? The prospect was appalling.

* "**Easy** is the descent to Avernus, but to retrace one's step is not so easy."—*Virgil.*

And it so appalled him, that again his mind gave way under it; and relapsed into the stupor of despondence.

It is not natural that one should sink at once into utter despair, without making an extreme effort. The instinct of self-preservation—common to the lowest animals—will nerve even the weakest spirit of man. That of Montagu Smythje was none of the strongest, and had given way at the first shock; but, after a time, a reaction came, stimulating him to make a fresh effort for his life.

Once more starting to his feet, he attempted to scale the steep walls that encircled him; but the attempt, as before, proved a failure.

In this last trial, however, he discovered that his exertions were greatly hindered by three special *impedimenta*—the tight fawnskin trousers that, moistened with perspiration, clung closely aroued his legs; his boots; but, above all, the straps that bound boots and trousers together.

To get rid of these obstacles became his next thought; and the execution of such a design might appear easy enough.

On tiral, however, it proved a most difficult undertaking.

From the confined space in which he stood, he could not get into a stooping attitude, so as to reach down to the straps and unbutton them; and so long as these remained buttoned, it was impossible to take off the boots. He could squat down tailor-fashion, as he had already done; but in that posture the straps became so tightened, that to unbutton them was clearly out of the question. The delicate fingers of the dandy were unequal to the effort.

"Necessity is the mother of invention." This adage held good in Smythje's case, for it just then occurred to him to unfasten his suspenders instead of his straps, and divest himself of his under garments all at once!

For this purpose he rose to his feet: in doing so, a better idea suggested itself, to cut off this fawn-skinned inexpressibles just above the knees; and thus free boots, straps, and pantaloon bottoms all together!

He had left his hunting knife by his brandy flask, and both on the ground of the bivouac. Fortunately, however, a penknife, which he carried in his waistcoat pocket, would answer even better; and, drawing it forth, he proceeded to execute his design.

A cross section of the fawnskins just above the knees was easily made; and then—by the alternate application of toe to heel—boots, trousers, bottoms and all, were cast simultaneously, and Smythje stood in his stockings!

He did not remain long inactive. Danger urged him to exert himself; and once more he essayed to scale the walls of his tree prison.

Alas! after many efforts—many oft-repeated, but unsuccessful clamberings—he was forced back to the appalling conviction that the thing was impossible.

He could get up within about four feet of the orifice; but there the surface, which had been long open to the atmosphere, was worn so smooth by the weather—besides being still wet and slippery from late rains—that he could find no holding place upon it; and at every endeavour to grasp the rotten wood, he lost his balance, and fell backward to the bottom.

These falls frequently stunned him, almost knocking the breath out of his body   They were from a considerable height—ten or twelve feet—and, but for the soft rubbish below, that modified the shock as he came down, one such descent would have been sufficient to cripple him for life.

Once more his spirit sank within him.   Once more he yielded to despair.

CHAPTER XLVII.

A TROPIC SHOWER.

WHEN reflection again favoured the unfortunate Smythje—which it did after a short time had passed over—his thoughts took a new turn. He made no further attempt at climbing out: the many trials already made had fully convinced him of its impracticability. He now felt satisfied that his only hope lay in the chance of Quashie or some one else coming that way. And this chance was grievously doubtful. Even should one pass near the dead wood, how was he to know that Smythje was inside it ? Who would suspect that the old tree was hollow ? and, least of all, that a human being was inclosed within its cylindrical cell—buried alive, as it were, in this erect wooden sarcophagus ?

True, a person passing might see the gun lying upon the ground outside ; but that would be no clue to the whereabouts of its owner.

There was no chance of his being *seen;* his only hope was that he might be *heard;* and the moment this thought came into his mind, he commenced crying out at the highest pitch of his voice.

He regretted that he had not done so before : since some one might have passed in the interim.

After falling in, he had shouted several times during the moments of his first surprise ; but while making his attempts to clamber out, he had desisted—the earnestness of his exertions having reduced him to silence.

Now that he had comprehended the necessity of making a noise, he determined to make up for his former remissness ; and he continued to pour forth scream after scream with all the power of his lungs,.

For several minutes, without ceasing, did he keep crying out ; but notwithstanding the loud clamour he was making, he was very anxious on the score of being *heard.* Even should people be passing near, could his voice reach them ? It was no thin shell that was around him. He knew from the diameter of the trunk, that a thick wall of solid wood was between him and the open air—to say nothing of the matting of vines and parasites—all calculated to deaden the sound.

As these facts passed before his mind, the suspicion that he might not be heard soon assumed the shape of a certainty ; and again the terrible phantom of despair rose up before him—grim and ghastly as ever.

For a moment it paralysed him—almost depriving him of the power of utterance. But necessity urged him to renewed efforts. His only chance of life lay in making himself heard ; and, convinced of this, he once more put forth his voice, its tones now varying from a scream to a groan.

For nearly an hour did he continue this melancholy *cavatina*, without receiving any response beyond the echoes of his own voice, which reveberated through the concavity in hollow, sepulchral tones—a mournful monologue of alternate groaning and howling, with pauses, at short intervals, as the utterer listened for an answer.

But no answer came; no change took place in his situation, except one that was calculated to make it still more deplorable and forlorn. As if his lugubrious appeals had invoked the demon of the storm, the sky above became suddenly overcast with heavy, black clouds, from which came pouring rain such as might have fallen during the forty days of the deluge!

It was one of those tropic showers, where the water pours down, not in single, isolated drops, but in long, continuous streams: as if heaven's canopy was one great shower-bath, of which the string had been jerked and tied down.

Though well sheltered from wind, the unfortunate Smythje had no roof—no cover of any kind—to shield him from the rain, which came pouring down upon his devoted head, as though the spout of a pump had been directed into the hollow of the dead wood. Indeed, the funnel-shaped orifice, which was wider than the rest of the concavity, aided in conducting a larger quantity of rain into it; and, but that the water found means of escape, by percolating through the mass of dry rubbish below, Mr. Smythje might have been in danger of a more sudden death than by starvation; since there fell sufficient water to have drowned him.

If not drowned, however, he got well *douched.* There was not a stitch of clothing upon his person that was not wetted through: the silk velvet shooting-coat, the purple vest, and what remained of the fawnskin trowsers, all were alike soaked and saturated. Even his whiskers had parted with their crisp rigidity; the curls had come out of the tails of his moustaches; his hair had lost its amplitude; and all three—hair, whiskers, and moustaches—hung dripping and draggled.

In that melancholy image of manhood, that stood shivering in the hollow tree, it would have required a quick imagination to have recognised Mr Montagu Smythje, the *dabonair* sportsman of the morning.

Lugubrious as were his looks they were nothing to compare with his thoughts. There were moments when he felt angry—angry at his ill-fortune—angry at Quashie—angry at Mr. Vaughan, for having provided an attendant so inattentive to his duties. There were moments when he felt spiteful enough to swear. Yes, in that fearful crisis Smythje *swore*—the owner of Mount Welcome and Quashie being alternately the object of his abjurations. Jamaica, too, came in for a share of his spite—its pigeons and Guinea hens, its trees, and, above all, its wild turkeys!

"The howwid island!" he cried in his anguish; would to his "Makeaw" he had never set foot on its "shaws!" What at that moment would he not have given to be once more in his "dwear metwopolis?' Gladly would he have exchanged his tree-prison for a chamber in the King's Bench—ay, for the meanest cell which the Old Bailey could have afforded!

Poor Smythje! he had not yet reached the climax of his sorrows. A new suffering was in store for him—one in comparison with which all he had undergone was but a mild endurance. It was only when that slimy thing came crawling over his feet, and began to entwine itself round his ankles—its cold clammy touch painfully perceptible through his silk stockings—it was only then that he felt something like a sensation of real horror !

He was on his legs at the moment; and instantly sprang upward, as if hot coals had been suddenly applied to the soles of his feet. But springing upward did not avail him, since it resulted in his dropping down again in the same spot; and, as he did so, he felt writhing beneath his feet the slippery form of a *serpent !*

CHAPTER XLVIII.

A DANGEROUS DANCE.

BEYOND the shadow of a doubt was Smythje standing upon a snake, or, rather, *dancing* upon one ; for as he felt the scaly creature crawling and writhing under his feet with a strong muscular action, it was contrary to human nature that he should remain at rest upon such a perilous pedestal.

For some moments he danced about upon this dangerous *deis*, expecting every instant to feel the sharp sting of a bite. Any one who could have looked on him at that crisis would have seen a face white with horror, eyes starting from their watery sockets, and his dripping hair and whiskers doing their best to stand on end.

Through his dark sky of dread a gleam of light flashed upon his spirits : he remembered having heard that in Jamaica there is no *poisonous* serpents.

Still it was but a spark of consolation. If the reptile could not *sting,* it could *bite ;* and, being such an enormous creature as to cover with its coils the whole floor of his *cylindric* chamber, its bite should be a formidable one.

Perhaps, after all, it was not a single snake ? Perhaps there was a whole family of serpents, crawling one over another, and wreathing fantastic figures of eight beneath his feet?

If so—and this was probable enough—he might be bitten by all ; repeatedly—torn to pieces—devoured !

What matter whether they were poisonous or not ? He might as well perish from their fangs, as by their teeth !

Fortunately it was for Smythje that the snakes—for his conjecture that there were more than one was correct—fortunate for him that they were still half asleep, else the danger he dreaded might have come to pass. As it was, the whole band of reptiles had just been aroused from a state of torpidity—the wash of cold rain having reached them in their crushed cave, and scattered the mutual coil in which they had been closely slumbering. Still only half awakened, in the confusion of their ideas, they could not distinguish friend or foe ; and to this was Mr. Smythje indebted for the circumstance that his skin. and even his silk stockings, still remained intact.

As it was, he escaped without a single bite—though without knowing the reason.

Notwithstanding his having remained so long untouched, his dread had by no means diminished. On the contrary, the thought of being eaten up alive—which succeeded that of being stung by poisoned fangs—still continued his terror, and incited him to fresh efforts to escape from his perilous position.

Only one mode suggested itself : to clamber up the " chimney" as far as he could go, and by that means get out of reach of the reptiles. On the instant of his conceiving this new design, he sprang upward, shaking the serpent coils from his feet ; and, after a few seconds of scratching and scrambling, he arrived at an elevation of some ten feet from the bottom of the tree.

Here a slight projection offered a tolerable support for his posteriors ; and setting his toes well against the opposite side, he did the best he could to sustain himself in position.

It was an irksome effort, and could not have lasted long—as to his consternation he soon discovered.

His strength would soon give way, his toes become cramped and nerveless ; and then, losing his hold, he must inevitably drop down among the monsters below—who, perhaps, in a second collision with him, would be less chary about using their teeth ?

The prospect of such a terrible fate stimulated him to put forth all his strength in preserving his balance and his place—at the same time that it drew from him cries of the keenest anguish.

His strength-could not have saved him, but his cries at this crisis proved his friend. The former was well-nigh exhausted, and he was on the point of letting go his hold, when, just then, an object came before his upturned eyes that determined him to hold out a little longer, even should his toes be torn out of their joints.

Above him, and half-filling the orifice of the hollow, appeared an enormous head, with a face black as Erebus, and two yellowish-white eyes shining in the midst of it. No other feature was at first seen ; but presently a double row of great white teeth appeared, gleaming between a pair of freshly-opened purplish lips, of a massive, cartilaginous structure.

In the confusion of his senses Smythje was, for the moment, inclined to believe himself between two demons—one below, in the shape of a monstrous serpent, and the other above him, in human form : for the grinning white teeth, and yellow eyeballs rolling in sockets of sable ground, presented an appearance sufficiently demoniac.

Of the two demons, however, he preferred the company of the one who bore something of his own shape ; and when a huge black man—like the trunk of a young tree—with the hand of a Titan attached to it, was stretched down to him, he did not decline to take ; but eagerly clutched at the gigantic paw thus proffered, he felt himself raised upward, as lightly as if elevated upon the extremtiy of a " see-saw !"

In another instant he found himself upon the summit of the dead-wood, his deliverer standing by his side.

So much light rushing all at once into the eyes of the rescued Smythje, instead of enabling him to see distinctly, quite blinded him · and it was

only by the touch that he knew a man was by his side—a man of colossal size, and nearly naked.

All this Smythje had surmissed by the *feel;* for so dizzy was he on emerging from the hollow tree, that the man had been compelled to hold him
some minutes in a sort of embrace to prevent his staggering over
Smythje, in groping about the breast of his gigantic deliverer, had come
in contact with various straps and strings, from which sundry horns and
pouches were suspended—and from this he concluded that the man was
a hunter.

Very soon Mr. Smythje's eyes became sufficiently strengthened to bear
the light; and then he saw, in full length, the individual who had rescued him from his perilous dilemma. He saw, too, that the man was not
alone ; for, on looking down from his elevated position, he beheld a dozen
others standing around the tree, all, or nearly all, with black skins—all,
with one or two exceptions, similarly armed, costumed, and accoutred.

They could not all be hunters? He had been mistaken in his first surmise? His deliverer was not a hunter, but a runaway negro—a robber?
He had fallen among a band of brigands—black brigands moreover ; for
what other kind could he expect to encounter in the mountains of
Jamaica?

" Wobbers they showly are !" muttered Smythje to himself.

If robbers, they appear at least to be a merry band ; for no sooner did
the sportsman stand erect on the summit of the stump—with the intention of descending—than a loud chorus of laughter hailed him from
below, in which his gigantic deliverer not only joined, but played first
trombone !

Although more than half believing that the joke was at his own ex
pense, Mr. Smythje was well pleased to find the robbers in this merry
mood. From such funny fellows he need not fear any ill-treatment, far
ther; perhaps, than to be stripped of his purse, arms, and accoutrements
His clothes, in their present condition, they would hardly covet.

The better to conciliate them by being beforehand with their demands
Smythje, as soon as safely landed on *terra firma,* pulled out his purse, and
commenced distributing its contents among his new acquaintances—giving to his deliverer, under whose special protection he now placed himself, a double share of the cash.

This free surrender seemed to have a happy effect. The robber no
longer laughed at their captive, but hastened to show him all the politeness in their power. One of them—a young fellow in light yellow
colour, who appeared to be their captain—even refused to accept any
thing, declining the proffered *douceur* with a dignified grace that somewhat astonished Smythje. The latter, however, was determined not to
be outdone in politeness, and suspecting that the gift was rejected on
account of its being *money,* immediately substituted for the coin his
handsome, London-made shot-belt and powder-flask, which, throughout
all his struggles, had clung to his shoulders. This proved a more ac-
ceptable offering to the robber chieftain—who, on receiving it from the
hands of the donor, acknowledged the present in a becoming and appropriate speech.

Smythje, now seeing that no further harm was likely to be done to him rapidly recovered his habitual equanimity; and, at the request of the robber chieftain, explained how he had got entrapped in the hollow tree, by giving a full account of his adventure, from the time he commenced stalking the "wild turkey," up to the moment of his deliverance.

His *bizarre* audience listened with a vivid interest—especially to that part of the story which gave them the information that there were *wild turkeys* in the woods of Jamaica—a point upon which they appeared rather incredulous.

As soon as Smythje had finished his narrative, the robber captain was seen making a sign, and whispering some words to one of his followers —the most diminutive of the band.

The latter, in obedience to the order thus given, proceeded to draw on a pair of large goatskin gloves, or gauntlets rather, that reached quite up to his elbows; and then, without further delay, he "speeled" up to the summit of the dead wood.

Fastening a cord, which he had carried up with him, around the top of the stump, he fearlessly let himself down into the dark, snake-tenanted chamber, which Mr. Smythje had been so glad to get out of!

The little fellow had not been more than half a minute out of sight, when a glittering object was seen projected above the top of the stump. It was of serpent form, and bright yellow colour. Wriggling and writhing, it hung, for a moment, suspended in the air; and then, yielding to the laws of gravitation, it came down with a thump upon the turf. Its large size, and its lines of black and gold, rendered it easy of identification as the "yellow snake" of Jamaica (*chilabothrus inornatus*).

Scarce had it touched the ground when a second and similar projectile was ejected from the hollow stump; and then a third—and another, and yet another, until no less than a dozen of these hideous reptiles lay scattered over the grass!

The blacks killed them as they came down—not from any particular spite at the serpents, nor even with the design of destroying them as "vermin." On the contrary, each, as it was deprived of life, was carefully stowed away in one of the wicker cutacoos, which carried the commissariat of these forest-rangers.

After the dead wood had been delivered of its last snake, an object of a far different character was seen to issue forth in a similar manner. It was a misshapen mass, of a dirty buff colour, and proved, upon inspection, to be one of Mr. Smythje's boots, still incased in its fawnskin covering! Its mate soon followed; and then, to the infinite amusement of the blacks, the "wild turkey," which had led the sportsman into his deplorable dilemma, and which now, with half its plumage gone, and the other half "drooked" and bedaggled, offered but a poor chance for the garnishing of his game-bag.

Smythje, however, too well contented with escaping with his life, thought no more of his game-bag, nor of anything else, but getting back to Mount Welcome by the shortest route possible.

His boots being restored to him, he lost no time in drawing them on, leaving the bottoms of his trousers in the companionship of the worthless "turkey," which the robbers, better acquainted with the ornithology of Jamaica, assured him was, after all, no turkey, but only a turkey-buzzard—a John Crow—in short, a stinking vulture!

To his grea' joy, and not a little to his astonishment, the bandits made no attempt to strip him of aught save his money ; and that he had delivered up without waiting for them to demand it. Even his valuable gold repeater was not taken from him; and not only was his gun restored, but a guide was furnished by the polite robber chieftain to conduct him on his road to Mount Welcome!

So grateful was the humiliated Smythje for the kind treatment he had experienced at the hands of these black-skinned but gentle brigands, that on parting company with them he shook hands with every individual of the band ; as he did so, promising one and all, that should he ever hear of them being in any danger of having their necks stretched, he would use his utmost influence to prevent that inconvenient catastrophe.

The Maroons (for these were the robbers into whose hands Smythje had fallen, Quaco being his deliverer), though somewhat mystified by the remark, graciously thanked him for whatever it meant; and, after once more shaking hands with their captain, the pseudo-sportsman took his departure.

CHAPTER XLIX.

QUASHIE IN A QUANDARY.

DURING all this time, where was Quashie? What was become of him? Mr. Smythje did not know, and no longer did he care. Too glad to get altogether away from the scene of his unpleasant adventure, he made no inquiry about his negligent squire; nor did he even think of going back to the place where he had left him. The road by which his new guide was conducting him led in quite another direction. As to the empty game-bag left with Quashie, the sportsman cared not what became of that; and as for his hunting-knife and brandy flask, no doubt the darkey would see to them.

In this conjecture Mr. Smythje hit the nail upon the head—at least so far as regarded the brandy-flask. It was by seeing too well to it, that Quashie had lost all thought of everything else—not only of the duties he had been appointed to perform, but of the whole earth and everything upon it. The buckra had not been twenty minutes out of his presence, when Quashie, by repeated application of the brandy-flask to his lips, brought his optical organs into such a condition, that he could not have told the difference between a turkey and a turkey-buzzard any more than Mr. Smythje himself.

The drinking of the *eau de vie* had an effect upon the negro the very reverse of what it would have had upon an Irishman. Instead of making him noisy and quarrelsome, it produced a tendency towards tranquility—so much so that Quashie, in less than five minutes after his last flask, coggled over upon the grass, and fell fast asleep.

So soundly slept he, that not only did he fail to hear the report of Smythje's gun, but the discharge of a whole battery of field-pieces close to his ear would not, at that moment, have awakened him.

It is scarce possible to say how long Quashie would have continued in this state of half-sleep, half-inebriety, had he been left undisturbed ; nor was he restored to consciousness by human agency, or living creature of any kind. That which brought him to himself—waking and partially sobering him, at the same time—was the rain, which, descending like a cold shower-bath on his semi-naked skin, caused him to start to his feet.

Quashie, however, had enjoyed more than an hour's sleep, before the rain began to fall; and this may account for the *eau de vie* having in some measure lost its influence when he awoke.

He was sensible that he had done wrong in drinking the buckra's brandy ; and as the temporary courage with which it had inspired him was now quite gone, he dreaded an encounter with the white " gemman." He would have shunned it, had he known how ; but he knew very well that to slink home by himself would bring down upon him the wrath of massa at Mount Welcome—pretty sure to be accompanied by a couple of dozen from the cartwhip.

After a while's reflection, he concluded that his most prudent 'plan would be to wait for the young buckra's return, and tell the best tale he could.

To say he had been searching for him, and that was how he had spent the time—was the story that suggested itself to the troubled imagination of Quashie.

To account for the disappearance of the cognac—for he had drank every drop of it—the darkey had bethought him of another little bit of fabrication—suggested, no doubt, by the mischance that had befallen the bottle of claret. He intended to tell the grand buckra—and " thrape" it down his throat if need be—that he, the buckra, had left out the stopper of the flask, and that the brandy had followed the example set by the " heel tap" of wine.

Thus fortified with a plausible scheme, Quashie awaited the return of the buckra sportsman.

The sky cleared after a time, but no buckra came ; nor yet, after a considerable spell of fine weather had transpired, did he make his appearance.

Quashie became impatient, and slightly anxious. Perhaps the English " gemman" had lost himself in the woods ; and if so, what would be done to him, the guide ? Massa Vaughan would be sure to punish him ? In fancy he could hear the crack of the cartwhip resounding afar off over the hills.

After waiting a while longer, he determined to put an end to his anxiety by going in search of the sportsman; and taking up the empty bag, along with the equally empty flask, and the hunting knife, he set forth.

He had seen Mr. Smythje go towards the glade, and so far he could follow his trail ; but once arrived at the open ground, he was completely at fault.

He had not the slightest idea of what direction to take.

After pausing to reflect, he took the right—that which would conduct him to the dead wood, the top of which was visible from the point where he had entered the glade.

It was not altogether accident that conducted him thither ; but rather because he heard, or fancied he heard, voices in that direction.

As he drew nearer to the decapitated tree, a glittering object on the ground caught his eye. He halted, thinking it might be a snake—a crea ture of which most plantation negroes have a wholesome dread.

On scrutinising the object more closely, Quashie was surprised to perceive that the glittering object was a gun ; and on a still nearer acquaintance with it, he saw that it was the gun of the buckra sportsman!

It was lying upon the grass near the bottom of the dead-wood. What was it doing there ?

Where was the buckra himself ? Had some accident happened to him? Why had he abandoned his gun ? Had he shot himself? Or had somebody else shot him? Or what on earth had befallen him?

Just at that moment the most lugubrious of sounds fell upon his ear It was a groan, long-drawn and hollow—as if some tortured spirit was about taking its departure from the earth! It resembled the voice of a man, and yet it differed from this! It was like the voice of some one speaking from the interior of a tomb!

The darkey stood horrified—his black epidermis turning instantaneously to an ashen-grey colour, quick as the change of a cameleon.

He would have taken to his heels, but a thought restrained him. It might be the buckra still alive, and in trouble? In that case he, Quashie, would be punished for deserting him.

The voice appeared to issue from behind the dead-wood. Whoever uttered it must be there. Perhaps the sportsman lay wounded upon the other side ?

Quashie screwed up his courage as high as it would go, and commenced moving round to the other side of the stump. He proceeded cautiously, step by step, scrutinising the ground as he went.

He reached the other side. He looked all over the place. Nobody there—neither dead nor wounded !

There were no bushes to conceal an object so large as the body of a man—at least, not within twenty yards of the stump. The groan could not have come from beyond that distance ?

Nor yet could a man be hidden under the trellis of climbing plants that hung around the underwood. Quashie had still enough courage left to peep among them and see. There was nobody there!

At this moment a second groan sounded in the darkey's ear, increasing his terror. It was just such an one as the first, long protracted and sepulchral, as if issuing from the bottom of a well.

Again it came from behind the stump; but this time from the side which he had just left, and where he had seen no one!

Had the wounded man crawled round to the other side while he, Quashie, was proceeding in the opposite direction ?

This was the thought that occurred to him ; and to determine the point, he passed back to the side whence he had come—this time going more rapidly, lest the mysterious moaner might again escape him.

On reaching the point from which he had originally set out, he was more surprised than ever. Not a soul was to be seen. The gun still lay in its place, as he had left it. No one appeared to have touched it—no one was there!

Again the voice—this time, however, in a shrill treble, and more resembling a shriek! It gave Quashie a fresh start ; while the sweat spurt ed out from his forehead, and ran down his cheeks like huge tears.

The shriek, however, was more human-like—more in the voice of a man; and this gave the darkey sufficient courage to stand his ground a little longer. He had no doubt but that the voice came from the other side of the dead-wood; and once more he essayed to get his eyes upon the utterer.

Still in the belief that the individual, whoever it was, and for whatever purpose, was dodging round the tree, Quashie now started forward with a determination not to stop till he had run the dodger to earth. For this purpose he commenced circling around the stump, going first at a trot; but hearing now and then the groans and shrieks—and always on the opposite side—he increased his pace, until he ran with all the speed that lay in his legs.

He kept up this exercise, till he had made several turns around the tree; when, at length, he became convinced that no human being could be running before him without his seeing him.

The conviction brought him to an abrupt halt, and a quick reflection. If not a human being, it must be a "duppy or de debbil hisself!"

The evidence that it was one or the other had now become overpowering. Quashie could resist it no longer.

"Duppy! Jumbé! de debbil!" cried he, as with chatteaing teeth, and eyeballs liko to start from their sockets, he shot off from the stump, and "streaked it" in the direction of Mount Welcome, as fast as a pair of trembling limbs were capable of carrying him.

CHAPTER L.

A SCARCITY OF TROUSERS.

FOLLOWING the guide which the robber captain had appointed to conduct him, Mr. Smythje trudged unhappily homeward.

How different his craven, crestfallen look, from the swell, swaggering sportsman of the morning! and the condition of his person was not more dilapidated than that of his spirit.

It was not the past either that was pressing upon it. He had suffered no material injury to grieve over. The damage done to his fine dress, or the coin he had been compelled to disburse among the bandits—as he still considered them—these were trifles to a rich man like him. His regrets were not on that score, nor retrospective in any way. They were directed to something before him, altogether prospective.

And what was that something? It was no longer the disgrace of returning with an empty game-bag, but the chagrin, which he expected to have to undergo, presenting himself at Mount Welcome in the "pickle" in which his adventure had left him.

He was now, when near the house, even in a more ludicrous plight than when he had parted from the jocose gentry of the forest: for the rain, that had long since ceased, had been succeeded by a blazing hot sun, and the atmosphere acting upon what remained of his wet fawnskin trousers, caused them to shrink until the ragged edges had crept up to mid-thigh; thus leaving a large space of thin knock-kneed legs between them and the tops of his boots!

With all his vanity about personal appearance, Smythje rathor suspected that he was defective in the legs. There lay his weak point. For that reason he had long since eschewed the habit of Hessian boots, the most graceful of all species of *chaussure*, excepting, perhaps, the sandal. Smythje hated the sight of them, as did every spindle-legged biped who was compelled to wear them, and hence their extinction. Smythje hated breeches, too, as leading to the same result—the exposure of his weak points.

No doubt it was that antipathy that had led to his innovation in the shooting dress already described ; and which on the present occasion had proved to be a grievous mistake.

Had the fawskins kept their place, and stood where he had cut them off, there would have been nothing particular to be remarked—at least, nothing so very ridiculous. They migh have resembled the "trews" of a Highlander, or even a pair of loose buckskin breeches—a costume becoming enough for a sportsman. But shrunk as they now were, and exposing the crooked skeleton-like form of the cockney's limbs, they made him the very *beau ideal* of a " guy."

Smythje was more than half aware of this ; and at that moment would have made a book-keeper on his estate of any man who should have pro· vided him with a pair of pantaloons. It was only these he wanted. The rest of his costume, though sadly deteriorated since starting out in the morning, was still well enough—at all events, it was not ludicrous. The trousers alone were likely to get him into disgrace.

It was an appaling prospect that lay before the *ci-devant* sportsman : for he was now fairly entitled to the qualifying phrase. Perhaps some would be disposed to use the less creditable appellation, *soi-disant*.

It was this that he dreaded. An empty game-bag—an absurd adventure, which had ended in placing him in such a ludicrous plight. Verily, the prospect was unpleasant—appalling. How could he appear before his friends at Mount Welcome ? For Mr. Vaughan he cared not so much; but *Miss* Vaughan—Kate—ah ! Kate—how was he to conceal his situation from her ? That was the secret of his solicitude—of his prospective chagrin.

Could he reach the house, and steal to his own chamber unseen ? What chance was there of his doing so ?

On reflection, not much. Mount Welcome, like all other mansions in Jamaica, was a cage—open on every side. It was almost beyond the bounds of probability that he could enter it unobserved.

Still he could try, and on the success of that trial rested his only hope. Oh ! for that grand secret known only to the jealous Juno—the secret of rendering oneself invisible ! What would Smythje not have given for a ten minutes' hire of that Carthaginian cloud ?

The thought was really in his mind ; for Smythje, like all young Eng lishmen of good family, had studied the classics.

The idea was suggestive. If there was no probability of being provided with the nimbus of Juno, there was the possibility of shadowing himself under the nimbus of night. Darkness once on, he might enter the house, reach his chamber unperceived, and thus escape the unpleasant exposure he so much dreaded !

Smythje stopped, looked at his guide, looked at the sun, and lastly at his naked knees—now from the enfeebled state of his limbs leaning against each other.

Mount Welcome was in sight. The guide was about to leave him; and, therefore, in whatever way he might act, there would be no witness. Just then the Maroon made his adieu, and Smythjo was left to himself. Once more he scanned the sun, and consulted his watch. In two hours it would be twilight. The crepusculous interval would enable him to approach the house; and in the first moments of darkness—before the lamps were lit—he *might* enter unobserved—or, at all events, his plight might not very plainly be perceived.

The scheme was feasible, and having determined to adopt it, Smythje cowered down in the covert and awaited the setting of the sun.

He counted the hours, the half-hours, and minutes—he listened to the voices coming up from the negro village—he watched the bright-winged birds that fluttered among the branches over head, and envied them their *complete* plumage.

Notwithstanding many rare sights and sweet sounds that reached him the two hours spent in his secret lair were not passed pleasantly—solicitude about the success of his scheme robbing him of all zest for the enjoyment of that fair scene that surrounded him.

The hour of action drew nigh. The sun went down over the opposite ridge, where lay Montagu Castle, his own domain; the twilight, like a purple curtain, was gently drawn over the valley of Mount Welcome. It was time to start.

Smythje rose to his feet; and, after making a *reconnoisance* of the ground before him, set off in the direction of the house.

He aimed at keeping as much as possible under cover of the woods; and this he was enabled to do—the pimento groves on that side stretching down to the shrubbery that surrounded the dwelling.

He had got past the negro village—keeping it upon his right—without being observed. To both the "quarter" and the sugar works he gave as wide a berth as the nature of the ground would permit. He succeeded in reaching the platform on which the house stood—so far unperceived.

But the moment of peril was not yet past: the dangerous ground still lay before him, and had still to be traversed. This was the open *parterre* in front of the house—for to the front his path had conducted him.

It was dusk, and no one appeared—at least he could see no one—either on the stair-landing or in the windows of the great hall. So far good. A rush for the open doorway, and then on to his own chamber, where Thoms would soon clothe him in a more becoming costume.

He started to make the rush; and had succeeded in getting half-way across the *parterre*, when all at once, a crowd of people, carrying large flaming torches above their heads, appeared coming from the rear of the dwelling.

They were the domestics and field hands of the plantation, with Trusty, the overseer, at their head.

One might have fancied that they were setting out upon some ceremonious procession; but their hurried advance, and the presence of Quashie trotting in the lead, proclaimed a different purpose.

Smythje divined their errand They were going in search of himself!

The sight filled him with despair. The torch-bearers had anticipated him. They had already reached the front of the house, and the glare of their great flambeaux illuminated every object, as if a new sun had sud·denly shot up athwart the sky !

There was no chance of successfully running the gauntlet under that bright flame : Smythje saw not the slightest.

He stopped in his tracks. He would have retreated back to the bush es, and there awaited the departure of the torch-bearers, but he feared that his retrograde movement would attract their eyes upon him ; and then all would be over—his adventure terminating in the most undesir· able manner.

Instead of retreating, therefore, he stood where he had stopped—fixed and immobile, as if pinned to the spot.

At that moment two figures appeared on the top of the stairway, in the brilliant light easily recognisable as the planter and his daughter. The maid Yola was behind them. Mr. Vaughan had come out to give some direction about the search.

All three stood facing the crowd of torch-bearers, and, of course, front·ing towards Smythje.

The planter was just opening his lips to speak, when a scream from Yola, echoed by his daughter, interrupted him. The sharp eyes of the Foolah had fallen upon Smythje, whose wan white face, shining under the light of the links, resembled those of the statues that stood at differ·ent places over the parterre.

Smythje was among the shubbery ; and as the girl knew that no statue stood there, the unexpected apparition had elicited her cry of alarm.

All eyes were instantly turned upon the spot ; and the torch-bearers, with Trusty at their head, hurried towards the piece of *pseudo*-sculpture.

There was no chance of escape ; and the unfortunate sportsman was discovered, and brought broadly into the light, under the fierce battery of eyes—among others the eyes of his lady love, that, instead of express·ing sympathy for his forlorn condition, appeared rather to sparkle with satirical delight !

It was a terrible catastrophe—to be contemplated in such a plight ; and Smythje, hurrying through the crowd, lost no time in withdrawing from observation, betaking himself to his chamber—where, under the consola·tory encouragement of the sympathising Thoms, he was soon rendered presentable.

CHAPTER LI.

HERBERT IN THE HAPPY VALLEY.

INAPPROPRIATE as Jacob Jessuron's neighbours may have deemed the title of his estate—the Happy Valley—Herbert Vaughan had no reason to re·gard it as a misnomer. From the hour in which he entered upon his situa·tion of book-keeper, it was a round of pleasures, rather than duties, that he found himself called upon to fulfil ; and his new life, so far from being laboriously spent, was one continued scene, or series of scenes, of positive pastime. Instead of keeping books, or looking after slaves—

or, in short, doing anything that might be deemed useful—most of his time was spent in excursions, that had no other object than recreation or amusement. Drives to the Bay—in which he was accompanied by Jessuron himself, and introduced to his mercantile acquaintances ; visits to neighboring penns and plantations with the beautiful Judith—and in which he was made acquainted with her circle ; fishing parties upon the water ; and pic-nics in the woods,—all these were afforded him without stint.

He was furnished with a fine horse to ride ; dogs and equipments for the chase ; everything, in short, calculated to afford him the life of a gentleman of elegant leisure. A half year's salary had been advanced to him unasked—thus delicately giving him the means of replenishing his wardrobe, and enabling him to appear in proper costume for every occasion.

Certainly, the prospects of the poor steerage passenger seemed to have undergone a change for the better. Through the generosity of his unexpected patron, he was playing a ' role' at the Jew's penn not unlike that which his fellow-voyager was, at this very time, performing at Mount Welcome ; and as there was not much difference in the social rank of the respective circles in which they were each revolving, it was by no means improbable that the two might meet again, and upon more equal footing than formerly.

To do Herbert Vaughan justice, it should be stated that he was more surprised than gratified by the luxurious life he was leading. There was something rather extraordinary in the generous patronage of the Jew— something that puzzled him not a little. How was he to account for such kind hospitality?

Thus for days after Herbert Vaughan had made the Happy Valley his home, matters moved on—smoothly enough to the superficial observer. Slight incongruities that did occur from time to time, were ingeniously explained ; and the young Englishman, unsuspicious of any evil design, with the exception of the unwonted hospitality that was being bestowed upon himself, saw nothing extraordinary in the circumstances that surrounded him. Had he been less the honoured guest of his Israelitish host, perhaps his perceptions might have been more scrupulous and discriminative. But the Arabs have a proverb—"It is not in human nature to speak ill of the horse that has borne one out of difficulty and danger;" and human nature in the East is but the counterpart of its homonym in the West. Noble as was the nature of the young Englishman, still was it human ; and to have " spoken ill of the bridge that had carried him safely over" from that desolate shore on which he had last been stranded, would have argued a nature something more than human.

If he entertained any suspicion of his patron's integrity, he zealously kept it to himself—not with any idea of surrendering either his independence or self-respect ; but to await the development of the somewhat inexplicable courtesy of which he was the recipient.

This courtesy was not confined to his Hebrew host. As Herbert had long been aware, his daughter exercised it in an equal degree, and far more gracefully. Indeed, among other transformations that had been remarked as occurring in the Happy Valley, the spirit of the fair Jewess seemed to have sustained a remarkable change. Though upon occasions the proud, imperious temper would manifest itself, more generally now was Judith in a sentimental vein—at times approaching to sadness. There were other times when the old spitefulness would show itself. Then the spiral nostrils would curl with contempt, and the dark Israeli‐ tish eyes flash with malignant fire.

Happily, these rather ungraceful exhibitions—like the tornadoes of her native land—were rare ; for a certain name—the cause that called them forth—was rarely pronounced in her hearing. Kate Vaughan was the name.

Her dislike for the young creole had originated in a mere rivalry of charms. Both enjoyed a wide spread reputation for beauty, oft discant‐ ed upon, and often compared, by the idle gallants of the Bay. These discussions and comparisons reached the ear of the Jewess ; and, to her chagrin, the decisions were not always in her favour. Hence the origin of her enmity.

Hitherto it had been only *envy;* and, with a toss of the head, and a slight curl of the nostril, the unpleasant theme would be dismissed. Of late, however, a stronger emotion that envy had begun to exhibit itself ; and, whenever the name of Kate Vaughan was introduced into the con‐ versation—no matter how incidentally or undesigned—the eye of the Jewess would light up with a jealous fire, her lips quiver as if muttering curses ; and she, who but the moment before seemed a very angel, would become all at once transformed into the semblance of a demon !

One would have supposed that the presence of Kate's cousin would have kept in check these unseemly exhibitions. On the contrary, it ap‐ peared rather the influence that invoked them ; for in Herbert's presence alone did the daughter of Jessuron put on such a seeming ; and if by any chance the young man spoke favourably of his cousin—to do him justice he never spoke otherwise—the fair Jewess would no longer confine her spleen to mere dumb signs, but would launch forth into the most bitter revilings. Then did Herbert listen to strange revelations. Then learnt he, and for the first time, that Kate Vaughan, his beautiful and accom‐ plished cousin, was the daughter of a quadroon slave !

Thus was he made to understand the *alias* of " lilly Quasheba," which Kate had been herself unable to explain ; and more than half compre‐ hended the plaint of friendless isolation which his cousin, in her inno‐ cent candour, had confessed to him.

Herbert, though little regarding all this, forbore to make denial or con‐ tradiction. Entirely ignorant of the past history of his cousin's life, neither against statements of fact nor insinuation of falsehood could he say a word in her defence. He scarce dared to defend her : for to say the truth, the imperious spirit of the Jewess had already gained a cer tain ascendancy over his.

It was only when Kate's name came uppermost that Judith was seen to frown—at least by Herbert Vaughan. At all other times her face was beset with smiles, sweetly seductive.

The behavior of the Jewess admits of easy explanation. *She was in love, and with Herbert Vaughan.*

The Jew Jessuron had commenced playing a game, with his daughter acting as decoy. Herbert Vaughan was the stake to be obtained. Whatever was its purpose, the game was a deep one, and, for the decoy, dangerous. If won, where would be the advantage ? What cbject could he have in desiring his daughter to entrap the heart of Herbert Vaughan? This was the mystery—the depth of the game. If lost, then lost too would be the lure ! Therein lay its danger. Cunning as he was, Jacob Jessuron may not have foreseen this danger. Having confidence in the habitual coldness, as well as the skilled experience of his daughter's heart, he had entered upon his play without apprehension.

Judith had herself began the game equally *insouciant* of consequences. Her notions differed from those of her father : for, indeed, it was not till a late period that she was fully informed of his—not until hers had become sufficiently strong to stimulate her to continue the play on her own account.

With her, at first, the motive was part vanity, part coquetry—blended however, with some serious admiration. Mingled also with this was a desire to vex Kate Vaughan ; for, from the first, she had suspected rivalry in that quarter. Even though she had been made aware of the very short interview between the cousins, she could not feel satisfied but that something had passed between them : and there was that bit of ribbon, which Herbert still cherished, and of the symbolism of which she had vainly endeavoured to obtain a solution.

Her suspicions did not die out, as it might be supposed they would, in the absence of any demonstration on Herbert's part towards his cousin. On the contrary, they only grew stronger, as her own interest in the young Englishman increased, for then she could not understand how a young girl—Kate Vaughan or any other—could have looked upon the man who had impressed her, without being themselves impressed.

And she had become impressed by him, not gradually, but rapidly and profoundly ; until her love had grown into a fierce passion, such as a tigress may be suspected of conceiving for her tawny mate.

Herbert Vaughan had passed scarce a week under the roof of the Jew's mansion when its mistress was in love with him—to the ends of her fingers—to the very extreme of jealousy !

As for the object of this fervent passion, the young man was at this time quite unable to analyse his own feelings ; still more difficult were they to be understood by an outside observer.

The knowledge of a few facts may facilitate their comprehension. In the short interview which he had had with his cousin Kate, Herbert Vaughan had looked, for the first time in his life, on one whom to look at was to love. The blue-eyed belle of his native village, the pretty barmaid at the inn, the sweet-faced chorister in the church, with other boyish fancies, already half obliterated by two months of absence, were swept instantaneously into the dust-bin of oblivion by that lovely apparition. He was face to face with a woman worthy of his love—one who deserved every aspiration of his soul. Intuitively and at the first glance he had felt that ; and still more was he impressed with it, as he pronounced those warm words on his painful parting. Hence the ardent proffer of the strong arm and stout heart—hence the chivalric refusal of the purse, and the preference of a piece of ribbon.

Not that he had any reason to regard the latter as a love-token. He knew that the kind words that had been spoken in that short but stormy interview—as well as the offer of gold that had ended it—were but the promptings of a pitying heart; and rather a negation of love, than a sign of its existence. Glad as he might have been to have regarded the piece of ribbon as a *gage d'amour*, he could only prize it as a *souvenir* of friendship—of no higher signification than the purse to which it had belonged, or the gold treasure which that purse had contained.

Though sensible that he had no claim upon his cousin beyond that of kinship—though not a word had been spoken by her to show that she felt for him any other kind of regard, Herbert, strange enough, had conceived a hope, that some day or other a more endearing relationship might exist between them.

Whence the origin of this pleasant expectancy? He could not himself tell: since there was nothing in her speech to betray aught upon which to build a hope. In her manner? There might have been something in that? Though ever so delicately outlined, Herbert *had* perceived an expression there that still lingered in his memory. Hence, no doubt, the fancy in which he had indulged.

Not for long was he cheered by the sweet remembrance. It was too transitory to stand the test of time. As day succeeded day, rumours reached him of the gay scenes that were transpiring at Mount Welcome. Especially was he informed of the contentedness of his cousin Kate in the society of her new companion, Smythje.

The effect of this information was a gradual but grievous extinction of the slight hope which Herbert had conceived.

The circumstances with which chance had now surrounded him may have rendered these regrets less painful. Though his cousin cared not for him, he had no reason to feel forsaken or forlorn. By his side, and almost constantly by his side, was beauty of no common brilliance, showering smiles upon him of no ordinary attractiveness.

Had he been the recipient of those smiles only one day sooner—before the image of Kate Vaughan had made that slight impression upon his heart—he might the more readily have yielded to their influence. And, perhaps, on the other hand, could he have known how *his* image had fallen upon *her* heart, and made lodgment there, he might have offered a sterner resistance to the syren seductions with which he was now beset.

But lover's hearts are not things of glass; and though at times they resemble mirrors mentally reflecting each other, too often, by the ruling of contrarieties, do the mirrors become reversed—turned back to back, with the reflected images facing darkly inward.

In such a dilemma was the heart of Herbert Vaughan. No wonder there was difficulty in effecting its analysis.

Nor was Kate Vaughan kept in ignorance of outward events. Her maid Yola was the medium by which she was made acquainted with them. Through this medium she had heard of Herbert's proximity—of his happiness and prosperity. The news would have given her joy, but that she had heard he was *too happy!* Strange that this should be a cause of bitterness!

In a condition somewhat similar to Herbert's was the heart of his cousin: though hers was easier to analyse. It was simply trembling under the influence of a first and virgin love. Two forms had been presented to it in the same hour, both in the blush of youthful manhood—one a distinguished gentleman—the other, an humble adventurer. The former had the additional advantage in priority of introduction; the latter was not even introduced. But the favourite does not always win. The earliest on the course may be the latest in the race; and though the heart of the young creole, on its pure virgin page, had received love's image at first sight, it was not that of him who first presented himself to make the impression.

The thoughts that succeeded—the hopes and fears—the dark doubts by day and by night—the dreams, often delusively bright—need not be detailed. There are none who have not known a first love; few who have not felt this chequered alternation of emotions.

As for the distinguished Smythje, he was not always in one mind. He, too, was troubled with an alternation of hopes and fears. The former, however, generally predominated; and, for the most part, he felt in his spirit the proud confidence of a conquerer. Often, with Thoms as his audience, might Smythje be heard exultingly repeating the somewhat boastful despatch of Cæsar :—" *Veni, vidi, vici !*"

CHAPTER LII.

IN SEARCH OF JUSTICE.

THE mutual spite between planter and penn-keeper was of old standing —dating, in fact, from their first acquaintance with each other. Some sharp practice between them, in the sale and purchase of slaves, had given origin to it; and circumstances were always occurring to hinder it from dying out. This was more especially the case since the Jew, by the purchase of the Happy Valley estate, had become the contiguous neighbour—and, in point of wealth, almost the rival—of the proprietor of Mount Welcome.

The enmity mutually indulged in by them was rather of the nature of an antipathy. Though keenly felt on both sides, it was generally concealed. Only upon very rare occasions had it found expression between them, and then only in the slightest manner. Not that either of them had succeeded in disguising his ill-will from the other. Each knew that the other hated him, as well as if the avowal had been made every day of their lives.

The dislike was rather intermittent than regular—that is, it was stronger or weaker according to circumstances; sometimes reaching the point of open hostility, and sometimes waning to mere unfriendliness, but never entirely dying out.

On the side of the Custos there had been for some time past another feeling mixed up with his antipathy to his Israelitish neighbour—a vague sense of fear. This was of modern origin—so late as since the execution of Chakra, the myal-man—and begotten of some remarks which as reported to Mr. Vaughan, the Jew had made in connection with that ugly incident.

If nothing had of late transpired to increase this fear on the part of the Custos, a circumstance had arisen to strengthen his hostility. The protection which had been given to his discarded nephew, and the parade which his neighbour was making of him, had proved to the Custos a scandal of the most irksome kind ; and almost every day was he made aware of some unpleasant bit of gossip connected with the affair. So irritated had he become with the reports, or rumours, constantly reaching him, that his hatred for the Jew had grown stronger than ever before ; and he would have given a dozen hogsheads of his best *muscovado* to any one who should have provided him with the means of humiliating the detested penn-keeper.

Just at this crisis chance, or fortune, stepped in to favour him, apparently offering him the very opportunity he desired ; and in a way that, instead of costing him a dozen hogsheads of sugar, was likely to put far more than that amount of property into his pocket.

It was the day before that on which Smythje had dropped into the dead-wood. The Custos was in his kiosk alone, smoking a plantation segar, and conning over the statutes of the "black code"—a favourite study with him, and necessary also : since he had arrived at the distinction of being the chief magisterial authority of the district. Just at that moment Mr. Trusty's shadow was projected into the summer-house.

" Well, Trusty, what is it ?"

" There's a man below wants to see your worship."

" On what business, pray ?"

" Don't know," answered the laconic overseer ; " he won't tell. Says it's important, and can only communicate to yourself."

" What sort of a man is he ? Negro or white man ?"

" Neither, your worship. He's a clear mulatto. I've seen him about before. He's one of the Maroons that have their settlement over among the Trelawney Hills. He calls himself Cubina."

" Ah !" said the Custos, showing a slight emotion as the name was pronounced ; " Cubina ! Cubina ! I've heard the name. I fancy I've seen the man—at a distance. A young fellow, isn't he ?"

" Very young ; though they say he's the captain of the band."

" What on earth can the Maroon want with me ?" muttered Mr. Vaughan half to himself. " He hasn't brought in any runaways, has he ?"

" No," answered the overseer. " Thanks to your worship's good management, we haven't any of late—not since that old schemer Chakra was put out of the way."

" Thanks to *your* good management, Mr. Trusty," said the planter, returning his overseer's compliment, not without a show of nervous excitement, which the reference to Chakra had called forth. " Then it's nothing of that kind, you think ?" hastily added he, as if desirous of changing the theme.

" No, your worship. It cannot be : there's not a runaway upon my list ;" replied Trusty, with an air of triumph.

" Gad ! I'm glad to hear it," said the Custos, rubbing his hands together as an expression of his contentment. " Well, I suppose the young fellow has come to consult me in my magisterial capacity. In some scrape, no doubt? These Maroons are alway getting themselves into trouble with some of our planters. I wonder who he's come to complain about?"

"Well, that much I think I can tell you," rejoined the overseer, evidently knowing more of the Maroon's errand than he had yet admitted—for Mr. Trusty was a true disciple of the secretive school. "If I should be allowed to make a guess, your worship, I should say it is something relating to our neighbour of the Happy Valley."

"What! the Jew?"

"Jacob Jessuron, Esquire."

"You think so, Trusty?" inquired Mr. Vaughan, with an earnest and gratified look. "Has the young fellow said anything?"

"No," answered the overseer; "it's not anything he has said. I heard something a day or two ago about a runaway the Maroons had got among them—a slave belonging to the Jew. It appears they don't want to give him up."

"Whom did you hear it from?"

"Why, not exactly from any one, your worship. I should rather say I overheard it, quite by accident. One of the Trelawney Maroons—a big fellow that comes down here occasionally after black Bet—was telling her something. I was passing Bet's cabin, and heard them talking about it."

"Don't want to give him up! And for what reason do they refuse?"

"Can't tell, your worship. I could only make out part of the conversation."

"So you think it's about that the young fellow has come?"

"I think it likely, your worship. He's close, however, and I couldn't get a word out of him about his business. He says he must see you."

"All right, then! You can show him in here—as good a place as any. And hark ye, Mr. Trusty! See Black Bet, and get out of her what you can. This is an interesting matter. A Maroon refusing to deliver up a runaway! There must be something in it. Perhaps the mulatto will tell me all about it; but, whether he does or not, you see Bet. You can promise her a new gown, or whatever you like. Show the young fellow up at once. I am ready to receive him."

Mr. Trusty bowed, and walked off in the direction of the works, where the Maroon had remained; while the Custos, composing himself into an official attitude, awaited the approach of his visitor.

"I'd give a good round sum," soliloquised he, "to learn that the old rascal has got into some scrape with these Maroon fellows. I shouldn't wonder," he added, in gleeful anticipation. "I shouldn't wonder! I know they don't much like him—less since he's taken the Spaniards into his pay—and I suspect he's been engaged in some underhand transactions of late. He's been growing grander every day, and nobody knows where all the money comes from. Maybe Master Maroon has a tale to tell; and, if it's against Jessuron, I'll take care he has an opportunity to tell it. Ah, here he comes! Egad, a fine-looking fellow! So, so! This is the young man that my daughter jokes Yola about! Well, I don't wonder the Foolah should have taken a fancy to him; but I must see that he doesn't make a fool of her. These Maroons are dangerous dogs among the women of the plantations; and Yola, whether a princess or not in her own country—princess, ha! ha! Well, at all events, the wench is no common nigger; and it won't do for Master Maroon to come humbugging her. I shall lecture him about it, now that I've got him here. I hope he has other business than that, though."

By this time the Maroon captain—equipped just as we have seen him in the forest—had arrived in front of the kiosk; and, making a deferential bow, though without taking off his hat—which being the *toqued kerchief*, could not conveniently be removed—stood waiting for the Custos to address him.

The latter remained for a considerable time without vouchsafing farther speech, than the mechanical salutation, "Good morning." There was something in the physiognomy of his visitor that had evidently made an impression upon him; and the gaze, with which he regarded the latter, was one that bespoke some feeling different from that of mere curiosity or admiration. It was a glance of keen scrutiny: as if the face of the young man had called up some *souvenir*—one, too, not altogether agreeable. This was indicated by a slight shadow that, at the moment, made its appearance upon the planter's countenance.

Whatever it was, he seemed desirous of suppressing it; and, making an effort to that effect, appeared to succeed: for the instant after the shadow cleared away; and, with a magisterial but courteous smile, he commenced the conversation.

CHAPTER LIII.

MAGISTRATE AND MAROON.

" WELL, young man," began the Custos, in an affable tone, " you, I think, are one of the Maroons of Trelawney?"

" Yes, worship," bluntly answered Cubina.

" The captain of a town, are you not?'

" Only a few families, worship. Ours is a small settlement."

" And your name is——?"

" Cubina."

" Ah! I've heard the name," said the Custos. " I think," added he, with a significant smile, " we have a young girl here on the plantation who knows you?"

Cubina blushed, as he stammered out an affirmative.

" Oh! that's all right," said the Custos, encouragingly. " So long as there's no harm meant, there's no harm done. Mr. Trusty tells me you have business with me. Is it about that?'

" About what, your worship?" inquired the Maroon, a little taken by surprise at the question so unexpectedly put to him.

" About your sweetheart?"

" My sweetheart, worship?"

" Ay, Yola. Is she not your sweetheart?"

" Well, Mr. Vaughan," rejoined the Maroon, " I'm not going to deny that something has passed between me and the young girl; but it warn't exactly about that I've come to see you, though now, bein' here, I might as well talk that matter, too, if it so please your worship."

"Very good, Captain Cubina; I'm ready to hear what you have to say. Go on!"

"Well, then, your worship, the truth is, I want to buy Yola."

"What! Buy your own sweetheart?"

"Just so, worship. . Of course, as soon as she were mine, I'd set her free."

"That is, you would change the bonds she now wears for the bonds of matrimony? ha! ha! ha! Is that it, Cubina?" And the Custos laughed at the conceit he had so neatly expressed.

"Something of that sort, your worship," replied Cubina, slightly participating in the worthy magistrate's mirth.

"And do you think Yola desires to become Mrs. Cubina?"

"If I didn't think so, your worship, I wouldn't propose to buy her. It would be nothing to me to own the girl, if she warn't agreeable."

"She *is* agreeable, then?"

"Well, worship, I think so. Not that she don't like the young mistress that owns her at present; but you see, your worship—but——"

"But there's somebody she likes better than her mistress; and that's yourself, Master Cubina?"

"Well, you see, worship, that's a different sort of liking, and——"

"True enough—true enough!" interrupted Mr. Vaughan, as if wishing to hasten the end of the conversation—at least, upon that subject.

"Well, Captain Cubina," he added, "suppose I was willing to part with Yola, how much could you afford to give for her? Mind you, I don't say I am willing; for, after all, the girl belongs to my daughter: and *she* would have something to say about the matter."

"Ah, sir!" exclaimed Cubina, in a tone of tender confidence, "Miss Vaughan is good and generous. I've often heard say so. I am sure she would never stand in the way of Yola's being happy."

"Oh, you think it would make Yola happy, do you?"

"I hope so, your worship," answered the Maroon, modestly dropping his eyes, as he made the reply.

"After all," said the planter, "it would be a matter of business. My daughter, even if she wished it, could not afford to part with the girl for less than the market price; which in Yola's case would be a large one. How much do you suppose I have been offered for her?"

"I've heard two hundred pounds, your worship."

"Just so; and I refused that, too."

"Maybe, Mr. Vaughan, you would not have refused it from another— from me, for instance?"

"Ah, I don't know about that! But could you raise that large sum?"

"Not just now, your worship. I am sorry to say I could not. I had rubbed and scraped together as good as a hundred—thinking that would be enough—when, to my sorrow, I learnt I had only got half way. But, if your worship will only allow me time. I think I can manage—in a month or two—to get the other hundred, and then——" .

"Then, worthy captain, it will be time to talk about buying Yola Meanwhile, I can promise you that she sha'n't be sold to anybody else. Will that satisfy you?"

"Oh, thank your worship! It is very kind of you, Mr Vaughan. I'll not fail to be grateful. So long as Yola——"

"Yola will be safe enough in my daughter's keeping. But now, my young fellow, since you say this was not exactly the business that brought you here, you have some other, I suppose? Pray tell me what it is."

The Custos, as he made this request, set himself to listen, in a more attentive attitude than he had yet assumed.

"Well, your worship!" proceeded Cubina, "I've come over to ask you for some advice about a matter I have with Mr. Jessuron—he as keeps penn close by here."

Mr. Vaughan became doubly attentive.

"What matter?" asked he, in simple phrase, lest any circumlocution might distract the speaker from his voluntary declaration.

"It's an ugly business, your worship; and I wouldn't bother about it, but that the poor young fellow, who's been obbed out of his rights, turns out to be neyther more nor less than the brother of Yola herself. It's a queer story altogether; and if it warn't the old Jew that's done the thing, one could hardly believe it."

"What thing? Pray be explicit, my friend!"

"Well, your worship, if you'll have patience to hear me, I'll tell you the whole story from beginning to end—that is, as far as it has gone: for it ain't ended yet."

"Go on!" commanded the Custos. "I'll hear it patiently. And don't be afraid, Captain Cubina," added he, encouragingly. "Tell me all you know—every circumstance. If it's a case for justice, I promise you justice shall be done."

And with this magisterial commonplace, the Custos resumed his attitude of extreme attention.

"I'll make no secrets, your worship, whether it gets me into trouble or no. I'll tell you all—leastwise, all that's come to my knowledge."

And with this proviso, the Maroon captain proceeded to detail the circumstances connected with the capture of the runaway; the singular encounter between brother and sister; and the mutual recognition that followed. Then afterwards the disclosures made by the young man: how he was an African prince; how he had been sent in search of his sister; the ransom he had brought with him; his landing from the ship, consigned by Captain Jowler to the care of Jessuron; his treatment and betrayal by the Jew; the branding of his person, and robbing him of his property; his escape from the penn; his capture by Cubina, already detailed; and, finally, his detention by the latter, in spite of several messages and menaces, sent by the Jew, to deliver him up.

"Good!" cried Loftus Vaughan, starting from his chair, and evidently delighted by the recital, somewhat dramatically delivered by the Maroon. "A melodrama, I declare! wanting only one act to complete it. Egad, I shall feel inclined to be one of the actors before it's played out. Ho!" exclaimed he, as if some thought had suddenly struck him; "this may explain why the old rascal wanted to buy the wench—though I don't clearly see his purpose in that. It'll come clear yet, no doubt."

Then changing from his soliloquised speeches, and addressing himself once more to the Maroon:

"Twenty-four Mandingoes, you say—twenty-four belonged to the prince?"

"Yes, your worship. Twenty regular slaves, and four others that were his personal attendants. There were more of the slaves, but they were the lawful property of the captain for bringing him over."

"And they were all carried to the Jew's penn?"

"All of them, with the others; in fact, the whole cargo came there The Jew bought all. There were some Coromantees among them; and one of my men Quaco, who had talk with these, heard enough to confirm young man's story."

"Ha! what a pity, now, that black tongues can't wag to any purpose! *Their* talk goes for nothing. But I'll see what can be done without it."

"Did your prince ascertain the name of the captain that brought him ever?" inquired the magistrate, after considering a minute.

"Oh, yes, your worship; Jowler, he was called. He trades upon the Gambia, where the prince's father lives. The young man knows him well."

"I think I know something of him too—that same Jowler. I should like to lay my hands upon him, for something else than this—a precious scamp! After all, it wouldn't do much good if we had him. No doubt, the two set their heads together in the business, and there's only one story between them.

"Humph! what are we to do for a *white* witness?" continued the magistrate, speaking rather to himself than his visitor. "That, I fear, will be a fatal difficulty. Stay! Ravener, you say, Jessuron's overseer, was at the landing of the cargo?"

"Oh, yes, your worship. That worthy took an active part in the whole transaction. It was he who stripped the prince of his clothes, and took all his jewellery away from him."

"Jewellery, too?"

"*Crambo*, yes! He had many valuable thing. Jowler kept most of his plunder aboard ship."

"A robbery! Egad, a wholesale robbery!

"Well, Captain Cubina," proceeded the custos, changing his tone to one of more business-like import, I promise you, that this shall not be passed over. I don't yet clearly see what course we may have to take. There are many difficulties in a prosecution of this kind. We'll have trouble about the testimony—especially since Mr. Jessuron is a magistrate himself. Never mind about that. Justice shall be done, even were he the highest in the land. But there can be no move made just yet. It will be a month before the assize court meets at Savannah; and that is where we must go with it. Meanwhile, not a word to any one—not a whisper of what you know!"

"I promise that, your worship."

"You must keep the Foolah where you have him. Don't, on any account, deliver him up. I'll see that you're protected in holding him. Considering the case, it's not likely the Jew will go to extremities with you. *He* has a glass house over his head, and will 'ware to throw stones —so you've not much to fear.

"And now, young man!" added the Custos, changing his tone to one that showed how friendly he could be to him who had imparted such gratifying intelligence, " if all goes well, you'll not have much difficulty in making up the hundred pounds for the purchase of your sweetheart *Remember that !*"

" Thanks, worthy custos," said Cubina, bowing gratefully; " I shall depend upon your promise."

' You may.' And now—go quietly home, and wait till I send for you. shall see my lawyer to-morrow. We may want you soon."

And Loftus Vaughan did see his lawyer on the morrow : for that was his errand to Montego Bay on the day that Smythje made his unlucky descent into the dead-wood.

CHAPTER LIV.

THE SMYTHJE ECLIPSE.

THE celebrated eclipse of Columbus, by which that shrewd navigator so advantageously deluded the simple savages of Don Christopher's Cove, is not the only one for which the island of Jamaica *should* be famous. It is my duty to introduce another : which, if not worthy of being recorded upon the page of history, deserves at least a chapter in our romance.

The eclipse in question, though, perhaps, not so important in its results as that which favoured the great world-finder, was nevertheless of considerable interest—more especially to some of the *dramatis personæ* of our tale, whose fortunes it influenced in no slight degree.

Occurring about two weeks after the arrival of the distinguished Smythje, it seemed as if the sun had specially distinguished himself for the occasion : as a sort of appropriate climax to the round of brilliant ' fetes' and entertainments, of which the lord of Montagu Castle had been the recipient. It deserves therefore, to be designated the " Smythje eclipse."

In the *finale* of this natural phenomenon, Smythje was not so fortunate as Columbus ; for, instead of rendering brighter some hopes he had hitherto held, it had served rather to darken them—like the sun itself, almost to a total extinction.

On the day before that on which the obscuration of the sun was expected to take place, the cockney had conceived a brilliant design—that of viewing the eclipse from the. top of a mountain—from the summit of the Jumbé rock !

There was something daringly original in this design ; and for that had Smythje adopted it. Kate Vaughan was to be his companion. He had asked, and, of course, obtained Mr. Vaughan's consent, and hers also, of course—for Kate had found of late, more than ever, that her father's will was to be her law.

Smythje was not without a purpose in the proposed ascent to the natural observatory of the Jumbé rock—more than one purpose was in his mind. The boldness of the idea—altogether his own—and a " dispway" of his knowledge of " astwonomy," which he intended to make, and for which he had prepared himself, could not fail to render him interesting in the eyes of the young creole—herself not much skilled in science.

But he had still another purpose—and one of a far more important character—which he had been cherishing and keeping back for some crisis occasion—just such a one as the expected eclipse was expected to offer. In that hour, when all the earth would be in *chiaro-oscuro*, as if shrouded under the pall of infinity—in that dark and solemn hour—Smythje had determined upon popping the question !

Why he had selected such a place and time—both pre-eminently sombre—must, I fear, remain a mystery. He may have been actuated in his choice by several considerations. He may have been under an impression that the poetical reputation of the place, combined with the romantic solemnity of the scene and the hour, might exercise a dissolving influence over the heart of the young creole, and incline her to an affirmative answer. Or, perhaps, *au fait* as he was to theatrical contrivances, he may have drawn his idea from something he had seen upon the stage, and chosen his climax accordingly.

With this resolve fully fixed in his mind, did Smythje await the coming of the eclipse ; an event which, by the laws of the solar system, should transpire on the following day—a little before the hour of noon. On that morning, Mr. Smythe awoke, the grand idea still uppermost in his mind. He had sufficient knowledge of astronomy to know that the sun would not play him false ; or rather the moon ; since in a solar eclipse, the planet is the principal performer. The sun was shining brightly. Not a speck could be distinguished on the azure arch of the West Indian sky. There need be no apprehension that any cloud would interfere to stay the execution either of Nature's design, or that of the enamoured Smythje. To all appearances, both were pretty certain to come off.

Some two hours before the expected contact between the limbs of the two great luminaries—in time to allow of leisurely walking—Smithje started out, of course accompanied by Miss Kate Vaughan. Attendants there were none : for the exquisite on such an occasion preferred to be alone , and had so signified—declining the sable escort which his host had provided.

The morning was one of the brightest ; and the scenes through which the path conducted Mr. Smythje and his fair companion were among the loveliest to be found in the domain of Nature.

Around the dwelling of Mount Welcome—in its gardens and parterres —the eye delighted to dwell upon a variety of vegetable forms, both indigenous and exotic—some planted for shade ; some for the beauty of their blossoms ; and others for their fruit. There could be seen the genip, the tamarind of Oriental fame, palms of several species, the native pawpaw,* and the curious trumpet-tree.† Distinguished for their floral beauties were the cordia, the oleander, and South Sea rose, the grand magnolia, and the perfumed Persian lilac.‡ Bearing luscious fruits, were the cashew, the mango, and Malay apple ; the sop, the guava, with every variety of the citron tribe, as oranges, lemons, limes, and the huge shaddock.

* Carica papaya.   † Cecropia peltata.   ‡ Melia azedarach.

Climbing the standard trunks, and twining around the branches were parasites of many species—rare and beautiful flowering plants : as the wax-like hoya carnosa, the crimson quamoclit, brassavolas, ipomeas, and other magnificent orchids.

It was a scene to stir the soul of a botanist to enthusiastic admiration ; resembling a vast botanical garden—some grand house of palms—having for its roof the azure canopy of heaven.

To the eyes of the young creole—all her life accustomed to look upon those fair vegetable forms—there was nothing in the sight of them to beget as tonishment ; and the cockney cared but little for trees. His late adventure had cured him of that inclination for a forest life ; and, in his eyes, a cabbage-palm was of no more interest than a cabbage.

Smythje, however, was not unmusical. Constant attendance at the opera had, to some extent, attuned his soul to song ; and he could not help expressing some surprise at the melody of the Western songsters —so much misrepresented and maligned.

In truth, upon that morning they appeared to be giving one of their grandest concerts. In the garden groves could be heard the clear voice of the banana-bird,* like the tones of a clarionet, mingling with the warbling tones of the blue quit.† There, too, could be seen the tiny vervain humming-bird,‡ seated upon the summit of a tall mango tree, trilling out its attenuated and fairy-like lay, with as much enthusiastic energy as if its little soul was poured forth in the song.

In the dark mountain woods could be heard other songsters—the " glass-eye merle"§ singing his rich and long-continued strain ; and, at intervals, the wild, plaintive cry of the " solitaire,"‖ uttered in sweet, but solemn notes, like the cadence chaunting of a psalm—in perfect keeping with the solitude which this singular songster affects.

Above all could be distinguished the powerful voice of the New World nightingale—the far-fame mock-bird,¶ excelling all the other music of the groves ; except when at intervals the rare May-bird** condescends to fling his melody upon the breeze, when the mock-bird himself instantly interrupts his lay, and becomes a listener !

Add to these sounds the humming of bees, the continuous " skirling" of grasshoppers, lizards, and cicadas—the metallic clucking of tree-frogs,†† the rustling of the breeze among the lanceolate leaves of the tall bamboos, and the sighing of a cascade among the distant hills—add these, and you may have some idea of the commingling of sounds that saluted the ear of Mr. Montagu Smythje, as, with his fair companion, he ascended the mountain slope.

Cheerful as were the birds and brisk the bees, Smythje appeared as cheerful and brisk as they. He was gay both in spirits and costume. Thoms had equipped him in one of his favourite suits ; and his spirits were elevated by his hopes.

These, for several days past, had been rapidly mounting higher, in the belief or fancy that Kate had been kinder. He had noticed on the part of the young creole a gravity of demeanour that had not shown itself on

---

* Icterus leucopterus. † Euphonia Jamaicus ‡ Mellisuga humilis.
§ Merula Jamaicensis. ‖ Phillogonys armillatus. ¶ See " Cassell's Natural History,"
** Turdus mustelinus. †† Hyladea. [vol. iii, p. 114]

their first acquaintance—a certain abstractedness, every day on the increase—which he, Smythje, could only explain by the supposition that she was in love. And who could she be in love with, but himself?

Thus did he interpret the altered air of Kate Vaughan; and thus did his vanity point out the cause. No wonder, then, he had come to the resolution of making a proposal, and had high hopes of receiving an affirmative answer.

It was quite true that the young creole appeared to be suffering Her gaiety was almost gone—at times, completely so—and in its place might be observed—long spells of abstraction, ending generally in sighs.

The sympathetic heart of Smythje could not permit this state of things to continue. It must be terminated. The sighs of Kate Vaughan must cease—her spirit's equanimity must be restored!

A word would accomplish all. That word should be spoken, and on that very day. So had Smythje resolved.

With this determination, he ascended the mountain slope, chattering gaily as he went—his companion walking rather silently by his side.

On arriving at the bottom of the ravine by which the path conducted to the summit, Smythje showed his courage by boldly advancing to scale the steep. He would have offered a hand to assist his fair companion; but in the climb he found full occupation for both; and in this ungallant manner was he compelled to continue the ascent.

Kate, however—who was accustomed to the path, and could possibly have given him assistance—found no difficulty in following; and in a few seconds both had arrived on the summit of the rock, and stood under the shadow of the palm.

The skeleton form, once chained to the tree, was no longer there to fray them. It had been mysteriously removed, as also a number of skulls, which a reckless dare-devil the of neighbourhood had carried up on some wild freak. The rock was untenanted by any living thing, except the solitary palm. No eye was there to see—no ear to hear the "popping of the question," save hers for whom it was intended.

Mr. Smythje consulted his repeater. They had arrived just in the nick of time. In five minutes the eclipse would commence; and the discs of the two great heavenly orbs would be in contact.

It was not this crisis, however, that Smythje had chosen for the cue to his important speech. Nor yet the moment of deepest darkness; but just when the sun should begin to reappear, and by his renewed-brightening symbolise the state of the lover's own feelings.

He had prepared some pretty things which he meant to say, by way of ushering in the declaration: how his own heart might be compared to the sun—now burning with passion—then darkened by the deep despair; and once more brightening up, with rekindled hope' at the prospect of Kate making him the happiest of "mawtals."

All these, and many other pretty speeches, a propos to the situation, he intended to make.

He had prepared them pit-a-pat the night before, and gone over them with Thoms in the morning. He had rehearsed them more than a dozen times—ending with a dress rehearsal just before starting out.

Unless the eclipse should in some way deprive him of the **use of his** tongue, there could be no danger of his breaking down.

With perfect confidence of success, the romantic Smythje restored his repeater to its fob; and, with sun-glass in hand, awaited the coming on of the eclipse.

CHAPTER LV.

A PROPOSAL POSTPONED.

SLOWLY, silently, and still unseen, stole the soft luminary of night towards her burning god—till a slight shadow on his lower limb betokened the contact.

"Thaw, it is !" said Smythje, holding the glass to his eye. "They awe just kissing, like two lovaws. How pwetty it is ! Dawn't yaw think so, fayaw Kate ?"

"Rather a distant kiss for lovers, I should say—some ninety odd millions of miles between them !"

"Haw, haw ! veway good, veway good indeed ? And in that sawt of thing, distance dawn't lend enchantment taw the view. Much bettaw to be neaw, just as yaw and I aw. Dawn't yaw thing so, fayaw Kate ?"

"That depends upon circumstances—whether the love be reciprocal."

"Wecipwocal !—yas, twoo enough—thaw is something in that."

"A great deal, I should think, Mr. Smythje. For instance, were I a man, and my sweetheart was frowning on me—as yonder moon seems to be doing with his majesty the sun—I should keep my distance, though it were ninety millions of miles."

Had Mr. Smythje at that moment only removed the glass from his eye, and turned towards *his* sweetheart, he might have read in her looks that the speech just made possessed a significance; altogether different from the interpretation which it pleased him to put upon it.

"Haw, haw ! veway pwetty of yaw, 'pon honaw. But yaw must wemembaw that yondaw moon has two faces. In that she wesembles the queetyaw called woman. Haw bwight face is tawned towards the sun and no doubt she is at this moment smiling upawn the fellaw. Haw fwowns, yaw see, awe faw us, and all the west of mankind ; thawfo' she wesembles a devoted queetyaw. Dawn't yaw think so, fayaw Kate !"

Kate was compelled to smile, and for a short moment regarded Smythje with a glance which might have been mistaken for admiration. In the analogy which the exquisite had drawn there was a scintillation of intellect—the more striking, that it was not expected from such a source. Withal, the glance was rather indicative of surprise than admiration though Smythje evidently interpreted it for the latter—his self esteem assisting him to the interpretation.   •

Before she could make reply, he repeated the interrogatory.

"Oh, yes," answered she, the smile gradually vanishing from her face ; "I can well imagine, Mr. Smythje that your simile is just. I should think that a woman who loves devotedly would not bestow her smiles on any other than him she loves; and though he were distant as yonder sun, in her heart, she would smile on him all the same."

The young creole as she spoke lowered her eyes, no longer regarding the eclipse, but as if involuntarily directing her glance downward.

"Ah, yes!" continued she, in thought, "and even if alike impossible for them ever to meet, still would her smiles be his. Ah, yes!"

For some seconds she remained silent and abstracted. Smythje attracted by the altered tone of her voice, had taken the telescope from his eye, and turned towards her.

Observing the abstracted air which he had often before remarked, he did not think of attributing it to any other cause than that which his vanity had already divined.

His sympathetic soul was ready to give way; and he was almost upon the point of departing from the programme which he had so ingeniously traced out. But the remembrance of the pretty speeches he had rehearsed with Thoms—and the thought that any deviation from the original design would deprive him of the pleasure of witnessing the effects which it must undoubtedly produce—restrained him from a premature declaration, and he remained silent.

It did not hinder him from some unspoken reflections.

"Po' queetyaw! evidently suffwing! Neithaw distance or absence make the switest impwession upon haw love—not the switest. Ba Jawvel aw feel maw than half inclined to bweak the spell, and reweive haw fwom haw miseway. But naw—it would nevaw do. Aw must wesist the temptation. A little maw suffwing can daw no harm, since the situation of the queetyaw wesemblcs the pwoverb : 'The dawkest houaw is that which is neawest the day.' Haw l haw!"

And with this fanciful similitude before his mind, the sympathetic and self-denying lover concluded his string of complacent reflections; and, returning the glass to his eye, once more occupied himself in ogling the eclipse.

The young Creole, seeing him thus engaged, withdrew to one side; and placing herself on the very edge of the cliff, stood gazing outward and onward. It was evident that the grand celestial phenomenon had no attractions for her. She cared not to look upon the sun, nor the moon, nor the stars, that would soon be visible in the fast darkening sky. Her eyes, like her thoughts, were turned upon the earth; and as the penumbra began to cast its purple shadow over the fair face of Nature, so could a cloud be seen overspreading her beautiful countenance.

There was now deep silence below and around. In a few seconds of time a complete change had taken place. The utterings of the forest were no longer heard. The birds had suddenly ceased their songs, and if their voices came up at intervals, it was in screams and cries that denoted fear. Insects and reptiles had become silent, under the influence of the like alarm. The more melancholy sounds alone continued—the sighing of the trees, and the sough of the distant waterfall.

This transformation reminded Kate Vaughan of the change which had taken place in her heart. Almost equally rapid had it been—the result of only a few days, or perhaps only hours: for the once gay girl had become, of late, habitually grave and taciturn. Well might she compare

her thoughts *t.* the forest sounds. The cheerful and musical were gone
—those that were melancholy alone remained !

For this change there was a cause, not very different from that which
Smythje had divined. He was right in assigning it to that passion—the
most powerful of a woman's heart.

Only as to the object of that passion did Mr. Smythje labour under a
misconception. His self-conceit had guided him to a very erroneous
conjecture. Could he have devined the thoughts, at that moment passing in the mind of his fair companion, it would have completely cured
him of the misapprehension that he was himself the maker of that melancholy.

The mansion of Mount Welcome was in sight, gaily glittering among
its gorgeous groves. It was not upon it that the eyes of Kate Vaughan
were bent ; but upon a sombre pile, shadowed by great cotton trees, that
lay in the adjoining valley. Her heart was with her eyes.

"Happy Valley!" soliloquised she, her thoughts occasionally escaping
in low murmurs from her lips. "Happy for *him*, no doubt! There has
he found a welcome and a home, denied him by those whose duty it was
to have offered both. There has he found hospitality among strangers ;
and there, too——

The young girl paused, as if unwilling to give words to the thought
that had shaped itself in her mind.

"No," continued she, unable to avoid the painful reflection ; "I need
not shut my eyes upon the truth. It is true what I have been told—very
true, I am sure. There has he found one to whom he has given his
heart!"

A sigh of deep anguish succeeded the thought.

"Ah!" she exclaimed, resuming the sad soliloquy ; "he promised me a
strong arm and a stout heart, if I should ever need them. Ah, me !
promise now bitter to be remembered—no longer possible to be kept ;
And the ribbon he was to prize so highly—which gave me such joy as
he said it ? Only another promise broken ! Poor little souvenir ! no
doubt, long ere this, cast aside and forgotten ! ah, me !"

Again the sigh interrupted the soliloquy. After a time it proceeded:—

"'We may never meet more !' These were among his last words.
Alas ! too prophetic ! Better, now, we never should. Better this, than
to meet him—with her by his side—Judith Jessuron—his wife—his wife
—oh!"

The last exclamation was uttered aloud, and with an undisguised accent
of anguish.

Smythje heard it, and started as he did so—letting the sun-glass fall
'rom his fingers.

Looking around, he perceived his companion standing apart—unheeding as she was unheeded—with head slightly drooping, and eyes turned
downward upon the rock—her face still bearing the expression of profound anguish which her thoughts had called forth.

The heart of Smythje melted within him. He knew her complaint—
he knew its cure. The remedy was in his hands. Was it right any
longer to withhold it ? A word from him, and that sad face would be
instantly suffused with smiles ! Should that word be spoken or postponed ?

Spoken! prompted humanity. Spoken! echoed Smythje's sympathetic heart. Yes ! Perish the cue and the climax! Perish the fine speech and the rehearsal with Thoms—perish everything to " welieve the deaw queetyaw fwom the agony she is suffawing !"

With this noble resolve, the confident lover stopped up to the side of his beloved, leaving a distance of some three feet between them. His movements were those of a man about entering upon the performance of some ceremonial of the grandest importance and solemnity; and to Mr Smythje such, in reality, it was.

The look of wild surprise, with which the young creole regarded them, neither deterred him from proceeding, nor in any wise interfered with the air of solemn gravity which his countenance had all at once assumed.

Bending one knee down upon the rock—where he had dropped the glass—and placing his left hand over the region of his heart, while with the right he raised his hat some six inches above his perfumed head, there and then he was about to unburthen himself of that speech studied for the occasion—committed to Smythje's memory and more than a dozen times already delivered in the hearing of Thoms—there and then, was he on the eve of offering to Kate Vaughan his hand, his heart—his whole love and estate—when just at this formidable crisis, the head and shoulders of a man appeared above the edge of the rock, and behind, a black plumed beaver hat, shadowing the face of a beautiful woman.

Herbert Vaughan!—Judith Jessuron!

CHAPTER LVI.

THE OBSCURATION.

" INTAWUPTED !" exclaimed Smythje, briskly restoring his person to its eiect position. " What an infawnal baw!" he continued, drawing out his handkerchief, and dusting the knee on which he had been kneeling. " Aw wondaw who are the intwoodaws ! Aw! ah ! It's the young fellaw, yaw cousin ? Shawly it is ; and—a—a pwetty girl with him—a doosed pwetty girl, ba Jawve !"

A satirical titter, loud enough to be termed a laugh, was heard issuing from between the white teeth of the Jewess. It somewhat discomfited Smythje, since he knew that the satire could only be pointed at the ridiculous *tableau* just broken up, and of which he had himself been the conspicuous figure. His *sang-froid*, however, did not quite forsake him, for the cockney possessed considerable presence of mind—the offspring of an infinite superciliousness. This at the moment came to his relief, bringing with it an idea, that promised to rescue him from his embarrassment. The spy-glass lying upon the rock suggested the idea.

· Dropping upon his knee—in an attitude similar to that from which he had just arisen—he took up the telescope, and once more rising to his feet, presented it to Kate Vaughan, as she stood bent and blushing.

The *ruse* was well intended, and not badly executed ; but Mr. Smythje had to deal with one as cunning as himself. It was of no use endeavour ing to throw dust in the keen, quick eyes of Judith Jessuron, and the laugh was repeated, only in a louder and more quizzical tone.

It ended in Smythje himself joining in the laughter, which, under the circumstances, was the very best course he could have pursued.

Notwithstanding the absurdity of the situation, Herbert did not seem to share in his companion's mirth. On the contrary, a shadow was visible upon his brow—not that produced by the gradually deepening twilight of the eclipse—but one that had spread suddenly over his face at sight of the kneeling Smythje.

"Miss Vaughan!" pronounced the Jewess, springing lightly upon the rock, and, with a nod of recognition, advancing towards the young creole and her companion; "an unexpected pleasure this! I hope we are not intruding?"

"Not at all—nothing of the sawt, aw ashaw yaw," replied Smythje, with one of his profoundest bows.

"Mr. Smythje—Miss Jessuron," interposed Kate, performing the duty of introduction with dignified but courteous politeness.

"We have climbed up to view this eclipse," continued Judith. "The same errand as yourselves, I presume?" added she, with a glance of quizzical malignity directed towards Kate.

"Aw, 'yas! sawtinly!" stammered out Smythje, as if slightly confused by the inuendo of the interrogative. "That is pwecisely the pawpose which bwought us heaw—to view this cewestial phenomenon fwom the Jumbé Rock. A spwendid obserwatowy it is, ba Jawve!"

"You have had the advantage of us," rejoined Judith. "I feared we should arrive too late. Perhaps, we are soon enough?"

The satirical tone and glance were reiterated.

Perhaps Kate Vaughan did not perceive the meaning of this ambiguous interrogatory, though addressed to her even more pointedly than the former; at all events, she did not reply to it. Her eyes and thoughts were elsewhere.

"Quite in time, Miss Jessuwon!" answered Smythje. "The ekwipse is fawst assuming a most intewesting phase. In a few minutes the sun will be in penumbwa. If yaw will step this way, yaw may get a bettaw standing-place. Pawmit me to offaw yaw the tewescope? Aw, haw!" continued he, addressing himself to Herbert. who had just come forward, " aw, how do, ma fwend? Happy to have the pwesyaw of meeting you again."

As he said this, he held out his hand, with a single finger projecting beyond the others.

Herbert, though declining the proffered finger, returned the salutation with sufficient courtesy; and Smythje, turning aside to attend upon Judith, escorted her to that edge of the platform facing towards the eclipse.

By this withdrawal—perhaps little regretted by either of the cousins— they were left comparatively alone.

A bow, somewhat stiff and formal, was the only salutation that had yet passed between them; and, even for some seconds after the others had gone aside, they remained without speaking to each other.

Herbert was the first to break the embarrassing silence,

" Miss Vaughan !" said he, endeavouring to conceal the emotion which, however, his trembling voice betrayed, " I fear our presence here will be considered an intrusion ? I would have retired, but that my companion willed it otherwise."

" *Miss* Vaughan !" mentally repeated the young creole, as the phrase fell strangely upon her ear, prompting her, perhaps, to a very different rejoinder from that she would otherwise have made.

" Since you could not follow your *own* inclination, perhaps it was wiser for you to remain. Your presence here, so far as I am concerned, is no intrusion, I assure you. As for *my* companion, he appears satisfied enough, does he not ?"

The rapid exchange of words, with an occasional cachinnation, heard from the other side of the rock, told that a gay conversation was going on between Smythje and the Jewess.

" I regret that our arrival should• have led even to your temporary separation. Shall I take Mr. Smythje's place, and permit him to rejoin you ?"

The reply was calculated to widen the breach between the two cousins.

It was indebted for its character to the interpretation which Herbert had placed upon Kate's last interrogatory.

" Certainly, if it would be more agreeable to you to do so," retorted Kate, in a tone of defiant bitterness.

Here a pause occurred in the conversation, which from the first had been carried on—defiance against defiance. It was Herbert's turn to speak ; but the challenge conveyed in Kate's last words placed him in a position where it was not easy to make an appropriate rejoinder, and he remained silent.

It was now the crisis of the eclipse—the moment of deepest darkness. The sun's disc had become completely obscured by the opaque orb of the night ; and the earth lay lurid under the sombre shadow. Stars appeared in the sky, to show that the universe still existed ; and those voices of the forest, heard only in nocturnal hours, came pealing up to the summit of the rock—a testimony that terrestrial nature was not yet extinct.

It was equally a crisis between two loving hearts. Though standing near, those wild words had outlawed them from each other, far more than if ten thousand miles extended between them. The darkness without was nought to the darkness within. In the sky there were stars to delight the eye—from the forest came sounds to solace the soul ; but no star illumined the horizon of their hearts with its ray of hope—no sound of joy cheered the silent gloom that bitterly embraced them.

For some minutes not a word was exchanged between the cousins ; nor spoke either to those who were their sharers in the spectacle. These, too, were silent. The solemnity of the scene had made its impression upon all ; and, against the dark background of the sky, the figures of all four appeared in sombre *sil-houette*—motionless as the rock on which they stood.

Thus for some minutes they stood, without exchanging word or thought. Side by side they were, so near and s. silent, that each might have heard the breathing of the other.

The situation was one of painful embarrassment, and might have been still more so, but for the eclipse; which, just then con.plete, shrouded both in the deep obscurity of its shadow, and hindered them from observing one another

Only for a short while did the darkness continue ; the eclipse soon re-assuming the character of a penumbra.

One by one the stars disappeared from the canopy of the sky—now hastening to recover its azure hue. The creatures of darkness, wonder ing at the premature return of day, sank cowering into a terrified silence and the god of the heavens, coming forth triumphantly from the cloud that had for a short while concealed him, once more poured his effulgence upon the earth.

The re-dawning of the light showed the cousins still standing in the same relative position —unchanged even as to their attitudes.

During the interval of darkness Herbert had neither stirred nor spoken ; and after the harsh rejoinder to which, in the bitterness of her pique, the young Creole had given words, it was not her place to continue the conversation.

Pained though Herbert was by his cousin's reply, he nevertheless remembered his indebtedness to her—the vows he had made—the proud proffer at parting. Was he now to repudiate the debt of gratitude, and prove faithless to his promise ? Was he to pluck from his breast that silken *souvenir*, still sheltering there, though in secret and unseen ?

True, it was but the memorial of an act of friendship—of mere cousinly kindness. He had never had reason to regard it in any other light ; and now, more than ever, was he sure it had no higher signification.

She had never said she loved him—never said a word that could give him the right to reproach her. On her side there was no repudiation, since there had been no compromise. It was unjust to condemn her—cruel to defy her, as he had done.

That she loved another—was that a crime.

Herbert now knew that she loved another—was sure of it, as that he stood upon the Jumbé Rock. That interrupted *tableau* had left him no loop to hang a doubt on. The relative position of the parties proclaimed the purpose—a proposal.

The kneeling lover may not have obtained his answer ; but who could doubt what that answer was to have been ? The situation itself declared consent.

Bitter as were these reflections, Herbert made an effort to subdue them. He resolved, if possible, to stifle his spleen ; and, upon the ruin of his hopes, restore that relationship—the only one that could now exist between himself and his cousin—friendship.

With a superhuman effort he succeeded ; and this triumph of virtue over spite, backed by the strongest inclinings of the heart, for a moment solaced his spirit, and rendered it calmer.

Alas ! that such triumph can be only temporary. The struggle upon which he was entering, was one in which no man has ever succeeded. Love undenied, may end in friendship ; but love thwarted or unreciprocated, never !

"Now, where the swift Rhone cleaves his way between
Heights, that appear as lovers who have parted
In hate, whose mining depths so intervene,
That they can meet no more, though broken hearted;
Though in their souls, which thus each other thwarted,
Love was the very root of the fond rage
Which blighted their life's bloom——"

Herbert Vaughan was perhaps too young—too inexperienced in the affairs of the heart—to have ever realised the sentiments so expressed; else would he have desisted from his idle attempt, and surrendered himself at once to the despair that was certain to succeed it.

Innocent—perhaps happily so—of the knowledge of these recondite truths, he yeilded to the nobler resolve—ignorant of the utter impracticability of its execution.

CHAPTER LVII.

AN ENCOUNTER OF EYES.

While Herbert Vaughan was making these reflections, the light began to re-dawn—gradually, as it were, raising the veil from the face of his cousin. He could not resist turning to gaze upon it.

During the interval of obscurity, a change had passed over the countenance of the young girl, both in its hue and expression. Herbert noticed the change. It even startled him. Before, and during the unhappy dialogue, he had looked upon a flushed cheek, a fiery eye, an air proud and haughty, with all the indices of defiant indifference.

All were gone. Kate's eyes still sparkled, but with a milder light; a uniform pallor overspread her cheeks, as if the eclipse had robbed them of their roses; and the proud air had entirely disappeared, replaced by an expression of sadness, or rather of pain.

Withall, the face was lovely as ever—lovelier, thought Herbert.

Why that sudden transformation? What had caused it? Whence sprang that painful thought that was betraying itself in the pale cheek and lips compressed and quivering? Was it the happiness of another that was making that misery? Smythje seemed happy—very happy, to judge by his oft-repeated "haw! haw!"

Was this the cause of that expression of extreme sadness?

So did Herbert interpret it.

Making a fresh effort to subdue within himself the same spirit which he believed to be actuating his cousin, he remained silent—though unable to withdraw his glance from that lorn but lovely face.

While still gazing upon it, a sigh escaped him. It could scarce have been heard by her who stood nearest; nor hers by him: for she also sighed, and at the same instant of time! Perhaps both were moved by some secret sympathetic instinct?

Herbert had succeeded in obtaining another momentary triumph over his emotions: and was once more on the eve of uttering words of friendship, when the young girl looked up and reciprocated his gaze. It was the first time during the interview their eyes had met: for up to that moment Kate had only regarded her cousin with furtive glances.

For some seconds they stood face to face—each gazing into the eyes of the other, as if both were the victims of some irresistible fascination. Not a word passed between them—their very breathing was stilled. Both seemed to consider the time too important for speech: for they were seeking in one another's eyes—those faithful mirrors of the soul—those truest interpreters of the heart—the solution of that, the most interesting enigma of their existence.

This silent interrogation was instinctive as mutual—uncorrupted by a shadow of coquetry. It was bold and reckless as innocence itself—unding outward observation. What cared they for the eclipse? for the sun, or the moon, or the waning stars? What for the universe itself? Less—far less for those human forms that chanced to be so near them!

Drew they gratification from that mutual gaze? They must—else why had they continued it?

Not for long : not for long were they allowed. An eye was upon them—the eye of that beautiful demon.

Ah! fair Judith, thy flirtation has proved a failure. The *ruse* has recoiled upon thyself!

The golden sunlight once more fell upon the Jumbé rock, revealing the forms of four individuals—all youthful—all in love, though two only were beloved!

The returning light brought no joy to Judith Jessuron. It revealed to her that glance of mutual fascination which, with a quick, sharp cry, she had interrupted.

A bitter embarrassment seemed all at once to have seized upon her proud spirit, and dragged it into the dust.

Skilled in the silent language of the eyes, she had read in those of Herbert Vaughan, as he bent them upon his cousin, an expression that stung her, even to the utterance of a scream!

From that moment the flirtation with Smythje ceased ; and the cockney exquisite was forsaken in the most unceremonious manner—left to continue his telescopic observations alone.

The conversation was no longer *dos y dos*, but at once changed to a *trio*, and finally restored to its original *quartette* form—soon, however, to be broken up by an abrupt separation of the parties.

The Jewess was the first to propose departure—the first to make it. She descended from the Jumbé rock in a less lively mood than that in which she had climbed up to it ; inwardly anathematising the eclipse, and the fortune that had guided her to the choice of such an ill-starred observatory.

Herbert Vaughan was, of course, compelled to accompany her. Gladly would the young man have continued that silent duet of the eyes—glad would he have been to stay longer on the summit ; but the partner of the excursion was, at least, in one sense, his *mistress;* and something more than mere courtesy required compliance with her wishes.

A certain air of hesitancy, as he stepped down from the rock, betrayed the irksomeness he experienced at that abrupt departure.

Perhaps, had their interview been prolonged, the cousins might have separated with a better understanding of each other, than was expressed in that cold, ceremonious adieu with which they parted.

Smythje and Kate Vaughan wero once more alone upon the summit of the rock; and the supercilious lover was now free to continue the declaration.

One might suppose that he would have instantly dropped back upon his knees, and finished the performance so vexatiously interrupted.

Not so, however. The spirit of Smythje's dream seemed equally to have undergone a change ; as if he, too, had seen something.

His air of high confidence had departed, as also the climax on which he had counted : for the sun's disc was now quite clear of the eclipse, and the pretty speeches, intended for an anterior time, would now have been pointless and inappropriate.

Whether it was this that influenced him, or a presentiment that the offer of his heart and hand might just then stand some chance of a rejection, can never be known : since Smythje, who alone could divulge it, has left no record of the reason.

Certain it is, however, that the proposal did not take place on the Jumbé rock on the day of the eclipse ; but was postponed, sine die, to some future occasion.

CHAPTER LVIII.

THE SMYTHJE BALL.

As if the eclipse had not been a sufficient climax to the round of 'fétes' got up for the express amusement of Mr. Smythje, only a few days—or, rather, nights—after, still another was inaugurated, to do honour to this young British lion.

Unlike the eclipse, it was a terrestrial phenomenon—one of the most popular of sublunary entertainments—a ball—a complimentary ball—Mr. Smythje the recipient of the compliment.

Montego Bay was to be the place ; which, notwithstanding its provinciality, had long been celebrated for its brilliant assemblies—from the time that fandangoes were danced by the old Spanish pork-butchers, down to that hour when Mr. Montagu Smythje had condescended to honour its salons by the introduction of some very fashionable steps from the world's metropolis.

The ball was to be a grand affair—one of the grandest ever given in the Bay—and all Planterdom was expected to be present.

Of course, Kate Vaughan would be there; and so, too, the Custos himself.

Mr. Smythje would be the hero of the night; and, as such, surrounded by the fairest of the fair—hedged in by a galaxy of beautiful belles, and beset by an army of match-making parents, all seeking success with as much eagerness as Loftus Vaughan himself.

Under these circumstances, it would be but simple prudence that Kate should be there to look after him : for the worthy Custos was not unacquainted with the adage, that " The sweetest smelling flower is that nearest the nose."

Mr. Vaughan would have rejoiced at the opportunity thus offered, of letting all the *monde* of Jamaica know the relationship in which he stood, and was likely to stand, to the distinguished individual to whom the entertainment was dedicated. He had no doubt but that Kate would be chosen as the conspicuous partner: for well knew he the condition of Mr. Smythje's mind upon that subject. To him the latter had made no secret of his affections ; and the cunning Custos, who had been all along warily watching the development of the passion, now knew to a certainty that the heart of Montagu's lord was not only smitten with his daughter, but was irretrievably lost—so far as such a heart could suffer love's perdition.

No doubt, then, Mr. Vaughan would have looked forward to the Smythje ball with pleasant anticipation—as likely to afford him a social triumph—but for a little circumstance that had lately come to his knowledge. It was the incident which had transpired on the 'Jumbé Rock'—the meeting between his daughter and nephew on the day of the eclipse.

The Custos had been the more particular in obtaining the details of that interview from his presumptive son-in-law, on account of a suspicion that had arisen in his mind, as to the inclinings of his daughter's heart. Something she had said—during the first days after Herbert's *brusque* dismissal from Mount Welcome—some sympathetic expression she had made use of—unguarded and overheard, had given rise to this suspicion of her father.

He was sufficiently annoyed about Kate having met Herbert on the 'Jumbé Rock'; and believed it quite possible that the latter had come there in the hope of encountering his cousin.

In Mount Welcome the name of Herbert Vaughan was no longer heard. Even Kate—whether it was that she had grown more sage—for she had been chided more than once for introducing it into the conversation—or whether she had ceased to think of him—even she never pronounced his name.

For all that, Mr. Vaughan was still vexed with some lingering suspicion that in that direction lurked danger ; and this determined him to prevent, as far as possible, any further interview between his daughter and nephew.

After the encounter on the 'Jumbé Rock,' he had taken his daughter to task upon this subject ; and using the full stretch of parental authority compelled her to a solemn promise, that she was not again to speak to her cousin, nor even acknowledge his presence !

It was a hard promise for the poor girl to make. Perhaps it would have been still harder, had she known Herbert's disposition towards her ?

There can be no doubt that her father, in extracting this promise, had in view the event about to take place—the grand Smythje ball. There an encounter between the cousins was not only possible, but probable ; so much so as to render Mr. Vaughan apprehensive. Judith Jessuron was sure to be present—perhaps the Jew himself; and Herbert, of course.

The nephew was now cordially disliked. Stung by the defiant speeches which the young man had made on the day of his arrival, his uncle even detested him; for the proud planter was himself too poor in spirit to admire this quality in any one else.

The Custos had heard all about the hospitality which his neighbour was extending to Herbert, and the kindness which the patron was lavishing upon his *protege*. Though not a little mystified by what was going on, he availed himself of the ordinary explanation—that it was done to vex himself; and, if so, the stratagem of the Jew was proving perfectly successful : for vexed was Mr. Vaughan to his very heart's core.

The night of the Smythje ball came round in due course. The grand ball-room of the Bay was decorated as became the occasion. Flags, festoons, and devices were hung around the walls ; and over the doorway a large transparency—supported by the loyal emblems of the Union Jack and banner of St. George, and surmounted by the colonial colours—proclaimed, in letters of eighteen inches diameter :— " WELCOME TO SMYTHJE !"

The hour arrived ; the band shortly after ; close followed by strings of carriages of every kind current in the island, containing scores—ay, hundreds of dancers. Twenty miles was nothing to go to a Jamaica ball. Mount Welcome, though more than ten (for Quashie's estimate of " fo' mile" was far wide of the mark) was near, compared with the distances which some of the dancers travelled to be present at the Smythje ball.

The grand barouche of Loftus Vaughan arrived with the rest, only fashionably behind time, bringing the Custos himself, his truly beautiful daughter, but, above all—as before all perhaps should have been mentioned—the hero of the night.

" WELCOME TO SMYTHJE !"

How his proud heart swelled in triumph under the magnificent ruffles of his shirt, as he caught sight of the flattering phrase! How conquering his smile, as he turned towards Kate Vaughan, to note the effect which the transparency could not fail to produce !

" Welcome to Smythje !" pealed from a hundred pair of lips as the carriage drove up to the door ; and then a loud cheer followed the words of greeting ; and then the distinguished stranger was ushered into the ball-room ; and, after remaining for a few moments in a conspicuous position—the cynosure of at least two hundred pair of eyes—the great man set the example by pairing off with a partner.

The band struck up, and the dancing began.

It need scarce be said who was Smythje's first partner. Kate Vaughan, of course. The Custos had taken care of that.

Smythje looked superb. Thoms had been at him all the afternoon His hay-coloured hair was in full curl—his whiskers in amplest bush—his moustache crimped spirally at the points ; and his cheek pinked with just the slightest tinting of vermilion.

His dress was that of a ball-room ' élégant' of the first water. A claret-coloured coat, lined through and through with white satin ; a vest of the same material as the lining of the coat, but richly embroidered with cord of gold ; breeches also of white satin ; spotless stockings of spun silk : and patent pumps with gold buckles. A white cravat around his neck, and a black crush-hat under his arm, completed his *costume du bal*—all perfectly ' en régle' according to the fashion of the time.

Remembering what has already been insinuated about Mr. Smythje's legs, this full dress might be supposed to have submitted his weak points to exposure. Not so, however ; Thoms had taken care to guard against

188 THE SMYTHJE BALL.

that; for both the small clothes and silk stockings were provided with padding underneath; and Smythje sported a pair of thighs, with calves to match, as large and rotund as the best-limbed man in the room.

This tendency towards elephantiasis might have interfered with his dancing, had he been an ordinary practitioner of the Terpsichorean art. But he was not. On the contrary, he was so perfectly *up* in every species of ball-room saltation, that he could, with grace, have gone through a waltz in the snow-boots of a Samoeid.

It would have been a disgrace indeed not to have danced well with such a partner; for the young creole, like all of her country and race, was a skilled and graceful dancer. In her simple dress of white silk—the outlines of her fine figure unbroken by the ungainly angles of corset or crinoline—she appeared the personification of that divine idea—the poetry of motion—by the Greeks termed Terpsichore—or rather might she have been likened to the goddess whom Terpsichore had taught to dance.

When the waltz came on in which Kate Vaughan had again the distinction to stand up with Smythje—and a splendid couple they appeared—

" So stately his form, and so lovely her face,
That never a hall such a galliard did grace."

There may have been finer forms on the floor than that of Mr. Smythje Acknowledged. But a lovelier face than his partner's there was not in the room.

And yet there were fair faces, too. Ay, many; and among the fairest that of Judith Jessuron.

Arrived a little late, the Jewess had not appeared in the first set. In the waltz she was conspicuous : not from her dress of rich purple velvet—not from the splendid tiara of pearls that glistened against the background of her glossy, raven hair—not from the dazzling whiteness of her teeth, that gleamed between lips like curved and parted rose leaves—not from the damask tinting of her cheeks; nor the liquid light that flashed incessantly from the black, Israelitish eyes—not from any of these was she conspicuous; but from all combined into one, and composing a grand and imperious picture.

It was a picture upon which more than one eye gazed with admiration; and more than one continued to gaze.

The partner of Judith was not unworthy to embrace such beauty. She was in the arms of a young man a stranger to the most in the room; but the glances bestowed upon him by bright eyes—some interrogative, some furtive, some openly admiring—promised him an easy introduction to any one he might fancy to know.

Not that this stranger appeared to be conceitedly conscious of the graces which nature had so lavishly bestowed upon him; or even sensible of the good fortune that had given him such a partner.

On the contrary, he was dancing with despondency in his look and a cloud upon his brow, that even the exciting whirl of the waltz was failing to dissipate.

The partner of Judith Jessuron was Herbert Vaughan.

*   *   *   *   *   *   *

A ball-room may be likened to a kaleidoscope—the personages are the same, their relative positions constantly changing. Design it or not, either during the dance or the interregnum—one time or another—you will find yourself face to face, or side by side, with every individual in the room.

So in the ball-room of Montego Bay came face to face two sets of waltzers—Smythje and Kate, Herbert and Judith.

The situation arose, as they were resting from the dizzy whirl of a waltz.

Smythje, flattening the opera-hat over his bosom, bent profoundly towards the floor—Judith, with an imperious sweep, returned the salutation \ —Herbert bowed to his cousin, with a half-doubting, half-appealing glance; but the nod received in return was so slight, so distant, that even the keen-eyed Custos, closely watching every movement of the quartette, failed to perceive it!

Poor Kate! She knew that the paternal eye, severely set, was upon her. She remembered that painful promise.

Not a word passed between the parties. Scarce a moment stood they together. Herbert, stung by Kate's salutation—unexpectedly cold, almost insultingly distant—warped his arm around the waist of his willing partner, and spun off through the unobservant crowd.

Though often again upon that same night Smythje and Kate, Herbert and the Jewess were respectively partners—so often as to lead to general observation—never again did the four stand *vis-a-vis* or side by side. Whenever chance threatened to bring them together, design, or something like it, stepped in to thwart the approximation!

CHAPTER LIX.

LOST AND WON.

Almost all the night did Herbert dance with the Jewess—no longer with despondency in his look, but with the semblance of a gay and reckless joy. Never had Judith received from the young Englishman such ardent attention; and for the first time since their introduction to each other, did she feel conscious of something like a correspondence to her own fierce love. For the moment her proud, cruel heart became dissolved to a true feminine tenderness; and in the spiral undulations of the waltz, as she coiled round the robust form of her partner, her cheek rested upon his shoulder, as if laid there to expire in the agony of an exquisite bliss.

She stayed not to question the cause of Herbert's devotedness. Her own heart, blinded by love, and yearning for reciprocity, threw open its portals to receive the passion without challenge or scrutiny—without knowing whether it was real, or only apparent.

A wild anguish would she have experienced at that moment, could she have divined what was passing in Herbert's bosom. Little did she suspect that his devotedness to her was only a demonstration intended to

act upon another. Little dreamt she that real love for another was the
cause and origin of that counterfeit that was deceiving herself. Happy
for her heart's peace she knew not this.

Herbert alone knew this. As the kaleidoscope evolved the dazzling
dancers one after another, often did the face of Kate Vaughan flit before
the eyes of her cousin, and his before her eyes. On such occasions, the
glance hastily exchanged was one of defiant indifference ; for both were
playing at piques ! The cold salutation had given *him* the cue, ignorant
as he was of its cause. *She* had begun the game only little later— on observing the attitude of extreme contentment which Herbert had assumed
towards his companion. She knew not that it was studied. Her skill in
coquetry, although sufficient for the pretence of indifference, was not
deep enough to discern it in him ; and both were now behaving, as if
each believed the love of the other beyond all hope.

Before abandoning the ball-room, this belief—erroneous as it might be
on both sides—received further confirmation. A circumstance arose that
strengthened it to a full and perfect conviction.

From the gossip of a crowded ball-room many a secret may be learnt.
In those late hours, when the supper champagne has untied the tongue,
and dancers begin to fancy each other deaf, he who silently threads his
way, or stands stiff among the crowd, may catch many a sentence not intended to be over-heard, and often least of all by himself. Many an involuntary eaves-dropper has fallen into this catastrophe. At least two in-
stances occurred at the Smythje ball; and to the two individuals in
whom, perhaps, we are most interested—Herbert and Kate Vaughan.

Herbert was for a moment alone. Judith, not that she had tired of
her partner, but perhaps only to save appearances, was dancing with
another. It was not Smythje, whom all the evening she had studiously
avoided. She remembered the incident on the Jumbé rock ; and feared
that dancing with him might conduct to a similar disposition of the partners, as that which had occurred on the day of the eclipse.

It was not flirtation in any way. On that night Judith had no need.
Confident in her success with Herbert, she was contented ; and cared
not to do anything that might hazard a rupture of the blissful chain she
believed she had woven around him.

Herbert was standing alone in the crowd. Two young planters were
near him engaged in conversation. They had mixed their liquor and
therefore talked loud.

Herbert could not help hearing what they talked of ; and, having
heard could not help heeding it. He was interested in the subject
though not from its singularity ; for it was the common topic of the ball-
room, and had been throughout the night. The theme was Smythje ;
and coupled with this name was that of Kate Vaughan.

On hearing these names. Herbert was no longer an involuntary listener. He strained his ears to catch every word. He had not heard the
beginning of the dialogue, but the introduction was easily inferred.

" When is it to come off?" inquired the least knowing of the planters,
from him who was imparting the information.

" No time fixed yet—at least, none has been mentioned. Soon, I suppose."

"There'll be a grand spread upon the occasion—breakfast, dinner, supper, and ball, no doubt?"

"Sure to be all that. The Custos is not the man to let the ceremony pass without all the 'eclat.' "

"Honeymoon tour afterwards?"

"Of course. He takes her to London. I believe they are to reside there. Mr. Smythje don't much relish our colonial life: he misses the opera. A pity: since it'll make one beautiful woman less in the island!"

"Well, all I've got to say is, that Loff Vaughan has sold his nigger well."

"Oh, for shame! to use such a word when speaking of the beautiful—. the accomplished Kate! Come, Thorndyke! I'm shocked at you."

Thorndyke, by the expression, had hazarded the punching of his head —not by his companion, but by a stranger who stood near.

Herbert curbed his indignation. Kate cared not for him! Perhaps she would not have accepted him even as her champion?

Almost at that same moment she, too, was listening to a dialogue painfully analagous. Smythje could not dance all the night with her. Too many claimed the honour of his partnership; and for a set or two she had been forsaken by him—left under the guardianship of the watchful Custos.

"Who can he be?" inquired one of two gentle gossips within ear-shot of Kate.

"A young Englishman, I have heard: a relative of the Vaughans of Mount Welcome; though, for some reason, not acknowledged by the Custos."

"That bold girl appears willing enough to acknowledge him. Who is she?"

"A Miss Jessuron. She is the daughter of the old Jew penn-keeper, who used to deal largely in blacks."

"Faugh! she is behaving as if she belonged to a——"

The last word was whispered, and Kate did not hear it.

"True enough!" asserted the other; "but, as they are engaged, that, I suppose, is nobody's business but their own. He's a stranger in the island; and don't know much about certain people's position I suppose. A pity! He seems a nice sort of young fellow; but as he makes his bed so let him lie. Ha! ha! If report speaks true of Miss Judith Jessuron, he'll find no bed of roses there. Ha! ha! ha!"

What causes merriment to one may make another miserable. That was true of the words last spoken. From the speaker and her companion they elicited a laugh—from Kate Vaughan they drew a sigh, deep and sad.

She left the ball with a bleeding heart.

"Lost! lost for ever!" murmured she, as she laid her head upon a sleepless pillow.

"Won!" triumphantly exclaimed Judith Jessuron, flinging her majestic form on a couch. "Herbert Vaughan is mine!"

"Lost! lost for ever!" soliloquised Herbert, as he closed the door of his solitary sleeping-room.

"Won!" cried the victorious Smythje, entering his elegant bed-chamber, and, in the fervour of his enthusiasm, dropping his metropolitan *patois*. "Kate Vaughan is mine!"

———

CHAPTER LX.

AFTER THE BALL.

THE time was rapidly drawing nigh when the ambitious scheme of the Custos Vaughan was either to be crowned with success, or end in failure. Of the latter he had little apprehension. Though Smythje, having lost the opportunity of the eclipse, had not yet declared himself, Mr. Vaughan knew it was his intention to do so on an early occasion. Indeed, the declaration was only postponed by the advice of the Custos himself, whose counsel had been sought by his intended son-in-law.

Not that Mr. Vaughan had any fear of Kate giving a negative answer. The stern father knew that he had his daughter too well in hand for that. His wish would be her will—on that point was he determined; and it was less the fear of a refusal than some other circumstances that had hindered him from bringing the matter to a crisis.

As for Smythje, he never dreamt of a rejection. Kate's behaviour at the ball had confirmed him in the belief that she was entirely his own, and that without him her future existence would be one of misery. Her pale cheek, and sad, thoughtful air, as she appeared next morning at the breakfast-table, told him too plainly that she would never be happy under any other name than that of Mrs. Smythje.

Again, upon that morning, it occurred to him that the proposal should be made. It would be an appropriate *finale* to the 'féte' of the preceding night.

His brow still glowing with the laurels that had bedecked it, like a second Antony he would approach his Cleopatra, triumphantly irresistible.

After breakfast, Mr. Smythje drew the Custos into a corner, and once more expressed his solicitude to become his son-in-law.

Whether, because Kate's behaviour at the ball had also impressed Mr. Vaughan with the appropriateness of the time, or for some other reason, Smythje found him agreeable. Only first, the father desired to have an interview with his daughter, in order to prepare her for the distinguished honour of which she was so soon to be the recipient.

Kate had gone out into the kiosk. There Mr. Vaughan sought her, to bring about the proposed preliminary interview. Smythje also stepped into the garden; but, instead of going near the summer-house, he sauntered along the walks at a distance, occasionally plucking a flower, or chasing the butterflies, bright and gay as his own thoughts.

Kate's countenance still preserved the air of melancholy that had clouded it all the morning; and the approach of the Custos did nothing to dissipate it. On the contrary, its shadows became deeper, as if the ponderous presence of her father, coming between her and the sun, was about to shut out the little light left shining in her heart.

From what she had heard that morning, she presumed that the time had arrived when she must either submit to the wishes of her father, and resign herself to an unhappy fate ; or, by the disobedience, brave his anger, and perhaps—she knew not what.

She only knew that she did not like Mr. Smythje, and never could. She did not hate the man—she did not detest him. Her feeling towards him was that of indifference, slightly tinctured with contempt. Harmless she deemed him ; and, no doubt, a harmless husband he would make ; but that was not the sort to suit the taste of the young creole. Far different was the hero of her heart.

Neither the lover, nor his prospective father-in-law, could have chosen a time more opportune for making their approaches. Although at that time Kate Vaughan felt towards Smythje more indifference—perhaps more contempt—than she had ever done, at that very hour was she wavering in the intention, hitherto cherished, of refusing him.

Though both lover and father had erroneously interpreted her air of dejection, it was nevertheless in their favour. It was not love for Smythje under which she was suffering ; but despair of this passion for another ; and in that despair lay the hope—the only hope—of the lord of Montagu Castle.

It was a despair not unmingled with pique—with anger ; that proud rage, which, painfully wringing the heart, prompts it to desperate resolves : even to the utter annihilation of all future hope—as if happiness could be obtained by destroying the happiness of the one only being who could give it !

Yes, the heart of Kate Vaughan had reached, or almost reached, that fearful phase of our moral nature, when love, convinced of its unrequital, seeks solace in revenge !

The Smythje ball, which had crowned the hopes of him to whom the compliment was given, had been fatal to those of Kate Vaughan.

Certain it was that she had conceived hopes that pointed to Herbert Vaughan. Love could scarce have been kindled without them. They were founded upon those fond words spoken at their first parting. Slight as was the foundation, up to that night had they endured : for she had treasured and cherished them in spite of absence, and calumny, and false report.

True, as time passed they had waxed fainter, with longer intervals of doubt, until the day in which had occurred the unexpected incident of meeting with Herbert on the Jumbé Rock.

There—notwithstanding the many circumstances that had arisen—calculated, as one would suppose, to produce an opposite effect—the hopes of the young creole, instead of becoming extinguished, had rather gained strength. Was it an instinct taught her that Herbert's tongue was less truthful than his eyes ? Perhaps it was an intuition founded upon her own feelings—for was not she also practising a similar deception ? Certain it is, that upon that occasion she had placed less faith in her cousin's words than his looks: for in that encounter of the eyes, already chronicled she had read something to cause a revival of her hopes.

They had lived with more or less intermission until that fatal night—the night of the Smythje ball—when they were doomed to utter extinction.

All night long he had come but once near her—only that once by the mere chance of changing positions. And then that bow—that single salutation, friendly as it might have been deemed, she could only remember as being cold, almost cynical !

She did not think how cold and distant had been her own—at least, how much so it must have appeared to him. Though her eyes had often ought him in the crowd, and often found him, she did not know that his were equally following her, and equally as often fixed upon her. Both were ignorant of this mutual espionage, for each had studiously declined esponding the glance of the other.

Never more that night had he come near—never again had he shown a desire or made an attempt to address her ; though opportunities there were—many of them—when no paternal eye was upon her to prevent an interview.

All night long had his attentions been occupied by another—apparently engrossed—and that other a bold, beautiful woman—just such a one as Herbert might love.

" He loves her ! I am sure he loves her !" was the reflection that passed often and painfully through the thoughts of Kate Vaughan, as she swept her eye across that crowded ball-room.

And then came the climax—that half-whispered gossip that reached her ear, falling upon it like a knell of death. They were to be married : they were already betrothed !

It needed no more. In that moment the hopes of the young creole were crushed—so cruelly, so completely, that, in the dark future before her, no gleam of light, not even a ray, arose to resucitate them.

No wonder that the morning sun shone upon a pale cheek—no wonder that an air of deep dejection sate upon the countenance of Kate Vaughan.

In this melancholy mood did the father find his daughter, on entering the kiosk.

She made no attempt to conceal it—not even with the counterfeit of a smile. Rather with a frown did she receive him ; and in her eyes might have been detected the slightest scintillation of anger, whether or not he was its object.

It is possible that just then the thought was passing through her mind that but for him, her destiny might have been different ; but for him, Herbert Vaughan, and not Montagu Smythje, might have been on the eve of offering for her hand, which would then have gone with her heart. Now, in the contingency of her consenting to the proposal she expected, would they be separated, and for ever .

Never more was she to experience that supreme happiness—the supremest known upon earth—and, perhaps, equalling the joys of heaven itself ; never more could she indulge in that sweet, delicious dream—a virgin's love—with the hope of its being returned. Her love might remain like a flower that had lost its perfume, only to shed it on the solitary air ; no more a sweet passion, but a barren, bitter thought, without hope to cheer it till the end of time.

Ah, Custos Vaughan ! proud, foolish parent ! Could you have known how you were aiding to destroy the happiness of your child—how you were contributing to crush that young heart—you would have approached less cheerfully to complete the ceremony of its sacrifice

CHAPTER LXI.

PAVING THE WAY.

"CATHERINE!" gravely began the father on stepping inside the kiosk
"Father!"
The parental appellative was pronounced in a low murmur, the speaker not uplifting her eyes from the object upon which she had been gazing.
The object was a small silken purse that lay upon the table. Stringless it was, though the broken ends of a blue ribbon attached to it showed that it had not always been so.
Loftus Vaughan knew not the history of that purse, neither why it lay there—what had stripped it of its string, or why his daughter was so sadly gazing upon it. All these circumstances, however, he noticed on entering the kiosk; and, but for the last, he might neither have thought of nor attempted to account for them."
"Ah, your purse!" said he, taking it up and examining it more minutely. "Some one has torn the string from it—a pity! who can have done it?"
Little did he care for the answer. As little did he suspect that the rape of that bit of ribbon had aught to do with his daughter's dejection, which he had observed throughout all the morning. The surprise he had expressed, and the question put, were only intended to initiate the more serious conversation he was about to introduce.
"Oh, papa! it don't signify," said Kate, avoiding a direct answer; "'tis but a bit of blue ribbon. I can easily replace it by another that will serve as well."
Ah, Kate! you may easily replace the ribbon upon the purse, but not so easily that peace of mind which parted from your bosom at the same time. When that string was torn, torn, too, were the strings of your heart.
Some such reflection must have passed through her mind as she made the reply; for the shadow stole deeper over her countenance.
Mr. Vaughan pursued the subject of the purse no further; but looking through the lattice-work and perceiving Smythje in chase of the butter-flies, endeavoured to draw his daughter's attention to that sportive gentleman.
This was the more easily done; as Mr. Smythje was at the momen humming a tone, and could be heard as well as seen.

"I'd be a butterfly,

sang Smythje—

And then, as if to contradict this pleasant prospectus of insect life, he was at that instant soon seizing a splendid *vanessa*, and " scrunching" the frail creature between his kid-gloved fingers!

" Isn't he a superb fellow?" said Mr. Vaughan, first gazing enthusiastically on Smythje, and then fixing his eyes upon his daughter, to note the character of the reply.

" I suppose he must be—papa—since everybody says so."

There was no enthusiasm in Kate's answer—nothing to encourage the Custos.

" Don't *you think so*, Kate?"

This was coming more directly to the point; but the response proved equally evasive.

" *You* think so, papa—and that should do for both of us."

The melodious voice of Smythie again interrupted the conversation, and turned it into a new channel.

Smythje singing—

> " I'd never languish for wealth nor for power,
> I'd never sigh to see slaves at my feet!"

" Ah, Mr. Smythje!" exclaimed the Custos, in a kind of soliloquy, though meant for the ear of Kate ; " you have no need to sigh for them —you have them ; five hundred in all. And beauties, too! Wealth and power, indeed! You needn't languish for either one or the other. The estate of Montagu Castle provides you with both, my boy!"

Smythje still chanted :

> " Those who have wealth may be watchful and wary,
> Power, alas! nought but misery brings."

" Do you hear that, Kate?   What fine sentiments he utters!"

" Very fine, and *apropos* to the occasion," replied Kate, sarcastically " They are not his, however ; but, no doubt, he feels them ; and that's just as good."

" A splendid property!" continued Mr. Vaughan, returning to what interested him more than the sentiments of the song, and not heeding the sarcasm conveyed in the speech of his daughter ; " a splendid property I toll you ; and with mine joined on to it will make the grandest establishment in the island. The island, did I say? In the West Indies—ay, in the Western World! Do you hear that, my daughter?"

" I do, papa," replied the young creole. " But you speak as if the two estates were to be joined together? Does Mr. Smythje intend to purchase Mount Welcome? or you Montagu Castle?"

These questions were asked with an air of simplicity evidently assumed. In truth, the interrogator knew well enough to what the conversation was tending ; and, impatient with the ambiguity, that was every moment growing more painful to her, desired to bring it to its crisis.

Mr. Vaughan was equally desirous of arriving at the same result, as testified in his reply.

" Ah, Kate! you little rogue?" said he, looking gratified at the opening thus made for him. " Egad! you've just hit the nail on the head. You've guessed right, only that we are both to be buyers. Mr. Smythje is to purchase Mount Welcome; and what do you suppose he s to pay for it? Guess that!"

" Indeed, father, I cannot! How should I know? I am sure I do not. Only this I know, that I am sorry you should think of our leaving Mount Welcome. Though I do not expect *now* ever to be happy here, I think I should not be happier anywhere else."

Mr. Vaughan was too much wound-up in the thread of his own thoughts to notice the emphasis on the word " now," or the double meaning of his daughter's words.

" Ha! ha! ha!" laughed he ; " Mr. Smythje's purchase won't dispossess us of Mount Welcome. Don't be afraid of that, little Katey. But, come, try and guess the price he is to pay ?"

" Father, I need not try. I am sure I could not guess it—not within thousands of pounds."

" Not a thousand pounds! no, not one pound, unless his great big heart weighs that much, and his generous hand thrown into the scale— for that, Catherine, that is the price he is to pay."

Mr. Vaughan wound up this speech with a significant glance, and a triumphant gesture, expressive of astonishment at his own eloquence.

He looked for a response—one that would reciprocate his smiles and the joyful intelligence he fancied himself to have communicated. He looked in vain. Notwithstanding the perspicuity of his explanation. Kate obstinately refused to comprehend it.

Her reply, was provokingly a " shirking of the question."

" His heart and his hand, you say ? Neither seem very heavy. But it it not very little for an estate where there are many hands, and many hearts, too ? To whom does he intend to give them ? You have not let me know that, papa ?"

" I shall let you know now," replied the father, his voice changing to a more serious tone, as if a little nettled by Kate's evident design to mis-understand him. " I shall let you know by telling you what I intend to give him for Montagu Castle. I told you we were both to be buyers in this transaction. It is a fair exchange, Kate, hand for hand, and heart for heart. Mr. Smythje freely gives his, and I give *yours*."

" Mine !"

" Ay, yours. Surely, Kate, I have not made a mistake ? Surely you are agreeable to the exchange ?"

" Father," said the young girl, speaking in a tone of womanly gravity, ' there can be no exchange of hearts between Mr. Smythje and myself. He may have given his to me. I know not nor care. But I will not de-ceive you, father. My heart he can never have: it is not in my power to give it to him."

" Nonsense !" exclaimed Mr. Vaughan, startled by this unexpected declaration ; " you are deceiving yourself, my child, when you talk thus. I do not see how you can fail to like Mr. Smythje—so generous, so accom-plished, so handsome as he is ! Come, you are only jesting, Kate ? You do like him ; you do not hate him ?"

" No, no! I do not hate him! Why should I ? Mr. Smythje has done nothing to offend me. I believe he is very honourable."

" Why, that is almost saying that you like him ?" rejoined the father in a tone of returning gratification.

" Liking is not love," murmured Kate, as if speaking to herself.
" It may turn to it," said the Custos encouragingly. " It often does—
especially when two people become man and wife. Besides, it's not
always best for young married folks to be too fond of each other at first.
As my old spelling-book used to say, 'Hot love soon grows cold.' Never
fear, Kate! you'll get to like Mr. Smythje well enough, when you come to
be the mistress of Montagu Castle, and take rank as the grandest lady of
the island. Won't that be happiness, little Kate?"

" Ah !" thought the young creole, " a cabin shared with *him* would be
greater happiness—far, far greater!"

It is needless to say that the "him" to whom the thought pointed was
not Smythje.

" As Mrs. Montagu Smythje," proceeded the Custos, with the design of
painting the future prospects of his daughter in still more glowing tints,
" you will have troops of friends—the highest in the land. *And remember, my child, it is not so now.* You know it, Catherine ?"

These last words were pronounced in a tone suggestive of some secret
understanding between father and daughter. The purpose was to bring
forcibly before the mind of the young girl a certain fact and thought—in
order that she might the more eagerly embrace the opportunity of escaping from that humiliating position, of late better known to her.

Whether the confidential speech produced the desired effect, he who
made it did not stay to perceive ; but continued on in the same breath to
finish the rose-coloured picture he had essayed to paint.

" Yes, my little Kate! you will be the observed of all observers—the
cynosure, as the poets say. Horses, slaves, dresses, carriages at will.
You will make a grand tour to London—egad! I feel like going myself!
In the great metropolis you will hob-nob with lords and ladies ; visit the
operas and balls, where you will be a belle, my girl—a belle ; do you
hear ? Every one will be talking of Mrs. Montagu Smythje! How do you
like it now ?"

" Ah, papa!" replied the young creole, evidently unmoved by these
promises of pomp and grandeur ; " I should not like it at all. I am sure I
should not. I never cared for such things—you know I do not. They
cannot give happiness—at least, not to me. I should never be happy
away from our own home. What pleasure should I have in a great city?
None, I am sure ; but quite the contrary. I should miss our grand
mountains and woods—our beautiful trees with their gay, perfumed
blossoms—our bright-winged birds with the sweet songs! Operas and
balls! I dislike balls ; and to be the belle of one—papa I detest the
word !"

Kate at that moment, was thinking of the Smythje ball, and its dis
agreeable souvenirs—perhaps the more disagreeable, that oftener than
once during the night she had heard the phrase " belle of the ball"
applied to one who had aided in the desolation of her heart.

" Oh! you will get over that dislike," returned Mr. Vaughan, " once
you go into fashionable society Most young ladies do. There is no
harm in balls, after a girl gets married, and her husband goes with her, to
take care of her—no harm whatever.

" But, now, Kate," continued the Custos, betraying a certain degree of nervous impatience "We must come to an understanding. Mr. Smythje is waiting."

"For what is he waiting, papa?"

"Tut! tut! child," said Mr. Vaughan, slightly irritated by his daughter's apparent incapacity to comprehend him. "Surely you know? Have I not as good as told you? Mr. Smythje is going to—to offer you his heart and hand; and—and to ask yours in return. That is what he is waiting to do. You will not refuse him?—you *must* not!"

Loftus Vaughan would have spoken more gracefully had he omitted the last phrase. It had the sound of a command, with an implied threat; and jarring upon the ear of her to whom it was addressed, might have roused a spirit of rebellion. It is just possible that such would have been its effect, had it been spoken on the eve of the Smythje ball instead of the morning after.

The incidents occurring there had extinguished all hope in the breast of the young Creole that she should ever share happiness with Herbert Vaughan—had at the same time destroyed any thought of resistance to the will of her father; and, with a thought of apathetic despair, she submitted herself to the sacrifice which her father had determined upon.

"I have told you the truth," said she, gazing fixedly in the face of her father, as if to impress him with the idleness of the arguments he had been using. "I cannot give Mr. Smythje my heart; I shall tell *him* the same."

"No—no!" hastily rejoined the importunate parent; "you must do nothing of the kind. Give him your hand; and say nothing about your heart. That you can bestow afterwards—when you are safe married."

"Never, never!" said the young girl, sighing painfully as she spoke. "I cannot practice that deception. No, father, not even for you. Mr. Smythje shall know all; and, if he choose to accept my hand without my heart——"

"Then you promise to give him your hand?" interrupted the Custos, in joy at this hypothetical consent.

"It is *you* who give it; not *I*, father."

"Enough!" cried Mr. Vaughan, hastily turning his eyes to the garden, as if to search for the insect-hunter. "I shall give it," continued he, "and this very minute. Mr. Smythje!"

Smythje, standing close by the kiosk, on the *qui vive* of expectation, promptly responded to the summons; and in two seconds of time appeared in the open doorway.

"Mr. Smythje—Sir!" said the Custos, putting on an air of pompous solemnity befitting the occasion. "You have asked for my daughter's hand in marriage; and, Sir, I am happy to inform you, that she has consented to your becoming my son-in-law. I am proud of the honour, Sir."

Here Mr. Vaughan paused to get breath.

"Aw, aw!" stammered Smythje. "This is a gweat happiness—veway gweat, indeed! Quite unexpected!—aw, aw!—I am shaw. Miss Vawns, I nevaw dweamt——"

"Now, my children," playfully interrupted the Custos—covering Smythje's embarrassment by the interruption—"I have bestowed you upon one another; and, with my blessing, I leave you to yourself."

So saying, the gratified father stepped forth from the kiosk, and wend
ing his way along the walk, disappeared within the door of his dwelling
We shall not intrude upon the lovers thus left alone, nor repeat a single
word of what passed between them. Suffice it to say, that when Smythje
came out of that same kiosk, his air was rather tranquil than triumphant.
A portion of the shadow that sate upon Kate's countenance seemed to
have been transmitted to his. One might have fancied him the recipient
of the " sack," but for the words that passed between him and his in·
tended father-in-law, as they met the moment after in the great hall.

" Well ?" anxiously inquired the latter.

" Aw! all wight; betwothed. Vewy stwaynge, thaw—inexpwicably
stwange !"

" How strange ?" demanded Mr. Vaughan,

" Aw, vewy mild. Aw expected haw to go into hystewics. Ba Jawve
naw : she weceived ma declawation as cool as a cucumbaw !"

She had done more than that : she had given him a hand without a
heart. And Smythje knew it ; for Kate Vaughan had kept her promise.

CHAPTER LXII

THE DUPPY'S HOLE.

On the flank of the " Mountain," that frowned towards the happy Valley,
and not far from the Jambé Rock, a spring gushed forth. So copious was
it as to merit the name of fountain. In its descent down the slope it was
joined by others, and soon became a torrent—leaping from ledge to ledge
and foaming as it followed its onward course.

About half-way between the summit and base of the mountain, a deep
longitudinal hollow lay in its track—into which the stream was precipitated, in a clear, curving cascade.

This singular hollow resembled the crater of an extinct volcano—in the
circumstance that on all sides it was surrounded by a precipice facing inward, and rising two hundred feet sheer from the level below. It was
not of circular shape, however—as craters generally are—but of the
form of a ship, the stream falling in over the poop, and afterwards escaping through a narrow cleft at the bow.

Preserving the simile of a ship, it may be stated that the channel ran
directly fore and aft, bisecting the surface of the valley, an area of several acres, into two equal parts—but in consequence of an obstruction at
its exit, the stream formed a lagoon, or dam, flooding the whole of the
fore-deck, while the main and quarter decks were covered with a growth
of indigenous timber-trees, of appearance primeval. The water, on
leaving the lagoon, made its escape below, through a gorge black and
narrow, bounded on each side by the same beetling cliffs that surrounded
the valley. At the lower end of this gorge was a second waterfall, where
the stream again pitched over a precipice of more than a hundred feet in
height; and thence, traversing the slope of the mountain, ended in becoming a tributary of the Montego River.

The upper cascade precipitated itself upon a bed of grim black boulders between which the froth-crested water seethed onward tɛ the lagoon below.

Above these boulders hung continuously a cloud of white vapour, like steam ascending out of some gigantic cauldron or gas-work. When the sun was upon that side of the mountain, an iris might be seen shining amidst the fleecelike vapour. But rare was the eye that beheld this beautiful phenomenon; for the Duppy's Hole—in negro parlance the appellation of the place—shared the reputation of the Jumbé rock; and few were the negroes who would have ventured to approach, even to the edge of this cavernous abysm. Fewer those who would have dared to descend into it..

Indeed, something more than superstitious terror might have hindered the execution of this last project; since a descent into the Duppy's Hole appeared an impossibility. Down the beetling cliffs that encompassed it, there was neither path nor pass—not a ledge on which the foot might have rested with safety. Only at one point—and that where the preci pice rose over the lagoon—might a descent have been made by means of some stunted trees that, rooting in the clefts of the rock, formed a strag gling screen up the face of the cliff. There an agile individual might possibly have scrambled down ; but the dammed water—dark and deep —would have hindered him from reaching the quarter-deck of this ship-shaped ravine, unless by swimming ; and this, the suck of the current to-wards the gorge below would have rendered a most perilous perform ance.

It was evident that some one had tempted this peril: for on scrutini-sing the straggling trees upon the cliff, a sort of stairway could be dis-tinguished—the outstanding stems serving as steps, with the parasitical creepers connecting them together.

Moreover, at intervals during the day, a tiny string of smoke might have been seen ascending out of the Duppy's Hole, which, after curling diffusely over the tops of the tall trees, out of which it rose, would dis-solve itself, and become invisible. Only one standing upon the cliff above, and parting the foliage that screened it to its very brink, could have seen this smoke ; and, if only superficially observed, it might easily have been mistaken for a stray waif of the fog that floated above the waterfall near which it rose. Closely scrutinised, however, its blue col-our and soft filmy haze rendered it recognisable as the smoke of a wood fire, and one that must have been made by human hands.

Any day might it have been seen, and three times a-day—at morning noon, and evening—as if the fire had been kindled for the purpose of cooking the three regular meals of breakfast, dinner, and supper.

The diurnal appearance of the smoke proved the presence of a human being or beings. One, at least, disregarding the superstitious terror at-tached to the place, had made the Duppy's Hole his home. By exploring the valley, other evidences of human presence could be found. Under the branches of a large tree, standing by the edge of the lagoon, and from which the silvery tillandsia fell in festoons to the surface of the water, a small canoe of rude construction might be seen, a foot or two of its stem protruding from the moss. A piece of twisted withe attach-ing it to the tree told that it had not drifted there by accident, but was moored by some one who meant to return to it·

From the edge of the lagoon to the upper end of the valley, the ground, as already stated, was covered with a thick growth of forest timber—where the eye of the botanical observer might distinguish, by their forms and foliage, many of those magnificent indigenous trees for which the *sylva* of Jamaica has long been celebrated.

There stood the gigantic cedrela, and its kindred, the bastard cedar, with elm-like leaves;* the ' mountain mahoe ; " † the "tropic bird ;"‡ and the world known mahogany.

Here and there the lance-like culms of bamboos might be seen shooting up over the tops of the dicotyledons, or forming a fringe along the cliffs above, intermingled with trumpet trees § with their singular peltate leaves, and tall tree-ferns, whose delicate lace-like fronds formed a netted tracery against the blue background of the sky.

In the rich soil of the valley flourished luxuriantly the noble cabbage palm—the *prince* of the Jamaica forest—while, by its side, claiming admiration for the massive grandeur of its form, stood the *patriarch* of West Indian trees—the grand *ceiba* ; the hoary Spanish moss that drooped from its spreading branches forming an appropriate beard for the venerable giant.

Every tree had its parasites—not a single species but in hundreds, and of as many grotesque shapes some twining around the trunks and boughs like huge snakes or cables—some seated upon the limbs or in the forking of the branches ; and others hanging suspended from the topmost twigs, like stream·rs from the rigging of a ship. Many of these trailing from tree to tree, were loaded with clusters of the most brilliant flowers, thus uniting the forest into one continuous arbour.

Close under the cliff, and near where the cascade came tumbling down from the rocks, stood a tree that deserves particular mention. It was a ceiba of enormous dimensions, with a buttressed trunk, that covered a surface of more than fifty feet in diameter. Its vast bole, rising nearly to the brow of the cliff, extended horizontally over an area on which five hundred men could have conveniently encamped; while the profuse growth of Spanish moss clustering upon its branches, rather than its own sparse foilage, would have shaded them from the sun, completely shutting out the view overhead.

Not from any of these circumstances was the tree distinguished from others of its kind frequently met with in the mountain forests of Jamaica. What rendered it distinct from those around was, that between two of the great spurs extending outwards from its trunk, an object appeared which indicated the presence of man.

This object was a hut constructed in the most simple fashion—having for its side walls the plate-like buttresses already mentioned; while in front a stockade of bamboo stems completed the inclosure. In the centre of the stockade a narrow space had been left open for the entrance—which could be closed, when occasion required, by a door of split bamboos that hung lightly upon its hinges of withe.

In front, the roof trendled downward from the main trunk of the tree —following the slope of the spurs to a height of some six feet from the ground. Its construction was of the simplest kind—being only a few

---

* Guasuma   † Hibiscus tiliaceus   ‡ Bursera.   § Cecropias.

poles laid transversely, and over these a thatch of the long ¡ imnate leaves of the cabbage palm.

The hut inside was of triangular shape, and of no inconsiderable size —since the converging spurs forming its side walls extended full twelve feet outwards from the tree. No doubt it was large enough for whoever occupied it; and the narrow platform of bamboo canes, intended as a bed-stead, showed that only one person was accustomed to pass the night under the shelter of its roof.

That this person was a man could be told, by the presence of some ar ticles of male attire lying upon the bamboo couch—where also lay a piece of rush matting, and an old, tattered blanket—evidently the sole stock of bedding which the hut contained.

The furniture was scanty as simple. The cane platform already mentioned appeared to do duty also as a table and chair ; and, with the exception of an old tin kettle, some calabash bowls, and platters, nothing else could be seen that might be termed a " utensil."

There were articles, however, of a different character, and plenty of them ; but these were neither simple, nor their uses easily understood. Against the walls hung a variety of singular objects—some of them ridiculous, and some of hideous aspect. Among the latter could be observed the skin of the dreaded galliwasp; the two-headed snake ;* the skull and tusks of a savage boar ; dried specimens of the ugly gecko lizard ; enormous bats, with human-like faces, and other like hideous creatures.

Little bags suspended from the rafters contained articles of still more mysterious import. Balls of whitish coloured clay ; the claws of the great eared owl ; parrots' beaks and feathers.; the teeth of cats, alligators, and the native aguti ; pieces of rag and broken glass ; with a score of like odds and ends, forming a medley as miscellaneous as unintelligible.

In one corner was a wicker basket—the cutacoo—filled with roots and plants of several different species, among which might be identified the dangerous dumb cane ;† the savanna flower ;‡ and other " simples" of a suspicious character.

Entering this hut, and observing the singular collection of specimens which it contained, a stranger to the island of Jamaica would have been puzzled to explain their presence and purpose. Not so, one acquainted with the forms of the serpent worship of Ethiopia—the creed of the Coromantees. The grotesque objects were but symbols of the African *fetisch*. The hut was a temple of Obi : in plainer terms, the dwelling of an *Obeah man*.

CHAPTER LXIII.

CHAKRA, THE MYAL-MAN.

THE sun was just going down to his bed in the blue Carribean, and tint-ing with a carmine-coloured light the glistening surface of the Jumbé Rock when a human figure was seen ascending the mountain path that led to that noted summit.

* Typhops. ‡ : † Caladium seguinum ↲. ‡ Echites suberecte.

Notwithstanding the gloom of the indigenous forest—every moment becoming more obscure under the fast deepening twilight—it could be easily seen that the figure was that of a woman; while the buff complexion of her face and naked throat, of her gloveless hands, and shoeless, stockingless feet and ankles, proclaimed her a woman of colour—a mulatta.

Her costume was in keeping with her caste. A frock of cotton print of flaunting pattern, half open at the breast; a toque of Madras kerchief of gaudy hues—these were all she wore, excepting the chemise of scarcely white calico, whose needle-embroidered border showed through the opening of her dress.

She was a woman of large form, and bold, passionate physiognomy; possessing a countenance not altogether unlovely, though lacking in delicacy of feature—its beauty, such as it was, being of a purely sensual character.

Whatever errand she was on, both her step and glance bespoke courageous resolve. It argued courage her being upon the "Mountain," and so near the Jumbé Rock, at that unusual hour.

But there are passions stronger than fear. Even the terror of the supernatural fades from the heart that is benighted with love, or wrung by jealousy. Perhaps this lone wanderer of the forest path was the victim of one or the other?

A certain expression of nervous anxiety—at times becoming more anguished—would have argued the latter to be the passion which was uppermost in her mind. Love should have looked more gentle and hopeful.

Though it was evident that her errand was not one of ordinary business, there was nothing about her to betray its exact purpose. A basket of palm wicker-work, suspended over her wrist, appeared to be filled with provisions: the half-closed lid permitting to be seen inside a congeries of young plantains, tomatoes, and capsicums; while the legs of a guinea-fowl protruded from the opening.

This might have argued a certain purpose—an errand to market; but the unusual hour, the direction taken, and, above all, the air and bearing of the mulatta, as she strode up the mountain path, forbade the supposition that she was going to market. The Jumbé Rock was not a likely place to find sale for a basket of provisions.

After all, she was not bound thither. On arriving within sight of the summit, she paused upon the path; and, after looking around for a minute or two—as if making a reconnoissance—she faced to the left, and advanced diagonally across the flank of the mountain.

Her turning aside from the Jumbé Rock could not have been from fear: for the direction she was now following would carry her to a place equally dreaded by the superstitious—the Duppy's Hole.

That she was proceeding to this place was evident. There was no distinct path leading thither, but the directness of her course, and the confidence with which she kept it, told that she must have gone over the ground before.

Forcing her way through the tangle of vines and branches, she strode courageously onward—until at length she arrived on the edge of the Duppy's Hole.

The point where she reached it was just above the gorge—the place where the tree stairway already described led down to the lagoon. From her actions, it was evident that the way was known to her; and that she meditated a descent into the bottom of the valley.

. That she knew she could not accomplish this feat of herself, and expected some one to come to her assistance, was also evident from her proceeding to make a signal as soon as she arrived upon the edge of the cliff. Drawing from the bosom of her dress a small white kerchief, she spread it open upon the branch of a tree that grew conspicuously over the precipice; and then, resting her hand against the trunk, she stood gazing with a fixed and earnest look upon the water below.

In the twilight now fast darkening down, even the white kerchief might have remained unnoticed. The woman, however, appeared to have no apprehension upon this head. Her gaze was expectant and full of confidence: as if the signal had been a preconcerted one, and she was conscious that the individual for whom it was intended would be on the lookout.

Forewarned or not, she was not disappointed. Scarce five minutes had transpired from the hanging out of the handkerchief, when a canoe was seen shooting out from under the moss-garnished trees that fringed the upper edge of the lagoon, and making for the bottom of the cliff beneath where she stood.

A single individual occupied the canoe; who, even under the sombre shadow of the twilight, appeared to be a man of dread aspect.

He was a negro of gigantic size—though that might not have appeared as he sat squatted in the canoe, but for the extreme breadth of his shoulders, between which was set a huge head, almost neckless. His back was bent like a bow, presenting an enormous hunch, partly the effect of advanced age, and partly from natural malformation. His attitude in the canoe gave him a double stoop : so that, as he leant forward to the paddle, his face was turned downward, as if he was regarding some object in the bottom of the craft. His long, ape-like arms, however, enabled him to reach over the gunwale without bending much to either side ; and only with these did he appear to make any exertion—his body remaining perfectly immobile.

The dress of this individual was at the same time grotesque and savage. The only part of it which belonged to civilised fashion was a pair of wide trousers or drawers, of coarse Osnaburgh linen—such as are worn by the field hands on a sugar plantation. Their dirty, yellowish hue told that they had long been strangers to the laundry ; while several crimson-coloured blotches upon them proclaimed that their last wetting had been with blood, not water.

A sort of *kaross*, or cloak, made out of the skins of the *utia*, and hung over his shoulders, was the only garment he wore. This, fastened round his thick short neck by a piece of leathern thong, covered the whole of his body down to the hams—the Osnaburgh drawers continuing the costume thence to his ankles. His feet were bare. Nor needed they any protection from shoes—the soles being thickly covered with a horn-like callosity, which extended from the ball of the great toe to the broad heel, far protruding backward.

, The head-dress was equally *bizarre*. It was a sort of cap, constructed out of the skin of some wild animal; and fitting closely, exhibited, in all its phrenological fullness, the huge negro cranium which it covered. There was no brim; but, in its place, the dried and stuffed skin of the great yellow snake was wreathed around the temples, with the head of the reptile in front, and two sparkling pebbles set in the sockets of its eyes to give it the appearance of life!

The countenance of the negro did not need this terrific adornment to inspire those who beheld it with fear. The sullen glare of his deep-set eyeballs—the broad gaping nostrils—the teeth filed to a point, and gleaming, shark-like, behind his purple lips—the red tattooing upon his cheeks and broad breast—the latter exposed by the action of his arms—all combined in making a picture that needed no reptiliform addition to render it hideous enough for the most horrid of purposes. It seemed to terrify even the wild denizens of the Duppy's Hole. The heron, couching in the sedge, flapped up with an affrighted cry; and the flamingo, spreading her scarlet wings, rose screaming over the cliffs, and flew far away. Even the woman who awaited him—bold as she may have been, and voluntary as her rendezvous appeared to be—could not help shuddering as the canoe drew near; and for a moment she appeared irresolute as to whether she should trust herself in such uncanny company.

Her resolution, however, stimulated by some strong passion, soon returned; and as the canoe swept in among the bushes at the bottom of the cliff, and she heard the voice of its occupant summoning her to descend, she plucked the signal from the tree, fixed the basket firmly over her arm, and commenced letting herself down through the tangle of branches.

The canoe re-appeared upon the open water, returning across the lagoon. The mulatta woman was seated in the stern, the man, as before, plying the paddle; but now exerting all his strength to prevent the light craft from being carried down by the current that could be heard hissing and groaning through the gorge below.

On getting back under the tree from which he had started, the negro corded the canoe to one of the branches; and then, scrambling upon shore, followed by the woman, he walked on towards the temple of Obi—of which he was himself both oracle and priest.

CHAPTER LXIV.

THE RESURRECTION.

ARRIVED at the cotton-tree hut, the myal-man—for such was the negro—dived at once into the open door, his broad and hunched shoulders scarce clearing the aperture.

In a tone rather of command than request, he directed the woman to enter.

The mulatta appeared to hesitate. Inside, the place was dark as Erebus; though without it was not very different. The shadow of the *ceiba*, with its dense shrouding of moss, interrupted every ray of the moonlight now glistening among the tops of the trees. The negro noticed the woman's hesitation.

"Come in!" cried he repeating his command in the same gruff voice. "You me sabbey—what fo' you fear?"

"I'se not afraid, Chakra," replied she, though the trembling of her voice contradicted the assertion, "only," she added, still hesitating, "it's so dark in there."

"Well, den—you 'tay outside," said the other, relenting; "you 'tay dar wha you is; a soon 'trike a light."

A fumbling was heard, and then the chink of steel against flint, followed by a fiery spark. A piece of punk was set ablaze, and from this the flame was communicated to a sort of lamp, composed of the *carapace* of a turtle, filled with wild hog's lard, and with a wick twisted out of the down of the cotton tree.

"Now you come in, Cynthy," resumed the negro, placing the lamp upon the floor. "Wha! you 'till afread? You de dauter ob Juno Vaghn—you modder no fear ole Chakra. Whugh! she no fear de debbil!"

Cynthia, thus addressed, might have thought that between the dread of these two personages there was not much to choose; for the devil himself could hardly have appeared in more hideous guise than the human being who stood before her.

"Oh, Chakra!" said she, as she stepped inside the door, and caught sight of the weird-looking garniture of the walls; "woman may well be 'fraid. Dis am a fearful place?"

"Not so fearful as de Jumbé rock," was the reply of the myal-man, accompanied by a significant glance, and something between a smile and a grin.

"True" said the mulatta, gradually recovering her self-possession; "true—you hab cause say so, Chakra."

"Das a fac', Cynthy."

"But tell me, good Chakra," continued the mulatta, giving way to a woman's feeling—curiosity—"how did you ebber 'scape from the Jumbé rock? The folks sez your skeleton is still up there—chain to de palm tree!"

"De folk 'peek da troof. My 'keleton am da, jess as dey say."

The woman turned upon the speaker a glance in which astonishment was mingled with fear, the latter predominating.

"*Your* skeleton?" she muttered, interrogatively.

"Dem same ole bones—da 'kull, de ribs, de joints, drumticks, an' all. Golly, gal Cynthy! dat ere 'pears 'stonish you. Wha fo'? Nuffin in dat. You sabbey ole Chakra? You know he *myal-man*? Doan care who know *now*—so long dey b'lieve um dead. Wha for myal-man, ef he no bring de dead to life 'gain? Be shoo Chakra no die hisself, so long he knows how store dead body to de life. Ole Chakra know all dat. Dey no kill *him*, nebber! Neider de white folk nor de brack folk. Dey may shoot 'im wid gun—dey may hang 'im by the neck—deymay cut off 'im head—he come to life 'gain, like de blue lizard and de glass snake. Dey *did* try kill 'im, you know. Dey 'tarve him till he die ob hunger and thuss. De John Crow pick out him eyes, and tear de flesh from de old niggar's body —leab nuffin but de bare bones! Ha! Chakra 'lib yet—he hab new bones, new flesh! Golly! you him see? he 'trong—he fat as ebber he wa'! Ha'! ha: ha!"

And as the niacous negro uttered his exulting laugh he threw up his arms and turned his eyes towards his own person, as if appealing to it for proof of the resurrection he professed to have accomplished!

The mulatta stood as if petrefied by the recital: every word of which she appeared implicitly to believe. She was too much terrified to speak and remained silent, apparently cowering under the influence of a super natural awe.

CHAPTER LXV.

CYNTHIA CONFESSED.

THE myal-man perceived the advantage he had gained; and seeing that the curiosity of his listener was satisfied—for she had not the slightest desire to hear more about the matter—he adroitly changed the subject to one of a more natural character.

" You've brought de basket ob wittle, Cynthy ?"

" Yes, Chakra—there."

" Golly! um's berry good—guinea-hen an' plenty ob vegable fo' the pepperpot. Anything fo' drink, g∢ Habent forgot daat, a hope? Iss da mose partickla ob all."

" I have not forgotten it, Chakr∴ There's a bottle of rum. You'll find it in the bottom of the basket ⸴ dad a deal trouble steal it."

" Who you 'teal it from ?"

" Why, master: who else? He have grown berry partickler of late—carries all de keys himself; and won't let us coloured folk go near de storeroom, as if we were all teevin' cat n"

" Nebba mind—nebba you mind, Cynthy—maybe Chakra watch him by'm-bye. Wa, now!" added he, drawing the bottle of rum out of the basket, and holding it up to the light. "De buckra preacher he say dat 'tolen water am sweet. A 'pose dat 'tolen rum folla de same excepshuns. A see ef um do."

So saying, the negro drew out the stopper; raised the bottle to his lip, and buried the neck up to the swell between his capacious jaws. A series of " clucks" proclaimed the passage of the liquor over his palate; and not until he had swallowed half a pint of the fiery fluid, did he with-draw the neck of the bottle from between his teeth.

" Whugh !" he exclaimed, with an aspirate that resembled the snort of a startled hog. " Whugh !" he repeated, stroking his abdomen with his huge paw. " De buckra preacher may ∴lk 'bout him 'tolen water, but gib me de 'tolen rum. You good gal, Cynthy—you berry good gal to fetch ole Chakra dis nice basket o' wittle—he sometime berry hungry—he need um all."

" I promise to bring more—whenebber I can get away from the Buff.'

" Das right, my picaninny! An' now, gal," continued the myal-man changing his tone, and regarding the mulatta with a look of interroga-tion ; " wha fo' you want see me dis night? You hab some purpiss par tickla! Dat so—eh, gal ?"

this she cares to make confession, only to him who has the right to hear it. Hence Cynthia's silent and hesitating attitude.

" Wha fo' you no 'peak ?" asked the grim confessor. " Shoo' you no hab fear ob ole Chakra? You no need fo' tell 'im—he know you secret a'ready—you lub Cubina, de capen ob Maroon ? Dat troof, eh ?"

" It is true, Chakra. I shall conceal nothing from you."

" Better not, 'cause you can't 'ceal nuffin from ole Chakra—he know ebbery ting—little bird tell um. Wa, now, wha nex' ? You tink Cubina no lub you ?"

" Ah ! I am sure of it," replied the mulatta, her bold countenance relaxing into an anguished expression. " I once thought he love me. Now I no think so."

" You tink him lub some odder girl ?"

" I am sure of it—oh ! I have reason."

" Who am dis odder ?"

" Yola."

" Yola! Dat ere name sound new to me. Wha d's she 'long to ?"

" She belongs to Mount Welcome—she Missa Kate's maid."

" Lily Quasheba, I call dat young lady," muttered the myal-man, with a knowing grin. " But dis Yola ?" he added : " whar she come from ? A nebber hear the name afo'."

" Oh, true, Chakra ; I did not think of tellin you. She was bought from the Jew, and fetched home since you—that is, after you left the plantation."

" Arter I lef' de plantation to die on de ' Jumbé rock'; ha! ha! ha! Dat's wha you mean, Cynthy ?"

" Yes—she came soon after."

"So you tink Cubina lub her ?"

" I do."

" An' she 'ciprocate de fekshun ?"

" Ah, surely! How could she help do that ?"

The interrogatory betrayed the speaker's belief that the Maroon captain was irresistible.

" Wa, then—wha you want me do, gal ? You want rebbenge on Cubina, 'cause he hab 'trayed you ? You want me put de *death-'pell* on him ?"

" Oh ! no—no ! not that, Chakra, for the sake of heaven !—not that !"

" Den you want de *lub-spell* ?"

" Ah ! if he could be made love me 'gain—he did once. That is—I thought he did. Is it possible, good Chakra, to make him love me ?"

" All ting be possible to ole Chakra ; an' to prove dat," continued he, with a determined air ; " he promise put de lub-spell on Cubina."

" Oh, thanks ! thanks !" cried the woman, stretching out her hands, and speaking in a tone of fervent gratitude. " What can I do for you, Chakra ? I bring you everything you ask. I steal rum—I steal wine—I come every night with something you like eat."

" Wa, Cynthy ; dat berry kind ob you ; but you muss do more dan all dat ?"

" Anything you ask me—what more ?"

" You must help in de spell. It take bof you an' me to bring im 'bout.'

" Only tell me how to do ; and trust me, Chakra, I shall follow your advice."

" Wa, den—lissen—I tell you all 'bout it. But sit down on da bamboos
dar. It take some time."

The woman, thus directed, took her seat upon the cane bedstead, and
remained silent and attentive—watching every movement of her hideous
companion, and not without some misgivings as to the compact which
was about to be entered into between them.

CHAPTER LXVL

THE LOVE-SPELL.

THE countenance of the myal-man had assumed an air of solemnity that
betokened some serious determination; and the mulatta felt a presentiment that, in return for his services, something was about to be demanded of her—something more than a payment in meat and drink.

His mysterious behaviour as he passed around the hut; now stopping
before one of the grotesque objects that adorned the wall, now before
another—now fumbling among the little bags and baskets, as if in search
of some particular charm—his movements made in solemn silence, only
broken by the melancholy sighing of the cataract heard from without:
all this was producing on the mind of the mulatta an unpleasant impression; and, despite her natural courage, sustained as it was by the burning passion that devoured her, she was fast giving way to indefinable
fear.

The priest of Obi, after appearing to have worshipped each *fetich* in
turn, at length transferred his devotions to the rum-bottle—perhaps the
most potent god in his whole Pantheon. Taking another long spell at the
neck, followed by the customary " Whugh!" he restored the bottle to its
place; and then, seating himself upon a huge turtle-shell, that formed
part of the plenishing of his temple, he commenced giving his devotee
her lesson of instructions.

" Fuss, den," said he, " to put de lub-spell on any body—eider a man
or a woman—it am nessary, at de same time, to hab de death-'pell 'long
wi' it."

" What!" exclaimed his listener, exhibiting a degree of alarm : " the
death-spell ?—ou Cubina, do you mean ?"

" No, not on *him*—dat's not a nessary consarquence. But 'fore Cubina
be made lub you, someb'dy else muss be made *die.*"

" Who," quickly inquired the mulatta, her mind at the moment rever
ting to one whom she would have wished to be the victim.

" Who you tink fo' ? who you greatest enemy you wish die ?"

" Yola," answered the woman, in a low, muttered voice, and with
scarce a moment of hesitation.

" Woan do—-woman woan do—muss be man ; an' more dan dat, muss
be free man. Nigga slave woan do. Obi god tell me so jess now. Buckra
man, too, it must be. If buckra man hab de death-'pell, Cubina he tak
de lub-spell 'trong—he lub you hard as a ole mule can kick."

" Oh! if he would!" exclaimed the passionate mulatta, in an ecstacy of
delightful expectation ; " I shall do anything for that—anything."

" Den you muss help put de death-'pell on some ob de white folk. You hab buckra enemy ?--Chakra hab de same."

" Who ?" inquired the woman, reflectingly.

" Who! No need tell who Chakra enemy—you enemy too. Who fooled you long time 'go ? who 'bused you when you wa' young gal ? No need tell you dat, Cynthy Vagh'n ?"

The mulatta turned her eyes upon the speaker with a significant expression. Some old memory seemed resuscitated by his words, and evidently anything but a pleasant one.

" Massa Loftus ?" she said, in a half-whisper.

" Sartin shoo, Massa Loftus—dat ere buckra you enemy an' mine boaf."

" And you would——?"

" Set de obea' fo' him," said the negro, finishing the interrogatory, which the other had hesitated to pronounce.

The woman remained without making answer, and as if buried in reflection. The expression upon her features was not one of repentance.

" Muss be him!" continued the tempter, as if to win her more completely to his dark project ; " no odder do so well. Obi god say so— muss be de planter ob Moun' Welc'm."

" If Cubina will but love me, I care not who," rejoined the mulatta, with an air of reckless determination.

" 'Nuff sed," resumed the myal-man. " De death-'pell ob de obeah sha' be set on de proud buckra, Loffus Vagh'u ; an' you, Cynthy, must 'sist in be workin' ob de charm."

" How can I assist ?" inquired the woman, in a voice whose trembling told of a slight irresolution " How, Chakra ?"

" Dat you be tole by'm-by, not dis night. De 'pelltake time. You de only one, 'sides one odder, who know ole Chakra still 'live. Odders know de ole myal-man in de mask, but nebba see um face, an' nebba suspeck who um be. Das all right. You tell who de myal-man am, den——"

" Oh, never, Chakra," interrupted his listener, " never !"

" No, berra not. You tell dat, Cynthy, you soon feel de death-'pell on youseff. Now, gal," continued the negro rising from his seat, and motioning the mulatta to do the same, " time fo' you go. I speck's one odder soon: no do fo' you to be cotch heaw when dat odder come. Take you basket, an' folla me."

So saying, the speaker emptied the basket of its heterogeneous contents ; and, handing it to its owner, conducted her out of the hut.

CHAPTER LXVII.

THE BARGAIN OF OBEAH.

For a while after the departure of Cynthia, the temple of Obi remained untenanted, except by its dumb deities : its priest having gone to ferry his neophyte across the lagoon.

In a few minutes he returned alone—having left the mulatta to make her way up the cliff, and homeward to Mount Welcome, where she belonged.

i

It was evident that the visit of the mulatta had given him gratifica
tion. Even in the dim light of his lard lamp an expression of demoniac
joy could be distinguished upon his ferocious visage, as he re-entered the
hut.

"One dead !" cried he, in an exulting tone, "anodder upon 'im death
bed ; and now de third, de las' an' wuss ob 'em all—ha ! ha ! ha !—he soon
feel de bengeance ob Chakra, de myal-man !"

Thrice did the wild, maniac-like laugh peal from under the spreading
limbs of the *ceiba*—reverberating with an unearthly echo against the cliffs
that hemmed in the Duppy's Hole. It startled the denizens of the dark
lagoon ; and like echoes came riding up the ravine the scream of the
crane, and the piercing cry of the wood ibis.

These sounds had scarce died away, when one of a somewhat different intonation was heard from above. It resembled a shriek ; or rather
as if some one had whistled through his fingers. Whoever gave utterance to the sound was upon the top of the cliff—just over the hut.

Chakra was not startled. He knew it was a signal, and given by the
guest he was expecting.

"Da's de ole Jew !" muttered he, taking the rum-bottle, and concealing it
under the bedstead. "You stay dere till I wants ye 'gain," added he
addressing himself in a confidential tone to this, the object of his greatest adoration. "Now for de nigga-dealer ! I'se hab news fo' him 'll tickle
'im in de ribs like a ole guana lizzard. Not dat Chakra care fo' him. No
—only, on dis voyage, boaf am sailin' in de same boat. Da he go 'gain !"

This last exclamation referred to a repetition of the signal heard further down : as if the whistler was advancing along the cliff, towards the
gorge at the lower end.

A third call proceeded from that point where the tree stairway scaled
the precipice—indicating to Chakra that his visitor was there awaiting
him.

Without further delay the ferryman—grim as Charon himself—returned to his canoe ; and once more paddled it across the lagoon.

At the same time, a man could be seen descending the cliff, through
the tangle of climbing plants, who, on the arrival of the canoe, stood
half-concealed among the bushes at the bottom, ready to step into it. The
moon shone upon a blue body-coat, with bright buttons ; upon a brown
beaver hat and white skull-cap ; upon tarnished top-boots, green goggles,
and an enormous umbrella.

Chakra did not need to scan the sharp Israelitish features of the man,
to ascertain who he was.

Jacob Jessuron was there by appointment : and the myal-man knew
both his presence and his purpose.

Not a word of recognition passed between the two, nor sign. Only a
caution from Chakra—as the Jew, swinging by a branch, let himself down
into the canoe.

"'Tep in lightly, Massr Jake, an' doan' push da canoe down 'tream.
'Tam jess' as much as I ken do to keep de ole craff out ob de eddy. She
get down da, an' den it am all up wif boaf o' us."

"Blesh my soul ! You shay so !" rejoined the Jew, glancing towards
the gorge, and shivering as he listened to the hoarse groaning of the
water among the grim rocks. "S'help me, I didn't know it was danger
ous. Don't fear, Shakra ! I step in ash light ash a feather."

So saying, the Jew dropped his umbrella into the bottom of the boat; and then let himself down upon the top of it, with as much gentleness as if he had been descending upon a basket of eggs.

The ferryman, seeing his freight safely aboard, paddled back to the mooring-place; and, having secured his craft as before, conducted his visitor up the valley in the direction of the hut.

On entering the temple of Obi, Jessuron—unlike the devotee who had just left it—showed no signs either of surprise or fear at its fantastic adornments. It was evident he had worshipped there before.

Nor did he evince a special veneration for the shrine; but, seating himself familiarly on the bamboo bedstead, uttered as he did so a sonorous "Ach!" which appeared as if intended to express satisfaction.

At the same time he drew from the ample pocket of his coat a shining object, which, when held before the lamp, appeared to be a bottle. The label seen upon its side, with the symbolical bunch of grapes, proved it to be a bottle of cognac.

The exclamation of the myal-man, which the sight of the label had instantaneously elicited, proved that equal satisfaction existed on his side at this mode of initiating an interview.

"Hash you a glass among your belongingsh?" inquired the Jew, looking around the hovel.

"No; dis yeer do?" asked his host, presenting a small calabash with a handle.

"Fush rate. Thish liquor drinksh goot out of anything. I had it from Capten Showler on hish last voyage. Jesh taste it, good Shakra, before we begins bishness."

A grunt from the negro announced his willing assent to the proposal.

"Whugh! he ejaculated, after swallowing the allowance poured for him into the calabash.

"Ach! goot it ish!" said his guest, on quaffing off a like quantity; and then the bottle and gourd being set on one side, the two queer characters entered into the field of free conversation.

In this the Jew took the initiative.

"I hash news for you," said he, "very shtrange news, if you hashn't already heard it, Shakra! Who dosh you think ish dead?"

"Ha!" exclaimed the myal-man, his eye suddenly lighting up with a gleam of ferocious joy; "he gone dead, am he?"

"Who? I hashn't told you," rejoined the Jew, his features assuming an expression of mock surprise. "But true," he continued, after a pause; "true, you knew he wash sick—you knew Justish Bailey was sick, an' *not likely to get over it.* Well—he hashen't, poor mansh!—he's dead and in his coffin by thish time; he breathed his lasht yesterday."

A loud and highly aspirated "Whugh!" was the only answer made by myal-man. The utterance was not meant to convey any melancholy impression. On the contrary by its peculiar intonation, it indicated as much satisfaction as any amount of words could have expressed.

"It ish very shtrange," continued the penn-keeper, in the same tone of affected simplicity; "so short a time since Mishter Ridgely died. Two of the three shustices that sat on your trial, good Shakra. It looksh ash if Providensh had a hand in it—it dosh!"

"Or de dibble, mo' like, maybe?" rejoined Chakra, with a significant leer.

"Yesh—Gott or the devil—one or t'other. Well, Shakra, you hash had your refenge, whichever hash helped you to it. Two of your enemies ish not likely to trouble you again ; and ash for the third——"

"Nor he berry long, I'se speck',' interrupted the negro, with a signifi- cant grin.

"What you shay?" exclaimed the Jew, in ar earnest under-tone. 'Hash you heard anythings ? Hash the wench been to see you ?"

"All right 'bout her, Massr Jake."

"Goot—she *hash* been?"

"Jess leab dis place 'bout quar'r ob an hour 'go."

"And she saysh she will help you to set the obeah shpell for him ?"

"Hab no fear—she do all dat. Obi hab spell oba her, dat make her dc mose anythin—ah! anythin in de world'—sartin shoo. Obi all-powerful wi' dat gal."

"Yesh, yesh!" assented the Jew; "I knowsh all that. And if Obi wash to fail," added he, doubtingly, "you hash a drink, goot Shakra—I know you hash a drink, ash potent as Obi or any other of your gotsh."

A glance of mutual intelligence passed between the two.

"How long dosh it take your shpell to work ?" inquired the penn- keeper, after an interval of silence, in which he seemed to be making some calculation.

" Dat," replied the negro, "dat depend altogedder on de sacomstance ob how long de spell am *wanted* to work. Ef 'im wanted, Dhakra make im in tree day fotch de 'trongest indiwiddible cla out o' 'im boots ; or in tree hour he do same—but ob coorse dat ud be too soon fo' be safe. A, spell ob tree hours too 'trong. Dat not Obi work—'im look berry like pison."

"Poison—yesh, yesh, it would."

" Tree day too short—tree week am de correct time. Den de spell work 'zackly like fever ob de teypos. Nobody hab s'picion 'bout 'um."

" Three weeks you shay? And no symptoms to make schandal ? You're shure that ish sufficient ? Remember, Shakra ; the Cushtos ish a strong man—strong ash a bull."

" No mar'r 'bout dat. Ef he ' trong as de bull, in dat period ob time he grow weak as de new-drop calf—I'se be boun' he 'taggering Bob long 'fore dat. You say de word, Massr Jake. Obi no like to nigga. Nigga only brack man ; he no get pay fo' 'im work. Obi 'zemble buckra man. He no work 'less him pay."

" Yesh—yesh! dat ish only shust and fair. Obi should be paid ; but shay, goot Shakra ! how much ish his prishe for a shpell of thish kind ?"

" Ef he hab no interest his self in de workin' ob de 'pell, he want a hunder poun' ob de island. When he hab interest, das diff'rent—den he takes fifty."

" Fifty poundsh ! That ish big monish, good Shakra ? In thish case Obi hash an interest—more ash anybody elsh. He hash an enemy, and wants refenge. Ish that not true, goot Shakra?"

" Das da troof. Chakra no go fo' deny 'im. But das jess why Obi 'sent do dar leetle *chore* fo' fifty'poun'. Obi enemy big buckra—'trong as you hab jess say—berry diff'cult fo' 'pell 'im. Any odder myal-man charge de full hunder peun.' Fack, no odder kud do de job—no odder but ole Chakra hab dat power."

"Shay no more about the prishe. Fifty poundsh be it. Here'sh half aown." The tempter tossed a purse containing coin into the outstretched palm of the obeah-man. "All I shtipulate for ish, that in three weeks you earn the other half; and then we shall both be shquare with the Cushtos Vochan—for I hash my refengo to shatisfy ash well as you, Shakra."

"Nuf sed, Massr Jake. 'Fore tree day de 'pell sha' be put on. You back come to do Duppy Hole four night from dis, you hear how 'im work. Whugh!"

The gourd shell was again brought into requisition; and, after a parting "kiss" at the cognac, the "heel tap" of which remained in the hut, the precious pair emerged into the open air.

The priest of Obi having conducted his fellow-conspirator across the lagoon, returned to his temple, and set himself assiduously to finish what was left of the liquor.

"Whugh!" ejaculated he, in one of the pauses that occurred between two vigorous pulls at the bottle; "ole villum Jew wuss dan Chakra—wuss dan de debbil hisseff! Doan' know wy he want rebbenge. Das nuffin' to me. I want rebbenge, an' by de great Accompong, I'se a g'wine to hab it! Ef dis gal proob true, as de odders did—she *muss* proob true—in tree week do proud, fat buckra jussis dat condemn me to dat Jumbé rock—' Cussos rodelorum,' as de call 'im—won't hab no more flesh on 'im bones dan de keleton he tink wa' myen. And den, when 'im die—ah! den, affer 'im die de daughter ob dat Quasheba dat twenty year 'go 'corn de lub ob de Coromantee for dat ob de yellow Maroon—maybe de lilly Quasheba sleep in de arms ob Chakra de myal-man. Whugh!"

As the minister of Obi gave utterance to this hypothetical threat, a lurid light glared up in his sunken eyes, and his white shark-like teeth were displayed in an exulting grin—hideous as if the demon himself were smiling over some monstrous menace!

Both cognac and rum-bottle were repeatedly tasted, until the strong frame of the Coromantee gave way to the stronger spirit of the alcohol; and, muttering fearful threats in his gumbo jargon, he at length sank unconscious on the floor.

There—under the light of the lard lamp, now flickering feebly—he lay like some hideous satyr whom Bacchus, by an angry blow, had folled prostrate to the earth!

CHAPTER LXVIII.

THE MYSTERIOUS MOTIVE.

THE original motive of the myal-man, in conspiring the death of the Custos Vaughan, would have been strong enough to urge him on without this new instigation. As we have seen, it was one of deadly revenge—simple and easily understood.

Not so easily understood was that which actuated the Jew. On the contrary, so secretly had he preserved his purposes, that no living man —not even Chakra himself—had been made privy to them. Up to this moment they may have appeared mysterious · and the time has arrived when it becomes necessary to reveal them. The explanation will show them to be only natural—only in keeping with the character of this crooked and cruel old man.

It is scarce necessary to say that Jacob Jessuron was no type of his race; nor, indeed, of any race. A German Jew by birth, it was not necessarily this that made him either slave-dealer or slave-stealer. Christians have taken their full share in both branches of the nefarious trade; and equally with both Jews and Mohammedans have they been guilty of its most hideous enormities. It was not, therefore, because Jacob Jessuron chanced to be a Jew that he was a trafficker in human flesh and blood—no more that he was a villanous man; but because he was Jacob Jessuron—a representative of neither race nor nation, but simply a character *sui generis*.

Without dwelling upon his general demerits, let us return to the more particular theme of the motive, or motives, which were instigating him to make a victim of his neighbour Vaughan—a death victim: for his conversation with Chakra showed that this was the very starting point of his intentions.

In the first place, he was well acquainted with the domestic history of the planter—at least, with that portion of it that had transpired subsequent to the latter's coming into possession of Mount Welcome. He knew something of Mr. Vaughan previously, while the latter was manager of the Montagu Castle estate; but it was only after the Custos had become his nearer neighbour, by removal to his present residence, that the Jew's knowledge of him and his private affairs had become intimate and accurate.

This knowledge he had obtained in various ways: partly by the opportunities of social intercourse, never very cordial; partly through business transactions; and, perhaps, more than all—at least, as regarded some of the more secret passages of Mr. Vaughan's history—from the myal-man, Chakra.

Notwithstanding his grotesque hideousness, the Coromantee was gifted with a rare though dangerous intelligence. He was *au fait* to everything that had occurred upon the plantation of Mount Welcome for a past period of more than forty years. As already hinted, he knew too much; and it was this inconvenient omniscience that had caused him to be consigned to the Jumbé rock.

For more than one purpose had the Jew made use of the myal-man; and if the latter was at present assisting him in his dark design, it was not the first by many, both deep and dark, in which Chakra had lent him a hand. The secret partnership had been of long duration.

The Jew's knowledge of the affairs of Loftus Vaughan extended to many facts unknown even to Chakra. One of these was, that his neighbour was blessed with an English brother, who had an only son.

An artist was the English brother, without fortune—almost without name. Many other circumstances relating to him had come to the knowledge of Jessuron; among the rest, that the proud Custos knew little about his poor English relatives, cared less, and scarcely kept up correspondence with them.

In what way could this knowledge interest Jacob Jessuron, for it did?

That we shall presently see. Indeed, the reason may be guessed at. It **has** been given already; though it may be here stated more fully.

As was well known, Loftus Vaughan had never been married to the quadroon Quasheba. That circumstance, however, would have signified little, had Quasheba been a white woman, or even a "quinteroon"— in Jamaica termed a *mustee*, and by some fanciful plagiarists, of late, pedantically styled "octoroon"—a title which, it may here be stated, has no existence except in the romantic brains of these second-hand litterateurs.

We repeat it—had the slave Quasheba been either a white woman, or even a *mustee*, the fact of a marriage, or no marriage, would have signified little—so far as regarded the succession of her offspring to the estates of the father. It is true that, if not married, the daughter would, by the laws of Jamaica—as by those of other lands—still have been *illegitimate;* but for all that, she could have inherited her father's property, *if left to her by will:* since in Jamaica no *entail* existed.

As things stood, however, the case was widely, and for the lilly Quasheba—Kate Vaughan — dangerously different. Her mother was *only a quadroon;* and, married or unmarried, she, the daughter, could not inherit —*even by will*—beyond the paltry legacy of £2,000 currency, or £1,500 sterling!

Kate Vaughan was herself only a *mustee*—still wanting one step farther from slavery to bring her within the protecting pale of freedom, and the enjoyment of its favours.

No will that Loftus Vaughan could decree, no testamentary disposition he might make, could render his daughter his devisee—his heiress.

He might will his property to anybody he pleased: so long as that anybody was a so-called *white;* but, failing to make such a testament, his estate of Mount Welcome, with all he possessed besides, must fall to the next kin—in short, to his nephew Herbert.

Was there no remedy for this unspeakable dilemma? No means by which the young creole might be saved from disinheritance?

The question has been already answered—there was.

Loftus Vaughan knew the remedy, and fully intended to adopt it. Every day was he designing to set out for Spanish Town, to obtain the *special act;* and every day was the journey put off.

It was the execution of this design that the Jew Jessuron of all things dreaded most; and to prevent it was the object of his visit to the temple of Obi.

Why he dreaded it scarce needs explanation.

Should Loftus Vaughan fail in his intent, Herbert Vaughan would be the heir of Mount Welcome : and Herbert's heart was in the keeping of Judith Jessuron.

So fondly believed the Jewess; and, with her assurance of the fact, so also the Jew.

The *love-spell* woven by Judith had been the first step towards securing the grand inheritance; the second was to be the *death-spell*, administered by Chakra and his acolyte.

CHAPTER LXIX.

THE DEATH-SPELL.

ON the night after that on which Chakra had given receptin to Jessuron, and about the same hour, the Coromantee was at home in his hut, engaged in some operation of an apparently important nature : since it engrossed his whole attention.

A fire was burning in the middle of the floor, in a rude, extemporised furnace, constructed by four large stones so placed as to inclose a small quadrangle.

The fuel with which this fire was fed, although giving out a great deal of smoke, burnt also with a bright, clear flame. It was not wood, but consisted of a number of black agglutinated masses, bearing a considerable resemblance to peat or coal.

A stranger to Jamaica might have been puzzled to make out what it was ; but a denizen of the island would have told it at a glance, that the dark-coloured pieces that appeared to be freshly piled upon the fire were fragments detached from the nests of the Duck-ants, which, often as large as hogsheads, may be seen adhering to the trees of a tropical forest.

As the smoke emitted by this fuel is less painful to the eyes than that of a wood fire, and yet more efficacious in clearing out the mosquitoes—that plague of a southern clime—it may be supposed that the Coromantee had chosen it on that account. Whether or not, it served his purpose well.

A small iron pot, without crook or crane, rested upon the stones of the furnace ; and the anxious glances with which the negro regarded its simmering contents—now stirring them a little, now lifting a portion in his wooden spoon, and carefully scrutinising it under the light of the lamp—told that the concoction in which he was engaged was of a *chemical* rather than *culinary* nature. As he bent over the fire—like a he Hecate stirring her witch-cauldron—his earnest yet stealthy manner, his cat-like movements and furtive glances, betrayed some devilish design.

This idea was strenghtened on looking at the objects that lay near to his hand—a portion of which had been already consigned to the pot. A cutacoo rested upon the floor, containing plants of several species ; among which a botanist could have recognised the branched *calalue*, the dumb-cane, and various other herbs and roots of noxious fame. Conspicuous was the "Savanna flower," with its tortuous stem and golden corolla—a true dog-bane, and one of the most potent of vegetable poisona.

By its side could be seen its antidote—the curious nuts of the "nhandiroba:"* for the myal-man could *cure* as well as *kill*, whenever it became his interest to do so.

Drawing from such a larder, it was plain that he was not engaged in the preparation of his supper. Poisons, not provisions, were the ingredients of the pot.

The specific he was now concocting was from various sources, but chiefly from the sap of the Savanna flower. It was the *death-spell of Obeah!*

For whom was the Coromantee preparing this precious hell-broth ?

* Fevillea cordifolia.

His mutterings, as he stooped over the pot, revealed the name of his intended victim.

"You may be 'trong, Cussus Vaugh'n—dat I doan deny; but, by de power ob Obeah, you soon shake in you shoe. Obeah! Ha! ha! ha! Dat do fo' de know-nuffin niggas. My Obeah am de Sabana flower, de branch calalue, and de allimgator apple—dems de 'pell mo' powerful dan Obi himself—dems de stuff dat gib de shibberin' body and de staggerin' limbs to de enemies ob dis here child. Whugh!"

Once more dipping the spoon into the pot, and skimming up a portion of the boiling liquid, he bent forward to examine it.

"'T am done!" he exclaimed. "Jess de right colour—jess de right sickness. Now fo' bottle de licka!"

Saying this, he took the pot from the fire; and, after first pouring the "liquor" into a calabash, and leaving it for some moments to cool, he transferred it to the rum-bottle—long since emptied of its original contents.

Having carefully pressed in the cork, he set the bottle to one side—not in concealment, but as if intended for use at no very distant time.

Then, having gathered up his scattered pharmacopæia, and deposited the whole collection in the cutacoo. he stepped into the doorway of the hut, and, placing a hand on each post, stood in an attitude to listen.

It was evident he expected some visitor; and who it was to be was revealed by the muttered soliloquy in which he continued to indulge The slave Cynthia was to give him another 'séance.'

"Time dat yella wench wa' come. Muss be nigh twelve ob de night. Maybe she hab call, an' a no hear her, fo' de noise ob dat catrack? A bess go down b'low. Like naf a find her da!"

As he was stepping across the threshold to put this design into execu tion, a cry, uttered in the shrill treble of a woman's voice, and just audible through the soughing sound from the cataract, came from the cliff above.

"Da's de wench!" muttered the myal-man, as he heard it. "A make sartin she'd come. Lub lead woman troo fire an' water—lead um to de debbil. Seed de time dat ar' yella' gal temp' dis chile. No care now. But one Chakra ebber care 'brace in dese arms. Her he clasp only once, he content—he willin' den fo' die. Augh!"

As the Coromantee uttered the impassioned ejaculation, he strode out-ward from the door, and walked with nervous and hurried step—like one urged on by the prospect of soon achieving some horrible but heartfelt purpose, he had long contemplated from a distance.

CHAPTER LXX.

THE INVOCATION OF ACCOMPONG.

THE canoe soon made its trip, and returned with Cynthia seated in the stern. She carried a basket on her arm as before, filled with comestibles, and not forgetting the precious bottle of rum.

As before, she followed the myal-man to his hut—this time entering

with more confidence, and seating herself unbidden upon the side of the
bamboo bedstead.

Still was she not without some feeling of fear: as testified by a slight
trembling that might be observed when her eyes rested upon the freshly-
filled bottle, that stood in a conspicuous place. The look which she
turned upon it told that she possessed some previous information as to
the nature of its contents—or perhaps she had only a suspicion.

" Da's de bottle fo' you," said the myal-man, noticing her glance, " and
tis hya," continued he, drawing the other out of Cynthia's basket, " dis
aya am do one fo'——"

He was about to add " me," but before he could pass the word out of
his mouth, he had got the neck of the rum-bottle into it; and the "gluck-
gluck" of the descending fluid was substituted for the personal pronoun.

The usual " Whugh" wound up the operation, clearing the Coromantee's throat ; and then by a gesture he gave Cynthia to understand that
he was ready to proceed with the more serious business of the interview.

" Dat bottle," said he, pointing to the one that contained his decoction,
" am de O'neah 'pell. It make Cubina lub you while dar's a tuff ob wool
on de top o' 'im head. Dat long 'nuf, I reck'n : fo' when 'im go bald, you
no care fr' 'im lub."

" Is that the love-spell you spoke of?" inquired the mulatta, with an
ambiguous expression of countenance, in which hope appeared struggling
with doubt.

" De lub-spell ! No—not 'zackly dat. De lub-spell am different. It
am ob de nature ob an ointment. Hya! I'se got 'im in de coco-shell."

As Chakra said this, he raised his hand and drew out from a cranny in
the thatch, about three-quarters of the shell of a cocoa-nut ; inside which,
instead of its white coagulum, appeared a carrot-coloured paste, resembling the pulp of the *sapata-mammee*—for this, in reality, it was.

" Das da lub mixture !" continued the obeah-man, in a triumphant tone ;
" das for Cubina !"

" Ah ! Cubina is to take that?"

" Shoo he am. He mus' take 'im. A gib it him, and den he go mad
for you. You he lub, an' he lub you like two turtle dove in de 'pring
time. Whugh !"

" Good Chakra—you are sure it will do Cubina no harm?"

The query proved that the jealousy of the mulatta had not yet reached
the point of revenge.

" No," responded the negro ; " do 'im good—do 'im good, an nuffin else.
Now, Cynthy, gal," continued he, turning his eyes upon the bottle ; " das
for de ole Cussos ob Moun' Welc'm—take um—put 'im in you basket."

The woman obeyed ; though her fingers trembled, as she touched the
bottle that contained the mysterious medicine.

" And what am I to do with it, Chakra?" she asked, irresolutely.

" Wha you do ? I tole you arready wha you do. You gib to Masar—
you enemy and myen."

" But what is it?"

" Why you ask daat ? I tole you it am de death-'pell."

" Oh, Chakra ! is it poison?"

" No, you foo'—ef 'twa pizen, den it kill de buckra right off. It no kill
'im. It only make um sick, an' den, preehap, it make 'im die. Das no
pizen ! You 'fuse give im !"

The woman appeared to hesitate, as if some sparks of a better nature were rising within her soul. If there were such sparks, only for a short while were they allowed to shine.

"You 'fuse gib 'im?" repeated the tempter, hastening to extinguish them. "If you 'fuse, I no put de lub-spell on Cubina. Mor'n dat—I set de obeah fo' you—you, youseff!"

"O no—no, Chakra!" cried she, cowering before the Coromantee; "I d: not refuse—I shall give it—anything you command me."

"Dere, now—das sensible ob you, Cynthy. Now I gib you de instrul ahin how fo' minister de 'pell. Lissen, an' 'member ebbery ting I g 'peak you."

As the hideous sorcerer said this, he sat down in front of his neophyte—fixing his eyes upon hers, as if the better to impress his words upon her memory.

"Fuss an' formoss, den, de grand buckra ob Moun' Welcome, ebbery night 'fore he go bed, hab glass ob rum punch. I know he used hab—he so 'till, eh?"

"Yes—he does,";mechanically answered the mulatta.

"Berry likely—dat ere am one ob de habits neider buckra nor brack man am like break off. Ebbery night, shoo?"

"Yes—every night—one glass—sometimes two."

"Gorry! ef twa me, me hab two—not sometime, but alway—'cept when a make um tree, ha! ha! Berry well, das all right; and now, gal, who mix de punch fo' 'im? You use do dat youseff, Cynthy?"

"It is still my business. I make it for him every night."

"Good—das jess de ting. Whugh! now we know how set de 'pell ob de obeah. You see dis yeer? It am de claw ob de mountain crab. You see de 'cratch—dar—inside ob de machine? Well—up to dat mark it hold jess de 'zack quantum. Ebbery night you make de punch you fill up dar out ob dis bottle. You pour in de glass—fuss de sugar an' lemon —den de water—den de rum, which am 'tronger dan de water out ob dis bottle; an' affer dat de 'pell, which am de 'trongest ob dem all. You 'member all a hab tell you?"

"I shall remember it," rejoined the woman, with a firmness of voice, partly assumed—for she dreaded to show any sign of irresolution.

"Ef you no do, den de 'pell turn roun' an' he work 'gin youseff. When de Obi once 'gins, he no 'top till he hab 'im victim. Now a go fo 'voke de god Accompong. He come when Chakra call. He make 'im 'pearance in de foam ob de catrack out yonna. Affer dat no mortal him lay not til: one die fo' de sacrafize. You 'tay in hya. De god muss not see no woman—you lissen—you hear um voice."

Rising with a mysterious air, and taking down from its peg an old palm-leaf wallet, that appeared to contain some heavy article, the myal-man stepped out of the hut, closing the door behind him, lest—as he informed the mulatta, in *sotto voce*—the god might set his eyes on her, and get into a rage.

Cynthia seemed to consider the precaution scarce sufficient; for, the moment the door was closed, in order to make herself still more secure against being seen, she glided up to the light and extinguished it. Then groping her way back to the bedstead she staggered down upon it, and sat shivering with apprehension.

As the myal-man had enjoined upon her, she listened ; and, as he had promised her, she heard—if not the voice of Accompong—sounds that were worthy of having proceeded from the throat of that Ethiopian divinity.

At first a voice reached her which she knew to be human: since it was the voice of Chakra himself. It was uttered, nevertheless, in strange and unnatural tones, that at each moment kept changing. Now it came ringing through the interstices of the bamboos, in a kind of long-drawn song, as if the myal-man was initiating his ceremonies with the verse of a psalm. Then the chaunt became quicker, by a sort of *crescendo* movement, and the song appeared transformed to a *recitative*. Next were heard sounds of a very different intonation, now resembling the shrill, harsh call of a cowhorn, or conch-shell, and gradually dying off into a prolonged bass, like the groaning of a cracked trombone.

After this had continued for some time, there ensued a dialogue—in which the listener could recognise only one of the voices as that of Chakra.

Whose could be the other ? It could only be that of Accompong. The god was upon the ground !

Cynthia trembled as she thought how very near he was. How lucky she had blown out the light ! If still burning, she must have been seen ; for both Chakra and the deity were just outside the door, and so near that she could not only hear their voices with distinctness, but the very words that were spoken.

Some of these were in an unknown tongue, and she could not understand them. Others were in English, or rather its synonym in the form of a negro *patois*. These last she comprehended ; and their signification was not of such a character to give solace to her thoughts, but the contrary.

Chakra chantant:—

> " Open de bottle—draw de cork,
> De 'pell he work—de 'pell he work ;
> De buckra man muss die !"

"*Muss die!*" repeated Accompong, in a voice that sounded as if from the interior of an empty hogshead.

> " De yella gal she gib 'im drink ;
> It make 'im sick—it make 'im srink,
> It send 'im to 'im tomb."

Him tomb " came the response of Accompong.

> " An' if de yella gal refuse,
> She 'tep into de buckra's shoes,
> An' fill de buckra's grave."

" *Buckra's grave!*" echoed the African god, in a sonorous and emphatic voice, that told there was no alternative to the hypothetical fate thus proclaimed.

There was a short interval of silence, and then the shrill, conch-like sound was again heard—as before, followed by the long-drawn bass.

This was the exorcism of the god—as the same sounds, previously heard, had been his invocation.

It was also the *finale* of the ceremony: since the moment after Chakra pushed open the door, and stood in the entrance to the hut.

"Cynthy, gal," said he, with a look of mysterious gravity, "why you blow out de light? But no matter for light. Its all oba. Did you hear de god 'peak?"

"I did," murmured the mulatta, still trembling at what she had heard.

"You hear wha him say?"

"Yes—yes."

"Den he 'peak de troof. Nuffin more'n dat. You take heed—I 'vise you, as you friend. You go troo wif de 'pell now 'im 'gun, else you life not worth so much trash ob de suga-cane. A say no more. Ebbery night, in um fuss glass, de full ob de crab-claw, up to de mark. Now, gal, come 'long."

The last command was the more readily obeyed : since the woman was but too glad to get away from a place whose terrors had so severely tested her courage.

Taking up the basket—in which the bottle containing the dangerous decoction had been already placed—she glided out of the hut, and once more followed the Coromantee to his canoe.

CHAPTER LXXI.

CHAKRA REDIVIVUS.

THE scene that had thus transpired in the depths of the Duppy's Hole requires some explanation. The dialogue which Cynthia had held with the hideous Coromantee, though couched in ambiguous phrase, clearly indicated an intention to assassinate the Custos Vaughan ; and by a mode which these arch-conspirators figuratively—almost facetiously — termed the *death-spell!*

In the diabolical design, the woman appeared to be acting rather as coadjutor than conspirator ; and her motive for taking part in the plot, though wicked enough, presents, in the language of French law, one or two " extenuating circumstances."

A word or two of the mulatta's history will make her motive understood, though her conversation may have already declared it with sufficient distinctness.

Cynthia was a slave on the plantation of Mount Welcome—one of the house-wenches, or domestics belonging to the mansion ; and of which, in a large establishment like that of Custos Vaughan, there is usually a numerous troop.

The girl, in earlier life, had been gifted with good looks. Nor could it be said that they were yet gone ; though hers was a beauty that no longer presented the charm of innocent girlhood, but rather the sensualistic attractions of a bold and abandoned woman.

Had Cynthia been other than a slave—that is, had she lived in other lands—her story might have been different. But in that, her native country—and under conditions of bondage that extended alike to body and soul—her fair looks had proved only a fatal gift.

With no motive to tread the paths of virtue—with a thousand temptations to stray from it—Cynthia, like, it is sad to think, too many of her race, had wandered into ways of wantonness. It might be, as Chakra had obscurely hinted, that the slave had been abused. Wherever lay the blame, she had, at all events, become abandoned.

Whether loving them or not, Cynthia had, in her time, been honoured with more than one admirer. But there was one on whom she had at length fixed her affections—or, more properly, her passion—to a degree of permanence that promised to end only with her life. The one was the young Maroon captain, Cubina; and although it was a love of comparatively recent origin, it had already reached the extreme of passion. So fierce and reckless had it grown, on the part of the wretched woman, that she was ready for anything that promised to procure her its requital—ready even for the nefarious purpose of Chakra.

To do Cubina justice, this love of the slave Cynthia was not reciprocated. To the levities and light speeches habitually indulged in by the Maroons, in their intercourse with the plantation people, Cubina was a singular exception; and Cynthia's statement that he had once returned her love—somewhat doubtingly delivered—had no other foundation than her own groundless conjectures, in which the wish was father to the thought.

Some friendly words may have passed between the Maroon and mulatta—for they had often met upon their mutual wanderings; but the latter, in mistaking them from words of love, had, sadly for herself, misconceived their meaning.

Of late her passion had become fiercer than ever—since jealousy had arisen to stimulate it—jealousy of Cubina with Yola. The meeting and subsequent correspondence of the Maroon with the Foolah maiden were events of still more recent date; but already had Cynthia seen or heard enough to produce the conviction that in Yola she had found a rival. With the passionate 'sang-melee', jealousy pointed to revenge; and she had begun to indulge in dark projects of this nature when Chakra chanced to throw his shadow across her path.

Cynthia was one of those slaves known as *night-rangers*. She was in the habit of making occasional and nocturnal excursions through the woods, for many purposes; but, of late, principally in the hope of meeting Cubina, and satisfying herself in regard to suspicion she had conceived of meetings that occurred between him and Yola.

In one of these expeditions she had encountered a man whose appearance filled her with terror; and very naturally; since it was not a man, but a *ghost* that she saw—the ghost of Chakra, the myal-man!

That it was the "duppy" of old Chakra, Cynthia on sight firmly believed; and might have continued longer in that belief, had she been permitted to make her escape from the spot, as she was fast hastening to do. But the long, ape-like arms of the myalman, flung around her on the instant, restrained her flight—and she became convinced that it was not Chakra's ghost, but Chakra himself, who embraced her !

It was not altogether by chance this encounter had occurred—at least, on the part of Chakra. He had been looking out for Cynthia for some time before. He wanted her for a purpose.

The mulatta made no revelations of what she had seen. With all his ugliness the myal-man had been the friend of her mother—had often dandled her, Cynthia, upon his knees. But the tongue of Juno's daughter was held silent by stronger ties than those of affection. Fear was one; and there was also another. If Chakra wanted Cynthia for a purpose, quick instinct told her she might stand in need of *him*. He was just the instrument by which to accomplish a revenge.

On the instant, mulatta and myal-man became allies.

This mutual confidence had been but very recently established—only a few days, or rather nights before that on which Cynthia had given Chakra the first 'séance' in the temple of Obi.

The purpose for which the myal-man wanted the mulatta—or one purpose, at least—has been sufficiently set forth in the dialogues occurring between them. He required her assistance to put the death-spell upon the planter, Loftus Vaughan. The character of Cynthia, which Chakra well understood—with the opportunities she had, in her capacity of housemaid—promised to provide the assassin with an agency of the most effective kind; and the pretended love-spell he was to put upon Cubina had given Chakra a talisman, by which his agent was but too easily induced to undertake the execution of his diabolical design.

Among many other performances of a like kind, it was part of Chakra's programme, some day or other; to put the death-spell upon the Maroon himself; to "obeah" young Cubina—as it was suspected he had the old Cubina, the father, after twenty years of tentation. It was but the want of opportunity that had hindered him from having long before accomplished his nefarious project upon the son, as upon the father—in satisfaction of a revenge, so old as to be anterior to the birth of Cubina himself, thought associated with that event.

Of course, this design was not revealed to Cynthia.

His motive for conspiring the death of Loftus Vaughan was without any mystery whatever; and this—perhaps more than any other of his crimes, either purposed or committed—might plead "extenuating circumstances." His cruel condemnation, and subsequent exposure upon the Gumbé Rock, was a stimulus sufficient to have excited to revenge a gentler nature than that of Chakra, the Coromantee. It need scarce be said that it had stimulated his to the deadliest degree.

The resurrection of the myal-man may appear a mystery—as it did to the slave, Cynthia. There was one individual, however, who understood its character. Not to an African god was the priest of Obi indebted for his resuscitation, but to an Israelitish man—to Jacob Jessuron.

It was but a simple trick—that of substituting a carcase—afterwards to become a skeleton—for the presumed dead body of the myal-man. The barracoon of the slave-merchant generally had such a commodity in stock. If not, Jessuron would not have scrupled to create one for the occasion.

Humanity had nothing to do in the supplying of this proxy. Had there been no other motive than that to actuate the Jew, Chakra might have rotted under the shadow of the cabbage-palm.

But Jessuron had his purpose for saving the life of the condemned criminal—more than one, perhaps—and he had saved it.

Since his *resurrection*, Chakra had pursued his iniquitous calling with even more energy than of old; but now in the most secret and surrepti-tious manner.

He had not been long in re-establishing a system of confederates—un-der the auspices of a new name—but only of sight, and with disguised form and masked face, did he give his clients rendezvous. Never in the Duppy's Hole, for few were sufficiently initiated into the mysteries of nyalism, to be introduced to its temple in that secure retreat.

Although the confederates of the obeah-man rarely reveal the secret of his whereabouts—even his poor *victims dreading to divulge it*—Chakra knew the necessity of keeping as much as possible *en-perdu*; and no out-law with halter threatening his neck, could have been more cautious in his outgoings and incomings.

He knew that his life was forfeit on the old judgment; and, though he had once escaped execution, he might not be so fortunate upon a second occasion. If recaptured, some surer mode of death would be provided—a rope instead of a chain; and in place of being fastened to the trunk of a tree, he would be pretty certain of being suspended by the neck to the branch of one.

Knowing all this, Chakra *redivivus* trod the forest paths with caution, and was especially shy of the plantation of Mount Welcome. Around the sides of the mountain he had little to fear. The reputation of the Jumbé Rock, as well as that of the Duppy's Hole, kept the proximity of these noted places clear of all dark-skinned stragglers; and there Chakra had the beat to himself.

Upon dark nights, however, like the wolf, he could prowl at pleasure, and with comparative safety—especially upon the outskirts of the more remote plantations; the little intercourse allowed between the slaves of distant estates making acquaintanceship among them a rare exception. It was chiefly upon these distant estates that Chakra held communications with his confederates and clients.

It was now more than a year since he had made his pretended resur-rection: and yet so cautiously had he crawled about, that only a few in dividuals were aware of the fact of his being still alive. Others *had seen his ghost!* Several negroes of Mount Welcome plantation would have sworn to having met the "duppy" of old Chakra, while travelling through the woods at night; and the sight had cured these witnesses of their propensity for nocturnal wandering.

CHAPTER LXXII.

MIDNIGHT WANDERERS

Once more under the *ceiba*, that gigantic trysting-tree, stood the Maroon and his mistress. Not, as before, in the bright noonday sun, but near the midhour of the night. The Foolah had dared the dangers of the forest to meet her beloved Cubina.

Ar.   .here were dangers in that forest, more to be dreaded than fierce beasts or ravenous reptiles—more to be dreaded than the tusks of the wild boar, or the teeth of the scaly alligator.   There were monsters in human form far more fearful to be encountered ; and at that moment not very distant from the spot where the lovers had made their rendezvous.

Love rocks little of dangers.   Cubina knew of none ; and, in Yola's belief, there was no danger while Cubina was near.

The moon was in high heaven, full, calm, and clear.   Her beams filled the glade with a silvery effulgence.   It was a moonlight that almost rivalled the brightness of day.   The flowers over the earth, and the blossoms upon the trees, appeared full blown : as if they had opened their petals to drink in the delightful dew.   Borne upon the soft silent breeze, the nocturnal sounds of the forest fell with a tremulous cadence upon the ear ; while the nightingale of the West, as if proud of the superiority of her counterfeit notes, in turns imitated them all.

The lovers stood in shadow—but it was the shadow of the *ceiba*. There was none in their hearts ; and had the moonlight at that moment fallen upon their faces no trace of a cloud could have been detected there.   \

It was a happy meeting—one of the happiest they had yet enjoyed. Each had brought good news to the other.   Cubina, that the brother of his beloved was still safe under his protection—safe and well ; Yola, that her young mistress had promised to bestow upon her her freedom.

Within the few days since they had last met, many things had transpired to interest both   Each had a tale to tell.

Yola related now the story of her brother's misfortunes, though strictly kept from the servants at Mount Welcome, had become known to her mistress ; how Miss Vaughan, on hearing it, had requested her father to grant her (Yola's) manumission ; and how the Custos had consented to the request.   Conditionally, it was true.   Her " free papers" were to be dated from a certain day—that on which her young mistress was to become a bride, but that day was supposed not to be far distant.

It was joyous news for the Maroon.   He might keep his hundred pounds for the plenishing of his mountain home !

This piece of intelligence might have taken Cubina more by surprise, but for the understanding that now existed between him and the Custos —whom he had of late frequently visited.   Certain conditions had become established between the magistrate and the Maroon, which rendered the latter less apprehensive about the future.   Mr. Vaughan had made some promises to himself in regard to the manumission of Yola.   It is true, these had also been *conditional* ; and their performance was to depend, to a great degree, on the success of the prosecution to be instituted against the Jew.   But, with the Custos himself as a prosecutor, Cubina felt sanguine that the conditions would be accomplished.

There were circumstances to be kept secret.   Even to his sweetheart the lover was not permitted to impart the knowledge of the affair.   Only did he make known to her that steps were being taken to cause the restitution of her brother's property ; but how, where, and when, could not be divulged until that day when war should be openly declared against the enemy.   So had the Custos commanded.

5

Cubina, nevertheless, could not help being gratified by the the intelligence which Yola had conveyed to him. The promise of Miss Vaughan had but one condition—her bridal day; and that was definite and certain.

"Ah!" said Cubina, turning with a proud look towards his sweetheart, "it will be a happy day for all. No, not for all," added he, his face suddenly assuming an expression of sadness; "not for all. There is one, I fear, to whom that day will not bring happiness!"

"I know one, too, Cubina," rejoined the girl, her countenance appearng to reflect the expression that had come over his.

"Oh, you know it, too? Miss Vaughan has told you then, I suppose? I hope she does not boast of it?"

"What she boast, Cubina?"

"Why, of breaking his heart, as you would do mine, if you were to marry somebody else. Poor young fellow! *Crambo!* If I'm not mistaken, it will be a sad day for him!"

The girl looked up in puzzled surprise!

"Sad day for him! No, Cubina; he very happy. For her—poor missa—that day be sad."

"*Vayate!* What do you mean, Yola?"

"No more dan I say, Cubina. Missa Kate be very sorrow that day she marry Mr. Mongew—she very sorrow now."

"What!" exclaimed Cubina, suddenly placing himself in an attitude of unusual attention; "do I understand you to say that Miss Vaughan don't wish to marry this Mr. Smythje?"

"She no love him, Cubina. Why she wish marry him, then?"

"Ha!" significantly ejaculated the Maroon, while an expression of joy seemed to steal over his countenance; "what makes you think she don't love him? Have you a reason, Yola?"

"Missa me say so; she me tell everything, Cubina."

"You are sure she has said that she don't love him?"

"She laugh at him—she no care for him. Girl no love one she laugh at —never."

"*Vaya!* I hope you will never laugh at me, then! But say, dearest; do you know why she is going to marry Mr. Smythje?"

"Massa her make marry. He Mr. Mongew very, very rich—he great planter. That why she him go marry."

"Ho?—he!" thoughtfully ejaculated the Captain of Maroons. "I suspected there was some compulsion," continued he, not speaking to his companion, but muttering the words to himself.

"Can you tell me, Yola," he asked, turning again to his sweetheart "do you know why your mistress does not like this grand gentleman? Has she told you any reason?"

"Very good reason, Cubina. She another love; that why she Mongew not like."

"Ah! she's in love with somebody else! Have you heard who it is Yola?"

"Oh, yes; you know him youself. He Missa Kate's cousin; she him love."

"Her cousin, Herbert Vaughan?"

"Yes, he name Herber'; he come once—never more come. No matter, she ℩ ve him first time—she him love ever more! Same I you, Cubina, I you love first time, all the same for ever."

" You are sure of all this ?" inquired Cubina, in his anxiety to know more, resisting the temptation to reciprocate the endearing speech ; "you are sure Miss Vaughan loves her cousin Herbert ?"

"Sure, Cubina ; Missa say so many time. She have very much grief for him. She hear he marry one fine, bad lady. You know old Jew—his daughter he go marry."

" I have heard so," rejoined Cubina, evidently keeping back from his sweetheart a more definite knowledge of the subject which he himself possessed ; " I have heard so. After all," he continued, speaking reflectingly, "it might not happen—neither of these marriages. There's a proverb, Yola, I've heard among the white folks—'*many a slip between the cup and the lip.*' I hope it won't be true of you and me ; but it might come to pass between young Master Vaughan and Miss Jessuron. Who knows? I know something. *Por Dios !* you've given me good news—I think, for somebody. But tell me, Yola ; have you heard them say *when* your mistress and this great gentleman are to be married ?"

"Massa he say soon. He tell Miss Kate he go great journey. When he come back they get marry ; he Missa Kate say so yesterday."

"The Custos going a journey ? Have you heard where ?"

"Spanish town, Missa me tell—a great big place far away."

" I wonder what that can be for ?" said Cubina to himself, and in a conjectural tone. "Well, Yola," he added, after a pause, and speaking more earnestly, "listen to me. As soon as Mr. Vaughan has set out on this journey, you come to me. Perhaps I may have a message for your mistress. Have you heard when he intends to take the road ?"

" He go to morrow morning."

" Ha ! so soon ! Well, so much the better for us, and maybe for somebody else. You must meet me here to-morrow night. Tell your mistress it concerns herself. No, don't tell her," he added, correcting himself, "she will let you come without that excuse ; besides, it might be that— never mind ! Come anyhow. I shall be waiting for you at this same hour."

Yola gave her willing promise to keep an appointment so accordant to her inclinations.

For some time longer the lovers conversed, imparting to each other the ordinary news of life—the details of common things—to be at length succeeded by words only of love of far diviner interest.

Cubina swore eternal truth—by the trees around—by the sky above— by the bright moon, and the blue heavens.

He had done the same a score of times ; and as often had he been believed. But lovers never tire of such vows—neither to near or to repeat them.

The African maiden answered with promises of faithfulness, alike free, alike fervent. She no longer sighed for her far Gambian home—no more mourned the fate that had torn her from a court to consign her to slavery

The dark hours of her life seemed to have ended ; and her future, as her present, was full of hope and bliss !

For more then an hour did the enamoured pair indulge in this sweet converse. They were about to close it with a parting kiss.

The Maroon stood with his strong arms tenderly entwined around the waist of his mistress, who willingly yelded to the embrace. Her slender form under the shadow of the *ceiba* looked like the statue of some Egyptian maiden in bronze antique.

The adieu had been spoken more than once ; but still the lovers lingered, as if loth to give the parting kiss. There had been more than one, but not that which was to end the interview.

Ere their lips had met to achieve it, the design was interrupted. Voices fell upon their ears, and two forms appeared emerging into the moonlight, at the lower end of the glade, rapidly advancing in the direction of the *ceiba*.

As if by a common instinct, Cubina and his mistress stepped silently and simultaneously back, retiring together between the buttresses of the tree. There it was dark enough for concealment. Only an eye bent on purposed scrutiny could have detected their presence.

The forms drew near. They were those of a man and a woman. The moonlight shining full upon them, rendered them easy of recognition; but their voices had already declared their identity. Both the intruders were known to both the lovers. They were the Jew Jessuron and the slave Cynthia.

"*Crambo!*" muttered the Maroon, as he saw who they were. "What on earth can *they* be doing together? At this time of the night, and here—so far away from any house? *Maldito!* some wicked errand, I warrant."

By this time the brace of midnight strollers had got opposite to the tree, and the Jew was delivering himself of a speech, which was plainly heard by those who stood concealed in its shadow.

"Now, Cynthy—goot wench!—you hashn't said yet why he hash sent for me? Do yoush know what it ish for?"

"I don't, Mass Jess'ron, unless it be——"

"Unlesh what, wench?"

"Somethin' 'bout the news I took him afore I come to you, when I went with his basket of provisions——"

"Ah-ah! you took him some newsh—what newsh, girl?"

"Only that Massr Vaugh'n am a goin' away in the mornin'."

"Blesh my soul!" exclaimed the Jew, suddenly stopping in his tracks, and turning towards the mulatta with a look of troubled surprise. "Blesh my soul! You don't shay that, dosh you?"

"Dey say so at the Buff, Massr Jess'ron. Besides, I know m'self he's a goin'. I help to pack up him shirts in de trabbelin valise. He's a goin' a hossaback."

"But where, wench? where?" gasped the Jew, in hurried and anxious speech.

"Dey say to 'Panish town—odder side ob de island."

"Spanish town! ach!" cried the pennkeeper, in a tone betokening that the words had conveyed some very unwelcome intelligence. "Spanish Town! S'help me, it ish! I knew it! I knew it! ach!"

And, as he repeated the aspirated ejaculation, he struck his umbrella fiercely into the ground, as if to render more emphatic the chagrin that had been communicated by the answer.

Only for a few seconds did he make pause upon the spot.

" Come on !" cried he to his companion, hurriedly moving off from the tree ; " come on, wench ! if that'sh the case, ash you shay, there'sh no time to be losht—not a minute, s'help me !"

And with this elegant reflection, he ended the brief dialogue, and strode swiftly and silently onward across the glade—the woman following close upon his heels.

"*Demonios!*" muttered the Maroon, as they went off. " That John Crow and his pretty partner are about some bad business, I fear? It appears to be the Custos they're conspiring against. *Crambo!* I wonder what they are after with him? What can the old Jew have to do with his going to Spanish Town? I must follow them, and see if I can discover. There appears to be some scheme brewing, that bodes no good to Mr. Vaughan. Where can they be going at this time of night? *From* the Jew's penn, instead of *towards* it !"

These interrogative reflections the Maroon made to himself. Then turning once more to his sweetheart, with a gesture that declared his intention to be gone, he said:—

" We must part, Yola, and this instant, love, else I may lose their trail. Adieu! adieu !"

And with a quick kiss, and equally hurried embrace, the lovers separated — Yola, returning to Mount Welcome, by a path well known to her, while the Maroon glided off on the track taken by the pennkeeper and his female companion.

———

CHAPTER LXXIII.

TRACKING THE STROLLERS.

THE Maroon was but a few moments in recovering the " spoor" of the two nocturnal strollers.

At the point where they had gone out of the glade, there was a path that led up the hills in the direction of the Jumbé Rock. It was a mere cattle track—used only very occasionally by bipeds. Being the only path that went that way, and judging moreover, that neither the Jew nor his follower would be likely to traverse the thicket at random, Cubina concluded that they had taken this path.

Throwing himself upon it, and advancing with a quick but silent step, he soon came in sight of them.

The shade of the gigantic trees—it was a primeval forest through which they were passing—was favourable to his design ; and without much risk of being seen, he was able to keep them in sight, and almost within earshot.

At that moment, the mind of the Jew was too pre-occupied to be suspicious ; and the mulatta was not likely to trouble her thoughts about whether they were followed or not. Had she known, however—had she even suspected—that her steps were dogged, and by Cubina the Maroon, it would, no doubt, have sharpened her senses.

" They appear to be making for the Jumbé Rock ?" mentally soliloquised Cubina, as they commenced ascending the slope of the mountain

"*Crambo*. That is odd enough! What do they intend to do there at
this hour of the night? Or at any hour, I might say? And who's the
he that's been sending for Jessuron? She took *him* a provision basket!
By that it ought to be some runaway? But what has the old Jew to do
with a runaway? To get out of his bed at this time of the night, and
tramp it three miles through the woods! For that matter, they say he
don't sleep much anyhow; and, like the owl, night's his favourite time I
suppose. Something's being cooked for the Custos; for that girl's a
very devil! Not *that* I should care so about *him* at any other time.
He's not much; and is only helping me in that matter for him; but
from what Yola's told me, I'd go to the world's end for his daughter.
Ha! I may do her a service yet. *Valga me Dios!* what's up now?
They've stopped!"

The Jew and his companion, about a hundred yards ahead, had suddenly come to a stand. They appeared to be scrutinising the path.

Cubina, crouching in the shadow of the bushes, stopped likewise; and
waited for the others to advance.

They did so after a short interval—hastening on as before; but in a
slightly divergent direction.

"Ho, ho!" muttered the Maroon; "not for the Jumbé Rock, but the
Duppy's Hole! I remember now. The path forks up yonder. They've
taken that which goes to the Hole. Well I it don't help me to comprehend
their purpose a bit clearer. *Carrai!* that Duppy's Hole. Didn't some of
my fellows tell me they've heard strange noises there lately? Quaco is
ready to swear he saw the ghost of the old myal-man, Chakra, standing
upon the edge of the cliff! They're going there, as sure as my name's
Cubina!"

And with this conjectural reflection the Maroon forsook the shadow,
under which he had been sheltering, and flitted forward along the path.

Another five hundred yards farther on his conjecture was confirmed.

The parties dogged by him had reached the edge of the precipice that
frowned down upon the Duppy's Hole, and there halted.

Cubina also made stop—as before concealing himself within the black
shadow of the bushes.

He had scarcely crouched down, when his ears were saluted by a
shrill but cautious whistle—not made by the lips, but proceeding from
some instrument: a reed or a common dog-call. It was plainly a signal,
sounded either by Cynthia or the Jew, Cubina could not tell which.

Only once was it given. And there was no answer—for that similar
sound, that came like an echo from the far forest, was a counterfeit. It
was the mimic-note of the mock-bird.

Cubina, skilled in these voices of the night, knew that, and paid no
heed to the distant sound. His whole attention was absorbed in watching the movements of the two individuals, still standing upon the edge
of the cliff. The white sky was beyond them, against which he could
see their dark *silhouettes* outlined with perfect distinctness.

After about a minute's time, he saw them once more in motion; and
then both appeared to vanish from his view—not wasting into the air,
but sinking into the ground, as if a trap-door had admitted them to the
interior of the earth!

He saw this without much surprise. He knew they must have gone down the precipice; but how they had perform 'his feat was something that did surprise him a little.

It was but a short spell of astonishment. In a score of seconds ho stood upon the edge of the precipice, at the spot where they had disap peared.

He looked down. He could trace, though dimly, a means of descent among the wattle of boughs and corrugated creepers that clasped the "façade" of the cliff. E' en under the fantastic gleam of the moor, he could see that human hands had helped in the construction of this natural ladder.

He stayed not to scrutinise it. An object of greater interest challeng ed his glance. On the disc of the lagoon—in the moonlight, a sheet of silver, like a mirror in its frame of dark mahogany—moved a thing of sharp, elliptical shape—a canoe.

Midships of the craft, a form was crouching. Was it human or demon?

The aspect was demon—the shape scarce human. Long, ape-like arms; a hunched back; teeth gleaming in the moonlight like the incisors of a shark; features anything but human to one who had not seen them before !

Cubina had seen them before. To him, though not familiar, they were known. If not the ghost of Chakra, he saw Chakra himself !

CHAPTER LXXIV.

CYNTHIA IN THE WAY.

THE heart of the young Maroon, though by nature bold and brave, was for a moment impressed with fear. He had known the myal-man of Mount Welcome—never very intimately—but enough to identify his per- son. Indeed, once seen, Chakra was a man to be remembered.

Cubina had, like every one else for miles around, heard of the trial of the Coromantee conjurer, and his condemnation to exposure on the Jumbé Rock. The peculiar mode of his execution—the cruel sentence —the celebrity of the scene where the criminal had been compelled to pass the last miserable hours of his existence—all combined to render his death even more notorious than his life ; and few there were in the western end of the island who had not heard of the myal man of Mount Welcome, and the singular mode of atonement that justice had demanded him to make for his crimes.

In common with others, Cubina believed him dead. No wonder, then, that the heart of the Maroon should for a moment misgive him on seeing Chakra seated in a canoe, and paddling himself across the calm surface of the lagoon !

Under any circumstances, the sight of the Coromantee was not calcu- lated to beget confidence in the mind of the beholder ; but his unexpect- ed appearance just then produced within the mind of the Maroon a feel- ing somewhat stronger than astonishment, and for some seconds he stood trembling upon the cliff.

Very soon, however, he remembered the statement which his lieuten
ant had made, aud which Quaco had put in the form of an asservation.

Quaco, like most of his colour, a firm believer in " Duppy" and "Jumbé," had believed it to be Chakra's ghost he had seen ; and under the
terror, with which the sight had inspired him, instead of making an
attempt to pursue the apparition, and prove whether it was flesh and
blood, or only " empty air," he had used his utmost speed to get away
from the spot, leaving the myal-man's ghost full master of the ground.

Cubina, less given to superstitious inclinings, only for a moment permitted himself to be mystified with the idea of a " Duppy." Quaco's experience, along with the presence of the penn-keeper and his companion
—there evidently for a purpose—guided him to the conclusion that what
he saw in the canoe was no spiritual Chakra, but Chakra in the flesh.

How the Coromantee came to be still living and moving, the Maroon
might not so easily comprehend ; but Cubina possessed acute reasoning
powers, and the presence of the Jew, evidently *en rapport* with the restored conjurer, went far towards explaining the mystery of the latter's
resurrection.

Satisfied that he saw Chakra himself, the Maroon placed himself in a
position to watch the movements, both of the man in the canoe, and those
who had summoned him across the lagoon.

In another moment the canoe was lost sight of. It had passed under
the bushes at the bottom of the cliff, where it was not visible from
above.

Voices ascended, which could be heard, but not distinctly.

Cubina could distingush three voices taking part in the conversation
—Chakra's, the Jew's, and, at longer intervals, the shrill treble of the
slave Cynthia.

He bent his ear, and listened with keen attention—in hopes of hearing
what they said. He could only catch an occasional word. The roar of
the cascade rising along with the voices hindered him from hearing
them distinctly ; and, notwithstanding his desire to do so, he was unable
to make out the matter of the conversation.

Only for a short while was he kept waiting. The *trialogue* came to a
close, followed by a brief interval of silence—at the end of which the
the canoe once more made its appearance upon the open water of the
lagoon. Two persons only were in it, Chakra and the Jew. Cynthia
had staid by the bottom of the cliff.

Cubina made this conjecture with some chagrin. It was a circum
stance that promised to frustrate the design he had suddenly conceived,
of following the myal-man to his lair. This he desired to do in order to
make himself acquainted with the hiding-place of the remarkable runaway.

That it was in the Duppy's Hole there could be no doubt ; and therefore the Maroon might at any time find him there.

This reflection would have contented him, but, on seeing the Jew
ferried across the lagoon, he conjectured that he and Chakra were bent
upon the completion of some horrid plot, which, by following, he, Cubina,
might have overheard, and, perhaps, have been enabled to counteract.

The Maroon was aware of the difficulty of descending into the Duppy's
Hole. He knew there was but one way—by the bushes that clustered

along the face of the cliff at his feet. Once, while on the chase, he had gone down there, swimming across the lagoon ; and, in search of game he had explored the wooded covert beyond. At that time, however, Chakra had not been *executed;* and the hunter had found no trace of hu man presence in the solitary place.

He knew, therefore, that he could have followed the canoe by swimming , but now that Cynthia barred the way, it would be impossible for him to reach the water unobserved.

To follow the conspirators farther was out of the question. His chance was cut off by the interposition of the slave. He could only remain upon the cliff and await their return.

He was reflecting upon what course to pursue, when a rustling sound reached him from below. It was made by some one moving among the bushes that grew against the face of the precipice.

He caught one of the branches ; and, supporting himself by it, craned his neck over the cliff. His eye fell upon the brilliant chequer of a *bandanna*, visible among the leaves. It was the toque upon the head of Cynthia. It was in motion ; and he could see that she was ascending by the tree stairway he had already observed.

Without staying to witness the ascent, he turned back into the underwood by the side of the path ; and, crouching down, he waited to see what the slave intended doing. Perhaps her part in the performance had been played out—at least, for that night—and she was on her way homeward ?

That was what Cubina conjectured, as well as just what he would have wished.

His conjecture proved correct. The mulatta, on mounting to the crest of the cliff, stopped only for a moment, to adjust upon her arm a basket she had brought up—from the half-open lid of which protruded the neck of a bottle. Then, casting her eyes forward, she struck off into the shadowy forest path, and was soon out of sight.

The moment after she had passed him, the Maroon glided silently forward to the edge of the cliff, and commenced descending the stair. Such feat was nothing to him ; and in a few seconds he had reached the edge of the lagoon.

Here he paused—to make sure that the canoe had arrived at its destination, and that its late occupants had disembarked from it.

After a moment spent in this *reconnoissance*—looking sharply, and listening with all his ears—he became satisfied that the coast was clear ; and, letting himself stealthily into the water, he swam for the opposite shore of the lagoon.

Upon only about two thirds of the surface of the lagoon did the moonlight fall—the cliff casting its shadow upon the other third. Keeping within the boundaries of this shadow, and swimming as silently as a fish, Cubina succeeded in reaching the opposite shore, without perceiving any sign that he had been observed.

Under the heavy timber with which the upper half of the ravine was covered the darkness was as deep as if not a ray of moonlight came down from the sky. Only on the stream itself, and here and there through a break in the umbrageous forest, could the moon beams reach the surface of the earth. Elsewhere, from cliff to cliff, the obscurity was complete.

Cubina conjectured, and correctly, that there was a path leading from the anchorage of the canoe; and to find this was his first purpose.

Keeping around the edge of the lagoon, he soon came upon the craft—empty, and anchored under a tree.

The moonlight entering here from the open water, showed him the *embouchre* of the path, where it entered the underwood; and, without losing a moment's time, he commenced moving along it.

Silently as a cat he stole around, at intervals pausing to listen, but he could only hear the hissing sound of the upper cascade—to which he was now making approach.

For a space in front of the waterfall the trees stood thinly, and this opening was soon reached.

On arriving at its edge the Maroon again stopped to reconnoitre.

Scarce a second of time did he need to pause. Light flashed in his eyes through the interstices of what appeared to be a sort of grating. It was the bamboo door of the Obeah hut. Voices, too, reverberated through the bars.

Within were the men upon whom it was his purpose to play eavesdropper.

In another instant Cubina was cowering under the cotton tree, close up to the door-post.

CHAPTER LXXV.

STRANGE DISCLOSURES

THE two plotters were palavering loud enough. In that place there was no need—at least, so thought they — for restrained speech; and the listener could have heard every word, but for the hoarse hissing of the cataract. This, at times, hindered him from distinguishing what was said; and only in detached portions could he pick up the thread of the discourse. Enough, however, heard he, to cause him astonishment—the greatest of all, that in the island of Jamaica, or upon the earth, existed two such villains as Chakra the Coromantee, and Jessuron the Jew!

He could see the conspirators as well as hear them. The chinks between the bamboos enabled him to obtain a view of both.

The Jew, slightly blown with his long walk against the hill, had dropped into a sitting attitude upon the truck-like bed-sted; while the Coromantee stood before him, leaning against the buttress of the tree which formed one side of his dwelling.

The conversation had commenced before Cubina came up. It could not have proceeded far. The lard lamp seemed recently lit. Besides, the Maroon knew he had only been a few minutes behind them. The plot, therefore, whatever it was, had not yet made much progress.

So reasoned the listener; but it soon appeared that it was the continuation of a plot, and not its first conception, to which he was to become privy— a plot so demoniac as to include *murder* in its design!

The Jew, when Cubina first got eyes on him, appeared as if he had just given utterance to some angry speech. His dark, weasel-like orbs were sparkling in their sunken sockets, with a fiendish light. The goggles were off, and the eyes could be seen. In his right hand the eternal umbrella was grasped, with a firm clutch, as if held in menace!

Chakra, on the other hand, appeared cowed and pleading. Though almost twice the size, and apparently twice the strength of the old Israelite, he looked at that moment as if in fear of him!"

"Gorry, Massr Jake!" said he in an appealing tone; "how ebber wa' J to know de Cussus wam a gwine so soon? A nebber speered ob dat; an you nebber tole me you wanted de death-'pell to work fasser dan wai safe. Ef a'd a know'd dat, a kud a fotch de dam Cussus out o' him boots in de shake ob a cat's tail—dat kud a did!"

"Ach!" exclaimed the Jew, with an air of unmistakable chagrin; 'he's going to shlip us. S'help me, he will! And now, too, when I wants more ash ever the shpell upon him. I'sh heard something from thish girl Cynthy of a conshpiracy against myself. Sheesh heard them plotting in the summer-house in the Cushtos's garden."

"Wha' dey plot 'gain you, Massr Jake? Who am dey dat go plottin'?"

"The Cushtos is one, the other ish that scamp son of Cubina, the Maroon—the young Cubina. You knowsh him?"

"Dat same a know well 'nuf."

"Ah! the proud Cushtos don't know—though he hash his susnpicions —that hish wife Quasheba was the mistress of a Maroon. Ha! ha! ha! And she luffed the mulatta better ash ever she luffed Vanities Vochan. Ha! ha! ha!"

"Dat am berry near de troof," observed the negro, with a thoughtful air.

"Little doesh the Cushtos think," continued Jessuron, without heeding the interpolation; "that thish young fellow, whosh a helping' him to conshpire againsht me is a sort of a son to hish consheited worship. Ha ha! ha!'

It was startling intelligence for the listener outside the door. It was the first intimation the young Maroon ever had as to who was his mother. Some vague hints had been conveyed to him in early childhood; but his memory recalled them as dreams; and he himself had never allowed them expression. His father he had known well—called as himself— Cubina the Maroon. But his mother, who or what she had been, he had never known.

Was it possible, then, that the quadroon, Quasheba—of whose fame he, too, had heard—was it possible she was his own mother? That "lily Quasheba," the beautiful the accomplished daughter of the Custos Vaughan was his half-sister?

He could not doubt it. The conversation that followed put him in possession of further details, and more ample proofs. Besides, such re-lationships were too common in the island of Jamaica, to make them matter either of singularity or surprise.

Notwithstanding, the listener was filled with astonishment—far more than that—for the revelation was one to stir his soul to emotions of the strangest and strongest kind. New thoughts sprang up at the announce-ment; new vistas opened before the horoscope of his future; new ties were established within his heart, hitherto unfelt and unknown.

Stifling his new-sprung emotions, as well as he was able—promising indulgence at some other time—he re-bent his ear to listen.

He heard enough to satisfy him that he had a sister- -a half-sister, it is true—but still a sister.

The next point determined on between the conspirators was equally calculated to startle and astonish him. It was no less than a design to render that sister *brotherless!*

"You musht put the shpell on *him*, too," said the Jew; "for hesh the principal in thish plot againsht me. Even if tho Cushtos wash out of the way, thish schamp, Cubina, will go to some other magistrate to carry out hish design. There will be plenty to help him. You musht shpell *him*, and soon ash you can, Shakra. There'sh no time to loose—not a minnit, S'help me.

"A do wha a can, Massr Jake; but a mout's well tell ye, dat it a'nt so easy to put de 'pell on a Maroon. It coss me more'n twenty years to put de Obeah on him ole fadder, and I'se a been trying' um on dis young Cubina fo' some time—ebber since him fadder die. A hate the young un same a hated de ole un. You knows why a hate boaf."

"I knowsh all that—I knowsh all. that."

"Wa, den! a do ma bess. Dat ar m'latta gib me no hope. She soon 'dminster de 'pell ef she hab chance—kase she think um de lub drink. She hab no chance, fo' Cubina he no let her come nigh of him. Nebber mind : Chakra he find opportunity some day; 'fore long he put de death 'pell on de son ob dat quaderoom."

"Perhaps not so soon!" was the mental rejoinder of him who listened to this confident declaration.

"It'sh less matter about him than the other!" cried the Jew, giving way to a fresh burst of rage. "S'help me! the Cushtos is going to shlip out of my fingers—the eshtate—all I Ach," he ejaculated as his disappointment came more palpably before him, "you hash pla ed me false, Shakra! I b'lief you've been playin' me false!"

As the Jew gave utterance to this conjectural speech, he started to his feet—taking a tighter hold upon his umbrella, and standing before his 'vis-a-vis' in a threatening attitude.

"No, Massr Jake," replied the myal-man, without altering the air of obeisance he had hitherto assumed. "No—nuffin of dat—any how, I'se can say, dar's nuffin ob dat. You yaseff sabbey well 'nuf, a hab as good ruezun as yaseff to make de 'pell work, an, I tell you *it shall worl!*"

"Yesh! when too late—too late! I don't care then. If the Cushtos get to Spanish Town—if he procuresh the shpecial act, I'm a ruined Shew! I don't care a shtraw if the death-shpell wash put on myshelf I don't!"

This speech was rather a soliloquy than addressed to Chakra, who lis toned to it without clearly comprehending its import: for the chief motive which was stimulating the Jew was still unknown to his fellow conspirator.

"I tell you," resumed Jessuron, still in threatening speech, "I believe you hash been fooling me, Shakra! You hash some interest of your own —perhaps with thish Lilly Quasheba. Ha! never mind! I tell you thish time--I tell you, Shakra, if the shpell dosh fail—yesh, if it fail, and the Cushtos reach the capital—where ho ish going—I tell you, Shakra, you may look out for shqualls! You loosh your monish I promised you. . Ay, you may loosh your life ash well. I hash only to shay a word, and the

Duppy's Hole will be searched by the houndsh of the law. Now will you do your besht, to keep the Cushtos from reaching the capital of the island ?"

As Jessuron finished the speech containing this hypothetical threat, he moved in the direction of the door, apparently with the intention of taking his departure.

The Maroon, perceiving the movement, stepped further back into the shadow of the cotton-tree—taking care to conceal himself effectually.

This change of position prevented him from hearing what subsequently passed between the two conspirators. Some more conversation there was on both sides—an interchange of it, which lasted for several minutes; but although the listener could hear the sound of the voices, he was unable to make out the words spoken.

What was said by the Jew was principally the repetition of his menace—in terms the most emphatic he could employ; while Chakra, with equal emphasis, repeated his promises to accomplish the nefarious purpose already agreed upon between them.

"A promise, Massr Jake," said the myal-man, in conclusion, "by the great Accompong, a do ma bess. Ef de Cussus 'trive 'scape, den you do wid ole Chakra whasomediver you hab mind to. 'Liver him, up ef you like! Ha! De Cussus no 'scape. Dis night Cynthy hab take bottle in her basket ob de 'trongest kind. It do de bizness in 'bout twenty-fo' hour. *Daat am de true death-'pell.* Whugh !"

"In twenty-four hours ? You ish shure, Shakra ? you ish shure ?"

"Shoo' as a 'm now in de Duppy Hole, Massr Jake. Doan' you bab no mo' doubt ob ole Chakra. He hab no lub fo' Cussus Va'han mo' dan youseff. P'raps he lub de Cussus' dau'ter, but dat am berry diffrent sort ob 'fecshun. Whugh !"

With this speech of fiendish signification the dialogue ended ; and the Jew was seen stepping outside, followed by his confederate.

Both walked away from the spot, Chakra taking the lead, the Maroon closely watching their movements.

On reaching the canoe the conspirators stepped abroad, and the craft was paddled over the lagoon.

Cubina waited for its return; and then, seeing Chakra safe within his hut, he hastened back to the water; and swimming, as before, under the shadow of the rock, he re-ascended the tree stairway, and stood once more on the summit of the cliff.

CHAPTER LXXVI.

A STORMY SCENE.

On emerging from the Duppy's Hole, the penn-keeper tracked it, as straight as the path would permit him, towards his own home. He walked with hurried steps, as if he had some purpose before him beyond that of going to bed. Late as was the hour—or early, it should rather be said, since it was getting on for day-break—in the eye of the old Israelite there was no sign of sleepiness ; but, on the contrary, a wide-awake ex

pression that betokened his intention to accomplish some desired object
before retiring to rest.

The mutterings which fell from his lips, as he moved onward among
the trees, told that his discontent still continued. Chakra's assurances,
that had, for the moment, partially removed his ill-humour, on reflection
failed to satisfy him. More than once before, the myal-man had given
him promises which he had failed in keeping; and so might it be with the
promise of the death-spell. With this thought was revived in full vigour the
apprehension that his enemy might escape ; and, consequently, his deep-
conceived scheme would result in ignominious failure.

The measures which the myal-man had taken for administering the
spell-medicine—that bottle of strong waters which Cynthia carried home
in her basket—had been revealed to the Jew. The revelation had been
made—as suited the subject—in a low tone of voice ; and it was this part
of the dialogue between the two conspirators which Cubina had not
heard.

But the Coromantee might be mistaken in his skill? The prescription
might fail in producing the desired effect? The slave might not find the
opportunity to administer it ?

Considering the early hour at which the traveler was to start—Jessuron knew the hour—Cynthia might not have a chance to give the *medicine?* Or frayed by contemplation of the fearful consequence, which she
now knew would follow almost instantaneously upon the act, she might
in the end shy from the dangerous duty? The intended victim might, in
the meantime, have become suspicious of the mixtures prepared by the
mulatta, and decline to drink the deadly draught?"

There were many chances that the Custos might escape.

"'There ish many a shlip between the cup and the lipsh,'" muttered
the wicked old man, quoting one of his favourite proverbs. "Ach I that
ish true," he added, with bitter emphasis, as the probabilities of failure
passed more palpably before his mind.

"S'help me I" continued he, with an attempt at self-consolation ; "I
shall not be deprived of my refenge—that ish certain—whether he goesh
to Spanish Town or shtays at home. Ach I" he exclaimed, again changing his tone to one of chagrin, "what dosh that signify, beshide the
other? If he could be shtopped, it wash a grand deshtiny for mice
Shoodith, for myself—me, old Shacob Shessuron I Mount Welcome wash
mine I It musht belong to thish young fellow—he belongs to Shoodith—
Shoodith belongsh to me I Ach I what a pity if my shkeme ish to fail—
after all I hash done to make it succeed I

"If it fail," he continued, the probabilities of failure presenting a new
phase to him, "if it fail, I'm a ruined man!—I am I Shoodith may want
to marry thish young fellow. I believe she luffs him—I'm afeerd she
doesh—and he hashn't the worth of the shoosh he shtands in. Blesh
my shoul ! I musht try to prevent it. It musht go no farther till I'm
shure of the Cushtos. Not a shtep—not a shtep. She musht be seen,
and thish very night. Yesh ; I musht see Shoodith before I shleep!"

Urged on by the desire of the interview thus announced, the Jew hastened his steps ; and soon arrived under the shadow of the dark pile that
constituted his penn.

Admitted by the black porter at the gate—for that of the court-yard, or slave enclosure, was always kept locked—he mounted the wooden steps, and stole as silently along the verandah, as if he had been a stranger in the house instead of its owner. His object, in this stealthy movement, appeared to be, to avoid disturbing some one who slept in a hammock near one end of the long gallery.

It was toward the other end, however, that he went—in the direction of a chamber, through the lattice-window of which a light was streaming. It was the sleeping apartment of the Jewess.

On arriving opposite the door, he knocked, not loudly, at the same time pronouncing, in a half whisper, the name "Shoodith!"

"That you, old rabbi?" inquired a voice from within; while a footstep passing across the floor told either that the Jewess had not yet sought her couch, or had sought, and again forsaken it.

The door was opened; and the worthy father of this wakeful daughter passed inside.

"Well," said she, as he entered, "I won't inquire what errand you've been on, my good papa Jessuron: some slave speculation, I suppose? But what have I to do with it, that you should compel me to sit up for you till this time of the night? It's now near morning; and I'm precious sleepy, I can tell you."

"Ach! Shoodith, dear," replied the father. "Everything ish goin' wrong! shelp me, everything!"

"Well, one might think so, from that doleful phiz of yours. What's troubling you now, my worthy parent?"

"Ach! Shoodith! Don't dishtress me by your speeches. I hash something of importance to shay to you, before I go to shleep."

"Say it quick, then: for I want to go to sleep myself. What is it, pray?"

"Well, Shoodith, dear, it ish this; you mushn't trifle any more with thish young fellow."

"What young fellow do you mean, my good man?"

"Vochan, of coursh—Mashter Vochan."

"Ho! ho! you've changed your tune. What's this about?"

"I hash reason, Shoodith; I hash reason."

"Who said I was trifling with him? Not I, father! Anything but that, I can assure you."

"That ish not what I mean, Shoodith."

"Well, then, what do you mean, old gentleman? Come now! make yourself intelligible."

"I mean thish, Shoodith: you mushn't let things go any farther with the young fellow—that ish, shoost now—till I knowsh something more about him. I thought he wash going to be rich—you know I thought that, mine daughter—but I hash found out, thish very night, that—perhaps—he may never be worth a shingle shilling; and therefore, Shoodith, you couldn't think of marrying him—and mushn't think of it till we knowsh more about him!"

"Father!" replied the Jewess, at once throwing aside her habitual badinage, and assuming a serious tone, "it is too late! Did I not tell you that the tarantula might get caught in its own trap? The proverb has proved true; I am that unhappy spider!"

"You don't shay so, Shoodith?" inquired the father, with a look of

"I do! Yonder sleeps the fly"—and the speaker pointed along the gallery in the direction of the hammock—"secure from any harm I can ever do him. And were he as poor as he appears to be—as humble as the lowest slave on your estate—he is rich enough for me. Ah! it will be *his* fault, not *mine*, if he do not become my husband!"

The proud, determined tone in which the Jewess spoke, was only modified as she uttered the last words. The conjunctive form of the closing speech, with a certain duplexity of expression upon her countenance, showed that she was not yet sure of the heart of Herbert Vaughan. Notwithstanding his attentions at the ball—notwithstanding much that had since occurred, there appeared to be a doubt—a trace of distrust that still lingered.

"Never, Shoodith!" cried the father, in a tone of determined authority. "You mushn't think of it! You shall never marry a pauper—never!"

"Pauper him as much as you like; father, he won't care for that, any more than I do."

"I shall disinherit you, Shoodith!" said the Jew, giving way to his spiteful feeling of resentment.

"As you like about that, too. Disinherit me at your pleasure. But remember, old man, it was you who began this game—·you who set me to playing it; and if you're in danger of losing your stake—whatever it may be—I tell you you're in danger of losing *me*—that is, if he——"

The hypothetic thought—whatever it was—that at this crisis crossed the mind of the Jewess, was evidently one that caused her pain: as could be seen by the dark shadow that came mantling over her beautiful brow.

Whether or not she would have finished the speech is uncertain. She was not permitted to proceed. The angry father interrupted her :—

"I won't argue with you now, Shoodith. Go to your bed, girl! go to shleep! Thish I promish you—and s'help me. I keepsh my promish! if thish pauper ish to be a pauper, he 'never marries you with my conshent; and without my conshent he never touches a shilling of my monish. You undershtand that, Shoodith?"

And without waiting to hear the reply—which was quite as defiant as his own declaration—the Jew hurried out of his daughter's chamber, and shuffled off along the verandah

CHAPTER LXXVII.

THE Maroon, after mounting to the summit of the cliff, paused for some moments to reflect upon a course of action.

In his bosom were many new emotions, springing from the strange revelations to which he had just listened. His mind was in such a state of chaotic confusion, that it required some time to determine what he ought to do next, or whither he should go.

The thought that thrilled him most, was that which related to the discovery of maternal relationship to Miss Vaughan. But this matter however strange it was, required no immediate action to be taken on his part; and though the semi-fraternal affection, now felt for the first time, strengthened the romantic friendship which he had conceived for the young lady--whom he had now seen several times—still from what he had overheard of the scheme of the conspirators, his new discovered sister did not appear to be in any danger. At least, not just then ; though some horrid hints darkly thrown out by Chakra pointed to a probable peril at some future time.

That her father was in danger, Cubina could not doubt. Some demoniac plot, had been prepared for the Custos, which was to deprive him even of life ; and from what the Maroon could make out of the half-heard conversation of the conspirators, action was to be taken upon it, so early as the following morning.

Mr. Vaughan intended a journey.

Yola had herself told him so ; and the confabulation between Jessuron and Chakra confirmed it. Cynthia, had been their informant ; and it was evident that upon that very night she had brought the news from Mount Welcome. Evident, also, that the piece of intelligence thus conveyed had taken both the conspirators by surprise—causing them to hasten some devilish plan that before that night had not been quite ripe for execution.

All this was clear enough to the mind of the Maroon.

Equally clear was it, that the plan was no other than an atrocious plot to murder the proprietor of Mount Welcome ; and that poison was the safe silent weapon to be used—for Cubina was not unacquainted with the signification of the *death-spell of Obeah.* Before that night he had reason to believe that his own father had fallen by that secret shaft, and reasons to suspect that Chakra had shot it. What he had just heard confirmed his belief and but that he saw the necessity of hastening to the rescue of the threatened Custos—and knew, moreover, that he could find Chakra at any time—he would, in all probability, have avenged his father's death before leaving the Duppy's Hole.

The young Maroon, however, was a man of mild character—combining prudence with an extreme *sang-froid*—that hindered him from bringing any event to an ambiguous ending. Though leaving Chakra for the time, he had determined soon to return to him.

The resurrection of the myal-man, though it at first very naturally astonished him, had soon ceased to be a mystery to the mind of the Maroon. In fact the presence of the Jew had at once explained the whole thing. Cubina conjectured, and correctly,that Jessuron had released the condemned criminal from his chains, and substituted the body of some dead negro—afterwards to become the representative of Chakra's skeleton.

For this the Jew, well known for wickedness, might have many motives.

The Maroon did not stay to speculate upon them. His thoughts were directed to the present and future rather than the past—to the rescue of the Custos, over whom a fearful fate seemed to impend.

.It need not be denied that Cubina felt a certain friendship for the planter of Mount Welcome. Heretofore it had not been of a very ardent character ; but the relations lately established between him and the Custos— t prospect of the process to be taken against their common enemy, the

penn-keeper—has, of course, occasioned a fellow-feeling between them.
The revelations of that night had strengthened the interest which the
Maroon had begun to feel for Mr. Vaughan; and it is not to be wondered
at that he now felt an honest desire to save the father of her whom he
was henceforth to regard as his own sister. To this end, then, were his
thoughts directed.

He stayed not long to speculate upon the motives—either of Chaloa or
Jessuron. Those of the myal-man he could guess to a certainty. Revenge
for the sentence that exposed him to that fearful fate on the Jumbé Rock

The motives of the Jew were less transparent. His deepest did not
appear in the confabulation Cubina had overheard. Even Chakra did not
know it. It might be fear of the approaching trial, which by some
means the Jew had become apprised of.

But no. On reflection, Cubina saw it could not be that: for the conversation of the conspirators betrayed that their plot had been anterior to
any information which the Jew could have had of the design of the Custos. It could not be that.

No matter what. Mr. Vaughan, the father of the generous young
lady—she who had promised to make him a present of his beloved bride,
and who now proved to be his own step-sister—her father was in
danger!

Not a moment was to be lost. Without regard to motives, measures
must be taken to avert that danger, and punish the miscreants who designed it.

Cubina continued to reflect upon what step should be first taken.

Should he go direct to Mount Welcome, and warn the Custos, by reporting to him what he had heard.

That was the first idea that presented itself to his mind; but at that
hour Mr. Vaughan would be a-bed, and he—a Maroon—might not be
admitted, unless, indeed, he could show, by pleading the urgency of his
errand, good cause for the Custos to be roused from his slumber.

This, undoubtedly, would he have done, had he known that the scheme
of the conspirators had been definitely arranged. But, as already stated,
he had not heard Chakra's concluding speech—referring to Cynthia and
the bottle of strong medicine; and all the rest only pointed vaguely at
some measures to be taken to frustrate the expedition to Spanish Town.

It would be time enough, thought he, to meet these measures by going
to Mount Welcome in the morning. He could get there before Mr.
Vaughan should start upon his journey. He could go at an early hour,
but one when his appearance would not give cause for any unnecessary
remark.

It did not occur to him to reflect, that the time of the traveller's departure from Mount Welcome—of which Cubina had not been apprised
—might be anterior to that of his arrival there. The Maroon, thinking
that the great Custos was not likely to inconvenience himself by early
rising, had no apprehension about missing him by being himself too late.

With this confidence, then, he resolved to postpone his visit to Mount
Welcome until some hour after daybreak; and, in the meantime, to carry
out the preliminaries of a programme, referring to a very different affair,
and which had been traced out the day before.

The first scene in this programme was to be a meeting with Herbert

Vaughan. It had been appointed to take place between them on the following morning; and on the same spot where the two young men had first encountered one another—in the glade under the great *ceiba*.

The interview was of Herbert's own seeking; for although neither had seen the other, since the day on which the runaway had been rescued, some items of intelligence had passed between them—Quaco acting as the medium of their correspondence.

Herbert had an object in seeking the interview. He desired a conference with Cubina, in hopes of obtaining from him an explanation of more than one circumstance, that had lately arisen to puzzle and perplex him.

His patron's suspicious story about the red runaway was one of these circumstances. Herbert had heard from Quaco that the slave was still staying with the Maroons in their mountain town; and had been adopted into their little community—in fact, had himself become a Maroon.

This did not tally with the account given by Jessuron. Of course, Quaco could not state the reasons. The secrecy enjoined by the Custos kept Cubina's tongue tied upon that theme; and his own men knew nothing of the design which their captain had conceived against the Jew.

This was not the only matter which mystified the young Englishman, and which he was in hopes of having cleared up by Cubina. His own position at the penn—of late developing itself in a manner to surprise and startle him—also needed elucidation. There was no one near of whom he could ask a question in regard to it, and never in his life did he stand more in need of a confidant.

In this dilemma he had thought of his old acquaintance, the Maroon captain. The intelligent mulatta appeared to be the very man. Herbert remembered the promise made at parting, his own conditional acceptance of it, which now appeared prophetic, since the contingency then expressed had come to pass. He had need to avail himself of the friendly proffer, and for that purpose had he made the appointment under the *ceiba*.

Equally desirous was the Maroon to meet with the young Englishman. He had preserved a grateful recollection of his generous interference in what appeared a very unequal combat; and, so far from having lost sight of his noble ally, he had been keeping him in mind—after a fashion that was calculated to show the deep gratitude with which Herbert's conduct had inspired him.

He longed for an opportunity of giving renewed expression to this gratitude; but he had other reasons for wishing to see the young Englishman just then; and the meeting with Yola on that same night had an object somewhat different from the mere repetition of love vows —already pronounced over and over again, upon a score of distinct occasions.

Now that the night hours had nearly all passed, and that the morning was nigh, the Maroon, instead of returning to his mountain home, decided on going back to the glade, spending the few hours of interval under the shadow of the *ceiba*.

Indeed, the time would not now allow of his returning home. The sun would be up in three or four hours. A little after sunrise was the appointed time for the meeting with Herbert Vaughan. Before that nour snould arrive, he could scarce reach his own "town" and get back again. The thing, therefore, was not to be thought of.

To sleep under a tree, or on one, was no new thing for Cubina. It would never occur to him to consider such a couch as inconvenient. In his hog-hunting excursions—often continuing for days, and even weeks— he was accustomed to repose upon the cold ground—upon the swirl of withered leaves—upon the naked rock—anywhere. Not much did it matter to a Maroon, to be sheltered by a roof—not much, whether a tree shadowed his slumbers, or whether on his grassy couch he saw shining over him the starry canopy of the sky. These were but the circumstan- ces of his every-day life.

Having come to the conclusion that his best plan would be to pass the few remaining hours of the night under the *ceiba*, he made no further delay by the Duppy's Hole; but turning into the path that led down the slope, he proceeded back towards the glade, where Herbert Vaughan was to give him rendezvous. He moved down the mountain road, slowly, and with some degree of circumspection. He went slowly, because there was no need for haste. It would be several hours before the young Englishman should be in the glade. As already stated, a little after sun- rise was the time agreed upon, through the messenger Quaco. There was no particular reason for Cubina's being in a hurry to get to the glade —unless he wished to have more time for his nap under the tree.

For sleep, however, he had but little relish just then. Wild thoughts, consequent on the strange disclosures he had listened to, were passing through his mind; and these were sufficient to deprive him even of the power to sleep.

He moved onward with circumspection from a different motive. He knew that Jessuron, in returning to his penn, must have taken the same path. Should the latter be loitering—since he had only started but a few minutes before—Cubina might overtake him; and he had no wish to see any more of the Jew for that night—or, at all events, to be himself seen by the latter. To avoid all chance of an encounter, he stopped at inter- vals, and reconnoitred the wood ahead of him.

He arrived in the glade without seeing either Jew, Christian, or living being of any kind. The penn-keeper had passed through a good while before. Cubina could tell this by an observation which he made on com- ing out into the open ground. A mock-bird perched on a low tree, that stood directly by the path, was singing with all its might. The Maroon had heard its melody long before entering the glade. Had any one pass- ed recently, the bird would have forsaken its perch—as it did on the ap- proach of Cubina himself.

On reaching the rendezvous, his first concern was to kindle a fire. Sleep in a wet shirt was not to be thought of; and every stitch upon his body had been soaked in swimming the lagoon. Otherwise, it would not have mattered about a fire. He had nothing to cook upon it; nor was he hungry—having already eaten his supper.

Kindled by a woodman's skill, a fire soon blazed up; and the hunter stood erect beside it, turning himself at intervals to dry his garments still dripping with water.

He was soon smoking all over, like freshly slaked lime; and, in order to pass the time more pleasantly, he commenced smoking in another

sense—the *nicotian*--his pipe and tobacco-pouch affording him an oppor
tunity for this indulgence.

Possibly the nicotine may have stimulated his reflective powers ; for
he had not taken more than a dozen puffs at his pipe, when a sudden and
somewhat uneasy movement seemed to say that some new reflection had
occurred to him. Simultaneous with the movement, a muttered soliloquy
fell from his lips.

" *Crambo!* ' exclaimed he, giving utterance to his favourite shibboleth ;
" say he should come an hour after sunrise—another we should be in getting to Mount Welcome. *Pordios!* it may be too late then ! Who knows
what time the Custos may fancy to set out?" he added, after a pause ; " I
did not think of that. How stupid of me not to have asked Yola !

" *Crambo!*" he again exclaimed, after another interval passed in a silent
reflection. " It won't do to leave things to chance, where a man's life is
in danger. Who knows what a scheme these John Crows have contrived?
I couldn't hear the whole of their palaver. If Master Vaughan was only
here, we might go to Mount Welcome at once. Whatever quarrel he
may have with the uncle, he won't wish to let him be murdered—no fear
of that. Besides, the young fellow's interference in this matter, if I mistake not, would be likely to make all right between them—I'd like that,
both for his sake and hers—ah ! hers especially, after what Yola's told me
Santa Virgin! wouldn't that be a disappointment to the old dog of a Jew !
Never mind ; I'll put a spark in his powder before Le's many days older.
The young Englishman must know all. I'll tell him all ; and after that if
he consents to become the son in-law of Jacob Jessuron, he would deserve
a dog's——Bah ! it cannot be ! I won't believe it till he tells me so himself ; and then——

" *Pordios!*" exclaimed he, suddenly interrupting the above train of reflections and passing to another. " It won't do for me to stay here till he
comes. Two hours after sunrise, and the Custos might be cold. I'll go
down to the Jew's penn at once ; and hang about till I see young Vaughan.
He'll be stirring about daybreak, and that 'll save an hour, anyhow. A
word with him, and we can soon cross to Mount Welcome."

In obedience to the thought, and without staying to complete the dry-
ing of his habiliments, the Maroon stepped out from the glade ; and
turning into the track—little used—that led towards the Happy Valley,
proceeded in that direction.

CHAPTER LXXVIII.

A DARK COMPACT.

On closing so abruptly the stormy dialogue with his daughter, Jessuron
proceeded to his own sleeping apartment—like the others, opening upon
the verandah.

Before entering the room, he glanced along the gallery, towards the
suspended hammock.

In that hammock slept Herbert Vaughan. His long sea-voyage had accustomed him to the use of a swing couch—even to a liking for it ; and

as the night was warm, he had preferred the hammock to his bed in the contiguous chamber.

Jessuron had a fear that the angry conversation might have been over-heard by the occupant of the hammock ; for, in the excitement of temper, neither he nor Judith had observed the precaution of speaking low.

The hammock hung motionless, oscillating scarce an inch ; and this only under the influence of the night breeze that blew gently along the véran-dah. Its occupant appeared to be in the middle of a profound slumber.

Satisfied of this, the Jew returned to his own chamber. There was no light, and on entering, he sat down in the darkness. The moon shining in through the window gave him light enough to discover a chair ; and into that he had flung himself, instead of seeking his couch.

For a time he displayed no intention either of undressing or betaking himself to bed ; but remained in the high-backed chair in which he had seated himself, buried in some reflection, silent as profound. We are permitted to know his thoughts.

" S'help me, she'll marry him !" was that which came uppermost. " She will, s'help me !" continued he, repeating the reflection in an altered form, " shpite of all I can shay or do to prevent her. She ish a very deffil when raished—and she'll have her own way, she will. Ach! what ish to be done ?—what ish to be done ?"

Here a pause occurred in the reflections, while the Jew, with puzzled brain, was groping for an answer to his mental interrogatory.

" It ish of no ushe !" he continued, after a time, the expression on his face showing that he had not yet received a definite reply. " It'sh no ushe to opposhe her. She'd run away with thish young man to a cer-tainty !

" I might lock her up, but that ish no good. She'd contrive to eshcape sometime. I couldn't alwaysh keep her under lock and key ? No—no, it ish imposhible !

" And if she marriesh him without the monish—without the great shugar eshtate ! Blesh me! that ish ruin!

" It musht not be. If she marriesh him she musht marry Mount Wel-come. She musht! she musht!

" But how ish it to be ? How ish he to be made the heir ?"

Again the Jew appeared to puzzle his brains for an answer to this last interrogatory.

" Ha!" he exclaimed aloud, at the same time starting from his chair, as if the solution had discovered itself; " I hash it!—the Spaniards? I hash it!

" Yesh," he continued, striking the ferrule of his umbrella against the floor, " theesh are the very fellows for the shob—worth a schore of Shakra's shpells, and hish bottles to boot! There ish no fear that their medishin will fail. S'help me, no! Now, ash I think of it," continued he, " that ish the plan—the very besht. There is no other safe and sure like that ish! Ha! Cushtos! you shan't eshcape yet. Ha! Shoodith, mine girl, you ish welcome to your way ; you shall have the young man after all!"

On giving utterance to those ambiguous speeches, the Jew dropped back into his chair, and sat for some minutes in silent but earnest medita-tion.

A DARK COMPACT. 249

The matter of his meditation may be known by the act that followed. " There ishn't an hour to be losht! muttered he, starting to his feet, and hurriedly making for the door; " no, not ash much ash a minute. I musht see them now. The Cushtos is to shtart at sunrishe. The wench hash said it. They'll joosht have time to get upon hish track. S'help me," he added, opening the door, and glancing up at the sky, " ash I live it'sh mesht sunrishe now."

Sticking his beaver firmly upon his head, and taking a fresh clutch of the everlasting umbrella, he rushed rapidly out of the verandah, crossed the courtyard, re-passed the porter at his own gate, and then, traversing the little inclosure outside, stood in the open fields.

He did not stand long—only to look around him, and see that the ground was clear of stragglers.

Satisfied on this head, he proceeded onward.

At the distance of three or four hundred yards from the outside stock-ade stood a detached cabin, more than half hidden among the trees.

Towards this he directed his steps.

Five minutes sufficed for him to reach it ; and, on arriving at the door, he knocked upon it with the butt of his umbrella.

" *Quien es?*" spoke a voice from within.

" It'sh me, Manuel—me—Shessuron!" replied the Jew.

" It's the ' Dueno' " (master), was heard muttering one of the other— for the cabin was the dwelling of these notable negro-hunters.

" *Carajo!* what does the old *ladron* want at this hour?" interrogated the first speaker, in his own tongue, which he knew was not understood by the Jew. " *Maldito!*" added he, in a grumbling voice ; " it's not very pleasant to be waked up in this fashion. Besides, I was dreaming of that yellow-skin that killed my dogs. I thought I had my *machete* up to the hilt in his carcase. What a pity I was only dreaming it !"

" *Ta-ta!*" interrupted the other; " be silent. Andres. The old *gana-dero* is impatient. *Vamos!* I'm coming, Senor Don Jacob!"

" Make hashte, then!" answered the Jew from without. "I hash im-portant bishness with both of yoush."

At this moment the door opened ; and he who answered to the name of Manuel appeared in the doorway.

Without waiting for an invitation, Jessuron stepped inside the cabin.

" Does your business require a candle, senor ?" inquired the Spaniard.

" No—no!" answered the Jew, quickly and impressively, as if to pre-vent the striking of a light. " It ish only talk; we can do it in the dark-ness."

And darkness, black and profound, was most appropriate to the con-versation that followed. Its theme was *murder*—the murder of Loftus Vaughan !

The plan proposed was for the two Spaniards—fit instruments for such purpose—to waylay the Custos upon the road—in some dark defile of the forest—anywhere—it mattered not, so long as it was on this side of Spanish Town.

" Fifty poundsh apeesh; goot island currenshy," was the reward promised—offered and accepted.

Jessuron instructed his brace of *entrepreneurs* in all the details of the plan. He had learnt from Cynthia that the Custos intended to take the southern road, calling at Savanna-la-Mer. It was a roundabout way to the capital; but Jessuron had his supicious why that route had been chosen. He knew that Savanna was the assize town of Cornwall; and the Custos might have business there relating to himself, Prince Cingües, and his two dozen Mandingoes!

It was not necessary to instruct the 'caçadores' in these multifarious matters. There was no time to use on any other than the details of their murderous plan; and these were made known to them with the rapidity of rapine itself.

In less than twenty minutes from the time he had entered the cabin, the Jew issued out again; and walked back with joyous mien and agile step towards his dark dwelling.

CHAPTER LXXIX.

STAKING THE SLEEPER.

CUBINA, on arriving near the precincts of the penn, moved forward with increased caution. He knew that the penn-keeper was accustomed to keep dogs and night watchers around his inclosure, not only to prevent his cattle and other quadrupeds from straying, but also the black bipeds that filled his baracoons.

The Maroon was conscious, moreover, that his own attitude towards the slave-merchant was, at this time, one of extreme hostility. His refusal to restore the runaway had been a declaration of open war between them; and the steps he had since taken in conjunction with the Custos—which he now knew to be no longer a secret to the slave-dealer—could not otherwise than render him an object of the Jew's most bitter hatred.

Knowing all this, he felt the necessity of caution in approaching the place; for should the penn-keeper's people find him prowling about the premises, they would be certain to capture him, if they could, and carry him before Jacob Jessuron, J. P., where he might expect to be treated to a little "justices' justice."

With this prospect before him, in the event of being detected, he approached the Jew's dwelling as cautiously as if he had been a burglar about to break into it.

It was towards the back of the house that he was advancing from the fields—or rather, the side of it, opposite to that on which lay the cattle and slave inclosures.

He had made a short circuit to approach by this side, conjecturing that the others would be more likely to be guarded by the slave and cattle watchers.

The fields, half returned to the condition of a forest, rendered it easy to advance under cover. A thick, second growth of logwood, bread-nut and calabash trees covered the ground; and nearer the walls the old garden, now ruinate, still displayed a profusion of fruit trees growing in wild luxuriance, such a guavas, mangoes, paw-paws, orange and lemon, sops, custard-apples, the akee, and avocada pear. Here and there a cocoa-palm raised its tufted crown far above the topmost spray of the humbler fruit trees, its long, feathery fronds gently oscillating under the silent zephyrs of the night.

On getting within about a hundred yards of the house, Cubina formed the intention not to go any nearer just then. The plan he had traced out was to station himself in some position where he could command a view of the verandah—or as much of it as it was possible to see from one place. There he would remain until daybreak. \

His conjecture was, that Herbert Vaughan would make his appearance as soon as the day broke, and this was all the more probable on account of his engagement with the Maroon himself.

The 'protégé' of Jessuron would show himself in the verandah on leaving his chamber. He could not do otherwise, since all the sleeping-rooms —and Cubina knew this—opened outward upon the gallery.

Once seen, a signal by some means—by Cubina showing himself outside, or calling the young Englishman by name—would bring about the desired interview, and hasten the execution of the project which the Maroon had conceived.

A slight elevation of the ground, caused by the crumbling ruins of an old wall, furnished the *vidette* station desired; and the Maroon, mounting upon this, took his stand to watch the verandah. He could see the long gallery from end to end on two sides of the dwelling, and knew that it extended no farther.

Though the house glistened under a clear moonlight, the verandah itself was in shade; as was also the courtyard in front—the old grey pile projecting its sombre shadow beyond the walls that surrounded it. At the end, however, the moonbeams, slanting diagonally from the sky, poured their light upon the floor of the verandah, there duplicating the strong, bar-like railing with which the gallery was inclosed.

The Maroon had not been many minutes upon the stand he had taken when an object in the verandah arrested his attention. As his eye became more accustomed to the shadowy darkness inside, he was able to make out something that resembled a hammock, suspended crosswise, and at some height above the balustrade of the verandah. It was near that end where the moonlight fell upon the floor.

As the moon continued to sink lower in the sky, her beams were flung farther along the gallery; and the object which had attracted the attention of Cubina came more into the light. It was a hammock, and evidently occupied. The taut cordage told that some one was inside it.

"If it should be the young Englishman himself!" was the conjectural reflection of Cubina.

If so, it might be possible to communicate with him at once, and save the necessity of waiting till the day-break?

How was the Maroon to be satisfied that it was he? It might be some one else? It might be Ravener, the overseer; and Cubina desired no conversation with him. What step could he take to solve this uncertainty?

As the Maroon was casting about for some scheme that would enable him to discover who was the occupant of the hammock, he noticed that the moonbeams had now crept nearly up to it, and in a few minutes more would be shining full upon it. He could already perceive, though very dimly, the face and part of the form of the sleeper inside. Could he only get to some elevated position a little nearer to the house, he might be able to make out who it was.

He scanned the ground with a quick glance. A position sufficiently elevated presented itself, but one not so easily to be reached. A cocoa nut palm stood near the wall, whose crest of radiating fronds overlooked the verandah, drooping towards it. Could he but reach this tree unobserved, and climb up to its crown, he might command a close view of him who slept in the swinging couch.

A second sufficed to determine him ; and, crawling silently forward, he clasped the stem of the cocoa-tree, and " swarmed" upward. The feat was nothing to Cubina, who could climb like a squirrel.

On reaching the summit of the palm, he placed himself in the centre of its leafy crown—where he had the verandah directly under his eyes, and so near that he could almost have sprung into it.

The hammock was within ten feet of him, in a downward direction. He could have pitched his tobacco pipe upon the face of the sleeper. The moonlight was now full upon it. It was the face of Herbert Vaughan !

Cubina recognised it at the first glance ; and he was reflecting how he could awake the young Englishman without causing an alarm, when he heard a door turn upon its hinges. The sound came up from the courtyard ; and on looking in that direction, Cubina saw that the gate leading out to the cattle inclosure was in the act of being opened.

Presently a man passed through, entering from the outside ; and the gate, by some other person unseen, was closed behind him.

He who had entered walked directly towards the dwelling ; and, mounting the steps, made his way into the verandah.

While crossing the courtyard, the moonlight, for a moment, fell upon his face, discovering to Cubina the sinister countenance of the Jew.

"I must have passed him on the path?" reflected the Maroon. " But no, that couldn't be," he added, correcting himself; " I saw his return track in the mud-hole just by. He must have got here before me. Like enough, he's been back, and out again on some other dark business. *Crambo!* it's true enough what I've heard say of him ; that he hardly ever goes to sleep. Our people have met him in the woods at all hours of the night. I can understand it now that I know the partner he's got up there. *Por Dios!* to think of Chakra being still alive !"

The Maroon paused in his reflections ; and kept his eye sharply bent upon the shadowy form that, like a spirit of darkness, was silently flitting through the corridor. He was in hopes that the Jew would soon retire to his chamber.

So long as the latter remained outside, there was not the slightest chance for Cubina to communicate with the occupant of the hammock without being observed. Worse than that, the Maroon was now in danger of being himself seen. Exposed as he was upon the cocoa—with nothing to shelter him from observation but its few straggling fronds— he ran every risk of his presence being detected. It was just a question of whether the Jew might have occasion to look upwards; if so, he could scarce fail to perceive the dark *silhouette* of a man, outlined as it was against the light blue of the sky.

That would be a discovery of which Cubina dreaded the consequences, and with reason. It might not only frustrate the intended interview with the young Englishman, but might end in his own capture and detention—the last a contingency especially to be avoided.

Under the apprehension the Maroon stirred neither hand nor foot ; but kept himself silent and rigid. In this attitude of immobility he looked like some statue, placed in sedentary posture upon the summit of the Corinthian column—the crushed crocus represented by the fronds of the palm-tree.

CHAPTER LXXX.

A MISSION FOR THE MAN-HUNTERS.

CUBINA for since time preserved his constrained position. He dared not derange it; since the Jew still stayed in the shadowy corridor—sometimes moving about; but more generally standing at the head of the wooden stairway, and looking across the courtyard, towards the gate through which he had come in. It seemed as if he was expecting some one to enter after him.

This conjecture of Cubina's proved correct. The great gate was heard once more turning on its hinges ; and, after a word or two spoken by the black porter outside, and answered by a voice of different tone, two men were seen stepping inside the court.

As they passed under the moonlight, Cubina recognised them. Their lithe, supple forms, and swarthy angular lineaments, enabled him to identify the Spanish *cacadores*.

They walked straight up to the stairway, at the bottom of which both stopped.

The Jew on seeing them inside the gate, had gone back into a room that opened upon the verandah.

He was gone but for an instant; and, coming out again, he returned to the top of the stairway.

One of the Spaniards, stepping up, reached out, and received something from his hand. What it was Cubina could not have told, but for the words of the Jew that accompanied the action.

" There'sh the flashk," said he ; " it ish the besht brandy in Shamaica. And now," he continued, in an accent of earnest appeal, " my goot fellish ! you hashn't a minute to shpare. Remember the big monish you're to gain ; and don't let thish runaway eshcape !"

" No fear about that, Senor Don Jacob," replied he who received the flask. " *Carraia !* he'll have long legs to get out of our way—once we're well on the trail of him."

And without further dialogue or delay, the *cacadore* descended the stair, rejoined his comrade, and both hurriedly re-crossing the courtyard, disappeared through the door by which they had entered.

" An expedition after some poor slave !" muttered Cubina to himself. " I hope the scoundrels won't catch him anyhow, and I pity him if they do. After all, they're no great hands at the business, spite of their braggadocio."

With this professional reflection, the Maroon once more bent his eyes upon the form that remained in the shadow of the verandah.

"Surely," conjectured he, "the old John Crow will now go to his roost? Or has he more of the like business on hand? Till he's got out of that I can't make a move. I darn't stir—not for the life of me!"

To the joy of Cubina, the Jew at that moment stepped back into his chamber—the door of which had been left standing open.

"Good!" mentally ejaculated the Maroon; "I hope he'll stay in his hole, now that he's in it. I don't want to see any more of him this night. *Crambo!*"

An exclamation indicated, that the congratulatory speech was cut short by the re-appearance of the Jew; not in his blue body-coat, as before, but wrapped in a sort of gabardine, or ample dressing-gown, the skirts of which fell down to his feet. His hat had been removed—though the skull cap, of dirty whitish hue, still clung around his temples; for it was never doffed.

To the consternation of Cubina he came out, dragging a chair after him; as if he meant to place it in the verandah and take seat upon it.

And this was precisely his intention, for after drawing the chair—a high-backed one—out into the middle of the gallery, he planted it firmly upon the floor, and then dropped down into it.

The moment after Cubina saw sparks accompanied by a sound that indicated the concussion of a flint and steel. The Jew was striking a light!

For what purpose!

The smell of burning tobacco borne along the gallery, and ascending to Cubina's nostrils upon the summit of the palm, answered that question. A red coal could be seen gleaming between the nose and chin of the Israelite. He was smoking a cigar!

Cubina saw this with chagrin. How long would the operation last? Half an hour—an hour, perhaps? Ay, maybe till daybreak—now not very distant?

The situation had changed for the worse. The Maroon could not make the slightest move towards the awakening of Herbert. He dared not shift his own position, lest his presence should be betrayed to the Jew. He dared not stir upon the tree, much less come down from it!

He knew that he was in a fix; but there was no help for it. He must wait till the Jew had finished his cigar; though there was no certainty that even that would bring the 'séance' to a termination.

Summoning all the patience he could command, he kept his perch, silent and motionless, though anxious and suffering from chagrin.

For a long hour, at least, did he continue in this desperate dilemma—until his limbs ached underneath him, and his composure was well nigh exhausted. Still the Jew stuck to his chair, as if glued to the seat—silent and motionless as Cubina himself.

The latter fancied that not only a first cigar, but a second, and, perhaps, a third, had been lighted and smoked; but in the sombre shadow, in which the smoker sat, he could not be certain how many. More than one, however from the time spent in the operation; for during the full period of an hour a red coal could bo seen glowing at the tip of that aquiline proboscis.

Cubina now perceived what troubled him exceedingly—the blue dawn breaking over the tops of the trees! By slightly turning his head he could see the golden gleam of sunlight tinting the summit of the Jumbé Rock!

Crambo! what was to be done? So ran his reflections.

If he stayed there much longer he might be sure of being discovered. The slaves would soon be starting to their work—the overseer and drivers would be out and about. One or other could not fail to see him upon the tree? He would be lucky now to escape himself, without thinking any longer of the hammock or him who slept within its tight-drawn meshes.

While considering how he might slip unperceived from the tree, he glanced once more toward the occupant of the chair. The gradually brightening dawn, which had been filling him with apprehension, now favoured him. It enabled him to perceive that the Jew was asleep !

With his head thrown back against the sloping upholstery, Jessuron had at last surrendered to the powerful divinity of dreams. His goggles were off; and Cubina could see that the wrinkled lids were closed over his sunken orbs.

Undoubtedly he was asleep. His whole attitude confirmed it. His legs lay loosely over the front of the chair—his arms hung down at the sides ; and the blue umbrella rested upon the floor at his feet. The last evidence of somnolency was not even counterbalanced by the stump of a cigar, burnt close, and still sticking between his teeth !

<hr />

CHAPTER LXXXI.

A STARTLING SUMMONS.

On the part of Cubina it was now a struggle between prudence and a desire to carry out his original programme—whether he should not go off alone, or still try to communicate with the sleeper in the hammock.

In the former case he could return to the glade, and there await the coming of Herbert Vaughan as at first fixed. But by so doing, at least two hours would be lost ; and even then, would the young Englishman be punctual to his appointment ?

Even against his inclination something might occur to cause delay—a thing all the more probable, considering the circumstances that surrounded him ; considering the irregularity of events in the domicile where he dwelt.

But even a delay of two hours ! In that interval Loftus Vaughan might have ceased to live!

These thoughts coursed quickly through the mind of the Maroon—accustomed as it was to perceptions almost intuitive. He saw that he must either go by himself to Mount Welcome, or awake the sleeper at once.

Perhaps he would have decided on the former course, but that he had other motives for an interview with Herbert Vaughan, almost as immediate in their necessity as that which related to the safety of the Custos. He had as yet no reason to believe that the peril in which the planter stood was so proximate as it really was: for it never occured to him that the departure of the two Spaniards had any other object than that which related to their calling—the capture of some runaway slave.

Had he suspected the design of the two ruffians—had he known the mission of murder on which the slave-merchant had despatched them—he would scarce have stayed for aught else than to have provided the means of intercepting their design.

In the dark about all this, he did not believe there was such necessity for extreme haste; though he knew something was on foot against the Custos which would not allow of much loss of time.

At that moment the occupant of the hammock turned over with a yawn.

"He is going to awake !" thought Cubina ; "now is my time."

To the disappointment of the Maroon, the limbs of the speaker again became relaxed ; and he returned to a slumber profound as before.

"What a pity !" murmured the Maroon ; "if I could only speak a word —— But no. Yonder John Crow is more like to hear it than he. I shall throw something down into the hammock. Maybe that will awake him ?"

Cubina drew out his tobacco-pipe. It was the only thing he could think of at the moment; and, guiding his arm with a good aim, he pitched it into the hammock.

It fell upon the breast of the sleeper. It was too light. It awoke him not.

"Crambo ! he sleeps like an owl at noontide ! What can I do to make him feel me ? If I throw down my *machete*, I shall lose the weapon ; and who knows I may not need it before I'm out of this scrape ? Ha ! one of these cocoa-nuts will do. That, I dare say, will be heavy enough to startle him."

Saying this, the Maroon bent downward ; and extending his arm through the fronds beneath him, detached one of the gigantic nuts from the tree.

Poising it for a moment to secure the proper direction, he flung the ponderous fruit upon the breast of Herbert. Fortunately, the sides of the hammock hindered it from falling upon the floor, else the concussion might also have awakened the sleeper in the chair.

With a start, the young Englishman awoke, at the same time raising himself upon his elbow. Herbert Vaughan was not one of the exclamatory kind, or he might have cried out. He did not, however, though the sight of the huge brown pericarp, lying between his legs, caused him considerable surprise.

"Where, in the name of Ceres and Pomona, did you rain down from ?" muttered he, at the same time turning his eyes up for an answer to his classical interrogatory.

In the grey light, he perceived the palm, its tall column rising majestically above him. He knew the tree well, every inch of its outlines ; but the dark *silhouette* on its top—the form of a human being *ouchant* and crouching—that was strange to him.

The light, however, was not sufficiently strong to enable him to distinguish, not only the form, but the face and features of his *ci-devant* entertainer under the greenwood tree—the Maroon captain, Cubina!

Before he could say a word to express his astonishment, a gesture followed by a muttered speech from the Maroon, enjoined him to silence

"Hush not a word, Master Vaughan!" spoke the latter, in a half whisper, at the same time that he glanced significantly along the corridor. "Slip out of your hammock, get your hat, and follow me into the forest. I have news for you—important! Life and death! Steal out; and, for your life, don't let *him* see you!"

"Who?" inquired Herbert, also speaking in a whisper.

"Look yonder!" said the Maroon, pointing to the sleeper in the chair.

"All right! Well?"

"Meet me in the glade. Come at once—not a minute to be lost! *Those who should be dear to you are in danger!*"

"I shall come," said Herbert, making a motion to extricate himself from the hammock.

"Enough! I must begone. You will find me under the cotton-tree."

As he said this, the Maroon forsook his seat—so long and irksomely preserved—and, sliding down the slender trunk of the palm, like a sailor descending the mainstay of his ship, he struck off at a trot, and soon disappeared amid the second-growth of the old sugar plantation.

Herbert Vaughan was not slow to follow upon his track. Some disclosures of recent occurrence—so recent as the day preceding—had prepared him for a somewhat *bizarre finale* to the fine life he had of late been leading; and he looked to the Maroon for enlightenment. But that strange speech of Cubina stimulated him more than all. "*Those who should be dear to you are in danger!*"

There was but one being in the world entitled to this description. Kate Vaughan! Could it be she?

Herbert stayed not to reflect. His hat and cloak hung in the chamber close by; and in two seconds of time both were upon him. Another second sufficed to give him possession of his gun.

He was too active, too reckless, to care for a stairway at that moment, or at that height from the ground—too prudent to descend by that which there was in front, though guarded only by a sleeper!

Laying his leg over the balustrade, he leaped to the earth below; and following the path taken by the Maroon, like him, was soon lost among the second-growth of the ruinate garden.

CHAPTER LXXXII.

BLUE DICK.

In making his hurried departure from the Happy Valley, Herbert Vaughan narrowly escaped observation. A delay of ten minutes longer would have led to his design being interrupted; or, at all events, to his being questioned as to the object of his early excursion; and in all probability, followed and watched.

He had scarçe passed out of sight of the penn, when he heard the jangling tones of a swing bell—harshly reverberating upon the still air of the morning.

Tho sounds did not startle him. He knew it was not an alarm; only the plantation bell, summoning the slaves to enter upon their daily toil.

Knowing that it must have awakened the sleeper in the chair, he congratulated himself on his good luck at getting away, before the signal had been sounded—at the same time that it caused him to quicken his steps towards the *rendezvous* given by the Maroon.

Cubina, though from a greater distance, had also heard the bell, and had in a similar manner interpreted the signal, though with a greater degree of uneasiness as to the effect it might have produced. He, too, had conjectured, that the sounds must have awakened the sleeper in the chair.

Both had reasoned correctly. At the first " ding-dong" of the bell, the Jew had been startled from his cat-like slumber, and rising erect in his seat, he glanced uneasily around him.

"Blesh my soul!" he exclaimed, spitting out the bit of burnt cigar that clung adheringly to his lips. " It ish broad daylight! I musht have been ashleep more ash two hours. Ach! theesh are times for a man to keep awake. The Cushtos should be on hish road by thish; and if theesh Spanish hunters do their bishness as clefferly ash they hash promise, he'll shleep sounder thish night ash effer he hash done before. Blesh my soul !" he again exclaimed, and with an accent that betokened a change in the tenor of his thoughts. " Supposhe they should get caught in the act? Ha! what would be the reshult of that? There ish danger—shtrike me dead if there ishn't! Blesh me! I neffer thought of it," continued he, after some moments spent in reflection of an apparently anxious kind. " They might turn Kingsh' evidence, and implicate me—me a shustice ! To save themselves, they'd be likely enough to do ash much ash that. Yesh: and eefen if they did'nt get taken in the act, still there ish danger. That Manuel hash a tongue ash long ash his *machete*. He'sh a prattling fool. I musht take care to get him out of the island—both of them—ash soon ash I can."

In his apprehensions the Jew no longer included Chakra : for he was now under the belief that the dark deed would be accomplished by the Spanish assassins ; and that to *steel*, not *poison*, would the Custos yield up his life.

Even should Cynthia have succeeded in administering the deadly dose —a probability on which he no longer needed to rely—even should the Custos succumb to poison, the myal-man was not to be feared. There was no danger of such a confederate declaring himself. As for Cynthia, the Jew had never dealt directly with her ; and therefore she was without power to implicate him in the hellish contract.

" I musht take some shteps," said he, rising from his chair, and making a feint towards retiring to his chamber, as if to adjust his dress. " What ish besht to be done? Let me think," he added, pausing near the door. and standing in an attitrne ? of reflection ; " yesh! yesh! that's it ! I musht send a messensher t Mount Welcome. Some one can go on ar excushe of bishness. It w   look strange since we're such bad neighbou.sh of late ? No matter for that. The Cushtos is gone, I hope ; and Rafener can send the message to Mishter Trusey. That will bring ish newsh. Here, Rafener !" continued he, calling to his overseer, who, cartwhip in hand, was moving through the court below, " I want ye, Mishter Rafener !"

Ravener, uttering a grunt to signify that he had heard the summons stepped up to the stairway of the verandah ; and stood silently waiting to know for what he was wanted.

" Hash you any bishness about which you could send a messensher to Mishter Trusty—to Mount Welcome, I mean ?"

" Hump ! There's business a plenty for that. Them consarned hogs of the Custos has got into our corn patch up the valley, and played pitch and toss with the young plants. Ye must have damages for it."

" That ish right--that ish right."

" Humph ! You won't say it's right when once you've seen the mess they've made. We'll have a sorry show at crop time, I tell ye."

" Neffer mind that—we'll have an action. Ish not let it pass ; but joosh now I hash other bishness on hand. You send a messensher to Mishter Trusty and tell him about it. And harksh you, Mishter Rafener ! I want this messensher to be discreet. I want him to find out whether the Cushtos ish at home—without making a direct ashking about it. I have heerd that he ish going on a shourney ; and I want to know if he hash set out yet. You understand me ?"

" All right," replied Ravener, with an air that betokened comprehension. " All right! I'll send a fellow that'll get an answer to that question without asking it. Blue Dick can do that."

" Ah ! true, Blue Dick ish the one. And harken you, Mishter Rafener ! tell him to try if he can see the mulatta wench, Cynthy." .

" What is he to say to her ?"

" He ish to tell her to come ofer here, if she hash an opportunity. I wants to shpeak with *her*. But mind ye, Mishter Rafener ! Dick is to be careful what he saysh and doesh. He musht talk with the girl *only in whishpers*."

" I'll instruct him in all that," replied the overseer, in a tone of confidence. " You want him to go now ?"

" Thish minute—thish very minute. I hash a reason for being in a Lurry. Send him off as soon ash you can."

Ravener, without further parley, walked off to dispatch his messenger : and a few minutes after he had gone out of the court, that yellow " complected" Mercury, known by the soubriquet of " Blue Dick" was seen " streaking" it along the path which conducted from the Jew's Penn to the mansion of Mount Welcome.

CHAPTER LXXXIII.

THE MYSTERIOUS ABSENCE.

THE brief conversation between Jessuron and his overseer had taken place *sotto voce :* as it was not desirable it should be overheard by any one —much less by the nephew of him who was its chief subject, and who was supposed to be suspended in a hammock not ten paces from the spot.

The hammock, however, was not visible from the front stairway—being hung in that part of the verandah that extended along the other side of the house.

On the departure of Ravener from his presence the Jew precooded with his original intention—to put his person in order for the day.

His toilet did not take long. After a very brief absence within his room, he re-appeared on the gallery in the same 'pocketed blue coat, breeches and tops, that served him for all purposes and occasions. The soat was buttoned over his breast, the whitey-brown beaver once more upon his head, and the goggles adjusted on the knife-back ridge on his nose. It was evident he intended a stroll. This was all the more certain as he had regained the umbrella—which had dropped from him during sleep—and holding it in his grasp, stood by the top of the stair· way, as if on the eve of starting out.

Whither was he going ?   For what purpose so early ?

His muttered soliloquy declared his design.

" It musht be to-day—yesh, I musht get them married thish very day ; and before any newsh can come. The report of the Cushtos' death might shpoil all my plans. Who knowsh what the young man might do, if he hash only a hint of hish good luck ?   After all, may be, Shoodith ish not so shure of him?   She hash said something lash night. Ha ! it musht be thish day. It ish no ushe going to the rector of the parish. He ish the Cushtos' friend; and might make some obsheckshun. That won't do —s'help me, no !   I musht go to the other. Hee'sh poor, and won't shtand shilly-shally. Besides, hish knot would be shoost as hard to looshe ash if it wash tied by the Bishop of Shamaica. He'll do; and if he won't, then I knowsh one who will—for monish ; ay, anything for monish !"

After this soliloquy, he was about setting foot upon one of the steps with the intention of descending, when a thought appeared to strike him; and turning away from the stair, he walked with shuffling gentleness along the gallery, towards that part of the verandah where the hammock was suspended.

" I supposhe the young shentleman ish shtill ashleep. Shentleman, indeed !   now he ish all that or will be, the next time he goesh to shloop. Well if he ish, I mushn't dishturb him. Rich shentlemen mushn t have their shlumbers·interrupted. Ach !"

The exclamation escaped from his lips, as on rounding the angle of the verandah, he came within sight of the hammock.

" 'Tish empty, I declare !   He'sh early ashtir. In hish room, I supposhe?"

Sans ceremonie, the Jew kept on along the gallery until he had arrived in front of his book-keeper's private apartment. There he stopped, look· ing inward.

The door was ajar—almost wide open. He could see the greater portion of the interior through the door ; the rest of it through the jalousies. There was no one in the room—either sitting, standing, or moving about!

" Mashter Vochan !   Are you there?"

The interrogatory was put rather by way of confirming his observation for he saw there was no one inside.

" Where are you, Mashter Herbert ?" continued he, repeating the inter
rogatory in an altered form—at the same time craning his neck into the
apartment and glancing all around it. " Ash I live, it'sh empty like the
hammock ! He musht have gone out. Yesh. Hish hat's not here—his
cloak ish not here and I see no gun. He alwaysh kept hish gun joosh
there. How hash he passed me without my hearing hish foot ? I shleep
so ash I can hear a cat shteelin' over the floor ! Hash he gone by the
shtairway at all ? Ash I live, no ! Blesh my soul ! there is a track where
somebody musht have shumped over the railing down into the garden.
S'help me, it ish his track ! There'sh no other but him to have made it.
What the deffil ish the young fellow after this morning ? I hope there
ish nothing wrong in it."

On missing the young Englishman out of his hammock and room, the
penn-keeper felt at first no particular uneasiness. His ' protégé' had, no
doubt, gone out for a stroll in the woods. He had taken his gun along with
him, to have a shot at some early bird looking for the early worm. He
had done so many a time before—though never at so early an hour.

The hour, however, was not enough of itself to cause any surprise to his
patron ; nor even the fact of his having leaped over the verandah railing.
He might have seen the owner of the house asleep in his chair near the
head of the stairway ; and, not wishing to disturb him, had chosen the
other mode of exit. There was nothing in all this to cause uneasiness.
Nor would the Jew have thought anything of it had it not been for
some other circumstances which quickly came under his notice—guiding
him to the suspicion that something *might be amiss.*"

The first of these circumstances was that Herbert, although having
taken his gun along with him, had left behind his shot-belt and powder-
flask ! Both were there in his room, hanging upon their peg. They did
not escape the sharp glance of the Jew ; who at once began to draw con-
clusions from their presence.

If the young man had gone out on a shooting excursion, it was strange
that he did not take his ammunition along with him ?

Perhaps, however, he had seen some sort of game near the house ;
and, in his hurry to get a shot at it, had gone off hastily—trusting to the
two charges which his gun contained. In that case he would not go far;
and in a few minutes might be expected back.

A few minutes passed, and a great many minutes—until a full hour had
transpired—and still nothing was heard or seen of the book-keeper :
though messengers had been dispatched in search of him, and had
quartered all the ground for half a mile around the precincts of the penn.

Jessuron—whose matutinal visit to the minister had been postponed by
the occurrence—began to look grave.

" It ish shtrange," said he, speaking to his daughter, who had now
arisen, and was far from appearing cheerful; " shtrange he should go
abroad in thish fashion, without shaying a word to either of us h ?"

Judith made no reply : though her silence could not conceal a certain
degree of chagrin, from which she was evidently suffering. Perhaps she
had even more reason than the " rabbi" to suspect there was something
amiss ?

Certainly, something disagreeable—a misunderstanding, at least, had
arisen between her and Herbert on the preceeding day. Her speech
had already given some slight hint of it; but much more her manner,

which, on the night before, and now unmistakably in the morning, betrayed a mixture of melancholy and suppressed indignation.

It did not add to the equanimity of her temper, when the house wench
- -who was unslinging the hammock in which Herbert had slept—announced it to contain two articles scarce to be expected in such a place
—a cocoa-nut and a tobacco-pipe !

The pipe could not have belonged to Herbert Vaughan : he never
smoked a pipe ; and as for the cocoa-nut, it had evidently been plucked
from the tree standing near.   The trunk of the palm exhibited scratches,
as if some one had climbed up it, and above could be seen the freshly
torn peduncle, where the fruit had been wrenched from its stalk !

What should Herbert Vaughan have been doing up the palm-tree,
flinging cocoa-nuts into his own couch ?

His unaccountable absence was becoming surrounded by circumstances still more mysterious.   One of the cattle-herds, who had been sent
in search of him, now coming in, announced a new fact, of further significance.   In the patch of muddy soil, outside the garden wall, the herd
had discovered the book-keeper's track, going up towards the hills ; and
near it, on the same path, the footprint of another man, who must have
gone over the ground twice, returning as he had come !

This cattle-herd, though of sable skin, was a skilled tracker.   His
word might be trusted.

It was trusted ; and produced an unpleasant impression both on
Jessuron and Judith—an impression more unpleasant as time passed, and
the book-keeper was still unreturned.

The father fumed and fretted ; he did more—he threatened.   The
young Englishman was his debtor, not only for a profuse hospitality but
for *money advanced.*   Was he going to prove ungrateful ? a defaulter ?

Ah ! little had that pecuniary obligation to do with the chagrin that
was vexing the Jew Jessuron.   Far less with those emotions, like the
waves of a stormy sea, that had begun to agitate the breast of his
daughter ; and which every slight circumstance, like a strong wind, was
lashing into fury and fome. .

*   *   *   *   *   *   *

Blue Dick came back.   He had executed his errand adroitly.   The Cus-
toe was gone upon a journey! he had started exactly at the hour of
daybreak.

"Goot !" said Jessuron ; " but where is hish nephew ?"

Blue Dick had seen Cynthia ; and whispered a word in her ear, as the
overseer had instructed him.   She would come over to the penn, as soon
as she could find an opportunity for absence from Mount Welcome.

" Goot !" answered the Jew.   " But where ish Mashter Vochan ? wheie
bash he betaken himshelf ?"

" Waere ?" mentally interrogated Judith, as the noonday sun saw the
black clouds coursing over her brow.

CHAPTER LXXXIV.

A SHADOWED SPIRIT

THE sun was just beginning to re-gild the glittering flanks of the Jumbé Rock, his rays not yet having reached the valley below, when lights streaming through the jalousied windows of Mount Welcome proclaimed that the inmates of the mansion were already astir.

Lights shone through the lattices of several distinct windows—one from the Custos' sleeping room, another from the apartment of Lilly Quasheba, while a brilliant stream, pouring through the jalousies in front, betokened that the chandelier was burning in the great hall.

From Smythje's chamber alone came no sign either of light or life. The windows were dark, the curtains close drawn. Its occupant was asleep.

Yes, though others were stirring around him, the aristocratic Smythje was still sleeping as soundly and silently as if dead, perhaps dreaming of the fair "cweeole queetyaws," and his twelve conquests, now happily extended to the desired baker's dozen, by the successful declaration of yesterday.

Though a light still burned in the sleeping apartment of the Custos, and also in that of Kate, neither father nor daughter were in their own rooms. Both were in the great hall, seated by a table, on which, even at this early hour, breakfast had been spread. It was not the regular matutinal meal, as certain circumstances showed. Mr. Vaughan only was eating; while Kate appeared to be present merely for the purpose of pouring out his coffee, and otherwise attending upon him.

The costume in which the Custos appeared differed from his every-day wear. It was that of a man about to set forth upon a journey—in short, a travelling costume. A surtout, of strong material, with ample outside pockets; boots reaching above his knees; a belt with pistol holsters around his waist—a guard against any chance encounter with runaway negroes: a felt hat, lying on a chair beside him, and a camlet cloak, hanging over the back of the same chair—all proclaimed the purpose of a journey, and one about to be entered upon within a few minutes of time.

A pair of large silver spurs, buckled over his boots, told also the mode of travel intended. It was to be on horseback.

This was further manifested by the fact that two horses were at that moment standing at the bottom of the stone stairs outside, their forms dimly visible through the blue dawn. Both were saddled, bridled, and equipped, with a black groom by their side, holding them in hand—himself in travelling toggery.

Valises, buckled upon the croup, and saddle-bags suspended across the cantle, showed that the travellers were to carry their luggage along with them.

The object of the intended journey is already known. Mr. Vaughan was about to put into execution a design long delayed—to perform a duty which he owed to his daughter, and which, if left unaccomplished, would seriously imperil the prosperity and happiness of her future life. He was about proceeding to the capital of the island, to obtain from the Assembly that special act of grace, which they alone could give;

and which would free his daughter from those degrading disabilities the Black Code had inflicted upon all of her unfortunate race. Six lines from the Assembly, with the governor's signature attached, though it might not extinguish the *taint*, nor the *taunt* of malevolent lips, would nevertheless, remove all obstacles to hereditament; and Kate Vaughan could then become the heiress to her own father's property, without fear of failure.

To sue for this act and obtain it was the purpose of that journey upon which Loftus Vaughan was on the eve of setting forth. He had no apprehension of a failure. Had he been only a book-keeper or small tradesman, he might have been less sanguine of success; but Custos of an important precinct, with scores of friends in the Assembly, he knew that he would only have to ask and it would be given him.

For all that, he was not setting out in very high spirits. The unpleasant prospect of having such a long and arduous journey to make was a source of vexation to him: for the Custos liked an easy life, and hated the fatigue of travel.

But there was something besides that dispirited him. For some days past he had found his health giving way. He had lost appetite, and was rapidly losing flesh. A constant and burning thirst had siezed upon him, which, from morning to night, he was continually trying to quench.

The plantation doctor was puzzled with the symptoms, and his prescriptions had failed in giving relief. Indeed, so obstinate and *death-like* was the disease becoming, that the sufferer would have given up his intention of going to Spanish Town—at least, till a more fitting time—but for a hope, that in the capital, some experienced physcian might be found who would comprehend his malady and cure it.

Indulging in this hope, he was determined to set forth at all hazards.

There was still another incubus upon his spirits, and one, perhaps, that weighed upon them more heavily than aught else. Ever since the death of Chakra—or rather since the glimpse he had got of Chakra's ghost—a sort of supernatural dread had taken possession of the mind of Loftus Vaughan. Often had he speculated on that fearful phenomenon, and wondered what it could have been. Had he alone witnessed the apparition, he might have got over the awe it had occasioned him; for then could he have attributed it to an illusion of the senses—a mere freak of his imagination, excited, as it was at the time, by the spectacle on the Jumbé Rock. But Trusty had seen the ghost, too! and Trusty's mind was not one of the imaginative kind. Besides, how could both be deluded by the same fancy, and at the same instant of time?

Turn the thing in his own mind as he might, there was something that still remained inexplicable—something that caused the heart of the Custos to tingle with fear every time that he thought of Chakra and his ghost.

This intermitent awe had oppressed him ever since the day of his visit to the Jumbé Rock—that day described; for he never went a second time. Nor yet did he afterwards care to venture alone upon the wooded mountain. He dreaded a second encounter with that weird apparition.

In time, perhaps, the fear would have died out, and, in fact, was dying out—the intervals during which it was not felt becoming gradually more extended. Loftus Vaughan, though he could never have forgotten the myal-man, nor the terrible incidents of his death, might have ceased to trouble himself with thoughts about Chakra's ghost, but for a circum stance that was reported to him on the day that Smythje sank into the deadwood.

On the afternoon of that day, as Quashie was making his way home-ward through the forest and over the hills, the darkey declared that, on passing near a noted spot called the Duppy's Hole, he had "see'd de gose ob ole Chakra!"

Quashie, on reaching home, announced the fact, with chattering teeth and eyes rolling wildly in their sockets ; and, though the loutish boy was only laughed at by his fellow-slaves, the statement made a most painful impression on the mind of his master—restoring it to the state of habit-ual terror that had formerly held possession of it, and from which it had become only partially relieved.

The circumstance related by Quashie—still fresh in the thoughts of the Custos—had contributed not a little to increase that feeling of dejection and discouragement under which he suffered at the moment of setting out upon his proposed expedition.

CHAPTER LXXXV.

THE STIRRUP-CUP.

IF Loftus Vaughan was in low spirits, not more joyful seemed his daughter, as she assisted at the early " déjûner."

On the contrary, a certain sadness overspread the countenance of the young creole ; as if reflected from the spirits of her father.

A stranger to the circumstances that surrounded her might have fan-cied that it was sympathy—at seeing him so dull and downcast—mingled with the natural regret she might have at his leaving home, and for so long an absence. But one who scrutinised more closely could not fail to note in those fair features an expression of sadness that must have sprung from a different and deeper source.

The purpose of her father's journey may, in part, explain the melan-choly that marked the manner of the young creole. She knew that pur-pose. She had learnt it from her father's lips, though only on the even-ing before.

Then, for the first time in her life, was she made acquainted with those adverse circumstances that related to her birth and parentage : for up to that hour she had remained ignorant of her position, socially as well as legally. Then, for the first time, was fully explained to her her own true status in the social scale—the disabilities and degradation under which she suffered.

It was to remove these disabilities—and wipe out, as it were, the de-gradation—that her father was now going forth.

The young girl did not fail to feel gratitude ; but perhaps the feeling might have been stronger, had her father taken less trouble to make her feel sensible of the service he was about to perform—using it as a lever to remove that reluctance to the union with Smythje, which still lingered.

During the few minutes that Mr. Vaughan was engaged in eating his breakfast, not many words passed between them. The viards, luxurious enough, were scarce more than tasted. The intended traveller had no appetite for the solids with which the table was spread, and seemed to care only for drink.

After quaffing off several cups of coffee, solely from a desire to quench thirst, and without eating bread or anything else along with it, he rose from the table, and prepared to take his departure.

Mr. Trusty entering, announced that the horses and the attendant groom were ready, waiting outside.

The Custos donned his travelling hat, and with the assistance of Kate and her maid Yola, put on his sleeved cloak : as the air of the early morning was raw and cold.

While these final preparations were being made, a mulatta woman was seen moving about the room—at times acting as an attendant upon the table, at other times standing silently in the background. She was the slave Cynthia.

In the behaviour of this woman there was something peculiar. There was a certain amount of nervous agitation in her manner as she moved about ; and ever and anon she was seen to make short traverses to different parts of the room—apparently without errand or object. Her steps, too, were stealthy, her glances unsteady and furtive.

All this would have been apparent enough to a suspicious person ; but none of the three present appeared to notice it.

The " swizzle " bowl stood on a side-board. While breakfast was being placed on the table, Cynthia had been seen refilling the bowl with this delicious drink, which she had mixed in an adjoining chamber. Some one asked her why she was performing that, her diurnal duty, at so early an hour—especially as her master would be gone before the time of swizzle-drinking should arrive ; usually during the hotter hours of the day.

" P'raps massr like drink ob swizzle 'fore he go," was the explanatory reply vouchsafed by Cynthy.

The girl made a successful conjecture. Just as the Custos was about to step outside for the purpose of descending the stairway, a fit of choking thirst once more came upon him, and he called for drink.

" Massa like glass ob swizzle ?" inquired Cynthia, stepping up to his side. " I've mixed for massa some berry good," added she, with impressive earnestness.

" Yes, girl," replied her master. " That's the best thing I can take. Bring me a large goblet of it."

He had scarce time to turn round before the goblet was presented to him, full to the rim. He did not see that the slave's hand trembled as she held it up, nor yet that her eyes were averted—as if to hinder them from beholding some fearful sight.

His thirst prevented him from seeing anything, but that which promised to assuage it.

He caught hold of the goblet ; and gulped down the whole of its contents, without once removing it from his lips.

" You've overrated its quality, girl," said he, returning her the glass

"It doesn't seem at all good. There's a bitterish taste abou: it ; but I suppose it's my palate that's out of order, and one shouldn't be particular about the stirrup-cup."

With this melancholy attempt at appearing gay, Loftus Vaughan bade adieu to his daughter, and climbing into the saddle, rode off upon his journey.

Ah! Custos Vaughan! That stirrup-cup was the last you were ever destined to drink. In the sparkling "swizzle" was an infusion of the baneful *Savanna flower*. In that deep draught you had introduced into your veins one of the deadliest of vegetable poisons.

Chakra's prophecy will soon be fulfilled. The death-spell will now quickly do its work. In twenty-four hours you will be a corpse!

CHAPTER LXXXVI.

THE HORN SIGNAL.

CUBINA, on getting clear of the penn-keeper's precincts, lost little time in returning to the glade ; and, having once more reached the *ceiba*, seated himself on a log to await the arrival of the young Englishman.

For some minutes he remained in this attitude—though every moment becoming more fidgety, as he perceived that time was passing, and no one came. He had not even a pipe to soothe his impatience : for it had been left in the hammock, into which he had cast it from the cocoa.

Before many minutes had passed, however, a pipe would have been to little purpose in restraining his nervous excitement ; for the non-appearance of the young Englishman began to cause him serious uneasiness.

What could be detaining him? Had the Jew been awakened? and was he by some means or other hindering Herbert from coming out? There was no reason, that Cubina could think of, why the young man should be ten minutes later than himself in reaching the *ceiba*. Five minutes— even the half of it—might have sufficed for him to robe himself, in such garments as were needed ; and then what was to prevent him from following immediately? Surely the appeal that had been made to him, —the danger hinted at to those dear to him, the necessity for haste, spoken in unmistakable terms—surely, all this would be sufficient to attract him to the forest, without a moment's hesitation?

Why then was he delaying?

The Maroon could not make it out: unless under the disagreeable supposition that the Jew no longer slept, and was intercepting his egress.

What if Herbert might have lost his way in proceeding towards the rendezvous? The path was by no means plain, but the contrary. It was a mere cattle track, little used by men. Besides, there were others of the same—scores of them trending in all directions, crossing and converging with this very one. The half-wild steers and colts of the penn-keeper ranged the thickets at will. Their tracks were everywhere ; and it would require a person skilled in woodcraft and acquainted with the *lay* of the country to follow any particular path. It was likely enough that the young Englishman had strayed

Just then these reflections occurred to Cubina. He chided himself
for not thinking of it sooner. He should have stayed by the penn—
waited for Herbert to come out, and then taken the road along with him.

"Not to think of that! Crambo! how very stupid of me!" muttered
the Maroon, pacing nervously to and fro; for his impatience had long
since started him up from the log.

"Like enough he's lost his way?

"I shall go back along the path. Perhaps I may find him. At all
events, if he's taken the right road, I must meet him."

And as he said this, he glided rapidly across the glade, taking the
back track towards the penn.

The conjecture that Herbert had strayed was perfectly correct. The
young Englishman had never revisited the scene of his singular adventure, since the day that introduced him to the acquaintance of so
many queer people. Not but that he had felt the inclination, amounting
almost to a desire, to do so; and more than once had he been upon the
eve of satisfying this inclination, but otherwise occupied, the opportunity
had not offered itself.

Not greatly proficient in forest lore—as Cubina had also rightly conjectured—especially in that of a West Indian forest, he had strayed from
the true path almost upon the instant of entering upon it; and was at
that very moment wandering through the woods in search of the glade
where grew the gigantic cotton-tree!

No doubt, in the course of time, he might have found it, or perhaps
stumbled upon it by chance, for—made aware, by the earnest invitation
he had received, that time was of consequence—he was quartering the
ground in every direction, with the rapidity of a young pointer in his
first season with the gun.

Meanwhile the Maroon glided rapidly back along the path leading to
the penn, without seeing aught either of the Englishman or his track.

He re-entered the ruinate fields of the old sugar estate, and continued
on till within sight of the house, still unsuccessful in his search.

Proceeding with caution, he stepped over the dilapidated wall of the
old orchard. Caution was now of extreme necessity. It was broad day;
and, but for the cover which the undergrowth afforded him, he could
not have gone a step farther without the risk of being seen from the
house.

He reached the ruin from which he had before commanded a view from
the verandah; and, once more stealing a glance over its top, he obtained a
full view of the long rambling corridor.

Jessuron was in it—not as when last seen, asleep in his arm-chair, but on
foot, and hurrying to and fro, with quick step and excited mien.

His black-bearded overseer was standing by the door as if listening to
some orders which the Jew was issuing.

The hammock was still hanging in its place, but its collapsed sides,
showed that it was empty. Cubina saw that, but no signs of its late occupant—neither in gallery nor about the buildings.

If still there, he must be in some of the rooms? but that one which
opened nearest the hammock, and which Cubina conjectured to be his
bed-room, appeared to be unoccupied. Its door stood ajar, and no one
seemed to be inside.

The Maroon was considering whether he should .stay awhile longer upon the spot, and watch the movements of the two men, when it occurred to him that if the young man had gone out, and up the right path, he must have crossed a track of muddy ground, just outside the garden wall!

Being so near the house—and in the expectation of seeing something there to explain Herbert's delay—he had not stayed to examine this on his second approach.

Crouching cautiously among the trees, he now returned to it; and, almost at the first glance, his eye revealed to him the truth.

A fresh footprint was in the mud, with its heel to the house and its toe pointing to the path! It was not his own; it must be that of the young Englishman?

He traced the tracks, as far as they could be distinguished; but that was only to the edge of the damp earth. Beyond, the ground was dry and firm—covered with a close-cropped carpet of grass, upon which the hoof of a horse would scarcely have left an impression.

The tracks, however, on leaving the moist ground, appeared as if trending towards the proper path; and Cubina felt convinced that, for some distance at least, the young Englishman had gone towards the glade.

That he was no longer by the house was sufficiently certain; and equally so that he had kept his promise and followed Cubina into the woods. But where was he now?

"He may have reached the glade in my absence, and is now waiting for me?" was the reflection of the Maroon.

Stimulated by this, as well as by the chagrin which his mischances or mismanagement were causing him, he started back along the path at a run—as if struggling in a match against time.

Far quicker than before he reached the glade, but, as before, he found it untenanted! No Englishman was under the *ceiba*—no human being in sight.

As soon as he had fairly recovered breath, he bethought him of shouting His voice might be of avail in guiding the wanderer to the glade; for Cubina now felt convinced that the young Englishman was straying— perhaps wandering through the woods at no great distance from the spot. His shouts might be heard; and although the stranger might not recognise the voice, the circumstances were such, that he might understand the object for which it was put forth.

Cubina shouted, first at a moderate pitch, then hallooed with all the strength of his lungs.

No answer, save the wood echoes.

Again and again: still no response.

"*Crambo!*" exclaimed he, suddenly thinking of a better means of making his presence known. "He may hear my horn? He may remember that, and know it. If he's anywhere within a mile, I'll make him hear it."

The Maroon raised the horn to his lips and blew a long, loud blast— then another, and another.

There was a response to that signal; but not such as the young Englishman might have been expected to make. Three shrill bugle blasts, borne back upon the breeze, seemed the echoes of his own.

But the Maroon knew they were not. On hearing them, he let drop the horn to his side, and stood in an attitude to listen.

Another—this time a single wind—came from the direction of the former.

"Three and one," muttered the Maroon; "it's Quaco. He needn't have sounded the last, for I could tell his *tongue* from a thousand. He's on his way back from Savanna-la-Mer—though I didn't expect him to be back so soon. So much the better—I want him."

On finishing the muttered soliloquy, the Maroon captain stood as if considering.

"*Crambo!*" he muttered, after a pause, and in a tone of vexation. "What has become of this young fellow? I must sound again—lest Quaco's horn may have misled him. This time, lieutenant, hold your tongue!"

So saying and speaking, as if the "lieutenant" was by his side, he raised the horn once more to his lips, and blew a single blast—giving it an intonation quite different from the other.

After an interval of silence, he repeated the call in notes exactly similar, and then, after another pause, once again.

To none of these signals did the "tongue" of Quaco make reply: but shortly after that worthy responded to the original summons by presenting himself 'in propriâ personâ.'

CHAPTER LXXXVII.

QUACO'S QUEER ENCOUNTER.

Quaco came into the glade carrying a large bundle upon his back—under which he had trudged all the way from Savanna-la-Mer.

He was naked to the breech-cloth—excepting the hog-skin greaves upon his shanks, and the old brimless hat upon his head. This, however, was all the costume Quaco ever wore—all, indeed, that he owned; for, notwithstanding that he was the lieutenant, his uniform was no better than that of the meanest private of the band.

His captain, therefore, exhibited no surprise at the scantiness of Quaco's clothing; but what did surprise Cubina was the air with which he entered the glade, and some other circumstances that at once arrested his attention.

The skin of the colossus was covered with a white sweat that appeared to be oozing from every pore of his dark epidermis. This might have been occasioned by his long walk—the last hour of it under a broiling sun, and carrying weight, as he was: for the bag upon his back appeared a fifty pounder, at least, to say nothing of a large musket balanced upon the top of it.

None of these circumstances, however, would account for that inexplicable expression upon his yellow eyeballs—the quick, hurried step, and uncouth gesticulations by which he was signalising his approach.

Though, as already stated, they had arrested the attention of his superior, the latter accustomed to a certain reserve in the presence of his followers, pretended not to notice them. As his lieutenant came up, he simply said:—

"I am glad you are come, Quaco."

"An' a'm glad, Captain Cubina, I've foun' ye har. War hurryin' home fass as my legs cud carry me, 'spectin' to find ye thar."

"Ha!" said Cubina; "some news, I suppose. Have you met any one in the woods—that young Englishman from the Jew's penn? I'm expecting him here. He appears to have missed the way."

"Han't met no Englishman, Cappin. Cussos Vaughan am that—I'se a met *him*."

"*Crambo!*" cried Cubina, "You've met Custos Vaughan? When and where?"

"When—dis mornin. Where—'bout fo' mile b'yond the crossin' on the Carrion Crow road. That's where I met *him*."

The emphasis upon the last words struck upon the ear of Cubina. It seemed to imply that Quaco, on his route, had encountered others.

"Anybody else, did you meet?" he inquired, hurriedly, and with evident anxiety as to the answer.

"Ya-as, Cappin," drawled out the lieutenant, with a coolness strongly in contrast with his excited manner on entering the glade. But Quaco saw that his superior was waiting for the coming of the young Englishman, and that he need not hurry the communication he was about to make.

"Ya-as, I met ole Plute, the head driver at Moun' Welcome. He was ridin' 'longside o' the Cussos, by way o' his escort."

"Anybody else?"

"Not jest then," answered Quaco, evidently holding back the most interesting item of news he had to communicate. "Not jess then, Cappin Cubina."

"But afterwards? Speak out, Quaco! Did you meet any one going on the same road?"

The command, with the impatient gesture that accompanied it, brought Quaco to a quicker confession than he might have volunteered.

"I met, Cappin Cubina," said he, his cheeks bulging with the importance of the communication he was about to make, while his eyes rolled like "twin jelly balls" in their sockets—"I met next, not a *man* but a *ghost!*"

"A ghost?" said Cubina, incredulously.

"A duppy, I sw'ar by the great Accompong—same as I saw before—the ghost of ole Chakra."

The Maroon captain again made a start, which his lieutenant attributed to surprise at the announcement he had made.

Cubina did not undeceive him as to the cause.

"And where?" interrogated he, in hurried phrase. "Where did you meet the ghost?"

"I didn't zacly meet it," answered Quaco, "I only seed it on the road afore me—'bout a hundred yards or that away. I wor near enuf to be sure o' it—and it was Chakra's ghost—jees as I seed him t'other day up thar by the Duppy Hole. The old villain can't sleep in his grave. He's about these woods yet."

"How far was it from where you met Mr. Vaughan?"

"Not a great way, cappin. 'Bout a quarter o' a mile, I shod **think**

Soon as it spied me, it tuck to the bushes ; and I seed no more on it. It was atter daylight, and the cocks had crowed. I heard 'em crowing at ole Jobson's plantation close by, and, maybe, that sent the Duppy a scuttlin' into the River."

" We must wait no longer for this young man—we must be gone from here, Quaco."

And as Cubina expressed this intention, he appeared to move away from the spot.

"Stop, Cappin," said Quaco, interrupting him with a gesture, that showed he had something more to communicate ; "You han't heard all. I met more of 'em."

" More of whom ?"

" That same queer sort. But two miles atter I'd passed the place where I seed the duppy o' the ole myal-man, who d'ye think I met nex'?"

" Who ?" inquired Cubina, half guessing at the answer.

"Them debbil's kind—like enuf company for the Duppy—them dam' Spaniards of the Jew's penn."

" Ah ! *Maldito !*" cried the Maroon captain, in a voice of alarm at the same time making a gesture as if a light had suddenly broke upon him. " The Spaniards, you say ? They, too, after him ! Come, Quaco ! Down with that bundle ! Throw it in the bush—anywhere ! There's not a moment to be lost. I understand the series of encounters you have had upon the road. Luckily, I've brought my gun, and you yours. We may need them both before night. Down with the bundle and follow me !"

" Stop and take me with you," cried a voice from the edge of the glade ; " I have a gun, too."

And at the same moment the young Englishman, with his gun upon his shoulder, was seen emerging from the underwood and making towards the *ceiba.*

CHAPTER LXXXVIII.

AN UNCLE IN DANGER.

" You appear to be in great haste, Captain Cubina," said Herbert, advancing in double quick time. " May I know what's the matter ? Anything amiss ?"

"Amiss, Master Vaughan ! Much indeed. But we shouldn't stand to talk. We must take the road to Savannah, and at once."

" What ! you want me to go to Savannah ? I'm with you for any reasonable adventure ; but my time's not exactly my own ; and I must first have a reason for such a journey."

"A good reason, Master Vaughan. Your uncle, the Custos, is in trouble."

" Ah !" exclaimed the young Englishman, with an air of disappointment. " Not so good a reason as you may think, captain. Was it him you meant when you said just now one who *should be* dear to me was in danger ?"

" It was," answered Cubina.

" Captain Cubina," said Herbert, speaking with a certain air of indiffe-

rence, " this uncle of mine but little deserves my interfeience."
" But his life's in danger !" urged the Maroon, interrupting Herbert in
his explanation.
" Ah !" ejaculated the nephew, " do you say that ? Is his life in danger,
then——"
" Yes," said the Maroon, again interrupting him, " and *others* too may
be in peril· from the same enemy—yourself, perhaps, Master Vaughan.
Ay, and maybe those that might be ·dear to you as yourself."
| " Ha !" exclaimed Herbert, this time in a very different tone of voice
" You have some evil tidings, Captain ? Pray tell me all at once ?"
" Not now, Master Vaughan, not now. There's not a moment to be
wasted in talk. We must take the route at once. I shall tell you as we
go along."
" Agreed then," cried Herbert. " If it's a life and death matter, I'm
with you—even to Savannah ! No *book-keeping* to-day, Master Jessuron
and——" (the speaker only mentally pronounced the name) " Judith may
well spare me for one day—especially for such a purpose as the saving
of lives. All right ; I'm with you, Captain Cubina."
" *Vamos !*" cried the Maroon, hastily moving off. " For want of horses
we must make our legs do double quick time. These skulking scoundrels have sadly got the start of us."
And saying this, he struck into the up-hill path, followed by Herbert—·
the taciturn lieutenant, no longer embarrassed by his bundle, keeping
close in the rear.
The path Cubina had chosen appeared to conduct to Mount Welcome.
" You are not going *there* ?" inquired Herbert, in a significant way, at
the same time stopping, and appealing to his conductor for an answer.
It had just occurred to the nephew that a visit to his uncle's house
might place him in a position both unpleasant and embarrassing.
" No !" answered the Maroon ; " there is no longer any need for us to
go to the house : since the Custos has left it long hours ago. We could
learn nothing there more than I know already. Besides, it's half a mile
out of our way. We should lose time ; and that's the most important of
all. We shall presently turn out of this path, into one that leads over
the mountain by the Jumbè Rock. That's the shortest way to the
Savannah road. *Vamos !*"
With this wind-up to his speech, the Maroon again moved on ; and
Herbert, his mind now at rest, strode silently after.
Up to this time the young Englishman had received no explanation of
the object of the journey he was in the act of undertaking ; nor had he
asked any. The information, though as yet only covertly conveyed—
that those dear to him were in danger—was motive enough for trusting
the Maroon.
Before long, however, it occurred to him that he ought to be informed
of the nature of that danger ; over whom it impended ; and what was the
signification of the step they were now taking to avert it.
These questions he put to his conductor, as they hastened together
along the path.
In hurried phrase the Maroon made known to him much, though not
all, of what he himself knew of the position of affairs—more especially of
the peril in which the Custos appeared to be placed. He gave an

account of his own descent into the Duppy's Hole ; of the conversation he had overheard there; and though still ignorant of the motives, stated his suspicions of the murderous plot, in which Herbert's own employer was playing a principal part.

It is needless to say that the young Englishman was astounded by these revelations.

Perhaps he would have been still more astonished, but that the development of these wicked dealings were only a confirmation of a whole series of suspicious circumstances, that for some days before had been constantly coming under his notice, and for which he had been vainly seeking an explanation.

From that moment all thoughts of returning to dwell under the roof of Jacob Jessuron vanished from his mind.   To partake of the hospitality of such a man——a murderer, at least by intent—was completely out of the question.   He at once perceived that his fine, sinecure situation must be given up ; and, despite the scandal his desertion might bring about, he could never again make his home in the Happy Valley.   Even the fascinations of that fair Judith would not be strong enough to attract him thither.

Cubina listened to these resolves, and apparently with great satisfaction. But the Maroon had not yet made known to Herbert many other secrets, of which he had become the depository ; and some of which might be to the young Englishman of extremest interest.   The communication of these he reserved to a future opportunity—when time might not be so pressing.

Herbert Vaughan, now apprised of the peril in which his uncle stood, for the time forgot all else, and only thought of pressing onward to his aid.   Injuries and insults appeared alike forgotten and forgiven—even . that which had stung him more sharply than all—the cold chilling bow at the Smythje ball !

Beyond the Jumbé Rock, and at no great distance from the by-path by which they were travelling, lay the proper country of the Maroons.   By winding a horn, it might have been heard by some of the band ; who at that hour would, no doubt, be engaged in their usual occupation—hunting the wild hog.

Cubina knew this ; and, on arriving at that point on the path nearest to the town, he halted, and stood for a moment reflecting.

Then, as if deeming himself sufficiently strong in the companionship of the robust young Englishman and the redoubtable lieutenant, he gave up the idea of calling any of them to his assistance; and once more moved forward along the route towards the Savannah road.

CHAPTER LXXXIX.

AN EQUESTRIAN EXCURSION.

Throughout the day the penn-keeper kept to his Penn.   The unexplained absence of his ' protégé' rendered it prudent to postpone his proposed visit to the minister ; besides, Cynthia was expected.

From the mulatta he hoped to obtain much information. Ier know-ledge of events must be fresher than even that of Chakra—else would he have gone up to the Duppy's Hole to consult the oracle of Obi.   Cynthia would be likely to know all. She could at least tell him whether the spell had been administered—how, and when.

These were facts worth knowing, and Jessuron stayed at home to await the advent of Cynthia.

Not so Judith. Devoured by spleen, inaction was too irksome. She could not content herself in the house; and resolved to seek outside, if not solace, at least distraction to her thoughts. Shortly after breakfast she ordered her steed to be saddled, and prepared to go forth.

Strange it was he should absent himself on that day above any other! Just after his uncle had departed on a journey? That was strange?

Judith summoned the herdsman who had discovered the tracks in the mud.

"You are sure it was the track of young Master Vaughan you saw?"

"Sartin sure, Missa Jessuron—one ob 'em war."

"And the other? What was *it* like? Was it also the track of a man?"

"Ya, missa; 'twar a man's track—leastwise, I nebber seed a woman track big as dat 'ere. Sartin de sole dat make it wor de fut ob a man, though it wa'n't de boot oba gen'l man like young Massa Vaughan."

Whip in hand, the Jewess stood reflecting.

A messenger might it be? From whom, if not from Kate Vaughan? With whom else was he acquainted? Such strange conditions of relationship! The mysterious mode by which the messenger must have approached him; for fresh mud upon the back of the tree told that he who had climbed up must have been the same who had made the foot-marks by the garden wall. The articles found in the hammock had been flung down to awake and warn the sleeper?

Clearly a secret message, delivered by a crafty messenger! Clearly a surreptitious departure?

And the motive for all this? No common one?—it could not be. No errand after game. The fowling piece was gone; but that was no evidence of an intention to spend the day in sporting. Herbert was in the habit of taking his gun, whenever he strolled out into the fields or forest. But the other and necessary paraphernalia had been left behind! A shooting excurtion? Nothing of the sort!

A messenger with a love message—a summons willingly accepted--promptly responded to!

"Oh, if it be!" cried the proud, passionate woman, as she sprang upon the back of her steed; "if it be, I shall know it! I shall have revenge!"

The horse came in for a share of this jealous indignation. A spiteful cut of the whip, and a fierce "dig" from her spurred heel, set the animal in rapid motion—his head towards the hills.

Judith Jessuron was a splendid equestrian, and could manage a horse as well as the best breaker about her father's penn.

In the saddle she was something to be seen and admired; her brilliant beauty, enhanced by the charm of excitement, exhibiting itself in the heightened colour of her cheeks, and the stronger flashing of her dark Jewish eyes. The outline of her form was equally attractive. Of full womanly development, and poised in the saddle with an air of piquant *abandon*, it illustrated the curve of Hogarth in all its luxuriant graceful-ness. Such a spectacle was calculated to elicit something more than ordinary admiration; and it required a heart already pre-occupied to

resist its fascinations. If Herbert Vaughan had escaped them, it could
only be from having his heart thus defended from a danger that few men
might have tempted with a chance of safety!

Galloping across the old garden, with a single leap she cleared the
ruined wall; and arriving at the spot where were still to be seen those
tell-tale tracks, she reined up, and leaned over to examine them.

Yes—that was his track—his small foot was easily distinguished'
The other? There it was—the footprint of a negro—pegged brogans
White men do not wear them. Some of the slave people of Mount Wel
come? But why twice back and forward? Was not once sufficient.
Had there been a double message? There might have been—a warning,
and afterwards an appointment !

Perhaps, to meet in the forest? Ha! perhaps at that moment!

The bitter conjecture brought her reflections to an abrupt ending ; and
once more plying whip and spur, the jealous equestrian dashed rapidly
on, up the sloping path that trended towards the hills.

The purpose of this expedition, on the part of the Jewess, was
altogether indefinite. It simply sprang from that nervous impatience
that would not permit her to rest—a faint hope that during her ride she
might discover some clue to the mysterious disappearance. Wretched-
ness might be the reward of that ride. No matter! Uncertainty was unendurable.

She did not go exactly in the direction of Mount Welcome, though
thither went her thoughts. She had never been a guest of the Custos,
and therefore had no colourable excuse for presenting herself at the
mansion—else she would have ridden direct to it.

Her design was different.

Though she might not approach the house, she could reconnoitre it
from a distance ; and this had she determined upon doing.

She had fixed upon the Jumbé Rock as the best point of observation.
She knew that its 'summit commanded a bird's-eye view of Mount Welcome estate, lying under the mountain like a spread map, and that any
movement by the mansion, or in the surrounding inclosures, might be
minutely marked—especially with the aid of a powerful *lorgnette*, with
which she had taken the precaution to provide herself.

With this intent did she head her horse towards the Jumbé Rock—
urging the animal with fierce, fearless energy up the difficult declivity of
the mountain.

CHAPTER XC.

SMYTHJE AMONG THE STATUES.

At that hour, when the heart of Judith Jessuron was alternately torn by
the passions of love and jealousy, a passion equally profound, though ap
parently more tranquil, was burning in the breast of Lilly Quasheba, in
spired by the same object—Herbert Vaughan.

In vain had the young creole endeavoured to think indifferently of her
cousin : in vain had she striven to reconcile her love with what her

father had taught her to deem her duty, and think differently of Mr Smythje—in vain. The effort only ended in a result the very opposite to that intended in strengthening her passion for the former, and weakening her regard for the latter. And thus must it ever be with the heart's inclinings, as well as its disinclinings. Curbed or opposed, it is but its instinct in both cases to rebel.

From that hour in which Kate had yielded to the will of her father, and consented to become the wife of Montagu Smythje, she felt more sensibly than ever the sacrifice she was about to make. But there was none to step forth and save her—no strong hand and stout heart to rescue her from her painful position. It had now become a compromise ; and, summoning all the strength of her soul, she awaited the unhappy issue with such resignation as she could command.

She had but one thought to cheer her, if cheer it could be called—she had not sacrificed her *filial* affection. She had performed the wishes of her father—that father who, however harsh he might be to others, had been ever kind and affectionate to her. Now, more than ever, did she feel impressed with his kindness, when she considered the errand on which he had gone forth.

Though thus resigned, or trying to feel so, she could neither stifle her passion for Herbert, nor conceal the melancholy which its hopelessness occasioned ; and during all that morning, after her father had left her, the shadow appeared upon her countenance with more than its wonted darkness.

Her lover—that is, her ' financé :' for Smythje now stood to her in that relationship—did not fail to observe her unusual melancholy, though failing to attribute it to the true cause.

It was natural that the young lady should feel sad at the absence of her worthy parent, who for many years had never been separated from her beyond the period of a few hours' duration, or, at most a single day. She would soon get used to it, and then all would be right again.

With some such reflections did Smythje account for the abstraction he had observed in the behaviour of his betrothed.

During all the morning he had been assiduous in his attentions—more than wontedly so. He had been left by the Custos in a proud position—that of *protector*—and he was desirous of showing how worthy he was of the trust reposed in him.

Alas ! in the opinion of Kate he was by far too assiduous.

The ' protegée' felt importuned; and his most well-meant attentions had the effect only to weary her. Too glad would she have been to be left alone to her sighs and her sadness.

Shortly after breakfast, Smythje proposed a stroll—a short one. He had no zest for toilsome excursions ; and, since the day of his shooting adventure, no zeal again to attempt any distant traverse of the forest.

The stroll was only to extend to the shrubbery and among the statues set there. The weather was temptingly fine. There was no reason why Kate Vaughan should refuse ; and, with a mechanical air, she acceded to the proposal.

Smythje discussed the statues, drawing largely from the stock of classic lore which his university had afforded him — dilating more especially on those of Venus, Cupid and Cleopatra, all suggestive of the tender sentiments that were stirring within his own romantic bosom, and to which, more than once, he took occasion to allude. Though narrowly did he watch, to see what effect his fine speeches were producing, he failed to perceive any that gave him gratification. The countenance of his companion obstinately preserved that air of pre-occupation that had been visible upon it all the morning.

In the midst of one of his scholastic dissertations the classical exquisite was interrupted by the advent of his valet, Thoms—who appeared coming from the house with the air of a servant who brings a message for his master.

The message was declared: a gentleman friend of Mr. Smythje—for he had now many such in the island—had called to see him. No particular business—merely a call of compliment.

The name was given. It was one which should be honoured by a polite reception; else the proud owner of Montagu Castle might have declined leaving the company in which he was upon so trivial a purpose. But the visitor was one of note—a particular friend, too. Miss Vaughan would not deem him rude, leaving her only for a moment?

"By no means!" said Kate, with a free haste that almost said as much as that she was only too glad to get quit of him.

Smythje followed his valet into the house; and the young creole was left among the statues alone—herself the fairest shape in all that classical collection.

CHAPTER XCI.

A STRANGE DETERMINATION.

For some moments after Smythje was gone, Kate Vaughan remained where he had left her—silent and motionless as the sculptured marbles by her side. Niobe was near; and, as if by accident, the eyes of the young creole turned upon the statue of the weeping daughter of Dione.

"Ah!" muttered she, struck with a strange thought; "unhappy mother of a murdered offspring! If thy sadness was hard to endure as mine, thy punishment must have been a pleasure. Would that I like thee were suddenly turned into stone. Ah, me!"

And finishing her apostrophe with a profound sigh, she stood for some time silently gazing upon the statue.

After a while her thoughts underwent some change; and along with it her eyes wandered away from the statues and the shrubbery. Her glance was turned upwards towards the mountain, and rested upon the summit —the Jumbé rock now glittering gaily under the full sheen of the sunlight.

"There," soliloquised she, in a low murmur; "upon that rock, and there only, have I felt one hour of true happiness—that happiness of which I had read in books of romance, without believing in, but which I now know to be real—to gaze into the eyes of him you love and think, as I then thought, that you are loved in return. Oh! it was bliss! it was bliss!"

The remembrance of that brief interview with her cousin—for it was to that her words referred—came so forcibly before the mind of the impassioned creole as to stifle her utterance, and for a moment or two she was silent.

Again she continued——

"An hour have I said? Ah! scarce a minute did the sweet delusion last; but had I my choice I would rather live that minute over again than all the rest of my past life—certainly, than all of it that is to come!"

Again she paused in her speech, still gazing upon the rock—wh)se sparkling surface seemed purposely presented to her eyes, as if to cheer her heart with the sweet souvenir it recalled.

"Oh I I wonder," she exclaimed at length, "I wonder how it would be were I but up there again! To stand on the spot where I stood! Could I fancy him, as then, beside me? Could I recall the looks he gave me, and my own sweet thoughts as I returned it? Oh! it would be like some delicious dream!"

Passion again called for a pause; but soon after her reflections found speech.

"And why should I not indulge in it? why not? What harm can it do me? Even if the souvenir should bring sadness, it cannot add to that which overwhelms me. No; I need not fear to tempt the trial; and I shall. This very hour shall I go up, and stand upon that same spot. There shall I invoke the past, and give to memory, to fancy, its fullest play. I need not fear. There will be no witness but the heaven above and the God who dwells in it—alike witness to the sa rifice of a broken heart made in the fulfilment of my duty."

On completing this impassioned speech, the young girl raised a kerchief of white cambric which she carried in her hand, and hastily adjusting it over the luxuriant plaits of her hair, glided towards the rear of the mansion.

She did not turn aside to enter the house, nor even to warn any one of her sudden determination but hastening on, soon reached the back of the garden.

There a small wicket-gate gave her egress into the woods—a path from that point trending in traverses, zigzag fashion, up the mountain slope.

It was the same path she had followed upon the day of the eclipse; but how different were the thoughts that row agitated her bosom from those she had indulged in on that memorable occasion! Even then, it is true, her spirits were far from being cheerful; but still there was hope ahead. She had not then arrived at the full knowledge of Herbert's indifference towards her—of his determination towards her more fortunate rival. The circumstances that had since transpired—the scenes that had come under her own observation—the rumors heard and too substantially confirmed—all had combined to extinguish that little gleam of hope so faint and feebly flickering.

Indeed, there was upon that very morning a new thought in her mind, calculated still farther to render her sad and humiliated.

The revelations which her father had made before starting on his journey—the admissions as to the inferiority of her race, and continity of her social rank, which he had been compelled to make—had produced, and no wonder, a painful impression upon the spirits of the quinteroon.

She could not help asking herself whether Herbert's disregard of her had aught to do with this? Was it possible that her own cousin was slighting her on account of this social distinction? Did he, too, feel shy of that *taint?* More than once during that day did she mentally put these interrogatories, without being able to determine whether they merited a negative or affirmative answer.

And what was her errand now? To resuscitate within her soul the memory of one moment of bliss—to weave still more inextricably around her heart the spell that was threatening to strangle it—to stifle the happiness of her whole life. But that was already gone. There could be no daring now—no danger worth dread. The zigzag path she ascended with free step and air undaunted—her fair, bright form gleaming,·meteor-like, amid the dark green foliage of the forest.

CHAPTER XCII.

A JEALOUS RECONNOISSANCE.

THE ravine leading up the rear of the Jumbé Rock—the only way by which its summit could be reached—though easily scaled by a pedestrian, was not practicable for a person on horseback. On reaching the base of the cliff, the jealous equestrian dismounted; made fast her bridle to the branch of a tree; and, after unbuckling the little spur and removing it from her heel, continued the ascent " à pie." Arrived at the summit, she took her stand near the edge of the platform, in a position that commanded an unbroken view of the mansion of Mount Welcome, its shrubberies and surroundings. Satisfied with the situation, she instantly commenced her reconnoissance. She did not, at first, make use of her *lorgnette.* Any human figure that might be moving around the house could be seen by the naked eye. It would be time enough to use the magnifying lens, should there be a difficulty of identifying them.

For some moments after she had taken her stand, no one made appearance near or around the dwelling. A complete tranquillity reigned over the spot. A pet *axis* deer skipping over the lawn, some pea-fowl moving amidst the shrubbery of the *parterre*—their purple gorgets gaily glittering in the sun—were the only objects animate that could be seen near the house.

Farther off in the fields, gangs of negroes were at work among the cane, with what appeared to be a white overseer moving in their midst. These had no interest for the observer upon the rock; and her eye, scarce resting on them for a second, returned to scan the enclosed space approximate to the dwelling, in the hope of there seeing something— form, incident, or scene—that might give her some clue to the mystery of the morning.

In respect to the former, she was not disappointed. Forms, scenes, and incidents were all offered in succession; and though they did but little to elucidate the enigma which had carried her to that aerial post of observation, they had the effect of calming, to some extent, the jealous thought that was distressing her.

First she saw a gentleman and lady step out from the house and take their stand among the statues. At the sight she felt a slight flutter of uneasiness; until through the *lorgnette* she looked upon hay-coloured hair and whiskers, enabling her to identify the owner as Smythje. This gave her a species of contentment; and her jealous spirit was still further tranquilised when the glass revealed to her the features of Kate Vaughan overspread with an expression of extreme sadness.

"Good!" muttered the delighted spy; "that tells a tale. She cannot have seen him? Surely not, or she would not be looking so woe-be gone?"

At this moment another figure was seen approaching across the *par-terre* towards the two who stood among the statues. It was that of a man in a dark dress. Herbert Vaughan wore that colour. With a fresh flutter of uneasiness, the *lorgnette* was carried back to the eye.

"Bah! it is not he. A fellow with a common face—a servant, I suppose? Very likely, the valet I've heard of! He has brought some message from the house? Ha! they're going in again. No, only the master. She stays. Odd enough he should leave her alone! So much for your politeness, Mr. Montagu Smeth-jay!"

And, with a sneering laugh as she pronounced the name, the fair spy again took her glass from her eye, and appeared for a moment to give way to the gratification which she had drawn from what she had succeeded in observing. Certainly there were no signs of the presence of Herbert Vaughan about the precincts of Mount Welcome, nor anything to indicate that he had had an interview with his cousin. If so, it must have ended just as the Jewess might have wished : since the expression observable on the countenance of Kate showed anything but the traces of a reconciliation. Pleased to contemplate her in this melancholy mood, her jealous rival again raised her glass to her eye.

"Ha!" she exclaimed on the instant. "Whatever is the nigger doing in front of the statue? She appears to be talking to it. An interesting dialogue, I do declare! Ha! ha! ha! Perhaps she is worshipping it? Ha! ha! She seems as much statue as it. 'Patience upon a monument, smiling'——Ha! ha! ha!

"Ah, now," resumed the hilarious observer, still gazing though the glass, " she turns from the statue. As I live, she is looking up this way! She cannot see me? No, not with the naked eye. Besides there is only my head and hat above the edge of the rock. She wont make them out. How steadfastly she looks this way! A smile upon her face! That, or something like it! One might fancy she was thinking of that pretty scene up here, the interesting tableau—Smythje on his knee. Ha! ha! ha!

"Ah! what now?" she continued, interrogatively; at the same time suddenly ceasing from her laughter, as she saw the young creole adjust the scarf over her head, and glide towards the back of the house. "What can it mean? She appears bent on an excursion! Alone, too! Yes, alone, as if she intended it! See! She passes the house with stealthy step—looks towards it, as if fearing some one to come forth and interrupt her! Through the garden!—through the gate in the wall! Ha! she's coming up the mountain!'"

As the Jewess made this observation, she stepped a pace forward upon the rock, to gain a better view. The *lorgnette* trembled as she held it to her eye: her whole frame was quivering with emotion.

" Up the mountain !" muttered she. " Yes, up the mountain ! And for what purpose ? To meet—Herbert Vaughan ?"

A half-suppressed scream accompanied the thought; while the glass lowered by her side, seemed ready to fall from her fingers.

CHAPTER XCIII.

A SPY IN AMBUSH.

You have seen a proud bird, whose wing has been broken by the fatal bullet, drop helpless to the earth ?

So fell the heart of Judith Jessuron from the high confidence that but the moment before had been buoying it up.

The sight of Kate Vaughan coming up the mountain path at once robbed it of exultation—even of contentment.

What errand could the young creole have up there, unless that of an assignation ? And with whom, but the man who was so mysteriously missing ?

Her surreptitious departure from the dwelling—the time chosen, when Smythje was out of the way—her quick gait and backward glances as she stole through the shrubbery : all indicated a fear of being seen and followed.

And why should she fear either, if bent upon an ordinary errand ? Mr. Smythje was not her father, nor as yet her husband. Why should she care to conceal her intentions from him: unless, indeed, they were clandestine, and pointing to that very purpose which the jealous Jewess had conjectured—a rendezvous with Herbert Vaughan ?

Judith felt convinced of it—so fully that, as soon as she saw the young creole fairly started up the sloping path, she glided to the rear edge of the platform, and looked down, expecting to see the other party to the assignation.

True, she saw no one : but this did little to still the agitation now vibrating through every nerve of her body. He was not in sight, but that signified not. Perhaps he was at that moment within hearing and might be seen, but for the forest screen that covered the " facade" of the mountain ?

Where was it their design to meet ? Where had they named their appointment ?

Judith did not doubt that there was design —jealousy did not stay to ask the question. She was convinced that an arrangement had been made and on that very morning. What else could be the meaning of the double message ? First, to demand a meeting ; secondly, to appoint the place. Yes, that would explain the repetition of those footmarks—that had gone twice to and fro.

What spot had they chosen for the scene of their clandestine encounter ?

A sudden apprehension seized upon the spy. She might lose sight of them ; and then they would enjoy their meeting in secret and uninterrupted. By Heavens, that must not be! Her spirit, now roused to the extreme pitch of jealousy, cared not for consequences. End as the scene might, she was resolved on its interruption.

The only chance of discovering the place of assignation would be to keep Kate Vaughan in sight. Perhaps Herbert was already there waiting for her? He would be there. The lover is always first upon the ground!

Obedient to this thought, the Jewess rushed back across the platform ; and once more directed her glance down the mountain.

She saw what she looked for: the snow-white snood easily distinguishable among the dark green foliage—now hidden as the wearer walked under the tall trees—again appearing at the open angles where the road zigzagged.

Most of the path could be seen from the summit of the rock: for, although rarely used, it had once been cleared by the axe, and formed an open track through the timber, narrow, but perceptible from above.

Judith, still marking the movements of the kerchief, swept the path with her glance and her glass—up to the point where it reached the base of the rock and ran round to the rear. Repeatedly she scanned the track, far in advance of the climber, expecting to see some one appear—Herbert Vaughan, of course.

If aught showed among the trees—a bird fluttering in the foliage, frayed by the approach of the gentle intruder—the heart of the jealous Jewess experienced a fresh spasm of pain. Though certain she was soon to see it, she dreaded to behold the first blush of that clandestine encounter. To see them come together, perhaps rush into each other's. arms, their lips meeting in the kiss of mutual love—oh, agony unendurable!

As she surmised the scene before her fancy, for a moment her proud spirit shrank, quailed and cowed within her and her form of bold noble development shook like a fragile reed.

*   *   *   *   *   *   *   *

Up the steep with springy step climbed the young creole, lightly as a bird upon the wing, unconscious that she was observed, and of all others, by the rival she had most reason to dread.

After completing the numerous windings of the path, she at length arrived within some twenty paces of the rock—here the road turned round to the rear. She knew the way; and, without pausing, kept on till she stood within the *embouchure* of the sloping ravine.

Up to this the Jewess had marked her every movement, watching her along the way. Not without some surprise had she perceived her intention to climb the Jumbé Rock—which by the direction she had taken was now evident.

The surprise soon passed, however, with a quick reflection. The summit of the rock—that place already hallowed by a love scene—was the spot chosen for the meeting!

On discovering Kate's determination to ascend the rock, which she had now divined by seeing her pass round to the rear, the Jewess stayed no longer upon the platform. That would have necessarily led to an encounter between the two. Not that Judith would have shunned it, however awkward, however *contratiempo*

It was not from any feeling of delicacy that she determined on leaving the place ; on the contrary, the action that followed betrayed a motive of a very opposite character.

Just where the ravine debouched upward on the platform, a lateral cleft opened to one side. Its bottom was but a few feet below the summit level ; covered with a thick growth of evergreen bushes, whose tops rising to an equal height with the table above, completely filled the hollow with their dense frondage.

The quick eye of Judith Jessuron at once detected the convenience of this covert. There concealed, she could see without being seen. From under the grim shadows of those dark evergreens, she could behold what was like enough to wring her heart: though she was now reckless of the result.

Watching her opportunity—when the eyes of the young creole were turned downwards—she glided into the lateral ravine, and concealed herself behind the curtain of leaves. Cowering within the covert, she awaited the ascent of her rival.

Amidst the tumult of her emotions, there was no chance to reason calmly. Suspicion of Herbert's perfidy—for it is not to be denied that the young man had shown her attentions, or, at all events, had passively permitted her to think so—suspicion of his faithlessness had now become certainty. There could be no mistake about the intended meeting between him and his cousin—at least, so Judith, blinded by her passions, believed.

There was Kate coming upon the ground, and Herbert—he would soon be after ! Strange he had not arrived first ! But that had not much significance. He could not be far off ; and, no doubt, would be there in good time—perhaps, overtake his sweetheart ere she could reach the summit of the rock ?

Thus ran the reflections of the rival.

She listened for Herbert's voice expecting every moment to hear him hailing from below.

She cast listless glances down the ravine, in the belief she should presently see him following franticly upon the footsteps of his cousin, and chiding himself for not being foremost at the tryst.

CHAPTER XCIV.

A FELL PURPOSE DEFEATED.

JUDITH had as yet traced out no definite plan of action—trusting to circumstances to suggest what course she should pursue.

Only on one thing had she come to a determination—to permit both to pass up on the rock before showing herself.

She resolved as long as possible, to restrain her instinct of revenge. She would see them meet—be witness of their mutual endearments—be sure of it ; and then would be her time to launch forth into the full torrent of recrimination.

Something of this kind was the course she had shaped out for herself —still but vaguely, still dependent on chance.

The young creole, little suspecting the proximity of her spiteful rival, ascended the ravine—close passing the spot where the latter was concealed. Altogether unconscious of being observed, she stepped upon the platform ; and crossing over, stopped near the opposite edge—precisely upon the spot where she had stood during the eclipse, hallowed by such sweet remembrance.

Undoing the slight knot that had confined the kerchief under her chin, and holding it in both hands, so as to shade her eyes from the sun, she stood for some time gazing into the valley below—not the one where lay the mansion of her father, but that in which dwelt a relative still dearer. As before, her eyes were bent upon the penn— that sombre \ pile which, despite the dim shadows that surrounded it, seemed to her the brightest spot upon the earth. The sun in the sky above was nothing in brightness to the light that circled there—the light of Herbert's love. What would she not have given to have lived in that light ? What to have been that favorite who now basked in it ?

" Would that I could see him once again," she murmured, " before that hour when we must meet no more: for then even the thought would be a crime ! If I could only see him once—only speak with him, I feel as if I should tell him all. Though he cannot love me, I am sure he would pity me. Even that, it seems to me, would soothe—it could not cure Oh ! why did he, upon this very spot—why those glances I can never forget ? I can see them now—his eyes as they were then, gazing into mine, as if something passed between us—something that sank into the very depths of my soul. Oh ! Herbert ! why did you so regard me ? but for that it might have passed. But now—never ! Ah, Herbert ! Herbert ! "

In her anguish the young creole pronounced the last words aloud.

Only the name was heard by Judith Jessuron ; but that fell upon her ear with fearful effect, piercing through her heart like a poisoned arrow. If she had any doubts about the purpose of Kate's presence, that word had decided them. The creole had now declared it with her own tongue !

On the instant a thought, dread and dire, commenced taking shape in the heart of the jealous woman. She felt her bosom stirred to a pur- pose bold and black as hell itself.

That purpose was nothing less than the destruction of her rival—the death of Kate Vaughan !

The circumstances suggested the mode. The young creole was stand- ing upon the escarpment of the cliff—scarce three feet from its edge. A slight push from behind would project her into eternity !

Not much risk either in the committal of the crime. The bushes be- low would conceal her body—at least, for a length of time; and, when found, what would be the verdict? What could it, but *felo-de-se ?*

The circumstances would give colour to this surmise. Even her own father might fancy it, as the consequences of his forcing her to be wed- ded against her will. Besides, had she not stolen surreptitiously from the house, taking advantage of an opportunity when no eye was upon her ?

Other circumstances equally favoured the chances of safety. No one seemed to know that Kate had come up to the Jumbé Rock; and not a soul could be aware that she, Judith, was there : for she had neither passed nor met any one by the way

No eye was likely to be witness of the act. Even though the forms of the actors might be descried from the valley below, it would be at too great a distance for any one to distinguish the character of the proceeding. Besides, it was one chance in a thousand if any eye should be accidently turned towards the summit of the mountain. At that hour the black labourers in the fields were too busy with their task to be allowed the freedom of gazing idly upon the Jumbé Rock.

With a fearful rapidity coursed these thoughts through the mind of the intended murderess—each adding fresh strength to her horrible purpose, and causing it to culminate towards the point of execution.

Her jealousy had long since become a strong passion, to which she had freely abandoned her soul. Already was it yearning for revenge; and now that an opportunity seemed to offer for gratifying it, she could no longer restrain herself. The chance was too tempting—the demoniac desire became uncontrollable.

Casting a glance down the ravine—to make sure that no one came that way—and another towards Kate, to see that her face was still turned away, Judith stole softly out of the bushes, and mounted upon the rock.

Silently, as treads the tigress approaching her prey, did she advance across the platform—towards the spot where stood her intended victim, utterly unconscious of the dread danger that was so nigh!

Was there no voice to warn her?

There was—the voice of Smythje!

" Nw-haw, deaw Kate! That yaw up there on the wock? Aw, ba Sawve! what a pwecious chase aw've had aftaw yaw! There isn't a bweath left in my body! Haw, haw!"

Judith heard the voice; and like a cheated tigress, was about to retreat to her lair, when Kate half facing about, compelled her to keep her ground. With the suddeness of a thought she had changed her terrific attitude; and as the eyes of the creole rested upon her, she was standing with her arms hanging negligently downward, in the position of one who had just stepped forward upon the spot!

Kate beheld her with surprise, not unmixed with alarm; for the wild look that still lingered in the eye of the disappointed and baulked murderess could not escape observation.

Before either could say a word, the voice of Smythje was again heard speaking from below.

" Deaw qeetyaw, I am coming! Aw shall pwesently be up," continued he; his voice constantly changing its direction, proclaiming that he continued to advance round the rock towards the ravine in the rear.

" I beg your pardon, Miss Vaughan," said the Jewess, with a sweeping curtsey and a cynical glance towards Kate; " most empathically, I beg your pardon. The second time I have intruded upon you in this delightful place! I assure you my presence here is altogether an accident; and to prove that I have no desire to interfere, I shall bid you a very good morning!"

So saying, the daughter of Jacob Jessuron turned towards the downward path, and had disappeared from the platform before Kate could command words to express either her astonishment or indignation.

" Ba Jaw-aw-ve!" gasped Smythje, breathless on reaching the platform

" Had yaw company up heaw ? Shawly aw saw some one gawing out fwom the wavine—a lady in a widing dwess ?"

" Miss Jessuron has been here."

" Aw, Miss Jessuwon—that veway remarkable queentyaw ! Gawing to be mawied to the—yaw cousin, 'tis repawted. Ba Jawve, she'll make the young fellaw a fine wife, if she dawn't want too much of haw awn way ! Haw ! haw ! what do yaw think about it, deaw Kate ?"

" I have no thoughts about it Mr. Smythje. Pray let us return home."

Smythje might have noticod, though without ccmprehending it, the anguished tone in which these words were uttered.

" Aw, veway well. A'm weady to go back. But, deaw Kate, what a womp yaw are, to be shawr ! Yaw thought to pway me a twick, like the young bwide in the misletaw bough. Haw ! haw ! veway amusing ! Nevaw mind ! Yaw are not so unfawtunate as that fair queetyaw ; saw yawr white scarf amid the gween trees, and that guided me to yaw seqwet hiding-place. Haw ! haw !"

Little suspected Smythje how very near had been his affianced to a fate as unfortunate as that of the bride of Lovel—as little as Kate that Smythje had been her preserver.

CHAPTER XCV.

CYNTHIA was not slow in responding to the summons of the Jew, who possessed an influence over her, which, if not so powerful, was also less mysterious than that wielded by the myal-man—since it was the power of *money*. The mulatta liked money, as most people do ; and for the same reason as most : because it afforded the means for indulging in dissipation, which with Cynthia was a habit.

Very easily did she find an opportunity for paying a visit to the penn —the more easily that her master was absent. But even had he been at home, she would have had but little difficulty in framing an excuse, or rather would she have gone without one.

In the days of which we write, slavery had assumed a very altered phase in the West Indies ; more especially in the island of Jamaica. The voices of Wilberforce and Clarkson had already reached the remotest corners of the island ; and the plantation negroes were beginning to hear the first mutterings of the emancipation. The slave-trade was doomed ; and it was expected that the doom of slavery itself would soon be declared.

The black bondsmen had become emboldened by the prospect ; and there was no longer that abject submission to the wanton will of the master and the whip of the driver, as had existed of yore. It was not uncommon for slaves to take " leave of absence" for days ; returning without fear of chastisement, and sometimes staying away altogether Plantation revolts had become common, frequently ending in incendiarism, and other scenes of the most sanguinary character ; and more than one band of·" runaways" had established themselves in the most remote fastnesses of the mountains ; where in defiance of the authorities, and despite the preventive service—somewhat negligently performed by their prototypes, the Maroons—they preserved a rude independence, partially sustained by pilfering, and partly by freebooting of a bolder kind. These runaways were, in effect, playing a ' rôle,' in complete imitation of what at an earlier period, had been the *metier* of the original Maroons ; while, as already stated, the Maroons themselves, employed upon the sage but infamous principle of " set a thief to catch a thief," had now become the detective police of the island.

Under such conditions of slavery, the bold Cynthia was not the woman to trouble herself about asking leave of absence, nor to be deterred by any slight circumstance from taking it : therefore, at an early hour, of the day, almost upon the heels of Blue Dick, the messenger, she made her appearance at the penn.

Her conference with Jessuron, though it threw no light on the whereabouts of the missing book-keeper, nor the cause of his absence, was not without interest to the Jew, since it revealed facts that gave him some comfort.

He had already learnt from Blue Dick that the Custos had started on his journey, and from Cynthia he now ascertained the additional fact, that before starting he *had taken the spell.* It had been administered in his *stirrup-cup* of " swizzle."

This intelligence was the more gratifying, in view of the apprehensions which the Jew was beginning to feel in regard to his Spanish ' employés.' If the spell should do its work as quickly as Chakra had said, these worthies would be anticipated in the performance of their dangerous duty.

Another important fact was communicated by Cynthia. She had seen Chakra that morning—just after her master had taken his departure. There had been an arrangement between her and the myal-man to meet at their usual trysting-place—contingent on the setting out of the Custos. As this contingency had transpired, of course the meeting had taken place—its object being that Cynthia might inform Chakra of such events as might occur previous to the departure.

Cynthia did not know for certain that Chakra had followed the Custos. The myal-man had not told her of his intention to do so. But she fully believed he had. Something he had let fall during their conference guided her to this belief. Besides, on leaving her, Chakra, instead of returning towards his haunt in the Duppy's Hole, had gone off along the road in the direction of Savanna.

This was the substance of Cynthia's report; and having been well rewarded for the communication, the mulatta returned to Mount Welcome.

Notwithstanding the gratification which her news afforded, it was far from tranquillising the spirit of Jacob Jessuron.

The absence of Herbert Vaughan still continued—still unexplained , and as the hours passed and night drew near, without any signs of his return, Jessuron—and it may be said Judith as well—became more and more uneasy about his disappearance.

Judith was puzzled as well as pained. Her suspicion that Herbert had had an appointment with his cousin Kate had been somewhat shaken, by what she had seen—as well as what she had *not* seen : for on leaving the Jumbé rock she had not ridden directly home. Instead of doing so, she had lingered for a length of time around the summit of the mountain, expecting Herbert to show himself. As she had neither encountered him, nor any traces of him, she was only too happy to conclude that her surmises about the meeting were, after all, but fancy ; and that no assignation had been intended. Kate's coming up to the Jumbé rock was a little queer ; but then Smythje had followed her, and Judith had not heard that part of the conversation which told that *his* being there was only an accident—the accident *of* having discovered the retreat to which the young creole had betaken herself.

These considerations had the effect of soothing the jealous spirit of the Jewess ; but only to a very slight extent : for Herbert's absence was ominous—the more so, thought Judith, as she remembered a conversation that had lately passed between them.

Nor did she feel any repentance for the dark deed she had designed ; and would certainly have executed, but for the well-timed appearance of Smythje upon the scene. The words which had fallen from the lips of Kate Vaughan had been a sufficient clue to her reflections ; and though he whose name she had mentioned was not present in person, the Jewess did not doubt that he, and only he, was the subject of that soliloquy.

There might have been remorse for the deed, had it been accomplished but there was no repentance for the design. Jealousy, bitter as ever in the breast of Judith, forbade this.

Judith's return did not make the matter any clearer to Jessuron. She had no story to tell, except that which she deemed it more prudent to keep to herself. Her not having encountered Herbert during her ride, only rendered his absence more difficult of explanation.

CHAPTER XCVL

A DAY OF CONJECTURES.

Towards sunset fresh inspection was made of the tracks, Jessuron going in person to examine them. The skilled herdsman was again questioned ; and on this occasion a fresh fact was elicited ; or rather a conjecture, which the man had not made, before, since he had not noticed the circumstance on which he rested it.

It was some peculiarity in the sole of the shoe that had made the strange track, and which guided the herdsman to guess who was the owner. In scouring the forest-paths of his cattle, he had observed that footmark before, or one very like it.

"If't be de same, massa," remarked he in reply to the cross-questioning of the Jew, "den I knows who owns dat fut. It longs to that ere cappen of Maroons."

"Cubina ?"

"Ah—that, jest the berry man.'

The Jew listened to this conjecture with marked inquietude ; which was increased as another circumstance was brought to his knowledge; that Quaco the Maroon—who had been arrested along with Herbert on the day of his first appearance at the penn—had been lately seen in communication with the latter, and apparently in a clandestine manner. Blue Dick was the authority for this piece of incidental intelligence

The penn-keeper's suspicions had pointed to Cubina at an earlier hour of the day. These circumstances strengthened them.

It needed but another link to complete the chain of evidence, and this was found in the tobacco-pipe left in the hammock : a rather unique implement, with an iron bowl, and a stem made out of the shankbone of an ibis.

On being shown the pipe, the herdsman recognised it on sight. It was " the cutty" of Captain Cubina. More than once had he met the Maroon with the identical instrument between his teeth.

Jessuron doubted no longer that Cubina had been the abductor of his book-keeper. Nor Judith, either ; for the Jewess had taken part in the analytical process that guided to this conclusion.

Judith was rather gratified at the result. She was glad it was no worse. Perhaps, after all, the young Englishman had only gone on a visit to the Maroon, with whom she knew him to be acquainted ; for Judith had been informed of all the circumstances connected with their first encounter. What was more natural than a sort of attachment between them, resulting from such an odd introduction ? Curiosity may have induced Herbert to accompany the Maroon to his mountain home ; and this was sufficient to explain his absence.

True, there were circumstances not so easily explained. The presence of the Maroon at the penn—his track twice to and fro—the hurried departure of Herbert, without any previous notice either to herself or to her father—all these circumstances were suspicious ; and the spirit of the jealous Judith, though partially tranquillised by a knowledge of the new facts that had come to light, was, nevertheless, not quite relieved from its perplexity.

The same knowledge had produced an effect on the spirit of her worthy parent altogether different. So far from being gratified by the idea that his book-keeper was in the company of the Maroon captain, he was exceedingly annoyed by it. He at once remembered how pointedly Herbert had put certain questions to him, in relation to the fate of the flogged runaway—the prince. He remembered, also, his own evasive answers; and he now foresaw, that in the case of the questioner being in the company of Cubina, the latter would give him a very different account of the transaction—in fact such a statement as could not fail to bring about the most crooked consequences.

Once in possession of those damning facts, the young Englishman—of whose good moral principles the old Jew had become cognisant—would be less likely to relish him, Jessuron, for a father-in-law. Such an awkward affair coming to his knowledge might have the effect, not only to alienate his much-coveted friendship—his equally solicited love— but to drive him altogether from a house, whose hospitality he might deem suspicious,

Was it possible that this very result had already arisen? Was the whole scheme of the penn-keeper to prove a failure? Had murder—the blackest of all crimes—been committed in vain? There was but little doubt left on the mind of Jacob Jessuron that the deed was now done. Whether by the poison of Chakra, or the steel of the 'caçadores,' so far as the Custos himself was concerned, that part of the programme would, by this time, be complete; or so near its completion, that no act of the 'instigator could stay its execution. How, when, and where was it done? And had it been done in vain? During the early part of that same night —and on through the midnight hours—thus interrogatively reflected the Jew. He slept not; or only in short spells of unquiet slumber, taken in his chair—as on the night before, in the open verandah. It was care, not conscience, that kept him awake—apprehension of the future, rather than remorse for the past. After midnight, and near morning, a thought became uncontrollable—a desire to be satisfied, if not about the last of these interrogatories, at least in relation to the former. In all likelihood Chakra would by that time have returned—would be found in his lair in the Duppy's Hole. Why he had followed the Custos, Jessuron could not tell. He could only guess at the motive. Perhaps he, Chakra, was in fear that his spell might not be sufficient; and failing, he might find an opportunity to strengthen it? Or, was it that he wished to be witness to the final scene? to exult over his hated enemy in the last hour of life? Knowing, as the Jew did, the circumstances that had long existed between the two men—their mutual malice—Chakra's deadly purposes of vengeance—this conjecture was far from improbable. It was the true one; though he also gave thought to another—that perhaps the myal-man had followed his victim for the purpose of *plundering him.* To ascertain that he had succeeded in the preliminary step—that of murdering· him—the Jew forsook his chair-couch; and, having habited himself for a nocturnal excursion, proceeded in the direction of the Duppy's Hole.

CHAPTER XCVIL

— **THE SICK TRAVELLER.**

AFTER passing beyond the precincts of his own plantation, and traversing for some distance a by-road known as the Carrion Crow, Mr. Vaughan at length reached the main highway, which runs between Montego Bay on the north, and Savannal-a-Mer on the southern side of the island.

Here, facing southward, he continued his route—Savanna-la-Mer being the place where he intended to terminate his journey on horseback. Thence he could proceed by sea to the harbour of Kingston, or the Old Harbour, or some other of the ports, having easy communication with the capital.

The more common route of travel from the neighbourhood of Montego Bay to Spanish Town, when it is desired to make the journey by land, is by the northern road to Falmouth harbour, and thence by St. Ann's and across the island. The southern road is also travelled at times, without

the necessity of going to the port of Savanna, by Lacovia, and the parish
of St. Elizabeth. But Mr. Vaughan preferred the easier mode of transit
—on board ship; and knowing that coasting vessels were at all times
trading from Savanna to the port on the southern side, he anticipated no
difficulty in obtaining a passage to Kingston. This was one reason why
he directed his course to the seaport of Savanna.

He had another motive for visiting this place, and one that influenced
him to an equal or greater extent. Savanna-la-Mer, as already stated, was
the *assize town* of the western district of the island—otherwise the
county of Cornwall—including under its jurisdiction the five great
parishes of St. James, Hanover, Westmoreland, Trelawney, and St. Elizabeth, and consequently the town of Montego Bay. Thus constituted,
Savanna was the seat of justice, where all plaints of importance must be
preferred. The process which Mr. Vaughan was about to institute
against the Jew was one for the consideration of a full court of assize. A
surreptitious seizure of twenty-four slaves was no small matter; and the
charge would amount to something more than that of mere malversation.

Loftus Vaughan had not yet decided on the exact terms in which the
accusation was to be made; but the assize town being not only the seat
of justice, but the head-quarters of the legal knowledge of the county,
he anticipated finding there the counsel he required.

This then, was his chief reason for travelling to Spanish Town *vid*
Savanna-la-Mer.

For such a short distance—a journey that might be done in a day—a
single attendant sufficed. Had he designed taking the land route to the
capital, then it would have been different. Following the fashion of the
island, a troop of horses, a numerous escort of servants, would have accompanied the great Custos.

*   *   *   *   *

The day turned out to be one of the hottest, especially after the hour
of noon; and the concentrated rays of the sun, glaring down upon the
white chalky road, over which the traveller was compelled to pass, rendered the journey not only disagreeable, but irksome.

Added to this, the Custos, not very well on leaving home, had been
getting worse every hour. Notwithstanding the heat, he was twice attacked by a severe chill—each time succeeded by its opposite extreme
of burning fever, accompanied by thirst that knew no quenching. These
attacks had also for their concomitant bitter nausea, vomiting, and a tendency towards cramp, or *tetanus*.

Long before night the traveller would have stopped—had he found a
hospitable roof to shelter him. In the early part of the day he had passed though the more settled districts of the country, where plantations
were numerous; but then, not being so ill, he had declined making halt—
having called only at one or two places to obtain drink, and replenish the
water canteen carried by his attendant.

It was only late in the afternoon that the symptoms of his disease became specially alarming; and then he was passing through an uninhabited portion of the country—a wild corner of Westmoreland parish, where
not a house was to be met with for miles along the highway.

Beyond this tract, and a few miles farther on the road, he would reach
the grand sugar estate of Content. There he might anticipate a distin

guished reception; since the proprietor of the plantation, besides being noted for his profuse hospitality, was his own personal friend.

It had been the design of the traveller, before starting out, to make Content the half-way house of his journey, by stopping there for the night. Still desirous of carrying out this design, he pushed on, notwithstanding the extreme debility that had seized upon his frame, and which rendered riding upon horseback an exceedingly painful operation. So painful did it become, that every now and then he was compelled to bring his horse to a halt, and remain at rest, till his nerves acquired strength for a fresh spell of exertion.

Thus delayed, it was sunset when he came in sight of Content. He did get sight of it from a hill, on the top of which he had arrived just as the sun was sinking into the Carribean Sea, over the far headland of Point Negrie. In a broad valley below, filled with the purple haze of twilight, he could see the planter's dwelling, surrounded by its extensive sugar-works, picturesque rows of negro cabins, so near that he could distinguished the din of industry and the hum of cheerful voices, borne upward on the buoyant air; and could see the forms of men and women clad in their light coloured costumes, flitting in mazy movement about the precincts of the place.

The Custos gazed upon the sight with dizzy glance. The sounds fell confusedly on his ear. As the shipwrecked sailor who sees land without the hope of ever reaching it, so looked Loftus Vaughan upon the valley of Content. For any chance of his reaching it that night, without being carried thither, there was none—any more than if it had been a hundred miles distant—at the extreme end of the island. He could ride no farther. He could no longer keep the saddle; and, slipping out of it, he tottered into the arms of his attendant!

Close by the road-side, and half hidden by the trees, appeared a hut surrounded by a kind of rude inclosure, that had once been the garden or "provision ground" of a negro. · Both hut and garden were ruinate—the former deserted, the latter overgrown with that luxuriant vegetation, which in tropic soil a single season suffices to bring forth.

Into this hovel the Custos was conducted; or rather carried: for he was now even unable to walk.

A sort of plantation, or *banquette*, of bamboos—the negro couch of the negro cabin—stood in one corner: a fixture seldom or never removed on the abandonment of such a dwelling. Upon this the Custos was laid, with a horse-blanket spread beneath, and his camlet cloak thrown over him.

More drink was administered; and then the attendant, by command of the invalid himself, mounted one of the horses and galloped off to Content. Loftus Vaughan was alone!

CHAPTER XCVIII.

A HIDEOUS INTRUDER.

LOFTUS VAUGHAN was not long alone, though the company, that came first to intrude on the solitude that surrounded him, was such as no man, either living or dying, might desire to see by his bedside.

The black groom had galloped off for help; and ere the sound of his horse's hoofs had ceased to reverberate through the unclayed chinks of the cabin, the shadow of a human form, projected through the open door-way, was flung darkly upon the floor.

The sick man, stretched upon the cane couch, was suffering extreme pain, and giving way to it by incessant groaning. Nevertheless he saw the shadow upon the floor ; and this, with the sudden darkening of the door, admonished him that some one was outside, and about to enter.

It might be supposed that the presence of any living being would at that moment have pleased him—as a relief to the lugubrious loneliness that surrounded him ; and perhaps the presence of a living being would have produced that effect. But in that shadow which had fallen across the floor, the sick man saw, or fancied he saw, the form of one who should have been long since dead—the form of Chakra the myal-man !

The shadow was defined and distinct. The hut faced westward. There were no trees before the door—nothing to intercept the rays of the now sinking sun, that covered the ground with a reddish glare—nothing save that sinister *silhouette* which certainly seemed to betray the presence of Chakra. Only the upper half of a body was seen—a head, shoulders, and arms. In the shadow, the head was of gigantic size—the mouth open, displaying a serrature of formidable teeth—the shoulders, sur-mounted by the hideous hump—the arms long and ape-like ! Beyond doubt was it either the shadow of Chakra, or a duplication of his ghost—of late so often seen !

The sick man was too terrified to speak—too horrified to think. It scarce added to his agony when, instead of his shadow, the myal-man himself, in his own proper and hideous aspect, appeared within the door-way, and without pause stepped forward upon the floor !

Loftus Vaughan could no longer doubt the identity of the man who had made this ill-timed intrusion. Dizzy though his sight from a disordered brain, and dim as it had been rapidly becoming, it was yet clear enough to enable him to see that the form who stood before him was no phantasy—no spirit of the other world but one of this—one as wicked as could be found amid the phalanx of the fiends of darkness.

He had no longer either fancy or fear about Chakra's ghost. It was Chakra's self he saw—an apparition far more to be dreaded.

The scream that escaped from the lips of Loftus Vaughan announced the climax of his horror. On uttering it, he made an effort to rise to his feet ; as if with the intention of escaping from the hut ; but finally, over-powered by his own feebleness, and partly yielding to a gesture of me-nace made by the myal-man—and which told him that his retreat was in-tercepted—he sank back upon the *banquette* in a paralysis of despair.

" Ha !" shouted Chakra, as he placed himself between the dying man and the door. " No use fo' try 'scape ! no use wha'somdever ! Ef ye wa' able get 'way from hya, you no go fur. 'Fore you walk hunder yard you fall down, in your track, like new drop calf. No use you ole tool. Whugh !"

Another shriek was the only reply which the enfeebled man could make.

" Ha ! ha ! ha !" vociferated Chakra, showing his shark-like teeth in a fiendish laugh. " Ha ! ha ! ha ! Shreek away, Cussus Vaughan ! Shreek

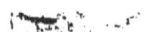

till you bust you windpipe. Chakra tell you it no use. De death 'pell am 'pon you--it am *in* you—an' jess when dat ar sun hab cease shine upon de floor, you go join you two brodder jussuses in de odder world, wha' you no fine buckra no better dan brack man. Dey gone afore. Boaf go by de death 'pell. Chakra send you jess de same ; only he you keep fo' de lass, 'kase you de grann Cussus, an' he keep him bess victim fo' de lass. De debbil him better like dat way."

"Mercy, mercy !" shrieked the dying man.

"Ha ! ha ! ha !" scornfully answered Chakra. "Wha' fo' you cry 'mercy ? D'you gib mercy to de old myal-man, when you 'im chain al dar to de cabbage-tree ? You show no mercy den—Chakra show none now. You got die !"

"Oh! Chakra! good Chakra!" cried the Custos, raising himself upon the couch, and extending his arms in a passionate appeal. "Save me ! save my life! and I will give you whatever you wish—your freedom—money——"

"Ha!" interrupted Chakra, in a tone of triumphant exultation. "Gib me freedom, would you ? You gib me dat arready, You money dis hya nigga doan' care 'bout—not de shell ob a cocoa. He hab plenty money ; he get what he want fo' de lub spell and de death 'pell. Whugh! de only ting you hab dat he care 'bout, you no can gib. Chakra take dat 'ithout you gibbin'."

"What ?" mechanically asked the dying man, fixing his eyes upon the face of Chakra with a look of dread import.

"Lilly Quasheba!" cried the monster, in a loud voice, and leering horribly as he pronounced the name. "Lilly Quasheba!" he repeated, as if doubly to enjoy the fearful effect which his words were producing. "De dawter ob de quaderoom! Da's only fair, Cussus," continued he, in a mocking tone. " You had de modder yourseff—dat is, after the Maroon! You know dat? It am only turn an' turn 'bout. Now you go die, Chakra he come in To' de dawter. Ha ! ha ! ha !

"Whugh !" he exclaimed, suddenly changing his tone, and bending down over the form of the Custos, now prostrate upon the couch. "Whugh ! I b'lieve the buckra gone dead ?"

He was dead. On hearing the name "Lilly Quasheba," accompanied by such a fearful threat, a wild cry had escaped from his lips. It was the last utterance of his life. On giving tongue to it, he had fallen back upon the bamboo bedstead, mechanically drawing the cloak over his face, as if to shut out some horrid sight ; and while the myal-man, gloating over him, was endeavouring to procrastinate his pangs, the poison had completed its purpose.

Chakra, extending one of his long arms, raised the fold from off his face ; and, holding it up, gazed for a moment upon the features of his hated foe, now rigid, blanched, and bloodless.

Then, as if himself becoming frightened at the form and presence of death, the savage miscreant dropped the cover quickly to its place ; rose from his stooping position ; and stole stealthily from the hut.

CHAPTER XCIX.

TWO SPECULATIVE TRAVELLERS.

THE sun was sinking out of sight into the bosom of the blue Carribean, and the twilight, long since extended over the valley below, was now spreading its purple robe around the summit of the hill, on which stood the hut. The shadows cast by the huge forest trees were being ex-changed for the more sombre shadows of the coming night; and the outlines of the hovel—now a house of death—were gradually becoming obliterated in the crepusculous obscurity.

Inside that deserted dwelling, tenanted only by the dead, reigned still-ness, solemn and profound—the silence of death itself.

Outside, were sounds such as suited the solemnity of the scene; the mournful *loo-who-ah* of the eared owl, who had already commenced quartering the aisles of the forest; while from the heaven above came the wild wail of the potoo, as the bird went across the fast darkening sky, in search of its insect prey.

To these lugubrious utterances there was one solitary exception. More cheerful was the champing of the steel bit—proceeding from the horse that had been left tied to the tree—and the quick, impatient stroke of his hoof, as the animal fretted under the stings of the mosquitoes, be-coming more bitter as the darkness descended.

The body of Loftus Vaughan lay upon the bamboo bedstead, just as Chakra had left it. No hand had been there to smooth that rude pillow —no friendly finger to close those eyes that were open, and saw not— those orbs glassed and coldly glaring from their sunken sockets!

As yet the attendant had not returned with that succour which would come too late.

Nor was it possible for him to get back in much less than an hour. Content, though in actual distance scarcely a mile from the hut, was full five in point of time. The slope of the mountain road was at an angle with the horizon of at least fifty degrees. There could be no rapid rid-ing on that road—neither up nor down, upon the most urgent errand; and the black groom was not going to risk life by a broken neck, even to save the life of a custos.

It would be a full hour, then, before the man would return. As yet only twenty minutes had passed, and forty more were to come. But it was not fated that even for those forty minutes the body of the Custos Vaughan should be permitted to rest in peace. Twenty minutes had scarcely elapsed after Chakra had stolen away from the side of the corpse, when there came others to disturb it, and with a rude violence almost sufficient to arouse it from the slumber of death! Had Chakra on leav ing the hut only taken the main road backward to Montego Bay—and that was the direction in which he intended going—he would have met two strange men. Not so strange but that they were known to him; but strange enough to have arrested the attention of an ordinary tra-veller. But among the proclivities of the myal-man, that of travelling along *main roads* was one in which he did not indulge, except under the most unavoidable circumstances. Following his usual practice, as soon as he had cleared the precincts of the negro cabin, he struck off into a by-path leading through the bushes; and by so doing lost the opportunity of an encounter with two individuals, who, although of a different nationality, were as great villains as himself. The brace of worthies thus described is already known. They were the man-hunters of Jacob Jessuron, Manuel and Andres—' caçadores do cimmarones' from the island of Cuba With the object with which they were journeying along the Savanna road, the reader is equally *au fait*. Jessuron's talk with them on starting them off, has plainly proclaimed the vile intent of his two truculent tools. All day long had these human bloodhounds been following upon the track of the Custos—now nearer to him—now farther off—according to the halts which the traveller had made, and the relative speed of horseman and pedestrian.

More than once had they sighted their victim afar off on the white dusty road. But the presence of the stout negro attendant, as well as the broad open daylight, had deterred them from proceeding in their nefarious purpose; and they had postponed its execution, till that time which gives opportunity to the assassin—the going down of the sun.

The hour had at length arrived; and just as the real murderer was hastening away from the hut, the intended assassins were hurrying towards it, with all the speed in their power!

"*Carrambo!*" exclaimed he who was the older, and in consequence the *leader* of the two, "I shouldn't be surprised, Andres, if the *ingeniero* was to slip out of our clutches to-night? Not far beyond lies Content, and the owner of that *ingenio* is a friend of his. You remember Senor Jacob said he would be like to put up there for the night?"

"Yes," replied Andres, "the old Judio was particular about that."

"Well! if he gets there before we can overhaul him, there'll be nothing done to-night. We must take our chance on the road between that and Savanna."

"*Carajo!*" responded Andres, with a somewhat spiteful emphasis; "if it wasn't for them ugly pistols he carries, and that big buck nigger by his side, we might have stopped his breath before this. Supposing he gets to Savanna before we can have a talk with him? what then, *compadre?*"

"Then," answered he thus godfatherly addressed; "then, our lines won't lie in pleasant places. Savanna's a big city; and it isn't so easy to murder a man in the street of a town as among these trees. People prowling about have tongues, where the trees haven't; and fifty pounds Jamaica money, ain't much for killing a man—more especially *a custos*; as they call him. *Carajo!* we must take care, or we may get our necks twisted for this simple trick! These custoses are like our *alcaldes*—kill one, and a dozen others will spring up to prosecute you."

"But what," inquired Andres, who, although the youngest of the two appeared to be gifted with a greater degree of prudence than his companion—"what if we don't find a chance—even in Savanna?"

"Then," replied the other, "we stand a good chance of losing our fifty pounds—shabby currency as it is."

"How that, Manuel?"

"How that? Why because the *ingeniero*, once in Savanna, will take ship and travel by sea. The 'ducno' said so. If he do that, we may bid adieu to him; for I wouldn't make another sea-voyage for five times fifty pounds. That we had from Batabano was enough to last me for my life. *Carajo!* I thought it was the *vomito prieto* that had seized upon me. But for the fear of another such puking spell, I'd have gone home with the rest, instead of staying in this nest of Jews and nigger-drivers; and how I'm ever to get back to Batabano, let alone making a voyage for the purpose of——"

The Cubano refrained from finishing his speech—not from any delicacy he had about declaring the purpose, but because he knew that the declaration would be superrogatory to an associate who already comprehended it.

"In that case," counselled the more sagacious Andres, "we must finish our business before Savanna comes in sight. Perhaps, *compadre*, by pushing on rapidly now, we may overtake the party before they get anchored in Content?"

"You're right, *hombre;* you're right about that. Let us, as you say, push on; and, if it suits you as it does me, let our motto be, '*Noche o nunca*' (this night or never)!"

"*Vamos!*" rejoined Andres; and the assassins increased their speed, as if stimulated by the fear of losing their prey.

CHAPTER C.

ÑO BLOOD.

THE sun had already hidden his red disc under the sea horizon, when the man-hunters mounted the hill, and approached the hut where Custos Vaughan had been compelled to make halt, and in which he was now lying lifeless.

"*Mira* Manuel!" said Andres, as they came within sight of the hovel and at the same instant saw the horse standing tied to the tree; "*un cavallo!* saddled, bridled, and with *alforjas!*"

"A traveller's horse!" rejoined Manuel, "and that very traveller we've been tracking. Yes! it's the horse of great alcalde of Mount Welcome. Don't you remember, when we saw them before us at mid-day, that one of the horses was a bay, and the other a grey. There's the grey, and it was on that very animal the Custos was riding."

"Quite true, *compadre;* but where's the other?"

"May be, among the trees? or tied round the other side of the hut? The riders must be inside?"

"Both, do you think, Manuel?"

"Of course, both; though where blackskin's horse can be is more than I can say. *Carrambo!* what's halted them here? There's nobody lives in the ranche. I know that; I came this way about a week ago, and it had no tenant then. Besides, the *injenio* where he was to put up for the night is just below. What in the name of Saint Mary has stopped them here?"

"*Por Dios, compadre!*" said the younger of the two 'cazadores,' looking significantly at the saddle-bags, still hanging over the cantle of the Custos' saddle. "There ought to be something valuable in those *alforjas!*"

"*Caval!* you're right; but we musn't think of that just yet, *camarado!* After the other's done, then, we shall have the opportunity——- I wonder whether they're both inside? It's very odd we don't see the negro's horse?"

"Ha!" rejoined Andres, apparently struck with an idea. "What if he's gone on to the plantation for some purpose? Suppose an accident has happened to the Custos' steed, or, *carrai!* suppose he's himself taken sick? You remember the man we met, who told us about them ugly pistols—he said that one of the travellers—the white man—looked sick. Didn't the fellow say he saw him puking?"

"*Por Dios!* he did. As you say, there may be something in it. If blackskin's out of the way, now's our time; for there is more to be feared from that big buck nigger than his master, when it comes to a struggle. If it should prove that the Custos is sick—I hope it is so—he won't be in a condition to make much use of his weapons; and *carrambo!* we must get hold of them, before he knows what we're after!"

"Hadn't we better go round first?" counselled the sagacious Andres. "Let us explore the back of the hut, and see whether the horse is there? If he's not, then certainly the negro's gone off on some errand? We can steal through the, bushes to the other side, and get right up to the walls without any danger of being seen?"

"That's our plan, *camarado.* Let's lose no time, then, for, if it be so that blackskin's abroad, we're in luck. We mayn't find such another chance—not between here and the world's end. Follow me, *hombre!* and set down your feet as if you were stepping upon eggs with young birds in them. *Vamos.*"

So saying, the chief of the two 'cazadores' skulked in among the trees, closely followed by his companion.

After making a circuit through the underwood, the assassins stole silently in towards the back of the hovel.

They saw no other horse—only the grey, which stood tied to the tree in front. The bay was gone, and in all probability his rider. Andres already congratulated himself upon his conjecture being correct: the negro had ridden off upon some errand. This was put beyond all doubt by their perceiving the fresh tracks of a horse, leading away from the hut along the road towards Content. The hoof-prints were so plain as to be visible at some distance. The turf on the road-edge was torn up, and deeply indented—where the negro groom had urged his horse into a gallop. The assassins saw, even without returning to the road; and were now satisfied that the attendant was gone away. It only remained to make sure that the traveller himself was inside the hut. Creeping cautiously up to the wall, the 'cazadores' peeped through the unclayed chinks of the cabin. At first the darkness inside hindered them from distinguishing any object in particular. Presently, as their eyes grew more accustomed to the obscurity, they succeeded in making out the

bamboo bedstead in the corner, with something that resembled the figure
of a man stretched lengthwise upon it. A dark cloak covered the form,
the face as well ; but the feet, booted and spurred, protruding from under
the cover, told that it was a man who was lying in that outstretched attitude—the man who was to be murdered !

He appeared to be sound asleep ; there was no motion perceptible—not
even as much as would indicate that he breathed !

Lying on the floor, at some distance from the couch, was a hat, and
beside it a pair of pistols, in their holsters—as if the traveller had un
buckled them from his belt, and flung them down, before going to sleep.
Even if awake, he could scarce get hold of the pistols, before his assail-
ants could spring upon him.

The assassins looked towards one another with a significant glance.
The fates appeared to favour their attempt ; and, as both on the instant
were actuated by the same sanguinary instinct, they leaped simultaneously to their feet, drew their sharp *machetes*, and rushed together through
the doorway.

" *Maleto ! maleto !*" (kill him !) cried both, in the same voice, each with
a view of encouraging the other ; and, as they uttered the cruel cry, they
buried their blades in the body of the unresisting traveller—stabbing it
repeatedly through the cloak.

Convinced that they had finished their bloody work, the murderers
were about to rush out again—probably with an eye to the saddle-bags
outside, when it occurred to them as strange that the victim of their
hired villany should have kept so quiet. In their frenzied excitement—
while dealing what they supposed to be his death-blows—they had not
stopped to notice anything odd in the behavour of the man whom they
were murdering. Now that the deed was done, and they could reflect
more coolly, a sudden surprise seized upon them—springing from the
circumstance that the wretched man had made not the slightest
motion—had neither stirred nor cried out ! Perhaps the first stab had
gone right through his heart; for it was so intended by Andres, who
had given it ? But even that does not produce instantaneously death, and
the man-hunters knew it. Besides, on the blade of Andre's *machete*, as
well as that of his comrade, *there was no blood.*

It was very strange. Could the cloak or under garment have wiped it
off ? Partially they might, but not altogether ? Their blades were wet,
but not with blood—of that they showed scarce a stain !

" It's a queer thing, comrade," exclaimed Manuel. " I could almost
fancy——, *Vaya.* Lift the cloak, and let's have a look at him."

The other, stepping close to the couch, stooped forward, and raised
the fold of the camlet from the face of the murdered man.

As he did so, his hand came in contact with the cold skin, while his
glance fell upon the stiffened features of a corpse—upon eyes whose dull,
blank film showed that the light had long since forsaken them !

The assassin stayed not for a second look. With a cry of terror he let
go the garment ; and rushed towards the door, followed by his equally
terrified companion.

In another moment both would have escaped outside ; and perhaps
have taken the back track, without thinking any more about the saddle-

bags; but just as Andres had set foot upon the door-sill, he saw before him something that caused him to pull up, and with a precipitancy that brought his comrade with a violent concussion against his back.

The something which had led to this sudden interruption was the presence of three men, standing in a triangular row scarce five paces from the door. Each was holding a gun, in such position, that its dark hollow tube was visible to the eyes of the assassin—pointing directly upon himself.

The three men, were of three distinct colours—white, yellow, and black; all three known to the man-hunter and his companion. They were Herbert Vaughan, Cubina, captain of Maroons, and Quaco, his lieutenant.

CHAPTER CI.

THE CAPTURE OF THE CAÇADORES.

THE black, though presumedly the lowest in rank, was the first to break speech.

"No, ye don't!" cried he, moving his musket up and down, while still keeping it levelled upon the foremost of the 'caçadores.' "No, Mister Jack Spaniard, not a foot d' you set outside that door till we see what you've been a-doin' 'thin there. Steady, now, or thar's an ounce of lead into yer garlicky inside! Steady!"

"Surrender!" commanded Cubina, in a firm, authoritative voice, and with a threatening gesture, which, though less demonstrative than that of his lieutenant, was equally indicative of determination. "Drop your machetes, and yield at once! Resistance will only cost you your lives."

"Come, my Spanish' worthies," said Herbert. "You know me? I advise you to do as you're bid. If there's nothing against you I promise you no harm——Ha! ware heels!" he continued in sharp haste, observing that the Spaniards were looking over their shoulders, as if intending to escape by the back of the hut. "Don't attempt to run away. You'll be caught, no matter how fast you go. I've got two barrels here; and each is good for a bird on the wing. Show your backs, and they'll be preciously peppered, I promise you."

"Carajo!" hissed out the oldest of the 'caçadores.' "What do you want with us?"

"Ay!" added the other, in a tone of innocent reproach; "what have we been doing to make all this fanfaron about?"

"What have you been doing?" rejoined the Maroon captain: "that's just what we desire to know, and are determined upon knowing."

"There's nothing to be known," answered the man, speaking with an air of assumed simplicity; "at the least, nothing that's very particular. We were on our way to Savanna—me and my comrade here——"

"Stach yer palaver!" cried Quaco, becoming impatient, and pushing the muzzle of his musket within an inch of the Spaniard's ribs. "Did ye hear the cappen tell ye to drop yer toastin'-forks and surrender! Down with 'em this minnit, I say, an' do yer jaw-waggon' atterwards!"

Thus threatened, a bullet between them, Andres sulkily let fall his *machete* upon the floor—an action that was instantly imitated by his senior and superior.

"Now, my braves!" proceeded the black lieutenant, still holding his huge gun to the Spaniard's breast; "lest ye mout be wantin' to gie us leg-bail, you muss submit to be trussed a trifle. Down upon yer behinds both o' ye; and keep that way till I get the cords and skewers ready."

The 'caçadores' perfectly understood the order; and, perceiving that there was no chance for disobedience, squatted down upon the floor—each on the spot where he had been standing. Quaco now picked up the two *machetes*, placing them beyond the reach of their *ci-devant* owners. Then, handing his great gun over to the care of Cubina—who with Herbert was left to guard the prisoners—he walked off to a short distance among the trees. Presently he returned, trailing after him a long creeping plant that resembled a piece of cord, and carrying a few short sticks, each about three feet in length. All this was accomplished with as much celerity, and in as brief a space of time, as if he had simply taken the articles from an adjacent store-room. Meanwhile, Cubina and Herbert had kept their guns still pointed upon the two 'caçadores:' for it was most evident that the villains were most eager to get off; and as it was now nearly night, had the least chance been allowed them, they might have succeeded in escaping through the darkness.

Their captors were determined they should have no chance: for although neither Herbert nor Cubina could see into the obscure interior of the cabin, and were as yet ignorant of the fearful spectacle that there awaited them, they had reason to suspect that the Spaniards had either intended some dark deed, or had already committed it. They had learnt something along the road of the progress of the 'caçadores,' and their mode of journeying, which, to more than one whom they met, had appeared mysterious.

The horse standing tied to the tree—caparisoned as he was for travel —that was the most suspicious circumstance of all. Though none of the three pursuers recognised the animal as belonging to Custos Vaughan, as soon as they had set eyes upon it, they had felt a presentiment that they had arrived too late.

The wild haste with which the Spaniards were rushing from the cabin when intercepted at the door, almost confirmed their unpleasant foreboding; and before any of the three had entered the hut, they were half prepared to find that it contained a corpse—perhaps more than one, for the disappearance of Pluto was not yet explained.

Quaco, habile in handling cordage of all kinds, more especially the many sorts of supple withes with which the tree of a Jamaica forest are laced together, soon tied the two Spaniards wrist to wrist, and ankle to ankle, as tightly as could have been done by the most accomplished gaoler. A long practise in binding runaway blacks had made Quaco an expert in that department, which, indeed, constitutes part of the professional training of a Maroon.

The captors had already entered within the cabin, now dark as death itself. For some moments they stood upon the floor, their eyes endeavouring to read the gloom around them. Silent they stood—so still, that they could hear their own breathing with that of the two prisoners upon the floor. At length, in the corner, they could dimly make out something like the form of a man lying stretched upon a low bedstead. Quaco, though not without some trepidation, approached it. Stooping down, he applied his hand to it with cautious touch.

"A man!" muttered he: "eyther asleep or dead.

"Dead!" he ejaculated the instant after, as, in groping about, his fingers chanced to fall upon the chill forehead—"dead and cold?"

Cubina and Herbert stepping forward, and, stooping over the corpse, verified the assertion of Quaco.

Whose body was it? It might not be that of Loftus Vaughan? It might be the black attendant, Pluto?

No! it was not a black man. It needed no light to show that. The touch of the hair was sufficient to tell that a white man lay dead upon the couch.

"Catch me one of those *cocuyos!*" said the Maroon captain, speaking to his lieutenant.

Quaco stepped outside the hut. Low down along the verge of the forest were flitting little sparks, that appeared to be a galaxy of stars in motion. These were the *lampyridæ*, or smaller fire-flies. It was not with these Quaco had to do. Here and there, at longer intervals, could be seen much larger sparks, of a golden green colour. It was the great winged beetle—the *cocuyo**—that emitted this lovely light.

Doffing his old hat-crown, Quaco used it as an insect-net; and after a few strokes succeeded in capturing a *cocuyo*.

With this he returned into the hut, and crossing over, held it near the head of the corpse. He did not content himself with the gold green light which the insect emits from the two eyelike tubercles on its thorax. The forest-craft of Quaco enabled him to produce a brighter and better. Holding open the elytra with his fingers, and bending back the abdomen with his thumb, he exposed that oval disc of orange light—only seen when the insect is on the wing. A circle of a yard in diameter was illuminated by the phosphoric glow. In that circle was the face of a dead man; and sufficiently bright was the lamp of the *cocuyo*, to enable the spectators to identify the ghastly lineaments as those of the Custos Vaughan.

CHAPTER CII.

A DOUBLE MURDER.

NONE of the three started or felt surprise. That had been gradually passing: for before this their presentiment had become almost a conviction.

Quaco simply uttered one of those exclamations that proclaim a climax; Cubina felt chagrined—disappointed in more ways than one; while Herbert gave way to grief—though less than he might have done, had his relative more deserved his sorrow.

It was natural they should inquire into the Custos' death. Now, firmly

*Pyrophorus Noctilucus.

believing he had been murdered, and by the ' caçadores, they proceeded
to make an examination of the body.

Mystery of mysteries! a dozen stabs by some sharp instrument, and
no blood! Wounds through the breast, the abdomen, the heart—all
clean cut punctures, and yet no gore—no extravasation!

" Who gave the stabs? you did this, you wretches!" cried Herbert
turning fiercely upon the ' employés' of Jessuron.

" Carrambo ; why should we do such a thing, master ?" innocently inquired Andres. "The alcalde was dead before we came up."

" Spanish palaver!" cried Quaco. "Look at these blades!" he contin-
ed, taking up the two *machetes*, "they're wet now! 'Ta'nt blood azzaot
ly ; but somethin'——. See!" he exclaimed, holding his *cacuyo* over the
wounds, and presenting one of the *machetes* to the light, " they fit to these
holes like a cork to a bottle. 'Twere they that made em', nothin' but
they an' you did it, ye ugly skinks!"

" By the Virgin, Senor Quaco!" replied Andres, " you wrong us. I'll
swear on the holy evangalists, *we* did'nt kill the alcalde—Custos, I mean.
Carrambo ; no. We were as much surprised as any of you, when we came
in here, and found him dead—just as he is now."

There was an air of sincerity in the declaration of the wretch that
rendered it difficult to believe in his guilt—that is, the guilt of him and
his companion as the real murderers, though their intention to have been
so was clear enough to Cubina.

" *Crambo ;* why did you stab him ?" said he to the two prisoners. " You
need not deny that you did that."

" Senor capitan," answered the crafty Andres, who in all delicate questions appeared to be spokesman, " we won't deny that. It is true—I confess it with shame—that we did run our blades once or twice through the
body."

" A dozen times, you John Crow!" corrected Quaco.

" Well, senor Quaco," continued the Spaniard, " I won't be particular
about the number. There may have been a thrust or two less, or more.
It was all a whim of my comrade, Manuel, here—a little bit of a wager
between us."

" A wager for what ?"

" Well, you see, master, we'd been journeying, as I've said already, to
Savanna. We saw the horse tied outside this little ranchio, and thought
we would go in and see who was inside. *Carrambo* what shculd we see
but the body of a dead man lying stretched out on the bamboos! *Santis-
sima Senoros,* we were as much startled as you."

" Terribly surprised, I suppose?" sarcastically spoke Cubina.

"Nearly out of our senses, I assure you, senor."

" Go on, you wretch!" commanded Herbert. " Let us hear what tale
you have to tell."

" Well!" said the ' caçadore,' resuming his narration, " after a while we
got a little over our fright—as one naturally does, you know—and then
Manuel says to me, ' Andres!' ' What is it, Manuel?' said I. ' D'you
think,' said he, ' that blood would run out of a dead body?' ' Certainly
not,' said I ; ' not a drop.' ' I'll bet you five pesos it will,' challenged my
camarado. ' Done !' said I ; and then to settle the thing, we—I acknowledge it—did run our machetes through the body of the Custos—of course,
a could do him no harm then."

"Monsters!" exclaimed Herbert; "it was almost as bad as killing him, What a horrid tale. Ha; you wretches, notwithstanding its ingenuity It'll not save your necks from a halter."

"Oh, senorito," said Andres, appealingly, "we've done nothing to deserve that. I can assure you we are both right sorry for what we've done. Ain't you sorry, Manuel?"

"*Carrai* that I am," earnestly answered Manuel.

"We both regretted it afterwards," continued Andres, "and to make up for what we had done, we took the cloak and spread it decently over the body—in order that the poor alcade should rest in peace."

"Liar!" cried Quaco, throwing the light of his cocuyo upon the corpse. "You did no such thing; you stabbed him *through* the cloak. Look there!"

And as Quaco gave this indignant denial, he pointed to the cuts in the cloth to prove the falsehood of the Spaniard's statement.

"*Carrai-ai-i;*" stammered out the confounded Andres. "Sure enough there's a cut or two. Oh, now I recollect: we first covered him up. It was after we did that, we then made the bet—didn't we, Manuel?"

Manuel's reply was not heard: for at that instant the hoof-strokes of horses were heard in front of the hut; and the shadowy forms of two horsemen could be distinguished just outside the doorway.

It was the black groom who had returned from Content, accompanied by the overseer of the estate.

Shortly after a number of negroes appeared on foot, carrying a stretcher.

Their purpose was to convey the sick man to Content.

Circumstances had occurred to make a change in the character of their duty.

CHAPTER CIII.

CHAKRA ON THE BACK TRACK.

Of the three magistrates who condemned the Coromantee, one had been slumbering in his grave for six months; the second, about that number of days; and the third—the great Custos himself—was now a corpse!

Of all three had the myal-man been the murderer; though in the case of the first two there had been no suspicion of foul play, or, at least, not enough to challenge inquest or investigation. Both had died of lingering diseases, bearing a certain resemblance to each other; and though partaking very much of the nature of a wasting intermittent fever, yet exhibiting symptoms that were new and strange—so strange as to baffle the skill of the Jamaican disciples of Esculapius.

About the death of either one Chakra had not felt the slightest apprehension—nor would he even had an investigation arisen. In neither murder had his hand appeared. Both had been accomplished by the invisible agency of Obi, that at this period held mysterious existence on every plantation in the island

With the assassination of the Custos, however, it was different. Circumstances had caused that event to be hurried, and there was danger—
as Chakra himself had admitted—that the spell of Obi might be mistaken
for a spell of poison. A death so sudden, and by natural causes inexplicable would, undoubtedly, provoke speculation, and lead to the opening and examining of the body.

Chakra knew that inside would be found something stronger than even
the sap of the Savanna flower or the branched *calalue;* and that in all
probability the malady to which the Custos had succumbed would be
pronounced *murder.* With this upon his mind, he was not without apprehension—his fears pointing to Cynthia. Not that he suspected the
honesty of his confederate ; but only that her *consistency* might be too
weak to withstand the cross-questioning of a coroner. Fearing this, he
had scarce got out of sight of the Custos's corpse before he commenced
contriving how Cynthia's tongue could be tied—in other words, how the
mulatta was to be made away with. Upon this design his thoughts were
for the moment bent. He had less, if any, apprehension about his other
accomplice in the crime. He fancied that Jessuron was himself too
deeply dyed to point out the spots upon his fellow-conspirator ; and this
rendered him confident of secrecy ôn the part of the Jew. Neither did
he dwell long upon the danger to be apprehended from Cynthia, and so
trivial a matter as the silencing of her tongue soon became obliterated or
blended with another and far more important project, to the execution of
which he was now hastening. On leaving the hut where lay the dead
body of his victim, he had taken to by-paths and bushes. Only for a
short time did he keep to these. The twilight rapidly darkening into
night left the highway free to him ; and, availing himself of this privilege, he returned to it—showing by his hurried steps, as he regained the
road, that he was glad to escape from a circuitous path. His face once
more set towards the Trelawney hills, he walked in silence, and with a
rapidity scarce credible—his long, ape-like legs, split trestle fashion to
the centre of his body, enabling him glide over the ground almost as fast
as a mule could mince.

When any one appeared upon the road before him, he adopted his customary plan of betaking himself to the bushes until they passed ; but
when travellers chanced to be going the same way—which more than
once did happen—he avoided an encounter by making a circuit through
the woods, and coming out far ahead of them.

The trouble thus taken to gain time, as well as the earnest manner with
which the myal-man was hastening forward, proved that the crime just
committed was not the crisis of Chakra's villanies ; but that some other
evil purpose—to him of equal or greater import—was yet before him ;
and soon to be achieved, or, at least, attempted.

Following back the main route between Savannala-Mer and the Bay,
he at length arrived at the Carrion Crow road, and, after traversing this
for some distance, came within view of the Jumbé Rock, now glancing
with viterous sheen in the clear moonlight.

Almost as soon as he had caught sight of the well-known land-mark,
he forsook the road ; and struck   a by-path that led through the
woods.

This path, trending diagonally up the side of the Jumbe mountain, and passing near the base of the Rock, was the same which Herbert Vaughan and the two Maroons had traversed on their way from the Happy Valley on the same morning.

Chakra, however, knew nothing of this; nor aught either of the design or expedition of Cubina and his comrades. Equally ignorant was he of the errand on which Jessuron had dispatched his Cuban emissaries—by way of having his bow twice stringed.

The Coromantee, fancying himself the only player in that game of mur·der, had no idea that there were others interested in it as much as he; and although once or twice during the day he had seen men moving suspiciously behind him along the road, it had never occurred to him who they were—much less that they had been deputed to complete his own job, should the "spell" fail to prove sufficiently potent.

A somewhat long detour—which he had taken after leaving the hut—had brought him out on the main road behind both parties; and thus had he remained ignorant of their proximity—at the same time that he had himself escaped the observation both of the villains who intended to assassinate the Custos, and the men who were pressing forward to save him.

Still continuing his rapid stride, Chakra climbed the mountain slope with the agility of one accustomed to the most difficult paths.

On arriving under the the Jumbé Rock, he halted—not with any intention of remaining there, but only to consider.

He looked up towards the summit of the cliff, in whose dark shadow he was standing; and then, raising his eyes still higher, he gazed for a short while upon the sky. His glance betrayed that interrogative scrutiny characteristic of one who, not being furnished with a watch, endeavours to ascertain the time. Chakra needed no watch. By day the sun was sufficient to inform him of the hour; by night the stars, which were old and familiar acquaintances.

The sinking of Orion towards the silvered surface of the sea told him that in two hours, or there-about, no stars would be seen.

" Kupple ob hour!" muttered he, after making the observation; " woan do—woan do. By de time I get to de Duppy Hole fo' de lamp, an' den back to de rock fo' fix um—It woan do! Adam an' his men be better part ob an hour 'fore dey ked climb up hya; an' den it be daylight. Daat woan do nohow. Muss be done in de night, else we git follered, an' de Duppy Hole no longer safe 'treat fo Chakra. Mussent risk dat, whasomebber a do.

" Whugh!" he continued, after reflecting a moment, and with a look of villanous chagrin overspreading his countenance; " 'tarn a piece of cuss crooked luck fo' me no' be hya 'bout two hour soona. Dat 'ud 'a been s'fishint to got 'em all up in time; an' dar wud den a been gobs o' time to 'complish de whole bizness.

" Nebba mind!" cried he, after a pause, and rousing himself from the attitude of reflection; " nebba mind, ye ole Coromantee fool! 'morra night do jess as well. Den dar be plenty ob time. 'Taint like dey get de dead corpus ob de Cussus back to de Buff afore two, tree day; an' ef dat ere niggar fotch de news, it do no harm. Maybe do good, in de 'fusion

it makes 'bout de place. Nobba mind. It be all right fo' 'm 'rr' night
'Fore dis time ob de mornin', de Lilly Quasheba—do beau'fut dauter ob
dat proud quaderoom—she sleep in de 'brace o' ole Chakra de myal-man.
Whugh!"

"Two hour 'fore day," added he, after a longer pause, in which he ap·
peared to gloat over his fiendish expectations ; "two hour. I'se jess hab
time go down to de Jew penn, an' den back to de Duppy Hole 'fore day.
light. Dat ole sinner, he want know what's a been done ; au' a want get
de balance ob dat fifty poun'. A mount stan' need ob de money, now a'
a-gwine to hab a wife, an' take to de keepin' ob a 'tablishment. Ha!
ha! ha!"

And as he gave utterance to the laugh, the prospective bridegroom once
more put his hideous form in motion, and followed the path leading to the
Jew's penn.

CHAPTER CIV.

THE VIGIL OF LOVE AND THE VIGIL OF JEALOUSY.

YOLA, true to her tryst, set forth to meet her beloved Maroon. The
hour of midnight was the time that had been appointed ; but, in order to
secure punctuality, she took her departure from Mount Welcome long
before that hour—leaving herself ample time to reach the rendezvous.

Of late these after-night expeditions had become known to Miss
Vaughan, and their object as well. To her young mistress the Foolah
maiden had confessed her *penchant* for Cubina—her belief of its being
reciprocated ; in short, had told the whole story of her love.

Common report spoke well of the young Maroon captain—Yola warmly ;
and as everything contributed to proclaim his intentions honourable,
Miss Vaughan made no objection of his meetings with her maid.

There was something in her own sentiments to incline her to this liberal
line of conduct. The young creole could sympathise with hearts that
truly loved—all the better that, by experience, her own heart had learnt
the bitterness of being thwarted.

At all times, therefore—so far as she was concerned—the brown-skinned sweetheart of Cubina had free leave to meet her lover.

On that particular night permission was granted to the maid more
freely than ever, since, for a certain reason, the mistress herself desired
the interview to take place.

The reason may be guessed without difficulty. On the previous night
Cubina had thrown out a hint, which his sweetheart had communicated
to her mistress.

She had spoken of some news he might have that would interest the
latter ; and although there was nothing definite in that, still the hint had
led to an indulgence in speculations—vague as dreams, it is true, but
tinged with a certain sweetness.

Kate knew something of the romantic friendship that had been es
tablished between Herbert and Cubina. Yola had long ago told her of
this—as well as the incident that had given origin to it. Perhaps that

knowledge may explain the interest, almost amounting to anxiety, she now felt to ascertain the nature of the communication which the Maroon had hypothetically promised to make.

It was only in the afternoon of the day—after her excursion to the Jumbé Rock—that the maid had imparted this piece of intelligence to her mistress ; and the altered demeanour of the latter during the rest of the evening proved how interesting it must have been to her. Her anxiety was scarce of the sorrowful kind, but rather tinged with an air of cheerfulness--as if some secret instinct had infused into her spirits a certain buoyancy—as if on the dark horizon of her future there was still lingering, or had suddenly arisen, a faint ray of hope.

Yola had not told all she knew. She said nothing of certain surmises that had escaped the lips of Cubina. With a woman's tact, she perceived that these, being only conjectural, might excite false hopes in the breast of her young mistress : for whom the girl felt a true affection. In fear of this, she kept back the allusion to the marriage of Herbert and Judith and its probable failure, which Cubina had so emphatically illustrated by a proverb.

Yola intended this reserve to be only temporary—only until after her next meeting with her lover—from which she hoped to return with a fuller power of explaining it.

Neither had she made known to her mistress the circumstance of having seen Cynthia in company with the Jew, and the conference that had occurred between them, overheard by herself and Cubina—much less the suspicions to which the latter had given expression.

Under the apprehension that a knowledge of these strange facts and suspicions might trouble her young mistress, she had withheld them.

The young creole had not retired to rest when Yola took her departure from the house, nor yet for long after. Anxious to know the result of the interview between her maid and the Maroon, she remained awake within her chamber—burning the midnight lamp, far into the hours of morning.

＊　　＊　　＊　　＊　　＊　　＊　　＊　　＊

Notwithstanding the more than permission that had been accorded to her, the princess-slave stole softly from the house—passing the precincts of the mansion, and traversing the grounds outside with considerable caution. This partly arose from the habit of that half-barbaric life, to which, in her own country and from earliest childhood, she had been accustomed. But there was also, perhaps, some suspicion of present danger, or, at all events, that fear of interruption natural to one on the way to keep an appointment of the kind towards which she was now betaking herself.

From whatever motive sprung her cautious behaviour, it was not sufficient to prevent her departure from being observed ; nor did it enable her to perceive that thing of woman's shape that, like an evil shadow, flitted after her across the fields, and went following her along the forest-path.

Whenever she turned it also turned, only not preserving an erect bearing, nor going in the same continuous gait; but every now and then pausing upon the path, sometimes in crouched attitude, as if seeking concealment under the shadow of the bushes—then gliding rapidly onward to make stop as before.

After having got beyond the surroundings of the house, and some distance into the pimento forest, the Foolah walked with more freedom—as if no longer fearing interruption. She was, therefore, less likely to perceive that ill-omened shadow, that still continued on her track—following, as before, by a series of progessive traverses, and in death like silence.

On reaching the glade, the young girl advanced towards the *ceiba*, and took her stand within its shadow—on a spot, in her eyes, "hallowed down to earth's profound, and up to heaven." She merely glanced round to satisfy herself that Cubina was not there. She scarce expected him yet. The hour, though late, was earlier than the time appointed. It had not yet gone twelve—else she would have heard the plantation clock announcing it. .

Allowing her eyes to drop to the ground at her feet, she stood for some minutes buried in a reverie of reflection—a sweet reverie, as befitted her situation of pleasant expectancy.

She was startled from this abstraction by the behavior of a bird---a scarlet tanager, that rose, fluttering and frightened, out of a small clump of bushes about ten paces from the *ceiba*, and in which it had been reposing.

The bird, uttering a cry of alarm, forsook the shelter, and flew off into the forest.

Yola could see nothing that should have caused the creature to make so abrupt a departure from its roosting-place. Her own presence could scarce have been the cause: since she had been some minutes upon the ground, and standing in tranquil *pose*. Some of its natural enemies had frayed the bird? Perhaps a rat, an owl, or a serpent? Thus reasoned she; and was satisfied.

If, instead of contenting herself with this conjecture, she had stepped ten paces forward, and looked into the little copse, she would have seen there something very different from any of the three creatures her fancy had conjured up. She would have seen the form of a woman crouching within the shadow, with features set in surpressed rage, and eyes glowing indignantly upon herself. Easily, too, would she have recognised the face as that of her fellow-slave, Cynthia! ' "

But she saw it not, though Cynthia saw her—though for hours did the two remain in this singular juxtaposition—one occupied with the vigil of love, the other absorbed in the vigil of jealousy. For long hours did the Foolah maid wait for the coming of her beloved Cubina—her ear keenly bent to catch any sound that might announce his approach; her bosom every moment becoming more and more a prey to painful impatience. Equally long stayed the spy in her place of concealment—equally suffering torture from jealous imaginings. To both it was a relief, when a footstep upon the path, and a rustling of branches proclaimed the approach of some one towards the spot. It was but a momentary relief, mocking the anticipations of both—thwarting the joy of the one, and the vengeful design of the other. Instead of the expected lover, a very different personage made his appearance; and almost at the same instant another, coming from the opposite side. Both, at the same time, advanced towards the middle of the glade; and, without exchanging a word, stopped face to face near the *ceiba*, as if they had met by appointment. They were out in the open-ground, and under the full light of the moon. Both were men, and the faces of both could be distinctly seen. Yola knew only one of them, and the sight of him hindered her from staying to look upon the other. She merely glanced at a countenance that was fearful—though not more fearful to her than the one she had already recognised, and which had at once determined her to get away from the ground.

Keeping the great trunk between herself and the new comers, and retreating silently under its shadow, she glided back into the underwood of the forest, and was soon far from the presence of the two intruders, who had brought her long and vain vigil to such an unsatisfactory termination.

Cynthia could not have followed her example, even had she been so inclined. The two men had stopped within six paces of the spot in which she lay concealed. On every side of it the ground was clear of cover, with the moon shining full upon it. A cat could not have crept out of the copse without attracting the attention of one or the other.

Cynthia knew both of the men—was the confederate of both—though not without fearing them.

At first sight of them she would have discovered herself, but disliked to come under the observation of her rival. Afterwards, when the two had entered into conversation, she was held in her place by a dread of a different kind. She had already overheard part of what they were saying ; and she feared they might punish her for eaves dropping, involuntary though it was.

Better for Cynthia had she then declared herself ; but dreaming not of discovery, or the fearful fate that might be involved in it, she determined to lie still, and listen the dark dialogue to its ending.

CHAPTER CV.

CYNTHIA IN TROUBLE.

THE two men who had thus interrupted the silent tableau by the *ceiba* tree where Jacob Jessuron and Chakra, the Coromantee,

Just at the time that Chakra parted from the Jumbé Rock to pay his nocturnal visit to the Jew the latter was leaving his penn to honour the Coromantee with a similar call.

As both were travelling the same path, and in adverse directions, it was more then probable—a necessity, in fact—that each should meet the other before reaching the end of his journey. Also, as the glade where stood the great *ceiba* was on the same path, and midway between the Jumbé Rock and the Jew's penn, it was natural this encounter should take place not far from that noted trysting place. In effect, it occurred within the glade : the two men having entered it almost at the same instant of time.

The Jew had got first into the open ground, and was first seen. The

myal-man might have had these advantages had he wished : he had been
the first to arrive on the edge of the opening ; but true to his instinct of
caution, he had kept under cover until making a reconnoisance, in which
he saw and recognised his advancing *vis-a-vis.*

They met near the middle of the glade, just outside the shadow of the
great tree, stopping face to face when within a pace or two of each other.
Not the slightest salutation was exchanged between the two men—any
more than if they had been two tigers who had just come together in the
jungle.   The secret compact between them precluded the necessity for
compliment or palaver.   Each understood the other ; and not a word was
spoken to introduce the dialogue except that which was pertinent to the
business between them.

" Well, good Shakra! you hash news for me?" interrogated the Jew,
taking the initiative in the conversation.   "You hash been in the direction of Savanna?   Ish all right on the road?"

" Whugh !" vociferated the myal-man, throwing out his breast and jerk-
ing up his shoulders with an air of triumphant importance.   "All right,
eh?   Well, not azzackly on de road, but by de side ob daat same, dar lie a
corp', wich by dis time oughter be as cold as de heart ob a water-millyum,
an' 'tiff as—'tiff as—as—de 'keleton ob ole Chakra.   Ha! ha! ha!"

And the speaker uttered a peal of fierce laughter at the simile he had
so much dfficulty in conceiving ; but which, when found, recalled the
sweet triumph of his vengeance.

" Blesh my soul !   Then it ish all over?"

" Daats all ober—Ise be bour'."

" And the shpell did it?   There wash no need——"

With a start the Jew paused in his speech, as if about to say something he had not intended ; and which had been very near escaping him,
" There wash no need—no need—for you to haf gone after?"

This was evidently not the question originally upon his tongue.

" No need !" repeated Chakra, a little puzzled at the interrogatory ; " no
need, so far as dat war consarned.   Ob coos de 'pell did de work, as a
knowd it wud, an' jess as a told you it wud.   'Twant fo' dat a went arter
but a puppos ob my own.   Who tole ye, Massr Jake, dad I wor gone
arter?"

" Goot Shakra, I washn't quite sure till now.   The wench Cynthy
thought ash how you had followed the Cushtos."

" Whugh ! dat 'ere gal talk too much.   She hab her tongue 'topped
'fore long.   She *muss* hab her tongue 'topp, else she gess boaf o' us in
trouble.   Nebba mind !   A make dat all right too—by-'m-bye.   Now, Massr
Jake, a want dat odder twenty-five pound.   De job am finish, an' de work
am done.   Now's de time fo' de pay."

" That ish right, Shakra.   I hash the monish here in red gold.   There
it ish."

As the Jew said this, he passed a bag containing gold into the hands
of Chakra.

" You'll find it ish all counted correct.   Twenty-five poundsh curren
shy.   Fifty poundsh altogether, ash agreed   A deal of monish—a deal
of monish, s'help me !"

Chakra made no reply, to this significant insinuation ; but, taking the bag depessited it in the lining of his skin *kaross*, as he did so giving utterance to his favourite ejaculation, " Whugh !" the meaning of which varied according to the accentuation given to it.

"And now, goot Chakra !" continued the Jew; " I hash more work for you. There ish another sphell wanted, for which you shall have another fifty poundsh; but firsht tell me, hash you seen any one to-day on your travels ?"

" Seed any one, eh ? Well dat am a quessin, Massr Jake. A seed a good wheen on my trabbels : more'n seed me, I'se be boun'."

" But hash you seen any one ash you know ?"

" Sartin a did—de Cussus fo' one, tho', by de gollies ! a hardly wud a knowd him, he wa' so fur gone—moas to de bone ! He am almos' as much a 'keleton as ole Chakra hisself. Ha ! ha ! ha !"

" Any body elshe that you hash a knowledge of ?"

" No—nob'dy—neery one as a know anythin' bout 'ceppin' de Cussus' 'tendant. A seed odder men on de road, but dey wur fur off, and a keep dem fur off as a cud. Oa ! yes, der wa' one who come near—mose too near—him I knowd. Dat wa' one ob dem 'ere Trelawney Maroon—Quaco dey call um."

" Only Quaco, you shay ? You hash seen nothing of hish capt'in, Cubina, nor of a young white gentlemansh along with him !"

" Neider de one nor de todder ob dem two people. Wha fo' you ask dat, Massr Jake ?"

" I hash a good reason, Shakra. The young fellow I speaksh of ish a book-keeper of mine. He hash left the penn thish very morning. I don't know for why or whither he ish gone ; but I hash a reason to think he ish in company with Capt'in Cubina. May be not, and may be he'll be back again ; but it looksh suspicious. If he'sh gone for good, the shpell will be all for nothingsh. S'help me, for nothingsh !"

" Dat's a pity ! I'm sorry fo' dat, Massr Jake. A hope he no gone."

" Whether or not, I mushn't go to shleep about it. There ish another shpell that will be more needed now ash ever."

" De Obi am ready. Who d' ye want um set fo' nex' ?"

" For this rashcal Cubina."

" Ah, dat ere in welkum. De god do him bess to 'pell *him*."

" He hash trouble for me. It ish not like to come so soon : now ash the Cushtos ish out of the way. But who knowsh how soon ? And better ash the shpell should be set at once. So, good Shakra, if you can manish to do for Cubina in as short a time ash you hash done the Cushtos, thore ish another fifty poundsh ready for you."

" A'll do ma bess, Massr Jake, to earn you money. A'll do ma bess— de bess can do no mo'."

" That ish true, good Shakra ! Don't you think this wench, Cynthy, can help you ?"

" Not a bit ob help from dat quar'r—not worth a 'traw for 'pellin' Cubina. He no let de m'latta come nigh o' 'm fo' no considerashun. He sick ob de sight o' her. Besides, dat gal, she know too much now. She one ob dese days fotch de white folk to de Duppy Hole. Dat nebba do. No furrer use now. She hab serb her turn, an' mus, be got rid ob—

muss go 'long wi' de odders—long wi' de Cussus. Da's my way—de only
way keep a woman tongue-tied, am to top 'um waggin' alltogeder.
Whugh!"

After uttering the implied threat, the monster stood silent a moment,
as if reflecting upon some mode by which he could make away with the
life of the mulatta.

" You think, Shakra, you ish likely to find somebody elshe to assist
you?"

" Nebba fear, Massr Jake. Leab dat to ole Chakra—ole Chakra an' ole
Obi. Dey do de bizness widcut help from any odder."

" Fifty poundsh, then, Shakra. Ach! I'd give twice the monish— yes
s'help me, ten times the monish—if I knew it wash all right with young
Vochan. Ach! where ish hé gone ?"

The expression of bitter chagrin, almost anguish, with which the vil-
lainous old Jew, for at least the tenth time on that day, repeated this interrogative formula, told that of all the matters upon his mind the
absence of his book-keeper was the one uppermost , and deemed by him
of most importance .

Blesh my sole! if he ish gone for good, I shall have all thish trouble
for nothing—all the cr-r——inconvenience."

It was the " crime" he was about to, have said ; but he changed the
word—not from any delicacy in the presence of Chakra, but rather to
still a shuddering within himself, to which the thought had given rise.

" Nebba mind, massa Jake," said his confederate, encouragingly ; "you
hab got rid ob an enemy—same's maself. Dat am someting, anyhow ;
an' a promise you soon got shot ob one odder. A go at once 'bout dat
berry bizness."

" Yesh! yesh! soon, good Shakra, soon as you can! I wont keep yoush
any longer. It ish near daylight. I musht go back and get some shleep.
S'help me! I hash not had a wink thish night. Ach! I can't shleep so
long ash he'sh not found. I musht go home, and see if there is any newsh
of him."

So saying, and turning on his heel, without " good night," or any other
parting salutation, the Jew strode abstractedly off, leaving Chakra where
he stood.

<hr/>

CHAPTER CVI

A FATAL SNEEZE.

" WHUGH!" ejaculated the Coromantee, as soon as his confederate was
out of hearing ; " dar's someting heavy on de mind ob dat ere ole Jew—
someting wuss dan de death ob de cussus Vagh'n. Wonder now wha'
cin be all 'bout? 'Bout dis yar book-keeper a nows it am. But wha'
'bout him ? A'll find out 'fore am many hour older. Daat a'll do. A'm
jess like de Jew masself—ha'n't had ne'er a wink dis night, nor de night
afore neider ; nor doant expeck get de half ob a wink morrer night. Ha!

morrer night; morrer night. Dat will be de night ob all odder. Morrer night, if all tings go well, Chakra he no sleep him 'lone—he sleep no more by hisseff- he hab for him bedfellow de beauty ob de island ob Jamaica. He sleep wid de Lilly ——"

Ere the full name of the victim threatened with this horrid fate had passed from his lips, the menace of the myal-man was interrupted. The interruption was caused by a sound proceeding from the little clump of bushes close to where Chakra stood. It sounded exactly as if some one had sneezed—for it was that in reality. Cynthia had sneezed.

She had not done so intentionally: far from it. After what she had heard, it was not likely she would have uttered any sound to proclaim her presence. At that instant she would have given all she possessed in the world—all she ever hoped to possess, even the love of Cubina— to have been miles from the spot, within the safe kitchen of Mount Welcome—anywhere but where she then was.

Long before the conversation between the Jew and Chakra had come to a close, she had made up her mind never to see the myal-man again— never willingly. Now an encounter appeared inevitable: he must have heard the sneeze?

The wretched woman reasoned aright—he had heard it.

A fierce " whugh!" was the ejaculation it called forth in response; and then the myal-man turning suddenly in the direction whence it appeared to have proceeded, stood for a short time silent and listening.

"By golly !" said he, speaking aloud ; " dat 'ere soun' berry like a 'neeze ! Some ob dem 'ere trees ha' been a takin' snuff. A'd jess like know wha' sort ob varmint made dat obstropolus noise. It wan't a bush —dat's sartin. Nor yet wa' it a bird. What-den ? It wan't 't all onlike tho 'neeze ob a nigga wench ? But what would a wench be a doin' in tha ? Dat's what puzzles me. Lookee hya !" added he, raising his voice, and addressing himself to whoever or whatever might have produced the noise ; "les hear dat ag'in, whosomebber you be ! Take anodder pince ob snuff—louder dis time, so I can tell whedder you am a man or whedder you be a femmynine."

He waited for a while, to see if his speech would elicit a response ; but none came. Within the copse all remained silent, as if no living thing was sheltered under its sombre shadows.

" You wan't 'neeze agin," continued he, seeing there was no reply ; " den by golly a make you, if you am what a 'speck you is—somb'dy hid in dar to lissen. No snake can't a 'neeze dat way, no' yet a lizzart. You muss be eyder man, woman, or chile ; an' ef you be, an' hab heerd wha's been say, by de great Accompong ! you life no be worth—Ha ! ha !"

As he entered upon this last paragraph of his apostrophe he had commenced moving towards the copse, which was only six paces from his starting point. Before the speech was completed he had passed in among the bushes , and, bending them over with his long, ape-like arms, was scrutinizing the ground underneath.

The exclamation was called forth by his perceiving the form of a woman in a crouching attitude within the shadow.

In another instant he had siezed the woman by the shoulder ; and with a quick wrench jerked her into an erect position.

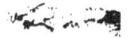

"Cynthy!" he exclaimed, as the light fell upon the countenance of the mulatta.

"Yes, Chakra!' cried the woman, screaming ere she spoke; "it's me, it's me!"

"Whugh! Wha' you do hya! Youb been lissenin'. Wha' fo' you lissen?"

"Oh, Chakra! I did not intend it. I came here——"

"How long you been hya? Tell dat quick?"

"Oh, Chakra—I came——"

'You hya 'fore we came in' de glade. Needn't ax dat. You an kud git hya atterwad. You heer all been said? You muss hab heer it."

"Oh, Chakra, I couldn't help it. I would have gone——"

"Den you nebba heer nodder word more. Won't do let you go now. You come hya; you stay hya. You nebba go out ob dis 'pot. Whugh!"

And giving to the monosyllable an aspirate of fierceness, that caused it to sound more like the utterance of a wild beast than a human being, the monster threw out his long dark arms, and rushed towards his intended victim.

In another instant his long muscular fingers were clutched round the throat of the mulatta, clamping it with the tightness and tenacity of an iron garotte.

The wretched creature could make no resistance against such a formidable and ferocious antagonist. She tried to speak; she could not even scream.

"Chak—r—a, de—ar Chak—r—r—a," came forth in a prolonged thoracic utterance, and this was the last articulation of her life.

After that there was a gurgling in her throat—the death rattle, as the fingers relaxed their long-continued clutch—and the body, with a sudden sound, fell back among the bushes.

"You lie da?" said the murderer, on seeing that his horrid work was complete. "Dar you tell no tale. Now for de Duppy Hole; an' a good long sleep to 'fresh me fo' de work ob de morrow night. Whugh!"

And turning away from the image of death he had just finished fashioning, the fearful Coromantee pulled the skirts of his skin mantle around him, and strode out of the glade, with as much composure as if medita-ting upon some abstruse chapter in the ethics of Obi.

CHAPTER CVII.

CHAKRA TRIMMING HIS LAMP.

Day was dawning when the tiger Chakra returned to his lair in the Duppy's Hole. With him night was day, and the dawn of the morn the twilight of evening. He was hungry: having eaten only a morsel of food since starting out on his awful errand, just twenty-four hours ago. The remains of a pepper-pot, still unemptied from the iron skillet in which it had been cooked, stood in a corner of the hut. To warm it up would require time, and the kindling of a fire. He was too much fatigued to be fastiduous; and drawing the skillet from its corner, he scooped up the stew and ate it cold.

Finally, before retiring to rest, he introduced into his stomach some thing calculated to warm the cold pepper-pot—the " heel tap" of a bottle of rum, that remained over from the preceding night; and then, flinging himself upon the bamboo bedstead, so heavily that the frail reeds " scrunched" under his weight, he sank into a profound slumber.

He lay upon his hunched back, his face turned upward. A protuberance on the trunk of the tree, of larger dimensions than that upon his own person, served him for a bolster—a few handfuls of the silk cotton laid loosely upon it constituting his pillow.

With his long arms extended loosely by his side—one of them hanging over until the murderous fingers rested upon the floor—and his large mouth, widely agape, displaying a double serrature of pointed shining teeth, he looked more like some slumbering ogre than a human being.

His sleep could not be sweet. It was far from being silent. From his broad, compressed nostrils came a sonorous snoring, causing the cartilage to heave outward, accompanied by a gurgling emission through his throat that resembled the breathing of a hippopotamus.

Thus slumbered Chakra throughout the live long day, dreaming of many crimes committed, or, perhaps, only of that—the sweetest crime of all—which was yet in abeyance.

It was near night when he awoke. The sun had gone down—at least he was no longer visible from the bottom of the Duppy's Hole—though some red rays, tinting the tops of the trees upon the summit of the cliff, told that the orb of day was still above the horizon.

Extended on his couch, Chakra saw not this. His hut was dark, the door being shut close; but through the interstices of the bamboos he could see to some distance outside, and perceive that twilight was fast deepening among the trees. The cry of the bittern, coming up from the lagoon, the shriek of the *potoo*, heard through the sough of the cataract, and the hoot of the great-eared owl—all three voices of the night—reaching his ears, admonished him that his hour of action had arrived.

Springing from his couch, and giving utterance to his favourite ejaculation, he sat about preparing himself for the adventure of the night.

His first thought was about something to eat, and his eyes fell upon the skillet, standing where he had left it, near the middle of the floor. It still contained a quantity of the miscellaneous stew—enough for a meal.

" Woan do eat um cold," he muttered, proceeding to kindle a fire, " not fo' de second time. Gib me de ager chills, it wud. Mus' fortify de belly wi' someting warm—else a no be fit do de work dat am to be done."

The kindling of the fire, warming up of the pepper-pot, and its subsequent consumption, were three operations that did not take Chakra any very great amount of time. They were all over just as the darkness of night descended over the earth.

" Now fo' get ready de signal," soliloquised he, moving about over the floor of his hut, and looking into crannies and corners, as if in search of some object.

" As de good luck hab it, dar be no moon to-night—least ways, till after midnight. After den dare be plenty ob dark fo' Adam to see de signal, and plenty fo' de odder bizzness at Moun' Wel'n'. Dar'll be light 'nuf 'bout dat ore 'fore we takes leab o' de place. Won't dat be a blaze? Whugh!

" Wha hab a put dat ere tellemgraff lamp ?" said he, still searching around the hut. " I'se fo'got all 'bout wha it am, so long since a use de darned ting. Muss be uner de bed. Ya—hya it am !"

As he said this, he drew from under the bamboo bedstead a gourd shell, of nearly egg-shape, but of the dimensions of a large melon. It had a long, tapering shank—part of the fruit itself, where the pericarp narrowed towards its peduncle—and through this a string had been passed, by which the gourd could be suspended upon a peg.

Holding it by the handle, he raised the shell to the light of his lard lamp, already kindled, and stood for some time silently inspecting it.

The gourd was not perfect—that is, it was no longer a mere empty shell, but a manufactured article, containing within a most singular apparatus. On one side appeared a hole, several inches in diameter, and cut in a shape nearly pyramidal, the base being above the thick end of the oval, and the apex, somewhat blunt, or truncated, extending towards the shank.

Up to the level of the opening the shell was filled with lard, in the middle of which appeared a wick of silk cotton staple ; and behind this were two bits of broken looking-glass, set slanting to each other.

The whole apparatus bore some resemblance to a reflecting lamp ; and that was in reality the purpose for which the rude contrivance had been constructed.

After a careful examination, its owner appeared to be satisfied that it was in good order ; and having " trimmed" it, by adding a little fresh lard, and straightening up the wick, he set the lamp aside, and proceeded with the preparation of some other paraphernalia necessary for the night's expedition.

A stick, some four feet in length, and a piece of strong cord, were the next articles procured ; and these were also put to one side,

To these succeeded a long-bladed knife, and a stout pistol, with flint lock which the Coromantee loaded and primed with great care. Both were stuck behind a belt which he had already buckled around his ribs, under the skin kaross.

" A doan 'ticipate," said he, as he armed himself with these formadable weapons, " dar a gwine be much need fo' eider ob 'em. Dar aint nob'by down dar am like show fight. Dat ere gran' buckra ob late came to Moun Welc'm' do say he be 'fraid ob de shadda ob daggar ; an' as fo 'de brack folks, de look ob dese weapon be suffishient fo' dem. Ef dat woan do, den a trow off my mask. De sight ob ole Chakra, dat dribe 'em into fits. Dat send ebbery nigga on de plantashun into de middle ob next week. Whugh !"

Another weapon appeared to be wanting, in the shape of a large black bottle, containing rum. With this the Coromantee soon supplied himself, drawing one out from its secret hiding-place, and holding it before the light, to make sure that it was full.

" Dis bottle, " said he as he thrust it into a pouch in his kaross, " I hab kep fo' dis 'pecial 'casion ; it am de bess weapon fo' my purpose. When dem fellas get dar dose ob de rum, dar'll be no back out in 'em den. Golly !" he added, glancing out, and seeing that it was now quite dark, " a muss be gone fro' hya. By de time ole Adams sees de tellemgraph an' gets 'cross dem 'ere mountains, it be 'ate 'nuf for de bizness to begin." Finishing with this reflection, the sable conjuror took up his "telegraphic apparatus,'" and, stepping over the threshold, hurried away from the hut.

———

CHAPTER CVIII.

SETTING THE SIGNAL.

THE short tropic twilight had passed, and night had descended upon the island of Jamaica. It promised to be a night of deepest darkness. The moon would not rise before midnight; and even then she might not be seen, as the canopy was covered with a thick curtain of black cumulous clouds, through which neither star nor speck of the blue sky was visible.

Alike lay valleys and mountains, shrouded in amorphorus darkness; and even the Jumbé Rock—the highest and most conspicuous summit for miles around—was wrapped in complete obscurity. Its vitreous flanks no longer sparkled in the light, since there was none; and its dark mass was so dimly outlined against the equally sombre background of the sky, as to be invisible from the valley below.

The form of a man groping his way up the narrow ravine that debouched upon the summit of the rock, could not have been distinguished much less the black hue of his skin, the deformity that marked his figure or the hideous aspect of his countenance. And yet a man so characterised climbed up there, about half-an-hour after the going down of the sun. It need scarce be said that that man was Chakra, the Coromantee. Who else would be seeking the Jumbé Rock at that hour? What was his errand up there? Let the sequal declare. On setting foot upon the platform, he undid the knot that fastened the skin mantle over his shoulders; and then taking off the garment, he spread it out upon the rock. The stick he had brought up with him he placed along one edge, and there made it fast with some pieces of string. When this was accomplished, he lifted both stick and cloak from the rock, and proceeding to the palm, he laid the stick transversely across the stem, at about the height of his own hand, and then lashed it fast to the tree. The karose now hung down the stem, in a spread-position, the transverse stick keeping it extended to its full width.

While arranging it thus, Chakra evidently had an eye to the direction —that is, the plane represented by the spread garment had one face fronting the valley of Mount Welcome and the cultivated lowlands between that and Montego Bay, while the reverse side was turned toward the " black grounds" of Trelawney—a tract of wild country in which not a single estate, plantation, or penn had been established, and where no such thing as a white settlement existed. In this solitude, however, there were *black* colonies of a peculiar kind; for that was the favourite haunt of the absconded slave—the lurking-place of the outlaw—the retreat of the runaway.

There, even, might the assassin find an asylum, secure from the pur-

suit of justice. There had he found it: for among those dark forest
clad mountains more than one murderer made his dwelling.

Robbers there were many—even existing in organised bands, and
holding the authorities of the island at defiance. All these circumstances
were known to Chakra; and some of the robbers, too, were known to him
.- —some of the fiercest who followed that free calling. It was to communicate with one of these bands that the preparations of the myal-man were
being made. Chakra was preparing the signal.

Satisfied that the skin cloak was extended in the proper direction, the
Coromantee next took up his reflector-lamp; and having attached it
against that side of the kaross facing towards the mountains, he took out
his flint, steel and tinder, and, after striking a light, set the wick on fire

In an instant the lamp burned brightly, and the light, reflected from the
bits of looking-glass, might have been seen from the back country to the
distance of many miles; while at the same time, it was completely screened from any eye looking from the side of the plantations. The projecting edges of the calabash hindered the rays from passing to either side;
while the interposed disc of the spread kaross further prevented the
"sheen" that otherwise might have betrayed the presence of the signal.

It was not meant for the eyes of honest men in the direction of Montego Bay, but for those of the robbers among the far hills of Trelawney.

"Jess de sort ob night fo' dem see it, muttered the myal-man, as with
folded arms he stood contemplating the fight. "De sky brack as de
debbil's pitch-pot. Ole Adam, he sure hab some 'un on de look-out. De
sure see 'im soon."

Chakra never looked more hideous than at that moment.

Stripped of the ample garment, that to some extent aided in concealing
his deformity; a scant shirt, of course crimson flannel, alone covering the
hunch; most part of his body naked, exposing to the strong light of the
reflector his black currugated skin; the aspect of his ferocious features
compressed by the snake-encircled turban upon his temples, the long-
bladed knife and pistol appearing in his waist-belt—all combined to produce a fearful picture, that could not fail to strike terror into whoever
should have the misfortune to behold it.

Standing immovable under the glare of the lamp, his mis-shapen figure
projected across the surface of the summit platform, he might easily
have been mistaken for a personification of the fiend—that African fiend
—after whom the rock had been named.

In this situation he remained, observing perfect silence, and with his
eyes eagerly bent upon the distant mountains, dimly discernable through
the deep obscurity of the night. Only for a few minutes was this silence
preserved, and the attitude of repose in which he had placed himself.

"Whugh!" he exclaimed, dropping his arms out of their fold, as if to
set about some action. "I know'd dey wud soon see um. Yonner go
de answer!"

As he spoke, a bright light was seen suddenly blazing up on the top
of a distant eminence, which was suddenly extinguished.

After a short interval another, exactly similar, appeared in the same
place, and in a similar manner went out again; and then, when an equal
interval had elapsed, a third.

All three resembled flashes produced by powder ignited in a loose heap.

The moment the third response had been given to his signal, the Coromantee stepped up to his reflector and blew out the light.

"Dar's no use fo' you any mo'," said he, apostrophising the lamp; "dar am some danger keepin' you dar. B'side, it am a gettin' cold up h.ya. A want my ole cloak."

So saying, he took down the reflector, and after it the kaross; and, separating the latter from the piece of stick, he once more suspended the garment around his shoulders. This done he moved forward to the front of the platform; and dropping his legs over, sat down upon the edge of the rock.

CHAPTER CIX.

THE CRY OF THE SOLITAIRE.

FROM the spot where he had seated himself, the mansion of Mount Welcome was in view—that is, it would have been, had it been day-time, or even a moonlight night. As it was, however, darkness veiled the whole valley under its opaque shadows; and the situation of the house could only have been guessed at had it not been for the light streaming through the jalousied windows. These revealed its position to the eyes of the Coromantee.

More than one window showed light—several that were side by side giving out a strong glare. These Chakra knew to be the side windows of the great hall, or drawing-room. Its front windows could not be seen from the Jumbé Rock: since they faced towards the valley and not to the mountain.

The myal-man knew all this. A forty years' residence on the estate of Mount Welcome had rendered perfectly accurate his knowledge of the topography of the place.

So much light shining out suggested the idea of cheerfulness, as if company were entertained within.

"Whugh!" ejaculated Chakra, as his eye caught the lights. "Doan look berry much like day war grievin'. Dey can't hab heer'd o' dat 'fair yet. P'raps de hab take de body to de plantashun ob Content? Leetle dey know down dar wha's been done. Leetle dey dream dat de proud massr ob dat ere Buff am jess at dis minnit a cold corpus. Da's no house ob mournin.' Dar's feas'in a gwine on da', a be boun'? Never mind! nebba mind! Patience, olo nigga! maybe you come in fo' share ob dem wittle 'fore de gits cold; and maybe you hab share ob de dishes on which do wittle am sa'v'd up—de forks an' de 'poons, an de silber plate gener-umly. Daat *will* be a haul. Whugh!

"But wha care I fo' de forks an' de 'poons? Nuffin! Dar's but one ting a care fo', an' dat am more dan silber, more na gold, more na Moun' Wel:'m, itself! Dat am de Lilly Quasheba. Whugh! A hab lub her fo' many long year—lub her more'n ebba; yes, a lub her wi' de whole 'trength ob my soul. Once a git dat bowfu' gal in dese arms, a no care for de forks and de 'poons. Ole Adam be welc'm take all dem rubbish. " No," continued he, after a pause, apparently relenting of his liber al

ity; " dat no do, neider. A soon need boaf de forks aud de 'poons. A'll want him fo' de housekeepin'. A'll want de silber an' de gold to buy odder ting. Muss hab m' share 'long wi'de ress.

" Wha am de bess place take my wife to ?" muttered the intended hus- band, continuing the same strain of reflections. " Muss leab de Duppy

'Iole. Dat place no longer safe. Too near de ole plantashun. Boun to be a debbil ob a rumpus after she carried 'way—daat are ef dey b'lieve she am carried away. Nebba mind. A know how manage dat!"

At this moment the reflections of the Coromantee were interrupted by a sound that caused him to draw his legs upon the rock, and assume an attitude as if about to spring to his feet.

At the repetition of the sound, he started up, and rapidly re-crossed to the opposite side.

At the point where the upward path debouched upon the platform, he stopped to listen. For the third time the sound was repeated.

There was nothing strange in it—at least, to ears familiar with the voices of a Jamaica forest. It was the common yet peculiar bird—the *solitaire*. The only thing strange was to hear it at that hour of the night. It was not the time when the soft and flute-like note of the *solitaire* should fall upon the ear of the forest wanderer. Hearing it at that hour was 'by no means strange to Chakra. It was not that which had startled him from his seat, and caused him to cross quickly to the other side of the platform. On the contrary, it was because he knew that which he had heard was *not* the note of the *solitaire*, but a counterfeit call from his confederate, Adam !

Chakra's private slogan was different—more mournful and less musical. It was an imitation of that melancholy utterance heard at night from the sedgy shores of the dark lagoon—the cry of the wailing bittern. With a small reed applied to his lips, the Coromantee produced an exact im- itation of this cry, and then remained silent, awaiting the result. At the bottom of the ravine could be heard a murmur of voices, as if several men were together, talking in guarded tones. Following this came a sound of scratching against the stones, and a rustling of branches, each moment becoming more distinct. Shortly after, the form of a man em- erged out of the shadowy cleft, stepping cautiously upon the platform. Another followed; and another, until six in all stood upon the sum- mit of the rock.

" Dat you, brodder Adam ?" said Chakra, stepping forward to receive the first who presented himself at the head of the sloping path.

" Ya—ya! Am it Chakra ?"

" Dat same ole nigga."

" All right, kommarade. We've see yar signal as soon as it war hoist- ed. We wan't long a comin', war we ?"

" Berry quick. A din't 'speck ye fo' half an hour mo'."

" Well, now we're hya, whart's the game ? I hope dar's a good big stake to play for ! Our stock of stuff wants replenishin' berry badly. We haven't had de chance of a job fo' more dan a month. We're a most in want ' wittles !"

" Wittles !" exclaimed the myal-man, laying a scornful emphasis on the
word. " Dar's a ting for ye do dis night dat'll gib ye mo' dan wittle—it
gib you wealth—ebbery one ob ye. Wugh !"

" Good !" ejaculated Adam, simultaneously with a chorus of like exclamations ; " glad to hear dat ere bit o' intelligence. Am it dat ere little
job you speak me 'bout last time I see you? Dat it, ole humpy?"

" Dat same," laconically answered Chakra, " only wi' dis diffurence,'
added he ; dat a call um de big job in'tead of de little un."

" Big or little," rejoined the other, " we've come ready to do it—you see
we hab ?"

The speaker, who appeared to be the leader of the party who accompanied him, pointed to the others as he made this remark.

The hint was scarce regarded by Chakra. Notwithstanding the murky
gloom that enveloped the forms of Adam and his companions, the myal-
man could see that they were all armed and equipped, though in the most
varied and uncouth fashions. The weapons of no two were alike. One
carried an old musket, red with dust; another, a fowling-piece, in like
condition. Others were provided with pistols, and nearly all had long
knives, or *machetes*. Thus provided, it was scarce probable that the job
for whose execution Chakra had summoned them could be one of a pacific
character.

Had a light been thrown upon the group that surrounded Chakra, it
would have revealed a collection of faces—each provided with a set of
features but little less sinister than those of Chakra himself. In not one
of them would have been found a line indicative of either peace or mercy
—for it was the band of black robber Adam, celebrated as the most notorious cut-throats in the island.

Chakra expressed no surprise at seeing them armed, nor felt any. He
had expected it; and the flourish which their leader had made of this fact
was only intended to make manifest that they were ready for the ordinary
requirements of their vocation.

Eagerly willing were they for the extremest action; but, in order to
make more certain of their compliance, Chakra thought it prudent to ply
them with a little rum.

" Ma friens," said he, in an affectionate tone, " you hab had de fatigue
of a long walk troo the darkness ob de night. A hab got hya a leetle
drop ob someting dat's berry good fo' keep de cold out ob you. 'Pose
we all take a wet from dis bottle ?"

To this proposition there was a general assent, expressed in varied
phraseology. There was no teetotaller in that crowd of worthies.

Chakra had not thought of providing himself with either drinking-cup
or calabash ; but the want was scarcely felt. The robbers each in turn
refreshed himself directly from the neck of the bottle, until the rum ran
out.

" Well, ole humpy," said Adam, drawing Chakra aside, and speaking in
that familiar phrase that betokened a thickness of thieves between them.
" I suppose the chance you spoke 'bout hab come round at las'?"

" Da's a fack, brodder Adam. I ha' come now."

" De great buckra gone from home?"

" He gone from home, and gone to house. Ha! ha!"

" Come, dat's a riddle. What you mean by gone to home?"

" To 'im long home. Da's wha' I mean."

" Ha!" exclaimed Adam; " you don't say the Cussos——"

" Nebber mind 'bout de Cussus now, brodder Adam. Dat you know
all 'bout atterwards. It am de Cussus silber plate dat consarn you now;
and dar's no time to was'e in p'laverin'. By de time we gets down da,
an' puts on de masks, dey'll be a gwine to bed. Better dey wa' gone to
bed ; but by dat time you see, de moon 'ud be up, an' fo' all dese clouds
mout shine out. Dat, as you know, won't nebba do. We must 'ticipate
de rising o'b de moon."

" True enuf. All right! I'm ready, and so are de rest."

" Den foller me, all ob you. We can plan de mode ob 'tack as we trabbel 'long. Plenty ob time fo' dat, when we find out how de land lie down
below. Foller me!"

And with this injunction, the Coromantee commenced descending the
ravine, followed by Adam and his band of burglars.

CHAPTER CX.

A SAD PROCESSION.

On that same evening, about half-an-hour before sunset, a singular procession was seen moving along the Carrion Crow Road, in the direction
of Mount Welcome. Its slow progress, with the staid looks and gestures of those who composed the procession, betokened it to be one of a
melancholy character.

A rude litter, carried upon the shoulders of four men, confirmed this
impression ; more especially when the eye rested upon a human form
stretched along the litter, and which could easily be identified as a dead
body, notwithstanding the camlet cloak that covered it.

There were ten individuals forming this funeral " cortége ;" though all
were not mourners. Two were on horseback, a little in advance of the
rest. Four followed carrying the litter ; while close behind these came
four others, two and two—the foremost pair being lashed arm in arm to
one another—each also with his hands tied behind his back, and both
evidently prisoners. The two that brought up the rear appeared to be
guarding them.

The individuals composing this mournful procession may be easily
identified.

The two riding in advance were Herbert Vaughan and the Maroon
captain ; the horses they bestrode being the same that had passed over
that road the day before, carrying the Custos and his negro attendant.
The prisoners were the Spanish caçadores—their guards, Quaco and the
before-mentioned attendant; while the four men bearing the body were
slaves belonging to the plantation of Content.

It need scarce be added that the corpse, stretched stark and stiff upon
the litter, was all that remained of the grand Custos Vaughan.

Strictly describing them, not one of the procession party could be
called a mourner. None of them had any reason to be greatly aggrieved
by the fate that had befallen the owner of Mount Welcome—not even

his relative. Notwithstanding this absence of a cause for grief, 'he faces of all—the prisoners excepted—wore a look of decent gravity becoming the occasion.

Perhaps the nephew would have more keenly felt the situation—for now that his uncle was no more, every spark of hostility had become extinguished—perhaps he might even have mourned, but for certain circum stances that had just come to his knowledge ; and which had the effect not only to counteract within his heart all tendency towards sorrow, but almost to overpower it with joy.

It was only with an effort, therefore, that he could preserve upon his features that expression of sadness, due to the melancholy position in which he was placed.

Despite the presence of death, his heart was at that moment filled with a secret satisfaction—so sweet that he could not deny himself its indulgence. The source of satisfaction may be easily traced. It will be found in the information communicated to him by the Maroon captain. During their journey of the preceeding day, their vigil of the night, and still further their long slow march of that morning, Cubina had made known to him many circumstances of which he had been hitherto ignorant; among other items of intelligence, one the most interesting that language could have imparted.

It need scarce be said what this was. It may be guessed at by recalling the conversation between the Maroon and his mistress Yola, occurring at the last tryst under the *ceiba*—that part of it which related to the Lilly Quasheba. Though Cubina's knowledge was only second-hand, it was sufficiently definite to inspire Herbert with hope—something more than hope ; and hence that secret joy whose outward manifestation he found it difficult to suppress.

Every word of the conversation that had passed between the Maroon and his mistress—every word that referred to *her* mistress—Cubina had been compelled to repeat over and over again ; till Herbert knew it as well as if he had been present during the dialogue. No wonder he was not in a condition to feel very profoundly for the sad fate that had befallen his uncle—hitherto only known to him as a relative harsh an l hostile.

Other secrets had Cubina disclosed to him—among the rest, the true character of his patron, Jessuron—which Herbert had already begun to suspect, and which was now revealed to him in all its hideous wicked-ness. The history of the Foolah prince—hitherto unknown to Herbert—besides his own experiences during the last twenty-four hours, were sufficient to confirm any suspicion that might point to Jacob Jessuron. Though it was plain that the two prisoners in the custody of Quaco had not actually assassinated the Custos, it was equally clear that such had been their intention, anticipated by a death of another kind. This both Cubina and Herbert conjectured to have proceeded from the same hand — the hand of Herbert's *ci-devant* host.

The phrase is appropriate. Long before Herbert had heard one half of Cubina's disclosures, he had resolved never more voluntarily to set foot in the Happy Valley—much less return to seek shelter under the roof of Jessuron.

If he should hereafter have aught to do with the Israelite, it would be

in the course of justice; as avenger of the death of his murdered relative. That Loftus Vaughan was the victim of assassination neither he
nor the Maroon for a moment doubted. The conversation which the
latter had listened to between Chakra and the Jew—and which, unfortunately, at the time he had not clearly comprehended—was no longer
mysterious; only its motive remained so. The deed itself had now furnished the terrible interpretation.

Neither Herbert nor Cubina had any idea of permitting the matter to
drop. An event of such fearful significance called for the fullest investigation; and they were now proceeding with the preliminary step—
carrying the body to Mount Welcome, in order that the authorities might
be called together, and an inquest instituted.

How different were the feelings of Herbert to those he experienced
on his former and first approach to the mansion of his haughty relative!
He was now the victim of emotions so varied and mingled as to defy
description!

CHAPTER CXI.

THE ABDUCTION.

To Chakra, viewing them from the summit of the Jumbé Rock, the well-
lighted windows of Mount Welcome had proclaimed the presence of
company within the mansion. In this, however, the Coromantee was
mistaken. In the past such an appearance might have had that signification, or up to a very late period—that is, up to the date of the arrival of
the distinguished Smythje. Since the latter had become the guest of
Mount Welcome, however, the illuminations of the mansion with chandelier and candelabra was not only not unusual, but had been the nightly
practice.

This was Mr. Vaughan's pleasure; which, in his absence, the house
steward had injunctions to carry out. The grand hall was only lit up as
usual, its lustrous floor glistening in the brilliant light, while the profusion of cut glass and silver plate sparkled upon the side-boards, loudly
proclaiming the opulence of the planter. There was no strange company
present—none expected—no one who did not belong to the family, except
Mr. Smythje; and he could scarcely be considered a stranger. Rather
might he be regarded—for the time at least—as the master of the mansion: since in that charge had the Custos left him.

The only individuals occupying this splendid apartment were Smythje
and the young mistress of Mount Welcome—both yet ignorant of what
had occurred upon the Savannah Road—that fearful event which had
left Kate Vaughan a fatherless orphan, at the same time depriving her of
the proud title we have just bestowed upon her.

Yola, her attendant, went and came at intervals, and Thoms occasionally presented himself in the apartment, in obedience to a summons from
his master.

Notwithstanding the absence of company, Smythje was in full evening
dress—body-coat, breeches, silk stockings, and pumps, with silver

buckles. It was his custom to dress, or be dressed, every evening—a custom so scrupulously observed, that had there been no one in the house except the negro domestics of the establishment, Smythje would have appeared in full fashionable costume all the same. With him the exigencies of fashion were as rigorous as to a holy friar would be the observances of his religion.

The gentleman was in high spirits—merry, indeed; and, strange to say, his companion was less melancholy than of late. No doubt this had given him his cue for mirth.

Why she had been enabled to escape from her habitual dejection was not known to Smythje; but he was fain to attribute the improvement in her spirits to the near prospect of that pleasant ceremony which in a few days must indubitably take place. In a week, or a fortnight at most, Mr. Vaughan might be expected back; and then it was understood by all—tacitly by the young lady herself—that the union of Mount Welcome and Montagu Castle should be no longer delayed.

Smythje had even begun to talk of the wedding *trousseau;* of the honeymoon tour—which was to extend to the grand metropolis; and as Kate, at his request, seated herself to the harp, suggesting a musical conversation, he commenced enlarging upon the theme of the grand " opwa," and its attractions—so dear and delightful to himself.

This sort of talk, upon other occasions, had invariably the effect of making the listener more sad; but, strange to say, on that evening, it produced no such a disagreeable consequence. Kate's fingers flitted over the strings of the instrument, drawing music from them that was far from melancholy.

In truth, the young creole was not listening to the *couleur de rose* descriptions of the "metwopolis," and its "opwa," which Smythje was so strenuously endeavouring to impart to her.

Though seated by the harp, and striking mechanically upon its strings, she was dwelling upon thoughts of a far different character—thoughts suggested by some further intelligence which Yola had communicated to her, and which was the true source of that joy—perhaps but a transitory gleam—that overspread her countenance.

Little did Kate Vaughan suspect that the corpse of her father—lying cold and lifeless upon a stretcher, and surrounded by strange mourners—was at that moment scarce five miles distant from where she sat, and slowly approaching the now masterless mansion of Mount Welcome!

Little did she suspect, while making that music for Smythje, that from another direction, monsters in human form were moving towards that mansion—their dark shadows projected across the glare of the window-lights—now stationary, now flitting stealthily onward—at each progressive movement drawing nearer and nearer to the walls!

She saw not these shadowy, demon-like men—had no suspicion either of their approach or intent—an intent which comprehended robbery, rapine of a far more fearful kind—murder, if need be.

Neither its mistress, neither Smythje, nor any one else of Mount Welcome, saw or suspected this mysterious circumvallation, until the movement had been successfully executed.

Not a word of warning, not a sign or gesture, was given to the occupants of the apartment, until, with wild unearthly yells, half-a-dozen fiend-like forms—men of horrid aspect—some with black masks—others with naked visage even more hideous to behold—burst into the grand hall, and commenced the work of pillage.

One of gigantic size, masked from crown to throat, and wrapped in an ample covering of skin—though not sufficient to conceal the deformity of a hunched back—rushed directly up to where the fair musician was seated; and, dashing the harp to one side, seized upon her wrist before she could disengage herself from her chair.

" Whugh !" came the ejaculation, in loud aspirate, from behind the mask, " I'se got ye at lass, ma Lilly Quasheba—atter many's de yea' ob longin' fo' hab ye. Ef de quaderoom, ya mudder, she 'cape and 'corn me, I'se take care de dauter doan' get the same chance. You come 'long wi' me !"

And as the ravisher pronounced these words, he commenced dragging his shrieking victim across the room, towards the stair entrance.

Smythje's half irresolute interposition was of no avail. With one sweep of his long flail-like arm, he in the skin cloak sent the exquisite sprawling upon the floor.

The terrified cockney no longer thought of resistance ; but after scrambling awhile over the polished planks at length succeeded in re-gaining his feet. Then, without waiting to receive a second knock-down, he shot out through the open doorway, and, descending the stone stairs, in a couple of skips disappeared in the darkness below.

Meanwhile, the alarm had been communicated to the kitchen, and all over the house. Shouts of surprise were succeeded by screams of terror. The domestics came running in from all directions ; but a shot or two from the muskets and pistols of the black burglars, fired for the purpose of increasing the confusion, scattered the whole establishment of servants, Thoms among the rest, and sent them in full flight towards the sugar works and the negro village beyond.

In less than a score of seconds, Adam and his confederates had the mansion to themselves.

It was but the work of a few minutes to fling open the buffets and side-boards, and plunder them of their most valuable contents. In less than a quarter of an hour the black burglars had finished their " job," and were ready to depart.

While his confederates were thus engaged, Chakra had secured his victim at the bottom of the front stairway, where he was impatiently awaiting the completion of the pillage. Though determined upon having his share of the booty, he cared less for that than for the gratification of that wicked desire that had so long possessed his savage soul—so long by circumstances restrained.

Notwithstanding his eagerness for this demoniac indulgence, he still possessed a certain degree of prudence. As soon as Adam and his associates made their appearance, loaded with spoils, he placed his prisoner under the charge of one of the robbers, and, commanding the others to follow him, rapidly re-ascended the stairway, and once more entered the plundered apartment.

In an incredibly short space of time the harp, the chairs, the ottomans, and other articles of light furniture, were piled up in the middle of the floor. The jalousies were wrenched from their fastenings, flung upon the heap, and then set on fire.

Quick as tinder the dry wood blazed up; and in five minutes the noble mansion of Mount Welcome was in flames!

In five minutes more, under the red glare, flung far out into the distant fields, the robbers were seen, slowly and laboriously seeking conceal-ment within the shadows beyond—six of them burdened with shining utensils, that gave back the gleams of the blazing mansion; while the seventh, the most formidable figure of all, carried in his arms an object of a far different kind—the body of a beautiful woman—the fainting form of Lilly Quasheba!

CHAPTER CXII.

BURGLARS! ROBBERS! MURDERERS!

In solemn pace the procession which accompanied the corpse of Custos Vaughan moved silently on along the lonely road. The Jumbé Rock was now in sight, encarmined by the last rays of the sinking sun. Beyond, lay Mount Welcome—a house to which that sad 'cortége' was about to carry the cue for wailing and desolation.

Ah! little dreamt they who composed it, that the demon was already there before them—if not of death, of a doom equally as dark.

Could Herbert only have known that at that moment the beautiful being he loved with his whole heart, and now more than ever—she who loved him, was struggling in the arms——

No matter. The terrible truth will reach him but too soon. It will meet him on his way. In another hour the sweet dreams in which, throughout that long day, he has been indulging, will meet with a dread dissipation.

At a turning of the road there stood several gigantic trees, offering a grand canopy of foliage. Under these the party halted, by the joint command of Herbert and Cubina, who at the same moment dismounted from their horses.

It was not the shade that had tempted them: for the sun had now gone down. Nor yet that the bearers might obtain rest. The men were strong, and the wasted form was far from being a heavy burden. It was not for that reason that the halt had been ordered; but on account of a thought that had suggested itself to Herbert, and which was approved of by Cubina.

It was the apprehension of the dread impression which their arriva-might produce at Mount Welcome—of course, on her whose father's corpse they were carrying.

They had stopped to consider what was best to be done.

A plan soon suggested itself. A messenger could be sent forward upon one of the horses to communicate the sad tidings to Trusty, the overseer, and through him the melancholy news might be more gradually made known to her whom it most concerned.

Herbert would have gone himself; but was hindered by certain delicate considerations, based on the conflicting emotions that were stirring within him.

It mattered little who should bear the melancholy tidings to Trusty ; and tho negro attendant was finally chosen.

The man received his instructions; and, having mounted his own horse, rode off at such speed as the darkness, now down upon the earth, would permit.

For another hour the party remained in the place where they had halted, to give time for the messenger to execute his commission. Then once more taking the road, they moved forward at a slow pace, Herbert alongside Cubina—now a-foot, and leading the horse upon which he had hitherto ridden.

Quaco alone guarded the prisoners ; a duty to which the Maroon lieu- tenant was quite equal, and which he had rendered the more easy of ac- complishment, by pressing into his service a piece of rope, attached round the neck of the one that was nearest, and which, held halter- fashion in his hand, enabled him to prevent either of them from straying in the darkness. Neither, however, made any attempt to escape : know- ing, as both did, that the slightest movement in that direction would cost them a " thwack" from a stout cudgel—an additional implement carried in the hands of Quaco.

In this way the ' cortége' had proceeded for some half-mile or so be- yond its last resting-place, when it was again brought to a halt by the orders of those in the lead.

The cause of this interruption was declared to all of the party at once. All heard the hoof-strokes of a horse coming rapidly along the road, and *from* the opposite direction to that in which they were moving.

Going as he appeared to be, in full gallop, in five minutes more, or in half the time, the horseman should be in their midst.

Was he a stranger ? Or could it be their own messenger coming back ? He had not been directed to return. It was deemed sufficient for him to see Mr. Trusty, and make known the news which he had been intrusted to communicate.

It was not without a feeling of surprise, therefore, as the horseman dashed forward upon the ground, and pulled up in front of the procession that Herbert and Cubina recognised the returned attendant.

He left them no time to speculate on the mystery of his re-appearance. The white froth upon the flanks of his steed, shining through the gloom, told of fast riding ; while the stammering and terrified accents in which the man proclaimed the purpose of his return, rendered more startling the news he had come to communicate.

Mount Welcome was, at that moment, attacked by a band of burglars, robbers, and murderers !

There were men in masks, and men without them—equally terrible to look upon. They were plundering the great hall, had murdered Mr. Smythje, were ill-treating the young mistress of the mansion, and firing guns and pistols at every one who came in their way !

The messenger had not stayed to see Mr. Trusty. He had learnt all this from the domestics, who were hurrying in flight from the mansion. Confounded by the shouting and shots he had himself heard, and thinking that the likeliest chance of assistance would be found in the party he had just left—and which he believed to be much nearer—he had galloped back along the road.

These were the main facts of the attendant's story---not communicated, however, with any regard to sequence, but in the most incoherent manner and liberally interpersed with exclamations of alarm.

It was a fearful tale, and fell with a terrible effect upon the ears of those to whom it was told—Herbert and Cubina.

Burglars — robbers — murderers! Mr. Smythje killed! The young mistress of Mount Welcome in the act of being abused! And Yola! She, too——

"Quaco!" cried the Maroon captain, rushing to the rear, and addressing himself to his lieutenant, "think you our men can hear us from here? Sound your horn on the instant: your blast is stronger than mine. There is trouble at Mount Welcome. We may need every man of them. Quick —quick!"

"The devil!" cried Quaco, dropping his hold of the halter, and raising the horn to his mouth, "I'll make them hear, if they're in the island of Jamaica. You keep your ground, ye pair of John Crows!" he added, as he held the horn an inch or two from his lips. "If either of you budge a foot out of your places, I'll send a brace of bullets through your stinkin' carcadges, and stop you thataway. See if I don't."

And with this emphatic admonition, the colossus applied the horn to his mouth, and blew a blast that might have been heard for miles.

In echoes it rang from the sides of the Jumbé Rock, and from many a peak lying far beyond. So loud and shrill rang it, that one might almost have believed in Quaco's affirmation : that it would be heard to the extremities of the island!

At all events, it was heard by some not so far off: for scarce had its echoes ceased to reverberate, when a half dozen similar sounds, proceeding from different directions, and apparently from different distances, came back in response.

Cubina waited not to hear their repetition.

"Enough!" cried he, " there are half-a-dozen of them anyhow. That will no doubt be enough. You Quaco, stay here till they come up, and then follow to Mount Welcome. Sound again, to direct them; and see that these two murderous villains don't escape you."

" Hadn't I better put a brace of bullets through them ?" naively inquired Quaco. "It'll save trouble if I do that. What say you, Capen Cubina ?"

"No, no! Quaco. Justice will settle accounts with them. Bring them on along with you ; and follow as soon as our men get up!"

Before Quaco could offer any further suggestions, the Maroon capatin had mounted the messenger's horse—Herbert having already leaped into the saddle of the other -and both, without further speech, rode forward as fast as their steeds could carry them.

CHAPTER CXIII.

DREAD CONJECTURES.

OBSERVING a profound silence, the two young men pressed forward. Neither liked to put question to the other. Each dreaded the answer the other might make—each was thinking only of the danger of her who was dearest to him.

They urged on their steeds with equal eagerness, for both were alike interested in the 'dénouement' of the dreadful drama, at that moment being enacted at the mansion of Mount Welcome.

Their reflections were similar, and similarly painful.

They might be too late? Ere they could arrive upon the scene the stage might be deserted—the tragedy played out—the players gone!

It needed not these thoughts to stimulate them to increased speed: they were already riding as if life or death rested on the issue. * *

They had neared the flank of the Jumbé mountain, and were heading for the ridge that separated the estates of Montagu Castle and Mount Welcome.

At this point the road debouched from the forest, and the ridge came in sight. At the same instant, a cry escaped from the lips of Cubina, as with a quick wrench he drew his horse to a halt.

Herbert echoed the cry of his comrade—at the same time imitating his action.

Neither thought of questioning the other. Both had halted under the same impulse. The evil omen had been seen simultaneously by both.

Over the summit of the ridge a yellow light glared, halo-like, against the sky.

" Fire !" exclaimed Cubina. " Just over Mount Welcome ! *Santa madre!* the mansion is in flames !"

" Oh, heavens !" cried Herbert; " we shall be too late !"

Not another word passed between the two horsemen. Stirred by the same instinct, they renewed their gallop ; and silently, side by side, urged their horses up the hill.

In a few minutes they had attained the summit of the ridge, whence they could command a full view of the valley of Mount Welcome.

The mansion *was* in flames!

There was no further utterance of surprise : that was past. It was scarce a conjecture which Cubina had pronounced, on seeing that glare against the sky, but a conviction ; and the crackling sounds which had assailed their ears, as they were riding upward to the crest of the ridge, had fully confirmed the event before their eyes looked on the fire itself.

There was no more a mansion of Mount Welcome. In its place a blazing pile—a broad sheet of flame, rising in gigantic jets to the sky, crowned with huge sparks and murky smoke, and accompanied by a con tinuous roaring and crackling of timbers, as if fiends were firing a *feu-de joie*, in the celebration of some terrible holocaust.

" Too late—too late !" muttered both the horsemen in the same breath ; and then, with despair on their faces and black fear in their hearts, they once more gave rein to their steeds ; and, riding recklessly down the slope, galloped on towards the conflagration.

In a few seconds' time they had crossed the inclosures, and halted in front of the blazing pile ; as near to it as their frayed steeds would con sent to carry them.

Both at the same instant sprang from their saddles ; and, with guns grasped and ready to defend themselves against whatever enemy, approached nearer and nearer to the building.

No one appeared in front of the house. They hurried round to the rear : no one was there. Equally deserted were the grounds and the garden Not a soul was to be seen anywhere—not a voice to be heard, except their own, as they called aloud ; and this only feebly, through the hissing and roaring of the flames.

Back and forth rushed the two men in eager haste, going round and round the house, and exploring every spot that might be expected to conceal either friend or foe. But in spite of their most eager search, and the constant summons of their shouts, not a creature appeared, and no response reached them.

For a moment they paused to consider.

It was evident the conflagration had been going on for some time. The upper storey—which was but a framework of light timber—was now nearly consumed, and only the stone-work below left standing. Over this the larger beams had fallen—no longer emitting flame, but lying transversely upon each other, charred, red, and smouldering.

On finding no one near the dwelling, Cubina and Herbert made for the works. These were all standing untouched ; and it was evident that no attempt had been made to fire them. Only the mansion had been given o the flames.

On arriving among the out-buildings, the two men again raised their voices ; but, as before, without receiving a reply.

Here everything was dark and silent as the tomb—a silence more expressive by contrast with the awe-inspiring sounds of the conflagration raging at a distance. Neither in the curing-house nor the mill, nor the mash-house nor the stable, could any one be discovered. Not an individual to be seen, not a voice to respond to their oft-repeated halloos.

On rushed they to the negro cabins ! Surely there some one would be found ? All could not have fled through fear of the robber-band ?

As the two men turned in the direction of the negro village, a figure started up in the path—having just emerged out of the bushes. In that semblance to the imp of darkness, seen under the distant glare of the conflagration, Herbert recognised his old acquaintance Quashie.

Quashie had already identified him.

" Oh, young massr !" cried the darkey, as he rose to his feet ; " de Buff em a blazin'! It be all burn up !"

" *Crambo !* tell us something w don't know !" impatiently demanded Cubina. " Who has set it on fire . Do you know that ?"

" Did you see the incendaries ?" hurriedly adde l Herbert.

" See who, massr ?"

" Those who set the house on fire ?" inquired Herbert, still speaking
with anxious haste.

" Yes—massr, I seed dem—when dey first rush up de front 'tair way."

" Well—speak quickly—who and what were they ? What were they
like ?"

" Law, massr, dey were like so many debbils. Dey were nigga men,
an' some had mask on dar faces. Folks say it war de Maroon ob de
mountains. Black Bet she deny dat, and say no. She say 'twar some
robbers ob de mountains, an' dat dey come fo' carry off——"

" Your young mistress ? Miss Vaughan ? Where ? where ?" inter
rupted Herbert, gasping out the unfinished interrogatory.

" And Yola, my lad ! Have you seen her ?" added Cubina.

" No, genlums," replied Quashie ; " I seen neider de young missa, no'
de brown gal Yola. Dey war boaf up in de great hall. I no go up dar
myseff. I'se feard dey'd kill dis chilo of he go up da. I stayed down
below, till I see Mr. 'Mythje a comin' down de stair. Lor—how he did
streak it down dem dere stone step. He run in under de arch below. I
guess he go hide dere. Den I took to ma heels, 'long wif de oder folk ;
an' we all go hide in de bushes. Massa Thom an' de house people dey
all run for de woods—dey none o'em nebber come back yet."

" Oh, heavens !" exclaimed Herbert, in a voice of anguish ; " can it be
possible ? You are sure," said he, once more appealing to the darkey,
" you are sure you saw nothing of your young mistress ?"

" Nor of Yola ?" asked the Maroon, equally as distressed as his com
panion.

" I decla' I didn't—neider o' 'em two," emphatically exclaimed Quashie :
" See yonner !" he added, pointing towards the burning pile, and speaking
in an accent of alarm. " Golly ! dey ant gone 'way yet—de robbers ! de
robbers !"

Herbert and Cubina, who, while in conversation with Quashie, had been
standing with their backs towards the fire, faced suddenly round. As
they did so they perceived several dark forms moving between them and
the bright background of the flames ; their shadows projected in gigantic
outlines up to the spot where the spectators stood. There were about
half-a-dozen in all—just about the number at which Quashie had roughly
estimated the incendiaries.

Both sprang forward regardless of consequences, resolved upon knowing the worst ; and, if their apprehensions should prove true, determined
upon death or vengeance.

CHAPTER CXIV.

SMYTHJE STILL LIVING!

WITH their pieces cocked, and ready for instant execution, Cubina and Herbert was pressing to get within range; when the notes of a horn, sounded by one of the men before the fire, came swelling upon their ears.

The sounds were re-assuring. Cubina new the signal of his lieutenant, and they were now near enough to recognise the colossal Quaco standing in the glare of red light, surrounded by some half-dozen of his comrades.

Quaco had left the corpse upon the road, also the prisoners well guarded by a couple of his followers; and—thinking he might be wanted at Mount Welcome—had hurried forward close upon the heels of the horsemen.

This accession of strength might have proved useful had the enemy been upon the ground. Where were the robbers—the incendiaries—perhaps the murderers? Where was Miss Vaughan? Where the maid Yola?

Had they escaped among the domestics? or ——

The alternative thought was too horrible for utterance. Neither Herbert nor Cubina could trust themselves to give speech to it; only in their minds did the interrogatory shape itself: *had they perished in the flames?*

Fearful as was the thought, it could not fail to be entertained; and in the solemn silence which the reflection produced, all stood hopelessly gazing upon the ruthless fire that was fast reducing the noble mansion to a shapeless and mouldering ruin.

At that moment the stillness was interrupted by a voice proceeding from an unexpected quarter. It appeared to come from out the great arched vault under the stone stairway, from a corner shrouded in comparative darkness. It was partly an exclamation, partly a groan.

Quaco was the first to seek an explanation. Seizing a fagot that still flamed, he rushed under the archway regardless of the scorching heat.

Herbert and Cubina quickly followed, and all three stood within the vault.

Quaco waved the torch in front of his body, to illuminate the place. The eyes of all three simultaneously rested upon an object—that, at any other time, might have elicited from them peals of laughter.

In the corner of the vault stood a half-hogshead, or large tub—its head covered with a heavy lid. Near the upper edge a large square hole had been sawed out; so that a hand containing a quart measure might be inserted, without the necessity of raising the lid. Inside, and directly opposite this opening, appeared the face of a man, with ample whiskers and

336

moustaches ; which face, despite the bedaubment of something that resembled treacle or tar, was at once identified as that of the aristocratic Smythje !

" Mr. 'Mythje !" cried Quashie, who had followed the others under the archway. " I seed him ——"

"Fact, ma fwenda, it's nawbody else but maseff," interrupted the ludicrous image within the hogshead, as soon as he recognised his ancient deliverer Quaco. " Aw took wefuge here fwom those howid wobbers. Be so good as waise the wid, and pawmit me to get out of this quoeaw situation. Aw was afwaid aw should be dwowned. Ba jawve aw bwieve it's tweakle ?"

Quaco, endeavouring to suppress his laughter, lost no time in throwing up the lid, and extracting the sufferer from his sweet, though unpleasant, position : for it was in reality a hogshead of molasses, into which the terrified Smythje had soused himself, and in which, during the continuance of the tragedy being enacted over his head, he had remained buried up to the neck !

Placed upright upon his legs, on the flagged floor of the vault, glistening from neck to heel with a thick coat of the slimy treacle, the proud proprietor of Montagu Castle presented even a more ludicrous appearance than when Quaco had last seen him upon the summit of the hollow stump.

The latter, recalling this scene to memory, and unrestrained by other sentiments, could no longer restrain himself from giving way to loud laughter, in which Quashie, equally free from sorrow, took part.

With Herbert and Cubina it was not the moment for mirth ; and as soon as Smythje had been fairly deposited on his feet, both eagerly questioned him as to the circumstances that had transpired.

Smythje admitted having fled—at the same time making an awkward attempt to justify himself. According to his own account, and the statement was perfectly-true, it was not till after he had been overpowered and struck down, that he betook himself to flight. How could he do otherwise ? His antagonist was a giant, a man of vast magnitude and strength.

" A howid qweetyaw," continued Smythje ; " a queetyaw with long arms, and. a defawmity—a pwotubewance upon his shawders, like the haunch of a dwomedawy !"

" And what of Kate, my cousin ?" cried Herbert, interrupting the exquisite, with contemptuous impatience.

" Aw—aw—yes ! yaw cousin—ma paw Kate ! A feaw the wobbers have bawn her off. A know she was bwought outside. Aw heard haw scweam out as they were dwagging haw down the staiw—aw—aw——"

" Thank heaven, then !" exclaimed Herbert ; " thank heaven, she still lives !"

Cubina had not waited for the whole of Smythje's explanation. The description of the robber had given him his cue ; and, rushing outside, he blew a single blast upon his horn—the " assembly" of his band.

The Maroons, who had scattered around the ruin, instantly obeyed the signal, and soon stood mustered on the spot.

" Upon the scout, comrades !" cried Cubina. " I know the wild boar that has been making this havoc. I know where the monster makes his den. *Crambo!* Ere an hour passes over his head, he shall answer for this villany with his accursed life. Follow me!"

CHAPTER CXV.

ON THE TRACK OF THE DESTROYER.

As Cubina pronounced this command, he faced towards the mountain, and was hastening to gain the wicket in the garden wall, when an object came before his eyes that caused him to halt. Amidst the gloom, it was a sight that gave him joy.

He was not the only one to whom it brought gladness. Among the Maroons that had come with Quaco was one who had been suffering anguish equally with Herbert and Cubina—one who had equal cause for grief—if not for the loss of sweetheart or cousin, for that which should be dear as either—a *sister*.

A sister for whose sake he had crossed the wide ocean—had been sold into slavery—robbed by ruthless men—branded as a felon—chastised by the cruel scourge—had suffered every indignity which man could put on man. In this individual may be identified the young Foolah prince—the unfortunate Cingües.

What was it that gave Cubina joy—shared thus by Cingües? It may be easily guessed. It was the sight of a female form, recognised by both—the sweetheart of the one, the sister of the other—Yola?

The girl was at that moment seen coming through the wicket gate. Once inside, she made no stop, but hastened across the garden towards the group of men.

In another instant she was standing between her brother and lover, sharing the embrace of both.

Her story was soon told, and by all listened to with breathless attention —by Herbert Vaughan with emotions that wrung blood-drops from his heart. It was short but far too long for the impatience of apprehension and revenge.

The girl had been in one of the chambers as the robbers entered the great hall. Regardless of consequences, she had rushed out among them. Like Smythje, she had been struck down, and lay for some minutes insensible, unconscious of what was transpiring.

When her senses returned, and she could look around her, she perceived that her young mistress was no longer in the room. The monsters were at that moment in the act of setting fire to the mansion.

A scream outside directed her. She recognised the voice of her mistress.

Springing to her feet, she glided through the open door, and down the stairway. The robbers were too much occupied—some with their booty, others with their scheme of incendiarism. They either did not observe or did not think it worth while further to molest her.

On getting outside, she saw her young mistress borne off in the arms of

a huge, mis-shapen man. He wore a mask over his face; but for all this
she could tell that it was the same individual she had seen upon the preceding night in company with the Jew. The masked man, whose attention seemed wholly engrossed by his precious prize, went off alone
leaving the others to continue their work of plunder and devastation.

The African maid, in her native land habituated to similar scenes, with
a quick instinct perceived the impossibility of rescuing her mistress at
that moment; and, abandoning the idea of making an idle attempt, she
determined to follow and ascertain to what place the robber was taking
her. She might then return to Mount Welcome, and guide those who
would be sent upon the pursuit.

Gliding silently along the path, and taking care not to show herself,
she had kept the robber in view, without losing sight of him for a moment. The darkness was in her favour, as also the sloping path—enabling her to see from below, while she was herself in little danger of being seen.

In this way had she followed the robber up the declivity of the moun
tain, and in an oblique direction across it, still keeping close behind him;
when all at once, and to her astonishment, she saw him suddenly disap-
pear into the earth—bearing her young mistress upon his arm—like some
monstrous fiend of the other world, who had stolen a sweet image of this,
and was carrying her to his dread home in the regions of darkness.

Notwithstanding the supernatural fear with which the sudden disappearance had inspired her, the bold maiden was not deterred from proceeding to the spot.

Both her terror and astonishment were in some degree modified when
she looked over a cliff, and saw the sheen of water at the bottom of a
dark abysm yawning beneath her feet. In the dim light, she could trace
something like a means of descent down the face of the cliff, and this at
once dispelled all idea of the supernatural.

She made no attempt to follow farther. She had seen enough to enable
her to guide the pursuit; and, instantly turning back upon the path, she
hastened down the declivity of the mountain.

She was thinking of Cubina and his Maroons—how soon her courageous sweetheart with his brave band would have rescued her unfortunate
mistress—when at that moment, in the light of the flickering fire, she recognised the very image that was occupying her thoughts.

Her story was communicated in hurried phrase to Cubina and his comrades, who, without losing a moment of time, passed through the wicket-
gate, and with all the speed in their power, commenced ascending the
mountain road.

Yola remained behind with Quashie and the other domestics, who were
now flocking around the great fire, looking like spectres in the flickering
light.

Cubina required no guide to conduct him. Forewarned by that wild
conversation he had overheard, as well as by the events of the preceeding day, he had already surmised the author of that hellish deed. More
than surmised in; he was satisfied that whatever head had planned, the
hand that had perpetrated it was that of Chakra, the Coromantee.

CHAPTER CXVI.

TOO LATE!

EAGER as hounds upon a fresh trail—quick as young, strong limbs could carry them—pressed the pursuers up the steep path that led to the Duppy's Hole.

Words could but feebly express the agony ranling in the heart of Herbert Vaughan. He knew not Chakra in person: but a full description of him, morally as well as physically, had been imparted to him by Cubina on the day before. It was not strange he should tremble with fear for the fate of her who was now in the power of a monster so fell and fiend-like —not strange that his soul should be filled with anguish.

That conditional phrase—" We may be too late!"—spoken as he urged his horse along the road ; repeated as he came within sight of the burning mansion—once more found utterance on his lips ; but now more emphatically and with a far more fearful significance.

His was a situation to stir the soul to its profoundest depths. Even had the victim of the vile abduction been no more than his consin, he could not have failed to feel keenly the danger that threatened her.

But now that he viewed Kate Vaughan in another and very different light—certain, from what Cubina had told him, that she reciprocated his love—under the influence of this sentiment, his distress was ten fold greater. So late, too, had he become possessed of that knowledge—so sweet had been the ecstacy it produced—that the sudden revulsion was all the more dreadful to endure.

While murmuring the words, " We may be too late," he dare scarce trust himself to give thought to the form of danger whose dread was thus hypothetically predicted.

Cubina, though, perhaps, a little less anxious than before, was equally earnest in the pursuit; and, indeed, every one of the Maroon band showed to some extent the feelings of painful apprehension that actuated their leader, whom they knew to be the friend of the young Englishman. No one showed a disposition to lag. All were alike eager to aid in the rescue of the unfortunate young lady, known to most of them, and honoured by those to whom she was known.

The horses had been left behind. On the steep and tangled path they would have been only an encumbrance.

Perhaps, never before, by man on foot, had that path been traversed in so short a space of time. There was no delay on account of the darkness. As if by divine favour, the moon had opportunely arisen, just as they were passing through the wicket-gate, and by her light they were able to proceed without pause or interruption. No stop was made anywhere, till the pursuers stood upon the edge of the Duppy cliff, and looked down into that dark abysm, where they hoped to find the spoiler and his victim.

Scarce a moment there, either. One after another they descended the tree stairway, Cubina going first, Herbert next, the others following, with like rapidity.

With the instinct of trained hunters all made the descent in silence. Only on arriving at the bottom of the cliff did an exclamation escape from the lips of their chief—Cubina.

The sight of a canoe, drawn up under the bushes, had elicited this exclamation—which expressed surprise mingled with disappointment.

Herbert saw the canoe almost at the same instant of time, but without drawing the inference that had caused Cubina to utter that cry. He turned to the latter for an explanation.

" The canoe !" whispered Cubina, pointing down to the little craft half hidden under the leafy branches.

"I see it," said Herbert, also speaking in a whisper. " What does it signify ?"

" They have gone out again."

" Oh, heaven !" cried Herbert, in an accent of anguish, the more expressive from the low tone in which the words were uttered. " If that be so, then we *are* too late—she is lost!—lost!"

" Patience, comrade ! Perhaps it is only Chakra himself who has gone out ; or, maybe, some one of the robbers who have been helping him, and who may be expected to return again. In any case, we must search the valley and make sure. Step into the canoe ! You can't swim in your clothes, while my fellows are not embarrassed in that way. Here, Quaco ! get your guns aboard this cockle-shell, and all of you take to the water. Swim silently. No splashing, do you hear ? Keep close under the cliff ! Swim within the shadow, and straight for the other side.

Without more delay the guns were passed from hand to hand, until all were deposited in the canoe. Cubina and Herbert had already stepped into the frail craft, the former taking possession of the paddle.

In another instant the little vessel shot out from the bushes, and glided silently under the shadow of the cliff."

Some half-dozen human forms, their heads just appearing above the surface of the water, followed in its wake—swimming with as little noise as if they had been a brood of beavers.

There was no need to direct the canoe to its old landing-place under the tree. Cubina knew that this had been chosen for a concealment. Instead of going thither, he made for the nearest point of the opposite shore. On touching land he stepped out, making a sign to his fellow voyager to imitate his example.

The Maroons waded out the moment after ; and once more getting hold of their guns, followed their captain and his companion—already on their route to the upper cascade.

There was no path from the point where they had landed ; and for some time they struggled through a thicket almost impervious. There was no danger, however, of their losing the way. The sound of the falling water was an infallible guide ; for Cubina well remembered the proximity of the hut to the upper cascade, and it was for this point they were making.

As they advanced, the underwood became easier to traverse ; and they were enabled to proceed more rapidly.

There was something lugubrious in the sound of the cataract. Cubina was painfully impressed by it, and equally so his companion. It sounded ominous in the ears of both; and it was easy to fancy sighs of distress, wild wailings of a woman's voice, mingling with the hoarser tones of the torrent.

They reached at length the edge of the opening that extended for some distance beyond the branches of the cotton tree. The hut was before their eyes. A light was shining through the open door. It cast its reflection across the ground shadowed by the great tree, till it met the surface silvered by the moon. Though faint, and apparently flickering, the light gave joy to the eyes that beheld it. It was evidence that the hut was occupied.

Who but Chakra could be there? And if Chakra, there too must be his victim?

Oh! was she his victim? Had the rescue arrived *too late?*

Cubina's bosom was filled with sad forebodings. Herbert's heart was on fire. It was with difficulty that either could control his emotion to approach with that caution that prudence required.

Making a sign to his followers to stay among the trees, the Maroon captain, with Herbert by his side, crept up towards the cotton-tree.

Having got fairly under its shadow, they rose to their feet, and with the silence of disembodied spirits, glided close up to the entrance of the hut.

In another instant the silence was broken by both. A simultaneous cry escaped them as they arrived in front of the open door, and looked in. It was a cry that expressed the extreme of disappointment. The hovel was empty!

CHAPTER CXVII.

THE CORPSE OF A COUSIN.

Yes, the temple of Obi was untenanted, save by those dumb deities that grinned grotesquely around its walls.

To ascertain this fact it was not necessary to enter within the shrine of the Coromantee pantheon. Nevertheless, Cubina and Herbert, as if moved by a mechanical impulse, rushed inside the door.

They looked around with inquiring glances. There were signs of late occupation. The lighted lamp was of itself sufficient evidence of this. Who save Chakra could have lit it? It was a lamp of lard, burning in the carapace of a tortoise. It could not have been long alight; since but little of the lard was consumed.

There was no doubt that Chakra had been there, with his captive. That added nothing to the knowledge they possessed already; since Yola had witnessed their descent into the Duppy's Hole.

But why had the robber so suddenly forsaken this apparently safe retreat? That the lamp was left burning betokened a hasty departure. And whither could he have gone?

"Oh, where?—on, where?" distractedly interrogated Herbert.

Cubina could make no answer. He was equally astonished at not finding the Coromantee within his hut.

Had he once more gone out from the Duppy's Hole? The position of the canoe gave colour to this conjecture. But why should he have done so? Had he caught sight of that agile-girl gliding like a shadow after him? and, becoming suspicious that his retreat might be discovered, had he forsaken it for some other at a great distance from the scene of his crime?

In any case, why should he have left in such haste, not staying to put out the light—much less to carry with him his peculiar penates?

"After all," thought Cubina, "he may still be in the Duppy's Hole! The canoe may have been used by some one else—some confederate? Chakra might have seen his pursuers crossing the lagoon, or heard them advancing through the thicket, and, taking his captive along with him may have hastily retreated into some dark recess among the trees."

His sudden abandonment of the hovel rendered this view of the case the more probable.

Quick as came the thought, Cubina once more rushed out of the hut, and summoning his men around him, directed them to procure torches and search every corner of the wood. Quaco was dispatched back to the canoe, with orders to stay by it, and prevent any chance of escape in that direction.

While the Maroons proceeded to procure the torchwood, their chief, accompanied by Herbert, commenced quartering the open ground in search of any trace which Chakra might have left. By the edge of the water, where the trees stood thinly, the moon afforded ample light to favour the investigation.

On advancing towards the cascade, an object came under the eyes of Cubina that caused him to utter a quick ejaculation. It was something white that lay by the side of the cauldron into which the stream was precipitated. Within the pool itself were broad flakes of white foam floating upon the water ; but this was not in the water, but above it, on one of the boulders, and all the more conspicuous from the black colour of the rock.

Herbert had seen the white object at the same instant of time, and both simultaneously ran forward to examine it.

A scarf !

It bore evidence of ill-usage. It was tossed and torn, as if it had fallen from some one who had been struggling !

Neither could identify the scarf, but neither doubted to whom it had belonged. Its quality declared it to have been the property of a lady. Who else could have owned it but she for whom they were in search ?

Cubina appeared to pay less attention to the scarf than to the place in which it lay. It was close up to the cliff, on the very edge of the pool into which the stream was projected.

Behind this pool, and under the curved sheets of the falling water, a sort of ledge ran across, by which one could pass under the cascade.

Cubina knew this : for, while on his hunting excursions, he had gone under it. He knew, moreover, that, half way across, there was a large cave or grotto in the cliff, several feet above the water in the pool.

As the scarf was found lying upon the ledge that conducted to this grotto, the circumstance caused the Maroon to remember it, at the same time that it guided him to the conjecture that Chakra might be there. Alarmed by their approach, there was nothing more likely than for the Coromantee to have chosen the cave for his place of retreat—the last place where any one, not aware of its existence, would have thought of looking for him.

Those reflections cost Cubina scarce two seconds of time. Quick as the conjecture had shaped itself, he ran back to the hut ; and, seizing a torch, which one of his men had prepared, he hurried back towards the cascade.

Then, signing to Herbert, and one or two others, to follow him, he glided under the canopy of falling waters.

He proceeded not rashly, but with due caution. There might be others within the cave besides Chakra? His robber confederates might be there ; and these the Maroon knew to be desperate characters— men of forfeit lives, who would die before suffering themselves to be captured.

With his drawn machete in one hand, and the torch in the other, Cubina advanced silently and stealthily towards the entrance of the grotto. Her bert was close behind, grasping his double barrelled gun, in readiness to fire, in case resistance should be offered from within.

Holding the torch in advance of him, Cubina entered first, though Herbert, anxious and eager, was close upon his heels.

The glare of the torch was reflected back from a thousand sparkling stalactites; and for awhile the sight of both was bewildered.

Soon, however, their eyes became accustomed to the dazzling corruscation; and then a white object, lying along the floor of the cavern, seen by both at the same instant, caused them to utter a simultaneous cry—as they did so, turning to each other with looks of the most painful despair.

Between two large masses of stalagmite was the body of a woman, robed in white. It was lying upon its back, stretched out to its full length—motionless; apparently dead!

They needed not to pass the torch over that pale face to identify it. It was not necessary to scrutinise those wan, silent features. On first beholding the prostrate form, too easily had Herbert rushed to the sad conclusion—that it was the corpse of his cousin!

CHAPTER CXVIII.

THE SLEEP-SPELL

During all this time where was Chakra?

As soon as he had seen the mansion of Mount Welcome fairly given to the flames, the Coromantee, bearing its young mistress in his arms, hurried away from the spot. Outside the garden wicket he made stop : only for a moment, which was spent in a hasty consultation with the chief of the black bandits.

In the brief dialogue which there took place between them, Adam was enjoined to carry the whole of the booty to his mountain home, where Chakra promised in due time to join him. The Coromantee had no intention to resign his share of the spoils ; but just then he was in no mood for making the division. He was at that moment under the influence of a passion, stronger than the love of plunder.

Adam was only too eager to accede to these terms ; and the confederates parted company—the robber and his followers at once shouldering their booty, and setting out for their forest dwelling among the far mountains of Trelawney.

Like the tiger who has killed his prey—and, not daring to devour it on the spot, bears it to his jungle covert—so Chakra, half dragging, half carrying Kate Vaughan, proceeded up the mountain path in the direction of the Duppy's Hole.

Lifeless as the victim of the ferocious beast, appeared the form of Lilly Quasheba, hanging supple and unconscious over the arm of the human monster—equally ferocious.

Her screams no longer fell upon the ear. Her terror had exhausted her strength. Syncope, resembling death, had succeeded.

It continued, happily for her, during the whole of the transit up the mountain. The wild forest path had no terrors for her: neither the descent into the dank solitudes of the Duppy's Hole. In the traverse over that dark lagoon, she was not frightened by the scream of the startled night bird, nor the threatening roar of the close cataract. She knew no fear, from the moment she was carried away in the arms of a hideous monster, on a path lighted by the blaze of the roof under which she had been born and reared: she experienced no feeling of any kind, until she awoke to consciousness in a rude triangular hut, lit by a feeble lamp, whose glare fell upon a face hitherto well known—the face of Chakra, the myal-man.

His mask had been removed. The Coromantee stood before her in all his deformity—of soul as of person.

Terror could go no further. It had already produced its ultimate effect. Under such circumstances reproach would have been idle; indig nation would only have been answered by brutal scorn.

Though she might not clearly comprehend her situation, the young creole did not think she was dreaming. No dream could be so horrid as that? And yet it was difficult to believe that such a fearful scene co ild be real?

O God! it was real. Chakra stood before her—his harsh voice was ringing in her ears. Its tone was mocking and exultant.

She was upon the bamboo bedstead, where the myal-man ad placed her. She had lain there till, on her senses returning, she discovered who was her companion. Then had she started up—not to her feet, for the interposition of the Coromantee had hindered her from assuming an erect position, but to an attitude half reclining, half threatening escape. In this attitude was she held—partly through fear, partly by the hopeless ness of any attempt to change it.

The Coromantee stood in front of her. His attitude? Was it one of menace? No! Not a threat threw out he—neither by words nor ges ture. On the contrary, he was all softness, all suppliance—a wooer!

He was bending before her, repeating vows of love! Oh, heavens! more fearful than threats of vengeance!

It was a terrible tableau—this paraphrase of the Beast on his knees before Beauty.

The young girl was too terrified to make reply. She did not even lis ten to the disgusting speeches addressed to her. She was scarce more conscious than during the period of her syncope.

After a time, the Coromantee appeared to lose patience. His unnatural passion chafed against restraint. He began to perceive the hopelessness of his horrid suit. It was vain to indulge in that delirous dream of love —in the hope of its being reciprocated—a hope with which even satyrs are said to have been inspired: The repellant attitude of her, the object of his demoniac adoration—the evident ' dégoût' too plainly expressed in her frightened features—showed Chakra how vain was his wooing.

With a sudden gesture he desisted, raising himself into an attitude of determination that bespoke some dreadful design--who knows what?

A shrill whistle pealing from without prevented its accomplishment, or, at all events, stayed it for the time.

"Tam de signal ob dat ole Jew!" muttered he, evidently annoyed by the interruption. "Wha he want dis time ob de night? 'Pose it some thin' 'bout dat ere loss book-keepa? Wa! a know nuffin 'bout him. Dere 'tam 'gain, and fo' de tree time. Daat signify he am in a hurry. Wha's dat? 'Foth time! Den dey be some trouble, su'tin. Muss go to him—muss go. He nebba sound the signal fo' time 'less da be some des p'rate casion fo' do so. Wonder what he want?

"Nebba mind, Li/ly Quasheba!" added he, once more addressing his speech to his mute companion. "Doan bex yaseff 'bout dis interupshun. De bisuess 'tween you 'n me 'll keep till a gets back, an' den, p'raps, a no find you so ob'tinate. You come—you 'tay out hya—you muss no be seen in dis part ob de world."

As he said this, he seized the unresisting girl by the wrist, and was about leading her out of the hut.

" Ha !" he exclaimed, suddenly stopping to reflect; "dat woau do, neider. De ole Jew mussn't kuow she hya—no account. She mout ruu back in de shanty, darfur she muss be tied. An den she mout 'cream so bo hear her, darfur she muss be gagged."

Still holding her wrist in his grasp, he looked around the hut as if in search of the means to put this design into execution.

" Ha !" he ejaculated, as if inspired by some new thought. " What hab a been bodderin' ma brains 'bout ? Dar's a better plan dan eider tyin' or gaggin'—better dan boaf put togedder ? De sleepin' draff. Dar's de berry ting keep her quiet. Wha's de bottle, a wonder ? 'Dar am be."

With this, he stretched forth his disengaged hand ; and drew something out of a sort of pockct cut in the palm-leaf thatch. It appeared to be a long narrow phial, filled with a dark coloured fluid, and tightly corked.

" Now, young missa !" said he, drawing out the cork with his teeth, and placing himself as if intending to administer a draught to his terrified patient: " you take a suck out ob dis hya bottle. Doan be 'feered. He do no harm—he do you good—make you feel berry comf'able, I'se be boun'. Drink !"

The poor girl instinctively drew back ; but the monster, letting go her wrist, caught hold of her by the hair, and, twisting her luxuriant tresses around his ebony fingers, held her head as firmly as if in a vice. Then, with the other hand, he inserted the neck of the phial between her lips, and, forcing it through her teeth, poured a portion of the liquid down her throat.

There was no attempt to scream—scarce any at resistance—on the part of the young creole. Almost freely did she swallow the draught. So prostrate was her spirit at that moment, that she would scarce have cared to refuse it, even had she known it to be poison!

And not unlike to poison was the effect it produced—equally quick in subduing the senses—for what Chakra had thus administered was the juice of the *calalue*, the most powerful of narcotics.

In a few seconds after the fluid had passed her lips, the face of the young girl became overspread with a death-like pallor—all through her frame ran a gentle, tremulous quivering, that bespoke the sudden relaxation of the muscles. Her lithe limbs gave way beneath her; and she would have sunk down upon the floor, but for the supporting arm of the weird conjuror who had caused this singular collapse.

Into his arms she sank—evidently insensible—with the semblance rather of death than of sleep !

" Now, den !" muttered the myal-man, with no sign of astonishment at a phenomenon far from being strange to him—since it was to that same sleeping-spell he was indebted for his professional reputation—" now, den, ma sweet Lilly, you sleep quiet 'nuff 'til I want wake you 'gain. Not hya, howsomedever. You muss take you nap in de open air. A muss put you wha de ole Jew no see you, or maybe he want you fo' him-seff. Come 'long, disaway !"

And thus idly apostrophising his unconscious victim, he lifted her in both arms, and carried her out of the hut.

Outside he paused, looking around, as if searching for some place in which to deposit his burden.

The moon was now above the horizon, and her beams were beginning to be reflected feebly, even through the sombre solitude of the Duppy's Hole. A clump of low bushes, growing just outside the canopy of the cotton-tree, appeared to offer a place of concealment; and Chakra was proceed-ing towards them, when his eye fell upon the cascade ; and, as if sudden-ly changing his design, he turned out of his former direction, and proceeded towards the waterfall.

On getting close up to the cliff, over which the stream was precipitat-ed, he paused for an instant on the edge of the seething cauldron ; then taking a fresh hold of the white, wan form that lay helpless over his arm, he glided behind the sheet of foaming water, and suddenly disappeared from the sight—like a river demon of old, bearing off to his subaqueous cavern some beautiful victim, whom he had succeeded in enticing to his haunt, and entrancing into a slumber more fatal than death.

In a few seconds the hideous hunchback reappeared upon the bank, no longer embarrassed by his burden ; and hearing the whistle once more skirling along the cliffs, he faced down stream, and walked rapidly in the direction of his canoe.

CHAPTER CXIX.

A NEW JOB FOR CHAKRA.

CHAKRA, on reaching the crest of the cliff, found Jacob Jessuron in a state of impatience bordering upon torment. The Jew was striding back and forth among the trees, at intervals striking the ground with his umbrella, and giving utterance to his favourite exclamatory phrases- "Blesh my soul !" and " Blesh me !" with unusual volubility.

Now and then also could be heard the Teutonic ejaculation," Ach !" proving that his soul was under the influence of some unpleasant passion, that was vexing him even to torture.

" Wha's de trouble, Massr Jake ?" inquired the myal-man, scrambling over the edge of the rock. " Dar's something go wrong, a 'pose from de way you had soun' de signal ?   A hear de whissel fo' time."

" There ish something wrong—a great deal ish wrong—s'help me, there ish !   What hash kept you, Shakra ?" he added, with a show of vexation.

" Golly, Massr Jake, a war asleep ; da's wha d'layed me."

" Hew then hash you heard the signal four times ?"

The query appeared slightly to puzzle Chakra.

" O—a—de signal fo' time," stammered he, after a pause of reflection. " Wa, ye see, a hear de fuss time in ma sleep—den de second time he wake me—de third a got to ma feet ; and when de fo'th——"

The Jew—either satisfied with the explanation, or too much hurried to hear the end of it—interrupted Chakra at " de fo'th."

" It ish no time for talk when Mount Welcome ish in flames. You knowsh that, I supposhe ?"

Chakra hesitated, as if considering whether to make a negative or affirmative reply.

" Of course you knowsh it. I needn't haf ashked. Who wash it ? Adam hash been there. Wash it him ?"

"Ole Adam hab a hand in dat ere bizness, I b'lieve."

"You knowsh it, Shakra; and I knowsh another that hash had a hand in it. That ish not my bishness, nor what I hash come here about. There ish worse than that."

"Wuss, Massr Jake?" inquired the myal-man, with an air of feigned surprise. It might have been real. "Wuss dan dat. Hab de young man no come back?"

"Ach! that ish nothing. There ish far worse—there ish danger; s'help me, there ish!"

"Danger!" Wha from, Massr Jake?"

"Firsh tell me where ish Adam now? I want him, and all his fellish."

"He am gone back to de mountains."

"Ach! Gone back, you shay? How long ish he gone? Can you over-take him, Shakra?"

"Possab'e a mout; dey won't trabbel fass. Dey am too hebby load fo' dat. But wha' fo' you want ole Adam, Massr Jake?"

"Bishness of the greatesht importance. It ish life and death. Blue Dick hash been over to Mount Welcome. He hash heerd shtrange news —ach! terrible news! A messenger who came in from the Saffana road hash brought the newsh of many dishagreeable things—among the resht that my Spaniards haf been made prisoners by Cubina and this ungrateful villain of a Vochan. They are accused of murdering the Cushtos. Blesh my soul!"

"What harm dat do you, Massr Jake? Wha's de danger?"

"Danger! Dosh you not see it, Shakra? If theesh hunters ish brought to trial, do you supposhe they would hold their tongues? S'help me, no they will turn shtate's efidence; and then I should be exshposed—! arreshted—ruined! Oh! why hash I ever trushted theesh clumshy fellish with a bishness of such importance?"

"Dey am clumsy fellas, jess as you say, Massr Jake."

"Aeh! it ish too late to shpeak of regretsh. It ish necessary to take some shteps to prevent thish terrible mishfortune. You musht go after Adam, and find him thish instant—thish instant, Shakra."

"All right, Massr Jake. A do whatebber you bid me, nebber fear. A soon track up Adam; but wha d'ye want me say to de ole nigga when a hab foun' 'im?"

"You needn't shay anything—only bring him back with you to the Shumbé Rock. I will wait there for you till you come. Don't keep me long in sushpense, Shakra. Make all the shpeed in your power. If you don't get back before sunrishe all will bo losht! I'll be ruined—I will s'help me!"

"Nebba fear, Massr Jake. A woan lose a minnit. A doan tink dat ere ole nigga's got far 'way jess yet. A soon obertake 'im. A go atter him at once. Whugh!"

As Chakra uttered the exclamation, ho turned on his heel, and was about to start up the mountain, in the direction of the Jumbé Rock, near which he would have to pass on his way towards the haunt of the black robbers.

"Shtay!" cried the Jew, "I'she going with ycu ash far ash the Shumbe Rock. I may ash well wait there ash anywhere elshe. It ish no ushe

my going home now. S'help me! I cannot resht till thish thing ish settled. And now, when I thinksh of it, you may ash well let Adam know
for what he ish wanted—so ash he may come prepared. Say to him he
ish to go shtraight to Mount Welcome—that ish, where it ushed to be.
Hesh not to show hishself there, but prosheed along the road, till he
meets the Cushtos' body, and them that ish with it   Then he ish to find
some way to rescue the Shpaniards, an' let them eshcape to me. You
musht go along with Adam and hish men, elshe they may shpoil all. He
mush bring hish fellish well armed; you may stand in need of them all.
The messenger said there were some negroes from the eshtate of Content.
Theesh won't signify. They will all run away ash soon as you show
yourselves; but the others may be inclined to make fight. There ish
Cubina, and the young raschcal of an Englishman, besides that giant.
Quaco, and the messenger hishself. You thinksh you can manage them,
Shakra?"

"Sure ob dat."

"You musht take them by an ambushcade."

"P'raps we kill some o' dem."

"Ash many ash you like. Only make shure to get the Shpaniards off."

"Be no great harm to kill dem too—atter de fool dey hab made ob
demselves, lettin' dem fellas take um pris'ner dat a way. Whugh!"

"No, no, goot Shakra!—we mushn't kill our friendsh—we may need
them again. You may promish Adam goot pay for the shob. I don't care
'or the cosht, so long as it ish clefferly done."

"All right, Massr Jake; leab dat to me an' Adam. We do de ting cleb-
berly 'nuf, I'se be boun'."

And with this assurance Chakra strode off up the mountain, the Jew
having set the example by starting forward in advance of him.

CHAPTER CXX

DEAD OR ASLEEP?

ON beholding what he believed to be the dead body of his cousin, the grief of Herbert Vaughan proclaimed itself in a wild cry—in tones of the bitterest agony. He flung his gun upon the rock—knelt down by the side of the corpse—raised her head upon his arm, and gazing upon that face, in death beautiful as ever, drew it nearer to his own, kissed the cold unconscious lips—kissed them again and again, as though he had hopes that the warmth of his love might re-animate the fair form over which he was bending.

For some time his frenzied caresses were continued—their fervour unchecked by the presence of his rude companions who stood around. Respecting the sanctity of his grief, all observed a solemn silence. Nor word nor sound escaped the lips of any one. Sobs alone proceeded from Cubina. The Maroon had also cause to sorrow at that sad spectacle—but these were not heard. They were drowned by a more powerful voice—the melancholy monotone of the cataract—that had been speaking incessantly since the creation of the world.

It was a long time before the heart of Herbert consented to his discontinuing these cold but sweet kisses—the first he had ever had—the last he was destined to have from those pale lips; long before he could withdraw his supporting arm from beneath that beautiful head, whose shining tresses lay dishevelled along the rock.

The torch held in the hands of Cubina was burning to its base. Only when warned by its flickering light, did the chief mourner rise once more to his feet; and then, making a feeble signal to those who stood around, he moved in solemn silence towards the entrance of the grotto.

His gesture was understood, and promptly obeyed. By the authority of his greater grief he had become master of the mournful ceremonies now to be observed.

The Maroons, quietly crossing their arms under the inanimate form

raised it from the rock; and following him, who had given them their
silent direction, they bore it to the hut—there placing it upon the cane
couch. With instinctive delicacy all retired upon the completion of their
task, leaving Herbert and Cubina alone with the body.

An interval elapsed before either essayed to speak. Both were under
the influence of a profound grief, that almost stiffled reflection. Cubina
was the first to have other thoughts, and to give expression to them.

"*Santa Virgen!*" said he, in a voice husky with emotion, "I know not
how she has died, unless the sight of Chakra has killed her. It was
enough to have done it."

This suggestive speech received no other answer than a groan.

"If the monster," continued the Maroon, "has used other violence, I
see no trace of it. There is no wound—no appearance of anything that
should have produced death. Poor young creature!—there's something
dark inside her lips—but it's not blood——"

"O God!" cried Herbert, interrupting the speaker with a fresh parox-
ysm of grief. "Two corpses to be carried home to the same house—
father and daughter—on the same day—in the same hour: both the
victims of villany. O God!"

"Both victims of the same villain, I have my belief," rejoined Cubina.
"The same hand that laid low the Custos, if I mistake not, has been at
the bottom of this horrible crime. Chakra is but the weapon. Another
has dealt the blow—you know who, Master Vaughan?"

Herbert was hindered from making reply. A dark form appearing in
the door, distracted the attention of both from the theme of their conversation.

Quaco had heard the melancholy tidings: and, relieved from his duty
by the canoe, had hurried back to the hut, he it was who now appeared
in the doorway, filling it from post to post—from step to lintle.

Neither his chief nor Herbert offered any remark. Quaco's presence
did not surprise them. It was natural he should come to the hut—if
only to satisfy his curiosity. Weighted with their sorrow, neither took
any notice of his arrival, nor of his movements after he had entered the
hut—which he did without waiting to be invited.

Having stepped inside, the colossus stood for some moments by the
couch, gazing down upon the sweet, silent face. Even on his features
was depicted an expression of sorrow.

Gradually this became more subdued; or rather appeared to undergo
a total change—slowly but surely altering to an expression of cheerful
ness.

Slight at first, and imperceptible on account of the large scale upon
which Quaco's features were formed, the expression was every moment
becoming more pronounced; until at length it attracted the notice of the
others, notwithstanding the abstraction cause by their poignant grief.

Both observed it at the same instant, and to both it caused a feeling of
annoyance—amounting almost to indignation.

"Lieutenant," said Cubina, addressing his subaltern in a tone of reproach, "it is not exactly the time for being gay. May I ask you what
is making you smile, while others around you are overwhelmed with
sorrow?"

"Why, cappen," rejoined Quaco, "I can't see what yar all a-greetin' bout. Can't be the Custos : since, sartinly, you've got over grievin' for him long afore this ?"

The reply—grotesque in character, and almost jovial in the manner of its delivery—could not fail still further to astonish those to whom it was addressed. Both started on hearing it ; and for some-moments bent their eyes on the speaker in an expression of wonder, mingled with indignation.

Had Quaco gone mad ?

"In the presence of death, sir," said the young Maroon captain, directing a severe glance upon his lieutenant, "you might lay aside that merry mood, too common with you. It ill becomes you——"

"Death, do you say, cappen ?" interrupted Quaco ; "who's gone dead here ?"

There was no reply to this abrupt interrogatory. Those to whom it was addressed were too much taken by surprise to say a word.

"If you mean the young buckra lady," continued Quaco, "I'd give all the barbacued hog I ever owned nebber to be more dead than she jess now. Dead i'deed ? Nonsense dat : she only sleep !"

Herbert and Cubina started from their seats, each uttering a cry of astonishment, in which might be detected the accents of hope.

"Who's got a piece o' lookin'-glass ?" continued Quaco, turning his glance interrogatively around the hut. "Good !" he exclaimed, as the sparkle of a piece of broken mirror came under his eye ; "here's the thing itself !"

"Now, lookee hyar !" resumed he, taking the bit of glass from the place where it had been deposited, and rubbing its surface with a piece of rag : "you see thar's ne'er a speck upon it ?"

The others, still held silent by surprise, made answer only by nodding their assent.

"Wal, now," continued Quaco, "watch me a bit !"

Placing the smooth surface of the mirror to the mute lips, he held it there for a minute or more ; and then turning, he raised it up, and held it close to the light of the lamp.

"Ye see," he cried, triumphantly pointing to a white filmy bloom that appeared upon the glass, partially obscuring its sheen, "that's her breath ! She no gone dead, else how she hab breath ?"

His listeners were too excited to make reply. Only by exclamations did they signify their assent to the truth of his hypothesis.

"Ho !" exclaimed Quaco, suddenly dropping the bit of glass, and clutching hold of a phial that lay upon the floor—now for the first time noticed.

"What we got here ?" continued he, drawing the cork with his teeth, and thrusting the neck up his wide nostril. "Sleepin' draugh ! I thought so. So this is the spell that's put the young buckra lady to rest. Well, there's another that'll wake her, if I can only find it. It's boun' be hya, somewheres about ; and if I can only get my claws on it, I'll make this hya young creetur' talk to ye in less than ten minutes.'

So saying, the colossus commenced searching around the hut, looking into the numerous chinks and crannies with which both walls and roof were provided.

Restrained by surprise, blended with hopeful anticipation, neither Herbert nor Cubina offered to interrupt his actions, by word or gesture. Both remained in their respective places—silently but anxiously awaiting the event.

CHAPTER CXXI.

QUACO TURNED MYAL-MAN.

To Herbert Vaughan it was a moment of tumultuous emotions—joy springing up in the midst of utter woe. That his cousin still breathed he could not doubt: that she lived he was only too ready to believe. Though mystified beyond measure by what appeared the perfect semblance of death, the words of Quaco had given him some clue to a remarkable mystery—at the same time inspiring him with the belief that in that motionless form the soul was yet present. Her breathing upon the mirror had made him sure of it.

The mystery to which Quaco's speeches had introduced him, was that of *myalism*. In this the Maroon lieutenant claimed to have skill almost equalling the regular professors of the art. In addition to being Cubina's deputy on all important occasions, Quaco was the doctor of the band; and in his medical experience he had picked up some knowledge of the system of Obeah—more especially of the trick by which, in the belief of the ignorant, a dead body can be brought to life again—that dread secret of the Coromantee charlatan, known in the West Indies as *myalism*.

"Only a sleep spell," said Quaco, still continuing his search; "nothin' more than that—a draught given her by the myal-doctor. I know it well enough; and I know's what'll make all right again; though 'ithout that she'd a come to of herself. A—ha! hyar it is! hyar's the anecdote!"

A small bottle glistened between his fingers; which in another instant was uncorked and brought in contact with his nostrils.

"Yes, dis is de stuff that's a'goin' to countrack that spell. In less'n ten minutes' time you see her wake up, brisk as ebber she been in her life. Now, young master, if you jess hold up the young lady's head while I spill a drop or two down her throat. It must go down to do any good."

Herbert, with joyful willingness, obeyed the request; and the beautiful head once more received the support of his arm.

Quaco, with all the gentleness of which his huge, coarse fingers were capable, parted the pale lips; and inserting the neck of the phial, poured out a portion of its contents into the mouth of the sleeper. This done, he held the bottle for some minutes to her nostrils; and then, laying it aside, he commenced chafing her hands between his own broad, corrugated palms.

With heart wildly beating, and eyes alternately scanning the face of Quaco and the countenance of the silent sleeper, Herbert made no effort to conceal his terrible solicitude.

It would have been far more terrible, but for the confident manner of the negro, and the triumphant tone in which he predicted the result.

Scarce five minutes had elapsed from the time of administering the antidote—to Herbert they appeared fifty—when the bosom of the sleeper was seen to swell upward; at the same time that a sigh, just audible, escaped from her lips!

Herbert could no longer restrain his emotions. With a cry of supreme joy, he bent his face nearer to that of the young girl, and pressed his lips to hers, at the same time gently murmuring her name.

"Be quiet, young master!" cautioned Quaco, "else you may keep her longer from wakin' up. Hab patience. Leave the annecdote to do its work. 'Tant a goin' to be verry long."

Herbert, thus counselled, resumed his former attitude; and remained silently but earnestly gazing upon the beautiful face, already showing signs of re-animation.

As Quaco had predicted, the "anecdote" was not long in manifesting its effects. The bosom of the young girl began to rise and fall in quick spasmodic motion, showing that respiration was struggling to return; while, at shorter intervals, sighs escaped her, audible even amidst the sounds, so similar, heard from without.

Gradually the undulations of the chest became more regular and prolonged, and the lips moved in soft murmuring—as when one is endeavouring to hold converse in a dream!

Each instant these utterances became more distinct. Words could be distinguished; and, among others, one that filled the heart of Herbert with happiness indescribable—his own name!

Despite the prudent counsel of Quaco, he could no longer restrain himself; but once more imprinting a fervent kiss upon the lips of his beloved cousin, responded to her muttering by loudly pronouncing her name, coupled with words of love and exclamations of encouragement.

As if his voice had broken the charm—dispelling the morphine from out her veins—the eyes of the young girl all at once opened.

The long, crescent-shaped lashes displayed through their parting those orbs of lovely light, brown as the berry of the *theobroma*, and soft as the eyes of a dove,

At first their expression was dreamy—unconscious—as if they shone without seeing—looked without recognising.

Gradually this appearance became changed. The spark of recognition betrayed itself fast spreading over pupil and iris—until at length, it kindled into the full flame of consciousness.

Close to hers was the face of which she had been dreaming. Looking into hers were those eyes she had beheld in her sleep, and with that same glance with which, in her waking hours, they had once regarded her—that glance so fondly remembered!

Again was it fixed upon her; but no longer in silence, and unexplained. Now it was accompanied by words of love—by phrases of endearment—spoken with all the wild *abandon* of an impassioned heart.

"Herbert, cousin!" she exclaimed, as soon as speech was restored to her. It is you? where am I? No matter since you are by me. It is your arm that is around me?"

"Yes, dearest cousin—never more to part from this sweet embrace. Oh, speak to me! Tell me that you live!"

"Live! Ah! you thought me dead? I thought so myself. That horrid monster! He is gone? I see him not here! Oh! I am saved! It is you, Herbert? you who have delivered me from worse than death?"

"Mine is not the merit, cousin. This brave man by my side—it is he to whom we are both indebted for this deliverance."

"Cubina! and Yola?—poor Yola? She, too, has escaped? Oh! it is a fearful thing. I cannot comprehend——"

"Dearest cousin! think not of it now. In time you shall understand all. Know that you are safe—that all danger is past."

"My poor father! if he knew—Chakra alive—that fearful monster!"

Herbert was silent, Cubina, at the same time, withdrawing from the hut to give some orders to his followers.

"Ah, cousin, what is that upon your breast?" inquired the young girl, innocently touching the object with her fingers. "Is it not the ribbon you took from my purse? Have you been wearing it all this time?"

"Ever since that hour! Oh, Kate, no longer can I conceal the truth. I love you! I love you! I have heard——. But tell me dearest cousin!—with your own lips declare it—do you return my love?"

"I do! I do!"

Once more Herbert kissed the lips that had given utterance to the thrilling declaration.

In that kiss two loving souls were sealed for ever!

CHAPTER CXXII.

THE RESCUE.

On starting off from the Duppy's Hole it had been the intention of the Jew to wait by the base of the Jumbé Rock for the return of Chakra with the robbers. Before arriving at the rock, a better plan presented itself.

In the absence of Chakra—which might be a prolonged one—it occurred to him that he might profitably pass the interval of time by making a reconnoissance of Mount Welcome and its precincts.

Before parting from Chakra, therefore, a new place of rendezvous was arranged between them—at a particular place upon the mountain slope, only a short distance from the rear of the garden.

This point being settled, Chakra continued on after the home-returning bandits; while his fellow conspirator, facing down the mountain, proceeded towards the valley of Mount Welcome.

He soon came upon the path habitually used in the ascent and descent of the mountain. Only for a short distance did he follow it, however. He conjectured that a pursuit would be already set on foot; and, apprehensive of encountering the pursuers, he preferred making his approach to the house by working his way through the woods, where no path existed. By this means he should advance more slowly, but with greater safety.

Favoured by an occasional flash from the smouldering fires—seen at intervals through the trees—he had no difficulty in guiding himself in the right direction; and in due time he arrived at the rearward of the garden.

Crouching behind the wall, and looking cautiously over its top, he could command a full view of the grounds—no longer containing a grand house, but only a smouldering mass of half-consumed timbers.

There was still sufficient flame springing up amidst the smoke to reveal to the eyes of Jessuron a terrible *tableau.*
Under the light could be seen a number of human figures grouped around an object resembling a rude bier. On this lay the body of a white man, whose ghastly visage—ghastlier under the glare of the unnatural light—betokened it to be a corpse.
A white man stood beside it, bent over the body, and looking thoughtfully on the face. Jessuron recognised in this individual the overseer of the estate. The others were blacks—both men and women—easily known as the domestics and field slaves of the plantation.
At a short distance from these was another group—smaller in individual numbers, but equally conspicuous.
Two men lay along the grass, in an attitude that showed them to be fast bound. They were white men in colonial phraseology, though their complexions of dark olive were but a shade or two lighter than those of the negroes who surrounded them. Jessuron easily identified them as his own 'employés,' the Cuban 'caçadores.'
Some three or four black men stood around them, apparently acting as guards. The costume, arms, and accoutrements of these last—but quite as much their bold, upright bearing—proclaimed them to be men of a different caste from the negroes who encompassed the corpse. They were the Maroons whom Quaco had left in charge of the prisoners.
As soon as Jessuron had finished making these observations, he returned to the place of rendezvous, where he was soon joined by Chakra and the robbers. The latter, on their homeward route, having halted for a rest not far beyond the Jumbé Rock, were there overtaken by the myalman, and brought instantaneously back.
The report of Jessuron was delivered to Chakra, who, along with Adam and his followers, advanced to the garden wall, and became himself a spectator of the scene already described.
The circumstances suggested the necessity of immediate action. It was evident that Cubina and the main body of the Maroons had gone off in pursuit of the incendiaries at once. No account was made of the presence of the plantation negroes; and the weak guard of the Maroons that had been left could be easily overpowered.
Such were the reflections of Chakra and Adam, acted upon almost as soon as conceived, and leaving Jessuron to await their return, they and their followers crept forward through the shrubbery of the garden.
A volley from their guns, fired from an ambush, was heard shortly after. It caused most of the Maroon guard to fall dead by the side of their prisoners, at the same time putting to flight the people of the plantation, with their overseer at their head.
Nothing then remained but to release the captives from their cords; and this being readily accomplished, both robbers and 'caçadores retreated up the mountain.
On nearing the Jumbé Rock, the confederates once more separated. Adam and his followers continued on towards their mountain home, while Chakra, accompanied by the Jew, and followed by Manuel and Andres, proceeded in the direction of the Duppy's Hole.
It was the design of Jessuron that the two Cubanos should remain in that safe asylum—as guests of the Coromantee—until such time as he

might find an opportunity for shipping them back to the country whence they had come.

Chakra's consent to this arrangement had not yet been obtained, and it was to this end that the Jew was now on his errand—for the second time that night—to the sombre solitude of the Duppy's Hole.

CHAPTER CXXIII.

DOWN THE MOUNTAIN.

THE midnight hour had passed ere the lovers forsook the solitude of the Duppy's Hole.

From mingled motives Herbert had lingered on that wild spot. He feared the dread development which he knew must take place on their return to the Mount Welcome. What a terrible blow to that young bosom, now in the full enjoyment of earth's supremest happiness! He knew the fatal truth could not long be concealed; nevertheless, he was desirous of keeping it back as long as possible—at least until his cousin had further recovered from the shock which her spirit had that night sustained.

In concert with Cubina, he had spent some time in reflecting how this temporary concealment might be effected.

Only one way suggested itself—to conduct his cousin to the house of the overseer; there to remain until, as she might suppose, her father could receive the news of the conflagration that had occurred, and return home again.

The young girl knew that the mansion was burnt down. Its blaze was before her eyes when they ceased to see—lighting her ravisher along the forest path. The roof that had sheltered her childhood was a ruin. She knew all that.

It was therefore but natural that a temporary home should be sought elsewhere, and in the house of the overseer. She could have no suspicion of any design in their taking her thither.

Neither Herbert nor Cubina knew whether the corpse of the Custos had yet reached its destination. Quaco, on hurriedly parting with it, had given no orders, either to the bearers or the Maroons left in charge of the two prisoners, to move forward.

The funeral ' cortége' might still be upon the road, where it had been left by Herbert and Cubina.

If so, it might be possible for them to pass the ruined dwelling, and reach the house of the overseer, without any news of the assassination being communicated to her—the only one likely to be profoundly affected by that dread disaster.

Once under the roof of Mr. Trusty, means could be taken to keep silent the tongues of those who should be brought in contact with her.

Such was the scheme, hastily concerted between Herbert and Cubina ; and which they now proceeded to execute, by conducting the young creole out of the Duppy's Hole and commencing their descent towards the valley of Mount Welcome.

Only the two accompanied her. The Maroons, under their lieutenant, Quaco, remained behind ; and for an important purpose, the capturing of Chakra.

Cubina would himself have stayed ; but for a certain impatience once more to enjoy the company of his beloved Yola, who had been left among the other domestics of the desolated establishment.

The Maroon captain had perfect confidence—both in the skill of his lieutenant, and the courage of his followers. He could trust them for an affair like this ; and as he parted from the Duppy's Hole he had very little doubt that by daybreak, or perhaps before that time, Chakra would be the captive of Quaco.

Slowly Herbert and his cousin moved down the mountain. The moon, now shining sweetly upon the perfumed path, favoured their descent ; but there was no need—no desire for haste. Cubina kept ahead, to secure them from surprise or danger. The young girl walked side by side with Herbert, leaning upon his arm—that strong arm, once so freely and affectionately promised. The time had arrived when the offer was accepted and welcomed—a proud time for the young Englishman—a happy time, as he walked on thrilled by the touch of that round arm softly pressing his own—at times more heavily leaning upon him, rot from any physical weakness on the part of his companion, but rather out of the pure fondness of her affection.

The strength of the young creole had become almost restored—the effects of the narcotic having completely disappeared. She had also recovered from the prostration of spirit which it had produced—perhaps all the sooner from the cheering presence of him who was by her side.

The terrible sufferings she had endured were succeeded by a happiness tranquil and profound. She now knew that Herbert loved her : more than once within the hour had he given her that sweet assurance.

On her part there was no coyness—not a shadow of coquetry. She had responded to his vows by a full, free surrender of her heart.

And her hand ? Was it still free ?

Herbert sought an answer to this question as they passed onward—only indirectly, and with all the delicacy that circumstances would permit.

Was it true what he had heard, that a promise had been given to Smythje?

With downcast eyes the young girl remained for some moments without vouchsafing any reply. Her trembling arm betrayed the painful struggle that was agitating her bosom.

Presently the storm appeared to have partially subsided. Her features became fixed, as if she had resolved upon a confession; and in a firm, but low murmured voice, she made answer—

" A promise? yes, Herbert, wrung from me in my darkest hour—then when I thought *you* cared not for me—when I heard that you also had made such promise—to another. Oh, Herbert! oh, cousin! believe me it was against my will; it was forced from me by threats, by appeals—"

" Then it is not binding!" eagerly interrupted the lover. " There was no oath—no betrothal between you? Even if there had been——"

" Even if there had been!" cried the young girl repeating his words, the hot creole blood mounting suddenly to her cheeks, while her eyes expressed a certain determination. " There was no oath. Even if there had been, it could no longer bind me. No! After what has occurred this night—in the hour of danger deserted by him—no, no! After that I could never consent to be the wife of Mr. Smythje. Rather suffer the charge of perjury, from which my own conscience would absolve me, than to fulfil that promise. Rather shall I submit to the disinheritance which my father threatens, and which upon his return he will doubtless execute. Yes, death itself, rather than become the wife of a coward!"

" How little danger of that disinheritance!" thought Herbert. " How shall I tell the fearful tidings? How reveal to her that she is at this moment the mistress of Mount Welcome? Not yet—not yet!"

For a while the young man remained silent, scarce knowing how to continue the conversation.

She noticed his air of thoughtful abstraction. It guided her to unpleasant conjectures.

" Cousin! are you angry with me for what I have said? Do you blame me——"

" No—no! " cried Herbert, impressively: " far from it. By the conduct of this man—woman, I should call him, were it not for disgracing the name—by his behaviour to you, you would be released from the most solemn of oaths—much more a mere promise given against your will. It was not of that I was thinking.'

" Of what, Herbert?"

As she put this question, she leant towards him, and gazed into his eyes with a look of troubled inquiry.

The young man was puzzled for a reply. His thoughtful silence was evidently causing her uneasiness that each moment increased. Her glances betokened some painful suspicion.

She did not wait for his answer; but, in a voice that trembled, put the additional interrogative—

" Have *you* made a promise?"

" To whom?"

" Oh, Herbert! do not ask me to pronounce the name. You must know to whom I allude."

Herbert was relieved by the interrogatory. It changed the current of his thoughts, at the same time giving him a cue for something to say. "Ha! ha!" laughed he; "I think, cousin, I comprehend you. A promise, indeed! Nothing of the sort, I assure you; though, since you have been good enough to make confession, neither shall I conceal what has passed between her to whom you refer and myself. There was no love between us—at least, none upon my side, I can assure you, cousin. But, I will confess that, stung by what I fancied was your coldness to me —misled by a thousand reports, now happily found to be false—I had nearly committed myself to the speaking of a word which no doubt I should have rued throughout all the rest of my life. Thank fortune! circumstances have saved me—saved us both, may I say?"

"Oh, happiness! Herbert—Herbert! then you will be mine—mine only?"

Yielding to the promptings of an all-absorbing passion, the young creole gave utterance to this bold interrogatory.

"Dearest Kate!" replied the lover, half delirious with joy, "my heart is yours—all yours. My hand—oh, cousin, I scarce dare to offer it. You are rich—grand—and I—I poor—penniless—even without a home!"

"Alas! Herbert, you know not. Were I rich—ten times as rich as you—believe me, you would be welcome to all. But no. Perhaps I may be poor as yourself. Ah me! you do not know; but you shall. I shall conceal nothing. Know, then, dearest cousin, that my mother was a quadroon, and I am only a *mustee.* I cannot inherit my father's property except by will; and not even that till an act is obtained from the Assembly. That is the errand upon which my father is gone. But whether he succeed or not matters not now. Too surely will he disinherit me; for never shall I consent to become the wife of the man he has commanded me to marry—never!"

"Oh, cousin!" cried Herbert, enraptured by the emphatic tone in which she had declared her determination "if you consent to become mine, I care not for your riches. Your heart is the wealth I covet—that will be enough for me. What matters it even should we both be poor? I am young. I can work. I can strive. We may yet find friends, or, if not, we can do without them. Be mine!"

"Yours for any fate!—for life, Herbert! for life!"

CHAPTER CXXIV.

AN ORPHAN.

THESE earnest utterances of love exchanged between the two cousins were suddenly interrupted. Sounds of woe broke upon the stillness of the night, and in the same place as before.

They had arrived within view of what was once the mansion of Mount Welcome.

Through the foliage that fringed the path, they could see glancing some remnants of red light, here and there flickering into a faint blaze. Now and then, as they descended the slope, they had heard the crash of falling timbers, as they gave way under the wasting fire.

A murmur of human voices, too, had reached their ears ; but only as of men engaged in an ordinary conversation ; or, at all events, not exhibiting excitement beyond what might be expected at the *finale* of such a scene as had there transpired.

All at once abruptly breaking upon this comparative tranquillity—at the same time interrupting the dialogue of the lovers—were heard utterances of a far different import: the cries of men, the screaming of women, shots and loud shouting!

All these sounds appeared to proceed from the spot that but a few hours before had echoed to the clangour of a chorus equally diabolical in its accents.

Cubina, who had been moving some paces in advance, sprang instantly back upon the path ; and with troubled look stopped in front of the lovers.

"What can it mean?" asked Herbert, equally showing signs of apprehension.

"The robbers! Master Vaughan! They have returned; but for what purpose I cannot guess. It must be they. I know that voice, louder than the rest. Do you hear it? 'Tis the voice of the brigand, Adam! Crambo! I'll silence it some day ere long—maybe, this very night. Hark! there's another, still louder and wilder. He! that, too, I can distinguish. It's the hellish shriek of Chakra!"

"But why should they have come again? They took everything, a robber would care for? What can have brought them back? There is nothing——"

"There is!" cried Cubina, with a quick gesture, as though the solution had just then presented itself to his mind. "There is Yola!"

As he said this he faced around, as if about to rush towards the fray, still strepitant—its noise rather on the increase.

For an instant he appeared to be undecided; though not from any fear of going forward.

No, it was another thought that had caused that indecision: which was soon made manifest by his words.

"Master Herbert Vaughan!" he exclaimed, in a tone of appeal; "I have helped you to rescue your sweetheart. Mine is in danger!"

The young Englishman stood in no need of this appeal. Already he had disengaged his arm from that of his cousin, and stood ready for action.

"Oh, Herbert!" cried the young girl, in wild accents of distress; "there is fearful danger! Oh, you must not go. Oh, do not leave me!"

Cubina looked as if regretting the challenge he had thrown out.

"Perhaps you had better not?" said he, with no sarcasm meant by the words. "There is danger, but you must not share it. Your life now belongs to another. I did not think of that, Master Vaughan."

"In the eyes of that other," replied Herbert, "my life would be worthless, as it would to myself, were I to play the poltroon. Brave Cubina! I cannot fail you now. Dear Kate! it is Yola who is in danger—Yola to whom we are both indebted. But for her I would not have known that you loved me, and then we should both——"

"Ah! Yola in danger!" interrupted the young creole, her affection for her maid half stifling the fear for her beloved. "Oh, Herbert! go if you will, but let me go with you. I should die if you returned not. Yes, yes; if death comes to you, it shall be mine also. Herbert, do not leave me behind!"

"Only for a moment, Kate! I shall soon return. Fear not. With right on our side, the brave Cubina and I can conquer a score of these black robbers. We shall be back before you can count a hundred. There I conceal yourself in these bushes, and wait for our coming. I shall call out for you. Behind the bushes you will be safe. Not a word, not a movement, till you hear me calling your name."

As he uttered these admonitions, the brave young man gently guided his cousin into the thicket. Causing her to kneel down in a shaded covert, he imprinted a hurried kiss upon her forehead, and then hastily leaving her, followed Cubina towards the fight.

In a few seconds they ran down to the garden wall, and passed rapidly through the wicket-gate, which they found standing open.

On through the garden, and straight towards the place from which they imagined the sounds had proceeded.

Strange enough, these had ceased as abruptly as they had arisen—the cries of the men, the screaming of the women, the shots, and the loud shouting!

All, as if by a simultaneous signal, had become silent; as though the earth had opened and swallowed not only the noises, but those who had been causing them!

Unheeding the change, Herbert and Cubina kept on; nor came to a stop until they had passed the smoking remains of the mansion, and stood upon the platform that fronted it.

There halted they.

There was still some fitful light from the burning beams; but the beams of the moon told a truer tale. They illuminated a *tableau* significant as terrible.

Near the spot was a stretcher, on which lay the corpse of a white man half uncovered, ghastly as death could make it. Close to it were three others, corpses like itself, only that they were those of men with a black epidermis.

Herbert easily identified the first. It had been his companion on that day's journey. It was the corpse of his uncle.

As easily did Cubina recognise the others. They were, or had been, men of his own band—the Maroons—left by Quaco to guard the prisoners.

The prisoners! where were they? Escaped?

It took Cubina but little time to resolve the mystery. To the practised eye of one who had tied so many a black runaway, there was no difficulty in interpreting the sign there presented to his view.

A tangle of ropes and sticks brought to mind the contrivances of Quaco for securing his captives. They lay upon the trodden ground, cast away, and forsaken.

The 'caçadores' had escaped. The affair had been a rescue!

Rather relieved by this conjecture, which soon assumed the form of a conviction, Herbert and Cubina were about returning to the place where they had left the young creole—whom they supposed to be still awaiting them.

But they had not calculated on the bravery of love—much less upon its recklessness.

As they faced towards the dark declivity of the mountain, a form like a white-robed sylph was seen flitting athwart the trunks of the trees, and descending towards the garden wall. On it glided—on and downward—as the snow-plumed gull in its graceful parabola.

Neither was mystified by this apparition. At a glance both recognised the form, with its soft white drapery floating around it.

Love could no longer endure that anxious suspense. The young creole had forsaken her shelter, to share the danger of him she adored.

Before either could interfere to prevent the catastrophe, she had pas-

ⵏⵏd through the wicket—a way better known to her than to them—and came gliding across the garden, up to the sod where they stood.

An exclamation of joy announced her perception that her lover was still unharmed.

Quick as an echo, a second exclamation escaped from her lips—but one of a far different intonation. It was a cry of the wildest despair—the utterance of one who suddenly knew herself to be *an orphan.* Her eyes had fallen on the corpse of her father

CHAPTER CXXV.

AN INVOLUNTARY SUICIDE.

ON seeing the dead body of her father, Kate Vaughan sank to the earth beside it; not unconsciously, but on her knees, and in an agony of grief. Bending over it, she kissed the cold speechless lips—her sobs and wilder ejaculations following each other in rapid succession.

Only the face of the corpse was uncovered. The camlet cloak still shrouded the body, and its gaping but bloodless wounds. ˙ She saw not these; and made no inquiry as to the cause of her father's death. The wasted features, now livid, recalled the disease under which he had been suffering previous to his departure. It was to that he had succumbed; so reasoned she.

Herbert made no attempt to undeceive her. It was not the time to enter into details of the sad incident that had transpired. The most mournful chapter of the story was now known;—the rest need scarce be told; Kate Vaughan was fatherless.

Without uttering a word—not even those phrases of consolation so customary on such occasions, and withal so idle—the young man wound his arms round the waist of his cousin, gently raised her to an erect attitude, and supported her away from the spot.

He passed slowly towards the rear of the ruined dwelling.

There was still enough light emitted from the calcined embers to make plain the path—enough to show that the little summer-house in the garden still stood there in its shining entirety. Its distance from the dwelling-house had saved it from the conflagration.

Into this Herbert conducted his ' protegé,' and, after placing her on a settee of bamboos, which the kiosk contained, seated himself in a chair beside her.

Yola, who had once more appeared upon the scene, followed them, and flinging herself on the floor, at her young mistress's feet, remained gazing upon her with sympathetic looks, that evinced the affectionate devotion of the Foolah maiden.

Cubina had gone in search of the overseer; and such of the domestics as might still have concealed themselves within a reasonable distance.

The Maroon might have acted with more caution, seeing that the second attack of the robbers had unexpectedly been made. But he had no fear of their coming again. The escape of the prisoners explained their second appearance—the sole object of which had been to rescue the 'cacadores.'

For awhile the three individuals in the kiosk appeared to be the only living forms that remained by the desolated mansion of Mount Welcome. The return of the robbers had produced even a more vivid feeling of affright than their first appearance; and the people of the plantation—white as well as black—had betaken themselves to places of concealment more permanent than before. The whites—overseer, book-keepers, and all—believing it to be an insurrection of the slaves, had forsaken the plantation altogether, and fled towards Montego Bay.

Among these panic-stricken fugitives, or rather at the head of them, was the late distinguished guest of Mount Welcome—Mr. Montagu Smythje.

On being left alone, after the departure of the pursuing party, he had made a rapid retreat towards the stables; and there, by the assistance of Quashie, had succeeded in providing himself with a saddled horse.

Not even staying to divest himself of his sacchariferous envelope, he had mounted and ridden at top speed for the port, announcing his fixed determination to take the first ship that should sail for his " deaw metwopolis."

Smythje had seen enough of Jamaica, and its "qweeole qweetyaws," and more than enough of "its howid niggaws."

Cubina, returning with Quashie—who again, imp-like, had started up in his path—the only living being the Maroon could discover, announced the fact that Mr. Smythje was no longer on the ground.

From those who occupied the kiosk, the intelligence elicited no response. Notwithstanding the many jealous pangs he had cost Herbert Vaughan, and the important part he had played in the history of the creole's life, the great lord of the Montagu Castle was no longer regarded even as a unit in the situation. Neither spoke of him—neither gave a thought to him. With perfect indifference, both Herbert and his cousin listened to the report that he was no longer on the ground.

But there was at that very moment one upon the ground, who might have been better spared—one whose proximity was a thousand times more perilous than that of the harmless Smythje.

As we have said, Cubina had no apprehensions about the return of the robbers ; but there was a danger near, and equally to be dreaded—a danger of which neither he nor any of the others could have had even the slightest suspicion.

The Maroon had delivered his report at the kiosk, and, with Quashie attending on him, had gone back to the spot where the dead body still rested. He had gone thither to ascertain which of his own men had fallen in the late struggle, and also the better to acquaint himself with the direction which the robbers might have taken.

Just as he had turned his back upon the kiosk, a human figure—gliding so softly that it might have been mistaken for a shadow—passed through the wicket-gate in the rear of the garden; and, with stealthy step, advanced in the direction of the summer-house.

Notwithstanding an ample cloak in which the figure was enveloped, its *contour* could be distinguished as that of a woman—one of boldly developed form.

The blaze of the still burning timbers was no longer constant. At intervals some piece—losing its equilibrium, under the effect of the consuming fire—would fall with a crushing sound: to be followed by a fresh glare of light, which would continue for a longer or shorter period of time, according to the circumstances that created it.

Just as the silent figure, approaching along the path, had arrived within a few paces of the summer-house, one of the sudden corruscations arose, lighting up not only the interior of the summer-house, but the whole inclosure to its farthest limits.

Under that light, had any one been looking rearwards across the garden, they would have beheld a beautiful face—yet disfigured by an expression of mingled rage and pain, that rendered it even hideous. It was the face of Judith Jessuron.

It is not necessary to explain why she was there. The fire of jealousy was still burning in her breast—more furiously, more bitterly than ever.

In another instant she had placed herself in a position that commanded a view of the interior of the kiosk.

What she saw there was not calculated to extinguish the fearful fire that consumed her. On the contrary, like the collision of the falling timbers, it had the effect of stirring it to increased strength and fierceness.

Kate Vaughan had raised herself from her reclining position, and was sitting upright on the bamboo settee. Herbert was by her side, also seated. Their bodies were in contact—the arm of the young man softly encircling the waist of his cousin. It would have been evident to the most uninterested observer that their hearts were equally *en rapport,* that between them was a tie—the strongest on earth—the tie of mutual love!

It needed no reasoning on the part of Judith Jessuron to arrive at this conclusion.

The tableau was typical. It was a picture that required no explanation nor did she who looked upon it ask for any.

She did not even stay to notice the brown-skinned damsel, who seemed to be guarding the entrance of the kiosk; but, springing past her, she stood in a defiant attitude in the presence of the lovers.

"Herbert Vaughan!" cried she, in a tone of bitter abandonment, "traitor! perjured villain! you have been false to me——"

"It is not true, Judith Jessuron!" cried the young man, interrupting her, and, as soon as he had recovered from his surprise, springing to his feet. "It is not true. I——I never intended——"

"Ha!" screamed the Jewess, her rage apparently becoming more fierce at the attempted explanation; "never intended what?"

"Never intended to marry you. I never gave you promise——"

"False!" cried Judith, once more interrupting him. "No matter now —it is all past; and, since you never intended to marry me; she at least will never be your wife."

The action that followed rendered the menace of the mad woman too easily intelligible.

As she gave utterance to it she passed her hand under the mantle in which her figure was enveloped; and, as she drew it forth again, a shining object appeared between her fingers.

It was a pistol, with silver sheen and ivory handle—small, but large enough to take life at such close quarters.

It was presented as soon as drawn, but not at Herbert Vaughan. It was towards his companion that its muzzle was pointed!

Scarce a second passed before the report was heard; and for a time, the kiosk was filled with smoke.

When this cleared away, and the shining light once more penetrated the apartment a woman was seen extended on the floor, her form quivering in the last throes of life. In another instant it was motionless—a corpse!

The shot had proved fatal; but the victim was not Kate Vaughan, but Judith Jessuron!

The transposition was due to the Foolah maid. Seeing the life of her mistress in such imminent peril, she had sprung up from her seat by the door; and, bounding forward with the supple quickness of a cheetah, had seized the wrist of the intended murderess, with the intention of averting her aim, and, in doing so, had directed it upon herself.

It was accident, therefore, and not from design on the part of Yola, that Judith Jessuron thus terminated her life by an involuntary suicide

CHAPTER CXXVI.

QUACO IN AMBUSH.

THE Maroon captain, before leaving the Duppy's Hole, had given official orders to his lieutenant about the capture of Chakra. There could no longer be any question of the absence of the myal-man from his haunt. The Maroons had continued their search after the discovery in the cave still thinking that he might be concealed somewhere in the wood. The bushes were well beaten—the trees, where it was possible for a man to have climbed, were all scrutinised; and the search had ended without their finding any other trace of the Coromantee than what had been already discovered.

Beyond doubt, Chakra had gone abroad—though in what direction, no one could guess; and to have attempted tracking him at night, and through a pathless forest, would have been labour lost.

The correct scheme for capturing him was for the Maroons to remain in the Duppy's Hole, against his return.; and by keeping in ambuscade until he should have re-crossed the lagoon, they would have him, as it were, in a trap.

This was the plan chosen—with the execution of which Quaco was in-trusted.

Indeed, the initiatory steps had been taken already; for ever since the search by torchlight had been abandoned, Quaco and his men had been placed in ambush.

Cubina perceived the error he had committed in causing the search to be made.

Chakra might have been upon the cliff above, where he could not have failed to see the light of the torches.

If so, there would not be the slighest hope of his returning for that night. After witnessing such an invasion of his secret haunt, his caution would be upon the *qui vive*—enough to hinder him from venturing down into the Duppy's Hole, notwithstanding the attractive lure he had there left behind him.

Cubina thus reflected with regret—with chagrin. The capture of Chakra had now become an object of primary importance.

After all, the apprehension that he had seen the torches, or in any way become aware of the intrusion of strangers upon his solitary domain may have been an idle one. If so, then he would be certain to come back. The presence of his prisoner was earnest of his return, and at no distant period of time.

To make sure of his capture, the Maroon captain had himself planned the ambush. Quaco and his men were placed under the great tree— where the myal-man was accustomed to moor his craft. Some of them were stationed on the tree, among its branches, with the design that they should drop upon the shoulders of the Coromantee, as soon as he should arrive at his anchorage.

The canoe itself was to be left at the bottom of the stairway, after being taken thither by the Maroon captain and his two companions, on their departure from the place. All this was done as designed. .

Before parting from the canoe, Cubina had taken the precaution to place it in the exact position in which it had been left by Chakra, so that the latter could have no suspicion that the craft had been used during his absence.

The Maroons were armed with guns, loaded and primed. Not that they intended to kill Chakra. On the contrary, Cubina's orders were to capture him. Criminal as was the outlawed myal-man, it was not their province to decide upon his criminality—at least, not so far as to the depriving him of his life. Free as was the license enjoyed by these mountain rovers, there were laws around them by which even they were bound to abide. Besides, there would be no danger of his escaping from the punishment that was his due. They knew that Chakra's capture would be but the prelude to his execution.

They had another reason for their being attentive to their arms. It was just possible the Coromantee might *not return alone*. They knew he had been in the company of others—Adam and his band of desperate robbers. These confederates might come back along with him. In that case, the quiet scheme of their capture might be transformed into a sanguinary encounter.

It was not necessary all should keep awake. One half of the little band were appointed sentinels, while the others went to sleep.

The lieutenant himself was among the number of those who was entitled to the latter privilege, since for two days and nights he had scarce slept a wink.

Speedily surrendering himself to the drowsy god, Quaco indulged in a profound slumber—snoring in such fashion, that, but for the louder into nation of the waters surging through the gorge below, his huge nostrils would have betrayed his presence to the expected Chakra—even before the latter should have set foot in his canoe.

As it was, however, the roaring of the cataract quite drowned the nasal music of the sleeping Quaco, and his companions suffered him to snore on.

CHAPTER CXXVII.

THE DOOM OF DESTINY.

UNTIL daybreak was Quaco permitted to continue his snoring and his slumber. Up to that time, no Chakra appeared ; but just as the red aurora began to tinge the tops of the forest trees, a dark form was distinguished upon the summit of the cliff, just over the tree stairway.

It had scarce made its appearance, when another was seen coming for-. ward by its side, and, in the rear of both, another—and then a fourth.

All four halted for a moment on the brow of the precipice. Whether they were in conversation could not be told. Likely they were, but their voices could not be heard above the mutterings of the moving water.

Presently, he who had first made his appearance commenced descending the cliff, followed by the others, apparently in the same order in which they had arrived upon its edge.

Cingües had already shaken Quaco from his slumbers. The other sleepers had also been aroused by their companions ; and, perceiving the numbers of the enemy, had grasped their guns with a firmer hold.

Though the day had now dawned, none of the four shadowy figures outlined against the façade of the cliff, could be identified. The dark rock and the bramble hindered them from being fairly seen. Not even when they had reached the bottom of the stair could they be recognised : for there also the frondage afforded them cover.

It was only after the two foremost had entered the canoe, and the craft was seen gliding out into the open water, that Quaco could tell who were the two individuals thus seeking the solitude of the Duppy's Hole.

"Chakra!" said he, in a whisper to Cingües. "The 'tother! Prince! if my eyes don't bamboozle me, it's your old acquaintance, the penn keeper!"

To the Fellatah this piece of information was superfluous : he had already recognised the well-known features of the man who had so deeply injured him.

The memory of all his wrongs now rushed into his heart, accompanied by a thirst for vengeance—keen, irresistible.

With a wild cry—and before Quaco could interpose—he raised his piece and fired.

The young African was a marksman of unerring aim ; and but for the upraised arm of Quaco, that had disturbed the level of that deadly tube, the hours of Jacob Jessuron would have been numbered.

And numbered they were. Despite the interruption—despite the accident that guided that leaden missile far wide of its mark—destiny had determined upon having its victim.

Neither of the occupants of the canoe appeared to have been wounded ; but as the smoke cleared away, it could be seen that the shot had not passed them without effect. Chakra's hands were empty ; the paddle had been struck by the bullet ; and carried clean out of them, was now seen on the surface of the water, fast gliding towards the gorge!

A shrill cry escaped from the lips of the Coromantee. He alone understood the danger to which the accident had exposed him. He alone knew of the whirl that threatened to overwhelm both himself and his campanion.

Instantly he threw himself upon his knees, and, with an arm extended on each side of the canoe, and his body bent down to the gunwale, he commenced beating the water with his broad palms. His aim was to prevent the craft from being drawn into the centre of the current.

For some moments the strange struggle was kept up—the canoe just holding its own—making way neither upwards nor downwards.

The Maroons watched the movement with mute surprise ; and no doubt would have continued to do so, but that the two men left by the bottom of the stairway—perhaps stirred by a like curiosity—had rushed forward to the edge of the water, and thus permitted their faces to be seen. At the same instant were they recognised by one who had an old account to settle with them.

"The Jack Spaniards!" cried Quaco, surprised beyond measure at the sight of his ci-devant prisoners. "They have got loose from our guard. Fire upon them, comrades! Don't let them escape a second time!"

The stentorian voice of the Maroon lieutenant, audible above all other sounds, at once awakened the caçadores to a sense of their dangerous situation ; and, like a brace of baboons, they commenced sprawling up the tangled stairway.

Too late had they taken this resolution. Before they had got a third way to the summit, half-a-dozen triggers were pulled ; and their bodies, one close after the other, fell with a heavy plunge into the water below.

Meanwhile, Chakra, in the canoe, had kept up his life and death struggle, now going against the current—and now the watery element appearing to prevail.

For the moment the Maroons could not have decided that strife. They were engaged in reloading their guns ; and the Coromantee was left free to continue his struggle without interruption.

Chakra's bitterest enemies could scarce have desired to bring that scene to a speedy termination. No avenger need have wished his victim in a more terrible situation than were Chakra and his confederate at that moment.

The former, acting under the instinct of self-preservation, had not yet given way to despair ; while the terrified look of the latter, who appeared to have already succumbed to it, might have restrained his deadliest foe from interference.

Between the long, sinewy arms of Chakra and the strength of the current, it was difficult to decide which would conquer. For many minutes the forces appeared to be equally balanced. But the strength of the man was declining, while that of the element remained the same. In the end the waters must prevail. Chakra at length appeared to become convinced of this ; and cast round him a glance of mingled inquiry and despair.

At that moment an idea seemed to strike him—some thought perhaps that promised him a chance of escape.

All at once he desisted from his hopeless efforts to stay the canoe, as if some resolution had suddenly become fixed; and, turning towards his companion, he bent down, as if about to whisper to him. His wild, dark look, however, declared his intention to be far different.

When fairly within reach, he threw out his long arms with a sudden jerk, and, clutching the Jew by both shoulders, drew him up into his embrace, like some gigantic spider seizing upon its prey.

Suddenly changing his hold, he grasped an arm and limb ; and, raising the body high in air, with an immense muscular effort, he projected it clear over the gunwale of the canoe.

One shriek from the Jew—emitted in the extremest accent of grief—was heard simultaneously with the plunge ; and then the body of the unfortunate man disappeared beneath the dark waters of the lagoon.

His hat and umbrella alone floated on the surface, both rapidly carried along by the current.

The wretched creature rose again, but not to discover any chance of saving himself from destruction. The only gratification he could have drawn from his temporary emergence was to perceive that his false confederate must perish as well as himself.

Chakra had hoped that by lightening the canoe he might contend more successfully with the current; but it soon became evident that his hopes would prove vain.

In disembarrassing himself of his *compagnon du voyage* he had lost way ; and, before he could recover it, the canoe was sucked into a charybdis, from which the power of the paddle could not have extricated it.

In less than ten seconds the craft entered the embouchure of the gorge, gliding downward with the velocity of an arrow.

It was but a despairing effort on the part of its occupant to seize upon a tree that grew horizontally from the rocks; though in his despair

Chakra clutched it. Even had the bush been firmly rooted, his strength would not have sustained him against the fierce, resistless flood.

: But it was not. The roots gave way; and, in another instant the Coromautee and his canoe were precipitated a hundred feet sheer among the rocks below!

His confederate had preceded him only by two seconds of time; and the dead bodies of both came once more in close contact—circling round and round, amidst the frothy spume that creamed over the cauldron below.

CHAPTER CXXVIII.

CONCLUSION.

ON the morning that succeeded the occurrence of these tragic events, one entering at the great gate of Mount Welcome estate, and directing his eye up the long palm-shaded avenue, would have beheld but a mass of black, smoking ruin.

On any other morning, twelve months after, the eye of a person looking in the same direction, would have been gladdened by a sight far different. Smiling in all its splendor, at the end of that vegetable vista, once more could be seen the proud mansion of Mount Welcome—*renaissant* in every respect—its stone stairway still standing—its white walls, and green jalousied windows looking as if they had sprung, phœnix-like, from the flames—every item of the architecture so closely in imitation of the former structure, that even the eye of an old acquaintance could have detected no trace of the transformation.

Outside, everything appeared as before. It was only upon entering the mansion that you might perceive a change, and this chiefly relating to its occupancy and ownership. Instead of a stout, red-faced, and somewhat plebeian personage, of over forty years old, you would see in the present proprietor of Mount Welcome a youth of noble mein, by age scarce claiming the privileges of manhood, but in aspect and demeanour evidently fit for the performance of its duties—deserving to be the master of that aristocratic mansion.

Near him—oh! certain to be near him—there is one upon whom the eye rests with still greater interest; one who had graced the old mansion—

yet more gracing the new—the daughter of its former proprietor, the wife of its present one.

She has not even changed her name—only her condition. Lilly Quasheba is no longer *Miss* but *Mrs.* Vaughan!

Both these personages may be seen seated in that great hall, with floor as smooth and furniture as resplendent as ever.   •

It is the hour after breakfast, and also, as of yore, the hour when the post may be expected. Not that either cared to look abroad for that diurnal messenger—more welcome to those around whom Hymen has not yet wound his golden chain.

Equally indifferent were those two happy individuals to the actions of the outside world : neither cared for its news. Their love, still in the fresh flush of its honeymoon, was world enough for them ; and what interest could either feel in the arrival of the mail?

But the post has no respect either for indifference or anxiety. It is transmitted alike to the grave and the gay. It brings joy to the heart heavy laden, and sorrow to that which the moment before its arrival may have been bounding with bliss.

In that great hall in the mansion of Mount Welcome there were two bosoms brimful of bliss, or a feeling near akin to it. Nay, why should we say *akin* to it, since they were two hearts in the enjoyment of mutual love? If that be not bliss, there is no other—either on earth or in heaven.

Without any attempt at concealment, the eyes of both betrayed their mutual delight. Gazing on each other, in sweet reciprocal admiration, they saw not that dark form—rudely centaurean—that approached up the long avenue.

Had they seen it, it would have created no surprise. It was only the post-boy, Quashie, on his shaggy cob, returning from the Bay.

After this speculative peroration, the reader may be apprehensive of some dire development springing from the letter-bag slung over the shoulders of the darkey.

Nothing of the kind. There was a letter, but not one that might be unwelcome. But for the postmark, it might have remained unopened.

But the impress was peculiar. It was African. The letter was stamped with the name of a port near the mouth of the Gambia. It was addressed to " Herbert Vaughan, Esq., Mount Welcome, Jamaica."

The young planter broke the seal, and rapidly ran over the contents of the epistle.

" From your brother, Cubina !" said he, though he knew he imparted no information by this. " He writes to say he is coming back again to Jamaica."

" Oh ! I am so glad of that. I knew he would never live contented among those wild people, notwithstanding he has been made a prince over them; but Yola——."

" She comes with him, of course. It is not likely he would leave her behind. She longs for her island home again. I don't wonder, dearest Kate. There is one spot on the earth hallowed beyond all others—the spot where heart meets heart, in the free confession of a mutual love.

No wonder the African maiden should desi e to return to it. Human nature is everywhere the same. To me this island is the elysium of earth!"

"Ah! to me also!"

On giving utterance to this mutual confession, the young husband and wife bent towards each other and pressed lips, as fervently as if they had never been married!

After this fond embrace, Herbert continued the reading of the letter.

"Oh!" exclaimed he, when he had perused another portion of the epistle; "your brother wants to know whether he can either become my tenant or purchase that piece of land that lies beyond the Jumbé Rock. The old king has given him a capital to start with, and he wants to turn coffee-planter."

"I am so glad he has such intentions. Then he will settle down, and be near us."

"He must not be permitted to purchase it. We shall present it to him since we have enough without it. What say you, Kate? It is yours, not mine to give."

"Ah!" returned the young wife, in a tone of playful reproach, "do not distress me with those sad *souvenirs*. You know that I gave it to you when I might have believed myself its mistress; and——"

"Stay, dearest. Do not distress *me* by such an appeal! You were its rightful owner, and should have been. Even had we not become joint proprietors, I should never have thought of disposessing you. Say, then, that the land shall be Cubina's?"

A repetition of that sweet embrace pronounced the consent of both to the proposal of Cubina.

Herbert resumed the reading of the letter.

"Good heavens!" cried he, on finishing its perusal, "what a singular story! The captain of the slaver, who brought Yola's brother over to Jamaica, has been back again to the coast. What a terrible retaliation!"

"What, dear Herbert?"

"Only that *they have eaten him!*"

"Oh, merciful Father!"

"Sad and terrible though it be, it is true; else Cubina would not have written it. Hear what he says:—

"'Jowler'—that was the name of the slaver's captain—'presented himself before old Foolah-foota, in search of a fresh cargo of slaves. The king, already apprised of the skipper's treason to Cingues, instantly ordered him to be seized; and, without trial or other formality, caused him to be chopped to pieces upon the spot. He was afterwards cooked and eaten, at the grand national feast, which was held on the celebration of my nuptials with the princess Yola. *Crambo!* it was a painful scene; and one might have felt sympathy for the unfortunate wretch, had he been anything else but a dealer in human flesh; but, under that reflection, I stood by without feeling any great anxiety to interfere in his behalf. In fact, my Fellatah father-in-law was so furious, I could not have saved the wretch from a fate which, after all, was perhaps not more than he deserved; and to which, no doubt, the poor victims he had carried across the

Atlantic would have been only to glad to have seen him consigned.'"

"It is well," said Kate, with a thoughtful air, "that Cubina had determined upon leaving a land where, I fear such scenes are too common. I shall be so happy to see them both once more in our dear, beautiful island. And you, Herbert, I am sure, will rejoice at their return."

"Most certainly I shall. Ah, Kate! did it ever occur to you how much we are indebted to them?"

"Often, Herbert—often. And were it not that I am a firm believer in destiny, I should fancy that but for them——"

"Nonsense, Kate!" playfully interrupted the young husband. "None of your creole superstitions. There is no such thing as destiny. It was not that which ruled my heart to believe you the fairest thing in creation—but because you *are* so. Don't be ungenerous to Cubina and Yola. Give them all the credit that is due to them. Say frankly, love, that but for them you might have become Mrs. Smythje, and I—I——"

"Oh, Herbert! speak not of the past. Let that be buried in oblivion, since our present is everything we can desire!"

"Agreed! But for all that, dearest, do not let us forget the gratitude we owe to Cubina and his dark-skinned bride. And to prove it to them, I propose something more than giving them the piece of land. Let us build them a house upon it; so that upon their arrival they may have a roof to shelter them."

"Oh, that would be a pleasant surprise for them!"

"Then we shall bring it about. What a lovely morning! Don't you think so, Kate?"

As Herbert put this interrogatory, he glanced out through the open jalousies.

There was nothing particularly fine about the morning—at least, for Jamaica; but Kate saw with Herbert's eyes; and just then, to the eyes of both, everything appeared *couleur-de-rose.*

"Indeed, a beautiful morning!" answered the young wife, glancing inquiringly towards her husband.

"What say you, then, to a little excursion, ' à pied ?'"

"I should be delighted, Herbert. Where do you think of going?"

"Guess now!"

"No—you must tell me."

"You forget. According to Creole custom, our honeymoon is to last for twelve months. Until that be terminated, you are to be master, sweet Kate. Where would you most like to go?"

"I have no choice, Herbert. Anywhere. In your company it is all the same to me. You must decide."

"Well, then, dearest, since you leave it to me, I declare for the Jumbé Rock. Its summit overlooks the piece of land we intend presenting to our brother, Cubina. While we are there we can select a site for his house. Is it agreeable to you?"

"Dearest Herbert," replied the young wife, entwining her arm around that of her husband, and gazing fondly into his eyes; "the very place I was thinking of."

"Why of it? Tell me, Kate?"

"Shame, Herbert! Must I tell you? You know that I have told you before."

" Tell me again. It gives me pleasure to hear you speak of that hour."

" Hour! scarce a minute was it, and yet a minute worth all the rest of my life! A minute in which I learnt that the language of your eyes was truer than that of your tongue! But for that belief, Herbert, I might, indeed, have yielded to despair. The memory of that sweet glance haunted me—sustained me through all. Despite all, I continued to hope!"

" And I, too, Kate. That remembrance is as dear to me as it can be to you. Let us seek the hallowed spot."

* * * * *

An hour after, and they stood upon the Jumbé Rock, on that spot so consecrated in their hearts.

Herbert appeared to have forgotten his purpose. Not a word was said about Cubina or the site of his dwelling. Not a word of the Happy Valley, or the unpleasant recollections it was calculated to call up. All the past appeared to be forgotten, except that one sweet scene ; and on this were concentrated the thoughts of both—their words as well.

" And you loved me then ?" inquired he only to enjoy the luxury of an affirmative anwer. " You loved me then ?"

" Oh, Herbert! how could I help loving you ? Your eyes were so beautiful then!"

" What! Are they not so now ?"

" How cruel to ask the question! Ah! far more beautiful now! Then I beheld them only with anticipation ; now I look into them with the consciousness of possession. That moment was pleasure—this is ecstacy."

The last word was perfectly appropriate—not a shade too strong to express the mutual feeling that existed between Herbert Vaughan and his cousin-wife. As their rounded arms became entwined, and their young bosoms pressed fondly together, the Maroons and all past dangers were forgotten, and both believed that even in this unhappy world ecstacy may exist.

THE END.

www.ingramcontent.com/pod-product-compliance
Lightning Source LLC
Chambersburg PA
CBHW021543110726
47902CB00004B/1006